DID SHE DARE TELL
THE TRUTH?

It was so easy for Kate to lie to her husband, Page Taggart. He was so overjoyed when she bore twin sons, Michael and Daniel. It never occurred to him that it was not he but Roger Templeton, thousands of miles away in England, who was their father.

But now Michael and Daniel were grown to manhood. And —like a ghost of the past who was all too alive—Roger had arrived with his family at the great Taggart estate of Beauvais.

Roger woke disturbing memories in Kate. But that was not what filled her with horror. It was the way her son, Michael, and Roger's daughter, Jane, looked at each other the moment they met.

God help them if they fall in love, thought Kate. *And God help me if I have to confess the truth that will be the only way to stop their sin. . . .*

HIGH
DOMINION

SIGNET Bestsellers You'll Want to Read

HIGH DOMINION

By
Janis Flores

A SIGNET BOOK
NEW AMERICAN LIBRARY
TIMES MIRROR

Publisher's Note

This novel is a work of fiction. Names, characters, places, and incidents are either the product of the author's imagination or are used fictitiously, and any resemblance to actual persons, living or dead, events, or locales is entirely coincidental.

SIGNET TRADEMARK REG. U.S. PAT. OFF. AND FOREIGN COUNTRIES
REGISTERED TRADEMARK—MARCA REGISTRADA
HECHO EN CHICAGO, U.S.A.

SIGNET, SIGNET CLASSICS, MENTOR, PLUME, MERIDIAN AND NAL BOOKS are published by The New American Library, Inc., 1633 Broadway, New York, New York 10019

First Printing, November, 1981

1 2 3 4 5 6 7 8 9

PRINTED IN THE UNITED STATES OF AMERICA

To Joel Francis Overholser,
who gave me footprints to follow

I

1

"Good heavens, Olivia! Isn't that Kate?"

Olivia Tremont froze in the act of pouring tea for herself and her dearest friend and neighbor, Maude Webster. The note of sly excitement in Maude's voice caused her heart to miss a beat, and she closed her eyes. Whatever Kate had done, or was doing now, Olivia didn't want to know. It was too much, she thought, for one woman to bear—especially at her age, which seemed to have leaped years forward during the ten months Kate had lived with her at Tremont Hall.

"It *is* Kate! I don't believe my eyes!" Maude turned, saw Olivia apparently engrossed in polishing a blemish from the shining silver tea service, and asked in exasperation. "Don't you want to see for yourself?"

Sighing inwardly, Olivia stood. Maude was like a terrier, she thought irascibly as she came to the window and looked in the direction Maude pointed; she never knew when to give up. "Can you see her?" Maude demanded.

Olivia could, indeed. She watched her niece galloping madly down the drive away from the house, and then her mouth tightened as she recognized the cause of Maude's excitement. She couldn't believe it herself: not even Kate would have the daring to don a pair of trousers—trousers!—and ride astride. For a horrible moment Olivia actually thought she was going to faint on the spot.

"Olivia? Olivia!"

Maude's voice was a screech in her ear, marshaling Olivia's swimming senses into some semblance of order. With an effort, she sat down again, and when she spoke, her voice, by some miracle, was actually calm. "More tea, Maude?"

"Is that all you have to say after witnessing that disgraceful exhibition?" Maude glared at her and then bustled stoutly over to the table, her doughy face alight with outrage. "Olivia, you simply must do something about that girl!"

1

"What do you suggest?" Olivia made herself lift her own cup. She drank without tasting, trying to maintain her composure. Glancing at Maude, she thought suddenly that while they were neighbors, supposedly the dearest of friends, they had never been close. In fact, Olivia decided abruptly, she really did not care for Maude Webster at all.

"That girl must have discipline, Olivia," Maude continued, too swept up in her own concerns to notice her friend's increasingly obdurate expression. "Heaven knows, she didn't receive any from her mother . . ."

Maude stopped abruptly. The name of Augusta Beauvais was not a subject mentioned in this house, and even Maude recognized that she had overstepped her bounds. Olivia's husband, Harold Tremont, had been Augusta's brother, and he had never forgiven his sister for bringing disgrace upon his family and his name. From the time she had defied him and had run off to London to become an actress, Harold had forbidden his sister's name to be spoken; even now, years after his death, the subject was avoided, for it reminded Olivia of too many painful memories.

It was not a pleasant time to remember for Olivia—those first months of her marriage, when her husband and his sister were at loggerheads. Augusta had battled continually against the stern control her older brother tried to exert, and Olivia had been disturbed and dismayed by the quick, mercurial temperament of her sister-in-law. Possessed of a calm and placid nature herself, born in a household where voices were never raised, Olivia could not understand the screaming and shouting, the slamming of doors, the very excess of emotion that Augusta seemed to thrive on. The conflict raging around her those first months had brought Olivia close to a nervous collapse.

When Augusta had stormed out one night at the very height of a blazing argument with her brother, even the charitable Olivia could not muster any sorrow that Augusta had gone. She could only feel a vast relief that her sister-in-law was away from the Hall. Suddenly everything was quiet and peaceful again, as though they had emerged safely from some tempestuous and turbulent storm. Olivia felt herself responding to that new serenity; and at first, it seemed that Harold did, too. The next weeks after Augusta's violent departure had been the best of Olivia's marriage—the only time, really, that she and Harold had been husband and wife. When the news filtered back to them that Augusta had become one of those depraved creatures—*an actress*—Harold had left immediately for London to bring his sister home before she could disgrace him further.

But Augusta had refused outright to return, and the strain and stress of that fateful journey had aggravated Harold's already failing heart. Neither Olivia nor Harold had realized until then how fragile was his health, and when a series of strokes after his return home had rendered him an invalid, Olivia had been forced to resign herself to the unsatisfactory role of shadow wife. Those brief halcyon weeks of happiness were gone as though they had never been, and when Harold finally died a year or so later, a young Olivia wondered if she had ever really been a bride.

Olivia had suspected that Harold would forgive his sister in the end, and she had tried to prepare herself for such an eventuality. She hoped only that her husband would leave her enough to live comfortably. To her shocked surprise, Harold's will made no mention of Augusta; everything had gone to his wife. In the absence of any male kin, Olivia had inherited Tremont Hall outright, and suddenly she found herself very well set indeed. Augusta and her natural heirs, if any, were to be forever excluded from the properties that comprised the estate, and if Harold had known of Kate's existence, he had carefully guarded the secret from his wife. Olivia had remained in blissful ignorance of her niece by marriage until some months ago. She had lived quietly until then, satisfied with her garden and her books and her petit point to occupy her time; she invited friends to call, and would drive out herself occasionally to visit. She had been content, or had believed she was, leading her sedate and uneventful existence. There were no upsets in her life; everything ran smoothly and well.

And then Kate had appeared, and suddenly Olivia's calm and ordered household had been turned upside-down with a vengeance.

Olivia had been totally unprepared for the sudden advent of Kate into her home. Oh, she had been approached by Augusta's solicitor after her death, delivering the letter asking Olivia to give Kate a proper home. But the man had told her to expect a young girl, and Olivia had foolishly taken him at his word. The young girl, whom Olivia had vaguely thought to be in her childhood, was, in fact, not a child at all. Kathryn Augusta Beauvais was a young woman of seventeen, with a temper to match her fiery hair, whose first words to the aunt she had never seen—the aunt who had expressly disregarded her own husband's last wishes never to give shelter to his niece—were: "Don't think I've come because I had nowhere else to go. I came because Augusta wished me to."

Even now, months later, Olivia could remember that scene clearly. She could even recall her complete and utter bewilderment at the ease with which her uneventful and quiet life had become a series of disasters and catastrophes as Kate proceeded to "set the house on its ear." And not only the house, Olivia thought now, but the entire neighborhood as well.

"Olivia? Olivia! I'm speaking to you!"

Olivia came back to the present with a start. She saw that Maude was about to launch into yet another violent discussion about Kate, and she lifted her hand, trying to halt Maude before she could begin. "I'll talk to Kate," she said crisply.

"You should do more than talk to her," Maude retorted darkly. "That girl is developing a reputation for being . . . fast. Soon the whole countryside will know. . . ."

"Know what?" Olivia felt a thrill of alarm. What had Kate done *now*?

Maude appeared uncomfortable for the first time. Looking away from her friend, she muttered, "Kate has set her cap for Roger Templeton. I thought you knew."

Olivia stared thoughtfully at her neighbor. Now she understood the reason for Maude's agitation. Maude desired a match between her own daughter, Amelia, and the very eligible Roger, and now it appeared that Kate had started out to snatch the quarry from under Amelia's prim little nose. Olivia smiled, suddenly feeling more energetic. There was much to deplore in Kate's behavior, she conceded privately, but perhaps the stolid Roger would have a calming influence on her hot-tempered niece. Yes, there were definitely some possibilities in this situation.

Maude, ever alert to her own interests, was quick to catch Olivia's smile. She snapped, "I fail to see anything humorous, Olivia!"

"I gather you don't approve of a match between Kate and young Templeton," Olivia replied calmly.

"I can't imagine anything more unsuitable!"

"Why is that?" Olivia inquired innocently.

Maude glared at her friend, wondering if Olivia could be baiting her. Surely Olivia knew the consequences of such a union. Why, it would be a scandal! She said so forcefully, hoping to shock Olivia out of this dangerous and inexplicable mood.

"Can you imagine the reaction if Roger Templeton, who is, after all, related to a peer, became involved with the . . . the illegitimate daughter of a London actress? Why, it would be a disaster!"

Carried away by her own emotion, Maude failed to notice the sudden icy contempt flash in Olivia's blue eyes. How Maude had found out the truth about Kate's parentage, Olivia didn't know. But even Maude should have had the decency to keep quiet about it, she thought; good manners, if nothing else, would dictate a discreet silence. Her estimation of Maude, never high at best, she realized suddenly, slipped yet another few notches.

"For whom would it be a disaster?" Olivia inquired sweetly.

"For whom! Olivia, have you lost your mind? For Roger, of course!"

"Oh, yes. For Roger. Of course." As Maude glared suspiciously at her, Olivia continued serenely, "Poor Roger might be disinherited if his father were displeased—is that what troubles you?"

"Of course not!"

"Thank goodness for that. I couldn't believe you would be concerned with a trifling thing like the Templeton inheritance. After all, Edwin, your husband, is certainly well-placed enough to—"

"That isn't it!" Maude was stung into replying furiously. She wasn't sure if Olivia knew about Edwin's slipping fortunes, but she certainly would never admit the precariousness of their position, even to her dearest friend. But in her haste to reassure Olivia, she went too far. To her horror, she heard herself say, "It isn't that at all. It's just that I had plans for Amelia . . ."

She stopped abruptly, her face turning fiery red at her verbal slip. She hadn't told anyone of her desire of a match between Amelia and Roger, not even Edwin. Her strategy had to be plotted very carefully; no one must know that such a marriage would help the Websters to recoup their financial losses.

Glaring at Olivia, daring her to ask what she had meant, Maude let out a breath when her friend seemed not to notice her awful error.

"Oh, yes: Amelia," Olivia said, and such was Maude's vast relief that she didn't even notice the fleeting expression of distaste that crossed Olivia's face. "Dear Amelia," Olivia murmured, thinking of Maude's daughter. She realized suddenly that she had never cared for Amelia, either.

"I don't like that tone, Olivia!" Maude was once more in command of herself.

"And I don't want to hear any more disparaging remarks about Kate, Maude," Olivia retorted calmly. "After all, she *is* my niece."

Still infuriated over her earlier slip, Maude was able to point out acidly, "Only by marriage. And Amelia is your godchild. She is closer to you than Kate is, surely. I simply don't understand how you can defend her, Olivia!"

In truth, Olivia thought, she didn't understand her own actions any more than Maude did. Why *was* she defending Kate? Only minutes ago she had been exasperated with the girl for causing her yet another embarrassment, and now she was championing her over Amelia, who had never done one unconventional thing in her entire prim little life. What was more, Olivia admitted, she was alienating Maude by her defense of Kate, and for what reason? Because her niece had shown her nothing but kindness and consideration? Hardly, she thought wryly. Kate was stubborn and defiant; she guarded her independence fiercely, professing not to care how others viewed her actions. She was willful and proud and quick-tempered—all qualities that Olivia viewed with some distaste, never once suspecting that since Kate's arrival, she had possessed not a few of these attributes herself. Outwardly Olivia might deplore Kate's behavior, but a treacherous part of her silently applauded her niece's grand disregard of the conventions that sometimes made life so unbearably . . . dull. Perhaps, thought Olivia sadly, if she had been just a little more like Kate, Harold wouldn't have felt his life had ended when Augusta went away.

Uncomfortable with that last thought, Olivia brought her attention forcibly back to Maude. Her neighbor was standing, gathering her things in preparation for an aggrieved departure.

"I'm sorry, Maude, that we had this disagreement," Olivia said contritely. She was suddenly ashamed of herself for her own inexplicable behavior. After all, Maude was her friend, and she had deliberately baited her with that business about Amelia and Roger.

"I'm sorry too, Olivia," Maude replied stiffly, in a tone that indicated she wasn't sorry at all. She gave Olivia the obligatory peck on the cheek before adding ominously, "I just hope that you come to your senses before it's too late. That girl—"

"I do wish you would not refer to Kate as 'that girl,' Maude," Olivia said irritably as they walked to the front door.

"All right, then," Maude said impatiently, "*Kate* needs a firm hand"—here Maude paused to fix Olivia with a gimlet eye—"before she does damage to more than her reputation."

"Maude!"

Maude lifted her hand. "Just remember, Olivia" she said, undaunted by her friend's scandalized tone, "if that girl finds herself in . . . trouble . . . you have only yourself to blame."

Before Olivia could gather herself enough to reply, Maude sailed down the front steps with the air of a woman who has done all she could to prevent complete disaster. Entering her waiting carriage, she waved perfunctorily before settling back with a grim expression. The vehicle rattled down the drive, and Olivia sighed as she turned back inside.

The butler, Wilson, a stately man who had somehow managed to maintain his calm dignity throughout the overturning of his orderly household, was hovering nearby, and Olivia addressed him. "Tell Miss Kate that I wish to see her in the drawing room immediately when she returns."

"Yes, madam."

Wilson's voice and manner were absolutely correct as he acknowledged the command, but when Olivia stepped by him, she thought she could discern the merest twinkle in his eye. She turned back severely. "Really, Wilson, it isn't amusing," she murmured.

"No, madam," Wilson returned gravely.

But their eyes met in the same instant, and with lips twitching, Olivia and her butler moved off in opposite directions.

2

Miles away from Tremont Hall, Kate reined in her horse at the top of a hill. She sat looking down at the pastoral scene as the horse blew and snorted from the fast gallop up the slope. Suddenly she laughed aloud. Her wide green eyes glinted as she imagined the things all those stuffy people below would say if they could see her now: her hair in a wild tangle about her face, wearing the breeches she had found in an attic trunk.

She laughed again, picturing all those pursed mouths, the moues of dismay, the knowing glances that were meant to indicate that she was no better than she should be, running around the countryside like a hoyden. She could imagine Maude Webster, for instance, looking down her long sharp nose and saying in that high, affected voice of hers: "Really, Kathryn, you should be ashamed of yourself. What will people think?"

But she didn't care what people would think, Kate thought defiantly as she slid out of the saddle and tethered the mare to a bush. Why should she care? Ever since her arrival, things had been whispered about her and her mother—cruel things, and vicious. The gossips thought they had been so discreet, that she hadn't heard. But she had heard. Oh, she had.

And what did they know about her mother? Nothing! Fiercely, Kate threw herself down on the grass. What could these people, so insulated in this tedious countryside, know about the great Augusta Beauvais—about the glamour of the stage, and the constant excitement of thunderous applause, of the standing ovations her mother had received night after night, of the hundreds of roses thrown at her feet?

Kate drew up her knees, her chin resting on her folded arms. But as she stared out across the hills, at the slopes cloaked with velvet grass, at the trees blowing gently in the breeze, she did not see the beauty before her. Instead, she found herself remembering her mother's last performance. Unbidden, the memory assailed her, and her mood of exhilaration vanished with the sudden sting of tears in her eyes. Raising one hand, she dashed the tears away. She had promised herself that she wouldn't think of that final night, and now she made a fierce effort to force the image from her mind. But the pictures continued to parade before her tightly closed eyes, and she saw her mother again as she had been that last, horrible night.

Gone was the fire that had been Augusta Beauvais at the height of her career. The flame had been extinguished as the craving for drink took over, until finally Augusta could not remember her lines, nor follow the cues her manager whispered urgently from the wings. In her befuddled state that last performance, Augusta did not even hear the hissing and the booing that followed her off the stage as the curtain crashed down in the middle of the scene.

She hadn't heard, but Kate, sitting in front of the stage, had heard. Oh, yes, she had heard it all. The sound was with her still. Sometimes in the night she woke, the noise of the catcalls ringing in her ears, as though she was reliving her mother's final humiliation all over again. It was a nightmare that had remained with her even after all these months, the horror magnified in her dreams.

But Augusta's last night on the stage had been only the beginning of the nightmare, Kate thought sadly. After that, Augusta's followers had disappeared one by one; the lavish parties were no more, and the luxurious hotel suites gave way to increasingly dismal accommodations as their money dwindled at an alarming pace. At the last, all that was left was a dreary back room with ragged carpets and battered furniture and the smell of cabbage in the air. And her mother, who seemed only a caricature of the beautiful woman she had once been: the flaming red hair faded, the once-perfect complexion sallow and lined as she staggered drunkenly about the small, ugly apartment.

Kate closed her eyes again, reliving the pain of that final scene. She had been out on some errand or another for her mother. When she returned . . . Flinging an arm over her eyes, trying to shut out the terrible picture, Kate was forced to see it again, as she had a hundred times before, a recurring nightmare that she would never be rid of: her mother lying dead, sprawled across the bed, the empty bottle of laudanum on the floor beneath her lifeless fingers.

There had been a note, a weary, sodden postscript to a life grown unbearable, instructing Kate to go to her aunt at Tremont Hall. There had been nothing else, no explanation. No mention of the father who had deserted his illegitimate daughter; no reason for Augusta's turning to drink at the height of her career. Alone in the world, Kate had sat for hours holding the crumpled note in numbed fingers, staring blindly in front of her.

With a sob, Kate lifted her head. She had to be free of these devils that tormented her, and she would ride— With a start she realized she was not alone on the hill. A pair of Hessian boots was planted squarely in front of her, and a deep voice asked with concern, "Is something wrong?"

More surprised than frightened, furious to be caught with tears on her face, even by a stranger, Kate ignored the hand extended to help her. She leaped to her feet unaided. "Wrong? Of course there's nothing wrong!" she answered haughtily. "What made you think there was?"

The stranger shrugged, not in the least abashed by her attitude. "I saw your horse, and you on the ground," he replied reasonably. "Naturally, I thought you had taken a fall."

"A fall?" Kate's tone was even more imperious. "I never fall. Please go away and leave me alone."

Perversely the man continued to stand there, and Kate studied him covertly as she pretended to brush grass from her shirt. She wondered who he was. She had never seen him before, and she would certainly have remembered him if she had, if only because he was so different from the pallid young men who abounded in this district. She judged him to be in his mid-twenties, even though he looked slightly older than that because of his self-assurance. He was tall, and handsome in a strong, unconventional way, with dark hair and skin that had been browned by the sun. His face was lean, with a high forehead and strong jaw, and he had an aquiline nose over a wide, full-lipped mouth. But it was his eyes that were his most arresting feature, Kate thought uncomfortably, as his glance rested on her: the irises were deep brown, so dark in color that they appeared almost black. Unfortunately, those eyes were now laughing at her, and Kate bristled.

"Why are you laughing at me?" she demanded.

He gestured toward the breeches that encased her long

legs. "Do you always wear trousers when you ride? I thought you were a boy."

"Hardly!" She stiffened, more uncomfortable by the minute. What had begun as a lark was fast becoming an embarrassment, a prank that had made her the source of amusement. She could feel her temper rising in response, and she wished futilely that she hadn't left her riding habit behind after all. There was nothing to be done about it now; she would just have to brazen it through.

Tossing her head, she became uncomfortably aware again of the tangle of curls about her flushed face, and her irritation increased. She wondered irately why he was still standing there with that ridiculous smile on his face, daring to laugh at her. Angrily she thought that he was rude and contemptible, and she hoped she never saw him again. Ever.

"I didn't mean to make you angry," he said, trying not to smile, which maddened her further. "But I really did think you might be hurt."

"Well, I'm not, and you're bothering me, so if you will just leave me alone, everything will be fine." Turning away abruptly, she made a grab for her horse's bridle. The perverse animal chose that moment to shy away from her, and Kate, enraged at being forced to prolong this embarrassing scene, muttered, "Blast!" She reached out again at the dangling rein.

"Here, let me help."

"I don't want your help! Oh, now look what you've done!" she cried unfairly as the mare reared back from both of them, freeing herself to trot down the hill.

"She won't go far. My horse is tethered in those trees," the man said, pointing.

Kate glared at him. "I hope you're right. I don't want to walk all the way home simply because you frightened my horse!"

Again she saw his amused expression, and she flushed in response. She wasn't being fair in her accusation; the fault had been as much hers as it was his, and they both knew it. That made her even angrier, and she started furiously down the hill. Seconds later she heard his footsteps behind her, and she turned around again. "Why are you following me?" she demanded rudely.

Instead of answering, he simply gestured to the copse of trees where his horse stood waiting for his return. It was impossible not to see the laughter in his eyes, and Kate's full mouth tightened. How she hated being laughed at! Whirling around again, she started down the hill once more. But her foot slipped on a stone, and the next minute, before she could catch herself, she was sprawling ignominiously on the grass.

He was beside her instantly. "Are you all right?"

"Of course I am!" She wasn't; her knee was scraped, but she was determined not to let him know. Oh, if only he would disappear! she thought angrily. First she had made a fool of herself by having him see her cry, and now she had completed the picture by falling flat on her face. She felt like bursting into tears of pure frustration and rage.

"Are you sure?"

There was no amusement now in the dark eyes anxiously regarding her, but for some unknown reason, this made her even angrier than his earlier laughter had. "Yes, I'm sure," she replied, gritting her teeth as she stood. Her abraded knee brushed painfully against the harsh fabric of the breeches she wore, and she was certain that she was bleeding.

He put a hand under her elbow to steady her, but she jerked her arm away as though she had been burned. "I can manage," she said icily.

"Why are you so angry?"

"I'm not angry!" she snapped back, thoroughly enraged.

"Perhaps we should begin all over again," he offered. "My name is Page Taggart . . ."

But Kate had left him standing. Hobbling as little as possible, she went to where her horse stood watching her innocently from behind the other. This time when she grasped the rein, she made sure she had it firmly in her hand; she wanted no repeat performance of the escapade on the hill. She had made a big enough fool of herself as it was.

She was in the saddle before he reached her. Looking down at the handsome face lifted to hers, Kate wished suddenly that she hadn't been so impossibly rude, that she hadn't completely lost her always treacherous temper. But her pride was battered, both by her tears and by her fall, and she refused to apologize. There was something about this man that disturbed her; something in his expression that was unsettling, as though he could read the thoughts she wanted kept hidden. With an unsteady hand she lifted the reins.

"Wait!" he said.

But Kate would not obey. She mistrusted this man who had aroused such confusing emotions within her. She had never experienced this feeling before—wanting to go and to stay at the same time, to listen to his voice, to feel the touch of his hand. She stared down at him for a moment, her eyes wide. Then she spurred her horse forward without thinking. She had to get away from him, away from the spell of those dark eyes that held hers.

The horse, startled by the sudden jab of her heel, leaped ahead, almost unseating her. Grimly she clung to the reins. It would be the final humiliation to fall, she thought; she absolutely would not give him the satisfaction of seeing her take a tumble, especially after she had been so haughty about her ability.

But while she had been thinking of not making a further fool of herself, the horse had taken the bit and was galloping madly down the hill and onto the lane she had ridden up. It was several miles before Kate regained control again, and by that time the spell, whatever it had been, was broken. Tossing her head, she chided herself for running away from him. Who was he, anyway? she asked herself disdainfully. Some young man out for a ride in the country, that was all. And not even a well-to-do one, at that, she thought contemptuously, remembering the old tweed coat and broadcloth breeches he wore. She tossed her head again, trying to dismiss him from her mind as she strove to bring her horse down from a gallop to a more sedate canter.

There was a woods ahead, and they entered the trees at a slower pace. Branches formed a shadowy green canopy over Kate's head, and the mare shied and snorted as a squirrel dashed across the track in front of them. Feeling better, as she always did after a wild ride, Kate gathered the reins firmly and set the horse at a fallen log beside the path. Horse and rider cleared it easily, and she glanced around for a more challenging obstacle. It was then that she noticed the single-horse gig coming toward her in the lane.

Kate's heart skipped a beat. She was sure that the horse belonged to Roger Templeton, and she urged her own mount ahead. At last! An opportunity to be alone with him, without that prim Amelia pursing her lips and acting affronted over everything Kate said!

But Roger was not alone. As the gig drew nearer, Kate saw Amelia Webster's blond and properly bonneted head beside his, and her eyes narrowed. How was she ever going to be

successful in her plans for herself and Roger if she never had
a minute alone with him?

And she had great plans for him; oh, yes, she had. She
would see that he got out from under his father's shadow, she
decided with determination—that was the first thing. She
would make him understand that he had to stand on his
own. He was too kind; that was the problem, and too generous. Roger never wanted to hurt anyone or be the cause of
any distress, Kate thought fondly, picturing his pale face with
its sensitive mouth and mild blue eyes. He had such a gentle
nature, easily wounded by others less kind and tolerant than
he, and Kate had felt protective of him from the moment he
had first bowed over her hand when they were introduced.
His courtly gesture had assumed almost noble proportions in
her mind since then, so that whenever she thought of it,
quick tears rose in her eyes. She had been so lost in grief for
her mother at the time, she remembered, and had felt so
alone. Roger's natural courtesy and gentle consideration had
made her feel less . . . . vulnerable, and he had moved her
more than he knew. She had thought then, and still believed,
that Roger Templeton was a man who would never hurt her,
who would never be unkind to her, or malicious. He would
defend her, and protect her, and she would never need to
fear vicious gossip again. Once they were married, and she
possessed the Templeton name, she would have the prestige
and the respect all that implied, and she would be able to
hold her head high with pride. No one would dare laugh at
her then—or call her mother names. She had loved Roger
from that first moment he had straightened and gently
pressed her fingers with his own, and she loved him now,
with all the reckless passion of her turbulent seventeen-year-
old soul.

And now . . . here he was, squiring that detestable Amelia
Webster about the countryside, too well-bred and courteous
to refuse her his company. Mouth tight, Kate moved her
horse directly onto the path, deliberately blocking the way.

Roger and Amelia had been deep in conversation until the
gig came to a halt in front of Kate. They both glanced up in
surprise at the sudden stop, and Kate noticed immediately
that Roger's pale face lighted with pleasure when he saw her.
She noticed, also, the sudden darkening of Amelia's pudgy
features, and she was pleased.

"Hello, Roger," Kate said gaily. "Amelia," she added carelessly, waving her hand vaguely in Amelia's direction.

Amelia had been well-trained. "Kate!" she exclaimed, forcing warmth into her voice. "How nice . . ." But even her mother's training failed to sustain her as her glance came to rest on the trousers Kate wore, and an embarrassed flush stained her round cheeks. "Why, Kate . . ." she said, in confusion.

"Yes, yes, I know," Kate answered nonchalantly. She raised her hand to brush away the windblown curls from her face, wishing again for the riding habit she had so scornfully left behind. But perhaps the situation could be saved, after all, she thought, smiling wickedly as she leaned forward toward Roger.

"I suppose you're shocked, too," she said, addressing him.

"Oh . . . no . . ." Roger lied gallantly. He cleared his throat. "I think . . . I mean . . . I don't believe I have ever seen a woman wearing . . . er . . ."

"Trousers? It's much more sensible when riding—don't you think?"

Roger nodded feebly, unable to take his eyes from that slim figure astride the horse. As Kate leaned toward him laughingly, her soft shirt outlined her breasts, and he swallowed painfully. He had never known anyone like Kate, not even when he had been at Oxford and more inclined to seek adventure—or say that he did. She made him uncomfortable and . . . nervous. Whenever he saw Kate, he realized dismally that the amorous escapades he thought of with such fondness during his school days hadn't been so exciting after all. Kate might make him uncomfortable, but there was a fascination about her that he had never felt with any other woman. It was an effort to jerk his attention away from the sight of her long, slender legs encased in those impossible trousers and look back to her face. He flushed deeply when he saw those deep green eyes regarding him with amusement, and he thought confusedly that a woman attired in masculine clothing had no right to appear such a magnificent sight. Beside him, Amelia stirred, but he hardly noticed. He was watching, with surprise, his hands shaking on the reins he held.

Kate laughed, that marvelous, catching laugh. "I promise," she announced gaily, "that the next time you see me, Roger, I shall appear the proper young lady. Stays and all," she added wickedly, for Amelia's reaction.

"Kate!" Amelia's cheeks were bright pink.

"Well, women *do* wear stays, Amelia. Unfortunately. As well as pan—"

"*Kate!*"

In spite of himself, Roger chuckled. Even though he knew he shouldn't encourage her, it was difficult not to be amused by Kate when she was in one of her reckless moods. She had such a grand disregard for conventional behavior sometimes that each meeting was like an adventure. He never really knew whether to be appalled or simply join in the fun. She was an enigma—a fascinating, devastating woman, even at seventeen—and Roger often envied the man who would be able to tame her.

Beside him, Amelia suddenly felt at a disadvantage, as though Roger and Kate were sharing some secret that she had only dimly grasped. Staring at both of them coldly, she wondered despairingly why Kate always made her feel so young and . . . stuffy. After all, *she* did all the right things; she was always demure and proper and well-bred and behaved. Why was it that Kate, who scorned all proprieties, should appear so vital, while she and her friends instantly became pale and colorless beside her? It wasn't fair, Amelia thought resentfully, glancing down at her gloved hands folded so primly in her lap. She looked up again, chancing to see Kate's long fingers, bare of covering, stroking her horse's mane, and Amelia's mouth tightened angrily. It simply wasn't fair, she thought again.

And why had Roger laughed? Amelia wondered irascibly. She stared at him in affront, but her glance was wasted: Roger seemed mesmerized by Kate, and totally unaware of her.

Amelia said, more sharply than she had intended, "Roger, it's getting late. Mama will be worried."

"What?" To her fury, Roger looked at her blankly. "Oh, yes," he said hastily when he saw her expression. "I'm sorry, Amelia. I wasn't thinking."

"I know. The time has simply *flown*, hasn't it?" Amelia fluttered her stubby eyelashes at him, simpering when she felt like pinching him to make him pay attention to her. Oh! If only Kate hadn't come along! They had been so happy together, making plans.

Roger turned apologetically back to Kate. "I'm afraid you'll have to excuse us, Kate. I must take Amelia home."

"What a pity," Kate answered, with a gleam in her eye that Amelia immediately mistrusted. "I had hoped that we could all ride back to the Hall together. We could have a late tea, if you like."

"Oh, we've already had tea," Amelia interrupted quickly, daring Roger to contradict her. "Haven't we, Roger?"

"A game of cards, then?"

"No, really, Kate," Amelia rushed on before Roger could answer. Why was she so afraid of what he would say? "I promised to be home early."

"Did you?" The green eyes impaled Amelia with a knowing glance, and Amelia flushed again. Kate waited a moment, then said carelessly, "Well, then. Another time, perhaps."

"Yes, of course," Amelia answered quickly for them both, desperate now to be gone. She turned to Roger. "Roger, if you will . . . ?"

Kate waved negligently as she wheeled her horse around before Roger could signal his own animal. Her laughter floated back to them as she spurred the lathered mare forward, gone in a flurry that was typically Kate.

Alone on the path, feeling as though they had emerged from some tempestuous storm, Roger and Amelia looked at each other in silence. Then Roger smiled—tolerantly, Amelia thought in outrage—over Kate's behavior, and clucked to the horse. The gig resumed its sedate, plodding pace in the wake of the hurricane that had been Kate.

3

Ahead of Roger and Amelia, and only when she was sure they couldn't catch up to her, Kate pulled her blowing horse to a walk. She was out of the wood and into the rolling green countryside, but she didn't see the velvet beauty around her, nor the clear blue sky above, darkening slightly now to

mauve as the afternoon waned. Her eyes were filled with
tears.

Distastefully she looked down at her shirt and breeches.
She had pretended a casual disregard for her attire in front
of Roger, but now all she could think of was how absolutely
feminine and . . . and *proper* Amelia Webster had looked in
the carriage beside him.

It served her right to be caught like that, she admitted,
furious with herself and the situation. Would she never learn?
she wondered despairingly. Was it really true, as Aunt Olivia
so often said, that she acted first and thought afterward, when
it was too late?

She knew it was, and the admission was galling.

"From now on," Kate said aloud, with new resolution,
"I'm going to be the perfect lady. Roger Templeton is going
to ask me to marry him if I have to . . ."

To what? Turn herself into another Amelia Webster?
Kate's lip curled at the thought. Surely she wouldn't have to
go quite that far. It would be difficult enough as it was, trying
to mold herself into one of these dreadfully demure and
downcast young ladies who abounded in this dreary neighborhood. Oh, how she sometimes longed for the excitement of
London, with its theaters and parties and crowded streets
teeming with all kinds of people! Even the noise and the dirt
and the smoke and the grime had been part of it, and she
had loved the city. Sussex and her aunt's home seemed far,
far away from her old life, and so dull.

Dispirited, Kate dropped the reins on the mare's neck and
allowed the horse to plod toward home at a leisurely pace.
She didn't belong here, she thought; that was the problem.
She had lived with Aunt Olivia for almost a year now, since
Augusta's death, and she still didn't belong, and never would.
Her friends in London had all been her mother's friends, far
older than she, and it was difficult for her to find any kind of
common ground with girls who were scarcely out of braids
and pinafores—she, who had been drinking champagne and
attending late-night theater parties since she was old enough
to toddle.

At first it had amused her to see the scandalized and bewildered expressions of the girls here when she told them stories
about her life with an actress mother. But her amusement
had quickly vanished when it became evident that these same
girls, who didn't even know, really, what she was talking

about, actually had the temerity to pity her. Pity her! It was insupportable. How could they, who had lived such sheltered and protected—such *entombed*—lives possibly understand what it was like to have been the daughter of Augusta Beauvais?

Sometimes, when Kate was low or depressed, she could forget the worst of that life and remember only the glamour and the excitement and the thrill of being even a small part of that magic circle, basking in all the admiration and adulation, a tiny satellite circling the star that had been Augusta Beauvais at the height of her career. It was then that she wondered if she wanted that life for herself. How would it feel to be the center of attention, the undisputed queen of the stage, the magnet that drew crowds from all over the world? Did she want that for herself? Could she make it hers?

No. No. Astride the tired horse, Kate shook her head decisively. No, as tempting as it was, she would never want to be another Augusta Beauvais. She had seen too much, witnessed too many painful realities when the fantasy could no longer be sustained, when time moved on inexorably. As much as she had loved and admired her mother, Kate had no intention of ending her life in a dreary little hotel room smelling of the laudanum that brought surcease from pain . . . and everything else. No; she wouldn't be faced with such a terrible choice, she vowed. She wouldn't allow it. She would marry Roger—eligible and rich and very safe Roger Templeton—instead.

"And I *will* marry him," she said aloud again, fiercely, to the horse. "I'll marry him if it's the last thing I do!"

Thus fortified, Kate touched the mare's flanks with her heels and turned her head in the direction of Tremont Hall. As they walked along, Kate began composing the apology she knew she would have to give her inexplicable and outrageous behavior this afternoon. But this time her apology would have more of a ring of truth than the others she had muttered in the past. *This* time, she vowed, she really would keep her promise to act more like a proper young lady. Her marriage to Roger Templeton was at stake, and she had no intention of relinquishing her claim to that puling Amelia Webster. She—Kathryn Augusta Beauvais—had finally learned her lesson. She had set her cap, as the saying went, for Roger, and no one would satisfy her but him.

But as she turned into the long drive toward the Hall, it

didn't occur to her to wonder why she wasn't thinking of the pale, fair-haired Roger—the man of her dreams. As she rode toward home, she was thinking instead of the dark, mocking features of the man she had met on the hilltop, and wondering, with a quick beat of her heart, if she would ever see him again.

4

Kate was so subdued that night at dinner that her aunt watched her anxiously from her position at the foot of the long, polished dining table. It was too much to hope, thought Olivia resignedly, that Kate's quiet demeanor indicated some penitence for her earlier misconduct that day: knowing Kate, as Olivia did all too well, she thought it probable her niece was plotting some further mischief. With an ominous sense of foreboding, Olivia raised the single glass of wine she allowed herself each day. Perhaps, she thought wryly as she tried not to gulp it down, she should increase her daily ration to two glasses. It might be easier, then, to cope with Kate.

Had Olivia realized the direction of her niece's thoughts, she would have despaired of coping with her at all. Kate wasn't dwelling on her indecorous behavior that day; she was recalling how Roger Templeton had looked at her that afternoon, and she was busily planning a way to steal some time alone with him. If only they could be by themselves for a while, Kate mused, she was sure then that she could find some way of encouraging him to forget about Amelia and to think just of her. She smiled to herself at this last thought, absorbed in her fantasy of a compliant Roger so obsessed with her that he wouldn't dream of looking at anyone else.

He was just shy, that was all, Kate assured herself. She had seen the admiration in his eyes today, as she had seen it several times before, and she knew that, given time, she could make Roger fall in love with her. But there was never any time to be alone with him, and Kate's frustration grew as she thought of how handsome he was, with his fair skin and blond hair and light blue eyes.

But it wasn't only his physical appearance that attracted her, she admitted dreamily; Roger had an inborn courtliness and gentle manner that set him completely apart from other young men his age. She could never imagine him being discourteous or harsh, not like . . .

Not like that impossibly arrogant man she had met this afternoon, she thought, frowning as an image of Page Taggart intruded rudely into her pleasant thoughts. Why was it now that she remembered the crisp way his dark hair grew back from a high forehead, or the direct and compelling gaze of his deep brown eyes? Uneasily she recalled the feel of strong, tanned hands helping her, and a faint flush crept up her cheeks as she remembered their brief physical contact when he had held her. His body had been powerful and hard; she had felt it in the strong muscles of his thigh against hers, in the breadth of his chest against her back. Remembering now, her flush deepening, she looked up in confusion when she realized that Olivia had been trying for some time to get her attention.

"Yes, aunt?" she said absently, her thoughts still with that awful man.

"Kate," Olivia said impatiently, "haven't you been listening to me at all? I don't think you've heard a word I've said for the past five minutes!"

"I'm sorry, Aunt Olivia," Kate answered contritely, wrenching herself away from her ridiculous preoccupation with Page Taggart's arresting face with its arrogant and mocking smile. Why was it that the contrast between the pale Roger and this horrible stranger seemed more evident the longer she thought about it? And why did Roger's blond fairness seem to suffer in the comparison? Had this other man bewitched her? Or was it just that he seemed to offer some kind of challenge she couldn't resist?

Kate started, realizing guiltily that Olivia had said something else to which she had paid no attention. "I'm sorry," she said again. "I was thinking of something else."

"Obviously," replied Olivia with asperity, wondering at the same time what it was that had Kate so bemused. She added sharply, "I certainly hope it had something to do with your appalling conduct today."

"Oh, it did," Kate answered meekly. She reached quickly

for the water goblet beside her plate to hide the blush that rose to her cheeks. Drinking, she looked covertly at her aunt over the rim of the heavy crystal, wondering what Olivia would say if she knew about Page Taggart. And then she knew very well what Olivia would say, and, Kate admitted, she couldn't blame her aunt for being outraged at her behavior that day.

She liked her aunt Olivia, Kate thought; really, she did. And often, after one of her "escapades," as Olivia called Kate's misdemeanors, Kate was truly sorry she had caused her aunt distress. It was just that Olivia Tremont, living all her life in this quiet and dull countryside, couldn't possibly understand Kate's restlessness, the boredom that drove her to create a little of her own excitement at times. It wasn't her fault that everyone disapproved of her actions; it was just that she couldn't compress herself into the mold of people whose idea of excitement was to decide between watercress sandwiches and seed cake for tea.

Still, Kate was fond of her aunt, who wore impossibly high-collared shirtwaists and who twisted her faded hair into a tight chignon that was sometimes oddly at variance with the sparkle in her hazel eyes or the quickly repressed twitch of her generous mouth. Looking at Olivia now, Kate wondered if her own temperament would have been more subdued if Olivia had been her mother instead of the mercurial Augusta Beauvais. Then, sighing, Kate supposed not. It seemed she was doomed to be forever burdened with the same fiery temper and curse of pride that her mother had been so famous for. Olivia Tremont, Kate knew, would never have dreamed of donning trousers in the first place—never mind riding abroad in such garb. She was much too dignified, and, Kate acknowledged resignedly, much too inclined to think things through first and act upon them later. Augusta would have found Kate's adventure as much a lark as had her daughter. Which was why, thought Kate now, as she took another drink of water, she was always in trouble.

"Aunt Olivia," she said slowly, putting the goblet down, "I met someone today—a neighbor, I suppose—and I was wondering if you knew him."

Olivia didn't know whether to be pleased or dismayed. "A neighbor?" she said cautiously when Kate hesitated. "Who was it?"

"His name was . . . let me see . . ." Kate knew very well

what Page's name was; she just didn't want to seem too anxious to ask about him. "It was an unusual name," she said musingly, pretending to think. "Page something . . . yes, Page Taggart. Do you know him?"

Olivia did not trust the innocent expression Kate turned to her. But she was distracted by the name Kate had mentioned. Page Taggart. Could it be the same young man? Excitedly Olivia thought that if it was, Page would be about twenty-two years old now. Twenty-two. It was hard to believe it had been that long since she had seen Andrew, Page's father. They been friends once—dear friends. Was it possible that Page was visiting his aunt at Green Eaves? She would have to find out.

Deliberately trying to control her excitement at the thought, Olivia turned a severe glance on Kate. She must remember her duties, no matter how stimulated she felt at the thought of seeing Andrew's son after all these years. "Kate," she said, "you haven't been talking to strangers, have you?"

"Well . . . not exactly," evaded Kate, avoiding her aunt's sharp gaze.

"What does that mean?" Olivia tried to maintain her curtness. It wouldn't do to let this pass. Her niece was a beautiful young woman, after all. That beauty might attract all manner of . . . unsavory characters, and even though this time no harm had been done, she didn't want Kate to think that all such encounters might be so harmless.

"Well, I had stopped to rest my horse and to admire the view . . ." Kate hoped this last would distract Olivia, who was always encouraging her to learn to appreciate her beloved countryside. This time the ploy had been unsuccessful; Olivia sat in stony silence, waiting for her to continue. ". . . and when I looked around, there he was."

"He simply . . . appeared, is that it?"

Kate winced at Olivia's obvious skepticism. Her explanation hadn't sounded believable even to her own ears, and yet that was what had happened. "He was very polite, aunt," she hastened to add, thinking privately and rebelliously that he hadn't been polite at all. He had been difficult and rude and impossible from the first word, and she disliked him all the more for making her defend him to her aunt.

"He . . . he had lost his way," Kate continued, making up the tale as she spoke. She wished heartily that she had never mentioned Page Taggart, but now it was too late. She had to muddle through somehow. "And he wanted to know how to get to the village," she said, unnerved by Olivia's stony silence. "I told him, and he thanked me, and that's all there was to it," she finished in a rush.

Olivia appeared completely unconvinced, but Kate managed to return her skeptical glance with an innocent look of her own, seething inwardly at the man about whom she had been compelled to dream up such lies.

Still, to Kate's relief, Olivia finally murmured, "Well, if that's all . . ."

"Oh, it was—truly!" Kate assured her, gritting her teeth. Why had she ever mentioned his name? she wondered irately; she didn't care in the least who he was, or anything about him.

Olivia was not taken in by Kate's earnest expression. "Really, Kate," she said sternly, frowning down the table at her niece. "In the future, you must be more circumspect."

Wryly Kate agreed this once with her aunt. Even now she felt her humiliation returning when she remembered that embarrassing scene on the hill. It was even more galling to admit that the entire episode could have been avoided if she had followed Olivia's wishes in the first place.

"I'm going to try, aunt," replied a chastened Kate. And this time she meant it.

5

Kate's vow was put to the test much sooner than she expected. The next afternoon, when she was changing her gown for tea—an amenity Olivia expected, but one which Kate found tiresome—she happened to glance out her window. She gasped. The next instant, she was hiding behind the curtain, peering out from behind the sheer panel to watch Page Taggart calmly riding up the drive.

How dare he come to call! she thought incredulously. Why, they hadn't even been properly introduced!

Eyes narrowed, unaware that she had taken refuge in one

of the conventions she so despised, Kate followed Page's progress toward the house. When he was met by the Hall groom and paused to swing down out of the saddle in front of the house, Kate shrank back a little behind the curtain in case he happened to glance up at her window. It would be totally humiliating to have him see her watching him; she could just imagine how self-congratulatory he would feel over that!

But why was he here? And even more important: would her aunt send him away?

Fingers flying, Kate threw down the tea gown she had already selected in favor of another, apple green with tiny pink roses on it. It also had an exasperating multitude of tiny buttons down the back, and as she struggled with them, she refused to ask herself why she was going to such trouble for a man she professed to dislike so thoroughly. If she despised him so, she shouldn't care if he saw her in sackcloth and ashes. Why, then, did she add her mother's strand of pearls and a dab of forbidden scent behind each ear?

Moving quickly to the mirror, she glanced critically at her reflection. "I don't care in the least what Page Taggart thinks," she assured herself, turning around to glance over her shoulder. The buttons marching in a line down her back were all properly fastened; her sash was perfectly tied. Tossing her head, Kate leaned forward again to examine face and hair. "It's just that he thinks he's so . . . so superior," she said, smoothing back an escaping curl, trying vainly to emulate her aunt's smooth—and mature—coiffure. But her hair, while not as red as her mother's had been, still possessed the same crackling life of its own, and the tendrils that framed her face refused to blend sleekly into a coil at the nape of her neck.

Frustrated, Kate stepped back from the mirror. Her eyes were bright—with anger, not excitement, she told herself—a deep jade enhanced by the green of her dress. There was no need to pinch her cheeks for color, for a faint rose already stained them, and her lips as well. The reflection that stared back at her was too vivid, too bold, and Kate sighed. There seemed to be no hope at all of her resembling the pretty and pale girls she had met so far; it was impossible to tone down her high coloring.

But there was nothing to be done about that now, and downstairs that abominable Page Taggart lurked. As Kate hurried toward the staircase, she wondered what her aunt would think of such an awful man. Then she smiled to herself. How thrilling it would be if Aunt Olivia simply refused to admit him! Or, better than that, suppose her aunt actually threw him out!

Olivia seemed delighted with their visitor. Kate saw her aunt's pleased expression the moment she entered the drawing room, and was immediately annoyed. As she hesitated in the doorway, surreptitiously trying to catch her breath, Olivia turned toward her and said with a smile, "Oh, there you are, Kate. Do come in and allow me to introduce Page Taggart. Mr. Taggart, may I present my niece, Kathryn Beauvais."

"We've met before, aunt," Kate reminded Olivia, mistrusting at once the look of amusement in Page's eyes as she crossed the room. What was he laughing at?

Glaring at him, she was about to say something that would demolish him completely, when she was distracted by the sound of Olivia's gay laugh. Astonished, Kate looked at her, forgetting what she had been about to say. It was so unlike Olivia to be girlish that Kate stared at her in amazement.

"Well, of course I know you've met before, Kate," Olivia was saying gaily. "Weren't we just speaking of Mr. Taggart last night at table, and you explained how he had lost his way and you gave him directions?"

Now she knew why he had been laughing at her. But had he given her away? Glancing anxiously in his direction, Kate wasn't reassured by the brief lift of his eyebrow. She glared at him again and raised her chin. As she looked away haughtily, she was annoyed to hear his quick cough that covered a laugh at her expense, and she sat down abruptly in the nearest chair, refusing to look at him again.

Olivia seemed not to notice this silent interchange between her niece and her guest, for she continued on blithely, "I meant, of course, that you should be properly introduced. A chance meeting on the road hardly qualifies as an introduction, does it?"

So he hadn't given her away after all! Why not? Her relief altered instantly into suspicion, and she looked at him covertly. But he was engaged in accepting a piece of cake that Olivia had offered him, and Kate couldn't tell from his expression what he was thinking. It wasn't until he sat back again and she was able to catch the look in his eyes that she realized he knew very well the focus of her concern and that he was laughing at her again because of it. Kate bristled.

"Your appearance is something of a surprise," she said, taking the offensive. She had had enough being the cause of his secret amusement; she would show him that she wasn't to be laughed at.

"Oh? And why is that?"

"Well, I would hardly have thought our chance encounter meant that you were automatically invited for tea," she said, laughing a little as if she were embarrassed for him.

If she had hoped to disconcert him by her attack, the ploy failed utterly, for to her annoyance he said at once, "Our encounter, as you call it, had nothing to do with my coming here today. In fact," he added with a wicked light in his eyes, "you weren't even the reason for my coming here, Miss Beauvais."

"Oh, really?" However much it cost her in control, she was determined to affect a disinterested tone. If he could sit there with that disgustingly smug expression on his face, then she could just as well appear to be utterly weary of this conversation. "How fortunate," she said, yawning. "Since we have nothing in common."

"Oh, but that isn't quite true," Olivia put in happily, as if unaware that her drawing room had become a battleground. Ignoring Kate's murderous expression, she said, "In fact, Mr. Taggart came today because of his father. Dear Andrew," Olivia said fondly, a smile of sad remembrance curving her lips. "We were all children together: Andrew and his sister, Mildred—who is now young Roger's mother, Kate—and Harold and I. Mildred is Mr. Taggart's aunt, and he has come after all these years for a visit."

"Then that means that you and Roger are cousins!" Kate exclaimed before she could stop herself.

"It does indeed, Miss Beauvais," Page admitted, grinning at the look of horror on Kate's face. "In fact, I'm staying at Green Eaves now with the Templetons." He turned again to Olivia. "Father told me how he had proposed to you, Mrs. Tremont," he said to a suddenly blushing Olivia. He smiled. "He also told me that you refused him outright, so he had no alternative but to run away, heartbroken, to America. I can see now why he was so devastated at your refusal."

Olivia was both pleased and embarrassed by the compliment, busying herself abruptly with the tea tray. It was true that she had refused Andrew's suit. But at the time, she had been so in love with the young Harold Tremont that there had been no one else in sight for her. She wondered now how different her life might have been if she had surrendered to Andrew's pleas to marry him. How different and how . . . exciting.

"I don't think that my rejection was as tragic for Andrew as he led you to believe," Olivia said, an attractive pink tinting her cheeks as she looked up again. "In fact, he probably came to regard it as a blessing in disguise. He emigrated to America after that, and it wasn't long before he met and married your mother. Eugenia Taggart was a beautiful woman, I've heard; the toast of New York, I believe."

"Yes, she was, at one time," Page agreed, setting down his cup and preparing to leave. "But even so, my father always spoke of you with a special fondness, Mrs. Tremont."

"Those days were long ago," Olivia said softly. "And now dear Andrew is gone. It's hard to believe."

"Yes. That's why I came to England—to settle Father's estate."

"Ah, yes," murmured Olivia. "Green Eaves."

Page stood. "I've taken enough of your time, I'm afraid. But I did remember Father saying that if ever I came to England, I must call upon Olivia Tremont and give her his warmest regards. I know he would have been pleased that we've met at last."

Olivia rose gracefully from her position on the sofa, offering Page her hand. "I hope that you will come again, Mr. Taggart—"

"Please call me Page, if you will."

Olivia inclined her head. "I hope you will visit again, Page. I would hate to think that your first call is also your last. Perhaps we can arrange a small soiree . . ."

Page bowed slightly over Olivia's hand, a courtly gesture that was not lost on Kate. So he could be courteous and charming after all, she thought with annoyance. But why not with her?

She was so irritated by this revelation that it was several seconds before she realized that Page and Olivia were looking expectantly at her. "I'm sorry," she said, not sounding apologetic at all, "but my attention wandered. Did you say something, Mr. Taggart?"

He nodded, obviously trying not to laugh at her pose. "I

uggested," he repeated, "that perhaps you and I might ride ogether tomorrow. The—"

"I can't imagine why you would suggest such a thing," Kate interrupted. "After all, we scarcely know each other."

"I hardly think that applies, Kate," Olivia protested. "Page s the son of a very dear friend, after all."

Gritting her teeth, Kate saw that Page was clearly enjoying aimself at her expense, and she loathed him for it. "I thought ou might be able to show me something of the district, Miss Beauvais," he said before she could think of any acid comment to make. "My father did spend his youth here, and as I am unfamiliar with the neighborhood, I would like—"

"I'm a stranger myself," snapped Kate. "I hardly qualify as a competent guide."

"Why, how can you say such a thing!" Olivia exclaimed. "You have lived at Tremont Hall nearly a year!"

"But—"

"And of course you're familiar with the main road at east," Page put in cleverly. "After all, you did direct me to he village when I had lost my way the other day."

Trapped in her own lie, Kate was defeated. She couldn't even suggest that as Roger was Page's cousin, perhaps *he* hould take on the task of showing Page around. But even hough she was cornered, she had no intention of giving in gracefully, and her eyes flashed when she said shortly, "All ight, then, Mr. Taggart. It seems as if I must be pressed into ervice as your guide, however inappropriate that is. But I aave no time tomorrow, nor the day after. Nor—"

"Next week will suit as well," said Page, smoothly interupting her objections. "Shall we say Tuesday week at ten o'clock?"

"No, I—"

"Tuesday next will be fine," Olivia said, firmly cutting off Kate's protest with a rare silencing glance in her niece's direction. "And thank you so much, Page, for coming to see ne. It was . . . very kind of you. Andrew was a dear friend, and I am so sorry to know he's gone."

"Thank you," said Page gravely, and with a bow that included both Olivia and Kate, he was gone.

Kate waited until she heard the front door close behind im. Rushing to the window, she assured herself that he was riding down the drive again, and then she turned rebelliously to her aunt.

"I don't want to go riding with him!" she declared mutinously. "I don't know why you insisted I should."

"Stop acting like a child, Kathryn," Olivia responded sharply. "And sit down, please. Pacing back and forth like that is most unbecoming."

Kate, who should have been warned both by her aunt's tone and by the rare use of her given name, ignored both. "I don't like him, aunt," she said. "And I think it was unfair of you to make me ride with him."

Olivia's seldom-aroused temper flared at the sight of her niece's indignant expression. Her headache, which had hovered all day and had only abated during the pleasant tea hour with Page, erupted into a thunderous pounding at her temples. She rose unsteadily, not even noticing the clattering of the tea service as her skirt brushed against the tray.

"Unfair!" she exclaimed in outrage. As much as Olivia detested a show of temper, having endured too much of that during the early months of her marriage, listening to the mother of this maddening young girl, now she couldn't control her own anger. Her face, when she rounded on her surprised niece, was pink, and her voice actually shook. "You dare to stand there and accuse me of being unfair! I can hardly believe even you could be so shallow and unfeeling!"

Taken aback, Kate tried to protest. "But, aunt, I only meant—"

Olivia cut off her niece's protest with an abrupt contemptuous slice of her hand. "No, Kate. This time I don't care what excuse you have to offer, or what explanation you decide to give for your outrageous behavior. *This* time you're going to listen to *me!*"

"But—"

"Be quiet!" cried Olivia. "Against the express wishes of my late husband, I took you into my home when you needed shelter; I fed you and clothed you . . ." As angry as she was, Olivia was still aware that she was being melodramatic, but she didn't care. So satisfying was the chastened look on Kate's face that she felt compelled to go on. ". . . and the first time, the very first time, that I ask you to do something for me in return, you refuse. It wasn't too much, was it, to ask you to sacrifice a single morning of your time to make the son of a dear friend of mine feel welcome? Surely I haven't demanded so much of you that you can object to such a small request of mine!"

Sheer indignation made Olivia pause for breath. "I knew you were willful and thoughtless, Kathryn," she said after a moment. "But I didn't realize you were selfish and cruel as well. I'm disappointed—very disappointed—in you. I tried to give you a home; really, I did. I welcomed you into my house and tried to make it yours, too. And now . . . and now . . ."

But Olivia's anger had run its course. She felt drained and exhausted and more than a little disappointed in herself. It was so unlike her to engage in scenes—especially something as distressing as this—that she was ashamed of herself. It was just that Page had looked so much like his father, she thought; the resemblance had stirred up so many memories . . . so many regrets . . . best left forgotten. Until she had received Page's note requesting an interview, she had believed herself successful in burying all those memories. Kate's stubborn and rude behavior toward his son had, for some reason, seemed like a slap in Andrew's face, and she had responded without thinking. Biting her lip, Olivia looked away.

Kate stood where she was, frozen with surprise and shock. Aware that she was responsible for Olivia's uncharacteristic display of temper, Kate was also uncomfortable with the realization that her aunt had spoken no less than the truth when she had accused her of being selfish and thoughtless. Now that she was no longer so indignant, she was ashamed that she had been so deliberately rude to a guest in Olivia's home and that she had embarrassed her aunt in front of Page. Contritely she approached her aunt.

"I'm sorry, aunt," she apologized in a low voice. "I don't know what is wrong with me sometimes. I didn't mean to be rude and inhospitable, truly!" It was impossible not to read the open disbelief in Olivia's face, and Kate rushed on. "I promise to be more considerate, aunt. Next week . . ." A vision of Page's mocking face flashed into her mind, but she resolutely brushed it away in a renewed effort to convince Olivia of her good intentions. "Next week when Page and I go riding, I'll be proper and polite—all the things you want me to be!"

Olivia, while she doubted that Kate could ever become the prim country miss, was still touched by her earnest ex-

pression. Gently she patted Kate's clinging hand and sighed.
"All right, Kate," she said. "I know you'll try."

"Oh, I will!" Anxiously Kate searched her aunt's face. "Do
you really accept my apology, Aunt Olivia? I . . . I don't
want you to be disappointed in me. I couldn't bear it!"

There was such a stricken look in Kate's eyes that Olivia
hastily revamped what she had been about to say in favor of
a kinder, more gentle approach. "I accept your apology,
Kate—yes. But you must also realize that you can be
thoughtless and headstrong at times, and you must work hard
to control these willful tendencies. If you don't, I'm afraid
you will face nothing but grief in the future. Do you understand what I'm trying to say?"

"Oh, I do—I do understand!" Kate assured her earnestly.
"And you'll be proud of me, you'll see!"

But while she reassured her aunt, Kate was thinking first of
Roger Templeton and his reaction to this new side of her.
For as much as she loved Olivia, it would be for Roger that
she would learn to curb her temper and control her tongue.
She wanted him to be so proud of her when they became
husband and wife that the shadow of Augusta Beauvais
would never come between them. So proud that when the
inevitable comparisons arose between Kate and her famous
mother, Roger would be able to say with utter conviction that
while Kate had inherited Augusta's beauty, she displayed
none of the terrible temper that had characterized Augusta
Beauvais's behavior. Kathryn Beauvais Templeton, he would
say fondly, was every inch the lady.

Kate's promises and dreams about Roger notwithstanding,
she could feel her temper rise the moment she saw Page Taggart riding up the drive a week later. He was hatless—
naturally, thought Kate indignantly; he hadn't even the
courtesy to dress the part of a gentleman!—and his black
hair glistened in the sun, lifting from his forehead as his
horse cantered forward. As annoyed as she was, Kate was
still forced to admire his self-assured posture as he sat easily
astride the horse, and a picture she had seen once of a cen-
taur striding through a woods flashed unbidden into her
mind. For some reason, the image embarrassed her, and she
quickly lowered her head, pretending to stroke her own waiting horse as Page rode toward her. What was the matter with
her? she wondered, blushing furiously. Centaurs, indeed!

But to her increasing confusion, the image persisted, and now she found herself remembering Page's broad shoulders under his brown riding coat, his long and muscular legs encased in polished Hessian boots. She also remembered how light his hands were upon the reins as he controlled his horse with ease, and without volition she wondered if those hands would have as light a touch on a woman's body. Then she blushed again, shocked that she could even imagine such things.

She was still crimson when Page reined in beside her, and she refused to look up when he greeted her from the saddle. "It's a beautiful day for a ride, don't you agree?"

Kate barely managed to remember her promise to Olivia. Her embarrassment, her annoyance at being coerced into taking this ride in the first place, and her irritation with Page for being the cause of such distracting thoughts all combined to make her feel thoroughly out of sorts. Irately she glanced up at him and thought how typical it was that he did not jump down to assist her. What was it about him, she wondered, that immediately set her teeth on edge? One minute in his company, and she could cheerfully slap that handsome face. He really was a maddening man, even without saying a word, simply staring at her as he was now.

"What are you staring at?" she demanded.

He started. "Was I?"

"Yes, you were," she said crossly.

"Oh. Well, then, I apologize."

To her astonishment, he waved away the approaching groom and leaped down to assist her before she could say more. Contrarily, now that he was about to help her, she wanted to refuse his aid. But then she caught sight of Olivia standing by one of the front windows with a pleased smile on her face, and she bit back the tart refusal she had been about to make. Instead, she gritted her teeth as Page took her elbow, and said, "Thank you, Mr. Taggart."

Gathering the reins to hold for her, Page held her arm to steady her as she stepped onto the mounting block. "It seems ridiculous for us to be so formal when your aunt has agreed to call me Page," he said as she settled herself into the saddle—this time a lady's demure side-seat instead of the jumping saddle she had used on her last disastrous ride. "Won't you do the same?"

Kate hardly heard the question. She was reacting con-

fusedly to the jolt she had felt when Page had taken her arm.
Scarcely had she recovered from that peculiar sensation than
she felt another similar thrill as he guided her booted foot
into the stirrup, holding her heel as he paused to gaze at her
questioningly.

Bewildered by the rush of emotion she had felt so unexpect-
edly, Kate gazed back at him. Their glances held, and for a
moment everything seemed suspended in time. They looked
into each other's eyes, and it was as though neither of them
was willing, or able, to break that heart-stopping contact.
Kate felt breathless, excited, mesmerized, as though she could
stare into those dark, depthless eyes forever.

And then, from somewhere beyond the edge of her vision,
something moved, distracting her from her confusing and
complete absorption. Someone asked anxiously, "Is everything all right, then, sir?"

Page started, turning to frown blackly at the groom, who
had apparently been hovering in the background. Neither
Kate nor Page had noticed the man, but Kate welcomed his
diffident intrusion with relief. Bending forward as Page answered the groom, Kate busied herself adjusting her snaffle
rein, and the spell—or whatever it had been—was broken.

Neither of them mentioned it as they rode together down
the drive, but Kate knew that Page was just as aware that
something had happened between them as was she. He still
sat easily in the saddle, but Kate noted with satisfaction that
his hands, which had been so light on the reins before, were
taut now, and gripped the leather tightly. Glancing down, she
saw that her own hands were the same, and she made a deliberate effort to relax. Whatever had been between them was
gone now, and she already knew from bitter experience that
with Page she would have to keep her wits about her. He
might have felt the same confusion as she had before, but
that did not mean he would give her any quarter now, and
she knew it.

"What would you like to see first, Mr. Taggart?" she asked,
assuming her role as guide at once. Somehow, it seemed safer
than allowing this silence to go on between them. "There is a
beautiful old church near the village, or—"

He turned to her, his eyes alarmingly intense as they rested
on her face. "Call me Page," he ordered. "And I'm not really
interested in churches, old or otherwise."

Kate laughed nervously, unable to pretend shock or dismay

in his statement. "No," she agreed. "I really didn't think you would be . . . Page."

Abruptly she turned to guide her horse past a fallen tree branch on the road. This role of guide might be the best thing after all, she thought; at least it would keep everything impersonal between them. There would be no more dangerous undercurrents that she didn't understand if they remained distant and formal.

"My horse is restless this morning," Page commented after they had sedately negotiated a small bridge spanning a stream. "I don't think he cares for this snail's pace."

Kate looked across at the gray Page was riding, and agreed with him. The stallion pranced under Page's firm control, pretending to shy at a shrub by the side of the road, starting at a bird that flew by. Her own horse was impatient as well, Kate noted. Unaccustomed to such restraint on their rides together, the mare was anxious to run.

Kate looked across at Page again, saw the challenge in his eyes, and immediately forgot every promise she had made to her aunt. It took only a touch of her heel to send the mare leaping ahead, and she didn't look back as the horse gathered speed. Behind her the chase was on; she could hear the gray thundering alongside, and she laughed with excitement. Bending forward, she urged the mare to a faster pace.

The wind brought tears to her eyes, loosening strands of hair that whipped about her face. She lost her hat, but she didn't care; it was too exhilarating dashing madly down the road to bother about it. Kate laughed again, in sheer joy.

The horses entered the woods at a furious pace, and when Kate dared to glance behind her again, she saw a grinning Page almost at her shoulder. Laughing back at him, she was about to turn ahead once more when his face changed. His sudden alarm startled her, and she hesitated a few precious seconds, gazing back at him, wondering what was wrong.

"Look out!"

Page's shout propelled her forward in the saddle. To her horror, there was a huge fallen tree directly in front of her, with a cutaway beyond. Some storm had eroded the natural curve of the land here, and the tree, old and dead, had fallen half into and half out of the deep jagged sluice made by the rush of forgotten rainwater. The tree was there in her path, a huge wall of jagged dead branches, menacing and dangerous and . . . inescapable.

Frantically, with only seconds to spare, Kate tried to assess the possibilities. If she slowed the mare, they would careen right into the tree; it was too late to turn the horse to one side. But if she set the animal to jump it, they might both break their necks, for twisted and bare branches poked skyward, and the breadth of tree and ditch was simply too much, even for the gallant mare.

Yet Kate had to decide something; she was speeding toward the obstacle with every horrified blink of her eyes, and in the space of a few seconds they would be upon it. There was no more time for debate; gathering her courage, grasping the reins in both hands, Kate set the mare for the jump.

Even afterward, when there was time to think about it, Kate was not sure how it had happened. One minute she was preparing to jump an impossible obstacle; in the next, she was flying violently sideways as the mare veered sharply to the left, almost unseating her. If she hadn't been such a superb horsewoman, she would have been thrown to the ground by the unexpected running-out of the horse. As it was, she pitched forward onto the animal's neck, losing one rein, forced to grab frantically for a handful of mane.

Grimly she clung to the mare. She had no idea where Page and his horse were; she only knew they were somewhere behind her and that if she fell she would be trampled before they could change direction to avoid her.

Fleetingly she wondered why her mount had veered out, and then, before she could even straighten from her awkward and dangerous position across the mare's neck, her blood froze at the hideous scream of an animal in pain.

Confusedly she looked down, expecting her horse to drop from under her, mortally injured—by what, she didn't know. But that awful sound hadn't come from her horse, and, fighting the mare for control, Kate looked back.

Eyes widening in horror, Kate took in at a glance what had happened, and without knowing it, her voice rose in a frantic cry. "Page! Oh, God! Page!"

There was no time for niceties. Grabbing a fistful of rein, Kate hauled the panicked mare's head around, using her heel savagely against its flank to turn it back. "Oh, God, don't let him be dead," she prayed. "Don't let him be dead. . . ."

She wasn't even aware that she was chanting that desperate litany over and over as she reached the spot where Page lay on the ground. Throwing herself from the horse, Kate closed her eyes to the sight of the stallion and the gaping wound across its chest where one of the branches had pierced it. Bright crimson blood gushed out of the chest, and it stood still, staring blankly around in shocked confusion.

But there was no time to worry about the horse; Page was on the ground in front of her, his face white, his breathing so shallow that she wasn't even sure she could see his chest move. Trying to hold back the hysteria clawing at her, Kate approached. Her heart was pounding so furiously she thought she would suffocate, and yet she made herself move forward. Why was he lying there so absolutely white and still? Had he been mortally injured? Was he dying? Or . . . already dead?

Kate closed her eyes and sank slowly to the ground beside Page, afraid to touch him, and even more afraid not to. Cautiously she opened her eyes again and reached out, tentatively touching his shoulder. He didn't move, and her hand shot back to her mouth. Biting a knuckle, she stared down at him, and knew that she would have to find the courage to turn him over onto his back.

I can't do it, she thought.

You must, came the answer.

He was heavy, much heavier than he looked or she had expected. It was an effort to move him, and when once he groaned, she almost panicked and let him roll back again. Biting her lip, she began struggling with him again, and because she had to concentrate on simply moving him, she lost much of her fear. By the time she had successfully stretched him out onto his back, she was able to take a deep breath and begin to try to assess the damage.

Quickly her hands moved over him—an act that normally she would have found embarrassing, but which now seemed only logical and necessary. Thankfully he didn't appear to have any broken bones, although there was a nasty gash on his forehead near his hairline, already matting the dark hair there with congealing blood. Sitting back on her heels, Kate thought that the blow to his temple might be the cause of his unconsciousness. If it was, she had no idea whether she would have time to run for help before he woke again, and she didn't want to leave him alone in case he was disoriented when he came to. Glancing nervously at his horse, she thought that she would have to do something about the stallion before long, although the animal seemed to be resting for now without too much distress. The blood from its chest glinted in the sun, a clotted mass that made her a little nauseous.

Why had this happened? *How* had it happened? One instant they were racing madly along, laughing at each other; the next . . .

Page's hand came up, grabbing her wrist so suddenly that she gave a cry of fear. His eyes were still closed, his face abnormally pale beneath his tan, but he said, "Are you all right, Kate?"

"Yes, yes, I'm fine," she answered quickly. "But you . . ."

"And my horse . . . is it hurt?"

Kate's glance flickered to the bleeding animal and then back to Page again. She couldn't reply, and Page's strong fingers tightened painfully about her wrist. "Is it hurt?" he asked again.

When he made a motion as if to sit up and see for himself, Kate answered hastily, "He . . . he has a nasty gash across his chest, but it . . . it's stopped bleeding now, so I think it will be all right once it's stitched." She hesitated as Page put his hand to his forehead, gingerly exploring his own wound. "But you," she said anxiously. "How do you feel?"

Opening his eyes, Page tried to smile at her, a lopsided attempt that made him grimace instead. He tried to sit up, but it took a second attempt, with Kate's help, for him to manage. Sitting with his head in his hands, he muttered, "Aside from a thundering headache and a few bruises, I think I'm all right."

Kate waited until he seemed more in command of himself. The deadly pallor was slowly disappearing from his face, and his eyes were no longer dazed. Aside from the mat of blood at his hairline, he appeared almost normal. But there was still the injured horse in the background, and as anxious as Kate was to see to the animal now that Page seemed a little recovered, she still wanted to know what had caused the accident. "What happened?" she asked.

Page looked at her. "What happened?" he echoed. "Don't you remember? You nearly got us both killed, and the horses as well!"

She stared at him. To her, his accusation was so unfair that for a moment she couldn't think what to say. And then she told herself to say nothing; he was probably still dazed by what had happened, and didn't really know what he was saying. Before she could collect herself, he was struggling to his feet, swaying a little as he tried to get his balance.

"What are you doing?" she asked sharply, still smarting at his earlier injustice.

"I have to see to the horse . . ."

He staggered as he took a step forward, and Kate struggled to her own feet. She ran to support him. "You shouldn't try to walk so soon," she said. "I don't think—"

"If you don't want to help, I can manage alone."

His voice was laden with arrogant impatience, and despite her good intentions, Kate bristled at that tone. "Don't be ridiculous," she snapped. "You can't possibly—"

He glared down at her. "I may have taken a bad fall—because of your foolishness, I might add—but I'm not helpless."

"Why do you insist that this was my fault?"

"If you hadn't wanted to race—"

"You wanted to as much as I!"

"I couldn't let you dash off by yourself, could I? What would your aunt have thought of that?"

"Leave Aunt Olivia out of this! I can't believe that you're trying to blame me for what happened! You might remember that I was going to take that jump—"

"Yes, and break your damned neck in the attempt!"

"I had to try! There was no other choice!"

"Yes, there was. You should have turned aside instead of setting the mare at such an impossible obstacle."

"There wasn't time! And besides, she veered aside herself. And you saw what happened! If I . . ." Kate stopped suddenly, only just now remembering Page's horse crowding her mare's hindquarters. It was almost as if it was trying to turn them to the side by the sheer bulk of its body. But everything had happened so fast, one horror blurring into another from the moment she had looked around and spied that gigantic tree, that she hadn't had time to sort it all out. Now she realized what she should have known in the beginning: Page had used his horse as a battering ram, deliberately putting himself in jeopardy in order to protect her. But why had he tried something so dangerous? Had he known that if she tried the jump, she wouldn't succeed? Was his act the necessary gesture of someone trying to prevent an accident? Or was it something deeper, a protective response of a man for a woman?

Kate felt a thrill at this last idea, but before she could examine it further, his impatient voice broke into her thoughts, scattering them in renewed temper at his tone. "Well, are you going to help me or not?" he demanded.

"I can see to the horse," she replied haughtily.

"I can see to my own horse," growled Page, trying to move forward as Kate deliberately held back.

For a moment they were engaged in an awkward pas de deux, Kate trying to hold him upright as he determinedly staggered forward. She could feel perspiration breaking out on her forehead from the exertion, and then, when she felt a seam rip as she braced his weight with hers, it was the last straw. Furiously she released his arm and stepped to one side.

"Oh, help yourself, then!" she cried, when he seemed determined to do without her. Reaction was setting in at last; she felt the sting of tears behind her eyes, and she lifted her chin, vowing not to cry.

Ignoring Page, whose own forehead was damp with sweat, Kate left him standing where he was and strode over to his horse.

It was standing by the tree, muscles quivering, watching her approach with rolling eyes. She murmured something soothing to it, and because she wasn't afraid, it allowed her to approach. The congealed blood on its chest and smeared across one shoulder repelled her, but Kate wasn't squeamish unless it suited her, and she bent close to examine the wound.

The amount of blood made it look worse than it was; she had seen more serious wounds in horse-car accidents on London's crowded streets. She sighed in relief. Softhearted and hardheaded, her mother had often called her, and while Kate never acknowledged the latter, she had long ago accepted the former; she hated to see anything hurt, especially an animal.

Patting the horse carefully on the neck to soothe it, Kate turned to ease off the saddle, which had slipped to one side and was in danger of sliding under the horse's belly. There was a deep slash in the leather, and Kate shuddered, realizing how fortunate both horse and rider had been. The saddle had taken the brunt of the accident, deflecting whatever branch had tried to pierce them. But another inch or so, and Page's leg would have been impaled. Kate shivered again; then she stiffened in surprise.

"Don't do that!"

She looked over her shoulder at Page, hands frozen in the

act of unbuckling the saddle girth. "Don't do what?" she asked, alarmed.

"Don't touch that horse!"

Puzzled, Kate looked from Page to the horse and then back again. "Why not?"

"He's injured, frightened. He might hurt you."

"Don't be ridiculous. You can see for yourself how calm he is now, and in any case, your warning is a little late. I've already—"

"I want you to move away from that horse!"

"Now, look here, Page Taggart!" Kate said sharply. "If you think that—"

The inevitable battle between their two strong and opposing wills might have escalated rapidly into open warfare but for the sound of hoofbeats on the road. Distracted immediately, Kate turned to see who it was, her relief that help was at hand so great that she forgot the quarrel with Page. Now there would be someone else to share the burden of getting injured horse and rider home without further mishap; she wouldn't have to do it all herself. Eagerly she scanned the road, waiting for the new arrival to come into view.

At sight of Roger Templeton's familiar plodding brown mare pulling the gig, Kate's joy and relief were so overwhelming that she almost let out an unladylike whoop. Running out onto the road, she began to wave wildly, trying to attract his attention.

There was no need for Kate's gesture. Roger had seen them and was urging his placid mare into a faster gait. The gig came roaring up to where Kate stood.

"My God!" Roger exclaimed, taking in the scene at a glance. "What happened? Kate, are you all right? Page?"

Looping the reins around the brake, Roger jumped down. He gripped Kate's shoulders tightly in concern, searching her face anxiously. "Kate, are you all right?" he asked again.

Kate felt like laughing and crying at the same time. With Roger's hands on her, she was determined to take advantage of this moment, and she was just trying to decide whether it would be better to burst into tears or to faint into his arms, when she happened to glance at the gig. Amelia Webster was sitting there, all pink ribbons and lace flounces and wide-eyed horror, her white-gloved hands gripping the seat. As soon as she saw Kate looking at her, she burst into tears. "Oh, Kate!

Kate!" she cried, struggling forward at once to step down. "You poor thing!"

Roger, of course, turned at once to assist her, and Kate lost her chance to do anything but glare murderously in Amelia's direction. But Amelia, occupied with climbing out of the gig, failed to see her, and before Kate could think of something to say to retrieve the situation, Roger had spied Page attending to the horse and sped off, leaving the two young women alone. Kate looked after him in total frustration.

"Oh, Kate, are you all right?"

Amelia was fluttering ineffectually around her, her shrill cries drowning out the much more interesting conversation across the way. Kate was able to hear Roger exclaim, "My God, Page, what the hell happened here, anyway?" She had to smile, Roger rarely used profanity of any kind to express himself; he must be very upset to use it now. Straining, Kate tried to hear Page's response, but with Amelia shrieking in her ear, it was impossible. Annoyed, Kate turned toward her in time to accept a scrap of lace handkerchief that Amelia pressed on her.

"Oh, dear!" cried Amelia. "I would leave my smelling salts behind today! But how was I to know I would need them? It seemed so silly, running all the way upstairs again, when Roger and I were only going to Green Eaves and then home again!"

"I don't need any smelling salts," said Kate impatiently. She was trying to fight the urge to slap away Amelia's fluttering hands.

"But of course you do! Why, Mama always says—"

"I'm all right, truly!" Kate didn't want to argue about smelling salts; she wanted to hear what Page had to say about the accident and his horse. Why wouldn't Amelia be still?

"Anyway," Kate said quickly, inspired, "Page would need them more than I. He's the one who was hurt."

"Oh, dear!" Amelia squealed in horror. "Is he badly injured?" She glanced fearfully in Page's direction, as if expecting him to be dripping with blood.

Kate saw her expression, and her lips tightened. "No, he isn't hurt badly," she said shortly. She was annoyed beyond endurance with Amelia, with Page, and with Roger—with the entire awful situation. "It was the horse that took the worst of it," she said. "Come and see."

Half-dragging the protesting girl over to where Page and Roger were deep in conversation, Kate was in time to hear: "The devil of it is that I really think she would have jumped it—or tried. The only thing I could think of was putting my horse in the way."

"You were damned lucky, you know. Both of you."

They began to turn around at the sound of the girls' approach, and as they did, the horse was exposed to Amelia's view. The sudden shriek she gave was enough to startle them all, and by the time Kate recovered, Amelia had pitched straight forward into Page's surprised arms. Sagging a little at the unexpected limp weight of the plump Miss Webster, Page looked up in consternation. "What happened?" he asked blankly.

"Oh, for heaven's sake!" Kate was torn between irritation over Amelia's squeamishness and envy that she hadn't thought of fainting herself. It was even more annoying that both Page and Roger were looking at her helplessly, and she snapped, "She's just fainted, that's all."

"Fainted?" Page looked down in utter bewilderment at the unconscious form he still held. "But why?"

"Well, how should I know?"

"What should we do?"

This last was from Roger, who was almost wringing his hands in despair. Kate uttered an irritated exclamation and wondered furiously why she had to do everything herself. "Here," she said, gesturing toward the ground. "Put her down on the grass. She'll be all right."

"Are you sure?"

"Yes, I'm sure," she answered Roger curtly. It didn't help her temper to see Page lowering Amelia gently to the ground, and when Roger whipped off his tan coat to spread under Amelia's head, Kate wished angrily to herself that the elegant garment would be completely ruined by grass stains.

She had no idea then how prophetic that wish was to become, nor how many times in the future she would recall this day with distress and even loathing. At this time, however, she was occupied solely with Amelia's timely swoon and Roger's reaction to it. Why, she wondered furiously, hadn't she been the one to faint like this? Roger's expression was openly alarmed, and even Page looked concerned as they all stared down at the prostrate Amelia. And Amelia, Kate thought in a rage, had never looked prettier or more feminine than she did right then, lying unconscious on the grass.

Kate couldn't stand there doing nothing. She bent forward when she saw Amelia's lashes beginning to flutter, and she began to slap her plump cheeks with just enough force to sting.

"Kate!"

She looked up into Roger's scandalized face just as Page reached down to stay her hand. "That's enough, Kate," he said.

Kate jerked her arm away from him. "It has to be done!" she snapped.

"Does it?"

Their eyes held, and to her annoyance, it was Kate who dropped her gaze first. Perhaps she had been a little rough, she conceded; it was just that she was so angry. After all, she thought resentfully, she was the one who had been through such a terrifying experience, not Amelia. And now the other girl was getting all the attention, and it just wasn't fair!

Amelia stirred, opening her eyes to look around blankly. "What . . . what happened?" she asked weakly.

Roger dropped to one knee beside her. "You fainted," he said kindly, rubbing her hands. "But you're all right now. Isn't she, Kate?"

He looked up for confirmation, and Kate was forced to nod. She didn't care at all for the sight of Roger helping Amelia to a careful sitting position, and it was an effort to swallow her jealousy. Only the quick glimpse she had of Page watching her intently kept her still when she wanted to rush forward and give Amelia's sausage curls a savage jerk. And as for Roger . . . Kate tossed her head. She absolutely would not betray her feelings of jealousy in front of Page. He saw too much as it was.

Glancing over at him again, she said curtly, "You're bleeding again."

"Am I?" Page took out his handkerchief to mop at the gash, asking Amelia at the same time if she felt all right. Once again Kate felt a stab of envy. He hadn't been that concerned about her, she thought resentfully. Why was it that everyone was so interested in Amelia!

Amelia took one look at Page's face and blanched. Looking away quickly, she glanced accidentally in the direction of Page's horse, and seemed in danger of fainting again. Eyes closed, she clutched Roger's hand tightly and whispered, "Oh, dear. How are we all going to get home?"

"Good question," Page commented, looking at Roger. "Any suggestions?"

"Well, we . . . we could . . ." Roger glanced doubtfully at the gig. The single seat, long enough for two, could not possibly hold the four of them; even three would be a crush. Besides the harness horse, there was Kate's mare, but clearly Page's mount was unridable, so riding home was out of the question, too. "Well, I suppose we could fit three in the gig," he offered finally.

"I guess that's the best solution," Page agreed. "Look, Roger, why don't you take the girls home in the gig, and I'll follow on Kate's—"

"Oh, no, you won't!" Kate objected at once. "Look at you—you're in no condition to ride, and you know it. No, I'll take my own horse, thank you, and go home by myself."

"Absolutely not!" Page said. "What would your aunt think if I allowed you to return home alone?"

"Why are you so concerned about Aunt Olivia?" cried Kate in frustration. "It isn't as if I've never gone riding alone, you know! And this time, there *are* circumstances—"

"I don't care. I won't allow you—"

"Allow me!" Kate's voice rose an octave. "Allow me! Who do you think you are? If I want to ride home alone, I will!"

"No, you won't."

"Kate . . . Page, please!" Roger interrupted hastily as the two combatants faced each other angrily. "Let's not quarrel about this," he said placatingly. "If you'll listen, I think I have a solution."

Page controlled himself visibly, turning away from Kate with an effort. "If you can suggest anything short of tying her onto the gig, I'm willing to listen," he said.

Kate responded to his frown with a haughty toss of her head. But before she could reply, Roger put in quickly, "I really think you should have that gash attended to, Page— and, the horse, as well. Perhaps, if Amelia doesn't mind"—here Roger shot a pleading glance at Amelia, who simply looked bewildered—"you and she could take the gig and tie your horse behind. Amelia's home is much closer than Green Eaves, and someone from the manor could go for the doctor."

"That's all very well, cousin," Page replied, trying to keep the impatience from his voice, "but if Amelia and I take the gig and two of the horses, how are you and Kate going to get home?"

Kate, who had been listening intently, was quick to sense this heaven-sent opportunity to be alone with Roger. And now that everything had been arranged so satisfactorily, she wasn't about to have her chances be ruined by hesitation or discussion. Before Page or Amelia could object, Kate was shepherding them both in the direction of the gig.

"I think Roger's suggestion is an excellent one!" she exclaimed, nodding at Amelia. "Roger is so clever, don't you think, Amelia? Now, you must take good care of Page—he won't admit it, but that was a nasty blow he took. You must see that he gets some attention for it right away!"

"Oh, dear!" said Amelia, confused by Kate's stream of chatter. "Kate, do you really think this is wise? I'm sure you could manage so much better than I."

Kate had no doubt of that, but she said firmly, "What nonsense! Why, the Webster women are known for their courage and resolve—Aunt Olivia told me that herself!"

"Well, yes, that's true," Amelia replied, responding to this outrageous statement with a new light in her eyes and a resolute expression. She didn't hear the quick cough Page gave, but Kate did, and she looked at him daring him to laugh aloud.

"I . . . I suppose I can try," Amelia said, smiling bravely at Kate, who had turned her back on Page.

"Well, then, it's all settled, isn't it?" Kate said, nodding encouragingly.

Thankfully Page had remained silent throughout this exchange, and now, his expression too solemn, he helped Amelia climb into the gig. As Roger carefully led the injured horse around to the back of the cart and tied it there, Page looked at Kate. "Is everything arranged to your satisfaction, madam?"

"I don't know what you mean," answered Kate with a toss of her head.

"Oh, you know exactly what I mean," Page replied. He glanced at Roger and Amelia, who were having their own conversation on the other side of the gig, and then he added, "Perhaps this ride didn't turn out so badly after all, did it?"

Annoyed that he seemed to see through her so easily, Kate

insisted, "I'm only thinking of you . . . and your horse. Why are you so suspicious?"

"Suspicion has nothing to do with it. Common sense does. And that seems to be a commodity in which you are sadly lacking."

"I don't know what you're talking about!"

"I think you do, Kate. And before you play with someone else's feelings, perhaps you should examine your own a little more closely. You need someone stronger, Kate—someone much stronger than—"

An instant before he said it, Kate knew what he was going to say. Betrayed by the fiery blush that rose to her cheeks, she reacted blindly. Her hand shot out to slap him, but he caught her wrist in midair, holding her easily while she struggled.

"How dare you assume to know what I need!" she hissed, abandoning the struggle only to avoid arousing Amelia's curiosity.

"Oh, I know," Page assured her with maddening confidence. "And if you're not careful, I won't be the only one to know what you want. It's there for any fool to see."

Dismayed that her intentions were so blatantly obvious, Kate tried to distract Page by insult. "Then you are a fool yourself to have interpreted mere friendship as something deeper," she said icily. "After all, my aunt and the Templeton family have been neighbors for years; it's only natural that I carry on that friendship."

"Friendship? Is that what it is?"

"Yes!" Why *did* she feel at such a disadvantage with this man? she wondered angrily. It was galling, and infuriating. "And further, not that it's any of your concern," she snapped, "Roger was very kind to me when I first came here."

"Roger is kind to everyone," said Page quellingly. "It's his nature."

"An attribute that is sadly lacking in yours!" Kate shot back furiously.

Fortunately the subject of their conversation interrupted them before Kate completely lost control of her temper. While she fumed and bit back another acid-tongued remark, Roger looked anxiously at the sky and said, "I think we should be away now. It looks like a storm building in the hills."

Kate glanced in the direction he pointed, and noticed for

the first time that the fluffy white clouds of the morning had become forbidding thunderheads moving rapidly toward them. She wasn't worried; she was always exhilarated by storms, but Amelia gave a little cry and said, "Oh, dear, I hope it doesn't thunder. Thunder frightens me so."

Page climbed briskly into the gig, lifted the reins, and while Kate looked on in disbelief, said kindly to the cowering Amelia, "Don't worry. We'll be home in good time, I promise. I never cared for thunder myself."

Kate was too nonplussed at this remark to think of any of her own. She didn't believe that Page was afraid of anything, least of all a storm, and she was about to say so derisively, when he looked at her blandly, promising a proper outing the next time. Before she could reply to that, he had bid goodbye to Roger and signaled the horse. The gig moved off, Page's horse following stiffly, and Kate looked after them with mixed emotions. Why was he so kind—even gentle—to that blubbering Amelia, and so awful to her? And what was it about him that made her want to find out?

Not that she really cared, she assured herself hastily, as the gig rolled out of sight; she was just curious, that was all. Page Taggart was nothing to her but an irritation, a thorn in her side. She didn't care about him in the slightest.

But why was she even thinking of Page when she was alone with Roger at last? After all the weeks of scheming and planning for just such an occasion, the opportunity had dropped into her lap, and she intended to make full use of the little time she had alone with him. And who knew? she thought deliciously: she might even let him steal a kiss or two. She felt a thrill at the thought, and looked across to where he was fetching her grass-cropping mare.

To her satisfaction, Roger's normally pale face had a high color as he turned toward her; it was as if he was as excited and thrilled about this encounter as she was. He led the horse to where she was waiting, and it wasn't until then that she realized she had forgotten to have Page exchange saddles with her.

All her glorious dreams of riding double with Roger vanished abruptly as she stared in dismay at the inglorious reality of the sidesaddle topping the mare. *Why* hadn't she asked Page to put his saddle on her horse? She had been so absorbed in the wonderful fantasy of being nestled in Roger's embrace as they rode home together that she had completely forgotten the practical arrangements that would make the dream come true.

Furious with herself over this lack of foresight, Kate could only smile blankly at Roger as he came up to her with the mare. But behind that smile, her thoughts were whirling madly, trying to find some solution to this untimely dilemma.

"Up you go," Roger said, smiling at her. Cupping his hands, he bent over so that she could put her foot there while he lifted her into the saddle.

Oh, this wasn't what she had imagined at all! How romantic it would be, she thought scathingly, with her towering over Roger from the saddle while he walked by the mare's head. What intimate and teasing things they could say, shouting at each other over the loud clopping of the horse! Kate could have burst into tears of sheer frustration.

"Is something wrong, Kate?"

Roger was staring at her, anxious over her hesitation. "No of course not," Kate said quickly. "It's just that I . . . I'm still a little unnerved over what happened, I guess."

"And no one could blame you for that! You were both lucky it wasn't worse."

"I know." Despite her preoccupation, Kate still shuddered when she thought of how narrowly Page had averted total disaster. She could still feel the mare swerving under her, still hear the stallion's scream of pain and fear. . . .

"Roger, would you mind if we both walked home?" she asked abruptly. "I . . . I really don't feel much like riding right now."

It was true; for once, the thought of climbing into the saddle held no joy for her. Roger's company notwithstanding, Kate was still shaken. The ground seemed suddenly infinitely safer than the back of a horse.

"But, Kate, it's miles to Tremont Hall!"

Kate ignored Roger's protest. "Then we should get started, shouldn't we?" she said brightly. She took the opportunity to link her arm with his, and when she smiled at him expectantly, he had no choice but to agree with her suggestion.

They started off the way she and Page had ridden earlier, but even before they emerged from the wood, it was clear that it was going to storm long before they reached home. The wind rose abruptly, and with it came the scent of rain. There was an ominous rumbling from the dark clouds massing overhead, and as they left the sheltering trees, Kate felt the first drops of rain on her face.

At any other time the idea of being out in a storm would have exhilarated Kate, but now she could only view the dark clouds with increasing dismay. Her outing with Roger, so fatefully arranged, was in danger of being ruined even before it began. She had to think of something to save the situation, but what?

As if his thoughts ran parallel to hers, Roger said, "I'm afraid we're in for it, Kate. Perhaps you should take the horse and ride back to Tremont Hall by yourself before the storm breaks."

For an instant Kate couldn't even think. Her romantic dreams of strolling arm in arm back to the Hall were fast disappearing in another spate of raindrops, and once more Roger urged her to take the horse. He was already pulling the reins over the mare's neck as she watched.

"But . . . but what will you do?" Kate asked, unable to think of a solution to this maddening contretemps.

"Oh, don't worry about me. I can hike across the hills in no time."

"But . . . but . . ."

Kate's half-formed protest was drowned in a startlingly loud roll of thunder directly over their heads. On a sudden inspiration, Kate gave a shriek and flung herself into Roger's arms. Burying her face against the rough tweed of his jacket, she clung to him. "I can't ride home alone in this storm," she cried. "Thunder frightens me—it has ever since I was a little girl!"

"But, Kate . . ."

She could feel him trying gently to disengage himself so that he could look at her. Clinging harder to him, she gave another little cry as the thunder rolled again. "Isn't there some place we can shelter until the storm passes?" she asked faintly. She willed him to think of the hay barn she had seen before, over the next rise. It was an old structure, and abandoned long since, but it would be cozy and warm, and while they waited for a break in the storm, they would be together. And alone. Kate felt a thrill of excitement at the thought, and wondered if Roger would kiss her. She hoped so; oh, she hoped so. Standing here with his arms comfortingly around her was wonderful; having him kiss her would be utter bliss.

But would he never think of that stupid barn? She was on the verge of mentioning it herself when he did.

"I think the old Lawson hay barn is somewhere over there," Roger said, motioning with his head. "It hasn't been used in some time, but I suppose it would serve as some sort of shelter." He grimaced and rubbed a hand over his already-damp hair. "It's better than standing out in the open and catching our death of cold."

"Well, whatever you think, Roger . . ." Kate said, deferring quietly to him while her pulse leaped with excitement. She was so thrilled at his suggestion that she had heard only what she wanted to hear: she hadn't listened to the note of hesitation in his voice, nor had she seen his reluctant expression. Both were mistakes she would bitterly regret in the weeks to come.

Now, though, such disappointment and rage were far in the future. She could feel a trickle of water sliding down her collar as they stood there, and she thought that if she didn't get under some sort of roof soon, she really would look a mess. Already her hair was clinging damply to her face, and she cursed the loss of her hat. Her hair, as heavy and long as it was, still displayed a maddening tendency to curl frizzily whenever it got wet. Another legacy from her mother, who had been flamboyant and haughty enough to use her red curls to advantage. It was only Kate who despaired at the unruly mass of her own hair, which seemed to have a mind and a life of its own.

But suddenly her hair didn't matter. With the horse trotting behind, Kate and Roger raced for the barn as the storm broke in earnest directly over their heads.

6

The barn door hung askew, held upright by only one rusty hinge when Kate and Roger arrived, breathless and drenched, from their mad dash over the fields. Kate gave the rickety structure only a passing glance before ducking quickly under to get out of the rain, but Roger was more cautious. He led the horse quietly in, soothing it when a barn owl, disturbed, gave its weird cry and relocated irately to another, loftier perch.

While Roger looked around for a place to tether the mare, Kate groped her way to a mound of straw on the floor and threw herself down, exhausted. A cloud of dust flew up, choking her and making her sneeze. Her sodden riding jacket felt cold and clammy against her neck, and her skirt was heavy and dripping with mud and water. Glancing down, she grimaced: her boots were ruined from the trek over the wet fields, and her silk shirtwaist would never be the same.

Thoroughly out-of-sorts, Kate had never felt more uncomfortable or unattractive in her life, and as she sneezed again, she felt like weeping in utter frustration. Gone were her thoughts of a romantic interlude while the storm raged over their heads; at the moment, all Kate wanted to do was go home and soak in a long, hot bath.

"Are you all right, Kate?"

Roger had evidently found someplace to secure her horse; right now, she didn't care. "Of course I'm all right," she answered crossly. "Why do you ask?"

"Well, you look so . . . so . . ."

"Miserable? Wet? Cold?" Angrily she tried to brush her wet hair away from her face, trying not to burst into tears at the ruination of all her romantic plans.

"No . . . I wouldn't say that, exactly . . ."

Kate paused in the act of running her fingers through the worst of her tangled curls. She looked up at Roger and saw that he was staring down at her with a bemused expression she had never seen on him before. As quickly as her anger had flared, now it faded away. Her heart began to pound, and she was almost afraid to speak.

"What would you say?" she whispered, staring at him with wide eyes.

Roger swallowed. "Sitting there like that, with your hair loose, you look . . . you look . . ."

He had dropped to one knee beside her, his face so close to hers that she could feel his breath fanning her cheek, could see that his light blue eyes were dilated to the point of appearing almost black.

It was dark here in this corner of the barn, dark and warm

and quiet. So quiet that the only sound she heard was another muted roll of thunder and the rain pattering on the roof and dripping from the eaves. She heard the swishing sound of the horse shifting its weight in the straw, and then there was only Roger Templeton and her own feelings for him as he lowered her gently to the ground.

Even then she could have stopped him, for despite the urgency she felt in him, she sensed a hesitancy as well. She could have stopped him; she *should* have stopped him. But she didn't. And by the time she realized that he meant to have more than a chaste kiss or two, it was too late. The passionate nature she had inherited from a tempestuous mother surged to the fore, and, as her mother had been, Kate was lost. When Roger kissed her, she responded with an abandon that was all the more exciting for her inexperience. A startled Roger was incited even further by her unexpected passion, and he kissed her again, losing himself in his own desire. When he touched her breast and she held his hand there, pressing his fingers against her flesh, Roger was swept away. He hardly knew what he was doing when he fumbled with the buttons of her jacket and those of her shirtwaist. Suddenly her breasts were bare, and Roger was arousing Kate in ways she had never even dreamed of. His lips on her, the glorious feeling of his weight as he slid over her, all excited her to fever pitch. She felt one brief, spasmodic pain when he entered her, and then there was only a pleasure so intense that she thought she would die of it. Clinging to him, she held him against her, and his cry of release joined hers, rising to the rafters of the old barn, where the joyous sound mingled with a sudden furious spate of raindrops against the roof.

It was over too soon. Kate felt Roger withdrawing emotionally from her even before he moved. She had been lying there, the straw pillowing her, in utter contentment, even drowsing a little from sheer exhaustion. When he made a move to get up, Kate tried to hold him there. She could have stayed this way forever, nestled in the straw and in Roger's arms, with the rain beating overhead, and the soft rustle of the birds sheltered in the rafters. It was so peaceful, so restful, after the wild release of emotion and pleasure only moments before, that she wanted to hold on to him, and to the feeling they had shared, as long as she could.

But Roger was insistent. Disengaging himself firmly, he pulled away from her and stood. When Kate lazily opened her eyes, she saw that he had moved off a few paces, and, with his back to her, was busily rearranging his disordered clothing. Dear Roger, she thought fondly; he seemed to be so embarrassed, and why? If anyone should be uncomfortable or ashamed, it should be she, and yet the only feeling she could summon at the moment was a delicious lassitude that threatened to make her fall asleep where she lay.

"Roger . . ." she murmured.

It was an effort to open her eyes again, but when he didn't answer her, she looked up, to see him standing off to the side, staring out the door, nervously twirling a wisp of hay in his hands.

"Roger," she said again, more loudly this time.

He spoke without turning his head. "The storm seems to be lifting."

Frowning, Kate sat up. From her position, she could see a patch of sky, gray clouds scudding across it, and the rain had stopped.

Before she could say anything, he spoke again. "We should get back, Kate. Your aunt will be worried about you."

What was wrong with him? Only minutes ago he had been her passionate lover, transporting her to heights she had only imagined, girlishly, before. Now she knew what it was to be a woman, and suddenly she felt a woman's bewildered impatience at this abrupt change in his manner. After such intimacy as they had enjoyed, she had expected . . . What? A sharing of hopes and dreams as they lay entwined in each other's arms? Yes. The beginning of their plans to marry? Definitely. For surely now that they had lain together, there was no question about marriage. And hadn't his eagerness for her, his desire and passion for her, proved that he wanted her for his wife? Oh, there was no question about it, Kate assured herself, staring in concentration at the man who was to be her husband. He was . . . embarrassed, that was all, she decided. Their lovemaking, as satisfying as it had been, hadn't been right because they weren't betrothed. He was probably thinking that he had taken advantage of her, using the situation they found themselves in to gratify his own desire without thinking of her.

Dear Roger! she thought lovingly. He was such a gentleman, so concerned with the feelings of others! She must assure him that she had wanted this to happen just as much as he had.

Quickly pulling down her skirt and holding the edges of her bodice together with one hand, Kate got to her feet. Her step light, she went to where Roger still stood by the swaying door, and on impulse, she put her arms around him. Pressing herself against him, she put her cheek against his back and sighed contentedly. "What is it, Roger?" She asked tenderly, enjoying the contact of their bodies. Her bodice had come open again, and the rough tweed of his coat scratched her, but she didn't care.

What she did care about was the sudden stiffening of his body when her arms went around him. Puzzled, she let go and came around to face him instead.

"What is it?" she repeated. "What's the matter?" Anxiously she searched his face.

His glance flickered to her open bodice and then back to her face again. He flushed painfully. "Cover yourself, Kate," he said harshly. "Suppose someone came?"

"You didn't care about that a few minutes ago," she teased.

His flush deepened to crimson, and he looked away from her. "That was a few minutes ago," he answered in a strangled tone. "I . . . I wasn't myself then."

"Roger . . ."

It was as though he had to force himself to turn back to her. "Kate, I . . . I'm sorry!" he burst out. Grabbing her hands, which had suddenly turned cold, he dropped them again, as if afraid to touch her. "I didn't mean . . . to take advantage of you."

"But you didn't—"

He overrode her protest, as if she hadn't spoken, saying what he had to say in a rush. "I did. I did take advantage of you!" he cried. "God knows I didn't mean to, but . . . but you were so beautiful sitting there, that I couldn't . . . I couldn't stop myself. Please say you forgive me, Kate! I couldn't bear it if you were to hate me because of this terrible mistake!"

"But I don't hate you, Roger," said the bewildered Kate. "I lo—"

He didn't allow her to finish. With a cry, he grabbed her by the shoulders, gripping her so hard that she winced. "Thank God for that!" he exclaimed. "I'm so glad you don't despise me, Kate. But I couldn't blame you if you did."

Kate didn't know what to say. She had never seen Roger

like this, and she was confused by the change in him, and by undercurrents in his behavior that she didn't understand. But before she could reassure him, he had released her, walking quickly to the horse to bring it forward.

"I've checked the bridle and girth," he said in a rush, allowing her no time to protest, even if she could have found the words to do so. In point of fact, she couldn't think of anything to say; she stared at him blankly, wondering what had happened to the warm intimacy they had shared. He was like a stranger now, awkward and uncomfortable, clearly anxious to be gone from this place.

Puzzled, she looked at him. And then she had the answer.

He was in such a terrible rush because he was concerned about her reputation! He knew that if anyone should see them emerging from the barn so long after the storm had passed, tongues would soon begin to wag, and he was concerned for her. Terribly concerned.

Kate was so warmed by his protective attitude that she didn't even protest when Roger bundled her onto the horse. How wonderful it was to be treasured by a man! she thought lovingly as she looked down at him.

"Kate," he said anxiously, restraining the mare by the bridle, "will you be all right?"

Kate laughed gaily. He was so *worried* about her! "Of course, silly!" she answered, bending down from the saddle in an effort to snatch one last kiss.

But either the horse moved just then or Roger stepped quickly back away from her; Kate was never sure exactly which. Surely the horse had moved; why would Roger deliberately avoid her?

In any event, her lips brushed air, and Kate immediately felt a little foolish over her gesture. She had wanted one last embrace, but Roger had lifted her so quickly into the saddle that there hadn't been time. Now it seemed as if she was going to be denied one final kiss; Roger seemed in such a hurry.

In fact, Kate realized with annoyance, there hadn't been much time for anything but that brief cataclysmic coming together. The whole affair had been rushed, hurried, almost . . . furtive.

"Kate, I'd go back with you to Tremont Hall, but I really should be getting home myself. Do . . . do you understand?"

Perhaps she understood a little more than she wanted to. But she pushed away the thought resolutely, denying as unworthy the nagging doubt that surfaced in her mind. She wasn't going to ruin everything by being shrewish or playing the outraged maiden, she vowed. Roger obviously needed more time than she did to adjust to their new relationship. Because she loved him, she would grant him all the time he needed, without pressuring him. Perhaps he was already planning how to tell his parents he wouldn't be calling on Amelia Webster anymore, but on Kate Beauvais instead! Perhaps he was trying to decide when to tell them he was going to marry her!

Kate looked down fondly, forgiving Roger his preoccupation. She had met his parents only once, but even that brief encounter had been enough for her to sense that the elder Templetons had never forgotten Augusta and her scandalous behavior. Like mother, like daughter, had been their attitude, and they had looked down their noses at her. Truly, Kate thought, Roger's parents were a formidable pair; she couldn't blame Roger for being apprehensive.

But once she was married to their son, things would be different, Kate thought. The Templeton family would close ranks, as such families always did, and she—Kathryn Augusta Beauvais Templeton—would be secure inside. And no one, thought Kate fiercely, would ever dare to condescend to her again!

"Kate?"

Kate came back to the present with a start. Realizing that Roger was waiting for an answer, she said, "Of course there's no need for you to come all the way back to the Hall with me. Look, the storm is passing, and I can certainly find my way home by myself. I've ridden these hills often enough!"

"If you're sure . . ."

Obviously Roger was relieved that he didn't have to accompany her, and again that nagging doubt surfaced. Just as firmly, Kated pushed it aside and asked, "When will I see you, Roger?"

She could have bitten her tongue the instant the words were out of her mouth. Would she never learn? Only seconds ago she had resolved to let him take the initiative, and now here she was, already forcing the issue.

Roger's embarrassment seemed acute. He coughed and shuffled his feet awkwardly, and Kate, her own face flaming, said hastily, "I mean, naturally, that I would be interested in knowing about Page, and the horse. I feel responsible, some-how."

"You shouldn't blame yourself for what happened, Kate," Roger said quickly, relieved at the change of subject. "It wasn't your fault."

"I know," she said slowly. "But still . . ."

"I understand. And of course you're concerned. Who wouldn't be?" Roger said, a shade too heartily. "Perhaps Page and I can visit one day for tea. How would that be?"

That wasn't what she wanted at all. But it was too late now; she was trapped by her own words. "All right, then," she said, too aware that Roger was anxious to be gone. "Any afternoon next week will be fine."

How formal they both were, she thought as Roger suggest-ed Wednesday. As if she cared what day he came to see her—just as long as he came. She could still see the indenta-tions their bodies had left in the mound of hay; her lips still felt bruised, her breasts tender where Roger had kissed her. And now he was making arrangements to come for tea, as if they were perfect strangers. Was he trying to spare her feelings, to make everything seem as normal as possible be-cause he thought she was embarrassed or humiliated by what had taken place between them? But she felt neither of these things, only a wild elation that her dreams were coming true at last. Didn't Roger feel anything himself? She wanted to ask him, but she knew he would be shocked by the question, and he was looking at her anxiously, eager to be gone.

And so should she be, Kate admitted reluctantly. The hour was late, and now that her euphoria was passing, she knew it was past time to ride home.

"Good-bye, Roger," she said, smiling lovingly down at him. "Until Wednesday, then. . . ."

Without waiting for an answer, Kate touched her heel to the mare. The horse started forward, and they cantered away from the barn and up the hill rise to the road. At the crest of the hill, Kate stopped to wave back at Roger. Turning the horse around, she lifted her hand in a farewell gesture that was halted in midair.

From this distance she could not see his expression, but as Roger leaned against the barn door, his face turned away from her, there was dejection in every line of his body. Frowning, sure that she was mistaken, Kate waited for him to look around and acknowledge her, but without even glancing her way, he suddenly squared his shoulders and began walking purposefully the opposite direction. He never once looked back, and even though Kate waited until he was a tiny figure disappearing in the distance, he did not turn around.

Only then, when she could no longer see him, did Kate realize she was still holding her arm high in farewell. Slowly she lowered her hand, her eyes on the place where Roger had disappeared over the hills.

It was a long time, and the rain was beginning again—hard drops that hurt her face when they struck—before she turned homeward herself. Gathering the reins, she sent the mare forward at a gallop. This time, though, there was no exhilaration or joy in her, and for the first time she wondered bleakly, and too late, if she hadn't made a terrible mistake after all.

7

To Kate's intense disappointment, indignation, and outrage, it was Page who came to tea the following week. He came alone, and Kate, who had waited out each day until Wednesday in a fever of impatience to see Roger again, greeted him in a tone that would have frozen a lesser man. Page, of course, was just amused, and that infuriated Kate all the more. She was so angry, in fact, that she abandoned all caution and demanded rudely to know why Roger hadn't come.

Page lifted a mocking eyebrow. "What? Not even a polite inquiry into my health? After all, we did have a slight mishap last week, if I recall."

Kate had the grace to be embarrassed by his comment. Page *was* wearing a bandage—albeit a small one—near his temple; she should have noticed it at once and made some reference. If she hadn't been so upset over Roger's absence, she would have. But then, she thought shrewishly, Page probably didn't even need a bandage at all. Undoubtedly he had worn it just to plague her. It was the horse who had been injured more seriously; she said so.

"The horse is fine," Page said. "You were right—a few stitches, and he is as good as new."

"Thank goodness for that!"

"Yes," he agreed soberly. "Especially since it's clear you are more concerned about him than me."

"As I recall, you were the one who insisted on making light of your . . . injury," she answered, hoping her sarcasm would annoy him. When she saw that it didn't, she finished waspishly, "And so naturally I assumed that it would embarrass you to speak of such a trivial thing now."

"Indeed not," he contradicted with a smile that set her teeth on edge. He touched the bandage. "In fact, I suffered from the most fearful headache for days afterward. I'm only just now returning to full health."

"Then you shouldn't have come all this way just to have tea with me," Kate said nastily. Especially, she thought angrily, when it was Roger she wanted to see in the first place.

"Oh, it was no bother; I wanted to come," said Page airily.

"Did you? I can't imagine why," Kate answered sarcastically. "If I was remiss earlier about inquiring after your health, I haven't noticed that you have displayed a great deal of concern over mine. I was involved in that accident, too, as you so charitably pointed out."

This time it was Page who flushed, and Kate felt a surge of triumph that she had pierced his armor at last. But her triumph was short-lived. *Where* was Roger?

Page seemed to have the disconcerting ability to read her thoughts—and at the most inconvenient times. "We seem to have strayed from your original inquiry," he said. "In answer to your question about Roger, we decided that since he wasn't able to come, I should accept the invitation in his stead, alone. *He* seemed to feel, at least, that I would be a worthy substitute."

Kate refused to be distracted from the subject of Roger's absence this time. Ignoring Page's last remark, she demanded, "But why couldn't he come himself?"

"You seem unduly concerned—"

"Naturally, I'm concerned!" Kate snapped. Then a sudden awful thought struck her. "Is he hurt?" she asked, alarmed.

"No, he isn't hurt."

"Then he must be ill!" she cried, giving away in the next breath more to the perceptive Page than she had intended. "It's the only thing I know that would keep him away!" She had a mental image of Roger tramping through the fields that day, suffering a chill because of the long walk back to Green Eaves in the storm. She was stricken with guilt. If something had happened to him, it would be her fault!

"He isn't ill—at least, not in quite the way you mean."

Page's hard voice cut into her whirling thoughts, his harsh tone like a dash of cold water. Kate looked at him. "What, then?" she demanded. Suddenly she didn't care for his expression at all.

Page shrugged. "My cousin seems to be suffering from some sort of malaise," he said unconcernedly, bending forward to give his attention to the plate of scones the maid had brought in with the tea. He took one, and then looked at the impatient Kate. "He really hasn't been the same since the day we had our little accident and he escorted you home."

It was only with an effort that Kate kept her expression under fierce control. Page had struck terror into her heart with his words, and, aware that he was watching her intently, Kate made herself pour tea. For the first time she was glad of the ceremony of passing cups and plates; it gave her something to do with her hands while her thoughts raced madly behind a poor semblance of calm. She wondered frantically how much Page knew—or guessed.

"A malaise?" she said finally. "What do you mean?"

"Oh, you know—the sort of nameless depression one suffers occasionally."

"But nothing serious?"

Again that keen gaze, and Kate flushed. But she held her ground, forcing herself to meet his eyes.

"I don't think it's serious," Page answered. "But perhaps you would know that better than I."

Kate laughed, a nervous sound of tension that echoed falsely even in her own ears. "I haven't the faintest idea what you mean," she said. "How would I know something like that?" But she was too aware of those dark eyes on her, and she put her cup down and went to the window, where he couldn't see her face. Nor she his. Why was it that his eyes made her so uncomfortable? Was it because he saw too much? Or because she felt so guilty?

No, no; she didn't feel guilty. Why had such a thing even occurred to her? She didn't know what to think; she was just so disappointed that Roger hadn't come that she wasn't thinking at all.

Determined to hide her disappointment from Page, Kate turned back from the window with a falsely bright remark on her lips. But Page, instead of sitting on the sofa where she had left him, was standing behind her instead. Whatever she had been about to say was forgotten as their glance met again.

As before, Kate was shaken by his expression. Her pulse began to race in response, and she felt light-headed. The traitorous thought stabbed through her: oh, if only Roger had looked at her this way!—and then she was horrified to find herself yearning to feel Page's arms around her.

What was the matter with her? she wondered wildly. Only days ago, she had lain in Roger's embrace, so ecstatically happy that she had believed herself totally fulfilled, desirous of nothing else. Now she was imagining what it would be like to be with Page—but this time her imaginings were flavored by her one too-brief experience. Now, instead of ignorant girlish fantasies, she was seeing Page as a woman sees a man, and she didn't know whether to be thrilled or ashamed by the thoughts that raced through her mind.

Confused by her conflicting emotions, Kate tried to look away from Page. She wanted to think of something—anything—to say, to break this pulsing silence between them, but the things she thought of could never be said. The most mundane topics leaped into her head: the weather, how beautiful the garden was this year, how cool the evenings had been, or how warm the days. All eminently sensible—and safe—subjects. But she couldn't speak, and she couldn't turn her head away when Page put his fingers under her chin and lifted her face to his.

The first touch of his lips on hers sent a shock wave through her entire body. For an instant she was too stunned to respond, too caught up in the intense emotion that single touch evoked. But when the pressure of his lips increased and his arms went around her, she began to panic. Some nameless fear leaped inside her, and she knew she had to get away from him before she was lost in the wave of shameful desire that blazed suddenly within her. Her allegiance was to Roger; it was Roger Templeton she loved, Roger she wanted—not this man who stirred up hidden passions in her that Roger Templeton had never touched. Dear God! she thought in frantic despair—what was wrong with her, that she could want two men at the same time!

"Oh, there you are! Dear me, I'm sorry for being late, but there was a crisis in the kitchen that demanded my attention, and so I was delayed."

At the sound of Olivia's voice, Page and Kate sprang apart. Kate was so shaken by what had happened that she couldn't have said a word, but Page murmured something appropriate, and the crisis was past. Glancing covertly at him, Kate was even more confused. Page seemed calm and unruffled; there was no evidence of the passion she had felt from him only seconds before, and she was mortified that she wasn't able to summon the same control.

Olivia bustled into the room, apparently oblivious of the tension. She glanced over the tea tray, frowned a little, and looked at Kate as she went to summon the maid. "Kate, dear, you really should have asked for another plate . . ."

Olivia paused, noticing for the first time that Page had come in Roger's place. "But I thought you said Roger Templeton was coming for tea," she said, addressing Kate.

"Roger was . . . indisposed," Page answered smoothly.

"Oh, dear, I hope it isn't serious," murmured Olivia as she took her place on the sofa.

Page glanced at Kate, who flushed. "We were just discussing that," he said. "I assured Kate that my cousin was in no imminent danger, but I believe she wanted to rush off, bearing broth and a soothing . . . er . . . manner to our invalid."

The mocking tone had returned to his voice, and Kate looked at Page in angry confusion. Where was the emotion that had vibrated between them? How could he act this way now, as if nothing had happened? Kate couldn't understand him, and because she felt like a fool who had only been imagining things, she reacted haughtily, trying to salvage her pride. "Don't be absurd!" she said coldly. "I merely expressed a natural concern for a friend."

If Olivia had been oblivious of the atmosphere before, she was certainly aware of the tension now. "Well, I'm glad it isn't serious," she said uncertainly. She didn't understand Kate's fiery expression, nor the sudden frown that crossed Page's face. But she was quick to sense that her niece was either close to tears or near to losing her temper—or both—and now she added quickly, "Won't you have another cup of tea, Page, and perhaps one more biscuit?"

There was something infinitely comforting about such commonplace ceremonies, Olivia thought as she passed a cup to the reluctant Page. One simply could not sustain an excess of emotion while balancing cup and saucer, and while Olivia didn't know what had caused this strain between Kate and Page, at least she had managed to distract them momentarily as they came forward to join her.

Lifting her own cup, Olivia glanced at Page over the rim and contemplated what sort of husband he would make for her volatile niece. It wouldn't be a bad match at all, reflected Olivia, passing the newly arrived plate of biscuits to the studiously polite Page and the thunderous Kate. He was a strong man—strong enough even for her willful niece, who was so drearily infatuated with that pallid Roger Templeton. Roger would bend before Kate's temper, but Olivia knew that Page would give until it no longer suited him, and then he would stand against her.

It was quite obvious, then, Olivia decided, that Roger was not the man for Kate and never would be. As much as it galled her to admit it, Maude had been right from the start: Roger Templeton would be the pérfect husband for the prim Amelia. Page Taggart, on the other hand, would be more than equal to the challenge that Kate represented. Their relationship might be tempestuous and stormy, but it would certainly never be boring, Olivia thought wryly; she could just imagine the raging quarrels that would resound throughout such a marriage. Oh, how exciting it would be, and how alive!

The only complication, thought Olivia now as she looked across again at Page, might be Page himself. For it was obvious that he cared a great deal for Kate—no, more than that, Olivia conceded, watching him. Page Taggart was head over heels, as the saying went, and Olivia wondered if he already loved Kate far too much for his own good . . . or hers.

8

Over the next few weeks, an alternately troubled and elated Olivia kept her own counsel about Page. If Kate had known what her aunt was thinking, she would have laughed derisively. Page Taggart in love with her? The very idea was absurd! On the contrary, she would have said: he seemed to take fiendish delight in provoking her at every opportunity, whether it was a musical evening at the Websters', or tea with Olivia, or following her when she wanted to ride alone. It seemed that he was always *there*, an unwelcome intrusion when she preferred to be by herself. They ended every encounter, accidental or otherwise, by quarreling, and Kate often thought there was nothing between them but animosity. She was content to have it that way, too. Page Taggart annoyed her, aggravated and irritated her; they had nothing in common, and never would. She disliked him intensely, and yet, as much as she tried to drive him away by sarcasm or rudeness or sheer bad temper, he continued to plague her— amusing himself, Kate would think furiously, at her expense.

And so, while Kate would have laughed scornfully at the idea of Page being in love with her, her laughter would have had a hysterical edge. It had been six weeks since the day she and Roger had sheltered from the storm, and something was terribly, hideously, irrevocably wrong.

At first she had put down her nausea to the berries in curdled cream she had eaten, or the extra portion of trifle, or the rich pudding she had overindulged in. But when she became ill at the very sight of her morning chocolate, a horrible suspicion began to surface. The day came when her waistline had thickened just enough so that she could no longer fit comfortably into her riding habit, and Kate knew she couldn't deny the evidence any longer.

Her face crumpling as she looked at her reflection in the mirror, Kate burst into tears and threw herself across the bed, weeping bitterly as she was forced to admit, finally, what she had been avoiding all these weeks.

What was she going to do?

In despair, she remembered all the times during these weeks when she had tried to see Roger—a Roger who was suddenly curiously, unavailable. Olivia had been amazed, Kate knew, when her niece had blossomed overnight into a social butterfly; Kate, who had scorned previous invitations, had begun to press her aunt to accept any that came. Olivia, of course, was delighted at this change, however inexplicable; she had long wanted her niece to make friends of the young people in the neighborhood, and she couldn't be happier to oblige Kate in her request. What Olivia didn't know was that Kate's sudden social whirl was brought on by desperation.

When Roger had failed to come that Wednesday afternoon for tea, Kate had been upset but not actively worried. But as time went on and she neither saw nor heard from Roger, her pique became concern, and then disquiet, and finally pure anxiety. Was Roger deliberately avoiding her? It seemed so, since he had not attended Abigail Wharton's soiree, and he had been noticeably absent from Maude Webster's musicale, an event Kate was sure he would attend, if only because of Amelia. But while Page had been maddeningly present at both functions, Roger had not been seen at all. And the most Kate could get out of Page without arousing his suspicions completely was that Roger was still suffering from that mysterious "malaise" that, to Kate, was becoming more dubious by the minute.

She had even taken to riding past Green Eaves lately, in the hope that she could catch a glimpse of Roger, but that ploy, too, had failed utterly. So far she hadn't dared to ride directly to the house and demand to see him, but now she knew she must take matters into her own hands and find a way to see him without delay. Already she had waited too long, and she could not, she *would* not, take the chance that someone would point to this child and whisper the same things about it that had been whispered about her. Augusta might not have cared, might even, in fact, have been amused by charges of her daughter's illegitimacy, but Kate cared; oh, yes, she did. She might have been thoughtless and indiscreet—wanton, even—that day with Roger, but their child was not going to suffer for it as she had done.

Kate cried until she was exhausted. Then, still shaking with the aftermath of her emotional storm, she put one arm across her eyes and rolled over onto her back, staring up at the ceiling. What was she going to do? She couldn't stay here weeping day after day; that would solve nothing.

Nor, she admitted, could she simply ride over to Green Eaves and ask to see the father of her child; she could just imagine the uproar that would ensue over that! No, there must be other courses she could pursue first, before such drastic measures were considered.

An idea occurred to her just then, and she wondered why she hadn't thought of it sooner. Throwing herself off the bed, she ran to the escritoire by the window. She rarely used the desk, being too impatient to sit for long hours as her aunt liked to do, writing letters or adding entries to her daily journal, but now she eagerly seized the stationery there. The inkwell was full, and snatching up a pen, Kate dipped the nib and bent to write.

But what was she going to say?

Hand hovering over the blank paper, Kate debated. She couldn't very well write to Roger that she suspected the worst from their liaison in the barn; anyone reading that would know instantly what she meant. And despite her earlier fantasy about riding up to Green Eaves and demanding to see her child's father, she knew it was just that: fantasy. She had no intention of anyone else discovering her secret, even after she and Roger were married. She would think of some excuse to explain the early arrival of the child, and no matter what anyone said or questioned, she would not deviate from that story. Whatever she decided, no one would ever know the truth.

But there was still this problem to be faced, and Kate nibbled on the end of the pen as she considered. She could invite Roger for tea, she thought. Then she rejected the idea. More than anything else, she wanted to avoid arousing suspicion, and an invitation from her and not from her aunt would certainly raise a few eyebrows in this community where the old rules still applied. Proper young ladies here did not invite young gentlemen for tea, even in dire emergencies. No, she would have to think of something else, she realized, for even if she dared issue an invitation of her own, there was always the possibility—no, the likelihood, Kate corrected herself crossly—that Roger would not come alone for tea. If she knew Page—and she did, all too well now—he would think nothing of assuming the invitation from her included himself as well.

"Damn that man!" exploded Kate, throwing down the pen in a fury. It hit the paper squarely and rolled to the back of the desk, leaving behind a wavering trail of ink. Kate exclaimed impatiently and reached for something to blot up the mess. Scrubbing away furiously, she wondered why Page had to visit his cousin now, at such an inopportune time. Why couldn't he have stayed in America where he belonged, and left her to pursue her plans in peace? If it hadn't been for him, she wouldn't be in the fix she was now.

Angrily she wadded up the ink-stained cloth and threw it away. Then, picking up the pen again, she selected a fresh sheet of paper and scribbled a few lines. Propelled by her anger at Page, Kate sanded what she had written and read the brief message defiantly. It stated simply, if a little imperiously, that she must see Roger alone about a matter of utmost importance. It was a dangerous demand, she realized, but there was no help for it; it would have to do.

Sealing the note, Kate thought that the only problem now was finding a way to send it to Roger. Frowning, she considered. One of the Hall's downstairs maids had a sister who was in service at Green Eaves, she remembered. She would ask the girl to take the note, pay her well, and hope that she was romantic, if not discreet.

The maidservant, whose name was Dolly, was indeed a romantic. Promising utter secrecy, she took the note that night. She had to go visit her sister anyway, she assured Kate with shining eyes and a barely repressed air of excitement. She would leave directly after supper, when her work was done.

Kate watched her go that night from an upstairs window. Dolly left by the kitchen door, walking with her head high, filled with such secret importance that Kate had to smile. Turning away as the girl disappeared into the night, Kate thought exultantly that she had solved a difficult problem with a minimum of fuss, and she began calculating how long it would take Roger to reply. Undressing for bed later, Kate was able to sleep well for the first time in weeks. Tomorrow afternoon at the latest, she thought drowsily, Roger Templeton would be beating down the door, anxiously demanding to know what was wrong.

9

Kate waited a week for a reply, or even a sign from Roger that he had received her message. After passing another two days in a taut state of nerves, Kate could no longer convince herself that he was just waiting for an opportune time to reply. Knowing how reckless it was, and not caring how she exposed herself, Kate finally summoned Dolly. She couldn't restrain her impatience any longer.

Wide-eyed, the girl entered the sitting room, where Kate had been waiting by the French doors, staring blankly out at the garden. Thinking that attack might catch the maid off-guard, Kate asked, without turning, "Why didn't you deliver the message I sent to Green Eaves?"

Dolly's face was ashen when Kate turned around and stared at her. The girl was only twelve years old, and the imperious Kate frightened her. "But I . . . I did, miss," Dolly stammered. "I did deliver it, just like you said."

"Are you positive?"

Was she positive? Yes, yes, of course she was. She had thought it so romantic then, delivering a secret message to the young master at Green Eaves, that she had hurried over that very same night, when her work was done. She had been tired, exhausted, she remembered, after fourteen hours on her feet, but it had been worth it, feeling—even for a moment—a part of the intrigue that surrounded the gentry, and especially the young miss. She had heard stories—oh, yes, she had heard stories. . . . But of course she couldn't tell Kate all this; she could only stand there terrified as Kate repeated her question, more harshly this time. "Well? Are you positive or not? Answer me!"

"Yes, yes, I'm sure I took it," Dolly answered in a rush. "I took it that night, like you said. On me own time, too, it was. I didn't go to Green Eaves until my work was done for the day, you can be sure of that." As eager as she was to please

69

Kate, Dolly was just as anxious to avoid angering Olivia Tremont, who employed her and treated her so well. The work might be hard, but the mistress was fair, and that was more than Dolly could say for other places, Green Eaves among them.

"And to whom did you give it?"

Dolly started at the curt question. Kate was staring at her coldly, and Dolly began to believe that something was very wrong, and worse, that she would somehow be blamed for it. What had started out as such a romantic adventure was quickly taking on a nightmarish quality, and Dolly didn't know what was expected of her or what to say.

Fighting back tears, the maid answered as best she could. "I gave it to my sister, miss. That was what you wanted, wasn't it? And she was to give it to the young master when . . . whenever she could slip it to him. On the sly, so to speak."

"I never said there was anything sly about that note!"

Dolly flinched at that tone, and wrung her hands. What was it that the young miss wanted her to say? she wondered desperately, trying not to cry.

Dolly didn't know that while she was trying to contain her tears, across the room from her Kate was battling for her own composure. If the maid spoke the truth, and Kate suspected that Dolly was too frightened of her not to, why hadn't Roger answered her? Thoughts racing, she considered; then felt a rush of fear as a horrible possibility occurred to her. What if Roger had no intention of answering her at all? Suppose he had received her note and had deliberately ignored it?

No, no, she was being absurd, letting her imagination run away with her because she was so anxious to see him. There had to be an explanation; there had to be.

Fixing the maid again with an angry stare, Kate said accusingly, "Well, if I'm to believe you, and you did give that note to your sister, then it was she who simply forgot to give Ro . . . Mr. Templeton the message."

As frightened as she was, Dolly immediately leaped to her sister's defense. Jane was only ten years old; she had been in service just under a year, and a slur like this could follow her the rest of her life, ruining her chances to make something of herself. And Dolly simply wasn't going to allow that to happen. Hadn't she worked hard herself, searching for the same opportunity? She wanted to be a nursemaid someday, and Jane—Jane had decided to become a lady's maid. Dolly was in awe of such ambition, and she knew she had to defend her sister, even at the expense of her own future.

"No, miss," Dolly stated, her voice trembling only slightly. "I know Jane wouldn't forget. Why, it would be worth her place not to remember something like that. She's only ten years old, but she's honest, and she wants to make something of herself." Dolly shook her head decisively, terrified at the same time that she had gone too far. But she couldn't stop now; there was Jane to think of. Trying not to see Kate's fiery expression, Dolly added positively, "Jane wouldn't forget, miss. You can be sure of that."

There was a silence in which Dolly did not dare look up from her riveted attention on the floor. She didn't see the variety of emotions that crossed Kate's face, nor Kate's sudden realization that she had only made matters worse by questioning Dolly so closely. Now, thought Kate bleakly, in addition to her other worries was one more: what would she say to her aunt if Olivia learned she had been sending smuggled messages to Green Eaves? How could she explain, without going into all the rest?

Groaning inwardly, Kate decided it was futile to pursue the subject. "All right, then," she said as severely as possible. "You may go."

She dismissed the confused and vastly relieved Dolly with a lift of her hand, and Dolly skipped out without another word, closing the door gratefully behind her. Kate stood where she was by the window, hugging her arms about her in despair. What was she going to do now?

A sense of urgency drove her, for she knew that the danger of discovery grew the longer she delayed. Somehow, she must find a way to impress Roger with that same urgency so they could make their plans. But how, when he hadn't come to see her?

Driving away the insidious thought that Roger had received her note and had chosen to ignore it, Kate forced herself to think of the practical instead. The primary opposition to their betrothal would come from his family, she was sure. Her aunt might object initially, but Kate hoped Olivia would be swayed by the assurance that her niece loved Roger and would consider no other. Mildred and John Templeton would be another matter altogether, and Kate grimaced at the thought of facing that formidable pair. Perhaps, she thought, she should leave that detail to Roger. She would only make things worse by losing her temper, which she was sure to do when the Templetons condescended to her, an act that was inevitable, no matter how she wished it were not.

But there was still the more immediate problem to be solved, and that was how to contact Roger. Frowning in concentration, Kate considered her few alternatives. Since Roger hadn't come to see her, and since sending the note had failed, there was only one thing left to do: she would have to ride over to Green Eaves herself.

Now that she had decided what to do, the idea became more attractive by the minute. It would be worth defying convention to see him now, without having to worry about errant messages or waiting for him to come to her. When she told him what she had to tell him, she had no doubt that he would act immediately, and once Roger took matters into his own hands, she could set aside this burden of responsibility and guilt that weighed more heavily on her with each day that passed. With Roger by her side, she could face anything.

And with luck, she thought as she went quickly upstairs to change, in seven months' time she could think of a convincing excuse to explain the new, and premature, Templeton infant. She only hoped that the senior Templetons would be so besotted by their first grandchild that they wouldn't care what excuse their daughter-in-law offered for its early arrival.

"Kate, is that you? Oh, Kate . . . you'll never guess!"

Kate paused at the head of the stairs, one hand on the rail. Olivia stood at the foot of the staircase, excitedly waving something at her, and in that instant Kate had a terrible premonition. The feeling of impending disaster was so strong that she trembled, and it was an effort for her to free the hand that seemed suddenly to be frozen to the banister.

"What is it?" She heard her voice with surprise. Instead of calling to Olivia in the harsh croak she had half-expected, she sounded almost normal.

But Olivia seemed not to notice Kate's white face, nor the stiff way she held herself as she slowly descended the stairs in response to Olivia's summons. When Kate reached her, Olivia thrust the heavily embossed and gilded announcement at her. "Read this!" she exclaimed. "It was just delivered. What do you think of . . . ? Kate, are you all right? You look as if you've seen a ghost! What is it?" Frowning anxiously, Olivia looked from Kate to the announcement she held, and then back to Kate's face again. "Oh, Kate! You didn't really think that Roger . . . that he would . . . ? Oh, dear, I'm so sorry . . ."

But Olivia's stammering voice was only a buzz in Kate's ear. She knew that her aunt was speaking to her, but she couldn't quite make out the words. There was a humming sound inside her head, and she felt dizzy. But it didn't matter; nothing mattered except her refusal to surrender to the blackness gathering behind her eyes. She would concentrate on fighting that instead of Roger's betrayal, and then maybe by the time this horrible faintness passed, she would have regained some semblance of control again.

Later, she thought; later, when she was calm and could reason clearly without feeling so utterly panic-stricken, she would think about the betrothal of Roger and Amelia Webster and what it meant to her. Right now, it was all she could do to stand here without falling to the floor in a dead faint.

"Kate, why don't we go into the drawing room?" she heard Olivia ask anxiously. "I'll ring for tea, if you like."

Tea! As if tea would soothe her! As if anything in the world would comfort her at this moment when her world had shattered at her feet!

Dazedly Kate looked at her aunt. They were almost the same height, and she could easily read the compassion and sympathy in Olivia's eyes. She looked away again, knowing that if she held Olivia's concerned glance, she would surrender to the terrible urge she felt to break into unrestrained sobbing. The desire to cry, to weep, to scream, almost strangled her; she felt as though a hand had closed tightly around her throat, a hand she had to claw away so that she could breathe again. She felt faint and weak and ill all at the same time, and she wondered how Roger could have done this to her. How could he have done such a terrible thing?

"Kate? Kate, please . . ."

Olivia was pulling gently at her arm, trying to lead her into the drawing room. Listlessly Kate tried to resist. "No, thank you, aunt. I . . . I really don't feel like having any tea just now, if you don't mind."

"Nonsense. A good strong cup is exactly what you need," Olivia said firmly. "And after that, we'll have a talk."

Kate had no will to refuse a second time. The tea service

appeared as if by magic, and Kate dutifully sipped at the hot, strong beverage Olivia brewed as she huddled in the high wing-back chair her aunt had guided her to.

There was no fire burning in the delicate marble fireplace, and Kate, who normally wouldn't have noticed during the day, now felt a chill, and shivered. It seemed that even the steaming tea could not warm her, and she felt like bursting into hopeless tears again. Closing her eyes tightly, Kate willed control.

Olivia had seated herself across from her. Now she reached over and put her hand on Kate's arm. "Kate," she said quietly, "I think we should discuss this, don't you?"

Kate knew that what little control she had summoned was too brittle to sustain for long. A vast, horrible emptiness had opened up inside her, and while Olivia was trying her best to be understanding, Kate realized it would be impossible to discuss feelings and emotions she hadn't sorted out herself. Was she ready to share her secret with Olivia? She wasn't sure that she could burden her aunt, and yet . . . Looming like a giant black presence at the edge of her mind was the question: what was she going to do? *What was she going to do?*

"Kate?"

Kate tried to pull herself together. Very carefully she said, "I'm sorry, aunt. But there really isn't anything to discuss."

Olivia was silent a moment. Then she said, "I think there is, Kate. Your reaction was . . . extreme. I thought for a moment that you might actually faint from shock."

Kate tried a laugh, a high, thin sound that was all nerves, and she knew it. "I admit I was surprised—no, more than surprised," she amended when Olivia looked askance at her. "I . . . I suppose I was stunned. Yes, that's it: stunned. I . . . I never thought of Amelia Webster as a choice for Roger."

Olivia glanced down at the cup she held, avoiding Kate's pleading glance until she could think of a reply that wouldn't hurt Kate too much. Kate might not have considered Amelia as a wife for Roger, Olivia thought sadly, but others had. Oh, yes; everyone else had. Including herself. But how to tell Kate? How to comfort her, support her, through this obvious blow?

"I'm sure the Templetons and the Websters had the match arranged for quite some time," Olivia said at last. "Perhaps even before you came here, Kate."

Olivia was unprepared for the violent start Kate gave. So

agitated was her reaction that the cup she had been holding clattered against the saucer and fell over, spilling tea in all directions.

"Oh!" Olivia jumped up and grabbed a napkin, trying to blot the stain that had spread across Kate's skirt to the brocade of the chair. "Kate!" she exclaimed, trying to restrain her impatience when Kate seemed not to notice what she had done. She sat there, absolutely still, her face blank, while Olivia scrubbed fruitlessly at the chair arm. Olivia felt a chill at the empty expression on her niece's face, and she paused, saying sharply, "Kate, are you all right?"

Kate started again at Olivia's tone, but to her aunt's relief, the emptiness faded from her eyes. Turning in the chair, she looked searchingly into Olivia's face. "Do you really think it was all arranged before I came to the Hall? Roger's betrothal to Amelia? Was it all decided before Roger even met me?"

Olivia didn't care for the underlying tone of hysteria in Kate's voice. She also didn't like it that her eyes seemed enormous, wide and staring in her white face. Her entire manner was one of desperation, and Olivia didn't know what to say. The right response was crucial, but what was it? Should she tell the truth? Or should she fabricate a lie, hoping to soothe Kate and bring some color back to her strained face?

"Why, I'm not sure, Kate," Olivia said slowly, trying to collect her scattered thoughts. What was it Maude had said on the veranda that day so long ago? Olivia couldn't remember. "I suppose it was arranged for quite some time," she continued cautiously, watching Kate as she spoke. "These things usually are."

"Yes, they are, aren't they? And sometimes the participants have nothing to say about it, do they? It's . . . it's almost like a business proposition, isn't it?"

Kate's rapid-fire questions disconcerted Olivia. But she saw with relief that some animation had returned to her face, and with it, a hint of her normal color. "Yes, business concerns sometimes initiate a match," Olivia admitted. "As do financial arrangements or family alliances. But, Kate," she pointed out, "there are also other reasons."

"What reasons?" demanded Kate.

Olivia hesitated again. But she knew what had to be said, and so she said it very gently. "Roger and Amelia could be in love," she suggested.

"In love!" Kate's laugh was utterly scornful this time.

"How could any man in his right mind fancy himself in love with Amelia Webster? Why, she's nothing but a pudding-faced little prig!"

"Kate!" As sympathetic as Olivia was, she could not allow Kate's remark to go unchallenged. "That was an uncharitable remark," she said severely. "And not worthy of you at all."

For once, it was a relief to see Kate become rebellious. Olivia thought for an instant that her niece might fly into a tantrum, and she had to admit that at this point such a display would be almost welcome. Anything would be better than seeing Kate so white-faced and taut, like a wire stretched to the breaking point. But although two spots of color burned still in Kate's cheeks, and her expression was mutinous, she muttered, "All right, then. I'm sorry."

"Thank you." Olivia inclined her head, thankful that another crisis had been averted. But she congratulated herself too soon; in another instant Kate had leaped up from the chair to pace back and forth. Then, abruptly, she stopped and stared at her aunt. "I'm going for a ride," Kate announced.

"A ride!"

Involuntarily Olivia glanced at the clock. "At this time of day?" she said, startled. For the first time she noticed that Kate already wore her riding habit. "But surely you're not serious!" she exclaimed. "Why, it's already after four!"

"I can't help it. I have to get away, if only for an hour or so. Please . . ." Kate dropped to her knees before her aunt, grasping her hands. "Please try to understand, aunt."

Olivia understood all too well. "All right, then," she said gently, knowing that someone with Kate's nature would be better off doing something rather than sitting and brooding. "But only for an hour, Kate, please."

Kate bestowed a quick grateful kiss on Olivia's cheek. "Thank you," she murmured, and was gone before Olivia could reply.

Jean Foster

know could any man in his right mind fancy himself in love
with Amelia Webster? Why, she's nothing but a pudding-

the . . . .

. . . .

10

In the stableyard, the groom took one look at Kate's face and
had her horse saddled in record time. Mounting, she had no
idea where she wanted to go, no real plan in mind. She only
knew she had to get away, to *ride*, before the emptiness inside her splintered into a thousand fragments and allowed her
to feel the pain of Roger's deception. She felt brittle, fragile,
as if the slightest thing would shatter the icy calm that had
descended upon her, and yet she couldn't think.

Spurring the willing mare into a canter, and from that into
a gallop, Kate took her down the drive and out onto the
road. As they raced along, Kate thought: Perhaps I'll fall,
and everything will be solved.

Immediately following that thought came a rush of shame,
and Kate bent her head over the horse's mane, gulping back
tears. What was she thinking of, to wish something so awful?
What kind of woman was she, to hope for such a thing?

But she wasn't a woman, she thought, dashing the tears
from her eyes with the back of one hand. Or at least she
didn't feel like a woman now. She was a young girl whom everyone had deserted, leaving her alone in a huge and dark
house full of ghosts and shadows. She was scared, frightened,
and there was no one to turn to.

Or was there?

The sudden realization made her sit up in the saddle.
There was someone, she thought, actually laughing aloud in
relief. And she should have thought of it long ago; if she
hadn't been so upset, so shaken, she would have seen the
logic of it at once. All she had to do was go to Roger as she
had originally planned; once he knew about the child, he
wouldn't hesitate to break his engagement to Amelia and announce sometime later that he was going to marry Kate instead. Oh, it would be awkward, explaining this sudden

reversal, but they would think of some way to get around it. They had to, Kate thought desperately.

They would go away for a while—that was it! She had never made any secret of the fact that she liked to travel, and she and Roger could take an extended honeymoon. By the time they returned, the strain of travel would have brought on the early birth of the baby, and everything would fall neatly into place.

Laughing somewhat hysterically at this clever solution to all her problems, Kate turned the horse in the direction of Green Eaves. How ironic that Roger's announcement, which had caused her so much needless anguish, should make things so much easier now. When she called upon the Templetons, she wouldn't have to contrive an excuse; everyone would simply assume that she had gone to congratulate Roger. And when Roger, upon seeing how brave she was at the thought of losing him, decided he was making a terrible mistake marrying Amelia, neither of them could be blamed for surrendering to such deep love. It was perfect, Kate thought, deliberately driving away any doubts.

But her laughter had a sharp edge, and her expression was white and strained when she urged the mare to a faster pace in the direction of Green Eaves.

"Why . . . Kate!"

Roger was obviously stunned to find her waiting in one of the Green Eaves drawing rooms. Kate smiled indulgently at his consternation, and then saw with dismay the dark smudges under his eyes. He had been ill, and no one had told her! This was the reason he hadn't replied to her message, why she hadn't seen him at any of the social events she had so miserably attended without him. Why hadn't Page told her?

Contritely she smiled at him and said quickly, "I'm sorry to burst in on you like this, Roger, but I had to talk to you."

"Oh . . . yes . . ."

There was something terribly wrong, Kate thought, alarmed. Roger seemed so distracted and ill-at-ease, so . . . so strained. What was the matter with him?

And then she realized that he must have been under great pressure to announce his engagement to Amelia, if he looked like that. How his family must have bullied and pleaded with him, to make him agree to this preposterous betrothal!

Clearly he was distressed and upset; she must feel her way very carefully. She didn't want to add to the burdens he already carried by rushing at him with demands of her own, she thought emotionally. Or at least, she amended practically, not right away.

"May I get you something, Kate? Tea or . . ."

"No, nothing, thank you. I know it's late, and not at all the proper hour for calling, but I had to see you." She laughed a little, feeling the tension herself. "Your butler—Grayson?—was a little shocked, I think, when he saw me at the door!"

"You're always welcome, Kate. You know that."

Was it her imagination, or was his manner too stiff and formal? But she was nervous herself; it was difficult to find the right words to say, especially when the memory of that day in the barn was like a barrier between them, all the more awkward because neither of them had mentioned it. Still . . . She was a little taken aback by Roger's aloofness; she had assumed that he would do something to greet her—a kiss or a quick embrace. Anything but stand all the way across the room staring at her as if he had never seen her before.

"Roger, I . . ."

"Kate . . ."

They both spoke at the same time, and it was Roger who solemnly gestured for her to go ahead. With a quick glance at his too-serious face, Kate plunged in before she could put a name to this vague uneasiness she was experiencing. She had felt it from the moment Roger entered the room.

"Roger, we received the announcement today about you and Amelia . . ."

Instead of reassuring her, as she had half-expected him to do, Kate was further dismayed when Roger winced and looked away. "I meant to talk to you about that, Kate," he said in a low voice. "I was furious when I learned that an announcement had been sent to Tremont Hall, but by then it was too late."

Then why didn't you ride over and explain yourself, instead of forcing me to come to you? The treacherous thought flashed unbidden into her mind, shocking her. Kate brushed it away. "It doesn't matter," she lied. "But what does—"

"Yes, it does matter!" To Kate's astonishment, Roger slammed one fist into the other. The violent gesture was so unlike him that she gaped. Hardly had she recovered from that surprise than she was amazed to see him almost leap across the room to the fireplace. He took a poker and began savagely to stir up the small fire there, as if he intended to turn it into a roaring blaze.

She had never seen Roger like this. He seemed to be under such extreme tension that her only thought was to comfort him, and so she went to where he was standing, still bent over the fire. Tentatively she touched his arm, and was appalled when he jerked away from her. Bewildered at his response, she said, "What is it, Roger? What's the matter?"

His back was to her, his face turned away so that she couldn't see his expression. But she saw his shoulders heave, and she was even more alarmed. Abandoning all caution, she put her arms around him, pressing her cheek against his back. "Everything will be all right," she whispered comfortingly. "You'll see."

Eyes closed, luxuriating in this forbidden contact, Kate was totally unprepared for the violence with which Roger thrust her away. So swift was his rejection that she stumbled and had to catch the back of a chair for balance. "Roger, what—?"

"Don't do that again, Kate!"

"But—"

"Don't touch me like that. My God! Suppose someone had seen you?"

She couldn't believe that he would speak so to her, that he could repudiate her so completely after what had taken place between them. She had tried to be understanding, had tried not to pressure him—had even, she realized appalled, made excuses for him. But the tension she had lived under the past few weeks, coupled with the strain of receiving that hideous announcement that afternoon, and now his behavior—all combined to take their toll. As he dared to stare at her in affront, her temper snapped.

"You didn't feel that way in the hay barn some weeks ago," she hissed. "As I recall, there was no mention at the time of anyone discovering us. There was only—"

Roger winced and shut his eyes. "Must you, Kate?" he asked in an aggrieved tone.

"Yes, I must," she replied, mimicking him. "Since it appears that you have forgotten—"

"I haven't forgotten," he said in a strangled tone. "But you have to."

She was about to demand furiously how he expected her to

forget what had happened when she had a constant, and growing, reminder of their folly. But something in his voice stopped her, and the first icy fingers of fear clutched her heart.

"What do you mean?" she asked sharply.

Roger tried to face her. A part of her mind noted, and was scornful of, the brief quivering of his lip, but she was too caught up in her own emotions to analyze this sign of weakness. "What do you mean?" she asked again.

Roger was distraught enough to be reassured by Kate's sudden icy calm. He took a deep breath and said, "I'm going to marry Amelia, Kate."

"Yes, so the announcement read," Kate said, marveling at how calm she sounded, when inside she was screaming at him in fury. "But I want to know one thing," she continued in that same strange tone even she couldn't recognize. "Why?"

Roger had tried to brace himself for the explosion he was sure would come. He had expected tears, rage, recrimination, and condemnation; but he had not expected Kate's quiet, almost detached question. Something was wrong, out of kilter, but Roger was suddenly too tired to put his finger on what it was. He was only wearily grateful that Kate seemed prepared to be reasonable.

"Why?" he repeated blankly, trying to dredge up the energy to explain what couldn't be explained.

"Yes," Kate said. "Why. Why are you marrying Amelia Webster after what happened between us?"

Involuntarily Roger glanced in the direction of the drawing-room door. In relief he saw that he had remembered to close it after he came in. Thank God, he thought. If anyone heard this conversation, he was lost. His father might sanction his taking down a maidservant or two, but he would never countenance his son's liaison with the niece of one of his oldest friends. If John Templeton ever discovered his folly that afternoon of the storm, there would be hell to pay, and Roger simply didn't feel well enough to face his father in one of his cold rages. The lethargy that had dragged at him for weeks past now seemed intolerable; he felt exhausted, spent. Somehow, he must get through this distressing interview with Kate; he did owe her some sort of explanation, after all. Hopefully he could think of one she would accept.

"Roger, I asked you a question," Kate said just then. "I think you owe me an answer."

Roger was unable to look at her. To Kate's disgust, he turned away and stared into the fire as he spoke. "I'm sorry, Kate," he said in a low voice, "awfully sorry if . . . if anything that happened between us led you to believe . . . to believe that there could be something more. The truth of the matter is that . . . that I love Amelia, and I'm going to marry her."

Kate couldn't believe her ears when she heard this faltering explanation. He was sorry, he had said. Sorry! As if that moment during the storm had been a momentary aberration, a lapse in control, a faulty judgment for which he could not be blamed or held accountable! As if . . . as if it had meant nothing to him.

She stared at him, willing him to look at her, to tell her that he didn't mean what he had said. But when he continued to stare abjectly into the fire, Kate felt a terrible rage building in her, an anger that almost blinded her, so that for a moment she could not speak.

Even then, she still might have saved the situation, might have swallowed the last of her tattered pride and confessed about the coming child. But Roger chose that moment to begin pleading with her, and all was lost. In later years, Kate would remember this scene and wonder how their lives might have changed if only she had spoken first. But now she was too choked with anger and disbelief to speak, and Roger plunged ahead instead.

"Kate, please try to understand my position," he begged. "Amelia and I have known each other for years, since we were children. Our parents have been close friends for longer than that. Our engagement isn't something that happened overnight; it has been understood between us for a long time now. I can't . . . couldn't ask her to step aside; I can't disappoint my parents, or hers. Don't you see?"

"I . . . I . . ." She couldn't speak over the closing in her throat. She couldn't even resist when Roger came to where she stood, taking both her icy hands in his for emphasis. She could only stand there woodenly, willing this nightmare to end; knowing that it wasn't a nightmare at all, but cold reality. He really was going to marry Amelia, she thought. He really was.

"Don't you see, Kate?" Roger said again, somehow encouraged by her strangled silence. "There are others to consider besides ourselves."

Why? she wanted to scream. Why did they have to think of anyone else but themselves? The injustice of it scalded her throat. She couldn't answer, and Roger pressed what he thought was his advantage. "I knew you would understand," he said in obvious relief. "I knew I could rely on you, Kate."

Understand! Rely! Did he think he was speaking to some dim-witted chit? Her temper, which had been such a detriment to her in the past, now came to her aid. The chill she had felt was gone; in its place was a blazing fury. "I understand very well," she said, her voice shaking with anger. "But I'm not sure how much you can rely on me, Roger."

"Kate, you wouldn't—"

Kate snatched her hands from his grasp, unable to bear his touch any longer. She wanted to hurt him, as he had hurt her, and so she said, "Wouldn't what, Roger? Tell Amelia? Or your parents? Don't be too sure of that." How satisfying it was to see the panic in his face—the same panic she had felt herself! "What's the matter?" she asked nastily. "Is it that you want to protect my reputation—or yours? Could it be that you want to guard Amelia's innocent opinion of you—until your wedding night, that is?"

"Kate!"

Roger was genuinely shocked, but Kate was too angry to care. Now she noticed that despite the situation, his glance kept going nervously to the clock and then back to her again. Her eyes narrowed. "Am I keeping you from something?" she asked dangerously. "Because if I am, please don't hesitate to tell me. I certainly wouldn't want this silly little discussion to detain you from more important matters!"

Roger winced again. "You do make things difficult, Kate," he said reproachfully.

Difficult! Difficult! Kate was tempted to show him just how difficult she could be. The urge to run out into the hall and scream the truth about Roger and the child was almost overpowering. It took an effort of will to remain standing where she was.

And there was Roger, staring blankly into the fire again, offering no consolation, no solution, no apology. Was he going to say nothing more?

Seizing his arm, she made him look at her. The abject misery in his face was both infuriating and appalling. "Is that all you have to say?" she cried.

Roger finally found the courage to answer her. Straightening, he looked at her with a little of the gentle compassion she had always admired so before, but which now only enraged her further. He said, "I'm afraid it is, Kate. I had hoped that you would understand that I can't abandon all my obligations, but . . ."

She didn't wait for him to finish. She had to get out before she did something awful, like picking up the poker and beating him senseless. Never—*never*—had she been so angry. Her fury was like a powerful tide rushing her along, enveloping her in a white rage. Whirling around, she headed blindly for the door.

Green Eaves' butler, Grayson, was hovering politely in the foyer when Kate burst out of the drawing room. She scarcely saw him; all her attention was focused on escaping Green Eaves and Roger before she lost all control and began screaming senselessly until she could scream no longer. The butler, seeing her in such a hurry, opened his mouth to ask her something, saw her expression, and abruptly closed it again. Abandoning all dignity, he leaped for the front door ahead of her, opening it as she swept through, and then he further surprised himself by actually shouting for the groom to come assist her with her horse.

But Kate had no intention of waiting for help. Before the startled man could come to her aid, she had mounted and wheeled the mare around. Digging her heels into the animal's flank, she sent the horse forward in a spray of gravel that made both butler and groom jump back. As she rode furiously down the drive, Grayson and the groom looked at each other in utter confusion, and then stared after her with identical expressions of complete bewilderment. They both felt as if they had been touched by a whirlwind, and neither knew why.

11

It wasn't until Kate had whipped through the huge iron gates leading to Green Eaves that she abandoned the desperate hope that Roger would come after her. Daring a look over her shoulder, she saw that the drive behind her was empty. He hadn't followed her after all, and a strangled sob burst from her when she admitted that he intended to let her go.

Oh, how she hated him! How she loathed and despised him! Beating her fist on the pommel of the saddle, Kate wept from frustration and hurt and rage. Duty, he had said. Responsibility. Obligation. Did he feel no duty or obligation to her? No sense of responsibility for what he had done?

Sobbing again, Kate sent the horse forward at a breakneck pace. It was almost dark now, and difficult to see; a last shred of common sense told her she should slow the mare, but she didn't listen. All she wanted to do was run home to her room at Tremont Hall, bury her head in a pillow, and cry until she couldn't cry anymore.

Blinded by tears, huddled over the horse's neck as she shook with sobs, Kate didn't see the figure looming out of the dark until it was too late. The mare swerved violently, she heard a startled shout, her own cry, and then she was falling through the air with the sickening thought that this had all happened before. But Page wasn't here this time to prevent her fall, and her last coherent thought was to kick free of the stirrup so that she wouldn't be dragged or crushed under the horse. And then everything went black.

"Kate, can you hear me? Kate!"

There was a stinging sensation against her cheek. Bewildered, she wondered why. She couldn't see anything, even though her eyes were open. Where was she? What had happened? *Why couldn't she see?*

Disoriented, terrified, she tried to sit up. The stinging

against her face resolved itself into a hand, and she clutched it, too grateful to be angry. She had known it was a hand because she could see it in the darkness: she wasn't blind after all! Her overwhelming relief at this discovery was followed by an even greater elation: Roger had followed her! He was just a dark shape bending over her; she could barely see him in the night, but so great was her joy that she flung herself into his arms.

"Roger!" she cried, burying her head against his shoulder. "I was so frightened!"

"Is that why you were racing down the road like a madwoman? You could have killed yourself, and me, as well. But perhaps that was your intention, since your first attempt failed. Tell me, Kate, are you going to make a habit of running me off the road?"

She had stiffened at the first word, recognizing his voice instantly. Vainly she tried to extricate herself, too angry to hear the relief in his voice.

"Let me go!" she cried. "And I was the one who was nearly killed! If you hadn't been in the way, I never would have fallen!"

"On the contrary," Page denied calmly. "If I hadn't taken that side of the road, your fall would have been much worse than it was. Listen."

As furious as she was, Kate could hear the rush of water in the direction Page indicated. She had seen the ravine on the way to Green Eaves earlier, had noted the collapse of the road to the side, and had ridden on, too anxious to see Roger to make note of being careful on her return. She had forgotten completely about that dangerous passage on her flight from Green Eaves just now, and was too embarrassed to admit it.

"You still startled my horse," she muttered sulkily, managing to free herself from Page's grasp at last.

"I'm sorry, madam, if I was so inconsiderate as to use the road when you wanted it to yourself. Next time I'll be more careful."

There was no mistaking the exasperated sarcasm in Page's voice, and Kate squirmed inwardly, knowing he was right to be impatient with her. At another time she might have muttered an apology, but now that she had recovered from the shock of her fall, her earlier misery came flooding back. To her horror, she was close to tears again.

It would be the final humiliation to have Page see her cry, she told herself, catching her trembling lower lip in her teeth in a vain effort to stop her tears. But despite her efforts, a sob shook her, and then another. Before she could control herself, she was weeping in earnest.

"Kate, you didn't . . . you aren't hurt after all, are you?"

The genuine concern in Page's voice made her cry all the harder. She tried to answer him through a fresh gust of tears, but only managed to alarm him even more when he couldn't understand her.

"Kate, tell me what's wrong!"

He gripped her shoulders tightly. His face was only a blur, and she couldn't see his expression, but there was no denying his anxiety, and she cried all the more. Sarcasm she could deal with, and mockery; his being kind was another matter altogether, and without knowing how it happened, she was enfolded in his arms again, sobbing against his shoulder while he awkwardly stroked her hair.

"I'm . . . not . . . hurt," she gulped between sobs. "It's just . . . it's just . . ." But she couldn't go on, even if she had been able to. Especially to Page, she couldn't confess the reason for her misery; she was too ashamed to tell anyone at all. And yet the specter of discovery loomed larger and more frightening the more she cried, and she wondered if it might be better to share this intolerable burden with someone else after all.

No, no; she couldn't tell anyone, no matter how tempting. She was hysterical, not thinking clearly—not thinking at all. It was just that she was so frightened, so unsure of what to do. Somehow, she must get hold of herself.

Finally the storm of weeping exhausted itself, and she was able to take the handkerchief Page offered her and dab at her eyes and face. "I'm sorry," she said, unable to look at him. "I don't know what made me cry like that. I suppose it was the shock of falling."

"I suppose so," said Page doubtfully. "But are you sure it was that, and not something else?"

Did he know? Kate felt a rush of panic and controlled it by sheer force of will, telling herself not to be absurd. Of course he couldn't know; if Olivia wasn't aware of the child she carried, then there was no reason to believe that Page Taggart suspected anything either. All the same, it was an effort for her to ask, "What do you mean, 'something else'?"

She could feel his hesitation, his reluctance to answer. But finally he asked, "You know about Roger and Amelia, don't you?"

Fortunately, they were both on their feet now, and Kate took the opportunity to brush the dirt from her skirt, willing the sudden lump in her throat to disappear so that she could answer. She might have made a fool of herself with Roger, but no one else would ever know—not if she could help it.

"You mean their engagement?" she was able to ask at last, proud that her voice shook only slightly. "I suspected it quite some time ago, didn't you?"

Clearly Page was taken aback by her response, and Kate blessed all the hours and hours she had spent as a child watching her mother practice an expression or a gesture until it was perfect. If she could fool Page, who saw too much and understood too many things, then she could fool anyone, she thought.

"I thought . . . I mean, I'm glad you feel that way, Kate."

It was refreshing to see Page at a loss for words for a change, and she pressed what little advantage she had. "You seem surprised, Page," she said. "Naturally I'm happy for Roger and Amelia. Why . . . shouldn't I be?"

Despite her bravado, Kate was glad of the darkness. If she couldn't see Page's expression, then he couldn't see her face, which threatened to dissolve any moment into another flood of tears. It was a miracle she had managed to speak at all when she felt so suffocated. Somehow she had to make her escape before he realized how much it cost her to act so casually.

To her dismay, Page insisted on accompanying her back to the Hall, and there was no excuse she could think of to dissuade him. Resigning herself, Kate rode silently and miserably beside him for a mile or so, until it occurred to her suddenly to wonder why they had met at this particular time on the road from Green Eaves.

Distracted from her preoccupation with Roger for the moment at least, Kate realized belatedly that Page hadn't seemed surprised to see her at all; in fact, it was almost as though he had expected to find her.

Turning abruptly in the saddle, she tried to study him. But the darkness that had successfully hidden her face before masked his expression now, and she couldn't tell what he was thinking, or even if he was looking her way.

Still, the question of their meeting gnawed at her, piquing her curiosity the longer she wondered about it, until finally, she knew she had to ask him. Any distraction was better than going over and over in her mind that humiliating scene with Roger, she thought, and so she demanded abruptly to know why Page had been looking for her.

"And what makes you think I was looking for you?" Page asked in response. "I might have been on my way back to Green Eaves after visiting someone. A young lady, perhaps. There are several who have invited me to call, you know."

Listening to the amusement in his voice, Kate cursed her curiosity. She should have known he would make her appear foolish for asking such a question, but it was too late now. Somehow she had to salvage a little of her pride. "I hadn't realized you were so eagerly sought out," she said shortly.

"Obviously, then, I have some admirable qualities you have ignored."

"I'm surprised that you haven't taken the trouble to point them out to me, then."

"I hoped you would notice for yourself."

Kate was in no mood for the quick repartee that normally would have exhilarated and challenged her. Absurdly close to tears again for a reason she couldn't define, she said, "The only thing I've noticed is your appalling behavior. My sympathies are with any girl who strikes your fancy, if you are as rude and inconsiderate to her as you have been to me!"

It was infuriating to hear the tremor in her voice. Despite her best efforts, she could feel the sting of tears behind her eyes, and she spurred her horse forward. She could think of nothing else but escaping Page and running back to the Hall, where she could surrender to the emotional storm she felt building inside her again. The threat of breaking into another flood of humiliating weeping was appalling; the journey home seemed endless, the privacy of her own room as unattainable as the moon. Oh, why had she met Page just now, when she wanted to be alone? At any other time she could have held her own with him; now she felt weak and defenseless, a stupid fool who had put her trust in a man who had let her down so badly she wondered if she would ever recover from it.

Feeling that nameless despair building inside her again, Kate urged the mare to a faster pace. It was then that she felt a sharp stab of pain lance through her. She gasped with the shock of it, but it was gone in an instant, disappearing so completely that she wondered then if she had felt it at all. But there wasn't time to think about it, for Page reached out just then and grabbed at the mare's bridle, slowing Kate's horse to pace beside his.

"Let go of my bridle!" Kate demanded.

"Absolutely not. I won't have you galloping madly off to run down someone else in another fit of temper."

"I didn't run you down!"

"Only because I saw you first."

Frustrated, still shocked and a little bewildered by what she had felt an instant ago, Kate cried, "You don't know anything about it at all!"

"Yes. I do."

Something in his tone made her pause in the act of reaching out to push away his hand. She stared at him as the horses slowed and stopped of their own accord. They were almost home; their mounts had carried them to one of the side entrances of the Hall as she and Page argued, and now they paused in the shadows.

Kate was hardly aware that she was home. Lamplight from a window illuminated Page's face, and she was so bemused by his expression that she didn't protest when he dismounted and came around to lift her down from her own saddle.

His hands were strong about her waist as he held her; when she put out her hands to balance herself, his shoulders were broad and powerful. Time stopped as they stared at each other, and when he lowered her to her feet, she couldn't move away from him. It was as though that same mysterious force held her there, a tie that had nothing to do with the strength of his hands still about her waist; a power that flashed from soul to soul, uniting them, despite their differences.

"Kate . . ."

She couldn't speak. It was all she could do to stand there, for her legs felt weak and her pulse was thunder in her ears. She didn't understand what was happening to her. She wanted to deny the power of her attraction to him, and couldn't.

The pressure of his hands increased. Slowly he drew her close to him until their bodies touched. She could feel his chest against her breasts, could feel the contact of her thigh against his. She drew in a sharp breath.

Page seemed as shaken as she was. He closed his eyes and held her even closer, until she was almost crushed against him. "Kate . . ." he whispered, his voice husky.

"Page, I—"

"No. Let me say it. I've wanted to tell you this for so long now, and you never gave me the opportunity. . . ."

She wanted to pull away from him, to put her hands over her ears to shut out the sound of his deep voice. It was all wrong, she thought frantically; all wrong, and too late. She didn't want to hear what he had to say, and yet she wanted to listen to him with all her heart.

"Kate, I've wanted you from the moment I saw you in those ridiculous breeches, crying on the hill that day. I want you now, with tears on your face, and another man's name on your lips."

She stiffened at this last, but he held her tightly. "It doesn't matter . . . it doesn't matter," he said. "I love you, Kate. I love you, and I want you to be my wife. Say you'll marry me."

"Marry you!" Her reaction was so violent that she succeeded in breaking away from him. "Marry you!" she echoed again stupidly. "I . . . I . . ." She was so distracted that she hardly knew what she was saying. "But . . . but that's impossible!"

"Why?"

Oh, how she wished he would stop staring at her like that! She couldn't think. Or, rather, her mind seemed to be leaping ahead of itself, racing into areas she didn't want to think about. But, insidiously, her mind turned to the coming child, and she thought that marrying Page might be the solution to her problem.

No! No! What was she thinking? Even to save her reputation, she couldn't marry Page. But was it her reputation she was thinking of, or of Page himself? She didn't know; she didn't know what her thoughts were. She was so confused, so sorry, so . . . so angry. Why hadn't Page spoken before now? If he had, she might have . . . No! she thought again. It was Roger she loved, not Page. It was Roger who was the father of the child she carried. It would be Roger she married, or no one at all.

Refusing to think of the consequences of that rash decision, Kate looked frantically at Page. "I can't marry you!" she said. "I can't!"

He reached for her, but she had already whirled away. She couldn't face him anymore; she couldn't!

"Kate, at least tell me why!" Page shouted after her. "Tell me why!"

"I'm sorry . . . I'm sorry!" she sobbed. She had reached the side door and was struggling with the handle. Another burst of pain from somewhere inside her nearly doubled her over, but she was so desperate to escape that she thrust the pain aside, to be dealt with later. All she could think of was getting away from Page. She had the frantic idea that if she were to face him again he would know the reason for her refusal. Page, with his dark eyes that saw too much, must never know about that day in the abandoned barn. No one must ever know.

The door yielded at last to her desperate efforts, and Kate rushed inside. But she had barely slammed it behind her before she was hit by another wave of pain. Gasping, she bent over, clasping both hands over her stomach, scarcely able to breathe over the sudden fire in her belly. Black spots danced before her eyes; she was dizzy and light-headed.

What was wrong with her? There was a strong rippling sensation inside her, and she barely had time to reach out and grab the back of a chair before a third shock of agony hit her.

She didn't know that she pulled the chair down with her when she fell, and that the noise brought two of the servants running. She wasn't even aware of it when she was carried upstairs, an anxious Olivia by her side. The doctor came and went, sworn to secrecy, but Kate never knew it. She was conscious only of the pain. It racked her body, crushing her in wave after wave, until she was too exhausted to fight it anymore. A hand smoothed her forehead, and she wanted to reach out and clasp it for comfort, but she could not even make that small effort. As she spiraled down to peaceful blackness, her last thought was that she had lost the child. She couldn't even be relieved or disconsolate at the thought, for there existed only herself and the pain that rushed after her, and Page, asking, "Why?"

12

When Kate opened her eyes, the first things she focused on were the lamp on the table and Olivia's concerned face bending over her.

"Here. Take a sip of this."

Obediently Kate sipped at the glass Olivia held to her lips. The liquid tasted bitter; it burned her throat, and she grimaced and pushed it weakly away. Olivia put the medicine on the bedside table and smoothed a compress over Kate's burning forehead. It felt wonderful, cool and soothing.

"Try to sleep now," Olivia whispered, smiling encouragingly at her.

Kate shook her head, a move she regretted an instant later, for it made every nerve jangle in protest. Reaching out, she grasped Olivia's hand. "What happened to me?" she croaked. "The pain . . ."

For the first time, distress showed clearly in Olivia's kind eyes. "We'll talk about it later, when you're stronger."

But Kate had to know. She couldn't rest without knowing. "Please . . ."

Olivia sat down on the side of the bed, clasping her hands tightly in her lap. "Why didn't you tell me, Kate?"

There was no accusation in her aunt's face, only a sad reproach, which made Kate feel even worse. "I didn't know how to tell you," she confessed, tears springing into her eyes. She had lost the baby after all, she thought. Was she relieved? In a way, she supposed she was, and then she was ashamed even of that private admission.

"Fortunately, Dr. Wilkins is an excellent doctor," Olivia was saying. "As well as a dear friend of mine. He won't betray you, Kate, if that's any comfort."

Kate moved her head on the pillow, forcing herself to meet Olivia's eyes. "I'm glad," she said. "For your sake. I'm sorry, aunt. I . . . I didn't mean for this to happen."

93

"Well, it has happened," Olivia said. "And now we must face the issue squarely and decide what to do."

Kate was confused. "But you said that the doctor wouldn't say anything."

"Even Dr. Wilkins can't hide the evidence for long, Kate."

"What . . . what do you mean?" But she knew what Olivia meant even before she said it. Listening to her aunt explain, Kate saw disaster rushing at her again.

"Of course we must decide what to do before your condition becomes evident," Olivia was saying gently. "What did you think I meant?"

Kate closed her eyes, fighting a surge of panic. "Then I . . . then I . . ." She swallowed, forcing herself to say it aloud. "I didn't lose the child, did I?"

"Why, no, Kate. I thought you realized that. I told you Dr. Wilkins is a skillful man."

A skillful man . . . a skillful man . . . The words chased themselves around her head until she thought she would scream. She could feel the pressure building behind her eyes, and knew that, given the slightest provocation, she could become completely hysterical. Only Olivia's next statement distracted her from the emotional storm about to break, and then Kate felt hysteria of quite another kind.

"Of course, Page Taggart is the father," Olivia was saying calmly. "Which is fortunate, really, since he . . . What's the matter, Kate? Why are you looking at me like that?"

Kate couldn't help it: she laughed. The sound burst from her like an explosion, and once started, she couldn't stop. Laugh or cry; it was one or the other, and she had shed far too many tears these past weeks.

"Kate!"

Olivia's voice was sharp, recognizing the desperation behind Kate's laughter as soon as Kate herself did. Hand over her mouth, Kate fought to control herself, and whatever had struck her as amusing vanished, leaving behind a fierce headache and the sobering realization that there were still problems to be faced. Involuntarily her hand went to her stomach under the blankets, and suddenly nothing seemed funny anymore.

"I'm sorry," she said in a low voice. "I don't know what came over me."

"I understand," answered Olivia sympathetically. "It must

have been a great strain, living under such tension these past weeks. The point now, though, is what are we going to do?"

Kate thought with a grimace of what had happened between her and Roger at Green Eaves, and she knew now that her earlier dreams of Roger renouncing Amelia for her had been the utmost folly. The reality was that she was all alone, and she would have to face whatever came by herself. She couldn't ask Olivia to share this problem with her; it wouldn't be fair.

"I think I should go away, aunt," she said finally. "I've brought you enough trouble as it is. With a child, everything will be more difficult, and I can't ask you to—"

"I want to help you, Kate," said Olivia firmly. "This is a family matter, and we will face it together."

Tears sprang into Kate's eyes again. Reaching for Olivia's hand, she grasped it tightly. But even though there was no doubting her aunt's sincerity, Kate could not in conscience ask Olivia to share in the certain scandal. Olivia had lived too long in this neighborhood, had presided over Tremont Hall too many years with a spotless reputation to be sullied now by her niece's thoughtless behavior.

"Thank you, aunt," Kate said gratefully. "But I can't accept your kind offer. Mama had many friends in London; I can stay with one of them until I decide what to do."

Olivia shook her head decidedly. "I can't allow that, Kate. I *won't* allow it."

"But it's the only solution, don't you see?"

"No. There is something else . . ."

"What?"

Olivia hesitated. "Does the father of the child know?"

Kate turned her head away, her expression bitter. "No," she answered briefly.

"Why not?"

It was some seconds before Kate could control herself enough to answer. "Because I couldn't tell him. There were . . . there were other considerations."

"What could be more important than your condition?" demanded Olivia. "No, I'm sorry, Kate; I don't mean to pry, but I think I have a right to know at least *some* of the circumstances. If you can't—or won't—tell me who the father is, then . . ."

Olivia stopped abruptly, comprehension dawning in her eyes. "It's Roger Templeton, isn't it?" she asked. Kate winced and looked away, and Olivia had her answer. "Oh, dear," she said, and sat back.

There was a silence that Kate was loath to break. Olivia seemed reluctant to speak, as well, and finally Kate dared a quick glance at her aunt. Olivia was deep in thought, and Kate couldn't tell from her expression what she was thinking. Perhaps, Kate thought hopefully, Olivia was reconsidering her offer to go to London.

"It's obvious that the child must have a name," Olivia said at last. "And it's equally obvious that the father is not going to marry you, so we'll have to find someone else."

"Someone else?" Kate echoed. Olivia made it all sound so simple. "I hadn't noticed that prospective husbands abound," Kate said morosely. "Especially when they discover they're going to be fathers even before they become bridegrooms."

Olivia ignored her. "You're assuming the man would know the situation beforehand."

Kate stared at her. "But he would have to know!"

"Why?"

"*Why!*" Kate couldn't believe she was having this conversation with her conventional, proper aunt. "Because . . . because it wouldn't be fair!"

"Whoever said life must be fair?" scoffed Olivia, startling Kate even more than before. She practically gaped at Olivia. "Was life fair to you when you were born out of wedlock and had to suffer for the misconduct of your mother?" Olivia continued, waving her hand at Kate's disbelieving expression. "Oh, I know all about your background, Kate; don't look so surprised. Did you think I wouldn't investigate before I invited a total stranger to my home—even if she was my niece by marriage?"

Kate couldn't reply. There was more to Olivia Tremont than she had ever suspected, she realized now. She thought of all the times she had been impatient with her aunt, had even, Kate admitted with shame, thought her somewhat of a fool. It was obvious now that Olivia was no fool and never had been. It was she, Kate, who deserved the title, for thinking herself so superior.

"I'm not going to be a prig and say something intolerably stupid like 'blood will out,'" Olivia was saying. "That would serve no purpose at all. But I will say this, and I want you to think about it very carefully, Kate. Sometimes it's better to

lie by omission than to insist on revealing a truth that will
only destroy. Do you understand what I'm saying?"

"Yes, I understand," Kate nodded slowly. "But . . . but
what happens when the truth is discovered at some future
date?"

"In that event, you have to hope that you're both mature
enough to deal with it. There are no easy answers, Kate,"
Olivia said, her expression softening at the misery evident on
Kate's face. "You can only do what you think is best at the
time, under the circumstances."

"And you think it's better to keep the husband—whoever
he might be—in ignorance about the child?"

Olivia didn't hesitate. "Yes," she said firmly. "I do."

Kate lay back on the pillows, trying to think. Was Olivia
right? Was it better to hide behind an omission of truth, if
not an outright lie? Kate didn't know. She was bewildered,
confused, not even sure how to tell right from wrong at this
point.

But at least she wasn't alone anymore, and she was grateful for that. What a relief it was to share this burden with
someone else! Especially when that someone was more experienced, wiser in the ways of life than she.

It was this final realization that swayed Kate. If she didn't
know what to do, Olivia obviously did. She would have to
trust that her aunt was right.

Managing a tremulous smile, Kate tried to speak lightly.
But there was still an underlying note of desperation in her
voice when she said, "Now all I have to do is find a husband."

"That won't be so difficult, will it?" asked Olivia serenely.

"Oh? Won't it? I suppose you already have someone in
mind," Kate spoke in jest, sure that Olivia was trying to ease
the tenseness of the situation by joking herself. But in the next
instant, she realized that Olivia wasn't joking at all, but
deadly serious, and she stared at her aunt, utterly appalled.

"I do have someone in mind, in fact," Olivia said. "Page
Taggart."

Kate's reaction was swift, violent, and unequivocal. Sitting
bolt upright in the bed, she thrust out one arm in total repudiation. "No!" she declared positively. "I wouldn't marry
Page if he was the last man on earth! I couldn't possibly . . .
I wouldn't do that to him! Absolutely not!"

But of course she married him. There wasn't really any other choice, she realized bleakly, feeling very much like a mouse caught in a trap. It was either marry Page or accept the responsibility of bearing an illegitimate child. And as repugnant as the thought of becoming Page's wife was to her, the idea of having no name for her baby was even more appalling. In the end, she was forced to accept the inevitability of her decision. Angrily, Kate swallowed her pride and endured the delighted satisfaction on Page's face when she ungraciously reversed her earlier position and accepted his marriage proposal after all.

They were married a week later, in a tiny registry in the north of England, by a special license that Page had somehow managed to procure on short notice. They had traveled north alone, because although Olivia regretted missing the wedding she had so carefully arranged, she insisted to Kate that the marriage must appear an impulsive action taken by two young people who had suddenly realized that they were very much in love.

And for one of the participants, it was no fiction: Page was too delighted at Kate's abrupt acceptance to question the speed with which she wanted to marry. He was so overcome by his sudden good fortune, in fact, that he saw nothing amiss in her wistful request that they return in time for Roger and Amelia's betrothal ball. Had he been older himself, or wiser in the ways of women, or had he even been a husband a little longer than a few hours' duration and able to see things more clearly, he might have wondered at Kate's wish. But if the bride was not quite ecstatic, the groom himself was too elated to refuse her anything. The newlyweds arrived home at Tremont Hall in time for the celebration. And in time for the first of many, many married quarrels.

13

As Kate stopped imperiously at the entrance to the ballroom at Green Eaves, no one looking at her would guess that she and Page had battled furiously only an hour before. She had wanted to appear the radiant bride, and she did; this night was important to her in more ways than one, and she was determined to savor her triumph to the fullest. The quarrel with Page would have to wait; it was all ridiculous nonsense anyway. She absolutely would not leave England, no matter what he said.

Olivia, sworn to secrecy concerning their announcement, had come ahead, and so only Kate and Page waited for Grayson to announce them. Page had whispered something in the butler's ear as they approached, and the normally imperturbable Grayson had exclaimed aloud in surprise, offering his congratulations at once in astonishment, confusion, and a large measure of admiration for Page. Then, pulling himself together, Grayson stepped forward. "Ladies and gentlemen," he intoned, his voice holding a note of excitement that had been noticeably absent before, "Mr. and Mrs. Page Taggart."

Heads turned, conversation slowed and then stopped, and as Kate moved regally forward, her hand on her new husband's arm, she felt a fierce pleasure at the shock and surprise she saw on so many faces. It was the most satisfying moment of her life.

There were five steps from the doorway to the ballroom floor, and Kate floated down every one of them, aware that all eyes were on her and the handsome man beside her. For the first time, she truly understood the elation her mother must have felt when making a grand entrance, and her head came up even higher. Augusta, thought Kate, would have been proud of her daughter tonight.

There was an awkward silence when they reached the floor, but Kate didn't care. This was her moment, and she

would enjoy it to the fullest. How satisfying it was to see all
these people at a loss; what a pleasure it was to know that
she had the upper hand at last! A smile curved her lips, and
she looked for Roger.

She found him at last, on the fringes of the crowd, his face
still mirroring his utter astonishment and confusion. Beside
him, Amelia looked angrily bewildered, aware that Kate had
stolen her party, helpless to think of something to steal it
back again.

Seeing them, Kate nodded. Ignoring Amelia, she met Roger's eyes and forced him to hold her gaze. At her side, Page
waited, and Kate knew without looking that he was smiling
with sardonic amusement at her little display, but she didn't
care about that, either. There was only one thing that mattered to her, and that was to see the profound regret on Roger's face when he realized what he had lost.

Satisfied that she had created enough tension, Kate turned
to Page. "We seem to have interrupted everything, darling,"
she said sweetly. "Do let's go and congratulate the betrothal
couple."

Her voice carried in the silent ballroom, as she had fully
intended it to do, and at the sound, Roger seemed propelled
forward, almost dragging the reluctant Amelia with him.

"It seems that congratulations are in order here, too," Roger said a shade too heartily as he and Amelia came up to
where Kate and Page were standing. "Page, you dog! Why
didn't you tell me?" He punched Page lightly on the arm,
grinning at him. But there was a sheen of perspiration on his
forehead, and his fingers shook as he grasped Kate's hands.
"Kate," he said, "you make a beautiful bride. Doesn't she,
Amelia?"

Amelia, thus dragooned into the conversation, had no option but to nod and smile and offer her congratulations, too.
Only Roger's pleading glance held her tongue; her plump
body was trembling with anger. This was *her* night, *her* betrothal ball! How *dare* that scheming Kate steal it all away
from her! And there was Roger, gaping like a moonstruck
idiot, not even caring that her night was ruined. Amelia could
have burst into tears on the spot.

Across the room, Maude Webster was staring at the scene
with narrowed eyes and tight lips. Oh, it was just like Kate
Beauvais to upstage her Amelia, Maude thought wrathfully.
If she knew Kate, she had planned it all, and Maude gritted

her teeth, forced to admit the girl's timing was perfect. All eyes were focused on her; her late entrance on the arm of a new husband—and Page Taggart, at that—had been flawless. But of course, Maude thought maliciously, she had had a good teacher, hadn't she? If anyone had known how to become the center of attention, it had been Augusta Beauvais!

"Edwin," hissed Maude to her husband, standing like a lump by her side. "Do something!"

"What would you like me to do?" Edwin replied, his glance still on the four young people in the middle of the room. "I say, they make a handsome couple, don't they?"

Maude had no need to ask which couple her husband meant. She glared at him in outrage, and Edwin, long familiar with the storm signs, sighed. Reluctantly he gestured to the confused musicians behind him on the dais, who were waiting for some signal to resume playing, and at the lift of his hand, they plunged with relief into the first strains of a dance.

Page heard the music with only part of his mind. He had been watching Kate's face with a puzzled expression of his own, and now that he allowed himself to realize what it was that bothered him, he couldn't deny seeing that look of triumph in his bride's eyes—a malicious kind of triumph that angered him. Now he knew why she had insisted on dashing back at such breakneck speed, and he cursed himself for acting like some fatuous fool and blinding himself to her motives before. She had wanted to steal the stage from Amelia—and to preen before Roger, who had rejected her. For a moment, Page wasn't sure whether to be amused or furious with his wife.

And then he glimpsed Amelia's face, and saw her determined effort not to cry, and suddenly he wanted to turn Kate over his knee and give her the spanking she so richly deserved. Abruptly he turned instead to Amelia and asked her to dance.

Kate gasped. Amelia herself stared at him in confusion, her cheeks turning pink. Roger swallowed, glancing hurriedly from Page to Amelia to Kate, and then back to Page again.

Before any of them could speak, Page stepped smoothly into the awkward breach. "I think it's only proper that you should have the first dance, Amelia," he said, smiling encouragingly and holding out his arm to her. "After all," he added with a quelling look in Kate's direction, "the ball *is* in your honor."

With a mighty effort, Kate took herself in hand. Amelia began stammering in bewilderment after another frightened glance at Kate, but Kate was determined to be equal to the situation. She was absolutely furious with Page, who had deliberately tried to ruin her moment of triumph, but she would have gone to the rack before admitting her humiliation. Dredging up a brilliant smile, Kate said at once, "Oh, but of course you must have the first dance! And who better to partner you, Amelia, than the cousin of your intended!" Turning to look up at Page, Kate increased the dazzle of her smile. "How chivalrous of you, darling!" she exclaimed brightly. "And how thoughtful, acting to put us all at our ease!" She could have killed him where he stood.

The admiring glance Page threw her as he led the distracted Amelia onto the floor was almost enough to assuage Kate's wounded dignity. Almost. Staring after them, Kate realized for the first time that the man she had married had depths to him that she hadn't known existed. She would have to be careful, she thought—much more careful—in the future. It was a little frightening that Page had discerned her innermost thoughts, and had understood her motives, even better than she.

Across the room from the suddenly thoughtful Kate, and the outraged Maude, and the stumbling Amelia, Olivia Tremont sat in a gilt chair that was half-hidden behind one of the floral arrangements dotting the ballroom. Sipping at a glass of champagne, she watched the scene in front of her with interest, and thought how unfortunate it was that the contrast between Amelia and Kate had never been so apparent. Amelia had chosen that night to wear a yellow gown with brown trim. Beside Kate's silver-and-white gauze just now, Amelia had resembled nothing so much as a plump little sunflower huddled next to a shimmering moonbeam. Yes, it was unfortunate, Olivia thought, but probably unavoidable, even if Kate had been wearing a grain sack. Her niece had the ability to outshine anyone, even in the worst of circumstances.

Sighing, Olivia sat back in the uncomfortable and spindly chair and wondered if she had done the proper thing, encouraging Kate to marry Page.

But she hadn't exactly encouraged them, had she? Demanded that they marry—that was more honest. She had practically ordered a desperate Kate to accept Page's proposal. Had she been right to do so? Only time would tell, Olivia thought as she sighed again.

It was odd how things had a way of working out, she mused, her thoughts taking another direction. If Page hadn't stopped at the Hall the night that Kate had dashed out, asking to speak to Olivia about marrying Kate, Olivia doubted that she would have had the courage to urge Kate to accept his proposal. How fortunate that he had declared his feelings before the crisis with Kate had demanded more immediate action. Somehow, that eased the guilt she felt about advising Kate not to tell him of the coming child. It wasn't right to keep such knowledge from him, Olivia knew. But there had been no other avenue open, and Olivia knew that, too.

They did make a handsome couple, she thought, observing them from her position across the room. The dance had ended, and Page had returned Amelia to a decidedly uncomfortable-looking Roger, who had finally, awkwardly, asked Kate to dance just as the music was ending.

Olivia sighed with pleasure as she saw Page bend attentively to Kate. His eyes rarely left her animated face as she responded gaily to the crowd of young people who came up to surround them, and Olivia could hear Kate's laugh above the music, a merry sound that was so rare from her, and so infectious, that Olivia had to smile in response. She could well imagine the adroitness with which Kate sidestepped those questions she didn't care to answer, and her lips quirked. She was glad someone else was on the receiving end of Kate in an elusive mood; heaven knew she had been in that position too many times herself in the past!

Page, Olivia saw as she sipped again at her champagne, spoke rarely. Instead, he stood back a bit and watched Kate. If he was curious about Kate's rather startling demand that they be married by the night of Roger's ball, he had never mentioned it—at least to her.

Frowning, Olivia watched him closely for a sign that he knew or suspected anything of Kate's condition. Was he aware, and chose to ignore it? Or was he so in love with Kate that it didn't matter?

Gazing at him as he turned to accept yet more congratulations from someone, Olivia decided that it was neither. If

Page Taggart knew that his bride carried another man's child, it would indeed matter a great deal to him. He was a proud man, and while he might love Kate to distraction, he could never ignore or pretend not to know the situation; he simply was not that kind of man. He might have married Kate anyway, thought Olivia, but not before he had made it clear that he knew the truth about her and accepted it in order to make her his wife.

So the only conclusion was that he didn't know, and once again that nagging doubt surfaced in Olivia's mind. Page *was* the son of one of her dearest friends, after all; had she the right to keep something so important from him? If she owed nothing to Page himself, didn't she have some sort of obligation to his father?

Guiltily Olivia bit her lip and stared at the crowd of young people surrounding Kate and Page. Seeing Kate's face, so alive, so bright, Olivia decided to put her doubts and misgivings out of her mind. Her first responsibility was to her niece, she reminded herself; what she had done in encouraging them to marry with this secret between them might not have been right in the moral sense, but it had been the only practical thing to do, and she wouldn't think about it anymore. All the problems had taken care of themselves, she rationalized; an unhappy situation had become instead an occasion for rejoicing, and Kate's dilemma had been solved to everyone's satisfaction.

Or rather, Olivia amended quickly, *almost* to everyone's satisfaction. A jealous Amelia might be close to bursting into tears, but an infuriated Maude was bearing down on her like a warrior about to do battle.

"Hello, Maude," said Olivia, taking the initiative. "Isn't this a lovely ball?"

Maude had screeched to a halt in front of her, taffeta skirts crackling with indignation and outrage. "How can you say such a thing?" Maude demanded, her face a fiery red that clashed unfortunately with the purple of her gown.

Olivia smiled innocently. "I don't know what you mean, Maude," she replied. "It *is* a lovely ball. I can't help it if you're not enjoying yourself."

"How can I enjoy myself when . . . when *your* niece has deliberately ruined the entire evening? Just look at her," she ordered, pointing in Kate's direction with an irate rustle of taffeta. "Standing there as if this were *her* party instead of Amelia's. Olivia, you have to do something!"

"What would you suggest?" asked Olivia serenely. "After all, Kate is a married woman now. She is no longer my responsibility." And thank heaven for that, Olivia thought privately with irreverence.

"Yes, and that's another thing!" Maude exclaimed. "I don't understand how you could condone such a hasty marriage! It isn't like you at all!"

Diverted from her daughter's problems for the moment, Maude sat down heavily on the chair next to Olivia and began to ply her fan vigorously to her red face. Then she stopped abruptly, turning to Olivia with a speculative glance. "Unless," she suggested with malice, "there was a reason. . . ."

Olivia was quick to reply. She had to stop that rumor before it began, or else it would all be for nothing. "I don't care for your implication," she said sharply to Maude. "If you're suggesting that Kate—"

"I'm not implying anything," Maude said hastily, retreating before Olivia's expression. "It just seemed . . . precipitate . . . of Kate to rush off like that. But then," she added placatingly, "I know how impetuous Kate is—"

"Indeed . . ." Olivia murmured.

"—and what a trial she has been for you. I mean," she added quickly, as Olivia shot another glance at her, "that it must have been difficult, trying to cope with a girl that age, thrust at you so suddenly. Heaven knows," Maude said with a heavy sigh, "it's hard enough with one's own daughter sometimes!"

"Yes," said Olivia sympathetically.

"So I suppose things turned out for the best, didn't they?" Maude said brightly. "Kate is married now, and no longer your responsibility, and she has managed to snare a' handsome husband . . ."

Maude could afford to be expansive now that she realized what Kate's hasty marriage meant to her and her daughter. With Olivia's troublesome niece safely out of the way, Amelia would no longer appear so pale and pallid and . . . ineffectual in comparison to Kate.

Maude's malicious gaze rested on the unsuspecting Kate, clearly enjoying herself as the center of attention, and her eyes narrowed. How that girl had caused her sleepless nights, worrying about whether she would snatch Roger from under Amelia's very nose! But no more, no more. Let her have her moment, thought Maude; it was worth it. From now on, Kate was Page Taggart's responsibility. And, Maude thought with satisfaction, he would certainly have his hands full.

14

"Oh, wasn't it wonderful?" Kate whirled ecstatically around the center of the apartment suite Olivia had prepared for them. It was long after midnight, and they had just returned from Green Eaves, but Kate wasn't tired. On the contrary, she seemed about to burst with energy as she danced jubilantly about the room. "Did you see Roger's face when we were announced? And Amelia! I thought she would faint on the spot!" She started to laugh again, but just then she glimpsed Page's face, and she realized her error. She wasn't going to give Page the opportunity to take her to task about ruining Amelia's ball; it was her own night of triumph, and she was going to enjoy it all, every minute.

Page tried to catch her as she danced by, but she eluded him with a laugh, whirling even faster. "Kate, if you don't stop, you'll make yourself ill."

"Never! Never! I feel wonderful!"

"Here, then. This should make you feel even better." Smiling in defeat, Page held out a glass of champagne.

"Champagne!" Kate stopped in delighted surprise. "Oh, I love champagne! What made you think of it?"

"This *is* our wedding night," he reminded her as she accepted the glass. "Or had you forgotten?"

She hadn't forgotten at all; she had just put it out of her mind. In the brief silence that followed, the clock struck twice, and Kate wondered if she could excuse herself, pleading sudden weariness and the lateness of the hour. Oh, why had she come in just now, dancing about the room like a fool? He would never believe such an excuse now, and she wouldn't blame him. A little desperately she emptied her glass and held it out for more. False courage, she knew, and thrust the thought away.

Page raised an eyebrow at her gesture, but he filled her glass again without protest. This time, though, he stayed her hand when she lifted the glass immediately to drink. He commented mildly, "I'd like to make a toast, if I may, before you drink the whole bottle."

Kate flushed, then laughed nervously as his glance held hers. What was the matter with her? Was she afraid of him? But what was there to be afraid of?

Suddenly her feelings of triumph over Roger evaporated; her euphoric mood of before seemed childish and immature. She had married Page voluntarily, after all; no one had forced her. Well . . . not really. And if she hadn't thought beyond attending the ball tonight, that wasn't Page's fault. She was his wife . . . his bride. It was their wedding night, and she was suddenly very nervous. Was it possible to drink oneself insensible on a single bottle of champagne? She wasn't sure, but she was determined to try.

Their glasses touched, the crystal chiming musically in the silence. She could hardly look at him, her heart was pounding so. She felt weak and breathless and totally unnerved. The house was still and silent, and she realized for the first time that she was alone with him. Alone with her husband. . . .

"To you, Kate," he said, raising his glass to her.

The clock ticked loudly on the mantel as they drank. Page put his empty glass on the table, took hers to set beside it. Her gauze skirts whispered silkily as he lifted her into his arms. Carrying her easily, he walked into the bedroom.

One of the maids had been in before them: the bedside lamp was aglow, the coverlet turned invitingly down. A finely embroidered lawn nightgown was laid carefully out on one of the plumped pillows; everything was ready.

Except Kate.

As Page set her gently on her feet again, her pulse began to hammer in her throat. This man was her husband, she reminded herself; they had every right to drink champagne together, to be alone, to shut the bedroom door. Why was she so nervous and apprehensive? After all, it wasn't as if she didn't know what was going to happen, as if she had never been with a man before. Hastily she thrust the thought of Roger from her mind. She couldn't think of him; she *wouldn't* think of him.

And then Page put his arms around her again and drew her close. Pressed against him, she was surprised to discover that his heart was pounding as hard as hers. He was trembling, in fact; she felt a tremor in his arms as he embraced her. Their lips met, and suddenly she forgot that Roger Templeton ever existed. Suddenly she wasn't nervous anymore.

Sometime later, when Page climbed out of bed to fetch more champagne, and became entangled in the voluminous skirt of the gown he had removed from her and thrown onto the floor, Kate giggled. His muttered cursing as he tried comically to free his foot made her laugh even more, and she sat up in bed to watch the ludicrous struggle. She felt wonderful, light and happy, fulfilled and . . . satisfied. Oh, yes: utterly satisfied. She wasn't tired at all, though it was nearly dawn, and they hadn't slept.

What a night it had been! Kate thought. And how shameless she had been during that night! The lawn nightgown lay on the floor, unwanted and unused—a mute reminder of forgotten modesty—while its owner languished between rumpled sheets, naked, and enjoying their silky feel on her bare skin.

Why had she been afraid? she wondered, watching Page kick free of the clinging gauze at last. Her husband might have been her fantasy lover come to life, so gentle and tender had he been, so passionate and demanding all at once.

Sighing, Kate lay back on the pillows. Even her experience with Roger had not prepared her for this night, she admitted wistfully, although she had been very careful, even at the height of their passion, to play the virgin. Now she wished she had been a virgin with Page; that furtive interval in the barn with Roger was in retrospect distasteful and degrading—an experience that might have been totally eclipsed by the events of this night, if it hadn't been for one constant reminder.

Unconsciously Kate pressed a hand to her belly. Impossible for her not to imagine the small bulge there, and yet Page hadn't seemed to notice a thing. In fact, remembering some of the things he had whispered to her during their frenzied lovemaking, Kate blushed furiously.

Page returned with two glasses and a fresh bottle of champagne that he had somehow managed to keep cold during the night. Handing her a glass, he walked over to the balcony

doors with his, and pulled aside the draperies, opening the
door to let in the cool, crisp air of dawn. It was almost sunrise, and Page was silhouetted in the doorframe, his body outlined in shadows. Looking at him, Kate marveled that this
was her husband: he was so handsome. Unashamedly she
stared, admiring his broad shoulders and strong back that ta-
pered to a trim waist and narrow hips. She had never seen a
man totally nude before, and while she suspected she should
look away in feminine confusion, she could not; she was utterly fascinated.

Page seemed completely unconcerned with his nakedness.
Turning, he saw her watching him, and smiled. She smiled in
return, but when he gestured for her to join him on the balcony, she shook her head. She was suddenly shy with him,
and unable to expose her own nudity.

His expression tender, Page joined her again in the bed. He
put his arms around her, drawing her close as they both
sipped their champagne and watched the sky change from
purple to mauve to rose. Outside the open door a bird woke
and chirped; another answered sleepily. It was a beautiful
morning, and lying against Page's chest, listening to his strong
heartbeat beneath her ear, Kate was utterly content.

And then Page spoke, and with a dismayed jolt Kate realized that the man she had married had no intention of being
swayed from his original course. The quarrel she had put out
of her mind resurfaced with a vengeance, and Kate knew she
had been a fool to think Page had surrendered or forgotten
about it.

"I've booked passage," he said calmly, "on a ship that
leaves for New York a week hence. Once we land, we'll leave
immediately by rail for Kansas, and from there we'll take a
coach to Colorado. I know you'll enjoy traveling in America;
the scenery there is so different from what England offers."

Kate stared at him throughout this blithe speech, too
shocked at what she was hearing to move away from him.
Lying there with his arms around her, listening to the soft
chirping of the birds, Kate had been almost asleep. Now,
with Page talking of ships and trains and coaches, she was instantly and appallingly awake.

Clutching the sheet to her, she sat up. "I thought we settled
that last night," she said.

Page shook his head. He finished the last of his champagne, put the glass carefully on the bedside table, and

turned back to her. "No," he said calmly. "You settled it. Or thought you did. I think your last words were something to the effect that you wouldn't go."

"Well, I won't! I'm not leaving England to go tramping around some country that doesn't even have a name yet!"

"The country is America, and while Colorado is still a territory, it will be a state very soon, I'm sure."

"How dare you lecture me as if I were a child in the schoolroom!" Kate cried, enraged at his paternalistic tone.

"Then don't act like a child," Page replied. "At any rate, this is all beside the point, isn't it? Colorado is where my home is, and that's where we're going."

"But my home is here!" wailed Kate.

"Your home is where your husband is."

Unable to think of a response to that logic, Kate immediately took another direction. "Well, why can't we live here?" she demanded. "You love England—you've told me so a hundred times! And Aunt Olivia would be ecstatic if we stayed at Tremont Hall!"

"Apart from the fact that I would never impose on your aunt, I don't need the offer of a home—I have one of my own. Of course, it isn't Tremont Hall, but—"

"Then why did you come here at all," Kate cried, not listening, "if you didn't mean to stay!"

"You know I came to settle my father's estate," Page replied patiently. But despite his tone, he was obviously trying to control himself; a muscle twitched in his jaw, and his eyes had darkened.

Kate was too angry herself to pay attention to these danger signals. Flouncing around in the bed, she turned her back on him. "I've made my decision," she said flatly. "I won't go!"

There was a silence. Then the bed rocked a little as Page threw back the covers and got up. She could feel him standing there looking at her, but she didn't turn around. Hurt that the tender lover of last night had dissolved into this unreasonable monster, miserable that they had quarreled, and infuriated over his stubbornness, Kate sat stiffly in injured dignity, refusing to look at him.

"It's time you learned that you can't have your way in everything," Page said quietly, enraging her even more by his calm control, when she felt like throwing something. "You accepted certain responsibilities when you married me," he continued. "And one of those is that you accompany your husband to his home, no matter where it is. I can't believe we're even discussing this; I thought even you would know where your duty lies."

"Don't talk to me of duty!" Kate said bitterly. "I know only too well what duty is!"

"What does that mean?"

But Kate had already said too much, and she knew it. "It doesn't mean anything," she muttered, trying fiercely not to cry.

"Let's not quarrel, Kate. . . ."

If she hadn't been so upset at the thought of leaving England, so afraid of going through a pregnancy without the support of her aunt, Kate might have accepted Page's attempt at apology. But because she was confused and unsure of herself, and suddenly very frightened of this unknown thing that was happening to her body, Kate jerked away from the hand Page put on her shoulder.

"Don't think you can apologize so easily," she said. "It wasn't fair of you not to tell me about going to America before we were married."

"Oh, and I suppose I should have spelled it out as a condition, just like you made me agree to the conditions you set forth. Is that it?"

Kate felt a chill, wondering if he was testing her. "You should have mentioned it at least," she said stubbornly.

"Why? Would it have made a difference?"

Was he testing her? And was she going to spend her entire married life wondering if he knew the truth about the child? Would she have to analyze every remark for a double meaning? She didn't think she could stand such a strain—years of walking a verbal tightrope. Those years stretched endlessly before her, fraught with pitfalls. She wondered bleakly if she could survive it all without at some point revealing the truth.

"Kate? Would it have made a difference?"

With an effort, Kate pulled herself together. "I don't know," she retorted crossly, praying that she sounded convincing. "You didn't tell me, so how can I guess?"

Fiercely she looked up at him then, and this time she didn't have to wonder if she sounded sincere; she meant every word. "But I'll tell you one thing, Page Taggart," she said decisively. "I'm not going to America, and that's final!"

But of course she went to America. There wasn't really any other alternative, she was forced to admit, enraged. If she hadn't agreed to go, Page would either have thrown her over his shoulder and carried her aboard or would have abandoned her, humiliatingly, on the dock. She had no doubt at all that he meant to carry out either threat, whichever applied at the time, and so they sailed a week later, surrounded by boxes and trunks and crates that numbered a set of sterling dinnerware from Roger and his intended; various household items, including embroidered linens and thick quilts; and as a wedding gift, Olivia's prized silver tea service.

Kate refused to speak to Page, and every time she thought of Olivia, she began to cry.

15

For Kate, the parting from her aunt had been such an emotional wrench that she was numb the entire journey from Tremont Hall to where the ship waited for them at Liverpool. She had broken down completely when Olivia had presented her at the last with the silver tea service, and she had tried to refuse the gift, knowing how much it meant to her aunt. Olivia had been adamant.

"I want you to have it," Olivia insisted. "Now, please don't argue, Kate; it would give me such pleasure to know that you and Page will have some use for it."

"But you have already given us so much," Kate protested, thinking of the vast assortment of sheets and towels and blankets and other things too numerous to mention that Olivia had packed for her. "And I know how fond you are of the set," she continued. "Why, you use it every day!"

"All the more reason for you to take it," Olivia said firmly. "It belonged to my mother, you know, and if I had had a daughter . . . well, it would have been hers. So I want you to have it, Kate, because I think of you as the daughter I never had. And when you use it in your new home, perhaps you can think of me . . ."

"Oh, I will!"

Aunt and niece had embraced through their tears, and when they had said their last good-byes on the wide front steps of Tremont Hall, neither could speak. Kate, who had rebelled so at the thought of coming to live with her aunt a year ago, was loath to leave her now. Olivia, who had viewed the impending arrival of her niece with alarm those many months ago, now had to fight for control at the thought of never seeing her again. A helpless Page stood by, watching his bride embrace the aunt who had been more of a mother to her than Augusta, and wondered where in the *hell* the carriage had gone to.

When finally it arrived to take them to the ship, Page bundled Kate inside, and, amid emotional promises from both women to write constantly, they were off, clattering down the wide drive for the last time. It would be many years before Kate saw Olivia again, and the silver tea service would be worn smooth from constant use.

It was a relief when they finally arrived at the docks. Page had been unable to offer Kate anything more than his handkerchief during the drive, for she sat silently in the corner of the carriage, refusing to speak to him, huge tears sliding down her white face. He himself had retreated into silence, feeling very much the villain for taking her away from her home, and not knowing how to handle this copious and quiet weeping. An enraged, quarrelsome Kate he could manage; this pale withdrawn young woman shrinking away from him was another matter altogether.

As soon as they arrived, Page busied himself with supervising the loading of their voluminous baggage; after enduring Kate's injured silence, it was a relief to be shouting orders about things men could understand.

Kate, left to her own devices, wandered around listlessly, cautioned by Page not to go too far out of sight. Every now and then she would glance back at him and glare murderously, hating him for insisting on this despicable journey. Anchored far out in the water, the ship seemed an alien thing, huge and clumsy and an utterly unreliable means of transportation across the vastness of the Atlantic. Kate hated it on sight. She was miserable and exhausted already, and her husband was so preoccupied that he wouldn't even notice if she pitched headfirst into the water.

Feeling very sorry for herself, Kate walked to the edge of the pier and looked down at the waves lapping at the dock. It was a mistake. The water here was dirty and oily; bits of unidentifiable garbage clustered on the surface, and her eye caught the rotten remains of a fish floating back and forth under her feet. Feeling nauseous at the sight, Kate turned away and was confronted by one of the roustabouts stuffing something into a sack, preparing to throw the baggage into the sea. As Kate watched in horror, a small ball of fur escaped from the sack, falling to the dock as the man heaved the bag far out into the water. He was about to scoop up the furry little thing to throw after the sack when Kate shrieked, "Don't you dare! Don't you dare throw that kitten into the sea!"

Rushing up to the startled man, Kate snatched the animal from him. She held it protectively against her as she glared at him. "How could you do such a thing?" she demanded. "What kind of man are you?"

Kate had disconcerted the man by her attack. The roustabout, who looked tough and coarse, well able to take on any man and win, found himself trying to explain an action he normally wouldn't have given a second thought. But there was something about Kate that held him there; she didn't know what a picture she made, with her flashing eyes and trembling mouth, holding the scruffy little cat to her breast. It had been a long time since the man had seen such a woman; he couldn't take his eyes off her.

"They was just strays, ma'am," he said. "They would've starved to death if I hadn't done what I did."

"Well . . ." said Kate doubtfully, glancing from the kitten to the roustabout and back again. The little animal *was* pitifully thin. "I suppose you only did what you thought was right," she conceded.

"Yes, ma'am." The man appeared about to say something more, but his eyes went to a point over her shoulder, and he gave his forelock a quick tug. "Thank you, ma'am," he said, and disappeared.

Kate hardly noticed his departure. The frightened kitten was clinging to her jacket like a leech, and she was busy disengaging its claws from her shoulder. Freeing herself, she held it out at arm's length while she inspected it. It was a calico, with a black patch over one eye and orange and black mingling with the dirty white of its coat. It mewed suddenly, piteously, screwing up its eyes, and Kate knew that it wasn't only frightened; it was hungry as well.

"Where did you get that?"

Kate turned. Page was standing behind her, and she was about to explain eagerly about rescuing the kitten when she remembered that she was still angry with him. "I found it, of course," she said coldly.

"Well, put it down. It's almost time to board the ship."

"I'm taking it with me."

"Oh, no, you're not."

They glared at each other, locked once again in a contest of wills.

"I'm taking it with me," Kate repeated. "If I have to be dragged halfway around the world to some barbaric place I've never even heard of, the least you can do is allow me this one simple thing!"

"The captain won't like it," Page warned.

"I," replied Kate loftily as she swept by him, kitten in hand, "will deal with the captain."

Captain Bain had no objection at all. After Kate had smiled her request about bringing the kitten aboard, and had flashed her green eyes at him, he would readily have consented to her bringing a cartload of kittens with her if it pleased her. So, the problem wasn't the captain at all; it was the ship itself. To her lasting mortification, Kate was not a good sailor.

The moment she stepped on deck and felt it roll under her, Kate was ill. It was all she could do to stand there exchanging inane pleasantries with the captain, for with every gentle pitch of the ship, her nausea increased. Once she made the mistake of glancing down at the water as they stood by the rail; that was even worse, for the dipping and swaying of the ship seemed accentuated. Closing her eyes, Kate took a deep shuddering breath, willing her nausea to pass.

"Kate, are you all right?"

Unwillingly she opened her eyes. Page was looking at her in concern. "Of course I'm all right," she forced herself to say. "What makes you think I'm not?"

"You're very pale. I think we should go below ..."

She was too ill to argue with him. As if from a long dis-

tance, she heard Page say to the captain, "I would like to see
our cabin now, captain, if you don't mind. Mrs. Taggart
seems a little . . . tired."

"Of course," Captain Bain murmured. Summoning the
steward to show them below, he added that he hoped they
would join him for dinner.

Kate didn't know what Page replied to the invitation; she
didn't care. The journey to the private cabin Page had engaged for them seemed interminable, and with each rolling
step, Kate was sure she would become violently ill. It was
only by the fiercest willpower that she negotiated the last few
steps without aid, and as soon as they were inside the cabin,
she looked around frantically, knowing she could hold back
her nausea no longer.

"Kate, are you sure. . . ?"

There was a small door opposite her. Praying that it wasn't
a wardrobe or storage of some kind, she dropped the kitten
on the bed and rushed over to it. To her relief, it was a water
closet, complete with small sink. There was a porthole over
her head, but that was the only thing she had time to notice.
Seconds after that she was bent over the sink, tears of mortification running down her face as she retched uncontrollably.

How long she stood there hunched over the bowl, she
didn't know. When the spasms finally passed, she was weak
and exhausted, forced to rest her head on her hands as she
leaned over the sink. It wasn't until then that she realized
Page was beside her, his arm around her waist, supporting
her. Had he been there the whole time? Kate was too sick to
care.

"Come along, love. Once you get in bed, you'll feel better."

She wasn't able to protest; her head rolled weakly against
his shoulder as he carried her over to the bed. She didn't even
object when he undressed her and tucked her between the
sheets. One of her trunks was stashed against the wall, but
she was too weary to ask for a nightgown, too ill to get up
and search for it herself. It was heaven, lying here in the
hard bed; if she was very careful and didn't move, the rock-
ing of the ship didn't seem so awful after all.

And then she knew how optimistic she had been: with a
lurch that shuddered through the entire vessel, the ship was
under way, and each time it rose to meet another wave,
Kate's stomach rose with it.

"Oh, Page," she sobbed, clutching miserably at his arm for

support as she surrendered to another bout of nausea. "I'm not a good sailor after all!"

Page smiled as he gathered her into his arms, stroking her hair as she wept weakly against his chest. "You're just sea-sick, Kate," he said tenderly. "It will pass, and you'll be well in no time."

"When?" wailed Kate, sobbing into his shoulder.

"Soon, darling. Soon."

Page went to dinner at the captain's table without her. The very thought of food brought on another attack of nausea, and when that had passed, Kate could hardly drink the weak tea Page had requested from the galley. It would settle her stomach, he told her, insisting that she drink it. But her stomach was queasy and tender; her whole body felt battered and bruised, and the tea, instead of producing the calming effect Page intended, only seemed to aggravate her nausea.

Finally, when she could no longer stand the sight of Page pacing back and forth in their cramped quarters, she insisted that he go to dinner without her. She couldn't rest with him staring at her all the time, she told him; and more than any-thing else, she wanted to go to sleep—to forget, even for a short time, how awful this ship was, and how horrible she felt. She refused to think about the fact that their journey had just begun; the idea that she might suffer like this for the entire voyage was too appalling to consider.

But even though she had practically ordered him to go, when the cabin door closed reluctantly behind him, Kate im-mediately burst into tears. Suddenly she felt abandoned and alone, utterly miserable, and so, so sick.

Oh, why had Page done this to her? she wondered wretchedly, clutching the sides of the bed as the ship rolled. Why had he made her come with him when she was so sick?

Roger wouldn't have insisted on this hideous journey, she thought suddenly. Roger wouldn't have dragged her off to America, making her leave everything behind to be violently ill on a ship she hated. He would have considered her feelings; he would have put her wishes before his, always. Roger, she thought with increasing resentment against Page, was a gentleman!

Yes, and if he was such a gentleman, why didn't he marry you?

Kate thrust the question aside, answering the nagging inner

voice irrationally by defending Roger. Aloud she said fiercely, "He would have married me if I had told him about the baby. He would have; I know it!"

Would he? Why didn't you tell him, then? Weren't you sure?

"Leave me alone!" Kate cried. "Oh, leave me alone!"

The ship gave another lurch just then, riding a swell before dropping nauseatingly into a trough between waves. Kate felt sick again, reaching for the basin Page had left by the side of the bed for such an emergency. Was this her punishment? she wondered tearfully as she wiped the streaming perspiration from her face. If it was, the sentence was aptly devised; she had never felt so wretchedly sorry in all her life.

Turning her face into the pillow, Kate began to cry with self-pity. She was exhausted, bruised, ill, and so weak that she couldn't have climbed out of bed if the ship were sinking. Which wouldn't be a bad idea, she thought bitterly, grabbing quickly for the sides of the bed as the ship rose sickeningly again. If it sank, at least this agony would be over with.

And where was Page? Forgetting entirely that it was she who had insisted that he go, she pictured him, resplendent in evening dress, having a wonderful time at table while she suffered in this dark and dismal hole. It wasn't fair, she thought resentfully. Why couldn't she have been a good sailor, too?

There was a sudden small rumbling sound next to her ear. Kate turned her head to look, and then began to cry at the sight of the kitten who had climbed up onto the pillow beside her. It was huddled into a little ball, watching her with wide eyes, purring mightily. To Kate, that purr was the most comforting sound she had ever heard, and she gathered the little cat close, nestling it against her cheek.

"At least you haven't abandoned me," she murmured, unashamedly glad of the kitten's company.

With the touch of her hand, the purring sound increased in volume, and finally, physically and emotionally spent, listening to the steady, comforting rumble by her ear, Kate fell asleep.

16

It was three days before Kate was well enough to put on a dressing gown and wander weakly about the cabin, almost a week before she felt strong enough to venture for the first time on deck. Despite the steady rolling motion of the ship, Kate immediately felt better when she stepped out into the open at last. The air was crisp and clean and bracing; the sky was blue, with a few scudding clouds; and the sea was deep green and relatively calm. She was standing by the rail, enjoying all this, when the captain came diffidently over to her.

"I hope you're feeling better, Mrs. Taggart," he said.

Kate turned to look at him, pleased by his concern. "Yes, thank you, Captain Bain. I'm much better now."

"Your husband has been so worried about you."

At the mention of Page, Kate's mouth tightened. "Has he?"

Captain Bain tried not to notice the sudden chill in her voice. "Oh, indeed, yes," he said enthusiastically. "Why, I thought at one point he would demand that I take the ship back to port!"

"How chivalrous of him," said Kate, her voice steely.

"Er . . . yes," the captain replied uncertainly. Glancing at her, he saw her expression and frowned. "Your husband is a fine man, Mrs. Taggart," he said.

Kate turned cool green eyes on him again. "And why do you make a point of that, captain?" she asked. "Do you think I am unaware of the kind of man I married?"

The captain was undecided how to interpret this remark, and Kate let him wonder what she had meant. Looking away from him, she gazed out to sea, and Bain decided he had business elsewhere. He excused himself.

"Of course, captain. I know how busy you must be."

Bain hesitated a moment more, wondering if he should speak to her about her husband. He himself had been mar-

119

ried some thirty years, and he knew how these things went.
Then, deciding that the Taggarts were engaging in a newly-
wed spat that was really none of his business, the captain
nodded at Kate and walked quickly away.

Kate hardly noticed his departure. She stayed at the rail,
enjoying the salt breeze on her face, and thought about Page.
Despite her disclaimer to the captain, did she really know the
man she had married?

They hadn't spoken for a week; they hadn't even slept in
the same cabin, not to mention the same bed. How Page had
managed other accommodations for himself, she didn't know,
and she had been too proud to ask just now. It had been un-
nerving enough, pretending not to notice the captain's speculative glance; she hadn't wanted to add to her humiliation by
admitting that she and Page had quarreled violently. And
over something so ridiculous as a spilled cup of chocolate.
Wincing at the memory, Kate could still vividly recall that
awful scene the first night on board when she had been so
sick and Page had accepted the captain's dinner invitation.

Kate wasn't sure how long she had slept with the kitten
purring in her ear, but she woke that night to the sound of
the cabin door unlocking. Startled and disoriented, it had
taken her a few seconds to remember where she was. When
she did remember, all her earlier misery came flooding back.
So, it hadn't been a dream, she groaned; she was still on this
nightmare ship after all.

"Kate, are you awake?"

It was dark in the cabin, too dark to see much more than
Page's outline as he stood uncertainly in the doorway. He
was carrying something, but she couldn't see what it was.

"Yes, I'm awake," she answered irritably. Why was it so
black in here? Where was the lamp? She couldn't remember.

Neither, apparently, could Page. He came cautiously in,
feeling his way carefully, trying to see ahead of him by the
dim light of the single sconce in the corridor outside. There
was a table bolted to the floor beside her bed; he began
making his way toward that.

Kate saw it coming an instant before it happened, but
there was no opportunity to warn Page. The kitten,
frightened by Page's sudden appearance, chose that moment
to leap off the pillow before Kate could grab it. The cat ran
for the door, colliding with Page in the process, startling him
because he couldn't see it in the darkness. He cursed, the cat

hissed, and somehow they became entangled. The next thing Kate heard was a crash. Yowling, the kitten changed direction and launched itself back toward the bed and straight into Kate's arms, where it huddled, shivering. The entire incident had taken place in a few seconds, but it would take days to undo the damage.

There was an ominous silence from Page. Kate could imagine him sprawled ignominiously on the floor, and as she reached hastily to light the lamp she now remembered seeing by the bed, she bit her lip to keep from laughing aloud. But the image she had of Page clashing with the kitten was too amusing; despite her efforts, she giggled.

She didn't laugh long. Lighting the lamp, she turned to look at Page, and was appalled. He sat on the floor, surrounded by broken china, his white shirtfront spattered with the hot chocolate he had been bringing to her, holding his bleeding right hand away from him.

"I hope," he said between clenched teeth, "that you're satisfied."

The look he gave her as he got to his feet would have quelled a lesser woman. It only had the effect of irritating Kate. "Satisfied!" she echoed. "What do you mean by that?"

"That damned cat nearly broke my neck!"

Kate clutched the kitten. "It wasn't the cat's fault," she said. "You frightened it."

"It had no business being here."

"Well, at least it was here to keep me company," Kate flared. "Which is more than I can say for you!"

Page looked at her. How he managed to maintain his arrogant dignity, splattered with chocolate and nursing a bleeding palm, she didn't know. For some reason, his poise in this ridiculous situation irritated her anew, and she glared at him as he took out his handkerchief and elaborately wrapped it around his hand for a bandage.

"As I recall," he said, "it was you who insisted I leave you alone. I didn't want to go to dinner; it was your idea."

He was right, of course, but Kate was too annoyed to concede the point. For a while she had been distracted from her misery, but now she was nauseated again, and dizzy. She felt as if she hadn't slept at all, and what was more, she was infuriated that Page could stand there so easily, adjusting his balance to the rolling of the ship, while she couldn't even get out of bed.

"You didn't have to go," she said unfairly. "You knew how sick I was."

Page didn't say anything for a long moment. She saw a muscle twitching in his jaw, and knew he was trying to control himself, but she didn't care that she had made him angry. "People don't die from seasickness, Kate," he said at last in that patronizing tone she hated. "It's uncomfortable—"

"Uncomfortable!"

"—but it passes."

"How dare you treat this lightly!" she blazed. "I wouldn't be suffering now if you hadn't forced me to board this hideous ship!"

"Let's not go into that again, shall we? I think we've already had that disagreement. Twice."

"We're going to have it again!"

"No," said Page. "We're not."

Very calmly he stepped over the broken china on the floor, grabbed a blanket from the foot of the bed, and started for the door.

"Where are you going?" Kate asked sharply.

"Does it matter? I thought you were more interested in that damned cat than you were in me."

"That isn't fair!"

"Isn't it?" His hand was on the door latch as he looked back at her. "Well, perhaps you need a little more time to yourself to think about it."

"How dare you talk to me like that! You're my husband—"

"And you're supposed to be my wife. When are you going to start acting like one?"

She was so furious she couldn't speak. "If you leave now," she said, her voice shaking with rage, "don't come back."

"Don't," he said as he jerked open the door, "tempt me."

Kate burst into tears as the door slammed shut behind him. There was a book on the bedside table, and she threw it furiously at the door, where it hit so forcefully that the binding parted, scattering pages like confetti as they fell to the floor. The sight made her cry all the harder, and as the kitten crept cautiously into her lap again, Kate picked it up and buried her face in its rough fur. "He'll be back," she sobbed. "He'll be back. I know it."

But Page hadn't returned that night, nor the next, nor the

one after that. And now it was a week since their quarrel, and Kate was miserable.

A shadow fell across her as she stood by the rail, and even before she looked up, she knew who it was. Her heart began to pound, and she cast about frantically in her mind for something to say.

Page took the initiative. "I see you're feeling better," he said neutrally.

"Yes. I am, thank you." As soon as she said it, she realized how ridiculous she sounded. How clever! she thought scathingly. *Yes. I am, thank you.* Was that all she could think of to say?

She had wanted to say something witty or devastating; she had wanted to tell him how lonely she had been, or . . . how much she had missed him. *Yes. I am, thank you.* She could have cringed.

"You're looking well yourself, Page," she said finally, to break the strained silence. Even now she could say none of those things that were closest to her heart; the words seemed to stick in her throat. She could barely look at him. "The sea seems to agree with you."

Forcing herself to meet his gaze, she realized she spoke the truth: Page did look tanned and hearty, and she felt a pang of envy at his robust health. Her mirror this morning had reflected a pale and drawn face with faint blue smudges under the eyes. She looked like a caricature of herself, while he had never looked better.

Dragging her eyes away from him, she pretended an interest in the blue-green water rushing by the stern. She was grateful at least that she could look down now without feeling so horribly nauseous. Hopefully, she was conquering this awful seasickness at last.

"Kate . . ."

Something in his voice made her pause. When she looked at him, she was stunned by his wistful expression. It was so unlike him that tears sprang to her eyes. Looking down again in a blur, she saw his hand reach for hers as she gripped the rail.

"Kate, don't you think we've quarreled long enough?"

His hand was covering hers; she could feel the strength and warmth of his fingers, and she turned her palm up, lacing her fingers with his. "I never meant to quarrel, Page," she said softly.

"I can't even remember what it was about."

Smiling through her tears, she glanced up at him again. "Neither can I," she said.

"Then can we start again?" He used his thumb to wipe away the tear that had spilled onto her cheek. "I'll even bring you another cup of chocolate, if you like," he said.

So he did remember! Laughing shakily, she shook her head. "No, but if you want to return to the cabin, I promise to keep the cat out of the way."

"How can I refuse an offer like that?"

The sunset that night was a marvel—a painting of rose and violet and gold that filled the sky with soft pink light. But neither Kate nor Page appreciated the wonder beyond their cabin porthole; they were too preoccupied with the wonder of each other. This time their lovemaking was even more satisfying than before, for joining passion and desire was the delight in finding and exploring each other again. Joyfully, they realized that their separation was truly over at last.

And afterward, basking in utter contentment with each other, they feasted on cold fowl and fruit, finishing with wine sent from the captain himself—a wise man who had sent the bottle unobtrusively along with the picnic hamper and instructions that the Taggarts were not to be disturbed.

Alone in the cabin, Kate and Page laughed and fed each other tidbits from their plates, kissed and made love again. The kitten munched its share from a safe place on a shelf, and as Kate fell into a weary sleep wrapped in Page's arms, she thought with drowsy satisfaction that now her honeymoon had truly begun.

And that time was a dream that Kate would always remember, a halcyon time of pleasure and fulfillment and contentment, when she and Page seemed to be in complete accord.

The weather held, except for one brief storm that Kate enjoyed immensely, free of any sign of seasickness as the ship pitched about, nestled in Page's arms in their narrow bed, listening to the rain outside. They spent hours on deck after that, sitting in the sun or walking by moonlight, enjoying the sweep of sky and water no matter what time it was. They dined by themselves when they felt like being alone, or joined the captain at his table, where Kate soon became a favorite for her sparkling laughter and quick wit. Page taught her to play the decadent game of poker, and she amused him in turn by reciting whole acts of plays she had learned by listening to her mother rehearse. And never once did Page mention his plans after they docked in New York.

Kate didn't ask. She was having such a wonderful time, enjoying herself and her handsome husband, that if she thought about an end to this blissful voyage, she put it out of her mind. So also did she try to forget her guilty secret, but that was much more difficult. Daily she examined herself for any physical sign that would alert Page to her condition, but to her profound relief, except for the slight thickening of her waist and a fullness to her breasts, her pregnancy was unnoticeable.

And so the days sped by, and the voyage that had begun so disastrously became instead a journey of discovery. Page was a considerate husband, a delightful and entertaining companion, and a demanding and satisfying lover. Kate thought that she had never been happier.

And then came the day that land was sighted, and with the first viewing of the New York skyline, Kate's handsome, thoughtful, and considerate husband turned into a monster before her eyes.

Kate was in the act of packing when the awful transformation occurred. She was just trying to fold one of her voluminous petticoats into her trunk when Page came in. She turned to him enthusiastically. "I'm so excited about seeing New York!" she exclaimed. "Just think! After hearing about it from Augusta all those years, I'm actually going to see it firsthand! Do you suppose we could go to the theater? Or the shops? And . . . Oh, I would love to have supper at Delmonico's! Do you . . . ?"

She stopped abruptly, only now becoming aware that Page's expression was a good deal less enthusiastic than hers. "What's the matter?" she asked uncertainly. "Did I say something wrong?"

"No, no, you didn't say anything wrong," Page replied uncomfortably. "It's just . . ."

"Just what?"

"I suppose I should have mentioned it before now," he said with reluctance as she frowned at him. "But I didn't want to spoil anything. . . ."

"Mentioned what? What are you talking about, Page?" She said it calmly, but behind that facade her heart was beginning to pound rapidly. She felt disaster rushing at her, and she didn't want him to say whatever he had to say. "Never mind!" she corrected quickly, wanting to postpone the awful moment, whatever it was. "I don't want to know."

She was too late. Helpless to stop him, she heard him say, "We won't have much time in New York, I'm afraid. I've already arranged for our train tickets, because we have to connect with the overland-stage line in little more than a week from now. I know it seems a rush, but—"

"A rush!" she echoed, still unable to believe what he was telling her. "I don't even know what you're talking about! Train tickets? Stage lines? Surely you're joking, Page!"

He seemed surprised. "Joking?" he repeated. "Of course not. We have to get to Colorado somehow, you know."

"But I thought . . ." Kate sank down on the side of the bed, petticoat in hand. "But you . . . you haven't mentioned Colorado in all this time! I thought . . . I hoped . . . you had reconsidered."

"I didn't want to mention it, that's true," he admitted. "I confess I didn't want anything to spoil our honeymoon."

"And so you deliberately let me think you had changed your mind about leaving directly for Colorado!"

"I didn't say that," Page protested mildly.

"No," Kate responded with a furious toss of her head. "You didn't say anything, did you? You *wanted* me to believe we would spend some time in New York! You *knew* how I detested the idea of going to that godforsaken place you call home, and so you let me think we could stay here for a while! Oh! How could you be so . . . so underhanded!"

"I'm sorry you look at it like that."

"How else should I look at it?" Kate shouted. Jumping off the bed, she faced Page with her fists clenched. "You tricked me!" she cried, her voice rising shrilly. She didn't care what she sounded like, she was too furious to lower her voice, even at his signal. Let the whole ship hear if they wanted; she was so angry she didn't care.

"I didn't trick you, Kate," Page said quietly.

"What do you call it, then? No, no . . . don't bother to answer; I wouldn't believe you anyway."

Whirling around, she took a deep breath, trying to regain some semblance of control. Behind her, Page tried to justify himself. "You didn't ask, remember that, Kate," he pointed out. "In all this time, you didn't ask me anything about leaving for Colorado."

"I trusted you," she said bitterly, turning back to him. "I trusted you, and now I see what a fool I've been. But let me tell you something, Page Taggart! I've fulfilled my part of the bargain. I said I would come to America with you, and I have. But I'm not going one step farther, no matter what you say! If you want to go to Colorado, please yourself. But you'll go without me!"

"Don't be ridiculous! Of course you'll go with me. You're my wife!"

"Not anymore! Not after the way you deceived me! You used me, Page, and I'll never forgive you for that. Never!"

"But, Kate—"

"I don't want to hear it! Find someone else to go with you, if you like!" cried Kate dramatically, almost in tears. "I'm not going to leave New York, and that's that!"

But of course she left New York. For despite her bravado on board ship, the busy, crowded city almost overwhelmed her as Page relented and took her sightseeing before they had to catch the train. After instructing the cabby to drive past some of the more famous mansions of Fifth Avenue, Page asked him to turn onto Broadway, where he pointed out to Kate the theaters, restaurants, salons, and shops. It seemed that there were hundreds of little shops tucked away here and there on that street.

Kate nodded through it all, craning her neck up at the tall buildings that towered over the smaller stores, staring with wide eyes at the congestion in the streets. Where was all her bravery now? she wondered, watching the milling people push past each other, all seemingly in a hurry to reach their destination and not caring whom they trod upon to get there. And what would she do if she were one of those people— where would she go, what would she do? So had no money, no friends; she didn't even possess the most rudimentary knowledge of the city itself. How could she possibly stay here alone? The noise itself would drive her mad within a few days, for with all the hurry and bustle of the pedestrians, there was also the constant din of clattering carriage wheels and the clopping of horses' hooves. And rising above it all were the cries of street vendors and the shrilling of urchins who tried to entice passersby into buying oranges or apples or flowers. There were traffic snarls on the crowded streets, and the piercing blasts of policemen's whistles, and even the frightening sound of a fire wagon in full flight, racing to put out a blaze somewhere in this swarming maze of a city.

Cursing her timidity, Kate clung to Page's arm, and the more alarmed she became at all the noise and confusion and din and bustle seething around her, the more angry she was with herself. What was the matter with her, that she should act like such a shrinking violet? This city was no different from London, she told herself; it was only in a different location, with different people. There was absolutely no reason to be afraid.

But it was different, and Kate knew it. The admission cost her a great deal of pride, and by the time they arrived at the train station, Kate felt both humiliated by her fright and enraged because she was such a coward.

Unfortunately, her ill temper was not soothed by the sleeping berth Page had arranged for them during their journey to St. Louis. Their quarters were cramped and uncomfortable, alternately too stuffy and too cold, so that one minute Kate felt as though she was suffocating with heat, and in the next fighting off a chill. Finally, halfway through the first night, she flounced out of the hard bed and dressed again, declaring in a fury that she would sleep in the passenger car. There, at least, she raged at the sleepy Page, she wouldn't have to worry about catching her death of cold or being thrown into the aisle every time the train took a curve.

Three exhausting days later, they arrived in St. Louis. But hardly had Kate caught her breath than Page was rushing her aboard a river steamer for the five-day journey up the Missouri River to Atchison, Kansas. And from Atchison, Kate learned discouragingly, they would board the stage for Denver.

Despite her initial weariness, Kate might have enjoyed the river boat. She might have, but for two things: she was determined to maintain her stony silence with Page; and the Missouri both frightened and repelled her. The river was deep and swift, and so muddy that to Kate it appeared bottomless. The current boiled and eddied around the boat, filled with drifting logs and even whole trees. Some of these, after being torn from the bank by floods, were thrown up again, to be planted afresh along a new section of bank. These were the most dangerous, for their tops might lurk just below or just above the surface of the water, forming a snag so dreaded by steamboat pilots. The entire time on the river, Kate lived in fear that they would either be impaled by one of these menaces or sunk entirely.

Consequently, it was with relief that she stepped off the boat at Atchison. She even accepted with delight Page's offer to take her out for her first sight of the high prairie. Excitedly she mounted one of the horses Page had obtained for them for the day, and she was so happy to be riding again that they had gone three or four miles before she really looked around her. She stopped, appalled, realizing for the first time what the open plains were truly like: vast, empty, barren, and except for the whir of grasshoppers in the dry grass and the sighing of the wind, completely silent. By straining her eyes she could just barely make out the white canvas of a moving wagon train, but that and a lone hawk floating high in the sky were the only signs of life for as far as she could see.

Raising horrified eyes to Page, she saw that he wasn't looking at her, but off into the distance, a private smile curving his lips. He looked tall and handsome and equal to any challenge, sitting there so easily in the saddle, and turning her head, Kate stared out at the endless expanse of land and sky in front of her. Her heart sank.

17

If Kate had hated Kansas on sight, she despised the overland stage even more. The flat, monotonous plainslands, the heat and the dirt and the dust and the grime she could put up with; the stagecoach itself was another matter entirely. When Page had told her, so casually that she should have been alerted, that their fares from Atchison to Denver included fifteen inches of seat space and what they could carry on their laps,

Kate had scoffed, sure he was joking. To her horror, it was
no joke.

In shock and total disbelief, she climbed inside the coach
the next morning and immediately found herself wedged
tightly between the wall of the coach and the obese man who
climbed in after her. Too stunned to speak, she watched her
fellow passengers—six others besides Page and herself and
the fat man—crawl in after them and jostle for position.
When the door was slammed shut and the driver shrilled a
whistle, Kate shut her eyes against her sudden feeling of
claustrophobia. She hadn't realized it was going to be so
crowded!

Page was sitting opposite her, his knees touching hers in
that cramped space. Next to him was a woman swathed in
black mourning, and beside her a boy of about twelve, who
appeared to be her son, for he wore a black armband and
held her arm comfortingly. In back of *them*, taking up the
third seat of the coach, was a trio of immigrants—mother, father and daughter—who spoke quietly among themselves in a
language Kate didn't recognize. She had only a glimpse of
the other man sitting beyond the fat man to her left; he wore
a black wide-brimmed hat pulled low over his eyes and sat
slouched in the opposite corner, apparently oblivious of everyone else.

The black-hatted man might be oblivious, Kate thought
with dismay, but she certainly wasn't. The thought of all nine
of them locked together in this tiny space while they careened
across the open prairie was enough to make her gasp. How
could she bear it for the time it took to reach their destination? Even now she despaired of getting to Denver in one
piece; already her legs felt cramped, and there was a sharp
protrusion of some kind digging into her spine.

Shifting position was impossible; she was jammed so se-
curely into the corner by the fat man's bulk that she could
hardly even breathe. And yet, before they started, she had to
find out what was poking her in the back; she knew she
would never be able to endure mile after mile of this constricted posture unless she had some relief from that sharp
projection. "Excuse me," she began, speaking to the man beside her. "But would you mind moving—"

She never finished her sentence. With a lurch and a forward jolt that snapped her head back on her neck, the stage
was under way.

Years later, Kate could laugh about her experiences on her first overland stage; she would even regale Colorado's governor with amusing tales of that initial ride. But that time was far in the future, when distance had mellowed her memory, and harsh recollections had been softened by the patina of passing time. Now the hard reality of it was that this ride was the most wretched and miserable experience of her entire life.

The cramped quarters inside the stage made the tiny train berth she had scorned seem in retrospect the height of luxury, the rolling and pitching of the ship that had made her so sick like being cradled in a cloud. After a few miles inside the stagecoach, Kate felt as if she was being shaken to pieces. It seemed that the driver took perverse pleasure in seeking out every chuckhole and rock in sight, and the coach crashed and jolted from one to the other until Kate thought her neck would simply break in two.

The only thing she could do was grit her teeth and hang on as best she could, abandoning all dignity in a frantic search for something solid to hold on to. She couldn't even complain to Page; the rattle and clatter of the coach made conversation, except for the most rudimentary kind, almost impossible. Not that complaining would have done any good, Kate reflected bitterly, casting dire glances upward in the direction of the driver she couldn't see; even if she had succeeded in getting Page's attention, there was no way to reach the driver. Unlike civilized English coaches and carriages, thought Kate scathingly, this hellish contraption had no speaking tube. Short of reaching out and dragging the driver off his high seat and throwing him into the cloud of dust he was deliberately creating, nothing was going to slow him down. And there was no way to ask politely.

Glancing covertly around, Kate clenched her teeth again. If no one else complained, then neither would she. The fat man next to her was actually dozing, she saw with amazement; his head was bouncing up and down on his fleshy neck every time the coach hit a rut. Nothing seemed to disturb him, and Kate couldn't believe that anyone could sleep through this awful clattering, jolting racket.

Looking across, Kate saw that the widow and her son had lapsed into a state of stupefaction, holding each other tightly; the three immigrants behind them were busily parceling out a breakfast of thick slices of bread topped by wedges of dark

yellow cheese. The woman, seeeing Kate's eyes on her, gestured with a chunk of bread she had in one hand, offering her
some with a smile. Kate smiled faintly in return, wondering
how anyone could eat in this appalling situation. She felt like
a pea in a cup, already nauseous.

Page seemed to have fallen into a brown study. He was
staring out the window, but Kate could see that he wasn't
really aware that they had left the outskirts of the town and
were heading out into the open prairie. He seemed preoccupied with thoughts of his own, his hands resting loosely on his
knees as he gazed absently out.

Later, when Kate felt the hand on her knee, she thought at
first it was Page, trying to get her attention. Turning away
from her own blank preoccupation with the barren landscape
rolling by outside, she looked down. Shocked, she saw that it
wasn't Page's hand at all, but one belonging to the dozing fat
man beside her. Too stunned to speak, she raised her eyes
and saw him leering at her, his head still down, staring at her
from under fat lids. When he saw her glance at him, he actually winked and squeezed her knee.

Kate was too repulsed to do anything for a few moments
but stare in horrid fascination at the doughy hand on her leg.
Then, when his fleshy thigh pressed against her and she felt
him deliberately rub against her leg, she was galvanized into
action. With no thought of calling Page, she raised her hand,
prepared to deal him a furious slap right across his sooty
face. But as her arm rose, she was amazed to see his head
snap up and his swinish eyes widen with real fear that her
own gesture couldn't possibly have caused. Startled, she
looked down, and froze.

"Take your hand off my wife."

Despite the constant clattering racket inside the coach,
Page could be heard clearly. But then, Kate thought hysterically, he had no need to raise his voice, for the gun he held
against the fat man's protruding belly spoke louder than
words. With every jolt and bounce of the stage, the barrel of
the gun sank deeper into that jellylike flesh, and the man
blanched and tried futilely to rear back and away from that
threatening pressure. But the bulk that had prevented Kate
from moving before, now held him prisoner in turn. There
was no place for him to go.

Wide-eyed, too frightened to speak, Kate turned a stiff
neck to look at her husband. She almost didn't recognize him;

the planes of his face looked as if they had been carved from granite. His eyes never left the fat man, and Kate had never seen such an implacable and dangerous expression on any man's face. She shivered. She had never seen Page look so . . . so merciless.

Where had he obtained the gun? she wondered wildly. And more important than that—where had it come from? One minute his hands had been empty, resting lightly on his knees; in the next, he was holding the weapon with a sureness and inflexibility that meant he knew what to do with it and wouldn't hesitate to do what had to be done. Would he actually use it? Kate wondered. Then, looking at his face again, she knew he would if he thought it was necessary. She shuddered again, proud and thrilled and frightened at the same time.

That fat man apparently knew that Page meant business. Very slowly he lifted his hand from Kate's knee, holding both hands squarely in front of him where Page could see them. Kate glanced down and saw that his sweaty palm had left a damp imprint on her skirt. Half-hysterically, she fought the urge to scrub furiously at it with her handkerchief. The sight revolted her.

"Hey, don't take offense, mister!" the fat man was saying, gabbling, as the gun against his middle didn't waver. "I didn't know the lady was your wife!"

"It shouldn't have mattered, should it?"

"Huh?" Clearly the man was taken aback by the question. "I don't . . . I don't think I heard you right, mister."

Page rammed the gun hard into that blubbery stomach. The man gasped from pain and fright, and the beads of sweat that had gathered on his forehead began running down his pasty face, dripping off shaking jowls onto his lapels. Kate wanted to turn away from the sight, but she couldn't. She was held in a kind of morbid fascination.

"I said"—the gun jabbed a little deeper, the barrel almost disappearing into the quivering flesh, the man sweating even more profusely now—"that it shouldn't have mattered if the lady was my wife or not. She's a lady, and that should have been enough."

"Hey, I didn't mean any harm. Honest! Please . . . please . . ."

Kate had the feeling that if there had been room enough, the man would have gone to his knees right there in the coach, blubbering an apology. He was almost in tears as it was.

Quickly she glanced across at Page. His eyes were on her. "What do you think, Kate?" he asked. "Should I accept his regrets and let it go?" The gun didn't move a fraction.

Kate didn't think she could stand the tension another minute longer. They were all sitting there frozen in position, waiting for Page to decide what to do. The stage bounced and jerked them and threw them from side to side, and still they all sat there stiff as statues.

"Well, Kate?"

"Please . . . put the gun away," she managed to say at last, her lips wooden. "I think an apology will be . . . sufficient."

"You got it, lady! You got it!" the man cried at once. He took out a large handkerchief and mopped his dripping face as Page slowly withdrew the gun from his middle. "And thanks!" he gasped, glancing hastily at Kate and then away again. "Thanks! I thought I was dead for sure!"

"Maybe next time you'll think before you try something like that," Kate said shortly, her terror evaporating now that Page had put the weapon away. Looking hastily across at Page, she was also relieved that that frightening merciless expression was fading from his face and eyes. That expression had scared her as much as had the gun. She had never seen him look like that before, and she fervently hoped she never would again.

"Never fear about me trying that again!" the fat man muttered. "Never fear! I've learned my lesson, I have!"

Slowly the charged atmosphere inside the coach reverted to what it had been before. The three foreigners finished their bread and cheese and began dividing huge slabs of cake; the widow and her son began comforting each other again. The fat man shifted his weight as far away as possible from Kate, and the silent man on the end with the haunted eyes pulled his black hat lower over his face. Kate leaned over and touched Page's arm in gratitude, suddenly feeling very protected and very proud, and he gave her hand a squeeze before he resumed his idle contemplation of the barren landscape outside. And beyond Kate's coach window, the silent and lifeless and hot and dusty Kansas plains rolled on. And on.

And always, there was Kate's fear of Indians that even Page's protective behavior couldn't quite dispel.

She hadn't been afraid until she had heard stories on the train about the Indian uprising near Denver a year or so before. In awful fascination she had listened to tales about the winter of 1864 becoming a reign of terror, with Indians destroying everything they could get their hands on from Julesburg to Denver. Every mile of stage route had been devastated; telegraph lines had been pulled down. Ranches, warehouses, and even forts had been fired; soldiers were killed and families mutilated. The hideous list had gone on and on, and Kate had listened with mounting horror, frightening herself into such a state of nerves that Page finally forbade her listening to any more. It was the first time she had ever willingly obeyed him.

Now, although Page assured her again and again that there was little danger, Kate could not rid herself of her fear. Every time the coach stopped for a change of horses or driver, or to give the passengers time to snatch something to eat at a stage house, or to stretch sore and aching muscles, Kate anxiously scanned the horizon for any sign of Indians. She had seen only a small band once, and those at a distance, but that one glimpse had been enough to strike terror in her heart. Painted, feathered, mounted on scrawny and rawboned little horses that nevertheless looked as though they could run for mile after mile, to Kate they had seemed . . . alien, and she was afraid. Suddenly the gun that Page carried, and which had seemed so huge in the crowded coach, now seemed pitifully inadequate in case of attack, and Kate wondered bleakly if they would actually arrive unharmed in Denver.

Five nerve-racking and wearying days after leaving Atchison, an exhausted Kate climbed out of the stagecoach for what she declared was absolutely the last time. She was bone-tired, shaken to pieces, desperately in want of a bath, and in a thoroughly bad temper. She hated everything and everyone around her, including Page, whose earlier championing had earned her gratitude and profound respect. All that was forgotten now, though; Kate despised him anew for dragging her into this hideous country where every mile was a threat to life and limb.

The past five days had been an eternity of hellish days and even worse nights; sleep had been impossible in the never-ending bouncing of the coach, and there hadn't been time to do more than pick at the indifferent meals the stage houses offered along their route.

Kate had been too wretched to eat anyway. After the initial excitement of Page challenging the fat man—who had decided to part company with them at the first rest stop and wait for the next stage—tedium had set in. The heat, the enforced confinement, the constant jolting of the stage, had all combined to make Kate thoroughly miserable. Because of her pregnancy, her hands and feet swelled; her fingers were often so swollen that she couldn't even see her wedding ring, and she had to unbutton her shoes to relieve her filled ankles. She had endured muscle cramps and sore shoulders and ferocious headaches from the interminable jouncing; she had swallowed what felt like acres of dust, and she had even found herself mumbling a prayer for an end to this torturous journey before she did something awful—like beating Page senseless with her useless parasol for making her follow him into this nightmare.

How she longed to stop for several hours to rest and to gather what little strength she had left! But even that was denied her: each time they stopped for a change of horses or driver, there wasn't time to do more than stretch aching muscles for a few minutes or to snatch something to eat before the call would come to board again. Then they would be racing off with a new team and a new driver, each worse than the last, and all of them, Kate was sure, determined to murder every one of his passengers by insanely reckless driving.

When at last she heard the shout "Denver ahead!" Kate felt like bursting into a chorus of hallelujahs. Eagerly craning her neck out the window, she tried to catch a glimpse of the city she was sure had existed only in everyone's imagination. But before she could see it through the cloud of dust they were raising, she was forced to pull her head in again. The driver had cracked the whip over his horses, driving them ahead in blithe disregard of the safety of his passengers. Hitting her head on the windowsill after a particularly vicious bounce, Kate held on grimly and cursed the fact that the entire stage could fall to pieces behind the driver; he probably wouldn't notice as long as he and his horses dashed into Denver smartly on schedule.

Desperately clutching at whatever handhold she could

grab, Kate happened to glance at Page's face during all this frenetic activity. He was grinning, actually enjoying this mad rush to the city! Kate could have boxed his ears on the spot—if she had had the courage to release her death grip on the seat long enough to do it.

How dare he enjoy this, she thought furiously, bouncing six inches off the seat as a wheel landed in yet another chuckhole. She came down with a crash, her hat resting on her nose, and then, with a final whistle of the whip and an elated whoop from the driver, they careened into Denver.

Their arrival was accompanied by the confusion of stamping, sweating horses, jingling harness, the excited cries of the three immigrants, who had obviously spied waiting family, and the renewed sobbing of the woman in mourning. Outside, the driver was already shouting hoarse unloading instructions; people, horses, carts, and carriages passing by added to the general delirium, and opposite her, Page was reaching for the door and exclaiming jubilantly, "We're here, Kate! We're here at last!"

There was a general exodus from the coach when Page flung open the door. All the passengers were anxious to get out; the final leg of their journey had taken almost three hours without stopping, for the driver had been determined to make up lost time. Although, Kate had reflected bitterly throughout those long, torturous hours, how he could have lost any time was beyond her: it seemed that they had all, horses and passengers alike, been pushed to the limit of their endurance these past five days.

But it was over at last, Kate assured herself, pushing her hat up out of her eyes. In the blessed silence that followed the departure of her fellow passengers, she dropped her hands to her lap and sat limply where she was for a few minutes, unmoving. The coach creaked and groaned as thoroughbraces and wood settled; the stage rocked back and forth a little as the horses stamped and jigged impatiently, anxious to be relieved of chafing harness. But after the violent bouncing and jolting she had endured these past days, such movements were almost like being rocked to sleep. And the silence! Kate closed her eyes, savoring it all.

How wonderful it was to sit here without having to hang on for her life, wondering if she was going to suffocate in the everlasting dust or be pounded to pieces by the never-ending jouncing of the stage! She could have sat here forever, just enjoying the cessation of such torture.

"Kate?"

Reluctantly she opened her eyes. Page was leaning into the open door, one foot on the step. "Aren't you coming out?"

Kate closed her eyes again. She ached in every muscle, her ears were still ringing, and her throat felt almost too dry to speak. "Only to a hot bath, a decent cup of tea, and a soft bed," she said, resting her head against the back of the hard seat.

"But, Kate . . ."

She opened her eyes slowly, recognizing that tone. Not even Page, she thought, could be so cruel and heartless. The only thing that had kept her going these past five days had been the thought of a long, steaming bath and a soft bed at the end of this hideous journey. And this time, she told herself positively, she was going to have her way. She had earned such consideration, she deserved it!

That was, she amended scathingly, if this appalling frontier town offered such basic amenities. As she glanced out the window, she wasn't sure; they seemed to be bordering on the edge of known civilization, from what she could see. But, oh—to be clean again! To wash away this gritty trail dust that seemed to have settled in every pore of her skin! To climb into an actual bed where she could stretch out full length and rest her head on a pillow instead of a wooden sill! She had thought of nothing else during every one of the six hundred and fifty miles from Atchison.

Kate looked at her husband. This time, she decided, there was no other choice, no argument, no discussion. If Page didn't agree, she wouldn't step one foot outside this stagecoach. She was firm, adamant. She would not leave Denver without her bath!

They stayed in Denver that night. And the next. Kate had her bath, her cup of tea, her soft bed, and more. Page was even able to obtain champagne that first night, and to accompany it, they had supper alone in their room. Candlelight and the wine, together with the steaming tub and the donning of her own comfortable dressing gown, soothed away the last of Kate's ill temper. They also had the effect of making her so drowsy that she might have fallen headfirst into her plate if Page hadn't picked her up and carried her over to the bed.

With a rueful laugh he tucked the quilt under her chin and kissed her good night. Exhausted, Kate was asleep almost before her head touched the pillow.

The next morning, Kate greeted Page with a chagrined expression, a pot of hot coffee, and an ardent nature that had been reawakened by her first restful sleep in over a week. Page didn't hesitate. Sweeping her into his arms, he banished her chagrin with the first kiss. The exploration of her ardent nature took longer, of course, and by the time either noticed it, the coffee had cooled to a chill, and the sun was long past the zenith. Page insisted then that Kate should have her first tour of the city.

To her relief, Denver was not quite the barbaric place Kate had imagined. The recent ending of the Civil War had opened the way for trade again, Page had told her, and the city had prospered. He took her to Stewart's Department Store, and Kate looked around in astonishment at costly silks, French-style beaver hats, dainty bonnets, satin cloaks, and lengths of cashmere. There were even copies of the newest Paris fashions, and a perfume called, appallingly, "Balm of a Thousand Bayonets." Kate was repelled as much by the name as by the scent.

After Stewart's, they walked past the Apollo Hotel with its own theater, called, appropriately, the Apollo Hall; she saw the offices of the *Rocky Mountain News*, Denver's daily newspaper. Along the main street were a meat market, a drugstore, a bakery, and a barbershop, and of course, interspersed with these prosaic establishments, the ubiquitous saloons and gambling halls. Kate managed to peek into one, and saw with amazement the long black mahogany bar, the oil paintings, velvet hangings, and shining imported glassware. If she hadn't seen if herself, no one could have convinced her that these things were available at what she considered an outpost of civilization. She told Page so, and he laughed, replying confidently that Denver was destined for great things once Colorado achieved statehood. Kate doubted it, no matter what he said.

All too soon, the two days Page had promised her were over. Trying to resign herself to the inevitable, Kate asked meekly how long it would take to journey to the ranch.

"The ranch?" Page repeated the question absently. He had been staring out the hotel window, looking up and down the street for the past half-hour, obviously watching for someone.

Now he dropped the curtain he had been holding back and looked over his shoulder. "Usually it's just a day's ride, but it probably will take us two this time."

"Two days!"

"Well, we have to take the wagon, instead of just the horses, so it will take longer." He came over to where she sat on the bed staring disconsolately at the floor. Dropping down beside her, he put his arm around her shoulders.

"It isn't far, Kate," he said. "And remember how many miles you've come already! Where's your spirit of adventure?"

"I left it on the ship, the first night I became ill," she said bitterly, trying to draw away from him.

Page laughed, giving her shoulder a squeeze before he stood up, restless again. "You'll enjoy camping out, Kate. I know you'll like it."

"That's what you said about the ship! And the train, and the riverboat."

"You liked the riverboat," Page pointed out as he went to the window again.

"*Like* is a relative term," she answered with heavy sarcasm. "In comparison to the train or that hideous ship, yes. But . . ."

"Well, then . . . you see? It hasn't all been so terrible, has it?"

Despite her promise to herself not to lose her temper—after all, they had been getting along so well these past two days—Kate was about to reply hotly to his remark. Then she noticed that he was glancing up and down the street again, not even paying any attention to her. "What are you *looking* for?" she cried, exasperated.

"Colin. He should have been here by now."

Colin Delaney was Page's foreman, that much Kate knew. She was also aware that the two young men were more friends than employer and hired hand, and now she saw that in spite of Page's apparent nonchalance, he was concerned about Colin's absence.

Her fear of Indians, never far from the surface, stabbed sharply through her at Page's worried tone. Had Colin been attacked? She glanced around despite herself, as if she half-expected to see painted savages appear suddenly in their room, prepared to murder them where they stood.

With an efford, Kate tried to tell herself she was being ri-

diculous, overwrought. Her imagination was working over-
time, fancying things that didn't exist or hadn't happened.
There was absolutely no reason to believe that Colin had
been waylaid by Indians, she assured herself stoutly. His
horse might have gone lame, or the wagon could have lost a
wheel—any number of things could explain his absence.

So she told herself. But the image of Colin fighting off an
Indian attack persisted; the tales she had heard of Indians on
the warpath—warpath! such a sinister word, she thought with
a shiver—haunted her, and she felt a chill. Hugging her arms
around her, she looked at Page and asked faintly, "What do
you think might have happened to him?"

"I don't know. I sent the telegram days ago, telling him
when we would arrive, and it isn't like him to be late."

"Do you . . . do you suppose . . . ?" But she couldn't
make herself say the awful possibility that had occurred to
her.

Page turned to look at her as she hesitated. He saw her
huddled on the bed and frowned. "Suppose what?"

"Well, I thought . . . it could be . . . Indians, couldn't it?"

"Indians!" Page was about to laugh when he saw her expression. Moving swiftly, he crossed to the bed again and
drew her to her feet. Clasping her icy hands in his, he said, "I
don't want you scaring yourself anymore about that, Kate. I
mean it."

"But . . . the uprising. And the—"

"That's enough," interrupted Page firmly. "The uprising
was over a year ago, and everything has been quiet since
then. There's absolutely no reason for you worry about it."

"Then what about Colin? If there hasn't been any trouble,
where is he?"

Page ran one of his hands through his hair, a gesture he
used only when he was worried or upset. "I don't know.
He—"

They were interrupted just then by a hesitant rap on the
door. Page's face cleared at once. "Maybe that's Colin," he
said, obviously relieved as he went to answer the door. "I
knew he . . ."

But it wasn't Colin. Page frowned as he opened the door
and saw a boy standing there with a grimy note in his hand.
The boy touched his cap. "Mr. Taggart, sir? Mr. Delaney
gave me this to give to you."

Page took the smudged envelope. As he slid his finger under the flap, he asked, "When did he give this to you?"

"Oh . . . I think it was last week or so. I been carryin' it with me ever since."

"Well, why didn't you give it to me before now?"

The boy swallowed at the exasperation in Page's voice. "I didn't know you were in town, Mr. Taggart. I . . . I must have missed the stage. Mr. Amos—he's the blacksmith—"

"I know who he is," Page said impatiently.

"Well, he . . . he works me pretty hard, and I guess I didn't see you come in. I'm sorry, sir, real sorry, if I did somethin' wrong."

Kate came forward at that point with a glare in Page's direction. The boy was almost in tears; he had pulled off his cap and was crushing it between his hands as he looked in misery at Page, who was frowning as he began to read the note.

"It's all right," Kate assured the lad. "I'm sure you did the best you could. Isn't that so, Page?"

At her tone, Page glanced up for a second from the paper in his hand. He grunted an assent and went back to reading. Reaching absently into his waistcoat pocket, he took out a coin and handed it across to the boy.

"Thanks, Mr. Taggart," the lad said hesitantly. "But are you sure . . . ?"

"He's sure," said Kate firmly with another glare in Page's direction. To her annoyance, he was still absorbed in the note and didn't see her. She turned to the boy again. "Thank you for bringing the message to Mr. Taggart," she said with a smile to make up for Page's rudeness.

"Oh, you're welcome, ma'am!" the boy said, touching his cap respectfully, his eyes wide as he stared at Kate. "I'll be glad to deliver a message to you anytime!"

Hardly were the words out of his mouth before he blushed furiously. Red to the roots of his hair, overcome with embarrassment, the lad turned without another word and sped down the corridor. Kate watched him go with another smile, until he had turned the corner with a skid. She could hear him clattering down the stairs with his heavy boots before she shut the door.

She looked at Page. "What is it?" she asked, gesturing toward the note he was tapping against his palm.

"What?" Page seemed preoccupied, and Kate gestured

again. "Oh." He looked down at the paper he was holding, as if he had never seen it before. "Colin can't meet us after all."

"Why not?"

Page folded the note and put it into his pocket. "Um . . . there's some business he had to attend to," he replied vaguely. "He left a wagon and two horses for us at the stable."

"Oh . . ." Kate wasn't sure what to say. What could be more important than meeting them in Denver, as Page had asked? she wondered. But she didn't voice the question, for there was a faraway look in Page's eyes, and an air of suppressed excitement about him suddenly that made her apprehensive. What *was* he grinning about?

"Are you sure that's all?" she asked cautiously, not sure whether she wanted Page to tell her or not. "There isn't anything else you want to say?"

Page shook his head. "What else could there be?" he replied, grinning that ridiculous grin again.

Kate definitely didn't trust that grin, nor the brisk way he bundled her out of the hotel and down to the livery after their valises were packed. Before she knew it, they were on their way out of Denver, sitting high up on the wagon, trunks and crates and boxes and the additional food supplies Page had hastily ordered stacked neatly behind them. And tucked here and there among the parcels and heavy sacks were the accoutrements for camping on the trail: coffeepot, skillet, tin plates and mugs, thick quilts, and a set of oilskins for each of them in case of rain. Kate had eyed these camping preparations askance as they were being loaded. But even the thought of sleeping out all night on the trail and cooking over a campfire did not make her as nervous as seeing that almost silly grin on Page's face. Was he happy about coming home at last, or did that grin signify something else entirely?

With an inward sigh, Kate tried to prepare herself for the worst.

18

Kate's first sight of what was to be her new home was so appalling that she couldn't speak. Page sat beside her on the wagon seat, proudly waiting for her to say something, but the words stuck in her throat. She sat riveted to the seat, staring in utter disbelief in the direction Page had pointed out, wildly hoping that it was some trick of the light, or her eyes, or even that he was joking. And as she looked, she even forgot the nagging backache that had become a sharper and sharper stab of agony with each passing mile; she forgot swollen hands and feet, and the pain in her legs and across her shoulders; even the pounding headache behind her eyes faded away. All the discomfort and weariness brought on by her pregnancy and the strain of travel these past weeks ceased to exist as she looked at what Page had enthusiastically called "the Taggart spread."

Hand to her throat, Kate told herself wildly that she hadn't expected another Tremont Hall. She hadn't even believed—not really—that Page had built a house comparable to those she had seen so briefly in New York. After all, she thought somewhat hysterically, his land wasn't near a sophisticated city in a civilized state; it was out in the middle of nowhere, two days' ride from a raw frontier town in what was called, ridiculously, a territory.

So she hadn't expected a fine mansion with lace curtains and Brussels carpets and imported furniture and a lawn in front with a proper garden and stables to the rear; she really hadn't. Or had she?

At this point, she didn't know what she had thought or expected. Staring transfixed at what was below her, she couldn't even remember what Page had said when she asked him to describe this place. She only recalled—too late—that he had answered her vaguely, saying that he wanted her to see it for herself.

Well, she was seeing it for herself, wasn't she? And what was she going to do now?

"Well, Kate? What do you think?"

She heard the pride in his voice, the sense of accomplishment and achievement, and for another instant she simply couldn't command her voice. Even simple speech seemed entirely beyond her.

"I . . . I . . ." Her throat working, she looked frantically away from him and gazed out again. Nothing, unfortunately, had changed in that brief glance away. The log cabin, with its few chickens scratching around the door and smoke curling lazily up from the fieldstone chimney, was the same. As were the lodgepole corrals to the side. There was a lean-to of sorts attached to the cabin along one outside wall; it was obviously a shelter for the four horses wandering aimlessly inside the enclosure. Kate's eyes automatically assessed the good breeding in the horses, but her glance slid away again, coming to rest, disastrously, on the shingled outhouse in back of the cabin. The sight was too much for her; before the astonished Page, she burst into tears.

"You never told me," she cried, sobbing more bitterly with each word, "that you were taking me to live in a . . . a *hovel!*"

Page had been trying clumsily to comfort her. Now he drew back a little. "It isn't a hovel," he said in an injured tone. "It's a cabin. And a well-built one, too. Colin and I built it ourselves—"

"I can see *that!*"

"—from the finest pines we could find. There isn't a crack or crevice anywhere in that cabin, Kate," Page continued more severely as she wept all the harder. "And any woman would be proud to live there."

"Find another one, then!" wailed Kate, trying vainly to find her handkerchief.

Page gave her his, saying in exasperation, "Be reasonable—"

"Reasonable!"

"Yes. I told you I couldn't give you Tremont Hall—"

"You certainly didn't lie about that!"

"—at least, not yet. But if you'll just be patient—"

"Patient! You're always telling me that, as if it's the solution to every problem!" She was trying to struggle down from the wagon, driven by some childish compulsion to get away from him—to run away. After traveling all these thousands of miles, and coming all this way—and for what? *To* what?

It was too much, she thought hysterically: too much to ask of her, to expect her to accept. She couldn't live here in the middle of this emptiness, in that ugly, barren cabin standing by itself—the only manmade structure for miles around. She couldn't!

Looking up, she saw the majestic Rocky Mountains rising awesomely toward the sky, snowcapped even at the beginning of July. She shuddered. She couldn't live under the shadow of those mountains. She felt hemmed in, pressed down on all sides. She had never seen such mountains, so high and huge and vast. She had never seen such country, so big, so . . . empty.

But why was she thinking of the country and the mountains? She had to get away before she broke down completely. She had to be alone so she could get a grip on herself and control the hysteria that threatened to overwhelm her. Then, when she was calmer, she would speak to Page. He would have to understand, she thought desperately; he would have to let her go, or take her back. She couldn't stay here; she would go mad—with fear.

"Kate, stop that!"

His harsh tone was like a dash of cold water, his strong hands like a lifeline as he pulled her back onto the seat. She fell against him, sobbing.

"Oh, Page! I'm so frightened!"

"There's nothing to be scared of, Kate," Page said gently, trying to stroke her hair away from her damp face.

"There is! There is!"

"What, love? Tell me what there is to be afraid of."

His tender tone was the final undoing. The weeks of travel, the physical drain of the pregnancy she had kept hidden, and now this last disappointment had been more of a strain than she had realized. She was exhausted in mind and body; she was unsure of herself in this new country; she felt incompetent and inadequate even for the simplest task.

And now, seeing that log cabin on the edge of nowhere, and realizing that Page expected her to live there with him, brought all this to the surface, and she cried, "The baby! I can't have the baby here—alone—with no one to help me! I don't know what to do, how to cope . . . Oh, Page, I'm so afraid!"

She was so distraught that she didn't even realize at first what she had said. It was some seconds before she saw that Page was trying to hold her away from him so that he could look into her face, and when she did lift her eyes to his, she was stunned at the blaze of excitement and pride she saw in his eyes.

"Baby?" he repeated unbelievingly. "*Baby*! You're going to have a child?"

The incredulity on his face would have been laughable if Kate hadn't been so appalled. She hadn't meant to tell him so soon; she had wanted to wait until the fact of her pregnancy was inescapable. Page could count as well as the next man, and she hadn't wanted even a hint of suspicion to cross his mind. Would he guess? she wondered in dread. And if he did, what would she say?

Pulse racing, Kate forced herself to look at him again. He was holding her at arm's length, staring at her. "Why didn't you tell me before?" he demanded.

Her heart skipped a beat. She made herself answer, calculating rapidly. "I . . . I thought it might be too soon," she said faintly. "I didn't want to tell you until I was . . . sure."

"And are you?"

She nodded, closing her eyes at the sudden joy in his face. Never had her guilt weighed more heavily on her than at this moment, when he swept her into his arms and kissed her delightedly. From somewhere deep inside of her, she thought: Forgive me, Roger! But the thought went winging away, and as Page held her close, she thought, again, with infinite regret: Forgive me, Page. . . .

19

The cabin was even worse than Kate had feared. She looked around with dismay after Page had gently handed her down from the wagon—a caution, Kate thought wryly, that came a

little late, after the way he had pushed to get here—and her
heart sank.

It wasn't so much that she had to pick her way carefully
past the pecking chickens near the door, raising her skirts and
walking cautiously lest she step on one of the stupid things; it
wasn't even that there was no real entry—no step, no mat,
just the wooden door. It was that the mountain grass grew
right up to that door, giving the cabin even more of an air of
being a usurper in this meadow. As if the encroaching grass
would eventually claim the log structure, and the meadow
would be pure again.

Kate shivered and tried to ridicule her runaway imagination. But somehow the image persisted, despite her efforts,
and she hurried ahead, stepping through the door Page
proudly held open for her.

Inside, the cabin was cool and not as dim as she had imagined it would be. The two windows set in each wall admitted enough light even to sew by; there was no need,
thankfully, for lamps during the day. Kate was relieved; she
had pictured herself huddled molelike next to a smoking lamp,
trying to see whatever she was doing.

But the daylight illumination was a two-edged sword.
There was also enough light for her to see how dismal the
rest of the cabin was. The floors—and at least there *were*
floors, Kate told herself; some of the stage houses she had
passed through had only dirt to walk on—were planked. But
the windows were bare, bordered only by wooden shutters,
and there were no rugs, no carpets, no curtains. Nothing,
thought a disconsolate Kate, to relieve the depressing sight of
chinked logs and bare rafters. The only color in the single
room that comprised the interior of the entire cabin was the
patchwork quilt on the bed and a length of calico hung in the
corner that served as a dressing room. She looked around
helplessly, and didn't know what to say.

"I know it's not what you're accustomed to," Page said
apologetically from somewhere behind her. "But it won't always be this way, I promise. In fact . . ."

A shadow fell across the open door just then, and as Page
turned and uttered a delighted exclamation, Kate had her first
introduction to the elusive Colin Delaney.

He was a big man, not so much tall as broad. Standing
there in the doorway, he filled it; his shoulders were immense,
his bare arms corded with muscle, his hands strong and

openly callused. He had black curly hair half-hidden under his hat, a wide jaw, straight nose, and the most piercing blue eyes Kate had ever seen.

Those eyes turned her way for an instant, and Kate felt a thrill down to her toes when they lit with appreciation. Then Colin turned to Page, and the two young men embraced with awkward affection, thumping each other on the back and shouting imprecations concerning the other's character.

Kate waited, watching the scene with amused impatience. But finally, piqued that her husband seemed to have forgotten her in the general delirium of being reunited with his friend, she was about to come forward herself when Page remembered her at last.

"And here," said Page, putting an arm out to draw her near, "is my wife, Kate."

There was no mistaking the pride in his voice, and Kate was mollified. She extended her hand. "I'm pleased to meet you, Mr. Delaney," she said, smiling into those startlingly blue eyes.

"Colin, please. And the pleasure is all mine."

Her hand disappeared in his bearlike one. Then, to her astonishment, he bent over it and brushed his lips across her fingers. For some absurd reason, the gesture made her blush.

"Thank you," she said faintly, wondering why he was staring at her so searchingly. It was almost, she thought, as if he were assessing her, judging her. But before she could say anything, it appeared as if he had made some kind of decision, for he straightened and glanced over his shoulder, in the direction of the curtain at the far end of the room. With a quick motion of his head, he gestured.

"And this," he said to the startled Kate, "is *my* wife. Her name is unpronounceable to the uninitiated, but it translates, roughly, to Hill Flower."

Colin turned then and said something in another language. Immediately the woman who had been peering out from behind the calico curtain came forward. Kate gasped. After all her nightmares about Indians, she was actually in the same room with one!

Terrified at the thought, Kate was in the act of reaching for Page, when she paused. Hill Flower wasn't quite the savage she had imagined, she realized suddenly. In fact, she seemed shy, and kind, and even beautiful, in her own way. She was an Arapaho, Kate learned later, a member of tall, swift-moving Plains Indians, and her heritage showed in every line and bone of her body. Not quite as tall as Kate, or as slender, Hill Flower appeared also to be a few years older—in her early twenties, perhaps, thought Kate, returning the shy smile the woman directed at her. She had a high forehead, wide cheekbones, a rather flat nose that didn't detract at all from her appearance, but somehow seemed to enhance it; and she had beautiful skin, a warm honey color that glowed. She was in full Indian dress, for her long jet hair was plaited and bound with beaver fur, and she wore white-fringed deerskin and beaded moccasins on her feet. Her coal-black eyes were soft and questioning as she looked from Kate to Colin and then back to Kate again. Silently she offered another hesitant smile.

Colin and Page had drawn away to one side, waiting, it appeared—but for what, Kate didn't know. When Hill Flower dropped her eyes and stared at the floor, Kate realized that she would have to take the initiative. Drawing a deep breath, she tried to collect both her poise and her manners as she stepped forward. "How do you do?" she said, holding out her hand.

"She doesn't speak English, Kate," said Colin abruptly. "In fact, she doesn't speak at all. She's been mute since . . ." He hesitated, glancing at Page, who shrugged.

"Tell her," Page said. "She'll have to know sooner or later."

"Are you sure?"

"*I'm* sure!" Kate snapped, feeling left out. "Tell me what you're talking about!"

Colin stared at her, measuring her again. Kate returned his glance evenly, her head high. Finally he answered her. "Hill Flower hasn't spoken since she was attacked by some white hunters. They . . . they hurt her, and killed her husband and child."

"My God!"

"Yes," said Colin bitterly. "My God. They left her for dead, too, and if I hadn't stumbled upon her, she might have died as well."

Kate had listened in horror, her vivid imagination supplying her too readily with terrible images of Hill Flower's ordeal. Then, because she was too appalled to think of something else to say, she blurted, "You could have said something, Colin! You could have warned me before I made a complete fool of myself!"

"If I had told you about Hill Flower being mute, it would have prejudiced you," Colin replied.

"You couldn't know that!"

He shrugged. "I've seen it happen before, Kate. I wanted you to form your own opinion before you knew."

Colin's voice was resigned, but as angry as she was, Kate saw the hurt in his eyes as well. She was about to say something to him, when Hill Flower, who had followed the conversation with her eyes, approached. Grasping Kate's hand in warm, smooth fingers, she gave it the slightest squeeze before she released Kate and stepped back with that beautiful, shy smile again. It was all the communication Kate needed to make her feel at home.

Head high, Kate swept haughtily by the two men, drawing Hill Flower after her. Ignoring their chagrined husbands, the girl who had been so terrified of Indians, and the Indian who had suffered so much at the hands of whites, spent the afternoon learning to speak to each other through the language of sign. For Kate, it was an education in more ways than one, and she would always be grateful to Hill Flower for such a warm welcome to her new home.

Kate's warm feeling of welcome lasted until after dinner that night. Then harsh reality set in with a vengeance.

Thankfully, Hill Flower had assembled the meal, managing the iron stove with such ease that Kate despaired of ever mastering the art herself. Then, after a supper of stew and cornbread, Hill Flower had insisted, with gentle firmness, on putting the dishes away. Kate was too weary by that time to argue. Gratefully she accepted the offer and went to sit in the hard wooden chair Page had drawn up to the fire for her.

The evening was chill, and Kate was glad of the fire's warmth. But her exhaustion at the end of this long and tiring day and the hypnotic quality of the leaping flames combined to make her so drowsy she could hardly keep her eyes open; she was almost asleep as she sat there listening vaguely to the quiet clatter of supper dishes being washed.

She hadn't been paying any attention to the muted conversation of Page and Colin, who were still at table finishing their coffee. She wasn't even listening, in fact, to what they were saying, until she heard her name mentioned.

Even then she might not have been alerted; it was so peaceful by the fire, so warm and restful, that she didn't want to be disturbed. But then Colin said something she couldn't quite catch, and Page answered, "I haven't told Kate yet. I thought she should be settled before I did. After all, with the child on the way, I didn't want her to be upset."

He had spoken just a shade too quietly. Listening, Kate felt the first stirrings of alarm. Hadn't told her what? she wondered. And why would she be upset if he had?

The ominous feeling grew. Kate turned her back abruptly on the fire and stared in the direction of the table. When both Colin and Page looked up guiltily, her alarm became dread. She wanted to turn back to the fire again and forget what she had heard, but it was impossible to ignore. Some morbid curiosity drew her on, and even though she suspected she would be sorry she asked, some compulsion made her ask the question. "What is it that you haven't told me, Page?"

Page glanced quickly at Colin, who shrugged resignedly and stood. "Come on, little Flower," he said to his silent wife "Why don't we take a walk?"

"No," said Page. "You don't have to leave, Colin."

"But—"

"Yes. Stay," said Kate, releasing her tight grip on the chair as she forced herself to her feet. "I have an idea this concerns you, too."

Colin sat down reluctantly again, leaving Kate and Page facing each other like wary antagonists. It was then that she learned about Page receiving the long-awaited government contract to freight goods from Fort Leavenworth to Salt Lake City, Utah. Appalled, Kate listened to her husband reciting facts and figures, cost estimates, tonnage, numbers of mules and wagons—everything, in fact, except how long such a trip would take.

"So you see, in one haul we can pay for the mules and the wagons," finished Page enthusiastically. "And from then on, it will be pure profit."

"If everything goes right, that is," put in Colin helpfully.

Page frowned at him. "Nothing will go wrong," he said shortly. "We've been over it a hundred times—"

"It isn't the same as doing it."

Still trying to comprehend that Page was actually leaving, Kate was only half-listening to the conversation. But she was quick to catch Colin's pessimism, and she looked up sharply.

"What does that mean?" she demanded. "Are you saying you've never done this before?" Her voice rose shrilly as she looked from one to the other. "Haven't you?"

"We've gone over the route before, of course," Page answered, clearing his throat. "What Colin means is that we've never been responsible for the train—we were just hired hands before."

Kate looked at Colin, who was suddenly interested in his empty coffeecup, examining it as if he had never seen it before. Appalled, she glanced back at her husband, who was trying his best to maintain his confident pose. "Do you mean," she said, enunciating each word clearly, "that you don't even know what you're getting into? What it's like to lead a train? I can't believe it!" She stopped abruptly as another thought occurred to her. "Starting a freighting business must be an expensive undertaking," she said suspiciously. "What—?"

Page stepped in easily. "The initial investment is already taken care of," he said with assurance.

"How?"

"You don't have to worry about that. It's my concern."

"It's mine, too!"

"No. It isn't."

Kate recognized that tone, and it made her even more furious. "Yes," she said, just as stubbornly. "It is my concern. If you're going to be gone, heaven knows how long, I have a right to know how you managed it."

They glared at each other. Kate saw the muscle working in his jaw, a sure sign that he was struggling to control his temper, and she tossed her head. She didn't care if he was angry or not. She was right this time, and she knew it.

Page obviously knew it too. His voice tight, he finally answered, "Why do you think I went to England after my father died? It was to—"

But Kate knew the reason even before he voiced it. "You didn't sell your inheritance, did you?" she asked, horrified at the thought. "Oh, Page, you didn't sell Green Eaves! Not for something that could fail miserably at any time! How could you?"

Page interrupted her then, his voice steely. "It's done, Kate. I'm not going to argue about it anymore."

"But—"

He overrode her protest. "Colin has been busy arranging

things since he heard—that's why he couldn't meet us in Denver. But everything is ready now, and we leave . . . as soon as possible."

"Why not go tonight?" asked Kate bitterly, beginning to cry despite her fierce effort to hold back her tears. She felt a soft touch on her shoulder, a comforting pat, and she looked up through a blur to see Hill Flower smile sympathetically at her before she disappeared through the door. Colin got up silently from the table and followed his wife, shutting the door behind him. Kate and Page were alone.

"Kate, listen—"

"Don't you *dare* touch me!"

She tried to struggle away from him, but his hands imprisoned her arms. He held her tightly, shaking her a little to make her look at him.

"Listen to me—"

"No! I won't!" she shrieked. If her arms had been free, she would have clapped her hands over her ears, shutting out his voice. "It's always what *you* want, Page! What pleases you! Well, I'm not going to listen this time. I'm tired of being expected to accede meekly to *your* wishes—"

"You never agreed meekly to anything in your life, Kate. And in this case, it doesn't apply anyway. I'm not doing this for myself—"

"How can you say that?" she cried. "We only arrived, and now you're planning to go off again on some disastrous venture that's probably doomed from the start!"

"I'm doing it for you, Kate."

"Oh, don't make me laugh!" She had succeeded in freeing herself at last, and now she moved away from him, putting the table between them. "You always do what pleases you, Page Taggart, and you know it."

It was then that Page finally lost his temper. Before Kate's startled eyes, he reached down and with one violent motion swept everything off the table. Salt and pepper cellars, sugar bowl, silverware, and plates went flying in all directions, raining down around them and clattering to the floor.

Kate was riveted to the spot. She had never seen Page even remotely close to losing control, and this sudden show of temper frightened her. She couldn't move.

"Do you honestly believe that it *pleased* me to bring you here—to this?" His arm swept out again in a vicious gesture that encompassed the entire cabin, and Kate shrank back, appalled by the blaze of anger in his eyes.

"Page, I didn't mean—"

But before she could finish, he had reached down again, flinging the table to one side as easily as if it had been a box of matches. It crashed to the floor on the other side of the room. Kate jumped back, terrified. "Page, please—"

"And do you think I *wanted* to bring you all this way, knowing that this was what I had to give you?"

He was shouting, advancing on her with every word. And each time he took a step forward, she moved one back. Her eyes never left his face. "Page, it doesn't matter—"

There was a chair in front of him. He kicked it out of the way with such force that it splintered.

"I didn't intend to marry until I had built a home worthy of a wife," he shouted. "This"—there was something else in the way; he threw it contemptuously aside—"this was just for Colin and me, until I had a reason to make it better."

With a final step, he reached her. She was pressed against the side of the fireplace in a vain attempt to get away from him. But there was nowhere to hide, no place to run. It was as if he filled the room with the bulk of his body, looming over her until she shrank away from him. She could feel the heat from the fire in the stones against her back; one of them bit sharply into her spine, but she couldn't move. She was almost afraid to blink. She had never believed Page capable of such a display of temper, and she didn't want to precipitate another scene of violence. Badly frightened, she made herself look up at him.

"I wasn't going to lose you, Kate," he said, holding her transfixed. He was staring down at her, so close that his breath fanned her cheek. She was mesmerized, unable to speak.

"I couldn't lose you—not while I raced back to build a proper home for you with money I didn't have. Can you understand that? Can you?"

She swallowed, trying not to flinch when his hands came up to either side of her face. His fingers went around her throat, thumbs along her jaw, tilting her head up.

"The freighting business is a gamble—dammit, don't you think I know that? But there's also a lot of money to be made for someone willing to take that chance. And I'm willing to take it, Kate. I thought you would be too."

She tried to shift position at that, but he held her firmly. His eyes bored fiercely into her. "I thought you were a gambler, Kate. You never gave a damn about anyone's opinion but your own—you were reckless and adventurous, and you had courage. God! You had courage. If I hadn't known before then that I wanted you for my wife, I would have known it that day you set your horse at that tree. I never saw a woman with such daring, so much spirit! And now . . ."

His fingers tightened on her throat, and for a wild instant she wondered if he intended to strangle her or to fling her aside as he had the table. His thumbs were pressing on the soft flesh under her jaw, raising her chin again. She tried to jerk her head back and away from the sight of his face, but again he held her too tightly to move. She could only stare up into those fierce dark eyes and wonder why she had ever been complacent about him.

"Tell me, Kate," he said softly, interrupting her thoughts, "tell me that I wasn't wrong about you."

The words were quietly put, but in a flash of intuition Kate realized that her whole future—*their* whole future—depended on her reply. If she answered negatively, she knew that would be the end. Page would let her leave—for Denver, or New York, or even England, if she wanted to go.

And did she?

Did she want to leave behind this huge, empty country that she hated and that frightened her so? Did she want to leave behind strange customs and rough people and raw frontier towns in favor of all that was familiar . . . and boring . . . and predictable?

Did she want to leave Page?

"Well, Kate? Was I wrong?"

She felt his hands tremble as he waited for her answer. The tension in the room was almost palpable; she sensed it vibrating between them like a force, making her breath short, her heart hammer in her throat. She knew that whatever she said now, her decision was irrevocable. Page would accept what she told him, but he would make her keep to it. And once rejected, he would not allow her to reconsider. He was too proud.

So she had to be sure—very sure. She took a deep breath. "How long," she asked clearly, looking directly into his eyes, "will you be gone?"

20

Page was gone nearly eight months. And during that horrible time of loneliness and drudgery and outright fear, Kate alternated between despair that something had happened to him and anger that he stayed away so long. He had promised to be home before the snow came, and yet, as the days and then the months dragged by with no sign and no word from him, Kate knew with a sinking feeling that he wasn't going to keep his pledge.

It had been difficult enough to let him go. Even now she remembered the panic she had felt the day Page kissed her good-bye, and despite her brave stand, she had wanted desperately to beg him to stay. It had taken all her will that cool July dawn to hold her tongue, but she had clung to him so tightly at the last that he hesitated, putting her at arm's length to study her face.

"We'll be gone only a few months, Kate," he said quietly when he saw her expression. "The time will go by before you know it."

Kate tried to control herself. Brushing away the tears that overflowed despite her best efforts, she said plaintively, "You promise you'll be back before the first snow?"

He laughed gently at her despondent tone. "Unless it comes intolerably early this year, yes."

"Oh, Page! What if the snow does come early? What will I do?"

He held her even more tightly. "You'll manage, Katie. I know you will."

"I'm not so sure," she answered bitterly, brushing away more tears so that he wouldn't see her cry.

"I am," Page said softly. Then he kissed her again, hurriedly this time, anxious to be gone. "I love you, Kate," he said gruffly. "No matter what happens, remember that."

Calling abruptly to Colin, who was engaged a few feet

away in his own leave-taking with Hill Flower, Page went to
his horse before the gruffness in his voice became even more
emotional. The silvery sound of his spurs rang clearly in the
hush of dawn as he mounted, and Kate ordered herself
fiercely not to burst into unrestrained weeping.

Somehow she managed to say good-bye to Colin; she even
raised her hand in farewell and smiled weakly as Page sat his
horse for a minute longer and looked down at her.

"Take care," she whispered. "Both of you."

Page appeared about to say something more. But then, as
if he didn't trust his voice, he nodded instead. With a lift of
his arm, he waved good-bye before he wheeled his horse
around. Then he and Colin were gone into the predawn
night.

Kate listened as long as she could to the measured sound
of the horses moving across the meadow. But when finally
the noise faded away and then disappeared altogether, she
was swept with such a sense of utter desolation that even the
magnificent sight of dawn breaking over the Rockies failed to
cheer her. Page was gone, she thought bleakly, and what was
she going to do until he returned?

It wasn't until Hill Flower came up softly behind her that
Kate was able to abandon her stiff pose by the door. But the
smile she gave the other woman was bleak, and once again
she wondered despairingly how she was going to endure until
Page came home again.

It wasn't until September that Kate had her first experience
with Indians other than Hill Flower. Contrary to Page's assurances the day he went away, the summer had dragged on
and on, and when Kate found herself stopping constantly to
search the horizon for any sign of Colin and Page, she tried
to make herself abandon the habit. Watching anxiously for
his return would not make it arrive any sooner, she would tell
herself firmly, bending to yet another task to take her mind
off Page. And then, a few minutes later she would find herself straining to see him coming over the hills, or up the
meadow, or along the creek.

Fortunately for her sanity, she was kept busy during the
day with the relentless chores of simple survival. And every
day, at one time or another, she would send up a silent
prayer of thanks for Hill Flower. Without her, Kate knew she
never could have managed alone.

To Kate's chagrin, it was Hill Flower who insisted on doing the heavy work, and even with only the two of them, there was much to be done: washing clothes and linens and dishes; scrubbing the stove and the table and the floor; ironing with the flat iron that was almost too heavy to lift. Then there was the cooking, hauling the corded firewood in for the stove, gathering eggs from the chickens, feeding and caring for the four blooded horses Page intended to use to start his own breeding stock, checking the small herd of cattle that was the fledgling beginning of the Taggart cattle ranch—the list seemed endless. And through it all, the two women worked side by side: Hill Flower teaching, Kate trying to learn how to cope with the myriad accomplishments expected of a frontier wife.

They went berry-picking, and Kate had her first experience making jam. They collected enough grease in the can at the back of the stove, and then Kate learned to make soap. Candle-making was next, and then drying fruit for the winter.

There was the day when they found the deer with the broken leg, and a horrified Kate learned that nothing was wasted: she watched Hill Flower calmly take the gun and shoot the animal behind the ear. Sickened, Kate made herself help with hauling the carcass back to the cabin, but even her formidable will quailed at the idea of assisting in the cleaning and quartering. Her first tentative touch of the slippery entrails was enough to send her running from the smokehouse, and even Hill Flower's gentle and understanding smile could not draw her back again to help.

Standing outside in the cool September dusk that day, Kate put a shaking hand to her hot forehead and tried not to think of Hill Flower serenely butchering the deer. Would she never become accustomed to this harsh land that demanded so much and gave so grudgingly in return? she wondered despairingly.

Propping herself wearily against the side of the cabin, Kate wrapped her arms about her and doubted it. It seemed that no matter how much Hill Flower taught her, no matter how much she learned and tried to learn, there were always a thousand lessons in front of her, each more difficult than the last. And she was so tired, she thought, raising one hand to brush a lock of hair back from her face; so tired.

But it was the nights that were the worst—the long quiet nights when she and Hill Flower sat together after supper.

She had found herself wishing uselessly that she hadn't given the kitten to that lonely little girl at the stage office in Leavenworth; at least a cat would be company, its antics provide some comic relief in the unendurable silence that surrounded her nights. At first the quiet had been deafening, Kate thought; she had developed the habit of getting up to stir the fire or to bang the coffeepot on the stove—anything to make a little noise and drown out that absolute silence. Then she had begun to chatter, to talk aimlessly—sometimes even to herself—just to hear the sound of a voice. Any voice, even her own. And that had frightened her badly. She had heard of a malady called "mountain madness": people who were alone too long simply went crazy, running amok or jabbering eerily to themselves as they sat on their heels and rocked back and forth, unable to cope any longer with crushing loneliness.

It was then that she had decided to teach Hill Flower to read and write.

So now their evenings were spent bent over books and the slate Kate had fortuitously brought with her, and Hill Flower was practicing writing her name against the day when Colin came home and she could proudly show him her accomplishment.

In return, although Kate hadn't asked, Hill Flower had begun to sew a beautiful infant wardrobe. Whereas Kate was impatient with her needle, Hill Flower excelled with hers, spinning out the most exquisite embroidery, the smallest stitches, the most invisible seams. Tiny smocks, dresses, bonnets, and coats blossomed under her agile fingers, and Kate blessed the wisdom that had led Olivia to pack the finest lawn and wool and linen in one of the trunks for just such use. Now, reflected Kate wryly, when the child was born, at least it would have something to wear.

So she was grateful to Hill Flower for more than she could ever repay, she admitted, resting her head against one of the sawed log ends that formed the corner of the cabin. Oh, yes, she was grateful, without doubt. If Hill Flower hadn't agreed to stay, Kate might have lost her mind from fear and loneliness and sheer ignorance. But, oh, how she longed for the sound of another human voice!

"We want . . . you give . . ."

The thick, guttural voice behind her startled her so badly that she jumped and half-fell against the cabin wall. For an instant she was confused enough to believe that she had imagined the sound, and as she groped her way upright again, she shook her head.

Ridiculous, she thought; there was no one within miles of . . .

But the thought froze in her brain as several shadows emerged seemingly from nowhere in the gathering twilight. Kate blinked and shook her head, trying to tell herself that her thoughts had not conjured up these images, that they hadn't magically appeared in response to her wish—that it was all some bewildering product of her fevered imagination. They weren't real; they couldn't possibly be real.

But they were.

And as Kate's wide, staring eyes went from one to the other, she knew that they weren't images at all, but real Indians. Five of them—all braves—and every one daubed with paint. War paint. Kate almost fainted on the spot.

Later, thinking about what had happened, Kate wasn't sure at all why she hadn't folded like a limp paper doll and simply sunk unconscious to the ground at their moccasined feet. Even then, she didn't know how she managed to face them, for her heart was thudding in her chest and her knees shook so badly that she had to reach behind her and hold on to the cabin just to stay upright.

What did they want? She was too frightened, too terrified to ask. All the stories she had ever heard about Indians raping, looting, murdering, and taking women for prisoners leaped through her mind like frightened birds before a squall, and she dug her nails into her palms to keep from screaming aloud in horror.

What had Page told her to do if Indians came to the cabin? She couldn't remember. She couldn't remember a thing. She was too scared, in fact, to recall that not twenty feet away, Hill Flower was calmly butchering the deer in the smokehouse.

One of the braves was holding his hand out, repeating in that guttural tone something that sounded like "choog . . . choog . . ." Woodenly Kate looked from his empty hand to his face and tried desperately to understand what he meant. Think! she told herself fiercely. Think! She had the horrible suspicion that unless she acted properly, he might be provoked into some unspeakable retaliatory action, and yet her brain seemed unable to deal with anything other than the sheer terror she felt. But she had to do something, anything. If she didn't, God alone knew what they might do.

The thought was enough to calm her. Where she found the courage, she didn't know; it was enough to be able to push herself away from the cabin wall and face them without flinching. Instinctively she knew that any show of fear would be disastrous, so even though she was more afraid than she had ever been in her life, she made herself raise her head and look the leader straight in the eye.

Chin high, and in her best, most precise, and clipped British voice she said, "This way, gentlemen. If you please."

Raising her skirts slightly, Kate went to brush by them. One of the braves reached out a hand as if to detain her, but Kate looked coolly at him until he withdrew. "Thank you," she said haughtily, and continued on.

The Indians might not have understood her words, but they correctly interpreted her proud tone. One by one, they followed her to the cabin door, where they paused, arms folded menacingly across their chests, watching her.

Kate didn't hesitate. She went straight to the kitchen, took down one of her best towels, and without pause tore it into five pieces. Then she went to the cupboard where the sugar tin was kept and brought it to the table in the middle of the room. Spooning out the sugar into five equal portions, Kate reserved some for herself, making sure that the Indians saw the gesture. Then she tied the five squares into packages, scooped them off the table, and brought them over to the waiting braves. Silently she gave each a packet and then stood back, praying she had done the right thing. Everything—perhaps even her very life—depended on it.

The leader seemed dissatisfied. With a frown he looked from the packet he held to the sugar tin on the table. He made a threatening gesture, indicating he wanted more.

As frightened as she was, Kate knew she had to hold firm. "No," she said clearly, shaking her head for emphasis. "You have yours. That is mine."

The Indian gestured again, more forcefully this time. Again Kate shook her head. "You have what you came for," she said with finality, beginning to close the door. "It's time for you to leave now."

Would the ploy succeed? Kate smiled pleasantly but firmly, praying that they wouldn't see how her lip trembled. She had no idea whether they would erupt with war whoops and murder her where she stood, and she was trying to steel herself, when suddenly the leader grinned. He held up his hand, palm toward her, the fingers splayed to show that he would grasp no weapon against her, and then he spoke rapidly in his own language. Kate had no idea what he was saying; she was too frightened even to try to interpret. The only thing she recognized was a grudging admiration in his tone, but she was too numb for the realization to penetrate.

The leader gestured to his companions, and an instant later they were gone, disappearing into the night as silently and abruptly as they had appeared, leaving Kate sagging against the table in relief.

She made herself walk forward and close the door. After her brave show of strength, she didn't want them to see her in this moment of jellylike weakness if they were still lurking outside watching her.

Her pose lasted long enough for her to shut the door. As soon as she had shot the bolt home, though, Kate collapsed. Sliding down the length of the door, she landed in a heap on the floor, sobbing and laughing at the same time. She had done it, she thought exultantly: she had beaten the Indians at their own game, and they had gone away, leaving her and Hill Flower in peace. She could hardly believe it yet.

She was still sitting on the floor when Hill Flower, finished with the deer, entered from the side door that connected the cabin and the smokehouse in back. As soon as she saw Kate huddled by the door, she rushed over, signing frantically to know what had happened. Kate managed to reveal that she wasn't hurt, but now that the crisis had passed, reaction was setting in. She began shivering uncontrollably, and even when the other woman helped her over to the fire and wrapped her in a blanket, her teeth chattered and her entire body shook with one tremor after another. Finally, exhausted, calmed by the herb concoction Hill Flower had slipped into her tea, Kate fell asleep. But it was a long time after that before she was able to tell the story of what had happened, and it was even longer before she wished so desperately to hear the sound of a human voice again.

The "Indian incident," as Kate came to call it, occurred in late September. October came and went without another appearance by the five braves, and after a while Kate was even able to go outside again without wondering fearfully if the

Indians were lurking somewhere just out of sight. When in early November they came again, Kate was able to handle both herself and the situation with a little more aplomb, and after that, the subsequent, sometimes monthly visits from various small Indian bands ceased to frighten her so badly. She was still cautious, careful to maintain an outward calm that betrayed none of her fear. The utter terror she had felt before never returned, and after a time she was even able to recognize different tribes and individual braves. The women never came, and sometimes Kate would wonder about that, but there was no one to ask, and she learned to accept the fact that the braves kept their squaws out of sight.

But there were other things to occupy her mind that fall. October, with its gorgeous display of falling leaves and fluttering aspen, passed almost unnoticed by Kate except for her continual surveillance of the sky. Storm clouds were massing; she could feel the brisk chill in the air that signaled the approach of winter, and when the first snowflakes fell, she became afraid. Page wasn't going to return home before the first snow after all, she acknowledged in despair, and she began to be sure something terrible had happened to him.

There were so many disasters that could befall a freight train, she knew—from harsh sun and alkali dust to driving rain and sucking mud that bogged down the entire train. The distance alone was a contest in endurance for man and animal, and sometimes sheer exhaustion took its toll even more than the whims of nature or marauding Indians. The more Kate thought about it, the more she became convinced that the worst had occurred—and just as frightening as that thought was the idea that she might never even know about it. Whole wagon trains had disappeared in the vast emptiness of the great West, never to be heard from again. Were Page and Colin destined to be two of the ghosts who roamed the plains, unheralded and unremarked, while she and Hill Flower waited and waited and never knew whether their vigil was fruitless or not?

As the snow grew thicker on the frozen ground, Kate became almost gaunt, with blue shadows under her eyes and hollows in her cheeks. She watched continuously from the cabin window for any sign of Page; every spare minute she had away from the daily chores she took on herself, she would wrap a thick shawl about her head and shoulders and walk clumsily to the head of the meadow to look for him.

But the pristine expanse of snow remained unbroken, and her despair grew.

By December, Kate was big with child. It was an effort for her to walk, almost impossible for her to bend. Even so, she insisted on doing her share of the work, or as much as she was able, trying to drown out her fear of delivering the child with only Hill Flower in attendance. She was afraid, and tried not to show it, but Hill Flower knew, and often Kate would glance up to find those great dark eyes on her, shining with gentle courage.

Christmas approached, and Kate roused herself to plan a small celebration. Determined to put away her fears, at least for a day, Kate even insisted on cutting down a small Christmas tree. Olivia, with her remarkable foresight, had given her a silver star and a gold bell for this occasion, and when the tree had been decorated with these and the candles Kate had helped make herself, she almost wept at the sight. The tiny pine stood bravely on a table in the corner, and the sight made her unutterably sad. Christmas morning they exchanged the gifts they had secretly made: Kate received a pair of beautiful moccasins, beaded and lined warmly with fur, and she gave Hill Flower the fringed shawl she had made of shimmering blue silk.

And all the while, she wondered where and how Page was spending his Christmas.

It wasn't until mid-January, when the snow was thickest, the wind most fierce, and the temperature cold enough to freeze the very air in her lungs, that Kate felt the first pain.

She was outside, in the lean-to shelter for the horses, doling out the dwindling supply of grain for the animals, when the pain struck. It was more of a surprise than an actual pain, like a sharp thud inside her, but enough of a shock to make her gasp and bend over.

When it came again a few seconds later, she had to reach out and take hold of the iced mane of the horse nearest her for balance. Breathing shallowly in anticipation of another, Kate held tightly to the horse and waited. Nothing happened. It was almost as if she had imagined the episode. Cautiously she straightened. Now she felt fine.

The thought was depressing. She had hoped that this would be the first signal, for she had been waiting anxiously two weeks and more. By her calculations, the child was sixteen days late, and she sometimes thought that if she had to carry this intolerable weight around much longer, she would go mad. But now she felt fine. She almost burst into tears.

She was just reaching awkwardly forward to retrieve the grain bucket she had dropped, when it happened again. This time there was no question that she had imagined it: the fiery pain lanced across the small of her back so sharply that she moaned.

Straightening again, she tried to call for help. But the rising wind tore the words from her mouth and whipped them away in the swirling snow. She knew that Hill Flower, inside at the stove making supper, couldn't possibly hear her, and yet somehow she had to get back into the cabin before the next pain struck. She would have to do it herself.

Groping her way from one handhold to the next, Kate paused at the entrance to the lean-to and looked out into the storm. As she measured the distance by eye from the shed to the cabin, she wondered why she had insisted on coming out to feed the horses herself; it seemed a foolish idea now. Especially since, as she watched, the snow was covering the footprints she had made on the way out. The storm was worsening.

And standing here was only prolonging the ordeal, Kate told herself. No one was going to carry her from the shed to the cabin; she had to walk it herself. Clutching the thick shawl closer about her throat, Kate took a deep breath and plunged out into that blank whiteness.

She hadn't gone six feet before she was floundering in deep snow. Without the shelter for protection, the wind tore at her, making her ponderous weight even more unbalanced, so that she lurched from side to side, struggling to make headway in the driving snow. Snowflakes clung wetly to her face and lashes, making it hard for her to see; if she hadn't known every inch of land between the cabin and the shed, she might have lost her way. Now, halfway to the cabin, she could scarcely see it; the structure was almost totally obscured by the blizzard. Looking up, Kate could have cried: the cabin seemed so far away, and she was already tired. She forced herself to struggle on.

The wind had clawed away her head covering by the time she arrived, panting, at the door. Her hair was white with clinging snow, and she could feel it beginning to creep icily down her neck. Her mittens were so stiff with ice that when she tried to grasp the door latch, her fingers slipped uselessly away. She could have cried with utter frustration: to be so near warmth and comfort, and yet so far away. It was a nightmare.

Weakly she beat at the door with freezing hands, begging Hill Flower to open it before she collapsed from sheer weariness. Panicked, she could feel the pain beginning to build inside her again, and when finally the Indian woman opened the door, Kate was only able to gasp, "The baby! I think it's coming!" before she pitched forward into the other woman's open arms.

Ever after, the only thing Kate remembered about that exhausting afternoon was the pain. It came in waves, building to a crescendo and then beyond, until she thought she would shatter with the force of it. The agony would ebb for a time, leaving her weak and breathless, and then it would build again, clawing at her with fingers of fire until she screamed. Her back felt like it was bending inward like a bow, and she wanted to stretch out, relieving that intolerable pressure before it crushed her. But the pain held her; she could only endure, letting it take her where it would. She was powerless to resist; too weak to try.

Finally, when she was sure she could bear it no longer, when she felt as though she was being torn in two, there was one last rush of agony, and then she heard an infant cry.

It was over. The child had been born, and she was too weak even to lift her head to look at it. Sweat ran into her eyes, almost blinding her, and she wondered briefly why she didn't feel empty.

Confused, spent, Kate lay back on the wet pillow and tried to catch her breath. Was something wrong? Why did she feel so . . . ?

Another burst of pain caught her off-guard. Arching back, she screamed and thrashed on the rumpled bed, sure she was dying. From somewhere, she felt Hill Flower's comforting hands on her, and then she thought deliriously that she heard another wailing cry.

She didn't care. She was truly dying, floating away on a blessed cloud of unconsciousness, and the only thing she could think of was how wonderful it was not to feel that crushing agony anymore.

As she faded away into the welcoming darkness, Kate was

unaware that she had given birth to twins, both boys. She couldn't know that the younger, fair-haired and placid by nature, was to be a source of comfort and strength to her in the years to come, or that the elder, the twin who had produced such agony that snowy January afternoon, was to cause another kind of pain in the far future. Black-haired and dark-eyed, Kate's firstborn would have a temper to match her own—and a proud nature that would not bend even when it caused suffering to those he loved most.

21

She named them Michael and David. And even if they had not been fraternal twins, and therefore dissimilar in coloring and looks, there would have been no question which was which. The elder, Michael, was from the first a handful. It was he who screamed loudest, who demanded more, who was never satisfied until he had his way. His brother, David, was calmer, quieter, content to wait his turn. Side by side they would lie in the single crib, and it would be Michael who struggled to raise his head, Michael who tried to turn over or pull himself up. David would lie quietly, gurgling to himself occasionally, following his brother's agitated movements with wide blue eyes, not making any of his own.

Kate watched them anxiously, wondering what Page would think when he saw them. Michael presented no problem, she assured herself; with his dark crown of hair and darker eyes, he looked astonishingly like Page himself. But David—David was so blond, so fair, so much like . . . Roger. Would Page see the resemblance too? And noticing it, would he wonder? Kate both anticipated and dreaded the day Page returned.

If he returned, Kate would think bleakly, turning to stare out the window at the white expanse of snow that covered everything but the tallest trees. The sky was a constant, depressing gray; there were always scattered snowflakes drifting down when it wasn't actively storming, and Kate had long ago abandoned all hope of seeing him before the spring.

But he would come then, Kate told herself time and time again; he would come then because he must. She hadn't endured this spirit-crushing winter for nothing—nor the agony of giving birth to the twins without him, or the days of utter silence, or the fear, or the loneliness. How many times, she wondered, closing her eyes, had she wished just for him to be near—to look up and see him there, or to feel his arms around her at night, warming the cold and empty bed?

Oh, he would come in the spring, she thought fiercely, or she would know the reason why!

He came in the middle of March, struggling up the slushy meadow on foot, leading a tired horse, both of them covered with mud.

Kate had gone outside to empty the pail of dishwater and to take a few minutes' rest in the welcome sun. After endless days of dreary skies, it was wonderful to feel the sunshine, weak as it was, on her upturned face. Propping the empty pail on one hip, Kate stood outside the open cabin door, threw her head back, and sighed contentedly.

One of the horses in the nearby corral nickered. Opening her eyes, Kate glanced in that direction and saw the five animals crowding the fence, looking down the meadow. Puzzled, she swung that way too, shading her eyes against the glare of sunlight on melting snow. She froze.

He looked older, and wiser; more lean than he had when he left. There were lines in his face that hadn't been there before, and he walked with a slight limp, favoring his left leg. But it was Page, just the same, and for a long minute, as he struggled up the streaming meadow, Kate couldn't believe her eyes. She was rooted to the spot, unable to move. She couldn't even call out to Hill Flower, inside with the twins, she couldn't speak over the stricture in her throat. She could only stand there foolishly and feel a wild exultation building in her at the sight of her husband coming home to her.

Page looked up just then, and from across the distance that still separated them, their eyes met. Kate couldn't breathe. She gripped the rim of the pail so tightly that the metal cut into her palm, and she didn't even notice. There was nothing in the world for her but the expression in Page's eyes and on his face; she didn't hear or see anything but him.

Then he grinned, and her trance was broken. Calling out to Hill Flower, Kate dropped the pail with a heedless clatter. Even before it hit the ground, she was off and away, lifting her skirts high and running pell-mell down the slope.

Page caught her in his arms, swinging her off the ground, whirling her around, and hugging her so tightly that she could hardly take a breath. She didn't care; she was laughing and crying at the same time, saying his name over and over again as if she couldn't believe it was really he.

"Well, Katie," he said, "I didn't make it back before the first snow, did I?"

He laughed a little then, and Kate saw the pain behind his eyes. Suddenly, all the things she had been about to say fled from her mind. "Where's Colin?" she asked quietly.

Page set her gently on the ground again. "Colin," he said, "didn't make it."

Kate would never forget the moment Page entered the cabin that day of his return; the scene was burned into her memory forever.

Scarcely had Page's shadow crossed the door than Hill Flower rose gracefully to her feet, waiting. Kate paused at the threshold, trying not to cry, and when she saw the Indian woman meet Page's eyes with calm understanding, she realized that Hill Flower had sensed for a long time that Colin wasn't coming home. And yet, thought Kate with a wrench, Hill Flower had gone about her work quietly, displaying none of the worry and fretfulness and scenes of temper that had characterized Kate's own behavior over the long winter. Now, Page didn't have to tell Hill Flower about Colin; the Indian woman merely nodded, as if she had known all along.

Kate, swept by emotion, went immediately to the other woman. But even before she approached, she sensed Hill Flower's withdrawal, the immense dignity and inner strength that enabled her to disengage herself from Kate's embrace gently and with a smile.

Helplessly Kate watched the woman who had been her friend in the truest sense walk to the door, where she paused. As she turned to look back, Kate saw that Hill Flower's great dark eyes were wounded, but without tears, and her admiration grew. Numbly she tried to return the smile Hill Flower gave her, but the woman's expression of fondness and deep affection was almost too much for Kate. Biting hard on her lip, Kate tried not to weep at the sight of Hill Flower nodding, once, to Page. Then, turning slowly, the Indian woman walked out the door.

For the first time since she had entered the cabin, Kate noticed that Hill Flower was wearing full Indian dress—the costume she had worn the day of Kate's arrival, and which she had worn only once since, at Christmas. And around her shoulders was the fringed blue shawl Kate had given her, which she treasured. Kate felt a terrible premonition.

Rushing to the door, Kate stared at the departing figure. Hill Flower had almost reached the trees at the edge of the meadow. In another moment she would disappear from sight.

"Hill Flower . . . wait!"

She was just lifting her skirts to run after her friend when Page checked her. "Let her go."

Kate looked uncomprehendingly down at the hand on her arm. Wild-eyed, she raised her glance to his face. "Are you out of your mind?" she cried. "She's had a terrible shock! There's no telling what she'll do!"

"She knows exactly what she's doing, Kate. Let her go."

"I can't!"

"You have to."

"But . . . but she's been a friend to me! The best friend I'll ever have, or want to have. You don't know what we've been through together! I can't just let her go!"

But there was no choice, and from somewhere deep inside her, Kate knew it. "Oh, God!" she sobbed in anguish as the full magnitude of what Hill Flower was about to do struck her. She beat her fists impotently against Page's chest as he tried to comfort her. "It isn't fair!" she cried. "It isn't fair!"

It was at that moment, when Kate was so devastated that her friend had gone, so appalled at what Hill Flower planned to do, that Michael gave a loud wail. It was as if he understood the magnitude of his mother's grief and wanted to join his voice to hers in mourning the woman who had brought him into the world and who had been almost as much a mother to him as had Kate.

Page stiffened. "What was that?"

And Kate, who had so dreaded this first confrontation between Page and her sons, forgot all the anxiety and the hundreds of times she had planned what to say. In the end, all her worry came to nothing; her thoughts still with Hill

Flower, Kate said the first thing that came into her head. "That," she said, "is one of your sons."

Page choked. *"One* of my sons?"

He rushed over to the crib, where Michael was now screaming lustily. Kate followed more slowly, brushing tears from her cheeks with her fingers. Hill Flower was gone; as horrible as it was, there was nothing she could do about it. Somehow, she had to pull herself together and forget that terrible scene; the next few minutes could affect Page and her and the twins for the rest of their lives. There would be time later to mourn for Hill Flower, and as she joined Page at the crib, Kate knew that Hill Flower would understand.

Trying to control her tears, Kate stood by her husband as he gazed down into the crib. She even managed a shaky smile when he looked at her again, almost fatuous with delight at the sight of the two infants. "The loud one," she said, pointing, "is Michael. The good one I named David."

Fondly she reached down and gave the blond David a pat. "I'm afraid there is a tendency to ignore him sometimes; he's so quiet, and Michael is so demanding, as you can see."

"David . . . Michael . . ." Page was staring at the twins as if he couldn't believe his eyes. Tentatively he reached out and touched the wailing Michael, who, to Kate's amazement, grabbed at Page's finger and ceased his screaming at once. Page laughed and reached out with his other hand toward David, who only looked back at him solemnly. He laughed again.

"We never talked about names," Kate said, watching Page, who seemed completely absorbed. "There didn't seem to be enough time before you went away to discuss much of anything." She couldn't keep the resentment from her voice, and Page glanced up.

"No, there wasn't time for much, was there?" he said soberly. "But Michael and David are fine names, Kate. And they're fine boys,'" he added, his eyes aglow with pride. "When were they born?"

Her heart missed a beat. Did he suspect anything? Was he asking as a proud father or as a suspicious husband? Kate swallowed, then bent down quickly to adjust the crib quilt so that Page couldn't see her expression. She was sure that her guilt was written loudly all over her face, and she felt a flush creeping up her throat to stain her cheeks a painful red.

Pretending a sudden absorption with Michael's smock,

Kate answered carefully. "They were born in January. I think the blizzard we had then brought on an early birth—I was out taking care of the horses when the first pain struck."

"You were outside? In a blizzard! My God, Kate, what were you thinking of?"

"I was making sure," she said evenly, "that your horses didn't starve to death. You might not have told me much, Page, but you did mention that those horses were to be the foundation of your ranch. I assumed that meant they were to be cared for."

Page winced at the sarcasm, but still he was firm. "No animal is worth risking your life and that of an unborn child, Kate. You should have—"

Her pain over Hill Flower, her guilt at deceiving her husband, her sudden outrage at his superior tone, combined to make her lose control again. But this time she didn't cry; she lost her temper. How dare he swagger in after so long an absence and tell her what she should or shouldn't have done? He had no right to use that tone, no right to speak to her as if she were a child herself, and a slightly stupid one at that. She was his wife, the mother of two sons, and she had survived the winter in a strange country without his help. She was furious.

"How dare you speak to me like that!" she said, her voice shaking with anger. "No one—especially you!—needs to tell me about *risk!* You weren't here, remember, to tell us how to manage when things went wrong—when one of your precious cows fell into a ravine and had to be pulled out, or when two of the horses were sick with colic and had to be walked all night! You weren't here when the Indians came, or when the spring stopped up, or when the bear got into the smokehouse—"

"Kate—"

She overrode him, her voice rising even more shrilly. "—so don't take that righteous tone and tell me what I *should* or *shouldn't* have done! I did the best I could—and we did what we had to, what was necessary. We *survived*, Page, and we . . ."

But she couldn't go on. Her tears were choking her, and she thought wildly that if she said another word, she would shatter into a thousand pieces. The strain had been too great, the time too long, the loneliness too debilitating. She hadn't realized it before, but she had been living on the edge of an

emotional precipice, and she was about to take that final step
over the line, when something stopped her. Now she could
only stand there helplessly with her fists clenched and tears
streaming down her cheeks, trying to hold on to the last ves-
tige of control before she became completely hysterical. Sob
after sob racked her whole body, and in the crib, both twins
began to whimper.

Page ignored the crying infants. He took Kate in his arms
and simply held her as she surrendered to the emotional
storm that had broken. "It's all right, Katie," he whispered
over and over again. "It's all right."

And then he took her to bed.

"It wasn't bad," Page said, much later. "Or at least, it
wasn't as bad as we thought it would be."

But it had been, thought Kate, twisting her head to look up
at him as they lay in bed. They were side by side under the
blankets, and Page's arms were around her. She had been
resting her head happily in the curve between his shoulder
and chest when he began talking of the freighting trip. Gazing up at him, Kate studied what she could see of his face,
and she knew that, contrary to what he had just said, it had
been awful, much worse than he was going to tell her.

After he had made love to her, gently with infinite tenderness, they had stayed abed, wrapped in each other's arms,
content to steal this day for themselves. Satisfied, drowsy in
the aftermath of lovemaking, they had talked of many
things—everything, it seemed, but the trip that had taken him
away for so long.

Page had obviously avoided the subject until now, and
Kate had aided him. She didn't want to know how Colin had
died; she never wanted to know. Because speaking of Colin
only made her think of Hill Flower, and Kate could still see
her walking slowly and majestically across the meadow
toward the trees, her head high and the fringed shawl fluttering in the breeze. Hill Flower had been more than a friend,
Kate thought sadly now; they had been women together, al-
lies against the lonely, soul-chilling winter. They had endured
so much with only each other to rely on, and now, when
Kate owed so much to her, she could never repay her debt.
A part of her would always remember and respect Hill
Flower's quiet strength, and a part of her would always
grieve over her loss.

And now, because Colin had been Hill Flower's husband, Kate felt that she had to ask. "How did Colin die?" she said softly.

Page shifted in the bed. Kate felt him tense at the question, and for a minute she thought he wasn't going to be able to answer her.

"You don't have to tell me if you would rather not," she said, almost hoping that he wouldn't.

"No . . . I suppose you should know." Page hesitated, steadying his voice. Then he continued, and Kate listened tautly, praying that the narrative would end before she had to beg him to stop. How she hated listening to the pain in his voice—the shock and the horror—as if he were reliving it all again as he told it.

There wasn't much to tell, in fact. Colin had died in a freak accident, trying to save a team of mules that would have been better plunging to destruction off the trail by themselves. The driver of the team had prudently jumped off the wagon when the axle broke, spinning the near back wheel down a steep gorge to shatter on the rocks below. The heavy wagon, unbalanced without that wheel, had slipped over the edge. The mules had scrambled wildly for purchase on the narrow ledge of the trail they were traversing, but they had been pulled inexorably back, foot by foot, unable to hold against the weight of the wagon.

Colin had seen what was happening, and before Page or anyone else could stop him, he had leaped off his horse, knife in hand to cut the traces and free the animals. In the dust and confusion and wild panic that ensued, Colin had somehow become entangled in the harness himself.

"And so," Page finished abruptly, his voice taut, "we all watched as it went sliding over the edge—mules, wagon, and . . . and Colin with it. There was nothing we could do to stop it."

"But you tried—"

"Oh, God, yes, we tried," said Page bitterly. "I even grabbed onto the harness with my bare hands, in some stupid attempt to hold back the wagon myself. It almost pulled me down with it."

"Is that how you hurt your leg?" Kate had seen the long jagged scar down his thigh. It was still an angry red weal, almost as painful-looking now as the injury must have been at the time. Kate hadn't dared to ask what had happened; judg-

ing from the scar and the limp Page exhibited even now, she
hadn't been sure she wanted to know.

"Yes," Page was saying briefly, as if it were of no importance. "That's how I hurt my leg. I was . . . dragged . . . a
little before I could get free."

"How horrible!"

"It doesn't matter. I was the lucky one, wasn't I? Poor
Colin never did get free. We found him at the bottom of the
ravine, under one of the mules he tried to save." Page's voice
broke on a sob, and he made a convulsive gesture with his
closed fist. "The goddamned . . . mules! It was such a waste,
Kate—such a damned waste! In the end, Colin was dead, and
we had to shoot both animals."

He turned his face away, but Kate felt the shudder pass
through his body. Intent only on trying to comfort him, she
murmured some soothing sound and went to put her arms
around him just as he turned back to her. Stricken, she saw
the glisten of tears in his eyes, the agony in his expression.

"I need you, Kate—I need you more than ever before," he
said, and then his mouth came down hard on hers.

Kate's response was as elemental as his demand. She answered his kiss with the same powerful urgency she sensed in
him, and this time there was no tenderness, no gentleness, in
their lovemaking. Fiercely they came together, driving toward
a thundering climax that rocked them both. It was as if, in
this turbulent and passionate union, they were seeking a desperate affirmation of life when death was all around them.
They were alive, they shouted; they had survived. But as their
sweating, writhing bodies pounded toward fulfillment, they
both knew, deep inside themselves, that their survival had
come at great cost to others, and that somehow this savage
and almost cataclysmic union was proof that the sacrifice had
not been in vain.

"Well, Kate, what do you think?"

It was mid-April. Page had been home a month, and they
had been to Denver twice: once to find a girl to help with the
twins and the housework; the second time to leave the girl, a
young French immigrant of eighteen named Ann-Marie Durand, in charge of the twins while Page took Kate on a
much-needed holiday. The Taggarts returned from Denver
rested and refreshed a week later, and the vague disquiet
Kate had felt about Ann-Marie disappeared when she discov-

ered that the twins had thrived in her absence and that the girl had cleaned the cabin from top to bottom.

Now, with the hardworking Ann-Marie taking much of the burden from her, Kate had begun to lose the gaunt, worn appearance she had developed during Page's absence. After a month of rest and shared responsibility, she was beginning to bloom again, and she had begun to look upon Ann-Marie as a godsend, even if the girl continued to disturb her occasionally by following Page with her bright brown eyes or flashing him a mischievous, knowing smile when he took one or the other of the twins from her capable arms. But Ann-Marie was French, Kate would remind herself, and everyone knew that Frenchwomen—or girls—were forward. Daily her mirror assured her that she had nothing to worry about, for she had regained her looks and her vitality, and Page seemed more in love with her than before.

Today, as she and Page reined in their horses at the top of a hill after an exhilarating ride from the cabin—one of Kate's first sojourns abroad on a horse—she looked as beautiful as she ever had, and she knew it: her color was vibrant once again, her eyes a sparkling deep green. Even her unmanageable red hair seemed to crackle with a renewed life of its own. She had nothing to worry about; Page had never even remotely looked at Ann-Marie as he looked at *her*; in fact, she thought with an inward smile, he seemed to regard the saucy Ann-Marie almost as a . . . a little sister. Yes, that was it. A little sister.

Now, as Page pointed, Kate smiled at him before following the direction of his hand. She was happy today, content; she had a handsome, loving husband and two beautiful sons. What more could she ask for, except perhaps a house? And then she saw what Page was pointing toward, and she gasped.

Below them, nestled in a beautiful green hollow of land that seemed made for it, with the towering Rocky Mountains serving as a spectacular backdrop and the lush tree-studded foothills sloping down to surround it protectively, was the house. Or rather, the beginning of it. The land had been cleared and the foundation laid; as Kate watched, several men—tiny figures from this distance—bustled around, working busily on the frame.

Dragging her glance away from the sight, Kate looked in wonderment at Page. Now she knew the reason for the secret smile he had worn all month, she thought dazedly: it hadn't been her improved appearance at all! Her eyes shone, and Page grinned at her expression.

"Surprised?" he asked.

"You know I am! Why didn't you tell me?"

"Oh, but I did."

"You did? When?"

"When I asked you to marry me. I told you then that I was going to build you a house—a proper home—someday. And this is the day."

"But . . . but I never suspected!"

"Of course not. I didn't want you to know about it until I was ready to tell you."

"Oh, Page!"

She was about to tear her eyes away from his face and look down at the house again when he reached across the saddle to take her hand. He held her fingers to his lips.

"I want to call it Beauvais," he said softly, his eyes intent. "The name itself means 'place of beautiful open spaces,' which is appropriate, I think. But that isn't the real reason I want to call it that, Kate."

"What is the real reason, Page?" Kate whispered.

"I want to name it after you, Kate. For all you've been through, for all you've done . . . for what you mean to me—my life itself. It's not nearly what you deserve, but it's all I have to give, to show you how much I . . . how much I love you. You're my treasure, and a treasure should have a proper setting. Beauvais will be built to honor you."

Kate was too emotional to speak. Tears filled her eyes, and she looked down at the house—her house—through a rainbow blur, listening to Page describe it as it would be. He painted a picture of it with words, and Kate could see it all as he spoke: the white three-story stone house, classic in simplicity, without towers or turrets; the veranda running the length of the house; the tall, clean columns rising to the roof; the floor-to-ceiling windows draped elegantly with rich brocade. There would be no white marble lions at the entrance, or cast-iron deer on the wide lawn; instead, Kate would have her English garden, or a facsimile of it, and in place of all the statuary that was beginning to be so popular, there would be only a profusion of flowers and green grass and tall trees that turned wonderful and vibrant colors in the fall. The gravel drive would curve gracefully to the front of the house and continue around to the side, where the stables would be built, and there would be a flagstone terrace at the back of the house, where they could sit and admire the lush pastures and paddocks that would be fenced for Beauvais horses.

And inside—inside the house, Page continued, his eyes glowing as they rested on Kate's rapt face, there would be brocade and velvet draperies, and Aubusson carpets and shining parquetry floors, and marble fireplaces. And filling the huge and spacious rooms—drawing rooms, sitting room, morning room, library, dining room—would be rosewood and pecan and walnut and oak furniture, all gleaming with polish and richness against silk-papered walls and gilded moldings. There would be bedrooms upstairs for a multitude of guests; there would be a huge master suite and a nursery, and later, bedrooms for the children. The attics would be comfortable for the servants, and down in the kitchen and pantry and dairy the cook would reign supreme amid copper pots and heavy silver and china so thin one could see the light through it.

And she would be the mistress of all this elegance, Page continued—the jewel in a graceful and refined setting.

"It's for you, Kate," he finished softly. "All for you."

"Oh, Page . . ." Kate couldn't say more; she was too moved. Instead, she looked down again at the house, and even through her tears, she did not see it as it was then, a hodgepodge of beams and struts and joists; she saw it as Page had said it would become: spacious, gracious, elegant—a home to be proud of, not because she was mistress of it, but because so much had been demanded in the building of it. She saw their children growing up in that house, safe and strong and secure, with no taint of suspicion surrounding their birth; she saw herself, and finally, she saw Page—the man who had promised that the ranch would be a moving force in Colorado one day. She had no doubt of it now, and her heart swelled with pride.

Still unable to speak, Kate reached blindly for Page's hand again. His fingers were warm and strong as he grasped hers, and, arms outstretched, holding hands tightly in a bridge that linked them and united them, Kate and Page sat motionless and watched the building of Beauvais.

22

Kate's third son was born a year after the twins, in the house christened Beauvais, with a doctor attending and Ann-Marie as the nurse. A distraught Page was present for the birth of his son, having returned early this time from another highly successful freighting contract. With his business expanded, Page had surrendered to Kate's demand that he delegate the actual hauling to a trusted subordinate while he managed the financial and other arrangements from closer to home. Reluctantly he had given up the excitement and danger of the trail, but he had seen the wisdom in acceding to a pregnant and ill-tempered Kate. Now, however, as she went into her eighth hour of labor, both of them wondered if it wouldn't have been better if he had gone out on the second haul that year. Banished to the upstairs hall outside the bedroom where Kate lay moaning, Page paced anxiously up and down until the new carpet had a path worn into it. Finally an irritated Kate had sent Ann-Marie outside to refer Page to his study, where she couldn't hear his agitated movements beyond her door, and Page escaped with profound relief. Sitting in the new leather chair, he fought the urge—almost successfully—to drink himself insensible.

Like his half-brothers, Rory Daniel Taggart entered the world on a snowy January day, but there the resemblance ended. Whereas Kate's first born, Michael, had been demanding and imperious from the first, and Michael's twin, David, shy and retiring, Rory was petulant and fretful from the outset. The child most like Kate in coloring, with his shock of red-gold hair and what were to become hazel eyes, Rory was least like his mother in temperament. Kate was forthright and open in her emotions and beliefs, but even as a young child, Rory was secretive, sly. He learned early on to manipulate people, even his mother, and almost from the crib, Rory and

Michael despised each other with a hatred that would one day rock Beauvais to its foundation.

But that day, of course, was far in the mists of the future. Right now Rory was a beautiful infant, strong and healthy, and Page was so proud of his wife and their new son that he extravagantly promised a weary Kate never to lead another freight trip.

"Do I have your word on that?" Kate asked.

As thin and tired as her voice was, her eyes were intent on his face as he sat holding her hand tightly by the side of the bed. The new infant had been taken away to the nursery, where a proper nursemaid was in residence and a freshly promoted Ann-Marie was watching the year-old twins and waiting impatiently for the day when she would become their governess in more than name alone.

Kate herself was pale and wan; this pregnancy and birth had been hard on her, coming so close after the twins, but to Page she was still the most beautiful woman he had ever seen.

"You have my word," he answered solemnly. No promise was too demanding for the mother of his sons.

Kate looked at her handsome husband, so eager to please her because she had given him another son, and she felt a sharp stab of guilt. He was so pleased, she thought, so proud and happy. How would he feel if he knew that Rory was in actuality his firstborn, his only son? What would he say then to the mother of that son? Kate shuddered inwardly at the thought, and closed her eyes, leaning back against the pillows heaped behind her.

"I've tired you," Page said at once. "I'm sorry, Kate. I didn't think."

He made a motion to get up, but Kate held his hand, keeping him there by her side a moment longer. "I'm glad," she whispered, "that you're not going away again."

Page released his hand, then bent and kissed her gently on the forehead, smoothing away a damp tendril of hair. "I never liked the trail anyway," he said softly, going to the door.

Kate opened her eyes as he tiptoed away. "Liar," she murmured.

Page turned. He saw her looking at him through half-open lids, struggling to stay awake. He grinned at her. "Just remember that it was your idea to make me stay home," he teased. "Somehow, whenever I'm around like this, we tend to have a baby the following year—are you sure you want me to stay?"

Kate frowned, pretending to think. "Well . . . since you put it that way," she said doubtfully, "perhaps we should also have you promise to stay on your side of the bed. What do you think?"

"I think," Page said solemnly, his eyes dancing, "that you're overtired, or you wouldn't dream of saying something like that. Stay on my own side of the bed, indeed! What do you take me for, you irresistible woman?"

"Oh . . ." Kate groaned, thinking of how she looked right now, tired and pale and utterly wretched. She threw the blankets over her head and muttered, "Go away, Page, go away. Come back when I can be a better adversary!"

Page laughed. Then he went out and gave all the servants—there were several by this time, for Beauvais, even unfinished, was already huge—half a day off in celebration of the new Taggart infant.

Then, unknown to anyone else except the watchful Ann-Marie, Page went to his study and silently raised a glass in his own private tribute to Kate. He was a fortunate man, he thought, as he went to the window to stare out at the swirling snow beyond the pane. He had three fine children, a beautiful home, and a wife who frustrated and annoyed and angered and irritated him, and whom he loved more than his life itself. And one day, he thought, one day the name Beauvais would be known and respected throughout the whole of Colorado. With a woman like Kate by his side, a man could do anything. Anything.

Proudly Page raised the glass again to his silvered reflection in the window. He thought of Kate and how much he loved her, and he drank deeply.

Kate's last child, the Taggarts' only daughter, was born almost two years after her brother Rory. A relieved Kate had escaped pregnancy for more than a year, although sometimes she would cross her fingers behind her back in a remembered gesture of good luck from her childhood, and ask to be spared another year, at least. She didn't have time for any more children just yet, she would say with a laugh; the three boys in the nursery now, and the running of Beauvais itself, took all the energy she had; she didn't have any to spare coping with another pregnancy. Consequently, when in the winter of 1869 she found herself pregnant for the third time, she wasn't sure whether to plunge into depression or dance with delight. At least, she consoled herself, this time she would deliver in the fall: somehow, it seemed an omen, and Kate was resigned, if not ecstatic, when she went through her wardrobe and ordered her gowns to be let out at the waist. And maybe this time, she thought hopefully, the baby would be a girl.

The baby was a girl. Adele Kathryn was born that October, as the leaves fell in a spectacular blaze of fall color. The timing was prophetic, for the new infant was a golden child, petite and delicate, with the striking combination of honey-colored hair, soft cream complexion, and dark brown eyes. From the first she was her father's darling, and knew it.

Kate, who had so wanted a girl in her household of boys, would have her hands full with her last child and only daughter: Adele's fragile appearance belied an iron will like her mother's, and an almost ruthless determination to have her own way. No one admiring the new baby then could have guessed that these strongest attributes of her character would bring disaster down on them all in the future; Adele was such a charming baby, everyone's favorite, a little golden doll with an enchanting smile. Kate was pleased, Page was ecstatic, and Adele's three brothers alternately jealous and indifferent.

23

In the summer of 1871, when Adele was almost two, Rory four, and the twins five years old, two events occurred that were to change the course of the future for everyone at Beauvais: they received a letter from Roger, and Page took a mistress. These two events, while not related directly, were nevertheless the cause and effect of one of the fiercest arguments yet in the Taggart marriage, the results of which would be felt for years.

It had begun innocently enough, as such things often do,

and afterward a furious and outraged Kate would wonder bleakly what had happened to cause such an appalling breach in their relationship. They had been getting along so well since Adele had been born: the only arguments they engaged in were about the horses, and that was because, Kate suspected, she had a better eye for horseflesh than Page, and he knew it. He had consulted her more and more these past two years about that part of the ranch operation, and more often than not, he took her advice on which horses to breed, which to cull and sell, and which to train. The horses, in fact, had become Kate's own project, and she was justifiably proud that due to her management, that part of Beauvais would show a profit this year.

Page was proud of her ability, too, she knew. But that didn't mean that they always agreed, of course. Many an evening was spent in spirited argument, discussing the relative merits of this mare or that, or the liabilities of one stallion or another as breeding stock. Kate believed that Page enjoyed these sessions as much as she, although he never admitted it. Of one thing she was sure: sharing in the building of the Beauvais horse ranch had brought them closer together than ever before.

And now that closeness was about to be shattered.

Kate was in her "office" when Page knocked on the door that warm August day. Having no use for a morning room where she sat and plied her despised needle, Kate had converted this particular room into a bright and cheerful place where she wrote her correspondence, went over household accounts, attended to the myriad details of running Beauvais, and charted the progress of her horse program. Disdaining the elegant and utterly inadequate Queen Anne desk Page wanted to give her, Kate had installed instead a huge and sturdy oak desk that took up the space of almost one wall in the small room. It was always cluttered, and Kate loved it.

But her office was more than a place of business; it was also her retreat, her place to be alone and to think. None of the children were allowed there, a foresight for which Kate was later to be profoundly grateful.

Now, however, she looked up with interest as Page entered. He had been away a great deal these past two months, having just returned two days ago from yet another business trip marketing Beauvais cattle. He had also sold several of her horses, and while Kate was pleased about that, she was a little worried about her husband. He looked tired and drawn, especially today, when he should have been rested. She wondered if the enormous time and energy required to paint the financial ledgers of Beauvais comfortably in the black might be too much for him to manage alone. She made a mental note to speak to him about a business manager of some kind to take part of the burden from him.

But there were other things to speak of first, and she was pleased he had come in to talk to her. There were several matters that required discussion—not the least of which, she thought with sudden sharp annoyance, was the subject of Ann-Marie. Their cheerful, willing Ann-Marie had seemed to change abruptly into a sullen, haughty young woman bent on disrupting the entire household. There had been a fracas just the other day in the nursery, Kate remembered; the nursemaid had been in tears, and she, Kate, had been forced to mediate.

It was ridiculous, really, she thought, Ann-Marie's sudden aversion to the twins. She favored Rory and Adele in the extreme, and Kate had spoken to her sharply about it more than once. If Ann-Marie didn't mend her ways, and quickly, Kate would have to dismiss her. It was absurd to continue to employ a governess who appeared to detest two of her charges, Kate thought irritably, but more than that, it was damaging to the boys themselves. Michael was a handful, she had to admit: he had lost none of that imperiousness that had characterized him from the first; he seemed daily to grow in pride and arrogance. But David—David, who so resembled his father that Kate could not look at him without a wrench—was a quiet boy, gentle and affable, eager to please. Kate doubted that he had ever given Ann-Marie a moment of distress or had even been a cause for concern. No, she simply didn't understand Ann-Marie's attitude. There was no reason for it that she could see, and it would have to change at once, or else.

"Page, I'm glad you—"

"Kate, I wanted to—"

They spoke at the same time, then laughed as each gestured elaborately for the other to continue. But despite her laughter, Kate was concerned over the faint blue shadows under Page's eyes, and she wondered if he wasn't ill and refused to tell her. It would be just like him, she thought indignantly, trying to quell her sudden alarm.

She had been sitting at the desk, and now she made a motion to rise, saying, "Why don't you sit down? I'll ring for some tea if you like. I've quite a list of things I want to discuss with you, and I'd like to be sure you're well fortified for it!"

Page didn't respond to her teasing. Instead, he sank wearily into the huge leather chair she always reserved for him when they discussed household details. He put his head against the back of it and closed his eyes.

Kate hesitated, knowing how Page detested questions about his health. Finally, she couldn't help it; she had to ask. "Is everything all right?" she said tentatively. "You look so . . . tired, Page."

He opened his eyes and shook his head in response to her question. "I'm all right," he said. "But there is something I want to talk to you about."

Kate sank back into her chair. "Of course. What is it?" Her manner might have been calm, but suddenly her heart began to hammer. He *was* ill. She knew it!

"It's about the twins."

"The twins?" she repeated blankly. "What about them?" Had something terrible happened? She was about to rush out in a panic to see for herself, when she was stopped abruptly by his next statement.

"You're going to have to change your attitude about them, Kate," Page was saying quietly, his expression grave. "Or else—"

"Change my attitude?" she echoed, frowning. "Or else . . . what?" Why was she parroting everything he said? She shook herself mentally. "What do you mean?"

Page leaned forward, resting his elbows on his knees, never taking his eyes off her face. "I mean," he said carefully, "that unless you stop favoring the twins over the other two children, they'll all be ruined. David I'm not too worried about; he has a forgiving nature. But Michael"—Page shook his head concernedly—"Michael is another matter altogether. Already he thinks he owns the nursery; if we're not watchful, soon he will become a bully, demanding his own way in everything just to see how far he can push people. I don't want that to happen, Kate; he has too much potential."

Kate had sat in silence, listening to him disbelievingly. She was outraged at this attack against her rearing of the children, and when he paused, she glared at him in affront. She said icily, "I don't understand a word you're saying! To imply that I favor the twins over Rory and Adele is absolute nonsense!"

"No, it isn't, Kate. I'm speaking the truth, and if you were honest, you would admit it, too."

"I'll admit no such thing!"

"You must. Because I'm not going to stand by and allow you to ruin those boys."

"How dare you!"

"I dare because I care about them." Page was unmoved by her display of temper. "Part of it is my fault, I admit."

"How very generous of you to say so!" cried Kate, enraged.

Page was not deterred. "I should have seen it long before now, I realize. But I've been away so much this summer—"

"And whose fault is that? No one asked you to leave Beauvais for weeks at a time!"

"Let's not lose sight of the point, shall we?" asked Page calmly, infuriating Kate all the more.

"And what *is* the point of this absurd discussion, may I ask?"

"The point, in case you've forgotten—or chose to ignore it—is the welfare of the children." At last Page was beginning to get angry himself. "You can't continually favor the twins and overdiscipline the other two; it just isn't right. Ann-Marie tells me—"

"Ann-Marie!" In his fervor, Page had gone too far. He recognized his mistake the moment the words were out, but then it was too late. Kate had leaped out of her chair, her eyes blazing. "How dare you discuss me with Ann-Marie!" she cried, outraged.

"I didn't discuss you with Ann-Marie," Page said, striving to maintain a reasonable tone. "As I recall, we were speaking about the children, and as Ann-Marie is both nursemaid and governess to them, it seemed logical to question her about what goes on in the nursery."

"Logical? You thought it more *logical* to discuss your children with their nursemaid than with their mother, your wife?" Kate's voice cut across the space between them like the blade of a knife. "And is that *all* you discussed—just the children?"

Page stared at her. "I don't know what you mean by that, Kate," he said evenly.

Kate came around the desk and leaned against the front of it, returning Page's stare with an icy one of her own. She gripped the edge of the desk, and her knuckles were white. "I've seen the way she looks at you, Page," she said. Her voice was tight with anger, and, though she wouldn't admit it, jealousy. "I saw it from the first," she continued with a bitter twist to her lips. "She was always so friendly, wasn't she? So helpful. So very much in evidence. I knew she would cause trouble one day; I knew it!"

"Ann-Marie hasn't caused any trouble at all!" Page said sharply. "She merely answered a few questions I put to her—and reluctantly, at that."

"Oh, yes." Kate sneered. "I can easily imagine how reluctant she was to be in conference with you. And it wasn't the first time, was it?"

Her sharp question had been a shot in the dark, but when Page was unable to hide his surprise, she knew she had hit the mark. Her eyes narrowed. "No, I see this wasn't the first little tête-à-tête you have had with our dear little Ann-Marie," she said, so angry her voice shook. "Tell me, Page, what else you and she have discussed—if anything."

Page looked at her. "I can't understand you, Kate," he said. "This sudden animosity toward Ann-Marie isn't like you at all."

Sudden? thought Kate, distracted by his words. But her dislike wasn't sudden at all, she realized; it had been building for a long time—ever since the first moment she had seen Ann-Marie's sharp brown eyes light speculatively on Page. Oh, she had tried to dismiss her uneasiness, her feeling of disquiet about the girl; she had tried to ignore her misgivings from the beginning, assuring herself that she was too suspicious. What could she have said, after all? That she was jealous of someone who took such exemplary care of her children, who never complained, who rarely even left Beauvais, except when Kate herself insisted the girl needed some time for herself away from the nursery and the children and the endless responsibility she assumed so readily and eagerly? Well, now she knew why Ann-Marie had been so reluctant to leave Beauvais, even for a day. Why should she leave? She had everything she wanted right here!

"Kate . . ."

She looked at him. And here was Page, she thought angrily, actually preparing to defend this chit of a forward, brazen girl who had set her cap for him! Was he flattered by this absurd competition between the nursemaid and his wife? Was he intrigued, dismayed . . . interested?

"Kate, you're not being fair," Page tried to say. "You're imagining things that simply aren't there."

"You can't deny that you have made more than one visit to the nursery!"

"But only for the children!" Page protested sharply. "It wasn't for anything other than that!"

"Oh, really? Then tell me—during your little domestic discussions with the children's nanny, was anything resolved other than the fact that Ann-Marie thinks I'm either incompetent about rearing my own children or just totally ignorant of their needs?"

"She doesn't think either thing, Kate. If you will just calm down—"

"Calm down! When you've been discussing domestic matters with one of my servants!"

"It's just that she's concerned—"

"Concerned! Does that imply that I'm not?"

"I didn't say that, Kate."

"No, you haven't said much beyond the fact that I'm an indifferent mother, an incompetent housewife, and a harsh martinet where the children are concerned! Is there any stone in my character that you and Ann-Marie have left unturned? Perhaps I should step aside and give *her* the keys to Beauvais! *Then* we would see just how competent our little Ann-Marie is!"

"Kate, please! You're not being reasonable."

"Oh, do forgive me! It was just that the idea of one of my own servants discussing me with her employer gave me pause. I quite apologize for straying from the subject, but if you don't mind, perhaps we can agree on one little detail before we end this illuminating analysis of my failures. I want our helpful Ann-Marie Durand dismissed and out of this house before the day is over!"

"Kate . . ."

She stared at him, her expression steely. "I will not," she said clearly, "be criticized by someone I employ. If Ann-Marie doesn't care for the way I treat my children, she can find a position elsewhere. Is that understood?"

They were both standing now, facing each other like combatants. Their eyes locked angrily, and finally Page said, "All

right, Kate. I won't argue with you about Ann-Marie, who
was only trying to help. But I will say this: if you don't stop
favoring the twins over Rory and Adele, I'll send Michael
and David away to school, out of your influence."

"Send them away! Don't be absurd! Why, they're only five
years old!"

"There are several good boarding schools in the East that
take children younger than the twins," replied Page inflexibly.
"I mean it, Kate. If you don't change, I'll put them on the
train myself."

"You wouldn't!"

"I most certainly would."

"I don't believe you!"

"Believe it, Kate. Or would you rather test me?"

For an instant she was tempted to say yes. Fortunately,
some last shred of common sense prevailed; she knew only
too well that when Page assumed that hateful obdurate expression, he meant what he said.

There was only one option left open to her. Gathering the
last vestiges of her pride, Kate tossed her head and swept regally by him. She opened the door, then paused, half-hidden
behind it as she turned to face him again. "When you care to
apologize for your appalling behavior today," she said haughtily, "I'll be upstairs. Until then, we don't have anything more
to say to each other."

"Don't expect me to apologize for telling the truth," Page
warned, ruining her dramatic exit. She glared at him furiously; then he enraged her more by adding, "I've let you
have your own way too long, Kate. From now on—"

But whatever he had been about to say was interrupted by
someone at the door. From where she stood, Kate couldn't
see who it was, and she herself was invisible to whoever it
was outside. But Page was directly in line with the doorway,
and as he glanced outside, Kate had time only to see the
chagrined expression in his eyes and to observe the quick
negative shake of his head. It was too late.

"Oh, there you are, Page!" Ann-Marie said brightly. "Did
you talk to Mrs. Taggart about the twins yet?"

Kate didn't take time to think. Absolutely livid at what she
had heard, she grabbed the door and flung it back so violently that it crashed into the wall. Ann-Marie—her devoted
employee, the woman to whom she had entrusted the care of
her children—stood framed in the doorway, her expression

suddenly not so pert, and her clever brown eyes wide with fright at the sight of Kate's face.

"Oh, Mrs. Taggart! I . . ."

Kate ignored the girl's frightened expression. "Do come in, dear," she said, gesturing in a sweeping motion with one arm. "How fortunate that you should arrive so conveniently, without being sent for!"

Ann-Marie swallowed. "Mrs. Taggart . . ."

"You're repeating yourself, dear. And we have several other more important matters to discuss."

"We do?" Hesitantly Ann-Marie entered the study. She almost skipped past Kate, as if she expected Kate to reach out and shake her. Kate smiled pleasantly. "We do," she said.

"About the children?" Ann-Marie said hopefully as she took a place several steps from Kate.

Kate nodded. "Oh, yes, about the children," she replied. "But especially about you."

"About me?" Ann-Marie repeated weakly. Her glance went involuntarily toward Page, then swung immediately back to Kate again. "I'm sorry, Mrs. Taggart, if I've given offense. I was only—"

"Trying to help?" suggested Kate with an encouraging smile.

"—concerned," finished Ann-Marie faintly.

"Oh, yes. So Page mentioned. In fact, it might please you to know that he was quite vocal about your 'concern.' "

"I didn't mean any offense," Ann-Marie said again, looking anxiously in Page's direction for help.

Kate saw that glance and had no intention of letting Page come to the girl's aid. "Of course you meant no offense, dear," she said. "Still, it seems that a woman of your vast understanding and expertise is utterly wasted here at Beauvais, which is so remote from the center of things. Page and I were just talking about that very subject when you so conveniently arrived. Weren't we, Page?"

"Kate . . ." began Page warningly.

She ignored him. "And we had just decided that it simply isn't fair of us to keep you to ourselves when there are so many other opportunities for you elsewhere." Kate's expression was sad but resigned. "So, reluctantly, we decided that the only proper course of action for us is to terminate your employment at Beauvais. Today."

Ann-Marie gasped. "But, Mrs. Taggart, I don't—"

"Oh, I understand how overwhelmed you must be, Ann-

Marie," Kate interrupted sympathetically. "But please—don't thank us. We gladly make the sacrifice for your sake."

"But—"

"I know how distressful this is for you, dear, so I can't see any reason to prolong this painful discussion." She glanced at the clock. "The morning is half over now, and unless you hurry along with your packing, you won't be away until afternoon. It's quite a distance to Denver, as you know, and you should get started as soon as possible."

Helpless, there was nothing Ann-Marie could do but try to fight back her tears until she escaped to her room. Hastily, her face already beginning to crumple, she sketched a quick curtsy and stumbled from the room. Her footsteps had scarcely faded away when Kate turned triumphantly to Page. But her triumph was short-lived.

"That was cruel and unnecessary, Kate," Page said tightly. "There was no need to humiliate her like that."

"Humiliate *her*! What about me?" demanded Kate. "I saw that look she gave you—as if she expected you to come rushing to her aid!"

"And why not?" retorted Page, as angry as Kate. "She was helpless against you."

"How dare you defend her, as if she were the injured party!"

"In this case, I think she was."

Kate couldn't believe that Page would say such a thing. She stared at him, her mouth working, but too furious to voice any words.

"And furthermore," said Page, taking advantage of his opportunity, "you won't have to arrange for someone to take her to Denver. I'll take her myself. If you insist on dismissing her so abruptly, it's the least I can do."

Kate was so stunned at this that again she couldn't even speak. Finally, her voice shaking with fury and indignation and another emotion she didn't care to identify, she said, "If you leave this house today, don't expect to come back as if nothing has happened!"

"I won't be threatened, Kate."

"And neither," said Kate haughtily as she swept out of the room, "will I."

She watched them go two hours later from her upstairs window, hiding behind the curtain like some shrinking culprit punished for an act of wrongdoing. But it was *she* who had been wronged, she thought pitifully, biting hard on a knuckle as her eyes followed them from the stables to the road and then to a curve that hid them from sight. Page hadn't been fair, accusing her of favoring the twins over Rory and Adele, she thought. It wasn't true; it simply wasn't true. Was it?

No, no; of course not. She treated all her children equally, and Page would have seen that for himself if he hadn't been swayed by that scheming Ann-Marie.

And now she was here alone, nursing her wounded pride, while Page and Ann-Marie rode off together for Denver. She despised them both; she was *glad* they were gone, *happy* that—

There was a knock on her door. Whirling around from the window, Kate said sharply, "What is it?" She didn't want to be bothered now, she thought angrily. Whatever crisis had developed could just go on without her. She wasn't emerging from this room for anyone or anything.

"There's a letter, Mrs. Taggart . . ."

"A letter?" It was ridiculous, trying to carry on a conversation through a closed door. "Very well," she said impatiently. "Bring it in." A maid entered, bearing an envelope, and as Kate took it, she asked crossly, "Where did this come from? Why didn't you give it to Mr. Taggart?"

"A rider dropped it off from Denver just now, ma'am. He was going by, he said. And . . . and Mr. Taggart just rode out with—"

"Yes, yes. That will be all." Kate hardly knew what she was saying as she dismissed the maid. With rising excitement she realized that the letter was from Roger, and her heart began to hammer as she opened the envelope. It was addressed to Page, but she didn't care; she couldn't wait to read it. It had been so long since she had seen him . . . so long. And so many things had happened.

Sinking down onto the chaise longue by the window, Kate was oblivious of anything but the letter she held. Her hands actually shook as she unfolded the single closely written sheet of paper.

Roger's letter was dry, prosaic, and even a little dull, but Kate read every line with a thrill. Seeing his handwriting, so precise and measured, seemed to bring Roger closer to her, so that as she read, it was almost as if he were in the room with her.

There was only one point at which she frowned, and that
was his reference to Amelia and what a wonderful, understanding wife she was, so sweet and considerate.

"I could have been sweet and considerate too," Kate muttered, skipping the next few lines with revulsion as Roger
went on lovingly about his wife. Suddenly she paused, uttering an exclamation. Roger and Amelia had a child!

Kate brought the page closer and read on with startled surprise. Somehow, during these past five years when she had
borne children herself, she had never imagined Amelia producing any of her own. Kate read with interest, eager for any
scrap of information affecting Roger.

The child had been a girl, and they had named her Jane,
Roger wrote. Kate smiled, detecting Roger's influence. If it
had been left to Amelia, Kate thought nastily, the baby
would very likely have been christened Hortense or Mehita-
bel. Amelia's imagination was a little fevered at times.

Reading on, Kate saw that Jane had been born the same
year as had Rory, and was a year younger than the twins.

The letter fluttered unnoticed to her lap as she thought of
Michael and David. What would Roger say if he knew that
he had not only a daughter but also two sons? Would he be
pleased? Dismayed? Appalled?

A little of each, probably, thought Kate as she smiled fondly. She pictured Roger, not as she had seen him last, utterly
wretched and almost weeping with despair, but as she had always wanted him to be: strong, decisive, forthright. She
smiled again, lost in her fantasy.

It had been a long time since she had allowed herself to
think of Roger. When she had left England, she had pictured
them as tragic figures kept apart by a malignant twist of fate.
She had imagined him pining for her as she had for him, but
as the months went by, she had forced herself to drive all
thought of him from her mind. Their situation was hopeless,
she had told herself; she had to pull herself together and try
to forget him. Very likely she would never see him again.

Now, with his letter in her hand, all her earlier dreams and
fantasies returned. She had a sudden wild urge to rush to the
nursery and enfold the twins in her arms, telling them that
there had been a letter from their father, and how happy she
was to hear something from him at last, after all these years
of silence.

But as quickly as it had come, the urge vanished. Harsh reality returned with a vengeance, and Kate wondered how she could have harbored such an insane and dangerous notion even for an instant. What was the matter with her? she wondered, staring blindly down at the letter she clutched in one hand. Did she want to risk her future—the twins' future—for something so absurd?

Very carefully she smoothed the creases she had made in the paper. Then she inserted the letter into the envelope again and put it in her pocket to take to Page's study. She would leave it on his desk, and if he asked why it had been opened, she would say . . . Oh, she didn't know what she would say, she thought impatiently. She would have to think of something if the occasion arose.

It wasn't until the letter was safely deposited under the blotter of Page's desk, and Kate had been drawn to the nursery to look at the sleeping twins, that she realized she could not put away her fantasies of Roger as easily as she had discarded his letter. She found herself thinking of him constantly, and this time, because of the blazing argument they had had, it was Page who compared unfavorably in her mind to Roger.

Roger would never have accused her of favoritism among her children, she thought indignantly. He would have realized only how devoted she was to them, and how much she loved them. And he certainly would never have championed a servant over his wife, she thought—no more than he would have dreamed of humiliating her by accompanying that servant away from Beauvais. Page was a monster, a hard unfeeling wretch, a brute, for disregarding her feelings and treating her so shabbily. Roger would have been kind, considerate; he would have understood that whenever she looked at the twins, she felt so guilty . . .

Kate's inner conversation halted abruptly at that last thought. Shakily she gave a little laugh, trying to convince herself that she was only being absurd. Why would she think such a thing? she asked herself mockingly. Guilty about the twins? Why should she be? She had given Page two children of his own, and he had never once betrayed the slightest doubt that Michael and David weren't his sons as well. So, she shouldn't feel guilty; she should feel . . .

But she didn't know what she should feel. She was confused and off-balance and out-of-sorts. It was all Page's fault. Compared to Roger, he was cruel and heartless, and she wished now that she had defied everyone and married Roger instead. Roger would never have put her in this degrading position of having to defend herself against this intolerable burden of guilt. And he certainly wouldn't have forced her to skulk behind her window while he calmly escorted a smirking Ann-Marie away from Beauvais. Oh, the humiliation of it! Kate thought in a rage. She didn't care if Page *never* came back from Denver!

Page returned two weeks later bearing a penitent expression, a guilty conscience, toys for the children, and a new engraved saddle for Kate. He found his house in an uproar, his wife hysterical, and two of his children missing. Michael and David had simply . . . disappeared.

"Disappeared?" he repeated blankly when he was told. "What do you mean, disappeared?"

Kate, who in the past two weeks had alternated between despair and fury over Page's continued absence, and who had planned a hundred times the exact icy tone and freezing words of greeting she would use when Page finally did come home, forgot all her plans. The moment she saw him, she burst into renewed weeping and flung herself into his arms.

"They've been gone since yesterday afternoon," she sobbed. "I've sent everyone out searching, and I've been out myself, but . . . but . . ."

Trying to control his own fear, Page took Kate by the shoulders and held her away from him, shaking her a little to make her look at him. "Start at the beginning," he ordered in a firm voice that belied his inner turmoil. There were so many things that could happen to young children. . . . Resolutely he shut his mind to everything but the immediacy of the moment, and told Kate to answer him. "What happened?" he demanded.

"I don't know!" Kate answered tearfully. "One minute they were here playing by the stables, and the next, they were gone!"

"Where in hell was the nursemaid? Why wasn't she watching them?"

"She was!" wailed Kate. "But Adele fell into the dirt, and Betty took her upstairs to change—"

"Why wasn't someone else sent to watch the boys, then?" shouted Page. "It wasn't too much to ask, was it?"

"Don't blame the nursemaid, Page; she feels as badly as we all do about this."

"A lot of good *that* does!"

"I just meant . . . Oh, Page! I'm so worried!" Kate's face had crumpled again, and she threw herself against his chest.

"It's all right . . . It's all right. We'll find them," he soothed. But she could feel his heart pounding, and she knew he was just as afraid as she was.

"They've been found! They've been found!"

There was a commotion at the door, and both Kate and Page turned with mixed expressions of eagerness and dread. When Kate saw Betty standing there jubilantly, holding a twin by each hand, she uttered a cry and sped across the room. Enfolding the two tired and dirty little boys in her arms, Kate laughed and cried at the same time, assuring herself that they were all right.

"Where were they found? Who found them?" she asked, holding each one away from her for a moment to look at them anxiously before she hugged them to her again.

Betty took a deep breath, obviously reluctant to say what she had to say. Page saw her hesitation, and with a motion of his head indicated that she should speak freely.

"I think, Mrs. Taggart," the nursemaid said unsteadily, "that you should ask Master Rory about that." Then she pulled the reluctant Rory from behind her skirts and pushed him forward.

Kate looked blankly at her third son and then back to the nursemaid again. "What do you mean, Betty? What could Rory possibly know—"

"I think I understand," Page said abruptly. "Take Michael and David upstairs, will you please, Betty? Rory will stay here."

"Yes, Mr. Taggart," replied the relieved nursemaid. She reached a hand out to the twins, anxious to escape.

"I don't want to stay, Papa," Rory said petulantly. "I want—"

Michael spoke for the first time. "I want," he said clearly, staring fiercely at his brother, "for you to tell Papa how you pushed David and me into that cave by the spring."

"The spring!" Kate exclaimed. Dear God, had they really gone that far? She felt faint at the thought.

But Michael didn't hear his mother's exclamation. His dark eyes were bright with childish fury as he shouted, "It was dark in there, and David was afraid. I hate you, Rory—I hate you!"

Before Betty could restrain him, Michael had launched his small sturdy body at his younger brother. Rory uttered a piercing cry as he crashed to the floor under Michael's weight, and then he began to scream as Michael began to pummel him with his fists.

"That's enough!" thundered Page, stopping both shrieking and pummeling by the sound of his voice. He reached down, grabbed both boys by their collars, and lifted them roughly to their feet. "I won't have any brawls in this house, no matter what the reason," he said firmly.

Michael tried to twist away from his father's grasp, still angry. Page held him firmly. "Is that understood?"

Michael glared upward at his father, his face rebellious. Page waited inexorably. Finally Michael looked down and muttered, "Yes, Papa."

Page turned to Rory. "Rory?"

"Yes, Papa," Rory answered sullenly.

Page released them. "Michael, I want you to go upstairs at once with Betty and your brother. Your mother and I will be up to see you shortly."

David, who hadn't spoken until now, and who rarely said anything to defend himself, turned back to look at Page as he was being led from the room. "It was only because Michael was angry for me, Papa," he said seriously. "Please don't punish him."

Page smiled at this too-quiet second son. "I'll think about it, David," he said solemnly. "But you run along. Your mother and I want to talk to Rory."

David, usually instantly obedient, hesitated again. "Michael told the truth, Papa," he said. His wide blue eyes were innocent and pleading.

Page nodded. "Run along," he said again gruffly.

The nursemaid had scarcely led the twins away before Rory began to cry. "I didn't mean it," he sobbed pitifully, his small shoulders shaking.

"That was a very foolish thing to do, Rory. And dangerous," Page said inflexibly, apparently unmoved by his son's sobs. "Do you know how worried your mother was?"

Rory sobbed even harder, and Page restrained Kate firmly by a hand on her arm when she wanted to go to comfort that small forlorn figure. She glanced angrily at her husband, but something in his face warned her to be silent.

"You were very wrong to do such a thing—do you know that, Rory?" Page asked sternly.

Rory's head lifted suddenly, and to Kate's astonishment, her son's expression was openly defiant as he faced his father. Tears still streamed down his face, but he had lost his woebegone attitude, and now he shouted, "I don't care! I never wanted them to come back!"

Kate was shocked. "Rory!"

Her son turned to her, his small body shaking now with sheer rage. "You love them best, Mama!" he screeched. "So I wanted them not to be here! I wanted to be first!"

The words were garbled, childish, but the meaning was all too clear. Aghast, Kate stared at Rory's convulsed face, and she knew, in that moment and with painful clarity, that Page had been right all along. Appalled, she turned away from the accusation in her son's eyes, her hand to her mouth as the full realization of what she had done struck her. If Rory had deliberately pushed the twins into that cave, hoping they would never be found, the fault was hers. It was as if, by favoring the twins as Page had said, she herself had guided Rory's hand. It was even more horrifying to know that it had taken something so serious, so frightening as this near-tragedy to make her see how foolish she had been.

Kate shut her eyes, chilled to the bone at how close she had been to losing everything that was important to her. If Michael and David had died . . .

Kate felt his hands on her shoulders. She forced open her eyes, dreading to see Page's face, making herself look at him. Whatever she expected to see in his expression, no blame was there. Instead, there was only compassion, and relief, and understanding in his dark eyes, and wordlessly they both turned to look at Rory.

The child was standing uncertainly in the center of the room, his hazel eyes overflowing with tears, his expression still grimly defiant, and his small fists clenched at his sides. When Kate gestured to him, he hesitated, but then when she smiled encouragingly, he came running. She bent down and gathered him comfortingly in her arms, murmuring some soothing sound that only a mother can make, and he wrapped his chubby arms about her neck, holding her tightly.

Over his red-gold head, Kate met her husband's eyes once

more. Was it too late to make amends? she seemed to ask
silently in that one glance. Had she already caused so much
damage that it could never be rectified? She shuddered at the
thought, picturing a bleak future in which her children
despised one another, in which Page blamed her for causing
such hatred, and in which she was obsessed with her guilt.
Was it too late? Was it?

The look in Page's eyes said no.

24

Kate looked at her reflection and sighed. It was the year
1881, she was almost thirty-two years old, and today she felt
every day of it. Where had the time gone? And more important than that, what had happened to her? Only yesterday, it
seemed, she had been a young girl; today she was a woman
who had been married fourteen years, who had four children
of her own and an adopted son, and who was mistress of a
beautiful showplace of a home and of a ranch that was
known for everything from fine horses to lavish hospitality. It
was springtime, and she should have felt renewed, as she always did after the long winter. Instead, she just felt tired . . .
and old. Sitting at her dressing table, she regarded herself
with gloom.

Only yesterday, Michael, who at fourteen had already
sprouted to six feet, had teased her and called her an old
lady. She had slapped his arm—halfheartedly, she had to admit—but he had laughed again; the blow hadn't fazed him at
all.

Which only underscored the passing of time even more,
Kate thought, resting her chin in her hands. It was almost impossible to believe that her three sons were so big; they all
topped her by half a head or more. Even eleven-year-old
Adele was quickly becoming a young lady, and as for Randall . . .

Kate's expression softened at the thought of Randall, who

had been such a godsend. If Page hadn't brought home the orphaned infant when he had, Kate wasn't sure what she would have done. She had been so depressed then, so grief-stricken.

That had been a terrible period for her, that time of 1871. It was almost ten years ago now, but she could remember it all as if it had been only yesterday: Ann-Marie's dismissal and that terrible battle with Page; the disappearance of the twins; her own appalling discovery of the enmity she had heedlessly fostered among her children.

She didn't want to think about that time, and yet it served as a constant reminder for her to be vigilant. She had worked hard to repair the damage she had caused, and somehow the rift between her and Page had been healed. When she had found herself pregnant again that fall, she had been overcome with joy. The coming child seemed to be an omen, a sign that everything was going to be all right again.

And then, that winter, when the first snow had iced the pond, David fell in and almost drowned. Kate had seen it happen from an upstairs window she had chanced to be passing by, and she had rushed outside and down to the pond, screaming for help. Somehow she had arrived before anyone else, and to her horror, saw Michael stretched out on his stomach, inching along the cracking ice, trying to reach his floundering brother. Kate barely noticed Rory standing so quietly at the edge of the pond; she only registered that he was in no danger. She didn't stop to think after that; with David near to freezing to death, and Michael perilously close to falling into the frigid water himself, Kate waded in and grabbed both boys, dragging them to safety as Page raced up to help.

She was in the water only a few minutes, but that had been enough. The boys recovered without incident, but Kate caught a chill that developed into a lung inflammation that almost killed her. There was nothing the doctor could do to prevent her subsequent miscarriage; it took all his skill simply to save her life.

Eventually she recovered—physically. But the shock and trauma of losing the baby that had become such a symbol of love between her and Page had plunged her into deep depression for months. Nothing Page or anyone else tried had shaken her melancholy; she had remained listlessly in her room, staring emptily into space until Page had been beside himself with worry. He feared for her sanity.

And then he had brought home the orphaned infant they named Randall, and that was all the medicine Kate needed. The baby had captured Kate's heart immediately. It was astonishing how much he resembled Page, with his black hair and solemn expression; even the fact that the baby's eyes were green and not dark brown like Page's did not detract from the resemblance.

If there was a question in Kate's mind about the likeness between Page and this adopted son of theirs, Kate buried it deep in her consciousness. She was so involved with this baby, so caught up in the wonderment of his appearance in her life, that she refused to allow any suspicion or doubt to surface. Page had been so attentive these past long months of her depression and illness that he had scarcely left Beauvais at all, and certainly never long enough to strike up a liaison that sustained itself long enough to produce a child. He was not a man for quick, brief encounters, Kate knew; he never had been. And as for Ann-Marie . . . well, Ann-Marie Durand had left Denver long before; discreet inquiries Kate had made before her illness assured her of that. So if the infant Randall bore a likeness to Page, it was a benevolent twist of fate, nothing more. After a while Kate even succeeded in convincing herself that they were fortunate that their youngest child resembled, even slightly, his adoptive father. Kate's vague doubts were consigned to oblivion, and she gave herself completely to the task of recovering from her long period of hopelessness and depression by immersing herself in the care of Randall. She wanted this baby; she needed him desperately after her loss. And Randall needed her. He was so tiny when Page brought him home, so frail. His cry was more a pitiful mewing sound than a robust wail; it was almost as if he knew he had been abandoned, and Kate was drawn to him in her own need.

And now Randall would be ten years old his next birthday, and during those years Beauvais had both prospered and survived one disaster after another.

In 1874 an outbreak of disease had decimated Beauvais's cattle. Fortunately, only the herds on the lower range were affected; those in the high country were safe from contact with the affected animals. But the acrid smell of burning hide and flesh and bone as the carcasses were destroyed hung like a pall over Beauvais, and to Kate and everyone else the odor had seemed to penetrate every corner for weeks afterward.

The following year there had been a terrible fire, and Kate's eyes always filled with tears whenever she thought of those terrifying two days when everyone had fought the blaze that nearly ignited Beauvais itself. Fortunately, although there were numerous burns and scrapes and cuts, no one was seriously injured. The house had been saved only by herculean effort, but even then the west corner had been charred before the fire could be turned. Several sections of timber had been decimated, acres of grass and hay had burned black, and two years' fodder had gone up in smoke. But worst of all had been the destruction of the barn and stables. Page had forbidden Kate to go near the blazing structure, but Kate had been beside him nevertheless as they and several others who could be spared worked frantically to free the horses trapped inside. Despite their heroic attempts, three of Kate's prize mares had burned to death before anyone could reach their stalls. Kate had heard their screams of pain for months afterward in dreams at night; she had been prevented from rushing in to save the suffering animals only because Page had literally thrown her to the ground and held her there until even she knew it was too late.

Somehow Beauvais had survived these catastrophes, but the financial losses had been heavy, the loss in fine cattle and good horseflesh even greater. When in 1875 Page took most of his dwindling capital and invested it in abandoned claims near Aspen and Leadville, there were those who either laughed outright or jeered at him behind his back. Those claims had been exhausted of gold long ago, everyone said; to invest in them now was like throwing good money after bad.

If Kate had any doubts about the wisdom of her husband's investment, she kept them to herself. He knew what he was doing, she would say to herself and to anyone who dared to ask; she trusted his judgment completely.

But that year had been a lean one for those at Beauvais. There had been no frills, no luxuries; there was barely enough for necessities. Most of the servants and hired hands stayed, out of loyalty or stubbornness, or perhaps a bit of both, and Kate, who had to squeeze her household accounts dry, thought back to the first year at the cabin and kept her own counsel.

Page never confessed any doubts to her, and even when

she saw the lines begin to deepen in his face, even when she heard the taut control in his voice, she wasn't concerned about anything but him. They seemed to have reached a new intimacy in their stormy marriage, a closeness and wordless affection and love that she was determined not to lose even if it meant she had to go back to living in a one-room cabin. But that wouldn't happen, she assured herself whenever she thought about it; she had every confidence in Page, and she believed he knew what he was doing. He always had, hadn't he?

In 1876, the year after Page had invested in his abandoned gold mines, Colorado became the thirty-eighth state. And with statehood, as Page had always maintained, came a period of great prosperity and phenomenal growth—wealth in which Beauvais shared.

That year, and those immediately following, were banner years for the Taggarts and Beauvais. Those who had scoffed before did not laugh anymore when silver was discovered at Leadville, and when one huge strike followed another, mockery became chagrin. Page was suddenly a rich man, and in the rush to follow in his footsteps, he made even higher profits by snaring freighting contracts to haul much-needed goods to the new boom towns blossoming where only mountain flowers had grown before.

Beauvais had become, as Page had predicted so confidently years before, one of the wealthiest and most respected ranches in Colorado. And Kate was proud to be a part of it.

Thoughtful, she rose from the dressing table and wandered over to the bedroom window. The majestic Rocky Mountains rising like huge sentinels all around no longer frightened her; now she loved the sight of the high peaks, snowcapped even in summer, and she had chosen this room as the master suite particularly because it had a beautiful view of the mountains from two windows. There was something comforting about the timelessness of the mountains, she thought now. The indestructible peaks, which had made her feel small and insignificant before, seemed by their very power to give her strength to endure. Or at least to cope, she thought wryly, smiling to herself.

Glancing away, Kate looked down into the yard and saw David and Randall walking together toward the creek behind the stables. Randall bobbed a fishing pole over his shoulder, and David, as usual, carried a book. David's fair head was bent as he listened solemnly to whatever the smaller Randall was saying, and as they disappeared around the corner of the barn, Kate smiled again. David and Michael might be twins, but two more opposite personalities could hardly be found, and this was exemplified in the scene she had just witnessed: David always had time to listen to the ten-year-old Randall; Michael had a tendency to ignore his adopted brother— unless he could help with a problem of some kind, or demonstrate a new invention he had succeeded with. Michael was a doer, as the cowboys said; David a listener.

Thinking about her two eldest sons now, Kate thought that David was as quiet and reserved as he had been throughout his entire childhood. He rarely spoke, but when he did say something, it was in a soft, measured voice that indicated he had devoted a great deal of thought to whatever it was he was about to say. He had never indulged in the rough-and-tumble games of boyhood, but it wasn't that he was afraid of being hurt or bested; it was simply that he preferred the academic to the physical. He could defend himself if necessary, Kate knew, because she had seen him do so; it was just that he rarely thought it necessary.

Michael, on the other hand, preferred to be actively engaged in something physical—either a sport, or a project, or anything that challenged the abundant energy he constantly generated. Seeing Michael now, working hard in the stable area at sinking a new snubbing post for training young horses to tie, Kate thought with secret pleasure that Michael was probably the cleverest of her sons: he always accomplished whatever he set out to do, whether it was taming a wild horse or constructing a water wheel in the creek to power a butter churn—both of which he had done by the time he was twelve. Now, at fourteen, Michael was handsome, self-assured, and bedeviled with the same faults that had plagued Kate herself for years: pride and temper. Watching him now, Kate shook her head ruefully; one day that arrogant pride was going to bring him trouble. She had tried to tell him so—who better than she should know? she asked herself wryly—but he was as she had been in her own youth: headstrong and willful, refusing to listen to anyone.

Kate shook her head again, her expression somber as she continued to watch Michael's struggle with the post. She was never able to look at either of the twins without feeling a sharp regret over the secret she had been forced to keep all

these years. And her guilt was not eased in knowing that
Page believed that the twins were truly his sons; the burden
seemed even heavier because he had never doubted it. She
had told herself again and again that it was better this way:
the twins accepted Page as their father, as he accepted them
as his own children, and they all were secure because of it.
So she had kept her silence, realizing that the truth, while it
would certainly relieve her conscience, would only hurt everyone involved and would accomplish so little except to
make her feel better.

But it was still so difficult sometimes, she thought with a
heavy sigh, especially when David reminded her so much of
Roger. Michael was different; if he was like either of his
parents, he was more like her—in temperament, at least. But
David . . . David would assume an expression sometimes, or
make a gesture that was so like his real father, that Kate's
heart would miss a beat as she wondered fearfully why Page
didn't notice the resemblance as clearly as she did. It was so
obvious to her—but then, perhaps it was only her guilty conscience that made it appear so.

Guilt . . . guilt . . . Sometimes it seemed that she was
overwhelmed with it. And never, never would she forget the
accusation in four-year-old Rory's eyes that day the twins
were found. That sight would haunt her always, for it was the
first time she realized what her obsession with blame had
caused her to do to her children. She had thought of that day
many times since then, and she often wondered at the para-
dox that bound her: if she told the truth about the twins, it
might destroy them, but in withholding the truth for their
sake, what injustice was she perpetrating where Rory was
concerned? Did he have a right to know he was really his father's firstborn? Or was that right superseded by the needs of
his older brothers? Kate didn't know. She could only go on as
she had before, and hope that Rory never discovered the
truth.

The object of her thoughts appeared just then, walking
purposefully away from the house. Rory's expression as he
strode across the yard was so petulant that Kate suspected
that he and his father had had "words" again, and she sighed.
Page was concerned about Rory's attitude, and so, she had to
admit, was she. There was something missing in this third son
of hers, she thought worriedly, something that made him cold
and unfeeling, and she had spent many sleepless nights in the

past wondering if she had caused this twist in his personality. Then she would tell herself no; no, it had always been there, this innate cruelty that had disturbed her from the time Rory was very young. It was just that now he was old enough to utilize it for his own ends: he had an almost uncanny ability to divine weakness or vulnerability in others, and sometimes, especially this past year, he had not been above using those uncovered weaknesses for his own purposes.

Following him now across the yard, Kate thought that it was difficult to believe Rory was only thirteen. He was a good-looking boy, not quite as tall as David, nor as lean as Michael, but handsome in his own way, with his fair skin and red-gold hair. It was just that the expression in his hazel eyes was sometimes too old for his years: there was a slyness and a calculation there that Kate didn't care for; it was as though Rory waited for his chance, and wouldn't hesitate to take it whenever it came—whatever it was.

Watching Rory stride out of sight, following the earlier footsteps of David and Randall, Kate thought that perhaps the only person who might save Rory from himself was David. Inexplicably, it was the kind and thoughtful David who had the most influence over this third son of hers. Rory would listen to David when he refused to heed anyone else, and while Kate knew what a terrible burden she was placing on David, she was helpless: she had to encourage the relationship, because it was the only alternative she had. She was frightened for Rory, and she didn't know why. Lately she had experienced a strange premonition of some disaster concerning Rory, and telling herself that she was only being fanciful and ridiculous didn't arrest her uneasiness. She found herself hoping that if—or when—David's help might be needed with Rory, his sphere of influence would be strong enough to avert the catastrophe, whatever it might be.

Turning away from the window again, Kate told herself wryly that she was becoming mystical in her old age. Disaster, catastrophe, premonition! What was the matter with her, anyway? She had never found that events could be changed by wishful thinking, and she wouldn't believe it was possible now. If such things did happen, the whole focus of her life would have been altered, for hadn't she wished desperately in those early days of her first pregnancy that her condition was merely the product of her imagination and not an inescapable fact of life? Hadn't she wished—?

Her musings were interrupted by a tap at the door, and then Page came in. Kate turned to him with a smile, thinking as she always did whenever she saw him how handsome he was. The passing years hadn't aged him so much as they had matured him. He was thirty-eight now, and the silvering just beginning to shadow his temples enhanced his distinguished appearance. He was just as lean as he had always been, but there was a new *ease* about him these past few years of his phenomenal success—a tendency to relax, to enjoy things, to laugh more. He came in now, smiling with amusement.

"I just had the most interesting conversation with your daughter," he said.

Kate lifted an eyebrow. "Why is Adele always *my* daughter when she's being impertinent, and *your* child when she's being clever about something?"

Page bent to kiss her briefly on the lips. "Because," he answered, "she inherited her impertinence from you . . ."

". . . and her cleverness from her father," Kate finished dryly. They had had this conversation before.

"Of course. But what do you think the little minx wants now?"

"I haven't the remotest clue," said Kate with a sigh. Whatever it was, Kate would probably have a difficult time talking Page out of giving it to her; he had the most maddening inclination to spoil Adele abominably.

"She wants a new horse."

Kate's eyebrow shot even higher. "But she has a perfectly good pony now," she pointed out. "Why does she want another?"

"She doesn't want a pony, she informs me. She wants a horse."

Kate sighed again, heavily. "Why?"

"Apparently ponies are passé for young ladies who desire to be sophisticated and elegant. Adele says it's *quite* impossible to be elegant when she is forced to ride a fat little pony whose main interest is snatching grass at the side of the road to make it even fatter."

"Well, I hope you told her that her request is *quite* impossible!"

"I said I would talk to you."

"Why did you tell her that? I thought we agreed Adele was to ride a pony until she was twelve."

"Well, that's only another year or so."

"Oh, Page, really! If I let you, you would spoil that child utterly!"

"I didn't say she could have a horse," protested Page mildly. "I merely said I would talk to you about it."

"Yes, and make me the villain when I refused her—as you knew I would!"

"She does have a point, Kate."

"And what point is that?" demanded Kate with asperity.

"She *is* old enough for a horse—and a good enough rider to handle one. After all, she is your daughter."

"Flattery won't change my mind," Kate said darkly. And in this case, she meant it. At eleven, her daughter was in danger of turning into a little prig, and Kate didn't like it. Sophisticated! Elegant! Adele was scarcely old enough to understand what the words meant, let alone emulate them! She could see that she was going to have to have a little talk with her daughter, who believed that because her father doted on her, everyone else should. Adele was becoming just a little too missish for Kate's taste, and that would have to be stopped quickly, or else their darling daughter would soon be completely insufferable.

Still, reflected Kate as she absently watched Page wander restlessly about the room, it *was* difficult to refuse Adele anything. At eleven, she was already a beauty, with her oval face and huge eyes. The honey-blond hair of her babyhood had darkened only slightly, and the color combination of light hair and dark eyes was devastating, even in one so young. Already she had learned how to use those eyes to advantage— just as she had learned when and how to use her shy smile. And behind both was the iron will Adele had evinced since early childhood. Adele might be small and delicately made, but there was nothing fragile about her determination to have what she wanted. Kate, who understood her daughter very well and was not as swayed by her wiles as were the males in the family, was often exasperated by her small daughter. She was also, when she allowed herself to be, a little frightened for her. Adele was so *intense*, she would acknowledge privately; things meant so much to her. And if she was faced one day with a will stronger than hers, Kate honestly believed her daughter would break before she would bend. And that made Kate all the more afraid for her.

Deliberately turning her thoughts away from such distressing contemplations, Kate thought more cheerfully that she would never be afraid for Randall. Behind that cherubic appearance, her adopted son was strong and resilient. He would be just ten years old soon, but already he possessed a quick and perceptive mind, a sharp intelligence, and a sunny disposition that drew people to him. Just as she had been drawn, Kate thought fondly; she had loved Randall as her own from the first.

She still believed that this youngest, adopted son of theirs bore an uncanny resemblance to Page, although she acknowledged that this could only be her imagination. She had so wanted another child at that terrible time in her life that she hadn't cared that Randall wasn't really theirs; she had just been grateful for the fact that they were able to adopt him. Still, Page and the boy had many of the same mannerisms, and that wasn't entirely her observation: others had mentioned it, too, despite Page's disclaimer. Page and this adopted son of theirs also had a similar way of looking at things, no matter how Page laughingly denied it: he and Randall approached every problem carefully and with much thought to the solution, and then, when either decided to solve whatever it was, they often did so with a hint of recklessness that saved them both from being pedantic and dull.

Randall had been born, it seemed, with a highly developed sense of justice that plagued him just as much as Michael's temper rode him. Randall was incapable of acting unfairly in any situation, and many times he had surrendered his own advantage simply because it was the right thing to do. Kate was proud of this trait in her youngest, for it reminded her so much of Page himself, whether he would admit it or not.

"Kate?"

She started. She had been so lost in her thoughts that she had almost forgotten Page was in the room. Looking up now, she saw that he had been roaming restlessly about, and had paused at her dressing table, absently fingering the silver-backed hairbrush he had given her for their tenth anniversary. It was made from the initial load of ore taken from the Vindication, the silver mine that had first struck for them. Kate was prouder of that hairbrush than of almost anything else Page had given her throughout the years of their marriage, and when now, four years later, he wanted to sell his interests at Leadville and Aspen, Kate encouraged him. His judgment had been vindicated before by the silver boom in Colorado; it would be again, she felt, when he said—to the same jeers he had received before—that the silver market would soon collapse of its own weight.

But it wasn't of silver and the mines Page wanted to speak. Restlessly he put down the hairbrush and walked to the window, away from her. He stood there looking out, absently fingering the curtain.

"What is it, Page?" Kate asked, her curiosity aroused. It was rare to see Page at a loss for words.

"How would you feel," he said cautiously, without turning around, "about a visit from my cousin?"

"Your cousin?" she repeated blankly. "Whom do you mean?"

Page turned to her then, his expression carefully neutral. "I mean Roger, of course."

"Roger!" She was so stunned that she could only gape at him. "But . . . but . . ."

"I've been thinking about asking him to come for a long time." Page spoke rapidly, and she could hardly speak at all.

"You have?" she said weakly.

"Yes. Yes, I have."

She wanted to ask why, but normal speech seemed to be beyond her. She tried to marshal her scattered thoughts into some semblance of order, but the shock was too great. She could only think: Roger here? At Beauvais? It was impossible!

"We've been exchanging letters for some time, as you know . . ."

"Yes, yes; I know," she said when he paused. And did she know? She wasn't sure of anything at the moment. Why, why, did Page want him here? she thought distractedly. Just when things were going so well, when she thought—hoped—that Roger was a part of her life that she could look back on with nostalgia and not longing. And now here was Page dragging in Roger's name again and asking her if he could invite him to Beauvais. It wasn't fair!

But she couldn't say any of the things that flew through her mind. How could she, and not betray herself? Trying to control a half-hysterical urge to break into shrill laughter, Kate realized abruptly that Page was still speaking, and she bent the whole force of her will on forgetting her conflicting emotions and concentrating on what he was trying to say. An instant later she found herself wishing even more hopelessly that they had never begun this conversation, that she had

never heard of Green Eaves or Roger Templeton, that she
was a thousand miles away where no thought was required.

Why, she asked herself despairingly, weren't they talking
about something safe and innocuous, like the Brussels carpet
she had ordered and had paid far too much for, or the new
colt she had bought from George Siddons, the rancher who
owned the land abutting Beauvais. The colt had been a bargain, even at the hard price Siddons drove, but . . .

*But why was she thinking about carpets and colts when her
entire life was disintegrating before her very eyes?*

". . . and so, while he hasn't actually come out and said
so, I think he wants to leave his humiliation behind and begin
a new life. I thought . . ."

Humiliation? Start a new life? What was he talking about?
In her distraction, she had missed Page's entire conversation,
and now she tried frantically to piece together the sense of
what he had said without admitting that she hadn't been listening.

"Yes? You thought what?" Kate tried to look expectant
and interested when he paused—neither of which was difficult. By now she was expecting the worst, and wondering
how she was going to deal with it. Then, to her horror, Page
told her his plans, and Kate felt herself sinking into emotional quicksand. Somewhat desperately, she tried to rally.

"You can't mean you want them to *stay* here!" she said,
her voice high. "I thought you said you wanted Roger and
Amelia to come for a visit!"

"Well, I do," admitted Page with reluctance. "But I
thought . . . I mean, if Roger liked it here, I might be able
to give him some kind of employment. A stewardship, perhaps. Or . . ."

"But . . . but . . ." She was stammering again. She made
another effort to control herself. It was not successful. "But
why do they have to stay here?" she wailed.

Page came to her, "I didn't think you would mind so
much," he said as he put his arms around her.

Oh, if only he knew! If only he knew! She shuddered at
the thought of Page discovering what had been between her
and Roger, and thankfully Page misinterpreted her reaction
and held her close, comforting her.

"I know you don't care for Amelia," he said soothingly,
"but perhaps you can tolerate her for a few weeks. I wouldn't

ask it of you, Kate, except that Roger really is in financial trouble, and since he is family . . ."

Trying not to reveal herself, Kate eagerly seized on the excuse Page had innocently offered her. As she sniffed into her handkerchief, she said in a small voice, "Well, since you put it that way, I suppose Amelia and I can get along for a while." She looked at him seriously. "I didn't realize Roger's situation was so dismal."

Page nodded. "He had to sell Green Eaves, Kate. When he first wrote to me about it, my inclination was to buy it back from him. I could now, but . . ."

He hesitated, and despite her own distress and confusion, Kate understood Page's reluctance. Buying back Green Eaves would be like a slap in the face, an outright admission that Roger was too incompetent to manage his own affairs. But if he couldn't take care of his own estate, how could he possibly act as steward for Beauvais? Feeling very much like a traitor to Roger in even asking the question, Kate asserted her practicality briefly enough to put aside her own emotions and say, "But if Roger lost Green Eaves, Page, why are you going to . . . to offer him such an important position at Beauvais?"

Page winced. "I'm not really sure myself," he answered. "After all, I'm very satisfied with McDermott, who can take over for me at any time. I suppose if I make Roger an assistant, or make sure I oversee exactly what he's doing . . . Oh, hell! I don't know! I'll think of something when the time comes, I suppose."

Kate considered. Loyalty to her ideal of Roger made her assure herself that some terrible catastrophe had occurred to make Roger sell his home. Surely it wasn't his fault; there had to have been something that made such a disastrous decision necessary. But the niggling little doubts remained in her mind, until she was distracted by Page again.

"You know," he said, "maybe it wasn't a good idea to ask Roger and Amelia to live here, if they decide to stay. It might be better all around if they found a place of their own—in Denver, maybe. What do you think?"

Kate's relief was so overwhelming that she almost laughed aloud. Instead, she lowered her eyes and said solemnly, "I'm sure Roger would prefer that, especially since he has had difficulties in the past. He might feel less . . . dependent . . . on you if he has his own home. And I'm sure," she added with what she thought was a brilliant touch, "that Amelia would prefer it as well. Don't you?"

Page laughed, relieved himself that he had handled a delicate situation so adroitly. "To tell the truth," he confessed, "I never could see you and Amelia living amicably together under the same roof! No, Denver seems a much better plan, I think."

"So do I. I'm so glad you thought of it, Page," said Kate demurely.

Page hugged her. "So am I. I'll write to Roger tonight and invite them for . . . let's see . . . how about the spring? Will that give you enough time?"

Nothing would give her enough time to prepare for Roger's visit, Kate thought. Even now she wasn't sure how she felt about seeing him again. Excited, apprehensive . . . a little frightened. All that, and more.

But she forced a smile for Page, and she answered with barely a tremor in her voice, "Springtime will be fine."

25

They came in May, when the new grass was tinting the hills apple green, and the mountain wildflowers were blooming in chaotic profusion, and Beauvais was at its most beautiful. The new leaves on the trees and the tiny buds on the flowers in Kate's garden spoke more eloquently than words that this was a season of renewal, a time of rejuvenation and restoration, and as Kate watched the carriage toiling up the long drive to the house, she wondered in trepidation what feelings and emotions this unwise reunion might resurrect.

She had deliberately begged off going to the station to greet Roger and Amelia; this first meeting after so many years was going to be difficult enough for her, and she wanted to be on home ground when she first saw him—them. And now the day was here, and she still felt unsure of herself.

All winter long she had tried to prepare herself for what

she had begun to think of privately as "the arrival." She had reminded herself that she was a mature married woman with five children; she had told herself that she loved her husband, her family, and her home with a bond she would be insane to break. Again and again she had assured herself that Roger Templeton was a part of the past that she remembered only with fond regret and nothing more. All these things she had repeated, time and again, like a litany—almost as if she were trying to convince herself through sheer repetition.

And now the day was here, and she was abominably nervous. Where were all of her assurances now?

She hadn't expected them to arrive until late afternoon, and as the day wore inexorably on, Kate found herself at once eager to see Roger again and dreading his arrival. What would she think of him? What would he feel about her? Would there be awkwardness, constraint . . . attraction? It had been almost fifteen years since they had last seen each other. Had the passing of time been kind or cruel?

Anxiously she examined herself in the mirror, searching for flaws and imperfections she knew he would see at once. She was as slim as she had been in her girlhood, but now there were new lines in her face that hadn't been there before, and her hair had darkened a little to a burnished auburn instead of the vibrant red it had been as a young girl. Would he notice these changes? Of course he would. Did she care? She wasn't sure. She didn't know how she felt about Roger Templeton; she only knew that their meeting after all these years would either fan the fire she had felt for him once or extinguish it completely. And which did she want it to be? The sane and logical part of her mind gave her the only answer that made any sense; another, more treacherous part wondered.

And now they were here at last, whether she was prepared or not, and as the carriage halted by the front door, Kate took a deep breath. Her heart was beating wildly, and for an instant she thought she might faint with sheer excitement and dread. In a few moments she would know whether her fantasies and dreams had sprung to life or whether they had withered away completely. Somewhat frantically she fanned her flushed face with her handkerchief and peered out from behind the drawing-room curtain for her first sight, after all this time, of the man who had been her first love.

Page stepped out as soon as the carriage stopped. He held

the door open without waiting for the coachman to jump down, and then he spoke to someone inside. He laughed, spoke again.

Watching breathlessly from her hiding place behind the curtain, Kate waited in an agony of impatience. What were they talking about? she wondered feverishly. Why didn't Roger step down?

And then she saw him. Her heart leaped, steadied, then leaped again as he emerged from the carriage and stood beside Page, staring in awe at the house.

Kate's first reaction was a startled *I remember him as being taller*. Her second was a dismayed *But he looks so much older!*

And then somehow her feet were carrying her forward, and she was crossing the drawing room, walking out to the entry, and greeting them all at the door with a smile on her lips, a pang in her heart, and a silent, anxious question: *What will he think of me?*

"Kate!"

His reaction was all she had desired, and more. Seeing her standing there silhouetted in the doorway with magnificent Beauvais surrounding her, Roger halted in mid-stride, his foot raised in the act of taking a step. His face cleared, and once again, for an instant, he assumed a boyish expression of utter delight. Standing at the bottom of the steps looking up at her, he thought that he had never seen a more beautiful, vibrant woman than Kate Taggart. She was even more striking than she had been in her girlhood, and something stirred in him. Posed in the doorway as she was, smiling at them all, she looked to Roger like a precious jewel in a polished setting, unattainable, unreachable, utterly desirable. He was speechless.

Page was a little staggered himself. Seeing his wife standing there so regally, so perfectly the mistress of his home, it was hard for him to believe that just yesterday she had been exhausted after the work of the past weeks, preparing for the Templetons' arrival. Now she looked as if she taxed herself no more strenuously than deciding which gown to wear for tea and which to dinner.

Yet Page knew, because he had been swept into the whirlwind himself, exactly how hard she had driven herself to prepare for this visit. Beauvais had been cleaned from top to bottom on her orders; everything had been waxed, washed, and polished to within an inch of its life—including the children, Page thought wryly. They had been drilled mercilessly in manners, conduct, and decorum, until even Kate was sure they would commit no dreadful faux pas before their visitors. She would *not*, she had declared more than once, be shamed by her children before Amelia Templeton. The children took note of that tone in her voice, and applied themselves studiously to their lessons.

If Kate had been hard on the children, she had been ruthless in other areas: the larder was stuffed, the smokehouse packed, the dairy overflowing, and the root cellar full to bursting. Beauvais had stocked enough food to withstand a full-scale invasion, and yet there were also new lavender sachets in all the wardrobes and fresh flowers in all the rooms. On the day of Roger and Amelia's arrival, Beauvais was the showplace it was meant to be, and Page was stiff with pride as he saw the mistress of all this splendor running lightly down Beauvais's wide front steps to take his arm and greet their guests.

"Roger! How wonderful to see you again!" Kate offered her face for his kiss, smiling brilliantly in welcome.

"Kate . . ."

Overcome, Roger reached for her hands, squeezing them tightly. As she returned the pressure, Kate saw the expression on his face, and her heart stumbled. There wasn't opportunity to do more than glance briefly at him again in the flurry of welcome, but when she saw the weariness and defeat in Roger's faded blue eyes, Kate was so appalled that she almost lost her composure. "Roger, are you—?" she began anxiously.

Fortunately for all of them, she was interrupted just then by a squeal from within the carriage, and as the three of them turned to look, Kate realized that she had completely forgotten about Amelia.

"Kate! Kate!" Amelia cried. "Oh, it's been such a long time!"

Roger turned to assist his wife, and Amelia emerged plumply from the carriage to throw her arms around Kate, engulfing her completely.

"Hello, Amelia," said Kate, trying to extricate herself. She felt a stab of jealousy at Amelia's stylish traveling costume and tried to repress it by telling herself that Amelia had grown even more stout over the years, so that she appeared stuffed into the pleated skirt and flared jacket. Still, it was ir-

ritating to feel provincial and outmoded in her new apricot
silk. She wished now that she hadn't disdained the bustle,
even though she had thought it ridiculous and had told the
seamstress so. Judging from Amelia's costume, it was still the
height of fashion, uncomfortable or not.

"Kate, you look absolutely wonderful!" Amelia exclaimed
enviously just as Kate was berating herself for being so drab
and out-of-date. "How do you stay so slender? I declare, you
don't look a day older than when we last saw each other at
my engagement ball! You were married that day, weren't
you?"

Stung, expecting malice in Amelia's wide blue eyes, Kate
searched her face. To her surprise, she saw behind the almost
feverish gaiety Amelia displayed to the worry and anxiety underlying her smile. And now that she took time to notice,
Kate was able to see the strain in Amelia's plump face, the
lines of weariness around her eyes. What had happened to
these two, to make them seem so tired and defeated?

"Yes, that was my wedding day," Kate said, still bemused
at what she had seen in Amelia's eyes.

"It was so long ago, wasn't it?" Amelia sighed.

"Yes. It was." It did seem so long ago, she thought now,
recalling that night when it had been so crucially important to her to make an entrance at Roger's betrothal ball. She
had wanted to impress him, to show him . . . What? That
she didn't care? That he would regret marrying Amelia? She
had acted out of spite and pique, and remembering it now,
she was ashamed.

But a third figure was emerging from the carriage as they
talked, and both Roger and Amelia turned to the girl with
the doting expressions of proud parents. Roger reached out a
hand and drew the girl forward.

"Kate," he said softly and with obvious pleasure, "this is
our daughter, Jane."

Astonishingly, Jane Templeton bore little resemblance to
either of her parents. At fourteen, she was tall for her age, a
good six inches over five feet—almost as tall as Kate herself—and she was very thin. She had small bones, beautiful
translucent white skin, fine straight black hair, and luminous
dark eyes. She was a beautiful child, quiet and reserved
rather than shy, and she already possessed a patrician air that
would, Kate thought with wry amusement, put Adele's
haughty little nose out of place. Adele was a wild mountain

rose—bold, splashed with vibrant color, and heady with fragrance; Jane was an English violet—soft, delicate, and elegantly refined.

Smiling to herself at the comparison between her vivacious daughter and the composed Jane, Kate was just about to welcome her when Michael, who had been engaged in some project or other, and who—contrary to his mother's express orders—was covered from hair to boot with grease and dirt, came around the corner of the house. His dark head was down as he studied a diagram he was carrying, and consequently he didn't notice the little group on the steps until it was too late for retreat.

Kate was so appalled at the sight of her eldest son looking like an itinerant beggar that she couldn't speak. It was Page who took one look at Kate's horrified face and broke the stunned silence with a roar.

"Michael!"

Frowning, still engrossed in what he was reading, Michael stopped. By chance, he had halted directly opposite the immaculate and fastidious Jane. They looked at each other, and Kate, who had finally gathered what remained of her dignity and was preparing to say something to her son, felt the words lodge in her throat.

In that instant before she spoke, Kate was stunned by Michael's reaction to Jane. It was as if he had suddenly come upon something of incredible beauty, something that fascinated and held him enthralled. The attraction was sudden, inexplicable, and so powerful that he stiffened. His eyes never left Jane's face, and when Kate dragged her glance away from him to look in Jane's direction, she was appalled to see the same bemusement lighting the girl's lustrous eyes. It was as if everyone else had ceased to exist for them; they stared at each other and saw no one else.

Kate was aghast. Dear God! she thought. They're only children!

But the look that flashed from Michael to Jane and back again was not childish at all, and when Kate saw that wordless communication, she groaned inwardly. Helplessly she stood there and watched brother and sister fall in love and felt disaster rushing at her with breakneck speed.

Somehow Kate got through the remaining introductions and ushered everyone into the house. Thankfully, it was not yet time for tea, and so she marshaled them all upstairs and into various guest rooms, insisting that they rest after their tiring journey. That duty performed, she rushed to her own apartments, where she collapsed on the chaise longue, her head in her hands. She had an hour to pull herself together, and the way she felt now, she would need every minute of it to recover.

Lifting her head, she dragged herself over to the dressing table and sank down onto the velvet stool. It was several minutes before she dared to look in the mirror, and when she did, she was surprised: she looked the same as she had only an hour or so before. She hadn't, as she had half-expected, suddenly become haggard, her hair white with shock.

Head in her hands again, Kate put her elbows on the dressing-table top and groaned aloud. How could this have happened? she asked herself despairingly. They were only children—how could they know, instantly and without preamble, that they had found . . . love? People spent their entire *lives* searching for someone to love; why had Michael and Jane found this elusive condition there on the front steps of Beauvais? Oh, it was awful!

Perhaps, she thought suddenly, lowering her hands to stare hopefully at herself—perhaps she was only being fanciful, imaginative . . . overwrought. She had been under such a strain lately, preparing for this visit; she might be overtired and seeing things that weren't there at all.

Her heart gave a wild leap at the thought, then steadied mournfully again. She wasn't mistaken; she knew she wasn't. She had seen it happen before her very eyes, and she couldn't dismiss it by reiterating that Michael and Jane were only children. If they fancied themselves in love, she would have to face it.

Face it! She made it sound so simple.

But unless she could think of some way to avert this impending disaster, they were all headed for a catastrophe. And she was the only one who could do something about it. But what? she wondered bleakly. What?

How could she possibly tell the truth at this late date? She couldn't just collect them all in the drawing room one day and announce over the teacups that Michael couldn't marry Jane because she was his half-sister. Shuddering, Kate could imagine the ensuing chaos from that pronouncement. And yet, if the situation continued—and knowing Michael as she

did, she was sure it would; he had been entranced, enthralled; he wouldn't give up easily—she would have to do
something. Even to protect herself and her marriage—her
marriage! God, she had forgotten about *that*, hadn't
she?—even to protect them all, she couldn't allow Michael
and Jane to marry. She would never be able to live with herself, knowing she had condoned an incestuous relationship by
her silence. Oh, what a coward she was! Why hadn't she told
the truth in the beginning? Now, when the denouement
came—and she was dismally sure it would, judging from the
look on Michael's face—the anger and hurt and humiliation
would be that much greater for them all.

Agitatedly she got up and paced about the room. It was no
use telling herself that Michael was only fifteen and Jane a
year younger; her eldest son was tenacious. He would wait,
years if he was forced to, for Jane.

Kate stopped abruptly. Maybe that was the answer, she
thought with a wild surge of hope. If it wasn't childish infatuation after all, and if they did decide they truly loved each
other, she would insist that Michael wait until he was at least
eighteen. That would give her a breathing space of three
years to decide on another plan, and in those three years she
would pray that the attraction between them waned and then
vanished altogether.

If it did not, Kate didn't know what the consequences
might be.

By teatime Kate had summoned her formidable will sufficiently to appear composed again. Now, passing cups and
plates and presiding over the silver tea service, she had time
to distract herself by studying Roger. She had been so upset
before that she had scarcely given him a thought, and now
she realized how ironic the situation was. For months, she
had hardly thought of anyone else but Roger; now that he
was here, she had almost ignored him totally.

Watching him covertly as she prepared a cup for him, she
saw that her first impression of him as a tired and defeated
man hadn't been far off the mark after all, and she was
shocked when she saw how pale and drawn he really was.
And then he smiled at her as he accepted the cup, and just
for an instant he was the Roger she had known. Their eyes
met, and her heart leaped treacherously in response. Fortunately, on the other side of her, Amelia chose that moment to

start chattering brightly about Olivia, and Kate dragged her eyes away from Roger and tried to concentrate on what Amelia was saying.

"She sends her love," Amelia said. "And also a few things for you and Page and the children. We have them in one of the trunks upstairs. I visited her at Tremont Hall before we left, you know, and I tried my best to encourage her to come with us."

"She wouldn't, of course." Kate sighed. "Every time I write to Aunt Olivia, I ask her to come for a visit. She has always refused, saying she can't leave England, even for me."

"Well, Kate," Amelia pointed out gently, "Olivia is getting on in years. And traveling is difficult enough as it is."

"I know. But now that the train comes directly to Denver, I thought I could persuade her to come. I would so like to see her again."

Amelia's eyes filled with sentimental tears. "She would love to see you, too, Kate. She told me how much she missed you."

"I miss her, too." Kate glanced fondly at the silver tea service Olivia had given her so long ago. She had always taken care of it, even in the early days at the cabin, when there hadn't been much opportunity to do more than polish it. Now it gleamed with the soft patina of age, and Kate reached out to touch it lovingly. When their second mine at Aspen had struck, Page had offered to have a new tea service made from some of the silver taken there. Kate had refused. She loved Olivia's gift; whenever she passed it reposing regally on the sideboard, she was reminded of her aunt, and she would never put it away to molder in some forgotten cupboard while some brash newcomer took its place.

Amelia helped herself to another biscuit. Chewing with appreciation, she glanced around Kate's elegant drawing room and said enviously, "You have such a beautiful home, Kate. You must be very proud."

Kate thought of all the pain and heartache that had gone into the building of this house; she thought of all the joy and pleasure and satisfaction Beauvais had given in return, and she answered, "Thank you, Amelia. Yes, we're very proud of it."

"And you have such beautiful children!" Amelia exclaimed, selecting another cake. "Michael is so handsome, and David so dignified—and at fifteen! One would hardly know they were twins, would one? They don't look at all alike!"

"No," Kate agreed, thinking of Michael's outrageous behavior that afternoon. "They couldn't be more opposite—as I'm sure you noticed today!"

Amelia giggled, well aware of Kate's reaction to the initial appearance of her eldest son. "Boys will be boys, I suppose," she said archly. "But four of them! What a relief it must be to have Adele. At least then you're not totally surrounded by males!"

"Well, sometimes I think rearing four boys is less difficult than raising one daughter," Kate said wryly. "Adele can be quite a handful."

"But those eyes . . . and that hair! Only twelve years old, and already Adele is quite a beauty. Imagine what she will be like in a few more years!"

Kate winced. "I'd rather not. It's difficult enough as it is." Then she smiled, returning the compliment with genuine warmth. "Jane is a beautiful girl, Amelia. You're very fortunate yourself."

Amelia sighed. "Yes. Sometimes I wish I had been able to have more children, but then I think what a comfort Jane is to me, and I know that if I could only have one child, I would want it to be Jane. Especially now, when things have taken such a turn for the worse with poor Roger."

Amelia stopped abruptly, and Kate paused in the act of pouring another cup of tea. It was out in the open at last, and Kate didn't know whether to be relieved or dismayed that the subject had been broached at last.

She looked across at Amelia, who said in obvious distress. "Oh, dear. I didn't mean to say that."

"Why not?" Kate asked matter-of-factly.

"Well . . . because . . ." Amelia glanced away from Kate's direct gaze, put down her cup on the polished table, and clasped her hands tightly in her lap. "I always thought discussing personal problems was a little . . . vulgar," Amelia said primly. "Didn't you?"

"Not always," replied Kate briskly. "Not unless one does it for effect. Sometimes it's the only practical thing to do."

"Oh, Kate, you always were unconventional!" Amelia said, suddenly close to tears.

"That has nothing to do with it."

"Oh, yes, it does! You were always able to *cope* so much

better than the rest of us—simply because you weren't bound
by all these ridiculous conventions! I honestly don't think you
would *mind* having to pinch pennies or trying to make do.
You would probably think it a lark, an adventure!"

Kate thought of that first hopeless year in the cabin, when
she didn't know if Page was coming home or not; she
thought of losing almost all their cattle; she thought of the
fire that destroyed the stables and incinerated her beautiful
horses; she thought of that terrible year when she had
squeezed the household accounts until there was nothing left,
and then squeezed some more, until Page struck it rich in his
silver mines. Had she thought these things an adventure?

"I understand more than you think, Amelia," she said finally, her voice low.

But Amelia was not convinced. "How could you?" she
cried. "Look at you and Page and how successful you've
been! You have everything you could possibly want! And
what do we have?" she asked bitterly. "I'll tell you! Nothing!
We have nothing! We don't even have Green Eaves anymore.
So don't tell me you understand, Kate, because I don't believe you!"

Kate shot a worried glance at Page and Roger, who had
retreated to the other side of the room. Thankfully, they were
deep in some conversation of their own, and were apparently
oblivious of the crisis over the teacups. She turned back to
Amelia, who was sobbing quietly into her napkin, and she
was about to say something comforting, when she stopped.
Was what Amelia said true? she wondered suddenly. Did she
really understand?

She and Page hadn't lost Beauvais, after all. They had
come close to losing it, but somehow they had managed to
hang on to it, even when things seemed so hopeless toward
the last. Now she thought that if Page hadn't been so strong,
so sure of himself and his judgment, and if he hadn't had
confidence in him, things might have turned out differently.
But Page *had* been strong, and she *had* trusted him. And in
the end, they had saved everything they had worked for.
They had endured.

Involuntarily Kate glanced at Roger. The half-formed
questions that rose in her mind as she looked at him disturbed her, and she tried to thrust them away, only to have
them return insidiously, demanding an answer she wasn't
prepared to give. If Roger had been more of a man, would

he have lost his home? If he had been stronger, would he have had to appeal to Page for help?

Kate shut her eyes briefly, rejecting her thoughts as both ludicrous and disloyal. Whatever the reason Roger had come to such a state, she was sure that he had done his best to keep the financial wolves at bay. Fate had been unkind to him, that was all; it hadn't been his fault, she was positive. Whatever had happened could have happened to anyone.

But as she turned to offer the weeping Amelia a fresh cup of tea, another insidious thought intruded, and this time Kate was unable to ignore the soft, insistent voice inside her that wondered: *It could have happened to anybody, couldn't it?* And then answered: *But it didn't happen to Page.*

26

Kate allowed it to go on for six weeks, trying to convince herself that Michael's infatuation with Jane was just that: infatuation. She told herself that she had overreacted at first, that Michael and Jane were just children, that their attraction was immature and fleeting. But as the weeks wore on and Kate saw them together constantly, she believed none of it.

The evidence was there before her eyes, so obvious that she wondered why no one else had seen it. But then, she was forced to admit, no one else had the knowledge she possessed, so why should anyone be concerned? If anything, there was an unspoken tendency to encourage such a match, for already Jane and Michael made a striking couple, even as young as they both were.

But as spring became summer, and the two adolescents were rarely apart, Kate began to worry in earnest. She knew only too well the compromises that passion demanded, and she knew, too, that there were times when youthful passion could not be denied. Hadn't she proved that herself that day so long ago in the hay barn? But in this case the consequences of such a union would be even more disastrous than her liaison with Roger. It would destroy Jane to know that she might have lain with her own half-brother, and a fearful Kate couldn't even guess what Michael's reaction might be.

But as if Kate didn't have enough to be worried about, there were other storm clouds on the horizon: Rory, who had always been envious of Michael, now seemed determined to challenge his older brother over Jane. As the weeks went by, tension between the two brothers increased, and their relationship, always strained at best, disintegrated even more. Jane's arrival seemed to have sparked a ceremonial rite as old as the passage of time: two males trying to outdo each other courting the same woman. In other circumstances Kate might have been a little amused at the jockeying for position that went on between the two brothers, but in this case the situation was too explosive to laugh about. Finally Kate couldn't stand it anymore; she decided she had to have a talk with Michael. What she would say when the time came, she had no idea; she would just have to pray for inspiration, she supposed, and hope that whatever she said made sense.

Once she decided she had to take matters into her own hands, she searched for an opportunity to talk to Michael alone, when they wouldn't be interrupted. She found it one morning at the end of June, when the house was quiet and she had risen at dawn because she couldn't sleep. Standing by the window, shivering a little in the cool morning air, Kate saw the light in the barn, and she knew Michael was there tending one of the foals that had sickened several days before and was now very weak. It was a valuable animal—or would be when it grew to maturity—and Michael had spent more time with it than anyone else. Dressing quickly, Kate wondered if he had been up with it all night. It would be like him, she thought as she went quietly downstairs; along with her temperament, Michael had inherited her love of horses.

The sky was just beginning to lighten when she crossed the yard. Hugging her shawl closer about her against the morning chill, Kate stopped for a moment, staring up at the magnificent sight of the Rockies catching the first rays of the sun. The high peaks seemed crowned with fire, and Kate drew in a breath, trying to draw strength from the sight. She stood there a moment more, wondering what she was going to say to her son, and then with a sigh she turned away from the mountains and hurried toward the barn.

Michael was inside, as she had known he would be, sitting

silently by the downed foal as the mare drowsed to one side. The loose box was piled high with straw, and the warm scent of hay and animals greeted Kate as she walked quietly up to the stall. She paused to stare at the scene before her, wondering why, of her five children, she secretly loved this boy the most. Was it because he was her firstborn? Or because he resembled her most in temperament? She didn't know. She only knew that she hated what she was about to do because it would hurt him. She had never wanted to hurt any of her children, but especially not Michael, for he felt things so deeply, and was too proud to show it. And now . . .

"Michael?" she said softly.

"Hello, Mother."

She smiled at his greeting. He had adopted the more formal "mother" several years ago, abandoning "mama" because he deemed it too childish. But it suited him to address her this way, even though it would have sounded strange coming from the other children, and it was one more thing that made him different from his brothers and sister.

But she had to keep her attention on the matter at hand, she reminded herself sternly; digressing from the real issue was only postponing the unpleasant task before her, and she had to begin before she lost courage completely.

That decided, she asked, "How is the foal this morning?"

Michael shook his head. "Not well, I'm afraid. It might not live."

Uttering a distressed sound, Kate opened the Dutch door to the stall and slipped inside, kneeling by the foal to touch it tenderly for herself. It barely moved at her touch, and she saw that its breathing was far too shallow. She looked up. "Perhaps," she suggested as gently as she could, "we should put it out of its misery."

Michael's response was exactly what hers would have been. "No!" he said fiercely. "If it dies, it dies on its own!"

Kate didn't argue; she only nodded in understanding and sat back on her heels, watching him and wondering how to begin.

Michael looked down at the foal lying so quietly between them. "You wanted to talk to me about Jane, didn't you?" he said, his voice low.

She was surprised by his perception, but then she realized she shouldn't have been. She and Michael had always understood each other, and many times they had communicated

without words—with only a look that flashed between them.
Now he raised his dark eyes to hers and looked at her
calmly, waiting for her answer.

"Yes," she said, wanting to reach out and brush back the
lock of hair that had fallen across his forehead. "I did want
to talk to you about Jane. How did you know?"

He shrugged, and she saw how broad his shoulders were
under his shirt. She thought of him as a boy still. But he was
almost a man.

"I know when you're upset by something—and you're upset by Jane and me, aren't you? What is it, Mother? Do you
think we're too young?"

Relieved that he had said it himself, Kate tried to answer
neutrally. "Well, you are only fifteen . . ."

"Yes," he agreed solemnly. "And fifteen is far too young to
be serious about someone. Is that what you think?"

"Well, I . . ."

"I agree." Thoughtfully Michael selected a wisp of hay. He
twirled it in his fingers while Kate looked at him in complete
astonishment.

"You agree that you're too young?" she said faintly. Oh, it
couldn't be as simple as this!

Michael threw down the hay. "Of course," he said. His
voice held only a hint of disdain for a mother who hadn't
given him credit for common sense. "What could I offer
Jane, anyway?" he continued as Kate sat in stunned silence.
"I don't have anything of my own—no home, no money."

"But your father . . ." Kate began, then stopped abruptly.
What in heaven's name was wrong with her? She had been
about to say something utterly absurd about Page never letting any of his children starve.

If Michael noticed Kate's appalled confusion, he gave no
sign of it. Fortunately for Kate, he was preoccupied with
thoughts of his own. "Yes, I know my father would give me
anything I asked for," he finished for her, frowning at the
idea. "But I don't want to ask for anything—it wouldn't be
right."

"But Beauvais will be yours one day—or part of it."

"Yes. And I'll be honored to accept it. But until then, I
have to do something on my own. Father did—no one gave
him Beauvais on a plate, did they? Why should I expect him
to hand it to me?"

"But . . . To Kate's consternation, she realized abruptly

that the conversation wasn't going at all the way she planned. She made a determined effort to drag them both back to the point. "And so," she said, dreading the answer, but forcing herself to ask, "what about you and Jane?"

"Well, I've thought about it, and we'll just have to wait. Probably three years—perhaps one or two more. I have plans . . ."

"Plans?" echoed Kate weakly. Judgment had been postponed, her secret was safe for a while, at least, and she didn't know whether to laugh or cry. She was so proud of Michael that she could have done both. "What kind of plans?" she asked.

But Michael only smiled to himself and didn't answer. Kate knew it would be fruitless to press him; he could be even more stubborn than she, and he would tell her what he meant when he wanted to. She should just be thankful that the confrontation she had dreaded so much was delayed. Now she would have a little more time to make her own plans—whatever *they* were to be.

She pulled herself together. Michael would think it strange if she didn't say something, and now that the immediate crisis had been taken care of, she could afford to become herself again. "Well," she said briskly, preparing to rise, "I'm glad you decided to be sensible."

Michael reached out, restraining her as she started to get to her feet. His hand closed around her wrist, and his dark eyes were hard on her face when he said quietly, "I'm going to marry her, Mother. It may not be soon, but I *am* going to marry her. I'll never want anyone else."

Alarmed all over again by his intensity, Kate protested, "You can't know that, Michael. People change."

"I won't. I'll never love anyone but Jane. And one day, she will be my wife."

"Michael—"

Whatever she had been about to say was forgotten, for just then the foal, which had been so motionless except for the slight rise of its small ribs, shuddered convulsively. As Kate and Michael watched, its legs thrashed weakly on the straw, and in the corner, the mare nickered in distress. But it was too late for anything but regret; with a last shuddering breath, the foal sighed, closing its eyes in death.

There was utter silence in the barn, and then Michael swore, one short expletive that gave vent to his anger and

frustration and sorrow over losing the foal he had tried so
hard to save.

And over the small, still body, Kate met her son's eyes and
tried not to think of it as an omen.

In the end, it was Kate herself who precipitated the crisis
she had tried so hard to avert. In one moment's reckless temper she lost everything: husband, son, and the dream that
should have died long ago. Her grief was even harder to bear
for knowing that it was all her fault, and yet if she had
known the terrible price she was to pay for her folly, she
would have carried her secret to the grave, no matter what
the consequences. But at the last, when it counted the most,
Roger could be only the man he was. He could not be the
man she had wanted him to be.

It began with a headache—so colorless an ailment to have
been responsible for ruining her life so completely. If she
hadn't been almost out of her mind with grief and worry at
the time, Kate might even have appreciated the irony of it:
her entire future had been destroyed because for once in her
life she had surrendered to a slight indisposition—she, who
hadn't given in to fire or blizzard, who had endured bone-
crushing weariness and real sickness, had been undone by a
simple little headache. It was enough to make her cry, if she
had had any tears left to shed after that terrible day when
confession caused such catastrophe.

The heat was oppressive that day in September when her
world fell apart. The temperature had been climbing steadily
all that morning as the rest of the family prepared for the
picnic Page had planned as a celebration. The high season
was over: cattle were sold and gone to market, hay had been
baled and stored for the winter, the spring crop of foals had
been culled and weaned from their mothers, and Roger had
rented a house in Denver after accepting the position of
business and financial consultant to Beauvais.

Page, who had worked long hours all summer buying and
selling stock, arranging freighting schedules for the coming
year, consulting with Kate over the new horse-breeding program, and attending to the thousand and one details of fur-
thering Beauvais's prosperity, was in a mood to celebrate.
With Roger soon taking so much of the daily burden of managing Beauvais, Page would be free to expand his interests
even further. Now that his silver mines had been sold, for in-

stance, he was considering copper mining in Montana, and there were new developments in orchard management in California he wanted to look into.

Kate had never seen Page happier or more content. He had been driving himself, it was true, but everything was going so well for him that he seemed relaxed in spite of the hard work he had put in these past weeks. He had even, to Kate's astonishment, come to her only the other day about a second honeymoon.

"A second honeymoon?" She was at her dressing table brushing her hair before they retired. At this suggestion, she paused, brush in midair, staring at him wide-eyed through the mirror.

"Well, it would really be a first," Page said, watching her. "We never did have a proper honeymoon, did we?"

"No, we didn't. You *were* rather in a rush to get here, if you recall."

Page winced at the memory of that lightning journey from England to Colorado. "I was afraid that if I gave you time to think, you wouldn't come with me."

"You were right about that!"

Page came over to the dressing table as they laughed together in shared intimacy. Kate had never forgotten the horrors of that journey, but at least now she could laugh about it.

But Page was suddenly serious as he stood behind her and put his hands on her shoulders. "What do you think, Kate?" he asked quietly. "Would you like to see England again? It's beautiful in the spring."

"Oh, Page!" Eyes shining, Kate threw down the hairbrush and jumped up to fling herself into his arms. "Do you mean it?"

"Of course I mean it. Do I ever say anything I don't?"

She held herself away from him. "But the children," she said doubtfully. "And the house . . . and the—"

"The children will be just fine right where they are. It will be good for them to assume a little extra responsibility. And Mrs. Cahill can manage the house alone for a few months, I know. She's been itching to get her hands on the household accounts ever since she began as our housekeeper."

But Kate was still doubtful. "We can't be gone that long! What about—?"

Page kissed her, silencing her effectively. "Stop worrying!"

he ordered. He lifted her in his arms and carried her over to the bed. As she slipped between the sheets, he turned out the lamp and then slid in beside her. "Well, what do you say, Kate?" He drew her close. "Yes or no?"

"Oh, yes! Yes! Yes!" Kate answered. "England in the spring!" she said blissfully. "I can't believe it!"

And then, as he began to kiss her and she responded with a passion that sixteen years together hadn't diminished in the slightest, but only seemed to enhance, she wondered why they needed a second honeymoon after all.

That had been last week, and a euphoric Kate had spent the next few days in utter bliss. Oh, how wonderful it would be to see England again—and her aunt! When next she saw Olivia, it would be sixteen years since that day they said good-bye on the wide front steps of Tremont Hall. Sixteen years! It was hard to believe that so much time had passed. What a lot they would have to talk about! She would have to have photographs taken of the children to show Olivia, and some of Beauvais itself. And she would have to . . .

And then Kate came back to earth with a thump. What was she thinking? She couldn't jaunt off to England and leave this business with Michael unfinished! He had promised to wait to marry, but what was a promise to his mother when Jane was here with him, soft and beautiful, and perhaps willing. Kate would never forgive herself if he did something rash while she was gone.

But you can't guard him forever, like a keeper.

The thought came from the recesses of her mind, demanding an answer.

No, she couldn't guard Michael, she had to admit; she couldn't control his feelings for Jane by the sheer weight of her disapproving presence. But what else could she do?

She was still wondering that day of the picnic. Page had planned, and because she had worried and fretted about it, she was pale and drawn—so much so that Page took one look at her and insisted that she spend the day resting while the family was gone. She was to do nothing more strenuous than sit in the chaise longue and read a book, he ordered. It had been too much for her, having guests for three months, and she was just worn out from the strain. With the family away, the house would be quiet, and she would have an opportunity to collapse by herself.

Kate didn't argue. She *was* tired, and while the reason wasn't entirely what Page believed, she allowed him to think so. It was a relief to see everyone off while she stayed home herself, and when they had all gone, she went directly upstairs to lie down in the peace and silence to take a nap.

She lasted almost twenty minutes before realizing that she was wide-awake and restless with nothing to do.

It was so quiet, so abominably hot and humid, as if there were a storm approaching, and she was simply unaccustomed to sleeping during the day. Irritation set in as she tossed and turned, trying to get comfortable, and finally she uttered an impatient exclamation and jumped up from the rumpled bed.

Now she wished that she had gone to the picnic by the lake with the rest of the family. Instead of resting, she was pacing back and forth, becoming more annoyed by the minute because she couldn't sit still. She even contemplated having a horse saddled and joining the celebration, despite her wretched headache, but then she rejected the idea. She had promised Page to stay and rest, and she would keep her promise, no matter how impossible it seemed.

Thinking that a book might distract her, Kate went downstairs to the library. The wide French doors leading from the library to the terrace and the garden were standing open when she entered the room, but so oppressive was the heat that not even a breeze drifted through. She could feel perspiration beading her forehead, and she went to the doors and looked out, wondering why it was so still and hot.

Far away over the mountains, storm clouds were forming. She could see the mass of thunderheads moving slowly in the direction of Beauvais, and she thought briefly of the picnickers. There was nothing to worry about, she knew; the approaching storm was a long way off, and from the looks of it, it wouldn't break until nightfall, long after everyone returned. But then it would be welcome, she thought. She could already feel the cool damp air the rain would bring, and she welcomed the relief it would be after this intolerable heat.

She had selected her book and was just turning away from the shelf when she heard a footstep on the terrace. Thinking it was one of the servants, she waited. To her surprise, it was Roger who came through the French doors and into the library. He stopped abruptly when he saw her.

"Roger! What are you doing here?"

She tried in vain to keep the note of dismay from her voice. Throughout his visit she had successfully avoided an encounter like this, and she didn't want to upset everything now. She still wasn't sure how she felt about him, and she didn't want to find out. That she was still attracted to him couldn't be denied—any more than she could explain it to herself. Beside Page, Roger was only a pale shadow, and yet . . . And yet, he had been her first love. Unhappily, she supposed that would always make him special, unique—no matter how much she loved Page.

But she didn't want to be attracted by this man; she didn't want to complicate her life by feelings she didn't understand and had no use for. So why did her pulse begin to race as he paused in the doorway to look at her?

"I thought you were at the picnic with the others," she said finally, aware that the silence between them had gone on too long. Why was he staring at her like that? His bemused expression made her nervous. "Roger?"

He blinked, jerking his head a little, as if startled out of a reverie. "What? Oh . . . I was at the lake. But I told everyone I was going for a walk."

"And you came back here? Why? Don't you feel well?"

He came into the library then, running one hand through his fair hair that had become streaked with gray. But when he looked at her again, his eyes were no longer a faded blue; they were almost black with some emotion Kate didn't care to identify. Suddenly the room seemed more stifling than before, the oppressive heat almost suffocating.

"No, I'm not ill," Roger answered in a low voice. "At least, not in the way you mean. I just had some . . . some thinking to do."

"Oh." Relieved, she saw her chance to escape this strange encounter. She didn't care at all for the way he was looking at her, and she wondered uneasily what he had meant. "I'll leave you, then," she said, clutching her book and starting for the door. "I just came down for something to read."

"No, Kate! Please stay."

She stopped, halted more by the tone of his voice than the actual words. Slowly she faced him again.

"I wanted a chance to talk to you alone before," he said rapidly. "But there never seemed to be any opportunity until now. There are always so many people about."

"Why did you want to see me alone?" Her heart was pounding, leaping inside her breast, and she didn't know if she wanted to hear his answer or not. Why was it so intolerably hot in here? She could hardly breathe.

"Oh, Kate!" This time there was real pain in his voice. He took a step toward her, and unconsciously she took one back. He stopped then, one hand stretched out toward her. "I've never stopped thinking about you, Kate," he choked. "I can't get that day out of my mind!"

"Roger . . ." Uneasily she glanced toward the door. Page had given all the servants the day off, but one never knew. And if anyone heard this conversation, it wouldn't be too difficult to piece together what he was talking about.

"Oh, I know it's wrong to talk about it—wrong even to think of it! But I can't forget, Kate. I can't! I've wanted you ever since—you've been in my thoughts constantly!"

He took another step toward her, and this time she was alarmed by the expression of open need on his face.

It was here now—the confrontation she had both desired and dreaded. And now that she was forced to define her own emotions, she realized with wonder that she didn't have any feeling for him at all. Whatever attraction she had felt for him had been dredged from the past; she had clung to the memory of him instead of facing the reality, and now that she was able to see him clearly, she didn't like what she saw.

"Roger," she said sharply. "Control yourself! You can't possibly mean what you're saying! What about Amelia . . . and Jane? You're a married man, with a family. And I'm a married woman."

Roger closed his eyes tightly. "I know," he groaned. "My God, I know!"

"Then you can see—"

"I can only see you, Kate. When we first discussed coming to Colorado, I hoped that you had changed—become fat or ugly, anything to destroy the image I had of you. And then I saw you on the steps of Beauvais, looking even more beautiful than you had when I last saw you, and I knew what a terrible mistake I had made letting you go. Oh, Kate, can't you see how I need you!"

She stood there in shock, unable to believe what she was hearing. How long, she asked herself, *how long!* had she waited to hear those words? How many times had she agonized over Roger's rejection, rationalizing it by telling herself that it wasn't his fault? How often had she pictured them in fantasy, reunited at last?

And now Roger was offering her everything she had dreamed about, and all she could think of was what a sniveling weakling he sounded. He was almost in tears, as he had been that day at Green Eaves so long ago, and she could only stare at him speechless, wondering what had ever made her think of him as anything other than what he was: weak, and weak-willed.

But Roger wasn't finished with his plea. Somehow he had approached her without her really being aware of it, and before she could escape, he had embraced her, crushing her to him so tightly that she couldn't move.

"Oh, Kate!" he cried, so caught up in emotion that he was nearly sobbing. "You loved me once; I know you did! But I was too concerned about what people would think to accept what you offered me! I was afraid that everyone would remember your mother, and . . ."

With every word he uttered, Kate's anger had grown. Now she was almost blinded by rage. The room shimmered in front of her eyes, but she saw only Roger, half-fallen across Page's desk, looking at her with shocked surprise. She didn't even remember pushing him away from her; she was shaking with fury.

"You rejected me because of my *mother?*" she cried. "My *mother?*"

Roger tried to pull himself together. Scrabbling for balance, he righted himself and then clung to the edge of the desk, leaning against it for support. "I . . . I . . ." He swallowed, almost cringing before the rage on Kate's face. She looked like an avenging goddess standing there, with her blazing green eyes and her hair a fiery halo about her head. "There was . . . talk, Kate," he whispered finally. "Your mother had a . . . reputation. There was bound to be talk . . ."

Kate thought of all the years—*years!*—she had wasted thinking of Roger and what might have been. And in all that time she had always thought of him as noble, self-sacrificing, obedient to duty, even when that obedience cost him his own happiness. And now, to discover that he had only been afraid of what the gossips would think . . .

Staring at him in utter repudiation, Kate felt her own dreams collapse with a crash, like a child's house of cards in a gust of wind. But that was exactly what those dreams had been, she thought with loathing: a house of cards built by a foolish child who had deliberately blinded herself to the truth. She hadn't even the wit to see what was in front of her eyes all this time; she had preferred to live in a fantasy world, trying to believe Roger was almost as much a man as Page.

Page! Her heart constricted at the thought of what she had done to her husband because of Roger Templeton. She had lied to Page, and deceived him, and for what? So Roger could come here years later and cry about what a mistake *he* had made?

Kate clenched her teeth in renewed rage, not even sure whether she was angrier at herself for concocting such a dream of lies, or at Roger, who was daring to approach her again.

"Kate, please don't look at me like that," he begged. "I know what I did was wrong, but—"

"It's a little late for apology, isn't it, Roger?" To her amazement, her voice was cold; she had expected every word to be singed.

"Oh, don't say that, Kate—please!"

To her horror and disbelief, he fell to his knees, wrapping his arms around her and burying his head against her waist. As she tried vainly to free herself, he cried, "I'm sorry, Kate! I didn't mean for it to turn out this way. I never dreamed you would marry Page!"

She couldn't believe this was actually happening to her. With a final wrench she pulled away from him and said sharply, "Get up, Roger! And what did you want me to do? Wait for you forever, pining away at Tremont Hall?"

Thankfully, he had scrambled to his feet again. "Well, I . . ." He hardly knew what he was saying. To her stupefaction, he actually blurted, "Well, I . . . I thought that after I married Amelia, you might . . . you might . . ."

But even in his extremity, he realized he had gone too far. The look on her face was enough to chill him to the marrow when he looked at her, and he backed away before such blind fury. The desk halted his retreat, and he stood there helplessly. "I didn't mean it, Kate, I never really thought . . . I don't know why I even said that—"

There was a sudden crash of thunder over their heads. Kate had heard the approach of the storm without realizing it; the rumbling of the thunder as it came closer was only a background noise to the clamor inside her head. A warning winged into her mind, and then rushed away again; she was too enraged to pay heed to any danger signal. It had been a long time since she had lost her temper, but with Roger staring at her so pitifully, she lost it completely now. Injured pride, wounded dignity, and the crushing realization of what a complete and utter fool she had been made her lose control. She had never wanted to hurt anyone as much as she wanted to annihilate this man who had taken what he wanted and had not been man enough to pay for it. If she had been a fool, he was a weakling, a coward, and she didn't know which was worse.

"Kate, please don't hate me!"

"Hate you!" she cried. There was another loud clash of thunder, almost drowning out her voice. But not quite. The absolute contempt in it was not lost on Roger, and he cringed. "How could I possibly hate you? Especially when we have so much in common?"

"What . . . do you mean?"

"I'll tell you what I mean!" she shrieked, oblivious of anything but Roger's face. How could she ever have imagined him as handsome? How could she ever have thought of him as kind and considerate? He was a disgusting caricature of a man, and she loathed even the sight of him.

"That day in the barn that you remember with such fond regret—surely you recall that particular day, Roger! I mean, it happened only once, didn't it?"

Roger shifted uncomfortably, unable to take his eyes away from her suffused face, not wanting to look at such contempt as he saw there. Neither of them heard the flurry at the front door as the picknickers came home early, drenched from the sudden downpour the thunder had brought. Neither of them was aware of Page approaching the library door, or of Michael following him, or of Rory hurrying behind to see what the noise was about. Kate and Roger were conscious only of each other and the terrible truth that could no longer be denied.

"I remember that day, Kate," Roger said, weak tears springing to his eyes. "How could I ever forget?"

"Well, I can't forget it either!" Kate said bitterly. "I have a constant reminder of that day—a memento of what a fool I was!"

"I don't understand . . ."

"I don't know why not! That was the day you became a father!"

Roger went white. "A father? But . . . but you never told me!"

"Why do you think I came to Green Eaves that day? Do you think I humiliated myself by coming to see you simply because of a whim? I came to tell you that I was going to have a child—or children, as it turned out to be!"

Kate was so enraged by the utter bewilderment on Roger's face that she wanted to rush over to him and beat him senseless with her bare hands. Didn't he understand what she was saying? Did she have to make it clearer than that?

"The twins are yours, Roger!" she screamed. "Michael and David are your sons—*yours*, not Page's!"

"My God! No!"

"Yes! Yes! Yes!" She was shrieking at him, unable to stop herself. "I've kept my guilty secret all this time, but you can share it with me from now on! Now *you* can live with the fear that someone will look at David and wonder why he resembles you instead of the man who is supposed to be his father! And now, whenever you talk to Page, you can think how fortunate it is that he doesn't know his wife was once your mistress!"

"That's enough!"

Page's quiet voice could be heard even over the sudden loud drumming of the rain on the flagstones outside. For an instant before she looked around, Kate thought that she would faint from utter shock. Her towering anger vanished in the smoke of fright, and the hardest thing she had ever done in her life was turn and face that door where her husband stood.

It was even worse than she had feared. Page stood there, almost filling the doorway, his face so convulsed that Kate thought he might murder them both on the spot. But standing behind his father—or the man he had believed was his father all the years of his young life—was Michael. And adding to Kate's horror was the sight of Rory's red-gold head as he stood to one side. Kate saw all three, but her whole attention was taken up with Michael's sheet-white face.

Their glances met—mother and son—and Kate's heart shriveled at the look of disbelief and utter contempt she saw in Michael's dark eyes. Then his lip curled in loathing and disgust, and he uttered one scathing denouncement as he turned on his heel. "Whore!" he spat.

Shoving Rory aside, he was out the front door and disappearing into the rain before Kate could recover.

But as desperately as Kate wanted to run after her son, whose hatred had stabbed her worse than the blade of any knife, it was to Page she looked first. "Page . . ." She faltered.

They looked at each other then, and Kate didn't know which of them was wounded more deeply. She wanted to hide from the bruised expression in his eyes, but she forced herself to stand there holding his glance. "Page, I . . ."

"Go after him," Page said finally, his voice choked.

"But—"

"Go."

Her legs felt like string as she started for the doorway; she thought hysterically that the floor had turned to quicksand, it was so difficult to move. Then somehow she was out of the library and almost to the open front door when she heard Rory's triumphant crow: "I knew it! I knew there was something wrong with him! All these years, I knew he didn't belong. I was right!"

She wanted to turn around and scream at him to be silent, but there wasn't time. Michael was out there somewhere in the growing darkness, and she had to find him.

Rory's voice rose triumphantly. "I'm glad he's going! I'm—"

But as Kate covered her ears against that jubilant cry, there was another sound—the ringing noise of a slap. Rory's voice was cut off in mid-sentence.

"Papa!" he gasped. Page had never slapped any of his children, and to Rory it was as though his father had suddenly become an ogre before his eyes.

"Go to your room."

"But—"

"Go to your room."

"Yes, Papa." Page hadn't raised his voice, but Rory turned meekly and went up the stairs, holding his cheek. Then he thought that his father might have slapped him for the first time in his life, but at least he had the satisfaction of knowing that the man who had struck him was truly his father.

The thought cheered him again, and taking the stairs two at a time, Rory forgot the stinging in his cheek and began to whistle. The way was clear, he thought exultantly; with his hated rival out of the way, he would have Jane and Beauvais, too. It was too good to believe! The sound of the door slamming to his room was the sound of victory, and Rory threw himself on his bed and began to laugh.

In the library, Page hadn't moved. Thankfully, Amelia and Jane had already retired upstairs—tactfully or not, Page didn't care. But Adele came running across the hall, startled by the sight of her mother rushing out into the rain, tears streaming down her face. Even more alarming was witnessing her father strike Rory, and she was frightened.

"What is it, Papa?" she asked, clinging to Page. Her dark eyes were huge. "What is it? Where is Michael going?"

"I'll explain later. Go upstairs now, Adele."

Adele might be her father's pet, but even she knew when not to balk. There were undercurrents here she didn't understand, but if her father had said he would explain, then he would. He had never broken a promise to her, and so she turned obediently away. But her fear took hold of her again, and she stopped. Looking over her shoulder at Page, she asked in a small voice, "Is everything going to be all right, Papa?"

Page hesitated for so long that Adele wasn't sure he had heard her. She was just about to ask again when he answered in a voice so low that she had to strain to hear, "I don't know, Adele. I don't know. You'll just have to trust me."

When Adele had gone, swept upstairs by a frightened maid who had had the foresight to keep Randall occupied, Page turned to Roger. His expression, which had been carefully guarded in front of his children, was murderous now, and Roger actually quailed before it.

"I didn't know, Page! I swear to God, I didn't know!"

There was no opportunity for Page to respond, for just then David came in by the French doors, his fair hair glistening with rain, his shoulders damp. "I saw these open, and I thought . . ." He paused, suddenly aware of the appalling tension in the room. "I'm sorry," he stammered, looking from one man to the other. "I didn't realize . . . Has something happened?" he asked anxiously.

"Yes, David, something has happened," Page said.

"Is it Mother? Or . . ."

"It has to do with your mother, yes," Page said, tight-lipped. "Roger will explain while I go after Kate. Won't you, Roger?"

"But, Page . . ." Roger cringed before the prospect of telling this tall young man the truth about his parentage. David's eyes were so clear, so steady, his expression so kind, that Roger wondered humbly how he had sired such a son. "Yes, you go ahead, Page," he said, pulling himself together at last, now that it was too late. "I'll talk to David, and then Amelia and Jane and I will leave."

"Yes," said Page. He didn't even care that the storm outside had broken in earnest. It would be a long, wet trip to Denver, but Page knew that unless Roger left immediately, he wouldn't be responsible. It was all he could do to keep from killing him now with his bare hands.

"Page," Roger said, his voice low, "I'm sorry. God! You don't know how sorry I . . ."

But Page had already gone.

And outside, in the driving rain, with the wind whipping her mud-sodden skirts about her and throwing her loosened hair into her eyes, Kate searched the growing darkness for her son, her beloved Michael, who was so close to her mind and her heart. The pain she had endured giving birth to him was nothing compared to the agony she felt now at losing him. Again and again she called his name, and each time, the rising wind tore the sound from her lips and threw it away into the lightning-pierced darkness. It was hopeless, and she knew it, but she had to keep trying.

Finally, exhausted, she sagged against one of the stone pillars that guarded the entrance to Beauvais. Tears streamed down her face, mingling bitterly with the rain that beat against her, as she was forced to admit defeat. For an instant she thought she couldn't bear the pain that gripped her at the thought of all she had lost that day; it reached out to crush her, to suffocate her, causing her to bend double with the agony of it. With one last effort before she collapsed totally, she clawed her way upright again, holding on to the pillar for support. The storm tore at her, the wind trying to drive her back to the house, where there was warmth and shelter and comfort. But she would never be warm again, and with a heavy heart, knowing how useless it was, she tried once more.

"Michael!" she screamed.

The sound echoed hopelessly down the meadow, ending on a strangled sob.

And only the rain answered.

II

27

Rory Daniel Taggart and Jane Elizabeth Templeton were married September 17, 1888, at the social event of the season, with almost all of Denver's elite in rapt attendance. To outward appearances, the wedding was a huge success: the hazel-eyed, red-headed groom was handsome, wealthy—or would be, when he inherited Beauvais's vast wealth—and he was clearly taken with his new wife; the bride was austerely beautiful with her porcelain complexion, fine bones, and expressive dark eyes. If anyone noticed the marked pallor of the bride or the bluish shadows under her fine eyes, it was generally understood that it was just nerves. Kate knew better. And so did the bride's mother. And both women watched Jane anxiously, remembering the day when she had finally agreed to accept Rory's proposal.

Kate, eyeing Jane from her position across the room, where she had been listening absently to someone prattle on about how beautiful the wedding had been, reflected that it had been a year ago—seven years almost to the day since Michael's disappearance—that Jane had told her and Amelia that she would marry Rory. It seemed so long ago now, and yet it might have been only the day before, because Kate could remember it so clearly. She had accepted Amelia's invitation to tea, having come to Denver from Beauvais to shop and to see a new play at the Tabor, and even now Kate recalled her alarm when Jane had opened the door to greet her that afternoon.

Amelia's daughter had always been pale, but on that day she had seemed almost ill, with a white face and bruised shadows under her eyes. Kate had exclaimed in dismay before she could stop herself. It had been several months since she had seen Jane, for Amelia and her daughter had lived in Denver from the day of Michael's disappearance and Roger's death only hours later.

Roger's suicide was never mentioned. The taking of his own life had been far more swift, decisive, and violent than his living had ever been, and there was something more appalling than ever about an ineffectual man like Roger Templeton accomplishing something so brutal at the last. Thankfully, Page had found him, so thay had all been spared the hideous sight of suicide by shotgun.

Page didn't discover until several days afterward that Roger had failed to provide for his wife and daughter. Enraged, infuriated, and preoccupied as he was with his own problems, he nevertheless found time to purchase the little house in Denver for Amelia soon after that. He had given the title to her, and had even, without her knowledge, designed an annuity for her in Roger's name. Then he had forbidden Kate to tell anyone of his generosity, and Kate had no choice but to honor his wishes, even though it was inevitably frustrating for her to listen to Amelia's praises of Roger, who had provided for his family so thoughtfully.

If Amelia had some inkling that everything was not as it was presented to be, she never mentioned it; she also never questioned the fact that, seven years after Roger's death, Page had not stepped once inside the modest brick house on Cherry Street, and why it was Kate who always came alone to tea.

Consequently, Kate was by herself that day when Jane opened the door for her, and when Kate saw how drawn and strained Jane appeared, she wondered if the girl was truly ill. "Hello, Jane," she said, trying to mask her dismay. "I hope I'm not too early . . ."

"Oh, no," Jane answered in her soft voice, leading the way into the small drawing room off the entryway. "You know you're always welcome, Aunt Kate."

Jane had called her Aunt Kate from the beginning, even though they were not related by blood, and Roger and Page had been cousins, not brothers. But the title had always seemed appropriate, because there had been a special closeness between Kate and Jane from the start. Kate knew that their affinity was due in part to their shared feelings about Michael, and Jane had been a quiet source of comfort for her during the long years of Michael's absence. But she would not, Kate told herself firmly today, think of Michael. She would concern herself with Jane, instead, who looked far too thin. Jane had always been slender, but now she appeared almost gaunt. Kate was worried enough to ask tentatively, "Jane, dear, you're so pale. Have you been ill?"

Jane turned to her with a brief smile as she shook her head. "No, I haven't been ill, Aunt Kate. And I've always been pale. You know that."

"It's just that you seem so . . . so quiet today."

Jane smiled again. "Perhaps it's the heat," she suggested. "It has been so warm for September, don't you think?"

Obviously Jane didn't want to be questioned, and so Kate murmured something in response. She seated herself in one of the chairs by the open doors leading to the small garden at the back of the house, and Jane said, "Mother will be down in a moment or two, but perhaps I should ring for tea while we wait."

"That will be fine," Kate replied, wondering why they were being so uncomfortably formal. It wasn't like Jane, who, although normally reserved, was not quite so distant with her as she often was with others, and Kate watched her covertly as she went to the other side of the room to summon their daily maid. There really was something wrong, Kate thought; she could feel it.

When Amelia's housemaid, Polly, appeared, Jane gave the order for tea; then she came again to sit by Kate. "You're looking well, Aunt Kate," Jane said with another small smile. "Every time I see you, which isn't often enough, you seem to grow more beautiful."

Kate might deny this, but what Jane said was true. Kate at forty was a lovely woman whose character showed in her face, in her gestures, in the way she held herself. She was even more slender than she had been as a girl, and if there were shadows in Jane's expression, Kate had them, too. Her once vibrant color had paled slightly, as had her manner. But there was a new maturity and poise about her, a quiet composure that was as attractive in its way as her earlier volatile temperament had been. It was rare to see her green eyes flash with temper now; Kate was more introspective, kinder, gentler. Michael's disappearance was a wound from which she had never recovered; the pain of that day and all those since would be with her always, but the wrenching experience had lent her a quiet dignity that had been lacking in young womanhood.

The strain of the past years had also left another, more startling change: her once red hair was burnished to a dark auburn now, and there was a single streak of white threading through the reddish strands from the peak at her forehead. It was the only real physical sign of the lonely vigil of these past years, and Kate accepted it, as she had accepted every-thing, else. She had learned, through one difficult lesson after another, that to think of Michael was to bring on a terrible feeling of desolation, a depression that she kept at bay only through an almost conscious effort. She would not think of Michael, or she would despair.

Smoothing her gloves, Kate was considering how to ac-knowledge Jane's comment when Amelia came rushing in. "Kate! How wonderful to see you!"

As always, she greeted Kate effusively, bending forward to wrap her in a plump embrace, kissing Kate's cheek as she ex-claimed delightedly. "Amelia," murmured Kate, trying to ex-tricate herself. "How well you look."

But the years had been kinder to Kate than to Amelia, who was only a year or so older but who appeared ten more than that. Amelia had not lost any of the roundness of her girlhood, but now her hair was frankly more gray than brown, and there were lines of anxiety marking her full face. She had also, in the past few years, developed some inflam-mation of the joints that the doctor called gout. Amelia re-fused to believe him, and would not give up the rich desserts she loved. In consequence, walking was painful for her at times, and often her hands and fingers were so swollen she could hardly move them. But through it all she maintained a sweet and kind disposition, and now she smiled fondly at Kate as she sat down to preside over the tea cart that had ar-rived with her.

"How is everything at Beauvais?" Ameila asked, passing a cup to Kate. "It's been so long since we've seen you that I'm afraid we're quite behind on all the news."

Kate took a sip of the tea. "Page is working too hard, of course," she replied, refusing the plate of scones Amelia of-fered her. "But I can't really say anything to stop him. After last winter . . ." Kate paused, remembering the sight of thou-sands of cattle starving to death. The winter of 1886–87 had been a hard one for Colorado; following two years of drought, it had been impossible for many of the stock to find enough feed. Beauvais had fared better than many of the other cattle ranches in the state because they had baled what-ever fodder they could find during the long, dry summers.

But even with that effort, thousands of Beauvais cattle had died, and all over Colorado, ranchers had been forced to watch helplessly as financial and stock losses mounted with dizzying speed. By the time spring finally arrived and the first few nourishing blades of grass appeared, many of the ranches had disappeared, their stock decimated, the owners bankrupt.

But not Beauvais, Kate thought with a sad kind of pride. Beauvais had endured once again. And it had endured because they were too stubborn to throw up their hands in surrender, as had so many of their neighbors and others across the state. More than one blizzard had seen Kate and Page struggling against the storm, pushing staggering, floundering horses through heavy snowdrifts in search of their cattle. They had almost frozen to death themselves several times, but there had been no thought of giving up; they had sacrificed too much to let it all go. And despite Page's angry protest, Kate had insisted on joining him in the fight. They were her cattle, too, she maintained, and her horses. She wasn't going to stand by and let Beauvais animals starve.

And so, because of their refusal to surrender, Beauvais had not only been saved, it was well on the road to financial recovery. Now Page, in addition to all his other expanded enterprises and interests, was looking into sugar beets. Sugar beets! What would it be next? she wondered. And once more Kate was filled with sadness when she thought of Page, her husband who was a husband no longer.

"Kate?"

Kate came back to Amelia's sitting room with a start. "I'm sorry. I must be woolgathering today. What did you say, Amelia?"

"I asked if you had heard anything from David."

A shadow flitted across Kate's face. Michael's loss might have been less devastating for her if she hadn't lost David as well, she often thought. David, the quiet and introspective twin, had decided to become a missionary several years before. A missionary. . . . Even now Kate could hear Page's thunderous incredulity when David had told them he was leaving Beauvais. Page had shouted, she had pleaded, but David, so obedient and respectful before, had been firm. He had departed, sadly but resolutely, for Africa, leaving behind a bewildered Kate, an infuriated Page, and a triumphant Rory, who saw David's departure as the removal of the final obstacle to his clear inheritance of Beauvais.

Even now, two years after David's departure, Kate could
not think of him without feeling guilty. As many times as he
had tried to assure and reassure her that his decision had
nothing to do with what had happened with Michael, Kate
had to believe otherwise. It was even more difficult for her to
think of her son living in some appalling hovel, existing under primitive and horrifying conditions, without believing that
she was somehow responsible, no matter what David said. In
every letter he reiterated how happy he was, how satisfied
and fulfilled he felt giving aid to others less fortunate, and
while Kate knew that David possessed the sacrificing and
selfless nature for such a task, she often wondered if he
would have been driven to such drastic measures if she hadn't
been at fault.

"Kate? Oh, dear, you *do* seem far away today!"

Once more Kate wrenched her thoughts away from her unhappiness. She tried to remember what Amelia had asked,
and she recalled that it was something about David . . . Yes,
a letter. "No, we haven't heard from him in several months,"
she said. "But the mail from Africa is so slow that it really
isn't surprising. I'm sure it won't be long before we receive
something. David is always so good about writing."

Jane spoke for the first time in several minutes. "You miss
David very much, don't you, Aunt Kate?" she asked quietly.

"Yes," Kate admitted with a sad smile, "I do."

Jane turned to look out the window. Her face was in sil-
houette, and Kate saw the girl's loneliness in every line of
that delicate profile. "I do, too," Jane said.

Her voice was barely audible, and yet Kate heard the awful sadness in that brief admission, and she knew, suddenly,
that it was not David to whom Jane referred. She looked
down at her hands, clasped tightly in her lap. How terrible it
was, she thought, when an accident of birth, a lie, an omission of truth, could affect so many lives. Jane suffered for
what could never be, and there was nothing that Kate could
say to comfort her.

"Jane!" Amelia said. "I won't have you mooning about like
this!"

Jane turned to her mother. "I'm sorry, Mama," she said.
"But I'm afraid I don't know what you mean."

"You know very well what I mean!" replied Amelia, her
voice rising shrilly. "And I won't have you acting like this!

It's unbecoming and . . . and melodramatic . . . and . . . and absolutely wicked!"

They both stared at her, Kate and Jane, so surprised at this uncharacteristic outburst that neither could think of anything to say. Avoiding their eyes, Amelia took out her handkerchief. "I'm sorry, Kate," she muttered, beginning to cry. "I didn't mean to say that in front of you. It's just that I'm . . . I'm at my wits' end!"

"I understand. . . ."

"Do you?" cried the agitated Amelia, crushing the handkerchief in her hand. "Do you understand? I wish I could! But I can't . . . I can't understand a girl pining away for her own . . . for her own brother! Her brother! It's wrong! It's evil! Michael is—"

"I won't speak of Michael!" Jane interrupted sharply. "I—"

"And why not?" Amelia shrilled, turning to her daughter. "Why won't you speak of Michael, since that's the only thing you think of! His name is always between us, just as he is here right now with the three of us! Why shouldn't we speak of Michael, when he rules all our lives?"

"Amelia—"

"Mama—"

Kate and Jane spoke at the same time, trying to reach Amelia, who had alarmed them both by the wild expression in her eyes. But Amelia, who had tried for so long to suppress her worry and concern over the daughter she loved so dearly and had never really understood, was not to be calmed. Springing up from the sofa, Amelia faced her daughter. Two bright spots of color burned in her round cheeks, and her eyes were bright with tears. "Why shouldn't we speak of Michael?" Amelia cried again. "I think it's time—past time!—that we did. The three of us! It's time we said what must be said, before you kill yourself longing for something that can never be! He isn't coming back, Jane—and even if he did, there could be nothing between you. For as much as we all try to ignore it and deny it and not speak of it, the fact remains that you and Michael have the same father. The same father! To think of Michael in any other way is wrong! It's sinful!"

Wild-eyed, Amelia looked from her daughter to Kate. "She's killing herself, Kate—mourning for him! You can see it, can't you? How thin and pale she is, how quiet. Michael is all she thinks about. I can see it in her eyes, and I can't go on with her like this! Roger's death was enough; I can't lose Jane as well!"

Before the appalled Kate could move, Jane was on her feet. Going to her mother, she gently forced her to sit down again, and then she sat beside her. As she held the now weeping Amelia, there was a new respect in Jane's face. "I'm sorry, Mama," she murmured over and over. "I never meant . . . I didn't realize how distressed you were . . ."

And then, for the first time since she had been a child, Jane's formidable composure failed. Her face crumpled, and soon she was weeping with her mother. She hadn't cried when she learned that Michael had gone without a word; she hadn't wept when she discovered why he had gone. Numb with grief, devastated by Michael's desertion, Jane hadn't even shed a tear when she was told of her father's suicide. Since that terrible night she had deliberately crushed all outward emotion from her life. Drawing a protective shell about her, she had lived in a private world of anguish. She had spoken, eaten, slept, and awakened, and she had done all these things mechanically, as though to do more, to feel more, would allow the pain to swamp her, upsetting the precarious balance she had barely managed to achieve. But the intolerable strain had told; it could be seen in her eyes and in her drawn face. It was only now that she realized her mother was more aware of her struggle than she had been herself.

They had spoken of Michael, she and Amelia, but they had never really talked about him at all. Amelia had avoided the painful subject of her daughter's involvement with her husband's son as studiously as Jane had kept silent about it herself. And now that it was in the open between them at last, Jane saw with terrible clarity that she had been cowering behind an illusion. It was time to stop causing her mother, and herself, such suffering. It was time to face reality: Michael was not coming back.

"I can't endure it anymore!" Amelia was sobbing as Jane reached this conclusion. "I can't endure seeing you like this. You're twenty years old—you should have a husband, a family, a home of your own. Instead, you're wasting your life and ruining your health, locked away, pining for something you can't have!"

Amelia's voice had risen again with each word, and Jane looked helplessly over her mother's shoulder to Kate, silently pleading for help.

Kate had sat in stricken silence during Amelia's startling outburst, but now she rose briskly and went to rescue Jane. "Amelia," she said firmly as she sat beside her, "listen to me. You'll only make yourself ill if you carry on like this."

Amelia looked up then, her face tear-stained, her expression bitter. "And what is Jane doing to herself, I wonder?" She shook her head. "I'm sorry, Kate. I've tried so hard to keep quiet about it, hoping it would pass, but it's been too long. Jane can't spend the rest of her life waiting . . ."

Kate searched Amelia's face, looking for blame. It wasn't there. She had always wondered why Amelia kept up their friendship, such as it was, and she was even more puzzled after Amelia's outburst just now. Did Amelia hate her for being the cause, indirect or not, of such misery? Did she hold her responsible? Kate couldn't have blamed her if she had, and yet it seemed that she did not, for Amelia's eyes were not accusatory, but pleading, as they held hers, and Kate didn't know whether to be relieved or not. Perhaps she would never know or understand, she thought. But whatever the reason for Amelia's actions, Kate felt that she owed it to her to try to help.

"How can I help?" Kate asked Amelia quietly.

"I think I know," Jane said, composed once more. Her tone was cold, and Kate turned to look at her in surprise. "Mother would like you to encourage me to marry, not Michael, but another of your sons, Aunt Kate." Jane looked at her mother for confirmation. Her expression was as cold as her voice. "Isn't that so, Mother?"

"Well, I . . ."

Amelia's painful flush betrayed her. Kate looked from one to the other, and wasn't sure what to say. Suddenly she felt very tired. How could she encourage Jane to marry Rory? she wondered dismally. How could she admit that although Rory was her son and she loved him, she still could not advocate such a marriage? How could she say that Rory was not the man for Jane, and never would be?

Glancing at Amelia's hopeful face, Kate knew that if she said any of these things, she would have to explain, for Amelia would never understand. And yet she couldn't explain without admitting that something about Rory was . . . not right. There was something missing in this third son of hers, some vital element that might have made him less calculating, less ruthless. Jane, thought Kate as she bit her lip, would be destroyed in a marriage with Rory, for she was too idealistic, and her standards were too high for Rory ever to attain, even if he would have wanted to try. No, she couldn't see Jane married to Rory, and yet . . . and yet, a marriage with Jane might be Rory's salvation. Jane would be a balancing wheel, a voice of the conscience Rory had always lacked. Jane would be good for Rory, but . . . but what would Rory do to Jane?

Kate sat there trying to think. She had known for a long time that her son desired Jane, that he had asked her more than once to marry him. But was it because he was in love with her, or did his desire stem from the fact that Michael had wanted her, too? The competition between Rory and Michael had always been intense, and Rory had always been happiest when he had taken something away from Michael. Was this another acquisition? Or was Rory truly in love?

Without realizing it, Kate turned her thoughts to David—a David who was far away from her, serving his life as a missionary to savages in Africa when his family needed him . . . when she needed him. David was the only person Rory had ever listened to; David was the one member of the family who could influence Rory or discover what he really thought about something. And now, when Kate wanted David near, he was gone. How she missed him and his quiet assurance. How grateful she was, and always would be, for his gentleness and his consideration that last terrible night when Michael had left Beauvais. David had come to her then, offering comfort when he had been devastated himself. David . . .

Her thoughts turning further inward, Kate was unaware of Jane's puzzled expression; she didn't see Amelia struggling to control a fresh burst of tears. Suddenly she was standing in the driving rain, hearing the awful echo of her scream sound down the meadow. So real was the picture in her mind that she could almost sense at her back the stone pillar that guarded the gate to Beauvais; so real was it that she could almost feel the rough stone under her fingers as she held on to it for support. Tears and rain mingled on her face, and her voice was hoarse from calling a boy who would never answer again.

She was desolate, bowed under the terrible weight of guilt and grief. Sheer will kept her standing there, for she wanted to sink down to the muddy, streaming ground and be washed away into oblivion.

But there were others to think of, and she had spent far too many years of her life thinking only of herself. Page, she thought with crushing remorse. She must find Page and try to tell him . . . try to explain . . . to make him understand . . .

But then she shook her head. She knew that there was no explanation sufficient, no excuse great enough for what she had done to him. It was too much to expect him to understand, to forgive. But she had to try. She must try.

She was just about to push herself away from the pillar and go back to the house again when she felt the hand on her shoulder. "Mother?"

For a wild instant, her heart leaped in her chest, thumping painfully against her ribs. Michael, she thought. But even before she heard the voice, she had glimpsed his blond fairness in the sleeting darkness, and she sagged against him, so grateful that he had come that she wasn't even able to cry; so disappointed that it was he and not his brother that she could have wept.

"David . . ."

"Come back to the house, Mother."

"David, I . . . I'm sorry. So sorry . . ."

The words were inadequate, inane, and yet it was hopeless to try to tell him how she felt. Finally she put her hand over his and simply held it there. The rain poured down on them, plastering their clothes to their bodies, their hair to their streaming faces, and still they stood there staring at each other in the flashing darkness.

At last David said quietly, "He isn't coming back, Mother."

Her head jerked up at that. Peering through the rain in an effort to see his face more clearly, she said, faltering, "You . . . you can't know that."

But he would know, she realized despairingly when he didn't answer. Staring up at her tall blond son, who was himself gazing emptily in the direction his brother had gone, Kate thought he knew even more surely than she did. She was Michael's mother, but David . . . David was his twin, as close to him as his own heartbeat. He would know.

"You're . . . sure?" she had asked.

David hadn't hesitated. "Yes," he answered briefly. "I'm sure."

He had taken her arm then, as if he was afraid that she, too, would run off into the pelting darkness. But he was wrong, she thought dully; she hadn't the strength to run anywhere. She could only stand there hoping he wasn't as certain as he sounded, knowing in her heart that he was, and that she had lost Michael—forever.

"Come on, Mother. Let's go back to the house."

She walked slowly, like an old woman, every step a battle against the hopelessness that weighed her down. David's arm was firm around her, and as the blurred lights of Beauvais came into view, Kate was glad of his support. Page was somewhere inside that house, and if she couldn't find the words to speak to her son, she wondered in despair what she was going to say to her husband.

"Kate?"

"Aunt Kate?"

They were both staring at her, Amelia and Jane, and for an instant Kate stared back, totally confused. She looked blankly at them, and they gazed in concern at her. Then she realized that she was in Amelia's sitting room, and there had been an argument about Michael. It was all this talk of Michael that had thrust her back in time; it had been so long since she had allowed herself to think of that scene with David, or the one that followed, because the memories brought with them such anguish. And now Amelia and Jane were looking expectantly at her, and she had to get a grip on herself and remember only that Amelia was depending on her for her help.

Drawing a deep breath, she tried to speak evenly. "I was thinking just now," she said, "of the night Michael ran away. Yes, Jane—ran away," she repeated harshly as Jane uttered a quick protest. "As much as I loved him . . . love him," she continued, still looking directly at Jane, "the fact remains that he ran away rather than face the truth."

"An unpalatable truth!" said Jane bitterly.

"Jane!"

"No, Amelia," Kate said when Amelia exclaimed. "Jane is right. It *was* an unpalatable truth—a difficult thing to face. I know that more than anyone. But David faced it—"

"David isn't as proud!" cried Jane. "It mattered much more to Michael!"

Kate's expression was harsh as she looked at Jane. "If you think that, then you're sadly mistaken. David feels things just as deeply as Michael ever did, perhaps more. It's just that he comes to terms with them in a different way. David," Kate said with emphasis, even though it hurt her to admit it aloud, "was always kinder and more considerate than Michael. He has a generous, forgiving nature. Michael . . . does not."

Jane sprang up, her fists clenched at her sides. Her eyes were a dark blaze in her white face, and both women looked at her in astonishment. It was so unlike Jane to be violent that they sat in stunned silence.

"How can you say such things about your own son?" Jane cried. "About Michael, especially! You're his mother, aren't you? You're supposed to love him!"

Love him? Dear God, thought Kate, closing her eyes. *Love him?* Her world had shattered the night he had gone; she was still picking up the pieces, forcing herself to go on, not to surrender to the terrible pain she still felt at her loss. She would have accepted anything—even that contemptuous epithet he had hurled at her that night—if she could have persuaded him to stay. He was her son, her firstborn, child of her heart and mind, so like her that they spoke without words. That was why his going was so hard to bear: she *knew* he would never forgive her—never! Just as she knew she would never stop loving him until the day she died. Love him? Oh, yes . . . and more.

With dignity, Kate looked up at the distraught Jane. "It's because I'm his mother and because I love him that I can say such things," she stated quietly. "I love Michael for what he is—"

"So did I!"

Kate shook her head. "No, you loved him for what you thought he was. I know, because I made the same mistake once myself about . . . someone else."

There was a silence. Jane stood still, staring at Kate, and beside her on the sofa, Amelia looked down at the floor.

"Was that . . .?" Jane began, white-faced.

Kate held her head high. "It was a long time ago," she said. "I was much younger than you are now."

Jane sank down onto a chair. The room was silent as they all wrestled with private thoughts and personal agonies. Finally Jane spoke.

A change had come over her as she sat there: her expression, which had been stormy before, had regained its normal composure. Now her eyes were calm, and her manner

icily serene. She said, "You're right, of course, Aunt Kate.
But then, you usually are, aren't you? I have been foolish—
and a fool, living a lie all these years."

Amelia looked at her daughter, struck by that chilly tone.
"Jane . . ."

"It's all right, Mother. I see now how stupid I was, and
how much needless worry I've caused you." Jane's eyes became even colder, so that they appeared like bits of coal,
hard and shiny. "I'm going to do as I should have done long
ago"—she nodded toward Amelia—"what you wanted me to
do, Mother. I've decided I'm going to marry Rory."

"Jane!" There was dismay in Kate's voice, pleased surprise
in Amelia's as they exclaimed together. Then Amelia rose
quickly and swept Jane into her arms, embracing her delightedly as she cried, "Oh, that's wonderful, darling! It's what
I've wanted for you for so long! And Rory will make an excellent husband for you, you know. He's so handsome, so
charming! Oh, I couldn't be happier—could you, Kate? It's
wonderful, wonderful!"

Kate made some strangled sound, trying to clamp down on
her instinctive protest. Looking at Jane, she wanted to beg
her to reconsider, to take time to think about what she was
doing. Jane didn't love Rory, Kate knew. She wanted desperately to tell her that she should marry only for love.

But her objection died unspoken. How could she advise
Jane to marry for love? She hadn't. She had been in love
with—or fancied that she loved—Jane's own father when she
had accepted Page's proposal. What a disaster if she had followed her heart and married Roger instead of Page! She had
been young and foolish and willful and immature during
those early days of her infatuation with Roger Templeton;
she hadn't realized for a long time—too long—that Page was
worth a hundred Rogers, a thousand. She hadn't known until
that awful night exactly how much she loved him. But by
then—as now—it was too late.

Too late for her, she thought, but perhaps not for Jane.
Thinking of all the mistakes she had made in the past, Kate
forced herself to be silent. She remembered her vow not to
interfere in the lives of her children after causing such a
disaster with David and Michael, and she was not going to
repeat that error with Rory or Adele . . . or even Jane. Jane
was a young woman. She had to make her own decisions.

And so while Amelia hugged her daughter and burst into

renewed weeping, this time for joy, Kate was quiet. She only hoped she had made the right decision, not to interfere.

It was then that Kate happened to glance up. Jane was looking at her, and in the instant their eyes met, Kate felt her uncertainty grow. Outwardly Jane might have been smiling determinedly in response to her mother's delighted cries, but Kate saw, with sad regret, that her smile was only on her lips. As she stared at Kate, Jane's beautiful dark eyes were resigned . . . and cold.

That scene in Amelia's sitting room had taken place a year ago, and now, today, was Rory's wedding day, and as Kate watched the newlyweds accept the congratulations of Denver's elite, she still wondered if she had made the right decision. Rory might appear delighted as he stood proudly by his bride, but Jane was so white. Kate wished suddenly that Rory hadn't planned to leave the city immediately after the reception, but it was too late to ask them to delay now. He had promised magnanimously—and with his father's financial assistance and the private rail car Beauvais now owned—to take Jane on a leisurely honeymoon to New York. The train left late that afternoon, and there would be little time for Jane to rest.

"What are you thinking, Mother? You look so far away."

Kate turned with a smile, pleased to see Randall by her side. "I was thinking," she said with a small laugh, "that Jane and Rory's journey to New York will certainly be different from your father's and mine when we first came to Colorado. What a trip that was!"

Randall laughed with her. He had heard the story many times, but he never tired of listening to Kate tell it—along with the tales of other arguments and adventures that had become family favorites over the years. "Father says he was in such a rush because he knew you wouldn't come with him if he gave you a chance to think about it," Randall said, enjoying the game.

"It was more than that," Kate said dryly. "He felt guilty about not telling me what he was bringing me to, and wanted to get it over with as soon as possible."

They laughed again, mother and adopted son, and Kate felt her spirits rise. Randall was such a handsome boy, now eighteen years old, tall like her other sons, and with an easy disposition that made him a favorite not only among his peers but also with adults. His green eyes seemed always to sparkle, and he usually had a smile for everyone, or a compliment. As they stood together watching the festivities from the sidelines, Kate thought of Randall as her own son, and not the boy she and Page had adopted so many years ago.

"Rory looks full of himself, doesn't he?" Randall said after a moment. "But then, I guess he has a right to. A man doesn't get married every day, especially to a beautiful girl like Jane."

"You've always liked Jane, haven't you?"

"Yes, I have. I admire her composure and her poise. Do you know, I've never seen her lose her temper, or even heard her raise her voice?"

Kate thought of that scene in Amelia's house a year before and said nothing. But her expression was troubled as she looked in Jane's direction again, and her private misgivings increased.

Randall was speaking again, and something in his tone made Kate forget her doubts and bring her attention back to him again.

". . . not like our Adele over there," Randall said, gesturing. "Some men find high spirits in women unfeminine, but I don't. I think it's more of a challenge. And there's one thing for certain," he added, laughing. "Adele would certainly be a challenge for any man, wouldn't she?"

"Yes, she would," agreed Kate somewhat grimly. But she thought to herself that she wouldn't call Adele's behavior at times mere high spirits. Like her mother before her, Kate had to admit, Adele was headstrong and willful, and absolutely infuriating on occasion. Having a daughter who vacillated from one emotion to another could be exhausting, and Kate had long since sympathized with Olivia's troubles over her. She only wondered how her aunt had managed to remain reasonably sane during that one stormy year Kate had spent at Tremont Hall. Sometimes, Kate thought ruefully, she just didn't know how to cope with this mettlesome daughter of hers.

And it certainly didn't help that Page had spoiled Adele abominably from the cradle on, Kate thought when she happened to see her husband deep in conversation across the room with some influential railroad men. Watching him, she was struck by how handsome he looked in his formal black, how good-looking and distinguished. His hair had silvered even more these past eight years, and it became him; he looked exactly what he was: a self-assured, confident man who wore wealth and power as easily as he wore that broadcloth suit. A proud man, Kate thought, and more than a little arrogant.

Deliberately Kate looked away from her husband and back to her daughter, now the center of an admiring crowd of young men, and now she thought that Adele, too, looked exactly what she was: the pampered, loved daughter of a wealthy man, volatile, mercurial, temperamental, and—Kate hated to admit it—a little too haughty.

Kate sighed, proud of her daughter despite herself. The promise of beauty in Adele as a child had blossomed into reality in Adele the young woman. At eighteen she was almost as tall as her mother, as slender, and displayed the high spirits Kate had shown at the same age. Her honey-blond hair had not darkened from the rich color it had been in childhood, and Adele's dark eyes were surrounded by a thick fringe of dark lashes, giving her face an even more arresting appearance. She knew how to use those eyes, flirting outrageously as she answered sallies with sharp wit that was sometimes, Kate thought, too quickly sarcastic. But Adele's laughter rang out just then, a silvery sound that turned heads all around, and beside Kate, Randall stirred restlessly.

Kate glanced at him and was surprised to see his expression as he stared across the room at Adele and her circle of admirers. Was that jealousy she saw in Randall's green eyes as he watched Adele? Looking away from him for an instant, Kate was further astonished to catch a glimpse of Adele, who had glanced their way and who wasn't looking at her, but at Randall. There was an exchange of looks between them, a private, shared smile, and then Adele laughed again, turning away. The whole thing happened so quickly that Kate wasn't even sure whether she had seen the interchange between Randall and her daughter or if she had only imagined it.

But she must have been mistaken, for just then Randall turned to her with an inconsequential remark and a parting laugh before he left her side. Kate wondered if he would go to where Adele was holding court across the room, and her eyes followed him as he moved easily away.

He didn't go to Adele. Instead, he went to the small cluster of girls who stood shyly to one side, and Kate watched him bow courteously to one of them, drawing her out for a dance. Kate smiled to herself: the girl was Emily Siddons, the daughter of George, who owned the land adjoining Beauvais. Kate had bought several fine horses from Siddons over the years, and she had always liked Emily, who was George's only child. From the age of twelve, when her mother had died, Emily had managed the Siddons household, and while at seventeen she could not be considered beautiful, Emily had a sparkle in her soft brown eyes, and a cheerful and uncomplicated personality.

Not at all, thought Kate, with another involuntary glance in her daughter's direction, like Adele, who was more perplexing by the minute. She sighed. She had tried to point out more than once to Page how spoiled Adele was becoming, how haughty and impossible to manage. She had warned him that he would regret his openhanded indulgence of her, but he had dismissed both Kate's protests and her warnings, asking her instead why she should complain when they had a beautiful, intelligent, and self-assured daughter. What more did she want? he had asked in that cold voice she hated.

What more did she want? Forgetting Adele, she let her eyes stray toward Page again, and her thoughts were even more bleak. She wanted what he had taken away, she thought; she wanted . . . him.

He had never been the same toward her since that night he had learned the truth about the twins. In one single revelation she and Page had lost the closeness they had struggled so hard to develop over the years of their marriage; they had lost the sense of caring, of sharing. They had lost everything. Page had withdrawn from her utterly, shutting her out of his life so effectively that sometimes she wished she could elicit any emotion at all from him—even hate. Anything would be preferable to this frozen vacuum of a marriage in which he never even spoke her name unless it was absolutely necessary.

Kate took a glass of champagne from a passing footman and drank it quickly, blessedly alone for the moment with her thoughts. Alone, she thought. She had been alone for too long. It was as if she and Page were complete strangers.

Oh, they lived in the same house, she admitted; they ate at the same table and sat in front of the same fire. But they didn't share the same bed, unless it was one of those rare occasions when Page came to her and then left again as soon as possible, and it was only in public that they acted the role expected of them. To outsiders, the Taggarts presented a united front. They might have had their troubles in the past, and their sorrows, but such trials had only drawn them closer together—or so it was said of them, Kate knew. That was the image they projected so carefully, thought Kate bitterly, and it was the role all their friends and acquaintances believed of them. To all appearances, Kate and Page Taggart were a fortunate couple: they loved each other and their beautiful children, and together they had built an empire called Beauvais—place of beautiful open spaces. Place of empty spaces. . . .

As she watched Page pause to talk with someone else who had come up to him, Kate's mouth twisted. She had everything—or so they all believed, these people—and she would trade it all for one smile of genuine warmth from Page, one loving touch of his hand.

There was a place behind a group of potted palms near the wall that was empty, she saw as she turned her head quickly away. She was suddenly very tired, and her jaws ached from holding a smile she didn't feel. Making her way there, she sank into a chair tucked away behind the plants and closed her eyes. Only half-aware of the music in the background or of the conversation swirling around her, Kate put her head back, utterly weary. All day long she had tried not to think of it, but the occasion of Rory and Jane's wedding had brought back too many vivid memories of her own wedding day.

Looking at Rory, who was so obviously the proud bridegroom, Kate was reminded poignantly of Page on her wedding night. And when she thought of him at that time, and then as he was now, other, more painful memories came flooding over her, making her remember despite her vow to put that horrible time out of her mind. Now when she looked at Page, she could only see him as he had been the night Michael had gone, the night David had helped her back to the house.

David had taken her as far as the master suite upstairs, Kate recalled, too weary to fight the images that crowded into her mind. They had stood outside the closed door for a moment, staring silently at each other, both hurt in different ways. Finally Kate had mustered the will to say, "I'm sorry,

David. So sorry. I wish I could tell you . . . I wish it had
been some other way . . ."

Her voice faltered, and she had to make a determined effort to speak again, to try to explain to her waiting son the
reason she had acted as she had. "We were all so young at
the time," she said hesitantly. "And I . . . I was so confused
and frightened. When I discovered that there was going to be
a child, and when your father . . . when Page asked me to
marry him, I couldn't think of anything to do but accept."

She stopped, then said, "Roger had already announced his
engagement to Amelia. There was . . . no question of his
marrying me."

David was silent for a long moment, gazing at her with
compassionate blue eyes that made her want to dissolve into
tears again. At last he said, with a wisdom far beyond his
years, "I can't judge you, Mother; no one should. I know you
did what you thought was right; you always have, and that's
what matters. I . . . I will always think of myself as a Taggart." He swallowed, becoming a young boy once again instead of the man he was trying valiantly to be. "That is, if
Father will let me. Now that I'm no longer . . . his son . . ."

"Of course you're his son!" Kate cried. She grabbed his
arm and shook him a little, adding fiercely, "You'll always be
his son, David—he loves you! No matter what I've done,
Page is still your father—the man who raised you and who
gave you his name and his home. It takes more than planting
a seed to be a father, David, and Page has been more to you
and Michael than Roger Templeton ever would have been.
You must believe me—Page is your father in the truest sense
of the word, and he always will be!"

David had gone away then, leaving Kate staring passionately after him, praying that she had convinced him.
Whatever happened between her and Page now, she knew
that she had said what Page would have to David. She only
hoped that David would believe her.

But there was still Page to face, and Kate sagged against
the door to the suite, trying to summon the strength and the
courage to enter. It was only when she realized that she was
soaking wet and shivering more from cold than reaction that
she knew she had to make an effort to get out of her wet
clothing. Somehow she had to force herself to move. And
then she had to find Page. She couldn't rest until she had

talked to him. Or tried to. She wasn't sure he would ever speak to her again, or even listen to what she had to say.

He was waiting for her when she entered the suite. She had known he would be there; her hesitation at the door had been only a weak ploy to delay what she knew she had to face.

Now, looking at him and feeling her courage falter, she knew that the delaying tactic had been futile. What could she say, after all?

They stared at each other in silence, and then Kate saw that Page's hair and clothing were as wet as hers. He had been out looking for Michael too. But before she could comment, she noticed also that he had a glass in his hand, a crystal tumbler from the set he kept in the library. Had he been drinking? Her heart sank at the thought of facing that, too.

He saw her staring at the glass he held, and abruptly, it was he who broke the silence. "No, I haven't had a drink," he said harshly. "As much as I would have liked to."

"Page . . ." His name was wrung from her. She couldn't bear the expression on his face; it was as though he despised her—and himself, as well.

He looked at her coldly, unmoved by the emotion in her voice. "I haven't had a drink," he said, getting to his feet from the deep armchair where he had waited for her, "because I thought I should have a clear head." He paused, holding the tumbler up to the light. The crystal prisms refracted the light, throwing out tiny rainbows of color. Kate hardly noticed; her eyes were riveted to Page's face. "Do you see this glass, Kate?" he asked, moving it back and forth so that the colors danced on the ceiling. He watched the display for a moment, apparently absorbed in the play of light over the ceiling. Then abruptly he dropped his glance to her.

"This glass," he said harshly, "was the one I used to raise a toast in tribute to you the day Rory was born. I congratulated you on giving me a son. I didn't know at the time that he was my *only* son!"

Page threw the glass so suddenly that Kate had time for only an instinctive protest. The crystal shattered into a thousand fragments against the marble fireplace, and the rainbows disappeared. When Page faced her again, his face was so congested and his expression so fierce that Kate actually shrank back.

"Why, Kate? *Why?*" he shouted, and his voice was filled

with such pain that Kate cringed. "You knew it would come
out sooner or later! You didn't hope to keep it a secret forever, did you? So, why?"

Kate sank into the nearest chair. Suddenly her legs refused
to hold her upright, and her head whirled. Miserably she
looked up at her husband, at the man she loved, and she
didn't recognize him.

"Answer me, dammit!" Page shouted. "What were you
thinking of, to try something so appallingly stupid?"

His contempt at last stung her into a reply. Jumping to her
feet again, her exhaustion forgotten, she cried in response, "I
was thinking of giving the child a name!"

"Oh, and since Roger so inconsiderately refused to give
you his, you thought mine would do as well? My God!"

"It wasn't like that—not really! I was frightened, confused.
Don't you see? I was thinking of the child!"

"Oh, how noble!" Page sneered, unmoved by the tears
streaming down her face. "You were thinking of the child,
were you? Don't make me laugh! You never thought of anyone but yourself, Kate, and don't try to make me believe otherwise at this late date! You were in a dilemma, and I
happened to provide a convenient solution to all your problems—wasn't that more the case? How relieved you must
have been," he jeered, "when I made my timely proposal of
marriage. A month or so later, and the game would have
been lost, wouldn't it?"

He turned away from her, contempt for her vying with the
loathing he felt for himself. "And to think I was in such a
hurry to marry you that I never questioned why you were in
such a rush yourself. God! What a fool you must have
thought me! How you must have laughed! I can see it all
now: the arrogant Page Taggart brought low by the oldest female excuse in the world. And you were concerned about the
child!" he said scathingly. "That's even more amusing than my
pitiful eagerness to have you marry me!"

"I *was* thinking of the baby!" cried Kate. So great was her
extremity that she blurted out her innermost fear, appalled at
what she was saying, and yet unable to stop herself. She had
never confessed this to anyone in the world before, not even
to Olivia, and yet she exposed herself to make him understand. She had to make him believe her. "Don't you see?" she
shouted. "I didn't want the child to suffer as I had. I wanted
it to be secure, happy. As I . . . as I never was. I wanted

to give it a chance to grow up with pride and dignity, to *know* that it belonged, to *know* that it had a mother *and* a father who loved it!"

She stopped, gasping for breath. In the silence that followed, the only sounds were the crackling of the flames in the fireplace and the muted drumming of the rain on the roof. She had forgotten it was still raining. She had forgotten everything but the terrible desire to make him understand.

They stared at each other, and finally it was Page who spoke. "You made a fool of me about the twins, Kate. I could forgive you for that. But I can't forgive you for pretending to love me all these years, living a lie because it was . . . expedient. I never realized . . ." His voice faltered, then went on, rough with pain. "I never realized how capable you are at deception, and I suppose that makes me the biggest fool of all."

She was drowning in tears, suffocating, trying to speak over the anguish in her heart and the buzzing in her ears. But she was unable to utter more than a strangled sound as Page turned on his heel and went to the door. She tried to call out to him; she tried to reach for him to bring him back. But suddenly the buzzing in her ears became a roar, and she half-fell against the chaise as the violent explosion of a gun being fired ripped through the house. She froze where she was, and Page stopped in mid-stride. They stared at each other in confusion, and then Page sprang for the door.

Dazed, Kate tried to clear her head. Stumbling, she followed Page, who had raced down to the library. But even before she reached the door, she realized numbly what had happened. Roger Templeton, in a spasm of guilt and self-accusation, had taken a shotgun and put it to his head. Thankfully, Kate never saw the hideous results of a cartridge fired point-blank into a brain, and because of Page's quick decision, neither did the rest of the family. Kate had time only to comprehend the horror of what had taken place before the whirling and buzzing in her own head forced her to lean against the wall for support. Standing there, she was helpless to fight the awful empty blackness that was rushing toward her. In the corridor beyond the library door, with the male servants running back and forth at Page's command, and the maids standing by in stunned silence, Kate managed to whisper Page's name before she collapsed.

She had caught a chill. The doctor said that it was a combination of nervous exhaustion coupled with running out into the storm and then the subsequent shock of Roger's suicide that left her prostrate for two weeks, alternately fighting cold chills and a raging fever. Kate didn't care what the cause was; by the time she had recovered enough to stagger out of bed, Page had moved to the guest bedroom near the study downstairs.

It was only that he had a reputation to think of, Kate knew, that prevented him from going to Denver and finding comfort in the arms and bed of some willing saloon girl. As it was, he locked himself in the study every night for the two weeks she was ill and proceeded to drink himself senseless. The house was silent, servants furtively came and went, Adele and Randall were studiously occupied by a white-faced tutor, and David kept to his room. Of them all, only Rory seemed unaffected by the taut atmosphere at Beauvais. He strode about the house and grounds as if he were already the master and everything was his. When Kate caught a glimpse of him, she was almost surprised that he wasn't running jauntily down the silent corridors of the house, whistling a merry tune. Instead, he went about with a sly smile that would have infuriated her at any other time.

But Kate lay upstairs in her lonely bedroom, unmoving in her empty bed, staring dry-eyed at the ceiling and unable to summon any emotion at all. And down in the study, a very drunk, unshaven, and disheveled Page stared emptily at the gray ashes in the cold fireplace grate and fought rage and pain and despair to a standstill. And in the whole house, only Rory smiled.

They had been like strangers after that, Kate thought, each following an unspoken agreement to preserve the fiction of their marriage. They had maintained separate bedrooms for a year, and Kate supposed it was vaguely assumed that the chill she had caught had brought on some undisclosed "female problem," necessitating Page's move to another bed. Whatever was assumed, Kate didn't care. She had lost her son, and it seemed that she had lost her husband as well. Her grief and sorrow were absolute; she was too despondent even to realize that both Michael and Page had been unjust: both had judged her without letting her defend herself or listening to any explanation. The former Kate would have asked—demanded—a hearing; this new Kate, pale and drawn and apathetic, asked and demanded nothing. Her world had come apart, and she felt she had only herself to blame.

Page came back to her bed after a year. Driven by the needs of his body, he claimed his rights as a husband. But that was all. Kate's brief flare of hope at a renewed loving relationship died almost before it was born; their lovemaking was no longer fulfilling, or even pleasurable; it was the union of two bodies trying to satisfy basic drives that could not be denied. Page came to her when he needed her as a male needs a female; he did not come to her as a man who needs a woman. He gave his body because he must, but he withheld his soul. These encounters, infrequent as they were, began to seem furtive to Kate, distasteful, and even degrading. And yet she could not refuse him; each time he came to her, she cherished the hope that this would be the time she had been waiting for—the time when he wanted her because she was his wife, the woman he loved, not because she was a receptive body in a convenient bed. It never happened.

She often wondered, during those long empty years after Michael went away, why Page didn't simply take a mistress. In her more despondent moments, such a course seemed more logical to her than enduring these brief encounters that must have been as unsatisfying to him as they were to her. But he seemed disinclined to take another woman, and Kate never asked him about it. She wanted no reopening of wounds that had scarcely begun to heal. The subject of mistresses and lovers was one to be avoided at all costs in the Taggart household, and so Kate held her tongue and wondered.

And so she and Page had remained polite strangers, and now, eight years later, Kate despaired that anything would occur to alter the situation. Once begun, this new relationship seemed to have cemented them into roles they could not break; the strain and tension between them had finally coalesced into an uneasy truce that allowed them to deal with each other on a surface level, but nothing more. And she endured it, Kate thought now as she abandoned her hiding place behind the palms, because she must. Rory and Jane were preparing to leave the hotel for the train station, and so Kate smiled at the people who came up to her, responding mechanically to whatever they said and wondering dismally why she had to play such an unsatisfactory role. Everything, she thought sadly, seemed so pointless without Page.

She hardly knew what she said in response to the congratulations and well-wishes; she was covertly watching her husband as he made his way across the room toward her. His progress was halted continually by influential guests who stopped him to have a word, and before he could reach her, Kate saw that Rory and Jane were approaching to say goodbye. Jane paused to speak to someone, and Rory came ahead then, and as Kate looked beyond him to Jane, she thought unhappily that Jane looked as wretched as she herself felt. But Rory's hazel eyes were triumphant as he came up to her, and his expression was self-satisfied. He smiled as he bent to kiss Kate's cheek. "I have a surprise for you," he said when he straightened again.

"A surprise?" Gazing up at this tall son of hers, Kate thought that Rory had never looked more handsome. The formal black of his suit contrasted sharply with his red-gold hair and fair complexion, and in the past two years or so his face had lost its boyish roundness and had become more defined, like a man's. Now his jaw was firm, hard, and there was a new—and disturbing—expression in his greenish eyes. Rory had always been an opportunist, Kate admitted reluctantly, but now she wondered if he had become something more.

She didn't know her son as well as she might, she realized, for Rory had taken a room in Denver this past year, abandoning Beauvais in favor, he maintained, of being closer to Jane. Kate hadn't seen him very often during these months; he was always too busy—he said—to come home for a visit. Now Kate thought that she should have paid more attention to how Rory was faring in the accounting firm where he had taken a position, at Page's insistence, learning how to keep Beauvais's books. She remembered Page telling her the other day in passing that he had settled a few of Rory's gambling debts—small ones, he told her—over this last year. Now, from that disquieting expression on her son's face, Kate wondered if there was more to Rory's smugness than his simply being married that day. What had Rory been up to?

Before she could pursue this disturbing thought, Rory said, "I know we all agreed that Jane and I would live at the house when we got back, but Pa and I were talking it over, and we thought . . ."

"Yes?" Kate was alerted at once by Rory's tone. She was

so intrigued, in fact, that she forgot to correct him for using the hated term "Pa," which she detested.

Rory's eyes gleamed. "Well, we thought," he said smoothly, "that perhaps Jane should have her own house instead. It's nothing against you, Mother," he added hastily when he saw Kate's expression, "it's just that Beauvais has only one mistress, and I know Jane would always feel out-of-place, as though she didn't really have a home of her own to manage."

"I see." In a way, Kate was relieved. She hadn't objected last year when Rory had assumed that he and his new bride would live at Beauvais. But then, thought Kate resignedly, she hadn't objected to very much of anything for a long time. Something seemed to go out of her the night Michael went away—some vital spark that had dimmed and then faded completely when Page had been lost to her as well. She had learned her lesson, she thought dully then; she had learned well. Before, she had cared too much; now she seemed not to care at all. Without Page, nothing mattered. Or so she had thought. Rory's next words were like a dash of cold water after a long sleep. Kate felt something stir in her at last, and with surprise, she realized it was indignation. No, her feelings were stronger than that, she thought as Rory chattered on. Listening to him, Kate felt something she had thought never to experience again. With a jolt, she realized she was angry.

Rory was saying with apparent unconcern, ". . . and so I thought we could tear down that old cabin and build right there. It's a natural setting, with that bit of meadow laid out in front, and the hills to the back—rather like a miniature Beauvais, don't you think?"

"Are you saying you want to *build* there?" Kate asked sharply.

Rory showed a trace of impatience. "Weren't you listening, Mother? Of course we would build there. I can't take Jane to that old cabin, can I?"

Rory's tone was sarcastic, and Kate flared. "I won't allow it. No one is going to destroy that cabin!"

Rory was surprised at her vehemence. "But, Mother," he pointed out, "no one ever uses that place, or even goes near there. I thought you would be happy giving it over. That falling-down old cabin is an eyesore, and you know it."

"I don't know any such thing!" snapped Kate.

Rory was silent, surprised again at the anger in her tone.

Kate hardly noticed his reaction; she was thinking of the
cabin and what it still meant to her, even after all these
years.

She still made pilgrimages to that cabin, saddling a horse
to ride alone through the hills and the tall stands of pine and
aspen to the sloping meadow that led up to the cabin's front
door. The entire setting—cabin, meadow, woods, and the
mountains beyond—held so many memories for her that she
would often pause without realizing it, remembering the
meadow covered with snow or seeing in her mind's eye the
blue smoke curling up from the stone chimney against the
clear cold air. Without looking, she could see the berry
bushes where she had gathered fruit for jam; she could picture delicate mountain flowers and ferns growing beside the
icy stream where they had piped their water.

And always she would remember Hill Flower and that first
winter they had spent together. It was so long ago now, but
Kate still recalled vividly the day Hill Flower had so calmly,
and with such dignity, walked out of her life. So many times
as Kate stood inside the abandoned and cobwebbed cabin,
she had sensed Hill Flower's presence, and she was comforted. She remembered her friend's thick black hair and her
even darker eyes; she could see her bent attentively over the
twins' crib, or hunched over the now splintered table, concentrating fiercely on learning how to write her name before
Colin came home. But Colin hadn't come home, and Kate
had lost Hill Flower, too. And now there was only the old
moldering cabin and her memories of that happier time.

She had often gone there to wander about sadly, touching
the table, the sagging chairs, staring at the cold and black-
ened fireplace or at the falling-down shelter where she had
kept Page's precious horses. It seemed, sometimes, that the
cabin and the memories it held gave her the strength to go
on; it seemed to offer comfort and solace, reminding her of
better days, when things were not so complicated, when . . .
when Page had loved her.

No, she thought now, she wasn't going to surrender those
memories for anyone, not even for Rory and Jane. The cabin
was hers; she had earned the right to it as no one else had.

"Mother . . .?"

"I'm sorry, Rory," Kate said, dragging her thoughts reluctantly from the past in order to deal with the present. She
looked at her son. "I'm sorry, but I can't allow you to destroy

the cabin. If you don't want to live at Beauvais, some other arrangements will have to be made."

"But Pa said—"

"Your father," interrupted Kate evenly, "should have discussed this with me first."

Rory looked thoughtful, another expression Kate didn't trust. She knew her son's character far better than he liked to think or wanted to admit, even though he had been away from Beauvais this past year. And yet, Kate thought consideringly, it seemed that while Rory might have lived on his own, his father was more involved in his affairs than was his mother. Page had obviously been subsidizing Rory, and that would have to stop. Rory was a married man now; he would have to learn to manage his finances more competently than he had in the past. He couldn't expect his father to bail him out when his indiscretion overcame what should have been his better judgment.

But she would speak to Page later about this disturbing financial assistance. It was clear that her son and her husband had been talking of other things besides money, and she would have to deal with this new development about building a house at Beauvais. "I take it," she said now, watching Rory's face, "that you have an alternative in mind."

Rory grinned, smiling his disarming, charming smile that fooled everyone but his mother. And, Kate suspected, Jane. She waited, unsmiling.

"Well, as a matter of fact," Rory admitted, "I do."

"I thought so," Kate said dryly. "Well, what is it?"

Rory turned up the smile another notch, moving Kate not one inch. Trying to ignore his mother's increasingly stubborn expression, Rory introduced a reasonable note into his voice that Kate mistrusted even more than the smile. "Well," Rory said, "Jane isn't really a country girl, you know. And I confess I like the city life myself. I just agreed about building at Beauvais to please Pa. But . . ."

He hesitated, and Kate, interested in finding out how he was going to extricate himself, took up her cue. "So you both would prefer to live in Denver. Is that it?"

Rory nodded. "Yes, it is. But neither Jane nor I wanted to hurt your feelings, so I didn't want to say anything until you mentioned it yourself."

Kate ignored Rory's dutiful expression. "How considerate," she said dryly. "And what, I wonder, would you have done if

I hadn't mentioned it at all? Never mind; I think I can guess.
So you want to live in Denver, do you? Do you think you
could manage it on your salary? Of course, you couldn't possibly think of buying a house, but I suppose if you searched
long enough, you might be able to find one to rent."

Rory cut in swiftly, trying to hide his dismay and his anger
at the same time. Anger won. "That wasn't what I meant at
all, Mother, and you know it! My *salary*," he added scornfully, "as it's so euphemistically called, barely keeps me in
pocket change. How could I possibly afford to buy a town
house with such a pittance?"

"A town house!"

"Of course a town house! Why do you look so surprised? I
can't allow my wife to live in . . . in a hovel!"

Kate suspected that it wasn't really Jane Rory was concerned about, but himself. But his use of the word "hovel"
had brought back a poignant memory, and she remembered
all too clearly the day Page had stopped the wagon on the
rise to show her the cabin he had built. He had been so
proud then, and she had been so . . . unfeeling. She recalled
even now with painful clarity how derisive she had been, how
scornful, as she had tearfully labeled the home Page had built
with his own hands a hovel.

Wincing a little at the memory of how shallow and insensi-
tive she had been, Kate wrenched her thoughts away from the
past again. She had been living far too much in the past
lately; she would have to learn to deal with the present and
somehow find a way to look toward the future. This maudlin
looking back all the time wasn't doing anyone any good—
least of all herself.

"Mother!" Rory was saying in exasperation. "Are you listening to me?"

"Of course I'm listening! It's just that you haven't said very
much yet except that you're dissatisfied with your salary and
want to buy a town house in Denver. What do you expect *me*
to do about it?"

"I don't expect you to do anything," Rory was stung into
answering. "And besides, when you say things like that, you
make it sound worse than it is."

Kate raised an eyebrow. "Oh, really? Then what should I
say? What I can't understand is why you waited until now to
make arrangements about where you want to live. Shouldn't
you have decided that long before your wedding day?"

Rory flushed at Kate's tone. "I didn't want to hurt your feelings by telling you that Jane and I didn't want to live at Beauvais," he said angrily.

"Oh, I see. And you thought that by telling me this in front of our guests, I wouldn't make a scene. Is that it?"

"No, it wasn't!" Rory retreated into an expression of injured dignity, not quite knowing how to deal with this new Kate. He had been accustomed for so long to his mother's unquestioning acceptance of his plans, her indifference to what he was doing, and her policy of noninterference in his life since his detestable half-brother Michael went away, that now he didn't quite know what to say. "Obviously, then," he said, "since you don't care about it, Jane and I are free to decide what to do ourselves."

Kate raised the eyebrow again. "Well, I certainly applaud that idea," she said, "but what exactly does it mean?"

"I wasn't going to tell you, but it seems I'm going to have to use my alternate plan now, so I suppose you should know anyway. You'll have to sooner or later, I guess."

"Alternate plan?" Kate decidedly didn't trust that particular gleam in Rory's eye. "What plan?"

But just then Amelia bustled up, solving Rory's problems with his mother so neatly that all he had to do was step back, smile, and nod at the appropriate moment. Amelia took care of the rest.

"Kate!" Amelia exclaimed as she rushed up to them. "Have you heard the news? Jane was just telling me, and I don't know how she's managed to keep it a secret all this time. Oh, I'm so happy I could cry!"

Kate had no doubt that Amelia's tears would begin to flow, given the slightest encouragement, and so she said quickly, "Then do share the excitement with us, Amelia! What is it?"

Kate had a glimpse of Rory's face as he stepped back a pace or two after Amelia had turned to give him a hug, and she was at once uneasy. He reminded her, uncomfortably, of a cat who had found itself, suddenly and without warning, alone in the dairy beside the cream. Speaking to Amelia, but with her eyes on Rory, she said, "Perhaps you should explain."

Amelia, unaware of the undercurrents between Rory and his mother, glanced coquettishly at her new son-in-law. "I don't know how you and Jane kept it to yourselves, but it's such a delightful surprise that I can't be angry with you!"

"Amelia, please!"

Amelia turned excitedly to Kate again. "Well, I was feeling so sorry for myself at the thought of Jane getting married and leaving me all alone while she went to live at Beauvais, you know. You can understand how miserable I was, can't you?"

"Yes, yes," Kate answered, trying vainly to keep the impatience out of her voice. She forced herself to smile.

"And yet, it turns out that I'm not going to be so lonely after all!" Amelia went on. "What do you think, Kate? Did you know that a long time ago Roger set aside some money as an inheritance for Jane? Isn't it wonderful?"

Kate was speechless. She stared at Amelia for an instant in complete bewilderment before she managed to say, "Yes . . . yes, it's wonderful, but . . ." She paused, wondering how to go on. Why hadn't Page, who had handled all of Roger's affairs since his death, ever mentioned this to her? But before she could think of something innocuous to say, Amelia was going on in delight. Kate listened with rising dismay and a growing suspicion that something was not as it should be.

"Jane had to explain it to me, too," said Amelia eagerly. "But according to her, it seems that this inheritance was designed especially as a wedding present—that's why she didn't find out about it until a little while ago." Amelia clasped her hands to her full breast, her eyes shining. "And do you know what Jane wants to do with it? She and Rory are going to buy a house here in Denver. It's what her father would have wanted, she told me just now. After losing Green Eaves, Roger always told us that owning a home was the most important thing in life . . ." Amelia broke off and glanced fondly at Rory. "And Rory, so kind and considerate as he is, has agreed to let Jane use the inheritance however she wants. Isn't that nice?"

"Oh, yes," agreed Kate dryly, narrowing her eyes at her son, who smiled innocently back. "Very nice, indeed."

But if Amelia wasn't aware of the expression behind Kate's eyes, Rory was, and he tried at once to extricate himself. "Well, if you will excuse me . . ."

"One moment, Rory, please," Kate said, halting his escape with a firm hand on his arm. He wasn't going to get away from her this time, she thought as she returned the innocent smile he had just given her. Looking up at him, she asked softly, "Tell me, dear, but how did Jane find out about this inheritance of hers?"

If Rory was taken aback by the question, he managed to hide it well. Instead, he merely looked abashed, like a small boy caught in a mischievous prank. "Oh . . . well, I . . . I'm afraid I told her about it," he finally admitted.

"Oh?" Kate turned to Amelia with a smile that hid her growing suspicions about the existence of Jane's inheritance, and she said sweetly, "Excuse us a moment, won't you, Amelia? There is something I must talk to Rory about, if you don't mind."

Amelia was too filled with her own happiness to notice anything wrong. "Of course," she said at once with a knowing glance. "I must speak to Jane before she leaves, as well."

With another delighted rustle of skirts, Amelia was rushing off again, leaving a determined Kate alone with her son. "Now," she said before Rory could free himself, "tell me about this sudden miraculous appearance of an inheritance for Jane. If I don't know anything about it, how did you possibly find out?"

"You mean you don't know about it?"

"Don't look so surprised, Rory. You may be a grown man, married now, but you're still my son, and I know when something is wrong. And something is definitely wrong with this!"

But Rory's expression was dismayed, and Kate wasn't sure whether it was honest or not. "Oh, Lord!" he exclaimed, frowning.

"And just what does that mean?"

"Well, I . . . I thought for sure that Roger would have . . . I mean, he wasn't a poor man, was he? And Jane was his only child. It just didn't make sense that he wouldn't have made *some* provision for her, did it?"

Kate stared at him, her own dismay genuine, whether his was or not. "Do you mean that you told Jane about an inheritance simply because you thought . . . you thought there should be one? Oh, Rory, I can't believe you would do such a thing!"

"Dammit! How was I to know Roger Templeton would be such a complete fool? I thought for sure that any man would have the . . . the decency and common sense to provide a dowry for his own daughter!"

As Kate tried helplessly to think of something to say to that, Amelia returned, her arm linked this time with her daughter's. Seeing Jane's questioning eyes on her, Kate tried to pull herself together. More than anything else right now, she didn't want to hurt or upset Jane, who looked so pale and tired. Even with her weariness, Jane looked beautiful; there was a delicate patrician air about her that was compelling, and the pale blue taffeta gown she had chosen as her wedding dress complemented her dark hair and eyes. But Kate saw that Jane's composure was forced; it seemed to her that Jane was exhausting herself just trying to hold herself together until this reception was over and she could get away to rest.

"Amelia was just telling me about . . . about your inheritance, Jane," Kate said, responding to the silent question in Jane's eyes.

Jane brightened for an instant. She glanced fondly at her mother, who was so obviously delighted, and then answered quietly, "Yes. When Rory first told me about it, I couldn't believe it. I knew my father set up the trust that bought our home and provided for us, because Uncle Page told me so a long time ago, but he never mentioned anything about a dowry. I suppose he wanted it to be a surprise—a present for my wedding day. But I never dreamed that my father planned something so wonderful for me; I can't tell you how proud I am."

Once more Kate was at a loss. She wanted to say gently that she didn't know anything about an inheritance, but before she could gather her thoughts, Amelia was saying, with tears in her eyes, "I'm so happy for Jane. Now that she has a dowry, it almost makes up for . . . Roger being gone. At least we know that he . . . that he thought of us at the last, despite what he did."

Kate was silenced by these remarks, and in the pause that followed, Rory finally seized his opportunity to escape. Taking Jane's arm possessively, he said, "We really must leave now, Jane, if we're to make the train on time. Why don't you say your good-byes now, while I find Pa?"

But Page had finally made his way over to their little group, and Kate was so relieved to see him that she clutched his arm. He glanced at her in surprise, and Kate laughed a little, embarrassed. "We were just talking about Jane's good fortune, darling," she said. "But of course you knew about it all along, didn't you?"

Page looked blank. "Knew what?" he asked.

"Jane, it's really time to go," Rory said hastily.

"Of course." Jane bent at once to kiss her mother good-bye, and in the confusion of leave-taking and trying to cope with Amelia's tears, Kate lost her opportunity to corner Rory and make him explain to his father what he had done. The newlyweds were gone in a flurry amid a chorus of well-wishes and congratulations, and Kate, caught in the press of the crowd of wedding guests, looked after the departing couple in frustration. She suspected, correctly, it turned out later, that they had all been manipulated quite cleverly by Rory, and that, in the end, he had gotten exactly what he wanted after all.

Her frustration was not tempered by the fact that, as she stood on the hotel steps with Page, Rory's eyes met hers. He was about to climb into the hack that would take him and his unsuspecting bride to the station, but he paused then to look at Kate. There was triumph in the hazel eyes that held furious green, and in that moment Kate knew that Rory had bested them all. They stared at each other for a moment, mother and son, and then Rory jauntily tipped his hat to her.

There was defiance in that gesture, and satisfaction as well, and Kate's misgivings grew as she watched the cab speed off. When the confrontation came with Rory—and now Kate was sure that it was inevitable somehow, someday—would she be strong enough to stand against him? Could she—against her own son?

It depended, she thought, both on the nature of the challenge and on the prize to be gained. She only hoped, as she watched the disappearing cab, that the challenge was not power, nor the prize Beauvais.

28

"Are you telling me you don't know anything about Jane's inheritance?" Kate asked. There was less incredulity than resignation in her expression as she looked at Page and waited for him to answer.

It was late that evening of Rory's wedding, and Kate was exhausted. They had finally retired to their suite upstairs at the hotel where the reception had been held, but there had been no time to talk to Page until now. As tired as she was, Kate had to know the truth, and when Page shook his head in response, she sank down in utter weariness on the sofa before the fireplace. Someone had been earlier to light the fire there, and Kate stared tiredly at the crackling flames.

"If you don't know anything about it," she asked, "who would?"

Page finished pouring the whiskey he wanted and came to sit by her. "No one would know," he replied. "You know I was the only one responsible for taking care of Roger's estate—what there was of it—after he killed himself. There was no money; I've told you that before, Kate. That's why I had to do what I have for Amelia and Jane. But what is all this dowry business about?"

Sighing, Kate told him. As she explained, Page's expression hardened, and when she had finished, he said, "I imagine Rory knew exactly what he was doing when he told Jane about this nonexistent money. He wanted a house in Denver, and he saw this as a way to get it."

"Yes. But what are we going to do about it? Oh, Page, if you could have seen Jane's face when she said how proud she was that Roger had remembered her after all!"

"I didn't have to see it to know," Page answered gloomily. "She loved her father very much, in spite of everything."

"Well, then, what are we going to do? If we tell the truth, Amelia's heart will be broken, and Jane will be devastated. But we can't let Rory get away with this, don't you agree?"

"Damn Rory!" Page exploded. "If he were younger, I'd give him the hiding he deserves!"

"Yes, but he's not a boy anymore," Kate pointed out as Page threw himself to his feet and began to pace back and forth in front of her. "He's a man—a married man, at that—and we have to decide what to do about this before he and Jane come back from their honeymoon."

Page stopped pacing. "What do you suggest?" he asked, looking hard at her. "That I buy the damned house for him?"

Kate stared evenly back. "Yes," she said, wincing when Page swore and began moving back and forth again. "That's one alternative," she added, wishing he would either sit down or stand still. "The other alternative is telling Jane and Amelia that Rory was mistaken—or that he lied, which is the truth—and I doubt that you would hurt Jane or Amelia like that."

"I should make Rory tell them himself," growled Page, downing the last of his drink in one gulp.

As he set the glass on the mantel, Kate noticed how tired he looked. There were lines in his face that she hadn't seen before, and bluish shadows under his eyes. At forty-six, he was even more attractive to her than he had been as a young man, and yet Kate saw now that he was much thinner, almost gaunt. She was alarmed at this, and stricken that she hadn't noticed until now.

But when had there been time to notice—or opportunity? she asked herself bitterly. Everyone at Beauvais had worked so hard this past year, recovering from the losses of the previous year, and she was tired herself. There had been the wedding to prepare for, and all the thousand details she had been called upon to help with. She might have been the mother of the groom, but the bride's mother had been so befuddled at times that Kate had been pressed into reluctant service more times than she could count.

And it wasn't, she thought, that Page was the husband he had been before. They lived together at Beauvais, but they really didn't live together at all. Last night, when they had arrived in Denver for the wedding today, and tonight, were the first two times they had spent alone in so long that Kate couldn't remember when last they had shared the same room for more than a few hours.

So, trying to console herself with the fact that they were both tired—she was exhausted herself, she admitted—she managed to quiet her fright over Page's appearance. Perhaps she looked the same herself after the past hectic months and the strain of the wedding and reception today, and she tried to reassure herself with the thought that if there was something seriously wrong, even Page wouldn't try to keep it a secret.

Forcing her attention back to the problem of Rory, Kate asked, "Are you going to insist, then, that he tell Amelia and Jane he was mistaken—or that he lied?"

Page glanced at her, his jaw tight. Then angrily he shook his head. "You know I can't do that," he muttered.

Despite the seriousness of the situation, Kate allowed herself a small smile. She had suspected that Page couldn't destroy Jane's illusions about her father, any more than she could herself. Page was just as fond of his new daughter-in-law as she was, and he had said more than once that he was glad Rory was marrying Jane; he hoped, with Kate, that such a marriage would give Rory the stability he obviously needed.

Rising, Kate went to where Page stood staring morosely into the fire. She put her hand tentatively on his arm and said, "I'm glad."

"Yes . . . well . . ." Unaccountably, Page seemed embarrassed by her gesture. He straightened and said firmly, "But young Master Rory—married man or not—and I are going to have a little talk when he comes strolling home. If he thinks I'm going to bankroll his marriage, he's sadly mistaken!"

"Oh?"

Kate couldn't keep the smile from her voice this time, and Page, seeing her expression, said, "Yes, 'oh.' I may buy Rory his house for the time being, but he's going to sign a note and pay back every single cent of the money—even if it takes his lifetime."

"It probably will," said Kate dryly. "Junior clerks don't make money hand over fist."

"That's *his* problem. If he channeled his energies into making a living instead of spending every cent he can get his hands on gambling—"

"Yes, that's another thing I wanted to talk to you about! He happened to mention today that you had helped him out again. And after you promised me some time ago that you weren't going to settle his debts again!"

"Well, I couldn't have him go to his wedding in debt, could I? Besides, I told him this was absolutely the last time—and he knows I mean it."

"Do you?" Kate asked, unable to keep the sarcasm from her voice. "It seems I've heard that before."

"All right—what would you have me do, Kate? Turn him away, refuse to acknowledge that he's my son?"

Kate looked up quickly at the pain in Page's voice. When she saw his expression, appalled and angry at the same time, she knew instinctively that he was thinking of Michael. He had been so proud of Michael, always interested in his experiments and projects and inventions; he had been so pleased that Michael had accepted his responsibilities at Beauvais eagerly and naturally. Michael, Page had believed, had been his son and heir, his firstborn, who would follow surely in his father's footsteps. Michael, so much the antithesis of Rory, who was careless and exigent and opportunistic, would have regarded Beauvais as the trust Rory never would. He loved the ranch as much as Page did, and more.

But Michael was gone. And David too. And now there was only Rory, who believed in . . . nothing. And hardest of all to admit was that Michael, by running away, had betrayed Beauvais after all.

"Oh, Page!" Involuntarily Kate's hand tightened on Page's arm. She wanted to comfort him, but it had been so long since they had comforted each other that she was almost afraid he would reject her if she tried. And yet she couldn't bear the anguish in his eyes, for it was mirrored in her own heart. "Oh, Page," she said again helplessly.

He clutched her hand. They rarely spoke of Michael anymore; the wound of his disappearance was too deep and agonizing, especially after their failure to find any trace of him. It was as if he had disappeared off the face of the earth after he walked out that night into the rain; even the men they had sent to find him—detectives from the famous Pinkerton Agency—had come back shamefaced and empty-handed after almost a year of search. So while Kate's feelings were an agonizing mixture of grief and guilt, Page had tried all this time to deal with the fact that he had failed utterly to find the boy he regarded—and always would—as his son. He had had such hopes for Michael, who was more a Taggart than Rory would ever be.

"Oh, Kate . . ." he murmured now, and his voice was weary.

Kate, who was almost afraid to comment on Page's gesture of holding her hand for fear he would remove it from hers, said softly instead, "It's late. Things will look better in the morning."

"Will they?"

She forced a smile. "Well, at least Rory's wedding will be behind us, and things can get back to normal again."

As she spoke, he had dropped his hand, and so she was about to turn away from him when he stopped her. Surprised, she looked up at him, and her heart seemed to slow and then stop altogether when she saw his expression.

It had been a long, long time since she had seen that look in his eyes—eight long, endless, empty, lonely years, in fact.

She was afraid to move, afraid even to breathe, for fear that his expression of longing would disappear. Slowly her heart began its painful beating again, and a thousand words died unborn on her tongue. She wanted to say so much, and she could say nothing.

"Kate, I—"

They were interrupted by a banging on the door, a giggle from the other side, a loud "Shhhh"; and then, without waiting for permission to enter, Adele burst laughingly into the room. Her eyes brilliant, her face flushed from too much excitement and champagne, Adele dragged a protesting, red-faced Randall behind her. Kate could have screamed in sheer frustration.

"Adele!"

Adele paused briefly at her mother's sharp tone. "I'm sorry, Mama," she giggled. "I know it's late, and we're disturbing you, but I couldn't wait to tell you the news."

Kate closed her eyes, trying to control herself. Short of hearing the news that they had lost Beauvais, Kate didn't want to listen to anything, from anyone. She and Page had been so close just now—as if the cold barrier that had separated them for so long was about to crumble at last, and she wasn't going to lose this opportunity to destroy that wall completely, if she could.

"Adele, this isn't the time . . ."

But Randall, sensitive as ever to atmosphere, had taken in the scene at a glance. One look at Page's thunderous face was enough to convince him to make as rapid an exit as possible, and he tried to do just that. "Come on, Adele," he said at once, tugging at the girl's arm. "We can tell them later."

Adele shook him off laughingly. "I want to tell them now," she said. "They'll want to know, I'm sure!"

"It isn't the right time—"

"If you two don't mind," Page cut in, breathing heavily, "you can carry on your discussion elsewhere. Your mother and I . . ."

Adele, in one of the lightning changes of mood which made her both intriguing and so exasperating, frowned stubbornly. Her cheeks were flushed now from temper as much as from champagne, and her eyes flashed. A few tendrils of honey-blond hair had escaped their high knot to curl about her face, and she lifted a hand to brush them back impatiently. Her color was vibrant, her manner imperious, but

there was something in her eyes . . . She looked, Kate
thought in that instant before the picture was destroyed utterly, like a beautiful girl poised on the threshold of full
womanhood. She looked, Kate realized suddenly, and too
late, like a woman in love.

And then Adele blurted out her "news," and nothing would
ever be the same. "Darling Mama and Papa," she said with
high drama. "You'll never guess what's happened. I thought
you would like to know right away, and so we've come to tell
you. You're the first to know. Randall has finally asked me to
marry him, and I've accepted." Abruptly her haughty manner
dissolved and she became an excited young girl again, just for
an instant. "Isn't it absolutely wonderful?" she cried.

There was a sudden silence, and then they all turned
toward Page, who had dropped the glass of whiskey he had
just poured. The glass shattered at his feet, spilling pungent
liquor in all directions, but he didn't notice. To Kate's
startled surprise, he was staring at them all with appalled disbelief, his face completely white.

Alarmed, Kate exclaimed, "Page! What is it? Are you ill?"

He shook his head, hardly aware that she had spoken. "I
can't . . ." His voice was a harsh rasp; he cleared his throat.
"I won't allow it!" he said, his voice becoming stronger and
stronger with each word, until he was almost yelling at them.
"I won't allow it!" he shouted again. "I absolutely forbid such
a marriage, and that's final. Do you all hear me? Final!"

They all looked at him with various expressions of shock
and disbelief, shaken by his violent reaction. It was Kate who
found her voice first, and yet she scarcely knew what she was
saying as she glanced quickly from the ferocious Page to
Adele and Randall, who hadn't moved. They both stood
there frozen, staring at Page. He had never used that terrible
voice before to either of them, and the announcement that
should have occasioned rejoicing had instead become some
kind of nightmare. Then, her face crumpling, Adele began to
cry. Randall tried awkwardly to comfort her, but his own
face was ashen as he glanced at Page.

"I think we're all tired," Kate said quickly, trying to collect
her wits long enough to shepherd her children toward the
door. She didn't understand Page's reaction any more than
did Adele or Randall, but she knew the wisest course would
be to send everyone away and try to talk to Page alone.

"We'll discuss this in the morning," she said. "When we're all rested and can sort things out properly."

"But, Mama . . ." Adele sobbed.

"Shhh." Putting an arm about her daughter's shoulders, Kate guided her gently to the doorway. "Randall will see you to your room, Adele," she murmured, glancing over her daughter's bowed head to the stricken face of her adopted son. Randall nodded, responding woodenly to Kate's silent plea, and she added in a low voice for him, "I'll talk to your father and try to find out why he is so opposed to this. It isn't like him."

Randall frowned, looking once more over his shoulder at Page, who had turned his back on them and was pouring himself another drink. "No, it isn't like him," Randall said soberly. "Do you think I should talk to him myself?"

"No, no," Kate said hastily. When Randall looked hurt, she added just as quickly, "I think it's better if I do. Now, don't worry"—she tried to smile at them—"I think it's a fine idea, your marrying. I couldn't be happier, truly. It . . . it just seems so sudden. I had no idea . . . and I'm sure your father didn't either, Adele. Perhaps you took him by surprise. You never gave us a clue, you know." But there had been clues, Kate thought suddenly; if only she had been astute enough to see them. She had seen the silent exchange between Randall and Adele this very afternoon during the wedding reception; she had noticed that special private communication, and had dismissed it. Oh, why had she been so stupid?

Thankfully, Randall took the initiative. "Mother's right, Adele," he said. "We shouldn't have burst in on them like that. After all, we're hardly used to the idea ourselves, you know!"

"But . . . but . . . this is supposed to be a happy time—a wedding announcement," Adele sobbed, her face awash with tears. "I don't understand. I don't understand at all!"

"Adele . . ." Kate began warningly. The last thing she wanted at the moment was a temper tantrum. And from the shrill note in her daughter's voice, she suspected that such a display was not far behind the tears.

Again, to her relief, Randall took charge. He put his arm firmly about Adele's shoulders and said, "Come on, Adele. I think we should all get some rest and talk about this in the morning, as Mother suggested. We'll all be calm then, and . . ."

Speaking soothingly, Randall led Adele away. Kate could still hear his quiet voice over her daughter's muffled sobbing as they went slowly down the corridor, and she shut her eyes for a moment, thankful that Randall had such a good head on his shoulders. If anyone could quiet Adele right now, it would be Randall. And as soon as she had talked to Page, she would go to Adele herself and try to explain. They weren't especially close, she and Adele, but there were times, Kate reflected, when a daughter needed her mother. Especially after the father, who had always pampered and spoiled and granted practically every wish that daughter wanted, had inexplicably refused this request that was more important to her than anything else.

Carefully Kate closed the door. Leaning against it for an instant, she tried to gather strength; then she turned back to the room. Page was standing by the window, staring blindly out at the night sky, and Kate paused to gaze longingly at him before she said anything. They had been so close only minutes before, and now they were worlds apart again. She knew it by the stiff set of his shoulders and the hard line of his profile.

And whose fault was it? Kate wondered dismally. Hers, for not speaking sooner? Adele's, for interrupting them? Randall, who only wanted to marry their daughter? Kate didn't know. Wearily she thought that it didn't really matter. Whatever opportunity she had been given had been lost tonight. Now there was only this cold, uncompromising man to deal with. It had been this way for eight years; it would be this way for eighteen more, or eighty more than that. Page would never forgive her; he was even prouder than she was. Their intimacy a while before had been an accident, a shared moment of weariness, a realization that the years had gone on without their being truly aware of it. Today they had witnessed the marriage of one of their children. Where had the time gone?

"Page?" she said.

He stiffened. "I don't want to talk about it," he answered tautly.

Kate hesitated, recognizing that tone. Then she thought of Adele's tearful face and Randall's stricken expression, and she said evenly, "Well, whether you want to talk about it or not, I think you at least owe me an explanation, and one to Adele and Randall, as well."

"I owe them nothing," Page said harshly. He still had not turned from the window. "I'm the . . . the head of this family, and I owe no one explanations for my decisions, not even you."

Kate gaped at him, unable to believe what she had heard. Other men might have taken such a high-handed attitude, but never Page. He had never been . . . *feudal,* she thought angrily, and he wasn't going to start now.

Indignantly she said, "I'm afraid you're mistaken, Page. If you don't deign to explain to me, you might think of Randall. Your refusal even to discuss this marriage has wounded him deeply, and even though he would never say it, I know he thinks your reaction has something to do with his background."

Page turned then, his expression so fierce that Kate was alarmed. "Why do you say that?" he demanded loudly.

Kate stared at him. His eyes were like black pits in his white face, and his expression was so ferocious that she had to make an effort to keep her own composure. What was the matter with him? He didn't look like himself at all.

"I only meant that . . . that Randall has always wondered about his real parents—who they were and—"

"How do you know that?"

His face, if possible, had paled even more; he was almost gray, and Kate was terribly frightened. Was he ill? What was wrong with him? She didn't know whether to answer him or not.

"It doesn't matter," she forced herself to say. "The only—"

"It does matter, goddammit!" Page shouted. "How do you know Randall has always wondered about his mother and father? Tell me!"

Kate couldn't understand Page's sudden obsession with Randall's parents. But because he looked so awful, she stammered, "Well, of course it was reasonable for him to ask about them; we've never made any secret that Randall was adopted, have we? It was only to be expected that he would be curious."

"Why didn't you tell me?"

"Because . . . because it didn't seem important . . ." She faltered. She had regarded Randall as her son as much as if she had given birth to him herself, and she had believed Page thought the same of him. It was only now, when she saw her husband's expression, that Kate wondered—and wondering, her first appalled suspicion surfaced insidiously and without warning.

She looked at Page, and by some trick of her overwrought imagination, she thought she saw Randall instead. They had the same physical build, tall and lean; they had similar facial characteristics: high, wide forehead, strong jaw and chin, straight nose, firm mouth. Randall's hair was dark brown instead of Page's crisp black, and at eighteen Randall had not yet fully developed the confident self-assurance of a man like Page, but so many other mannerisms were the same . . . The same.

It was the eyes that had fooled her; she had never really looked beyond the eyes. Randall's were green, and so cheerful and uncomplicated that she had never really compared the two. Page's eyes were always so intense and compelling, so magnetic. She had been mesmerized by those black eyes for so long that she hadn't seen anything else.

Kate sank abruptly into a chair, aghast at her own foolishness. She had been blind, she thought—deliberately blind. It had been years—eighteen years—since she had allowed herself to see things clearly; she had been so stricken by her own guilt that she had turned a blind eye to what was there before her. She had allowed herself to comment on Randall's likeness to Page, but she had shied away from realizing what she really meant. Desperate to preserve the surface calm of her marriage, she hadn't wanted to probe too deeply into something that might bring her own sins to light. And then, even after her worst fears had been realized and the twins were admitted to be Roger's, she had been too burdened with guilt and misery to think of anything else.

But now . . . now she could no longer deny the evidence that had been before her from the beginning. The self-deceiving gauze was stripped from her eyes, and as she stared appalled at Page, she saw him finally, not as her husband, but as Randall's father. *He was Randall's father.*

Page saw the sudden awful comprehension in her eyes, for he took a step toward her. "Kate, listen to me . . ."

Springing up from the chair, Kate recoiled from him, suddenly unable to bear the thought that he might touch her. A thousand things to say raced through her mind, but she rejected them all. Horrified, Kate gazed at him, and saw, not

the husband she had loved and needed so desperately only
minutes before, but the man who had put her through eight
years of hell, knowing that his sin was just as great as hers.
The awfulness of it was almost too much to bear; she felt like
laughing hysterically at the irony of it, or screaming at the
absolute unfairness of it all.

To think that she had endured his cold and silent condemnation all this time without offering any defense or making
any demands! To think that she had accepted his righteous-
ness without demur because she believed she deserved it!
Deserved it! Oh, God, what a fool she had been!

He had made her feel despised and contemptible and
despicable, and she had accepted it all because in her heart
she had known she had been wrong. Oh, yes, she thought
wildly, she had suffered because of him, and she had accepted that as her punishment because she felt she could
never make up for the injustice she had done him.

But she had endured all this because she was the guilty
one, and she knew he was the innocent victim of her deception. Page would never betray *her*, she had thought—oh, no,
not Page, who was so honest, so just, so fair. Page would
never deceive her; he prided himself on his honesty, his sense
of justice and fair play.

Kate ground her teeth. To think how glad she had been
that Randall exhibited these same characteristics she had so
admired in Page. Little had she known that he had inherited
them rightfully!

But now it seemed that Page had betrayed her after all,
and she, who had trusted him, realized she had never known
him at all. Their entire marriage had been a lie, and now bitterness was like an acid eating away at her as they stared at
each other across a gulf that widened with every heartbeat.

Kate forced herself to stay where she was. She wanted to
turn and run—run away from the shattered dreams and the
terrible knowledge that this time there would be no patching
together of their marriage. The fabric of their relationship
was rendered, torn, and nothing could mend it again.

Somehow she made herself speak. The words came slowly,
forced past stiff lips and the searing pain of betrayal that
burned her throat and left her too empty even to cry. "Were
you punishing me with Randall?" she asked. "Was he the
punishment for the twins?"

Page's eyes were dark bruises in his face as he looked away

from her. His expression was agonized, tortured, and yet Kate felt no mercy. She felt nothing at all, only the barren void opening up endlessly before her.

Page took a step toward her. "Stay away from me!" she cried. She couldn't bear it if he touched her; she felt the slightest contact with him would cause her to splinter into a thousand fragments, and then she would never know anything at all. And she had to know. More than anything else, she had to know why.

He had paused, halted more by the shrill tone of her voice than the words themselves. Now he tried again, searching for words to explain, when there was no explanation at all.

"It . . . it wasn't like that, Kate," he said finally, his voice choked. "I . . . I didn't mean to punish you at all."

"Oh?" She wanted to hurt him, to slash at him, to injure him as mortally as she had been injured. "Well, then, what *did* you intend? It worked out neatly, didn't it? Here you brought me *your* child to take care of, when I had given you mine to raise before. How cleverly we used each other—and how easily I fell into the same trap I laid for you! It must have been so amusing for you all these years, punishing me so ingeniously by committing the same sin you condemned me for! How you must have laughed to think how blind and stupid I was for not seeing something so blatantly obvious!"

"Kate, please listen—"

"Listen?" she asked, and her voice was like a knife. "To what? You don't have to devise another lie to explain this, Page. I can see clearly now—for the first time in eighteen years. It *was* Ann-Marie, wasn't it?"

She saw by his face that her sudden inspiration was right, and then she laughed shrilly at his surprised expression. "Oh, don't humiliate me by asking how I knew," she said scathingly. "It's humiliating enough to realize that I should have seen it long ago, that day Ann-Marie didn't know I was in the office with you. She called you by name then, do you remember? And what else did she call you, my darling, when I wasn't around?"

"There was nothing between me and Ann-Marie when she was at the house," Page said hoarsely. "It wasn't until . . . until I took her to Denver after you dismissed her that I . . . that we . . ."

He couldn't finish, and so Kate asked brutally, "Do you really expect me to believe that you were suddenly swept

away by her beauty, or her charms, or whatever it was that
attracted you to her, on the way to Denver? Come now,
Page, I may have been a fool, but I'm not completely stupid!"

"There was nothing," Page repeated, "between us at the
house. As much as she would have liked there to be."

"Oh, I see. It was *she* who threw herself at *you!* You were
only the helpless bystander, I imagine!"

"Well, in point of fact, that's true."

"Oh, Page!" It was strange, she thought, but while she felt
like screaming and shrieking at him and not making any
sense at all, instead she was acting calmly and even ration-
ally. In the midst of all this chaotic emotion that threatened
to overwhelm her, she was still able to concentrate totally on
Page. She saw, with absolute clarity, the way he looked, the
gestures he made, even the careful way he stood, as if reluctant to move for fear she would run away.

In the silence, the clock ticked loudly on the mantel, the
logs crackled noisily in the fireplace, the gas jets hissed, and
outside, city life went on. Kate waited, watching him. She
had, she thought in sudden icy calm, all the time in the
world.

"Tell me," she said, "about Randall."

It was a long time before Page spoke. But finally he said
quietly, "Do you remember that winter when David almost
drowned in the pond, and you were so . . . ill?"

Did she remember? Kate's mouth twisted. Would she ever
forget? She had saved David, but at such a terrible price—the
life of her unborn child. Thinking about it now, so many
years later, Kate reflected bitterly that philosophers and cler-
ics might better spend their time if, instead of debating how
many angels could dance on the head of a pin, they could answer satisfactorily a mother's timeless heart-wrenching cry:
which child to save? Was it the one who lived, or the one
about to receive life? It was a question that echoed mournfully down through the ages whenever mothers had to sacrifice one for the other. And no one had ever answered the
plea. In the end, she had only done what she was able to do,
and that was no comfort at all."

"Yes," she said at last. "I remember that winter."

"Then you recall how despondent you were when you lost
the child."

"Yes," she said briefly again. "I remember that, too."

Page looked at her, asking silently for her to understand. "I was so worried about you, Kate. I was at my wits' end, wondering what to do. The doctor said that unless you came out of that terrible depression, you might . . . you might . . ."

"Lose my mind? finished Kate coldly. "Take my own life? Oh, don't look so surprised, Page. I may have been despondent, but I knew what the doctor said. But aren't we straying from the point? I thought we were discussing Ann-Marie."

"I don't care to discuss Ann-Marie—now, or at any other time. That episode is over—finished. I was a fool; I admit it. I don't even know how it happened—*why* it happened. I only know it was over almost before it began, and—"

"And there was Randall," said Kate cuttingly. "But how did you find out about Randall? Ann-Marie left Denver long before she could have delivered her child. Did you want her so much that you followed her?"

"No! *I* was the one who sent Ann-Marie away! I gave her money to leave. Don't you see? After that disastrous encounter, I never wanted to see her again!"

"Then how did you know about Randall?" Kate's voice was steely; she wasn't going to give Page an inch.

"She wrote me, of course!" Page exploded. "Damn her! She left Denver, all right, but she came back to tell me that she didn't want Randall, that she would give him up to an orphanage if I wouldn't take him. She would have abandoned him without a moment's thought, Kate! I know she would have!"

"And so?"

"And so, there was Randall . . . and there was my wife, almost out of her mind with grief over losing a child. Is it any wonder that I thought of bringing you both together—a child in need of a mother, and a woman so desperately in want of a child?"

Kate was silent. Then she spoke, and all the anger and hurt and disillusionment she felt were reflected in her voice. "No, Page," she said without mercy. "It's no wonder that you brought us together. The wonder is that you dared to do it, and then punish me years later for having committed the same sin. Tell me," she added, her expression relentless, "how you justified that in your own mind—you who pride yourself on fairness and justice?"

But Page couldn't answer, as she had known he couldn't,

and suddenly she had to get away from him before her bitterness overwhelmed her.

Very calmly she walked to the door. But once there, with her hand on the porcelain knob for support, she turned back to Page. His face, in the harsh gaslight, was haggard, his eyes bleak. He started to say something, but fell silent at her expression. Where the strength came from to stand there and say what must be said, she didn't know. She was only grateful that there was some reserve left in her to tap—something that made her strong, when she wanted to sink into a huddled miserable heap on the floor. She wouldn't allow herself to be affected by Page's obvious misery, for then her own unhappiness would swamp her, and there were still things to be done, plans to be made. But it amazed her that she could feel pity for Page after what he had done to her, and she despised herself for it. If there was anyone to pity, she thought coldly, it was Randall, who didn't understand why Page had acted as he did; and Adele, who was crushed and heartbroken by her father's inexorable refusal. Kate would think of Randall and Adele, and of no one else—not even herself.

"I imagine," she said, "that you will want to speak to Randall about this."

Page took a deep breath, and Kate knew that he was thinking that it had all come full circle: she had been in the same position eight years ago with her sons; now Page must face his. She allowed herself an acid smile. At least, she thought remorselessly, Page would be given a chance to try to explain. He was a man, after all, and allowed such lapses. Women were judged more harshly. In similar circumstances, men were excused their indiscretions. Women, Kate thought with sharp remembered pain, were called whores.

Page saw the gall in her expression, and he said, "I'll speak to Adele, as well, if you like. If you think that's best."

For an instant, Kate was tempted to allow it. But then she thought of her daughter, and she knew that she had to try to explain this to Adele herself. Later, perhaps, when there had been time for them to try to adjust to this change in their lives, she would send Adele to Page, but not now. Instinctively Kate knew that it was too soon for father to confront daughter; Page would have difficulty enough facing Randall.

And why, she asked herself bitterly, was she concerned about Page's difficulties? Why was she concerned about him at all? She was the one who had been wronged—she and Adele and Randall. Why was she thinking of Page?

It was just that she couldn't let go—not yet. She felt so empty . . . so drained. It was an effort to stand here, grimly clutching the door for support, trying to dredge up the strength even to say that she hated Page, that she despised him—not for what he and Ann-Marie had done, but for his punishment of her. She wanted to tell him that she understood how such a thing had happened—who better than she would understand? she wondered—but she wanted even more to ask why he had treated her with such contempt these past years, when all he had to do was look at Randall and know that while what she had done was wrong, he had been wrong, too.

It was so monstrously unfair of him that she felt like she had been trapped in some hideous nightmare, that she had stepped suddenly into some other world where nothing made sense and there were no rules of conduct—just random impulse and confusing reactions. Whatever else had happened in her life with Page, Kate had trusted him because she had believed in his honesty. And now it was all a lie, and she was so shaken that she didn't even know what to say to end it.

Somehow she managed to scrape together a few fragments of dignity. "I'll speak to Adele myself, Page," she said with only a slight tremble in her voice. "And then . . . and then . . ." She had to pause. There were tears gathering behind her eyes, and she could hardly speak over the lump in her throat. But the words had to be said, no matter how hurtful to either of them. She would never be able to live with herself if she didn't speak, and yet she wondered emptily how she was going to endure living after she did.

Swallowing hard, she forced herself to look directly at him. His expression was even more desolate than she felt, but she made herself say, "I think after that it would be best if Adele and I went away for a while."

"Away?"

She could not endure the pain in his voice. So she spoke quickly, the words tumbling over each other—talking rapidly so that he wouldn't talk himself. She couldn't bear it if he spoke. "Yes," she said, "away. I think that Adele will need time—distraction—to get over this . . . this situation. And I need time myself, to think. To decide if I want to come back to Beauvais."

He was shaken, she could see. It hadn't occurred to him that she would actually leave Beauvais—or that she would wonder if she wanted to return. The thought made her angry, and she was just about to say something when he spoke.

"I don't want you to go, Kate," he said, his voice deep with emotion. His eyes were so intense as he looked at her that they appeared coal black. "Whatever it is, we can work it out here."

"And what about Adele?" Kate said, welcoming her growing anger, because it gave her flagging courage a boost. Now she could face him with her head high and no trace of tremor in her voice. "And what about Randall? What do we say to them?" she demanded. "How will they feel, seeing each other every day, and knowing . . . ?"

"They'll have to face it, Kate. Just as we have to face it."

"Oh, how glibly you talk of facing things!" cried Kate. "How easy it is for you to stand there and act so righteous— as if *you* were the one who was wronged! But then, you've had so much practice acting the part of the long-suffering husband, haven't you? Eight years of it, to be exact! How smug and self-satisfied you sounded just then, Page! Facing it! As if things could ever be so simple as that!"

"I only meant that running away would solve nothing."

But Kate, now that she had broken through that emotionless state that had held her before, gave her anger full rein. "And who says I'm running away? Or are you so busy thinking of yourself that you can't spare a thought for anyone else?"

"That's not fair, Kate, and you know it!"

"Not fair!" she cried incredulously. "Not *fair*? You actually have the gall to stand there and accuse me of that? And what were you, pray tell, all these years you so cleverly hid the fact that Randall was truly your son?"

Provoked by her attack, Page responded, "You're not so innocent in that regard yourself, Kate. You did the same thing with the twins."

"Yes!" she shouted back at him. "I'm as guilty as you are—I admit it! But I've paid for it every day the past eight years—every day, when you treated me like a stranger in my own home, like a glorified bookkeeper or housekeeper, an employee who just happened to be your wife! And the nights, Page—the nights! Wanting you to come to my bed, and hating it when you did come, because I knew—I *knew*—I was just a convenience, an outlet for drives you couldn't deny, no matter how hard you tried. I wondered why you never took a mistress—oh, yes, I wondered—and now I know the reason why, don't I? You didn't need to take a mistress because you already had one!"

"That's not true! Except for those two weeks in Denver with Ann-Marie, there has never been another woman but you since we married. I swear it!"

"Oh, don't make me laugh! You had to—"

"No! No, don't think that I—"

"What do you want me to think, then?" she screamed at him. "Tell me! Tell me so that I'll know just what was on your mind these past eight years!"

"I thought if you knew about Randall, you would leave me," Page said, his expression haggard. "I wouldn't have blamed you if you had, and yet every day of those eight years I was afraid you would guess, or someone else would." He took a deep breath, trying to control his voice. "And as time went on," he continued doggedly, while Kate looked at him in contempt, "my secret seemed almost safe, and instead of being relieved, I felt more guilty, more ashamed." His eyes burned into hers, and still she stood with her head high, her mouth a tight, disbelieving line. "Even then I couldn't stay away from you, Kate. Even then, when I knew what I had done and was doing to you because of it, I couldn't stay away. I wanted to tell you, to confess, to be done with that agony of uncertainty, but I thought if I told you, I would lose you completely. I could stand anything, Kate, but I couldn't take that."

She would not allow her pain to stop her. The battle was with words now, and if the wounds were more agonizing than if they had been fighting with rapiers or stabbing each other with swords, she still had to go on. Knowing that they were hurting each other beyond repair, she was unable to halt the hateful flow of words. "And so because you felt guilty, you made me pay for it!" she cried.

"No! I . . ." But he stopped at the absolute contempt written on her face. "Yes," he said.

"And I paid for it, Page," she said bitterly, so angry at his admission that she was shaking. "I still pay for it every day that Michael is gone and no one knows where he is or what happened to him. I pay for it whenever I think of David so far away, giving his life to savages that don't even care about the sacrifices he's making for them. I pay whenever you look at me as if you hate me. But the highest price I've paid is knowing now that you punished me for the same sin you committed yourself. I'll never forgive you for that, Page. Never!"

In the silence that followed, Kate looked at the man she had loved and admired and respected more than any man she had ever met, and she knew that no matter what was said between them now, nothing would ever be the same. They stood staring at each other across an endless barren landscape of misunderstanding and deception and stubborn pride, and suddenly Kate knew that there was nothing to say anymore, after all.

Blindly she reached behind her and opened the door. Without looking back, she stepped outside and closed the door behind her.

But outside in the corridor, alone in the ringing silence, she leaned against the door she had just shut, too exhausted to move any farther. Looking up, she felt the sting of tears behind her eyes—tears that wouldn't come. She was too empty.

With a great effort she pushed herself away from the door. Wearily she started toward Adele's room, her head bowed under an intolerable weight of guilt and responsibility. She felt old, and unutterably tired, and as she walked slowly down the corridor, she thought brokenly: Dear God, what have we done to our children?

And then, weighing even more heavily on her, so that it seemed almost impossible to raise her hand to knock at Adele's door, there came another thought, a cry from her heart and soul.

What, she wondered, agonized, had they done to each other?

Somehow Kate managed to hold herself together during the hurried preparation for the trip to England. She even maintained a brittle control during the long journey across half a continent and a rough Atlantic Ocean all the way from Beauvais to Liverpool and beyond, enduring the trip for her white-faced and silent daughter's sake.

It wasn't until the hired carriage had passed through the tall iron gates of Tremont Hall and they were nearing the house itself that Kate allowed herself to realize the terrible strain she had been living under these past weeks. Tears came to her eyes as the vehicle halted in front of the wide steps she remembered so well, and she blinked rapidly, trying not to cry. Reaching for Adele's cold hand, she squeezed the girl's fingers reassuringly, but before she could react to her daughter's lack of response, the coachman had opened the carriage door, and Kate saw Olivia waiting for her.

The two women stared at each other across the expanse from doorway to carriage, and Kate saw at once how little and how much her aunt had changed. Olivia's hair was completely silver now, and she seemed to have become smaller. But there was still the same subdued sparkle in her hazel eyes, and the same wry smile on her lips. She stood framed in the doorway of the first real home Kate had ever known, and as she saw Kate's expression, Olivia's smile became sad. Wordlessly she held out her arms.

Kate didn't hesitate. With only a brief assist from the coachman, she was out of the carriage and flying up the steps, a girl once more, coming home to the wise reassurances of a loving mother.

They looked at each other for only an instant when Kate reached her, but in that single moment Olivia saw and understood, as she always had, the pain and hurt in those deep green eyes shining suddenly with all the unshed tears Kate had withheld for so long.

"Oh, Kate," said Olivia softly, and enfolded her in comforting arms.

29

". . . and so I made arrangements to leave immediately with Adele," Kate said, much later, to Olivia. She had unpacked by that time, and had rested—the first sound sleep she had had in weeks. Olivia had given Kate her old room, and after wandering about nostalgically, touching things she remembered so well, Kate had finally thrown herself down on the bed and slept the afternoon away, physically spent and emotionally exhausted.

Olivia had sent one of the maids to wake her in time for a late tea, and Kate was astonished to find that it was almost sunset. She couldn't remember the last time she had napped during the day; there was always so much to do at Beauvais. And then, she thought as she hurriedly changed her gown, she hadn't been able to sleep at all since that horrible scene with Page.

Now, as she gave herself a final quick inspection in the mirror, she admitted that the rest had been good for her; the weariness she had felt since Rory's wedding day was gone, and she didn't look so drawn and tired. When she went downstairs to the drawing room where Olivia waited, Kate felt rested and refreshed. Sitting opposite her aunt, watching Olivia pour her a cup of tea, she felt almost like herself. Until they had begun talking of Page.

Looking down, she saw that her hands were tightly clenched in her lap, and she had to make a considerable effort to relax when she accepted the cup Olivia passed across to her.

"And how," asked Olivia gently, when Kate had finished explaining briefly the events that led up to her fleeing Beauvais, "did Page like your leaving?"

Kate tightened her lips. "Page accused me of running away."

"But you don't see it like that?"

"No. I thought we all needed time to accept—or at least to try to adjust. Beauvais, big as it is, seemed suddenly too small. And Adele . . ." Kate paused, glancing around with a frown. "Where *is* Adele? Hasn't she come down yet?"

"Oh, yes. She couldn't rest, she said, so we had a nice chat while you were asleep."

"You did?" Kate was surprised. Adele had been silent and withdrawn these past weeks, changing almost instantly from a lively and vivacious girl into an unreachable, unapproachable, bitter young woman. Kate had often watched her on the long journey to England, wishing there had been some way she could comfort her daughter—or offer consolation or understanding. But Adele had become more wooden with each passing day, more apathetic and indifferent, and Kate was forced to accept, finally, that her daughter had withdrawn into her own world of pain and that she was not going to emerge until she could deal with the hurt and disillusionment she had suffered. In a way, Kate couldn't blame Adele; she had been tempted to retreat so herself.

But if she wasn't able to reach Adele, Kate was glad that Olivia had been able to draw her out. Adele needed someone to confide in, someone who could offer comfort and wise understanding. Someone, Kate thought wryly, who wasn't her mother.

"You have a beautiful daughter, Kate," Olivia said, bringing Kate back to the present. "She reminds me so much of you."

"Does she? But we don't look anything alike!"

"Oh, I agree that you don't have the same coloring. But the temperament is there. You're both so proud . . . and so stubborn." Olivia paused. "And you both feel things so deeply. You're both so easily hurt."

Kate put down her cup. "Yes," she said. She got up to walk restlessly over to the French doors. Opening one, she stood there smelling the crisp October air with its tinge of decaying leaves and pungent wood smoke. Down in the spent garden, idly watching a young gardener sweep the flagstone path free of debris, was Adele. Kate watched her sadly for a moment. There was something forlorn about her as she stood there among the last of the flowers, and Kate's mouth twisted when she saw her daughter's lost expression. If only there was some way to help her, she thought again; if only there was something she could do for Adele other than stand by helplessly while her daughter retreated farther and farther behind the wall she had built.

Kate thought suddenly of Jane, who had been through the same crisis Adele was enduring now. If Jane were here, she might be able to help, because she could offer comfort and understanding—an empathy based, not on a mother's protectiveness, but a sympathy of shared emotion because she had suffered the same way herself.

But Jane wasn't here. She was somewhere in New York, and across the ocean at Tremont Hall there was only Kate to help Adele. And Olivia, who was wisest of them all.

Turning away from the door, Kate looked at her aunt and asked, "Was I really like that, aunt? Are Adele and I so much alike?"

Olivia smiled slightly at Kate's plaintive tone and patted the sofa beside her. "Come and sit down," she said. And when Kate had obeyed, she took her niece's cold hand in her own warm one and asked softly, "Why did you really leave Beauvais?"

Kate stared at her. "I told you why!"

"Did you?"

"Of course I did!" Kate answered. But she couldn't meet Olivia's eyes.

"Kate, look at me," Olivia said. And when Kate had reluctantly lifted her eyes to Olivia's face, her aunt said, "Didn't you leave Beauvais because you expected more of Page than he could give, and when he failed to live up to the high standards you set, you simply couldn't bear the disappointment?" Olivia paused, searching Kate's face. "Didn't you leave because you felt . . . betrayed?"

Kate was stung. "Of course I felt betrayed!" she cried. "I *was* betrayed! And I wasn't the only one who set standards, you know! Page expected so much of me, too!"

"And you resent that?"

"No, no! It was just that . . . that I . . . that he . . ." Kate stopped to draw an agitated breath. She went on, "He *lied* to me, Aunt Olivia! Can't you understand that?"

"But didn't you do the same thing to him, years ago?" asked Olivia gently.

"If you mean with the twins—yes! But Page was an expert in exacting a price from me for that! He—"

"Yes. You've told me how . . . empty your life has been over the past few years. But aren't you trying to make him pay the same price in a different way?"

"What do you mean?" cried Kate, outraged. She tried to pull her hand away from Olivia's grasp, but her aunt held her firmly.

"I mean," said Olivia with quiet insistence, "that you might consider the real reason why you escaped to England."

"I didn't 'escape,' as you so kindly put it!"

"Didn't you? What do you call it, then?"

"Well . . . I didn't think of it as an escape," Kate muttered.

"No, I don't suppose you did. You were hurt, and you only thought of getting away. Perhaps I can't blame you—"

"Well, thank you for that, at least!"

"—but you might think why you left your home in such a rush."

Kate tried again to justify herself. "I honestly thought we

all needed time to . . . to . . ." But she faltered again before the look in Olivia's calm hazel eyes, and she couldn't go on. Finally, her head bowed. Kate whispered, "You're right, aunt. I did want to punish him. I wanted to hurt him as he hurt me."

"And so you took away the one thing he valued most."

"Yes," Kate admitted, her voice low. "I took away Adele."

Olivia's fingers tightened on hers, forcing her to look up again. "No, Kate," Olivia said softly. "You took away yourself."

Kate's reaction to this was swift, almost violent. Jerking her hand away from Olivia's, she sprang up again. Her eyes were bright with unshed tears as she stared at Olivia, and her voice shook. "As wise as you are, aunt, you have misjudged the situation utterly if you think Page was upset when I went away! He might have been concerned about Adele, but certainly not about me—except where his pride was concerned! It's a little difficult for a man to explain why his wife went away, isn't it? Why she left *him*! But if he cared about it, that's why. He hasn't cared about *me* for a long, long time!"

"I'm sorry Kate, I just don't believe that's true."

"Well, whether you believe it or not, it is."

"Page does care about you," Olivia insisted. "He—"

Kate laughed shrilly. "If he does, he has a peculiar way of showing it, doesn't he? Either that or I simply invented the hell he put me through these past years! I made up the entire story, like a child creating fairy tales—is that what you think?"

"Of course not!"

"Then I ask you—if Page valued me so highly, why did he act like he despised me all this time? Why did he withdraw from me? Why did he take away the one thing *I* valued most—himself? Oh, God, *why?*"

"Because," came a bitter voice from the doorway, "he loves you."

Kate whirled around. Adele stood at the threshold, regarding her coldly. She came into the room, pausing a few feet from her mother. "He loves you, Mother," Adele repeated stonily.

"Don't speak of things you know nothing about, Adele," Kate said harshly.

"You don't think that I'm qualified to know anything about

love—is that it?" Adele asked, with eyes like flint. "Because I
fancied myself in love with my brother, does that make me
suspect? I think you're judging me a little harshly, Mother,
don't you? After all, how was I to know about Randall, when
you were ignorant of the circumstances yourself?"

Kate wasn't sure what to say. This was the first time that
Adele had spoken openly of Randall since Rory's wedding
night, and she didn't want to stop what might be a healing
flow of words. During the entire journey to Tremont Hall,
Kate had tried to probe gently, encouraging Adele to talk
about her feelings. But Adele had rejected every attempt, and
finally Kate had given up in despair.

But now, even as her hopes rose and she tried to swallow
her anger over Adele's insolence, Adele said coldly, "But we
weren't talking of Randall and me, were we? We were talking
about you and Father, and you were saying that I had no
right to talk about that, either."

"I didn't say that at all," Kate corrected as firmly as she
dared. "I only meant—"

"Oh, I know what you meant, Mother. You always think
you're right and everyone else is wrong, don't you?"

"Adele!" Kate didn't know whether to be more angry at
her daughter's rudeness or at what she had just said. "I'm
sorry, Adele," she said evenly, "but I don't agree with you. I
have often in the past admitted I was wrong, but that isn't
really the issue here."

"No," Adele agreed with that frigid expression that made
Kate despair of ever getting through to her. "The issue was
whether Father cares for you or not. You said just now that
he didn't love you, but if he loves anyone, Mother, it's you.
He told me so himself."

Kate couldn't imagine Page revealing himself so openly to
one of his children, even to Adele, his favorite. He was such
a private man, so open and generous about everything but
what he really felt, that Kate was doubtful. "And when did
he tell you that?"

"He told me the day before we left for England. We went
riding that day, to the cabin."

This time Kate couldn't speak. Page at the cabin? She was
sure she was the only one who visited the place. If anyone
had asked her, she would have been positive that Page had
forgotten all about the cabin—except, as Rory had so deri-

sively stated, to think of it as an eyesore that should be torn down.

Adele was quick to see her mother's surprise. "Oh, yes," she said. "Father goes quite often to the cabin. You didn't know that, did you?"

"No." Kate couldn't believe it now. Why did he go there? Was it because he yearned for better days, too? But why hadn't he mentioned it all these years? Why hadn't he ever said anything?

Why hadn't she?

Adele was watching her, and Kate saw that her daughter's expression was hard and cold. "There are a lot of things you don't know about Father," she said. She closed her eyes tightly for an instant, then opened them again. "There were a lot of things I didn't know either, weren't there?"

Adele looked down and away from Kate's troubled expression and Olivia's open sympathetic glance. She looked about to cry, but Kate saw the fierce effort she made to control her tears. She had said once that tears were for foolish women, and she had been too much of a fool already.

There was a glass figurine by her hand. Kate watched her pick it up and look at it. It was an image of two children, a boy and a girl, looking down into a wishing well. The boy held a penny, and the expressions of both children were wistful. They looked like they didn't know whether to throw in the penny or not. As Adele stared at it, her mouth twisted, and very carefully she put the figurine back on the table.

"Why do you look at me like that, Mother? Is it so strange that I agreed to go riding with my father? I wanted to hear what he had to say, you know. In fact, I wanted to hear how he would justify himself."

Kate did not care for Adele's harsh tone; it worried her. But even less did she like the derisive manner in which Adele spoke of Page, who was still her father. "I don't believe your father had to justify himself to you or to anyone else," Kate said sharply.

Adele stared at her, unmoved. "Of course you would say that, wouldn't you? Even after all he's done, you still defend him. I knew you would. Just as I knew he would defend you."

"What do you mean by that?"

"Oh, nothing. It's just that you both are so predictable. On the one hand you correct me about him, and on the other

he tells me that while he has been wrong about Randall, what
he has done to you is unforgivable." Adele paused, her eyes
narrowing. "I suppose you know," she said sarcastically,
"what he meant by that."

Despite her anger, Kate caught her breath. The sharp pain
she felt at her daughter's words caught her off-guard, and she
couldn't speak. Page sorry? But it was too late. . . .

Or was it?

When Kate looked up again, she was startled at the condemnation in her daughter's eyes. "It's all your fault, you
know," Adele accused before Kate could speak. "If you
hadn't lied about David and Michael, none of this would
have happened!"

"Adele!"

But Adele was gone after this blistering indictment, turning
on her heel and running from the room.

"Adele!" Kate called to her again, starting to follow.

Olivia, who had been silent from the beginning, stopped
her in mid-flight. "Let her go, Kate."

Kate glanced wildly at her aunt. "How can you ask such a
thing!" she cried. "I—"

"She doesn't mean what she said, Kate. Not really."

"But—"

"She's young, dear. And she's hurt. She wants to lash out
at something, and you're a convenient target. She wants to
hurt you because she doesn't understand."

Kate sank into a chair. "I don't understand, either!"

"No, I don't suppose any of us does—least of all Page
himself. But we all do things that are inexplicable."

Kate frowned. "I'm afraid that isn't much comfort!"

"No," agreed Olivia. "But that's the way things are, and
since you can't change it, you'll have to learn to accept it."

Biting her lip, Kate was silent. At last she said despairingly, "But what about Adele? I can't reach her—I've tried!
She's not the same girl she was, and I'm so worried about
her! I don't want her to become so bitter and withdrawn that
she denies herself any chance of happiness. She has so much
to offer, if she can forget . . ."

Olivia rose from her place on the sofa. As she came to
where Kate sat, the cameo she wore at her throat caught the
last of the late sun and threw a rosy glow up to her face. She
paused with her hand resting gently on Kate's shoulder, and
as Kate looked up at her, she realized more certainly than be-

fore that while Olivia had aged in years, she hadn't become old. The calm hazel eyes that gazed back at her were filled with wise understanding, and even, Kate thought in surprise, with a subtle wry humor—as if Olivia could laugh at human failings because she had seen so many of those failings herself: foolishness repeating itself in an endless cycle, so long as there were people who cared for each other and took a chance on love.

For an instant, staring into those compassionate eyes, Kate felt the weight of all her problems lifting from her. And then she thought of Page and Adele and Randall, and all her misery came flooding back again. "Oh, aunt!" she said helplessly, close to tears again.

Olivia squeezed her shoulder. "I'll talk to Adele," she said. "If you like."

"Would you?" Kate clutched Olivia's hand. "I would be so grateful if you did! It's obvious," she said bitterly, "that she won't listen to me."

Olivia smiled. "That's because you're her mother. I, however, am only a doddering great-aunt, and therefore not of much consequence."

"You're much more than that, Aunt Olivia," Kate said fervently, rising to give Olivia a grateful kiss.

"Well, we'll see if Adele feels the same, won't we?"

Kate never knew what it was that Olivia said to Adele, but later that night, after Kate had excused herself from going down to dinner on the plea of a headache, a chastened Adele came to her mother's room.

Kate had been sitting staring emptily into the fire she had lighted more for comfort than for warmth, and she started when she heard the soft tap at the door. "Who is it?" she called, expecting Olivia to answer.

"It's Adele, Mother. May I talk to you?"

When she entered, her eyes were red from weeping and she held herself stiffly, as if afraid to lose control again. Seeing her, Kate was immediately forgiving, but before she could say anything, Adele began to talk. She spoke quickly, as if she had rehearsed what she was going to say and wanted to get it over with as soon as possible.

"I'm sorry, Mother, for the awful things I said earlier. It was rude and unfair, and I'm ashamed of myself for acting like such a child."

"We all act childishly at times, Adele." Kate smiled briefly and gestured toward the other chair by the fireplace. Adele took it, staring morosely at the floor. "It seems to be human nature to make fools of ourselves, doesn't it?" Kate asked quietly.

Adele stirred. "You never felt like a fool!" she said, glancing up quickly. "You're always so . . . so confident, so in control of everything!"

Kate felt a hysterical urge to laugh outright. In control of everything? If only it were true!

"When I was small," Adele continued in a low, bitter voice, "I used to stand before that portrait of you in the drawing room—you know the one I mean, over the fireplace?"

"Yes, I know," Kate said. Page had commissioned that portrait in happier times, and she had worn one of his favorite gowns for it, a white gauze shot through with silver thread that emphasized her vivid coloring.

"Anyway, I used to stand there and just look at it, thinking how beautiful you were," Adele said, swallowing hard as if it were painful for her to speak, to remember. "And when I became a little older, I realized I wasn't the only one who thought that. I began to see how everyone doted on you, how sought-after you were. We always had guests at Beauvais, you know—important people, I recognized, and every one of them came to see you."

"That isn't true!" Kate protested. "They came because your father is an influential man, because he—"

"Oh, yes. They came *because* of father, I agree. But they came to *see* you. Kathryn Beauvais Taggart, who made Beauvais such a showplace; Kate Taggart, who is one of the most beautiful and lovely women in the whole of Colorado. Don't deny it, Mother. It's true. It must be; I've heard it said often enough!"

"Adele, you sound so . . . so . . ."

"What? Jealous? Envious?" asked Adele with a twisted smile. "Oh, no; I was proud of you, Mother—proud to be your daughter." Glancing away from Kate, Adele stared at the flickering fire. "I knew from the very beginning that I could never be as beautiful as you, as accomplished. I knew that as much as I wanted to be like you, it was impossible from the start. The portrait told me that. I just couldn't compete."

Kate was horrified. "But I didn't want you to compete! I wanted you to be yourself, Adele. I thought you believed that! Why, you're popular with all the young people; you're always surrounded by beaux. What do you mean, compete?"

Adele shifted in the chair again, her honey-colored hair catching the light and making a soft gold frame for her face. But her dark eyes were bleak when she said, "I wanted you to be proud of me, Mother."

"But I am!"

"And I knew that you would want a popular daughter—a girl who flirted and teased and always had plenty of admirers."

Kate stared at her, aghast. Was this what Adele really thought? She was so appalled that she couldn't speak.

"Randall understood," Adele was saying now, her voice suddenly so low that Kate could hardly hear her. "He used to ask why I had to pretend all the time, why I didn't just take a book and go off in a corner somewhere and read. But the truth is, I *did* enjoy all that attention; I *did* want people to like me, to admire me as much as everyone admired you."

As Kate stared helplessly at her, Adele got up and stood by the mantel, leaning against it with her fists clenched. "I don't know," she said. "I just don't know anything anymore, Mother."

"Adele . . ." Kate got up too, just as Adele's face crumpled. Reaching her, she put her arms about her daughter and drew her close. With one hand she stroked the thick honey hair, trying to ease a pain that she had not known existed, and which might never be erased. "It's all right, darling," she said. "I understand . . ."

"Oh, how could you understand?" sobbed Adele. "How can you possibly understand?"

"Because . . ." Kate held Adele away from her, one hand under her chin, forcing her to look up at her. "Because," she repeated, "I thought that same thing when I was a girl. I wanted to be like my mother, too—my mother, who was so beautiful that she could stand onstage and hold an entire audience in the palm of her hand without saying a word. My mother was the center of attention wherever she went and whatever she did, Adele, and I wanted to be just like her. I wanted her to be proud of me, and to love me."

"And did she?"

Kate hesitated. "I don't know," she admitted finally. "I

suppose she did, in her own way. But not," she added
fiercely, "the way I love you! I never wanted you to be like
me, darling! I want you to be yourself!"

"Oh, it doesn't matter now, does it?" Adele asked bitterly.
"Everything is ruined now, anyway."

"Adele," Kate murmured sadly, holding her daughter close
again. "I wish there was something I could do for you, some
way to help you through this . . . this disappointment." She
hesitated as Adele tensed, but it had to be said. "Why didn't
you ever tell us your feelings about Randall, darling? Your
father and I had no idea . . ."

Adele pulled away from her then, holding herself so stiffly
that she rejected any offer of comfort. For a long minute she
didn't answer, and Kate was afraid she had said too much.
But finally, her voice choked, Adele answered.

"Randall and I used to . . . to joke about how funny it
was that we should love each other when we were brother
and sister. Siblings were only supposed to tolerate each other,
you know? Not love each other like we did. But of course it
was all right for us, because we really weren't related by
blood at all—we had just been raised that way. How we used
to laugh about that. . . . But it wasn't very funny, was it?"

Her voice broke, and Kate reached instinctively for her,
but Adele moved away. "Do you remember how I used to
follow Randall around when I was small? I always wanted to
be with him—to know what he was doing or where he was
going. Whatever it was, I wanted to be there too."

"I remember," Kate acknowledged, wondering now why
she had never thought about it before. She wished uselessly
that she had paid more attention, but if she had thought
about it at all, she had assumed that Adele was close to Randall because he was the one nearest her in age—the brother,
Kate realized abruptly, who had never repulsed his sister, or
tormented or teased her, as had the others at one time or another. Even David, Kate remembered now, had sometimes
been impatient with his little sister, but not Randall. Never
Randall.

Kate looked at Adele. "But that doesn't explain why you
never said anything. Why neither of you ever indicated by so
much as a word that you were thinking of marriage."

Adele glanced away. "It was a kind of game we played,"
she admitted in a choked voice. "I don't know how to explain
it, except to say that what we had was so . . . so precious

that we didn't want anyone to know about it until we were ready. Can you understand that?"

"Yes," Kate said softly. "But . . ."

"It wasn't wrong, Mother!" Adele cried. "Nothing we did was wrong!"

"Of course it wasn't . . ."

But Adele wouldn't give her mother the opportunity to comfort her. In one of her lightning changes of mood, she had altered from a daughter confiding in her mother to a cold and withdrawn young woman again. And Kate, gazing at Adele's proud expression, knew that whatever flame of understanding had flared between them was extinguished now. Adele was retreating, in bitterness and humiliation and defeat, behind the high emotional wall she had built for her own protection, and there was nothing Kate could do to stop her. She couldn't even blame her daughter for hiding from something so painful; she had done the same thing, Kate thought bitterly, almost all her life.

30

Three weeks after that scene with Adele, Kate still hadn't made up her mind what she was going to do about her own problems. It was mid-November by that time, and far away in America, everyone would be looking forward to celebrating Thanksgiving. Standing by her bedroom window upstairs at Tremont Hall, Kate stared out at the lifeless garden and the bare branches of the trees, idly watching the few scattered snowflakes drift down from a cold, leaden sky. She thought to herself that she was glad she wasn't at Beauvais now. There was little to be thankful about, unless it was the fact that after twenty-three years of marriage she and Page had no more secrets from each other.

But if they had nothing to hide, they seemed to have nothing else either, and it was time—past time—for her to come to some sort of decision about her and Page. She couldn't hope to stay with Olivia for the rest of her life, tempting as the idea was. She couldn't avoid the problem of her marriage by pretending it didn't exist.

Turning away from the window, Kate went to the wardrobe and took out the riding habit she had brought with her. Because her aunt had sensed her restlessness, she had borrowed riding horses for her and Adele several days before. There had been only the old carriage horse for the Hall in the stable before that, and Kate had quickly tired of trotting out sedately in the pony trap. But she hadn't wanted to ask about riding; it was imposition enough to have extended her visit this long, as it was.

But now, because Olivia was still adept at discerning her moods, there was a horse waiting for her, and Kate thought it was a good time to make use of it. She had been indoors too long; she needed fresh air and a brisk ride to clear her head. She would return, she told Olivia downstairs a few minutes later, before she went out, in time for tea.

"All right, dear," Olivia said, glancing up from where she was cozily embroidering something in the drawing room by the fire. Her eyes sparkled and she smiled. "But don't be late."

Kate stopped in the doorway, frowning a little in puzzlement. Olivia seemed excited about something, and doing her best to hide it.

"What is it, aunt?" Kate asked. "Has something happened?"

"Why, no, dear. Why do you ask?"

"Well, you seem so . . . pleased about something."

"I am! I'm pleased you're going out. You've been so restless lately, so irritable!"

"Why, thank you!"

Olivia waved a hand. "Oh, you know what I mean! It's just that I think you've been confined too long. You need to get out, like you used to."

"Oh . . . well, if you're sure . . ."

"Yes, I'm sure. Go along now, Kate. I don't want you to be late for tea."

Kate would have hesitated again, still puzzled by Olivia's manner, but with her aunt waving her out and smiling, she decided she had been making something of nothing. Olivia was just pleased, as she had said, that Kate was making use of the horse she had borrowed.

Once out on the road, however, with the chill November wind whipping color into her cheeks and the horse moving swiftly into a canter, Kate forgot about Olivia's puzzling behavior and began to enjoy herself for the first time in weeks. Riding had always calmed her, and as the horse gathered speed, she felt her tension slipping away. It was wonderful to be out in the fresh air again, wonderful to leave behind—however briefly—all her problems.

Unfortunately, her initial euphoria disappeared as rapidly as it had come, and Kate found that she hadn't left anything behind at all. To her dismay, she discovered that she had only put it all out of her mind for a time as she reveled in the brisk gallop down the road. Now, with the horse slowing, insidious thoughts intruded again, and she knew she had to face all the unanswered questions.

Reluctantly she slowed the horse to a walk and thought of Adele, who had become more despondent than before. In desperation Kate had suggested a visit to London, thinking it would be a distraction if nothing else, but Adele had listlessly refused. She didn't want to go anywhere or see anyone, she declared, and she never—never—wanted to return to Beauvais. They had had words about this last only the night before, when for the third day in a row Adele had refused to come down to dinner.

"Leave her alone, Kate," Olivia had said when she and Kate had seated themselves at the table, only to discover that Adele had sent yet another message excusing herself from the meal. "I'll send up a tray for her."

Kate had very carefully folded the napkin she had taken from the silver holder and put it back on the table beside her plate. "No," she said, rising. "I know Adele has had a terrible experience, Aunt Olivia, but she can't go on this way. She may fancy herself in a decline, but I don't. This has got to stop!"

Reluctantly Olivia had agreed with her, and Kate had marched upstairs to Adele's room. Barely waiting for her daughter to answer her knock, Kate had flung open the door and said, "Your great-aunt and I would appreciate it if you would join us for dinner."

Adele had been sitting by the window. Now she turned to Kate, her face stubborn. "I'm not hungry."

"Whether you are or not, you will join us at table. I won't

have you skulking about this room, refusing to see anyone and worrying your aunt."

Adele turned away, her huge eyes scornful. "Great-Aunt Olivia isn't worried about me; she understands. I thought you did, too."

"I understand that you can't spend the rest of your life acting the martyr," replied Kate sharply.

"Is that what you think I'm doing—acting?"

Kate was unmoved by her daughter's outraged tone. "Whatever it is, I think it's gone on long enough. When we get back to Beauvais—"

"I'm not going back to Beauvais."

Kate stared at her. "That's ridiculous! Of course you're going back. Beauvais is your home!"

"Not anymore."

Kate lost what little patience she had been clinging to. She had been standing on the threshold to Adele's room; now she came inside and shut the door.

"What do you mean," she asked, "not anymore? Beauvais is your home, and it always will be."

Stubbornly Adele shook her head. "No. I can't go back there."

Kate took a deep breath, trying to hold on to her temper. "Well, then," she asked, "what do you expect to do instead? Find yourself a garret somewhere and eke out a miserable existence hunched over a cold grate? Where exactly do you think you'll live?"

Adele had winced at this sarcasm, but she tried to answer haughtily. "I'm sure Great-Aunt Olivia will let me live here with her."

"Oh?" Kate was more sarcastic than before, but now a thought occurred to her, and she added sharply, "You haven't asked her, have you?"

"No, no. I was going to after I talked to you."

"Oh, I see. First you were going to honor your mother by telling her first. Then you were going to ask your aunt. How nice."

"Well, I *was* going to ask you!"

"All right, Adele. You've asked me; we've discussed it. And the answer is no. You're not going to live at Tremont Hall; you're coming home to Beauvais."

"But, Mother . . ."

Kate had opened the door again. "And furthermore," she

added in a tone that meant no further discussion at all, "you're coming down to dinner. You can apologize for keeping your aunt waiting when you get there."

Adele had obeyed sullenly, and the meal was so strained and tense that Kate was sorry she had insisted on her daughter joining them. It was a relief when after dessert they could all abandon the dining room, and this time Kate didn't object when Adele excused herself smartly and went back upstairs.

Thinking about the scene now, with the horse plodding slowly down the road on a loose rein, Kate sighed. She was sure she hadn't heard the last of the argument from Adele; her spoiled daughter was too accustomed to getting her own way not to balk over this.

But not this time, thought Kate grimly. Adele might have suffered a blow about Randall, but she was not going to live out her life hiding at Tremont Hall. She was young yet; she would recover, in time.

Just as Randall would recover, Kate hoped sadly, remembering her adopted son's face the day before she and Adele had left for England. Randall had come to her that day when she had taken a few minutes from her frantic packing to sit by herself on the terrace. The terrace at the back of the house was another of her favorite places at Beauvais, for from this point she could gaze out at the neatly fenced horse paddocks beyond the stables, and from there to the magnificent backdrop of the Rockies. Together, the two were a restful sight to Kate—the mountains that gave her strength, and the horses that gave her such joy. Whenever she had a spare minute to herself, she would often come out to sit by herself, enjoying the sight of such beauty.

Randall had found her there that last day, and when he approached, Kate smiled a welcome and held out her hands. She drew him down to sit beside her on the marble bench and anxiously searched his face.

It had been several weeks since Rory's wedding, and Randall had stayed with friends in Denver all this time, trying to avoid the inevitable awkwardness with Adele. But he had come out to the ranch today to say good-bye, and Kate saw now that in the interim he had grown noticeably thinner. There were hollows in his cheeks and shadows under his eyes. But he returned Kate's smile when he saw her worried expression.

"How are you, Mother?" he asked quietly.

Kate bit her lip. "Oh . . . better, I suppose. And you, Randall? How are you?"

He looked down. When he glanced up again, there was such pain in his eyes that Kate involuntarily tightened her grip on his hands. "I'm not sure," he said, his voice low. "It's a little difficult to get used to, I guess. But we all have to go on . . . somehow."

"Yes. I suppose we do. Randall—"

"Mother—"

They spoke at the same time, each trying to reassure the other. Kate smiled a little and gestured for Randall to speak first.

"I just wanted to say that I'm glad you're taking Adele away for a while," Randall said.

"Are you?"

"Yes." He looked away from her, gazing out across the paddocks to the mountains, finding comfort in the sight, just as she did. They had often sat here together like this in the past, Kate thought sadly. But they had all been happier then. She wondered bleakly if anyone here would ever be happy again. "Adele might not show it, Mother," Randall continued after a moment, "but she feels everything so deeply. She acts as if things don't matter to her, but they do. They do." Randall paused again, swallowing. "So I'm glad you're taking her away," he said at last. "It will be easier for her if you go."

"And what about you, Randall? How easy will it be for you?"

He didn't answer for so long that Kate thought he was going to avoid the question entirely. But finally, his voice even deeper than before, he replied, "I'll stay until you and Adele come home. I . . . I owe that much, at least, what with everyone gone now. But then I think it would be better if I left—"

"No!" Kate's cry was instinctive. "Oh, Randall, I can't lose you, too!"

He looked at her, his green eyes stark in a pale face. "I can't stay, Mother. You know that."

"But . . . is it because of Adele, or because of . . . your father?"

"Both, I suppose," Randall answered honestly. "But mainly because of Adele. I don't want it to be difficult for her, or embarrassing. So I think it would be better all around if I left."

"But where will you go?"

"I don't know. I haven't thought that far ahead." He stood then, freeing himself from her clutching hands. Bending, he kissed her cheek, and it was all Kate could do not to burst into tears. "I won't leave like Michael did," he said quietly. "You'll know where I am, what I'm doing."

"Do you promise?"

Randall smiled gently at her mournful tone. "Yes, I promise." He began to turn away, but he paused once again to look back at her. "I've tried to talk to Adele, but she won't listen to me," he said, and the pain had returned to his voice, making it rough and harsh. "Tell her that she can't shut herself off, that she should find someone else—some man who will love her and cherish her . . . almost as much as I do."

His voice broke completely then, and he hurried away, leaving a desolate Kate staring after him.

Now, so many thousands of miles away from the terrace at Beauvais, Kate flexed her icy fingers on the reins and urged the horse to a trot. The sky was leaden, the wind chill, but she didn't want to go back to Tremont Hall just yet. Thinking about that scene with Randall and what he had said, Kate had to agree with him. It would be better for both him and Adele if he left the ranch, and yet . . . Kate swallowed back tears. Dear Randall, she thought; he had been such a comfort to her. How could she lose him, too?

But she couldn't think of herself; she had to think of Randall and Adele, who were so young, and so intense. It would be too difficult for them both if Kate begged him to stay. They had to be apart to ease the pain, to help the separation, to give them time to find someone who would console and comfort and give them the love that they were denied each other. They had their lives in front of them, and in time, the hurt would disappear.

But would her own hurt disappear? Would she, too, heal in time? Would she find someone else to help ease her pain?

But there was no one else for her but Page. There had never been anyone else but him. She knew the most influential men in Colorado—governors, senators, congressmen, powerful ranchers, wealthy businessmen—and none of them had ever attracted her as much as her own husband. Looking at him even from across the room and after more than twenty years of marriage, Kate could still feel her pulse race as it had when she was a girl. She could still become breathless when he glanced up and smiled at her; she still knew a thrill when he took her arm or held her hand.

But it had been a long time since he had smiled that particular smile or sent her a private look across a room; it had been even longer since a touch had been a caress.

Someone else? Even now the thought didn't even tempt her. She only knew that after Page, every other man was only a pale imitation, a caricature. If she couldn't have Page, then she wanted no one else.

Even after what he had done?

The question shot at her from the recesses of her mind, and she examined it. Enough time had passed for her to consider Page's actions with less emotion and more thought; she was far enough away from Beauvais to think about what had happened without anger.

Was she still hurt? she asked herself.

Unquestionably, yes.

But was the pain she felt enough to make her sacrifice everything else?

Ah, yes. That was the question, wasn't it?

Without Kate really being aware of it, the horse had left the road and was following a track up a hill. Kate realized with a start that it was the same place she had ridden that day so long ago—a young, defiant girl in breeches, hurt deeply by her mother's death, wounded by the gossip that she heard everywhere, determined to hide her feelings, and about to set her cap for Roger Templeton. What a fool she had been!

Was she an even bigger fool now, some twenty years later?

Deep in thought, Kate slid from the saddle and tethered the horse to a shrub. Walking a little ways away, she stood for a moment looking out over the countryside she had hated so when she first came to Tremont Hall, and which now she loved almost as much as she loved Beauvais.

Biting her lip, Kate sank to the ground on the crest of the hill. The dead November grass felt dry and brittle under her hands, the ground too cold for comfort. Yet she sat there, her knees drawn up, resting her chin on her folded arms as she looked out across the valley. It was fitting somehow, she thought bleakly, that she had come to this particular place. It was where she had first met Page, and now, twenty-three years later, it was where she would decide whether to say good-bye to him.

Tears filled her eyes at the thought, and dropping her head onto her folded arms, she began to cry. She had controlled her tears for so long, and now she could hold them back no longer.

Sitting huddled on the breast of the hill, with the countryside spread out before her and the cold wind cutting through her coat to chill her to the bone, Kate neither saw nor felt anything but the terrible pain of her loss. Sob after sob shuddered through her, and yet, the more she cried, the more agonized she felt.

Scenes from the past flashed randomly through her mind, and she saw how smug she had been, and how self-satisfied. She had been proud and stubborn and temper-ridden—and she saw these traits now, not as the strengths they had been when she needed to be strong, but as weaknesses, flaws, that had brought her to such a terrible decision now. Seeing the person she had been, Kate hated herself, and she wept even more.

And now it was too late to change things, to change herself, to tell Page she had been wrong about so many things. Olivia was right: she had expected more of him than he could give. She had wanted him to be everything to her, and for a while, he had been. But she had wanted more; she had wanted him to be perfect, and he was not.

Misery flooded her, utter wretchedness. She had held happiness in the palm of her hand, she wept, and she had let it drift away, like the gossamer thing it was. And now she would never know such happiness again, and she had only herself to blame as she thought of all the years of empty loneliness ahead of her. She could go back to Beauvais, but nothing would ever be the same, because she had left it in anger. And she had been angry and hurt and disillusioned because she had demanded more of Page than she had asked of herself. She had exacted from him a higher price than she herself was willing to pay.

She had, she thought, declared that she would never forgive Page for what he had done. She hadn't wondered if she herself needed to be forgiven, too.

"Is something wrong?"

Kate froze in mid-sob. The voice came to her out of the past, so real that for a moment she was sure she had only to open her eyes and she would see a pair of Hessian boots planted before her. It was how they had met, alone on this very hill. She had been crying then, she remembered, and he had found her. She recalled it all, the entire scene, as if it were yesterday instead of so long ago. Did he remember, too?

"Wrong?" she whispered, not daring to raise her head. "Of course there's nothing wrong. What makes you think there is?"

"I saw your horse, and you here on the ground. Naturally, I thought you had taken a fall."

Her heart was beating so wildly that she could hardly breathe. Her eyes were filled with tears, so that when she finally dared to lift her head to look, she could only see him as a blurred figure standing in front of her. This time, so many years later, he was wearing, not Hessian boots, but city shoes, and his hair wasn't the crisp black it had been then, but was now streaked with silver.

But his eyes—his eyes were the same. Fierce, black, commanding . . . and filled with an expression she had thought never to see again.

"A fall?" she said, gazing up at him, hardly daring to believe that he was really here. "I never fall. Now, will you go away and leave me alone?"

Page smiled at her then, a twisted smile of blame and guilt and regret . . . and love.

"Never," he answered softly, helping her to her feet. His black eyes shone with the tears mirrored in hers. "I'll never leave you alone again, Katie," he said.

And then he kissed her.

31

Of course it wasn't so simple as a kiss on a cold November afternoon on a hillside; both of them had known it wouldn't be. If it had been that easy, it wouldn't have been worth the pain of their separation, or the joy of their reunion. But it was a beginning, and they were grateful for that.

In the days that followed, Page and Kate began the agonizing process of coming to terms with their differences. Page reported that if it hadn't been for Adele, Randall would have been pleased—relieved, in a way—to know that Page was truly his father. But Adele . . . Adele was another story. From the moment she saw him at Tremont Hall, she had refused to speak to him, confining herself to her room despite Kate's alternating pleas and threats that she come out and listen to her father. Finally, even Kate had been forced to admit defeat, and Olivia had quietly suggested that Adele just needed more time to adjust.

Page agreed, but Kate could see that he was hurt by his daughter's attitude, and she was torn. On the one hand, she could almost understand Adele's withdrawal; on the other, she suffered for Page. But nothing, she reminded herself, was easy, and there were still their own compromises to be worked out.

"Rather like two warring factions sitting at a conference table," Kate said one morning as they lazed in bed drinking coffee and watching the light snowfall outside the window.

Page smiled sadly and reached out to draw her close. She put her head against his chest, contented.

"Except," Page murmured, his lips against her hair, "not all treaties end so amicably, with both parties in bed."

Kate looked up. "Perhaps they should, then," she suggested. "There might be less war, and considerably more talk of peace!"

"Only if beautiful women like you were involved."

Smiling at the compliment, Kate put her head back against his chest. She could hear his heart beating steadily under her ear, and she knew that he was as happy with their reconciliation as she was. He said so, in the next instant, as if he could read her thoughts.

"I missed you, Kate," he said softly, stroking her shoulder. "God, how I missed you!"

Kate thought of all the wasted years and shut her eyes tightly. This was one subject that neither of them had mentioned, and yet it had to be discussed. If she didn't ask, she would always wonder why, and she would not allow the acid of doubt to erode their peace again. They had come so far; they had only to talk about this last, and then be done with it forever.

"Why, Page?" she asked quietly. "Why did you shut me out for so long?"

He tensed, and she had the frantic thought that it was happening all over again: his anger, his rejection, his withdrawal. She wanted to protest, to beg him not to go away; she wanted to take back what she had said, pleading with him to ignore such a senseless, stupid question. She wanted to say that it didn't matter.

But it did.

And so, while she wanted to say all the things that chased themselves through her mind, she said nothing at all. Her heart in her throat, she waited for him to speak, wondering if she had crushed all her hopes again; knowing that, given the choice, she would have to ask the same question.

Page sat up. The movement put her away from him, and she shifted position herself, leaning back stiffly against the tumbled pillows. There was a roaring fire in the fireplace opposite the bed, but Kate was suddenly chilled by a cold that had nothing to do with the snow outside. Clutching the bed's thick comforter to her, she waited.

It was a long time before Page said anything. When he did speak, he turned to look at her first, and as she looked back at him, she saw how difficult it was for him to speak. She tried to smile in encouragement, but her face felt wooden, her lips stiff. She could only gaze at him and watch him struggle for words she didn't have, either.

He looked away from her once more, staring out the window. Kate realized that he wasn't seeing the swirling snow, but some inner vision of his own.

"I always knew," he said at last, "that you were infatuated with Roger. I saw it from the first—it wasn't difficult to see, since while I never could take my eyes off you, you were blind to anyone but him. I thought for a while that he might actually ask you to marry him." A smile curved his lips briefly, then was gone. "I used to lie awake nights thinking what I would do to him if he ever got up the courage to propose to you. I needn't have worried; he didn't have any courage after all. He asked Amelia instead—as his family ordered him to do. Roger always did everything he was supposed to do, you know—except that one time. How ironic that he should be found out, and with such awful consequences, the single time he did something on his own, without asking Mama or Papa."

Kate was afraid to move, to comment, for fear of interrupting. She had never heard Page talk like this about Roger or anyone else, and she was too absorbed even to feel the age-old guilt about the twins.

"Of course, I didn't know about that when I asked you to marry me," Page continued musingly. "But I used to wonder, after I found out about the twins, if it would have mattered. I was so in love with you that sometimes I think I would have accepted anything so long as you agreed to marry me."

"But it did matter to you," Kate put in quietly. "Otherwise you wouldn't have . . ."

"Otherwise I wouldn't have been such a bastard to you all these years?"

Kate didn't wince at the epithet, or claim that it wasn't true or that it didn't matter. She looked directly at him and answered simply, "Yes."

Page got up then, belting a dressing gown about his lean, hard body. He went to the fireplace and stirred up the fire, leaning one arm against the mantel and staring down into the leaping flames. "I was a bastard," he admitted. "But it wasn't because of you, Kate. Not really."

"Then why?"

He straightened, still staring at the fire, shoving his hands into his pockets. Kate could see that under the heavy silk of the dressing gown his hands were clenched into fists.

"I was so angry when Michael ran away," he said at last, his voice filled with pain. "So angry, and so hurt that he could leave like that—without giving anyone a chance to explain or to work things out. He was my son—I always thought of him as that, even after I knew differently. He was my son, the boy who was going to follow after me and take care of what we had built, Kate, because he loved Beauvais as much as you or I."

Page looked at her then, tears glinting in his dark eyes, his face agonized. "I couldn't believe that he could leave like that—that we would never hear from him again! I can hardly believe it now, after all these years. Dammit, Kate, he was my son, and I loved him! God, how I loved him!"

Kate threw herself out of bed and ran to him then, realizing at last that Page had suffered Michael's loss as much as she had, if not more. He blamed himself for Michael's going just as much as she blamed herself, and the two of them were helpless against the tide of pain that was Michael. Reaching Page, she clung tightly to him, and he held her close, as a drowning man clutches a raft.

"I thought you blamed me for not knowing how to stop him," Page said finally, his voice harsh with emotion. "And when I realized that there was nothing I could do to bring him home, I blamed myself. I should have thought of something; I should have done something! God, Kate, he was only fifteen years old! I should have gone after him—"

"But you tried, Page," Kate cried. "We both tried, that night. But there were so many things to see to that night—the children . . . David . . . Roger . . ."

"Yes," said Page grimly. "And then there was Roger."

He drew her down to sit beside him on the chaise before the fire. There was a shawl along the back of it; he unfolded it and draped it around her shoulders, holding her protectively against his side.

"If Roger hadn't killed himself that night, I might have murdered him myself," Page said. "I was so enraged . . ."

"But he wasn't totally to blame," Kate forced herself to say.

"No, but he wasn't man enough to face what he had done. And it galls me still to think how readily he accepted my invitation to visit Beauvais. He didn't even hesitate when, like the fool I was, I offered him employment."

. "But all these years you've taken care of his family," Kate said gently. "If you felt like that about him, why did you see to Amelia and Jane?"

"They had nothing to do with Roger. And I couldn't stand by and do nothing for them; it wouldn't have been right. They were helpless women, with no means of support. Roger, true to form, hadn't even the backbone to see that his wife and daughter were taken care of before he killed himself. They didn't even have a home to return to in England," Page said disgustedly. "Roger had lost everything by then, you know, and Amelia's family were all dead."

"You're a good man, Page," Kate said softly into the silence that followed.

Page's arm tightened around her shoulder. He shook his head. "No. I'm not," he denied. "If I was, I wouldn't have put you through the past eight years. I would have told you how I felt . . . I would have said something about Randall . . . I would have done so many things differently, if I hadn't been so . . . so guilty and so inadequate . . ."

"I would have too," replied Kate sadly. "I would have too."

They sat quietly after that for a long time, preoccupied with their own thoughts. Outside, the snow fell softly, frosting the windows and icing the bare branches of the trees. But inside, the fire crackled cheerfully, and the room was warm with a renewed intimacy, a feeling of sharing and closeness that Kate treasured all the more because they had lost it for so long.

Page felt it too, for after a while he said, "I love you, Kate. I've always loved you, and I know I always will. You're the only woman I've ever said that to, and I . . . I was lost without you."

And after twenty-three years of marriage and five children and all the trials and suffering and joys and victories that had accompanied those years, Kate still felt that glorious hard pounding of her heart, that wonderful thrill of anticipation when Page lifted her in his arms and carried her to the bed. They were young once more in that moment, and for a while, at least, they could forget a recalcitrant Adele, a desolate Randall, and a spendthrift Rory and unhappy Jane. Slipping between the sheets, they loved each other again, and the future spread out rapturously before them.

32

The future was not quite so rapturous when, four months later, Kate and Page returned home after a delayed and blissful European honeymoon. They had visited the great Worth salon in Paris, had walked through the Colosseum at Rome, stood awed before the great sphinx, and had feasted on grape leaves in Greece. But they went back to Beauvais without Adele, and if going home without one adamant and wooden-faced daughter wasn't enough, they returned to find an absent Randall, a defiant Rory, and a silent Jane.

There was no sign of what awaited them as they stepped off the train that morning in early April. Rory, displaying no trace of remorse or chagrin, was waiting for them, tall and

big and handsome in the weak spring sunshine, and while
Page was pleased at this sign of filial devotion, Kate was instantly suspicious. She was even more mistrustful of the easy,
charming smile Rory directed toward them when they
alighted from the Taggart car, and as he hurried toward
them, Kate wondered what had brought Rory to meet them
instead of Randall.

"Well, well! The prodigal parents return at last!" Rory exclaimed, relieving Kate of the hatbox she carried and kissing
her briefly on the cheek. He took Page's valise and shook his
father's hand. "Did you have a good time? You must have—
you were gone long enough! I see that we sent the car to
fetch you in time!"

Rory laughed, and despite her growing suspicion that he
was hiding something, Kate stopped to admire this son of hers
who was so different from her other children. Even at the beginning of April, when the snow had all but disappeared,
there was a chill to the air, and Rory wore a heavy tweed
coat over his gray suit; both were cut without fault, and fitted
him perfectly. He was hatless, and his red-gold hair shone in
the sun, a fiery halo that gave no indication of his true character.

Kate started, reacting guiltily at such a disloyal thought
about her son. She looked closely at him, seeing now the almost feverish brightness of his hazel eyes and the tense lines
about his smiling mouth with the strong white teeth. No, she
hadn't been wrong. Despite his angelic manner, Rory was no
angel, and had never been. Something was obviously, maddeningly wrong.

Kate glanced across at Page, who seemed to notice nothing
amiss, and for a moment she was tempted to ignore her fore-
bodings. Page had been so happy these past few months—
they had been so happy together. Did she want to ruin a
wonderful homecoming after such a glorious time away by
demanding to know what Rory was hiding? Wouldn't they
discover it soon enough without her asking? Gloomily Kate
supposed they would.

"Hey!" Rory said, glancing around. "Where's Adele? Did
she run off with some dashing Englishman after the debacle
here?"

"I wrote everyone," Kate answered curtly, glimpsing the
pain in Page's eyes at Rory's thoughtless remark, "that Adele
had elected to stay in England for a while with Aunt Olivia.

She did not run off with anyone," she said with a frown, praying that she wouldn't have to recall her words at some future date. In the mood Adele was in now, anything could happen.

"Aw, I was just teasing," Rory said quickly. "And we did get your letter, Mother. I just thought . . . I mean, it's hard to believe that you would let Adele stay in England alone."

"She isn't alone," Page said. He had glimpsed Kate's fiery expression. "Adele is staying at Tremont Hall in the very capable hands of Olivia Tremont. I think even your sister will have a time fooling her great-aunt Olivia." He glanced again at Kate with a determined smile. "Your mother never could, after all, could you, Kate?"

"That's true," Kate answered, forcing herself to respond lightly to Page's remark. "There isn't much that escapes her, even now."

As they talked, they had been walking toward the waiting carriage. In the years since Kate had endured the long, jolting wagon ride from a fledgling Denver to what was to become Beauvais, the railroad not only had come to the city but also had added a spur that cut the additional journey from the station to Beauvais to less than an hour. Now, as they greeted one of the hands, who acted as their driver, Kate wished suddenly that they had stopped in Denver after all. There was something odd—tense and strained—about Rory as he shepherded them quickly inside the coach, and Kate reluctantly decided to abandon this polite pose and demand to know the reason why.

"You haven't given me a chance to ask, Rory," she said when they were settled inside the carriage and were starting off. "But how is Jane?"

Rory didn't miss a beat. His hazel eyes clear and direct, he smiled and answered readily, "Jane is fine, Mother. Why do you ask in such a suspicious tone? Do you think she's left me already?"

"Has she reason to do so?" Kate responded sharply, abandoning pretense in favor of a more aggressive attack.

Rory hesitated, and in that infinitesimal pause, Kate's suspicions were confirmed. "What is it?" she asked more sharply than before. "Is something the matter with Jane?"

"No, no, of course not!" Rory said reassuringly. "She's at Beauvais, in fact, waiting to welcome you home."

He turned his attention to his father then, and while the

two of them began a business discussion about Beauvais, Kate listened with only part of her attention. Watching Rory as he talked figures with Page, she was more dissatisfied than before with her son's response to her questions, and more distrustful of his innocent demeanor.

It was a terrible thing not to trust one's own son, Kate thought, turning her head to gaze out the window at the countryside she had missed so much. But as awful as it was, she had to admit it: she didn't trust Rory, and she never had, from the time he was a small child. Now, his reassurances to the contrary, Kate knew that something had happened, something that had made Rory make the effort to meet them at the train, something that had kept Randall away and accounted for Jane's absence, as well.

As the miles rolled by under the carriage wheels, Kate continued to stare out at her beloved mountains, trying to draw comfort and strength from them as she had so often in the past. Gone was the euphoria of homecoming; in its place was a growing dread that whatever it was that Rory was holding back would destroy the new relationship she and Page had so carefully revived during the past months in Europe.

Was she so insecure about that relationship, so uncertain? Yes.

No.

She didn't know; she only knew that she didn't want anything to imperil what she and Page had built together again between them. After long, empty years without him, she wouldn't lose him again. She would not.

She was silent during the drive, wrestling with her thoughts, doing the best she could to offer the proper responses whenever an infrequent question was directed at her. She knew she should pay attention to what Rory was saying; everything that happened at Beauvais concerned her, too. But she couldn't keep her mind on facts and figures, stock totals and crop projections, and the myriad other details that were Beauvais; she was too preoccupied with thoughts of Page, who was closer to her heart than even Beauvais.

As the stone pillars guarding the approach to the house came into view through the trees, Kate reached involuntarily for Page's hand. He was a little surprised at the fierceness of her gesture, the possessiveness, but he squeezed her fingers in return and smiled at her.

Kate smiled back, but as she turned again to look at the

house she could see more clearly, her smile faded and her expression became set and determined. Whatever Rory had done, Kate thought, or whatever it was that had happened while they were gone, she was not going to let it destroy the love that she and Page shared once more. She would sacrifice them all for Page.

They were greeted urgently at the door by Mrs. Hardesty, the housekeeper who had been with them the past ten years. Elvira Hardesty had been more than an employee to Kate over the years; she had become something of a friend as well. Now, as Kate hurried up the steps to the open front door, she was not reassured by the anxious look in the housekeeper's light eyes, or by her greeting.

"Welcome home, Mrs. Taggart!" exclaimed Mrs. Hardesty as Kate swept by into the house. "Oh, it's so *good* to have you home again!"

"Thank you, Mrs. Hardesty," Kate answered, thinking that they never had abandoned the more formal way of addressing each other for something less intimidating. But even after all these years and many shared midnight conferences, Kate could no more imagine calling Mrs. Hardesty "Elvira," than the housekeeper would have been comfortable calling her "Kate."

But why was she thinking of such irrelevancies when something was obviously wrong at Beauvais? Turning back to the housekeeper, Kate was just about to ask her into the study for an explanation that Elvira seemed just as anxious to give, when she glimpsed a shadowy figure out of the corner of her eye. Distracted, Kate looked in that direction instead and saw that it was Jane who was approaching. She started to call out a greeting, but just then Jane moved more fully into the light, and the words lodged in Kate's throat. As her eyes met the troubled gaze of her daughter-in-law, Kate's heart sank. Whatever it was, she realized bleakly and with a sort of numbing despair, it was worse than she had imagined.

Rory did not give them an opportunity to speak privately. He seemed determined to remain effusive as he led the way to the drawing room, for he greeted Jane elaborately with a kiss and a fond embrace, and he chatted constantly as he put an arm about her waist and drew her along beside him down the corridor. But Kate noticed that Jane held herself stiffly, even more than was customary for her in her habitual reserve, and she was worried anew.

In the drawing room, Kate saw Olivia's tea service gleaming on the table, and she went directly to it, wondering why she had ever been so scornful of the ceremony that occupied her hands and gave her time to gather her strength and her wits. More thankful than ever that she hadn't abandoned this part of her English heritage, Kate seated herself behind the tea tray and for the next few minutes everyone was busy passing cups and plates back and forth. It wasn't until Kate had drunk one cup and was reaching to pour another that she knew she could not avoid the subject any longer. She had to know why Rory was so bright, Jane so tensely silent, and Randall so inexplicably absent.

But Page anticipated her. As Kate looked at him in surprise, he put down the teacup he had taken to please her and raised the glass of whiskey he had poured for himself when they first came in. Taking a careful swallow, he looked at Rory over the rim of the glass. "All right," he said. "What happened?"

Rory was startled. "What do you mean?"

"You've been nervous as a cat from the moment we arrived. I want to know why."

Jane stirred then. "You haven't told them yet," she said, and her tone was not accusatory but resigned. All eyes were on Rory, who had flushed uncomfortably. "I was going to tell them," he said defensively to Jane. "There just hasn't been time yet."

"There's time now," Page said. "So what is it?"

Rory recognized that particular tone of voice and knew he could delay no longer. So while Jane sat tense and strained, Kate and Page listened in appalled silence as Rory poured forth the whole sorry tale about how he had gambled away the house Page had resigned himself to buying for the newlyweds.

". . . but it really wasn't my fault," he finished plaintively. "It was that John Leeds and Derry Sawyer who lured me into the game! Before I knew it, I was in too deep to pull out, and I had to risk it. Dammit, Mother, don't look at me like that! It isn't as if I've committed some heinous crime, after all! Derry's friends have the deed—they said I could get it back by paying up. That's why I was so anxious for you to come home. You'll lend me the money, won't you, Pa?"

In the tense silence that followed Rory's feverish plea, Kate didn't dare look at Page. She glanced instead at Jane and was alarmed by her pallor and absolute stillness. She looked, Kate thought anxiously, like a marble statue about to topple over at the slightest touch.

Jane saw Kate looking at her, and she closed her eyes, turning her face away in shame. Even the cords on her neck stood out, straining against her white skin as she struggled to control her emotion.

"That isn't all," Jane whispered.

"Good God! You mean there's more?" Page sprang up, his eyes blazing.

Frantically Kate signaled him; she had seen Jane cringe at Page's explosion, and she was truly alarmed by Jane's demeanor. The girl had to clutch the arms of the chair simply to hold herself upright.

Page saw Kate's gesture, and as she rose quickly and went to Jane, he made a visible effort to control himself. Taking a deep breath and avoiding looking at his son, he said, "I'm sorry, Jane. I shouldn't have shouted like that. But"—now he did glare in Rory's direction—"you will have to admit that this . . . this situation is a little . . . trying."

Kate had knelt by Jane's chair. Taking one of her hands, she was further dismayed at how cold it was. Jane's fingers were like ice, her hand lifeless in Kate's. "What is it, Jane?" she asked quickly. But as she gazed into the girl's still and strained face, Kate already knew the answer.

"I . . ."

But Jane couldn't finish. And before she could gather strength to speak again, Rory interceded. With that odd mixture of plaintiveness and aggressiveness in his voice that was so typically Rory at a disadvantage, he said, "What Jane is trying to say, Mother, is that she's going to have a baby." He turned abruptly to his father. "So you can see why I must have that loan, Pa."

"I see nothing of the kind," Page said, glancing away from Jane to stare hard at his son.

"But . . ."

Page's face was like granite. "I don't see any purpose in continuing this discussion here. I will meet you privately in the library, after you allow me a few moments with your wife. I must admit that at this point I don't know whether to offer her my congratulations or my sympathies."

The entire house reverberated with the row between Page and Rory. Jane retired, white-faced, to her room, and as Kate supervised the unpacking upstairs in the master suite, she tried to ignore both the shouting match below in the library and the fierce headache that pounded at her temples because of it.

Finally, because neither she nor her maid could keep their minds on what they were doing, Kate dismissed the girl and went out onto the balcony for some fresh air. Closing the balcony doors firmly behind her, Kate put her hands to her temples and closed her eyes, trying to shut out the fierce argument raging below her.

It was a mistake to have come out. Standing at the rail, Kate could hear not only the general sounds of battle, but a few specific words and phrases as well. She didn't want to hear any of it, and she was just about to go back inside when something Rory shouted stopped her. She froze, listening despite herself. Michael. Rory was saying something about Michael, she realized incredulously.

Despising herself for what was, after all, eavesdropping, Kate stood where she was. A minute more, and she wished she had gone back inside, but now she was caught—unable to stop herself, feeling the pain of Rory's accusation as if it were directed at her instead of at Page.

". . . know you wouldn't refuse if it was Michael!" Rory shouted.

"Michael would never have been in such a deplorable position!" Page roared back.

"How do you know? You don't know what he would or wouldn't have done! You don't know anything about Michael!"

Whatever Page said to that was lost. Kate strained to hear, gripped with a sort of horrible fascination, leaning farther out over the balcony rail.

"No, you don't!" cried Rory, as enraged as his father. "Michael was always so goddamned perfect, wasn't he? Michael always did everything right, didn't he? Well, if he was so blasted perfect, why did he run away? He was a coward, that's why! A sniveling coward who couldn't take the truth about himself!"

"That's enough!"

"No, it isn't!" Rory's voice was high and shrill. "It won't be enough until you and Mother accept the fact that Michael was no saint! At least I had the guts to stay and face you. *He* didn't!"

Kate had heard enough. Hands over her ears, she ran inside and threw herself across the bed, one arm over her eyes. Michael . . . Michael . . . Would his shadow stay forever, affecting all their lives? Would his ghost never be laid to rest, as it should have been years ago? Michael was gone . . . lost. But would any of them ever forget it?

Kate never knew what else was said between Page and his son. She didn't dare ask when, sometime later, Page came up to the room, still in a towering rage. His voice clipped, he said only, "Rory and Jane are going to stay at Beauvais until the child is born. After that . . . we'll see. I told him it depends on how he conducts himself in the coming months."

As dismayed as she was at the prospect of a sullen Rory sulking at the ranch, Kate didn't object to the plan. She couldn't, in conscience. It was past time, she knew, to make Rory take responsibility for his actions. As disheartening as it was, she and Page had to admit that while Rory might be a man in years, he was still a child in many ways. Would becoming a father change that? Kate could only hope that it would.

"You aren't going to buy back the note on the house for him, are you?" she asked.

Page shot her such a look of indignant rage that she added hastily, "No, no, I didn't think so. I just wanted to be sure."

"Well, you can be sure," said Page grimly.

There was a liquor cabinet on one wall, and Page went to it now, opening a decanter with such force that the amber liquid inside splashed down the sides. He poured himself a generous measure, and Kate bit her tongue. He was drinking too much, she thought. But it was difficult to blame him; she felt like joining him, as well. The homecoming they had anticipated with such pleasure had been totally ruined by Rory's destructive behavior, and Kate suddenly felt defeated. It was hard to believe that only that morning she and Page had sat side by side in the railroad car, eagerly watching the miles roll by as the train sped through Colorado, taking them home to Beauvais. They had been so happy then, so content. And now . . .

"Where's Randall?" she asked abruptly.

Page slammed the empty glass on the table at her question,

startling her. "And that's another thing!" he growled. "It seems that Rory, instead of coming home to Beauvais with his tail between his legs at his despicable behavior, returned instead as the lord and master. He and Randall apparently had a terrible row, and naturally, Rory got what he wanted—again."

Kate felt a stab of fear. She swallowed, her mouth suddenly dry, and it was an effort to ask, "Randall isn't . . . he didn't . . . ?"

Page saw her fright and came at once to hold her tightly. "No, no," he said quickly, trying to soothe her. "He didn't leave, Kate. I'm sorry. I didn't mean to frighten you."

She sagged against him, so relieved that she could hardly speak. Page continued to hold her comfortingly, and finally her heart stopped its frantic pounding.

Page seemed calmer, too, for after a minute he held her away from him and said, "Randall is at the Siddonses' ranch, according to Rory. George had a heart attack while we were gone, and Randall went to help out." He paused to search her face, adding gently, "It seems the best thing for a while, don't you think?"

Kate bit her lip, torn between wanting Randall home and wondering if his being away from Beauvais was really the solution for them all for the time being. Then she thought of George's daughter, and she wondered if Emily might be just the medicine Randall himself needed. Emily, having lived too lonely a life for a young girl—young woman, Kate corrected herself—might welcome the companionship of someone her own age.

No, she had to be honest, Kate told herself firmly. It wasn't only companionship she wished for Emily and Randall; it was something deeper, more lasting. Emily was so much the opposite of Adele—so much less intense and complicated. She had a lively, pert personality, and she wasn't so . . . self-absorbed. If anyone could, Kate thought, Emily Siddons would be the one to help Randall forget.

"I think it's a wonderful idea," Kate said, smiling as she came to her own conclusions.

"Are you thinking the same thing I am?"

"What? That as sorry as I am for George's illness, it might be a blessing in disguise?"

Page smiled broadly. "I've often thought that Emily would be the perfect wife for Randall."

Kate was startled. "You have?"

"Don't sound so surprised. Women aren't the only ones who think such things, you know."

"But what made you think of Emily?"

Page shrugged. "I don't know. I've always been fond of her, I suppose. And despite all the responsibilities she's had from such a young age, she's always managed to be . . . gay. I think that might be what Randall needs just now—a little gaiety."

Kate stared at him. Would she never cease to be surprised by this man? It seemed that whenever she was sure she knew him totally, he would say or do something that made her realize she didn't know him at all.

They smiled at each other, enjoying one of those brief moments of silent communication that made everything else worth the pain and the bother and trouble. Then Page became serious again. "You don't mind having Rory and Jane here for a while, do you? I know I should have discussed it with you first, but I was so infuriated with Rory and his damned arrogant attitude that I just ordered him to stay."

"No, I don't mind," Kate said honestly. "In fact, I think it might be the best thing for Jane. She doesn't look well, and I'm afraid that this pregnancy is going to be hard on her." She hesitated. "Do you think she would feel more comfortable if we invited Amelia to stay, too? We could explain to Amelia about Rory somehow."

Page laughed and hugged her again. "How like you, Kate!" he said fondly. "Determined to do the best thing for Jane, despite the fact that you dislike her mother."

"That's not true! Or at least," she amended, "it isn't true anymore. In fact," she added, piqued by Page's renewed laughter, "Amelia and I get on very well now. It's been years since she annoyed me with all that ineffectual fluttering."

"Well, you'll be happy to know that in our absence, Amelia has mended her ways."

"Mended her ways? What do you mean?"

Page's eyes danced. "It seems that Amelia was so lonely after Jane married and went on her honeymoon that she decided to turn her home into a boarding establishment."

"A boardinghouse!" Kate couldn't have been more astonished if Page had told her Amelia had suddenly decided to become a saloon singer.

"And doing quite well, too, if Rory is to be believed. Of

course, our snobbish son looks down his nose at such enterprise, but he did offer it as one explanation for his and Jane's retreat to Beauvais." His eyes twinkled again. "There simply wasn't room for them," he said solemnly, "at Amelia's Room and Board for Genteel Women."

"Is that the name of it? Oh, my!" Kate giggled. "I hope she doesn't have to have stationery printed!"

They collapsed with laughter onto the bed, choking and sputtering with an amusement that really didn't have anything to do with Amelia's venture—which they admired—and really didn't have to do with amusement at all. After such a disastrous welcome home and the problems with their children, it was a relief to laugh about anything, and as they rolled together on the bed, their laughter finally stilled and became passion instead.

Looking into Page's eyes as he held her close, Kate knew that her fears about him were groundless and that they had existed only foolishly in her imagination. The love they had nurtured and somehow kept alive through joy and sorrow, through pain and tears and final victory, sustained them now in this crisis and in whatever would follow. They had been through doubt and suspicion and guilt and betrayal, and had emerged anew, stronger together than they had been before.

33

To Kate's surprise, and Page's grim satisfaction, Rory proceeded during the next months to mend both his fences and his attitude. Suddenly he became a considerate husband, a hardworking part of Beauvais, and a model son. If Kate hadn't witnessed this startling transformation herself, no one could have convinced her it was true.

Not that she really trusted Rory, she assured herself. But it was a relief to see him this way, even for a while. And in her most optimistic moments she was even hopeful that Rory had finally decided to recognize his responsibilities as a husband

and father-to-be and to accept that he was no longer a care-free young man running up debts he was sure he could cajole his parents into paying.

She said so one day to Page when they were sharing a quiet moment on the terrace. And when his expression was so openly derisive at her statement, she had to laugh. "Well, we can always hope, can't we?" she said.

"I think I'd prefer to see something a little more concrete than hope," Page replied darkly. "After that last debacle, Rory will have to prove a great deal more to me than he has up to now."

"Well, you have to admit that he hasn't put a foot wrong in months," Kate pointed out, thinking at the same time how odd it was for her to defend Rory to Page. In the past their positions had always been reversed: she had accused, and Page had championed their errant son.

"He has been careful, hasn't he?" Page said. "I must have put the fear of God into him, if nothing else. That, or he just hasn't had a chance to do anything wrong. I haven't let him leave the ranch for weeks, unless someone goes with him." He grinned at her, then sobered again. "But all the good behavior in the world isn't going to put a dent in the money he owes me for that note. I told him he had to repay me for saving his house, and it seems for once that he believes me."

"And is he going to repay you?" Kate asked. "Every cent?"

Page looked sheepishly away. "Well . . ."

"Page Taggart!" Kate flared. She had been prepared for this, or so she thought. But now her eyes flashed as she glared at him. "If you cancel that debt of his, I'll never speak to you again!"

"Now, don't get upset—"

"Upset! If you . . ." Kate stopped, suddenly aware of the laughter in Page's eyes. "You tricked me! You never had any intention of canceling that note, did you?"

Page shook his head. "I just like to see you flare up some-times—when I haven't done anything to deserve it myself. Do you know that your eyes get very green when you're angry?"

"Oh, really!" She tried to act affronted, but it was impossible with Page grinning boyishly at her. "So you are going to expect Rory to honor his obligations?" she asked, blushing despite herself at the look of appreciation on Page's face.

Page became serious again. "If he has to pay the full amount, Kate, he'll be at Beauvais for the next hundred and fifty years. Are you sure you want him underfoot all that time?"

They had been sitting together on the marble bench. Kate rose now and walked restlessly to the edge of the terrace, her expression thoughtful. "I don't know," she answered. "If Adele comes home, and I think she should," she added, frowning at the thought of her daughter, who had gone with Olivia's misgivings to visit some new acquaintances in Brighton, and who had insisted on prolonging her stay despite Olivia's protests, "the house will be full again, and I'm not sure that would be best for Jane—all the confusion and noise. You know how Rory and Adele are together, always quarreling even when they aren't angry with each other." Kate looked over her shoulder, her voice dropping even more. "I'm not concerned about Rory or Adele, but I am worried about Jane. I wonder what would be best for her."

Page joined her as she turned to look somberly out at the mountains, which were crowned with the fire of afternoon sun. "Jane doesn't look well, does she?" he said quietly as he put his arm about her waist.

Kate shook her head, thinking now of her daughter-in-law, who had grown more pale and quiet as the months went by. The child was due in several weeks, and while Jane's once slender body was cumbersome in late pregnancy, it was more her manner that worried Kate. She was apathetic and lethargic, and the dark shadows under her eyes indicated that more was wrong than the physical strain of being pregnant. She rarely spoke; she seldom even left the suite of rooms Kate had given her and Rory. Because Kate was so concerned, she would often make up a pretext for visiting Jane upstairs, encouraging her to join the rest of the family for tea or meals, or simply sitting with her in the drawing room, sewing. But it was rare that she could persuade Jane to join her, and while she and Amelia were actively worried about the listless Jane, there was nothing they could do. Jane would just look at them both with those huge dark eyes and insist that nothing was wrong.

When pressed, Jane would only admit that she didn't feel well, and when Kate had confronted Rory in desperation, Rory had only looked astonished that she was concerned.

"Why are you so anxious, Mother?" he had said, infuriating Kate with his apparent unconcern when she was so worried. "Some women just have a more difficult time than others carrying a child, isn't that true? Jane is just one of the unlucky ones, I guess."

Kate had attempted to swallow her anger, trying to be reasonable. "I think you might display a little more consideration than that, Rory," she had said.

Rory infuriated her even more then by appearing hurt. "I am being considerate," he insisted. "Doesn't Jane have everything she wants here? Doesn't she have the best care, and when the time comes, the best doctor? Even when her own mother came out and practically begged her to stay with her during these last months, Jane refused. So she must be all right, don't you think? I do."

Rory's tone was both persuasive and impatient, and Kate wondered in exasperation if he honestly couldn't see how thin Jane was despite her pregnancy, or how drawn and strained. But before she could say anything more, Rory had patted her arm and added, "I think you worry too much, Mother. Jane has never had the strongest constitution, but she tells me she's fine, and I believe her. You should, too."

But Kate didn't believe either of them. Something was wrong with Jane, and if it wasn't her physical condition, it was something far worse. Jane seemed to be afflicted with some malaise of the spirit, a sickness that was far more debilitating than any physical illness would ever have been, and Kate remained concerned.

She turned to Page now, answering his earlier question by saying quietly, "No, she doesn't look well at all, Page." She moved restlessly in the circle of his arm. "If I thought it would do any good, I'd ask the doctor to come again and examine her."

Page shook his head. "I've already asked her if she wanted to see the doctor."

Kate was startled. "You have?"

"Why do you always look so surprised when I say something like that? Did you think I hadn't noticed how little we see of Jane? Or how pale and silent she is when you can persuade her to join us?"

"I wasn't surprised, not really," Kate said, leaning against him again. "It's just that you always do such thoughtful things and then never say anything to anyone about them."

"But why should I?" It was Page's turn to be surprised.

"Because . . ." But Kate knew from long experience that whatever she said on the subject would be ignored. Page was his own man—thoughtful, considerate, generous . . . and quiet about it. He would never change, and, Kate thought with love, she didn't want him to.

"What did Jane say when you asked her about having the doctor in?" she asked instead, anxious again.

Page gazed out across the horse paddocks, filled now with valuable Beauvais mares and their foals. "She refused, of course. She insisted that she was all right." He paused. He had always loved Jane; long before she married his son, he had considered her another daughter—a gentle, troubled daughter he would have given anything to help. "But she isn't all right, is she, Kate?" he asked finally, his voice low. "She isn't all right at all."

To their sorrow, Page's solemn words that day were more prophetic than they knew. In early autumn, only days before her first wedding anniversary, Jane gave birth to a son. Todd Templeton Taggart was born on a hot, sultry day in September, when the grass was dry, the wind still, and a hush was in the air. It was 1889, and an arid Colorado waited for rain. Six hours old, Todd cried for the mother he would never know.

They buried Jane at Beauvais, the place she had loved because it held so many memories of her first and only love. The doctor was at a loss to explain to a bewildered Rory why Jane had died. The birth had been difficult, and long, but it had not been life-threatening, he was sure. It was just that Jane had seemed to . . . slip away. He didn't know what had happened; he insisted that he had done everything he could to save her.

But while the doctor might not have understood what had taken Jane, Kate knew. As she dressed the day of the funeral, Kate thought sadly of Jane, who had come to her only the week before—calm, resolute, and with a new expression lighting the dark eyes that had been so empty these past worrisome months. She had appeared at the sitting-room door one quiet afternoon when Kate had been morosely stitching on a baby dress for the new infant.

"Aunt Kate? May I talk to you for a moment?"

Kate had glanced up at once, forcing a smile that hid how dismayed she felt at the sight of Jane's drawn face. "Of course," she said, patting the seat beside her. Looking critically at the embroidery in her hand, Kate grimaced as Jane sat down; she folded the little garment quickly and stuffed it with relief into the work basket at her feet.

"I hope I didn't interrupt," Jane said.

"Not at all. In fact, if you hadn't rescued me just now, I probably would have ripped the thing to shreds in sheer exasperation." Kate pulled a face, trying to make Jane smile. "It was a smock for the baby, but I don't think I'll force it on you after all. I'm a terrible seamstress, you know!"

When Jane didn't answer, Kate abandoned her light tone. Taking the girl's cold hands in hers, she asked gently, "What is it, dear?"

Jane swallowed. Despite her pregnancy, she had grown so thin that Kate saw the cords in her throat convulse at the movement. Trying to keep a tight rein on her alarm, Kate squeezed the icy fingers reassuringly in hers and waited.

Finally, after a silence, Jane said, "I . . . I never should have married Rory. It was a mistake . . . a grave mistake. I know that now."

Kate wasn't sure what to answer. Jane had turned her face away from her and was struggling to control her emotion, and Kate herself was at a loss for words. Should she admit that she agreed, or would that make Jane feel worse? She didn't know, so at last she just said quietly, "What do you mean, Jane, a mistake?"

"I never should have allowed Mama to push me into marrying him," Jane said, as if Kate hadn't spoken. "I didn't love him, you know."

Once again, while Kate wasn't alarmed by Jane's words, she was concerned by her manner. She was speaking so mechanically, almost without inflection, her tone dead. It was frightening, in a way, and Kate took a grip on herself. She wouldn't help Jane by becoming hysterical, she told herself sternly. So she said simply, "I know you didn't love him, Jane."

The girl turned, searching Kate's face, as if she thought Kate might blame her, or be condemning. But Jane saw only a sad regret and nothing more, and she sighed, nodding. "You knew."

It was a statement more than a question, and now Jane gently pulled her hands from Kate's and stood. Walking slowly over to the window, she stood there a moment gazing out. Then she said softly, "I've always loved Beauvais. I loved it from the moment I first saw it." She looked briefly over her shoulder at the silent Kate, then out the window again. "It seemed right somehow, like Michael, who was so strong, and so much a part of the land . . ."

Her voice drifted away then, and Kate was just about to rise and go to her when Jane spoke again. Turning away from the window, she said, "If something happens to me, will you see that the child is taken care of? I don't want it to grow up solely under Rory's influence. I'm . . . sorry if that hurts you, but I . . . I can't help it."

"It doesn't hurt me, Jane," Kate answered. "Or, at least, not in the way you think." Now she did get up and go to Jane. "But nothing is going to happen to you," she said reassuringly, with her arm about Jane's thin shoulders. "You're young and healthy, and—"

Jane interrupted, her dark eyes almost fierce as they rested on Kate's face. "Will you promise, Aunt Kate? Will you see that you or Mama takes the baby?"

And so, as uneasy as she had been, Kate had given her promise. Now, standing beside the freshly spaded earth, gazing sadly down at the mound of flowers that covered the grave, Kate was neither surprised nor shocked at Jane's death. She was only numb.

Lifting her eyes, Kate looked beyond the clustered group of mourners to the house some distance beyond. Involuntarily her glance went to the nursery-floor window. Jane's child—and her first grandchild, Kate reminded herself—was there with his shock of russet hair and blue eyes, thriving already under the care of a hastily imported wet nurse. Jane had died giving him life, and Kate thought how sad it was that Todd would never know his mother, who had been good and kind, and so desperately in love with the wrong man.

Kate looked away from the house, her glance seeking Rory's bent head. Watching him, Kate wondered what he was really thinking as he stood there and listened to the minister read the service. His handsome face was creased into lines of sorrow, his red-gold hair even more fiery than usual in the hot September sun. From the moment he had been told of Jane's death, he had acted the bereaved husband: solemn, silent, grief-stricken. But to Kate, who knew him so well, something had been missing—something not quite right about his reaction. Grieving herself, it had taken her several days to realize what it was that troubled her about him. And then she knew.

Rory had said the proper things, had done the proper things, had acted correctly in everything he did. And that, Kate had finally realized, was the clue. Rory had been acting. And his performance had been so polished that it had even fooled her for a while. Oh, she was sure that he felt some sorrow and regret over Jane's death—as much as he was able to feel about anything, Kate thought. But as she gazed at him now, she wondered if Rory was really capable of honest emotion at all. Sadly, she doubted it. Some vital ingredient—compassion, understanding, the ability to love—was missing from his personality, and nothing seemed to touch him.

Except, thought Kate with a sense of despair, where greed and the conquest of power were concerned. Rory would always see to Rory; if others were hurt or helped along the way, it didn't matter. The only person who mattered in Rory's life was Rory himself. As a mother, Kate hated to admit it; but as a woman, she knew it to be true.

And so had Jane known, Kate recalled with a sharp sense of loss. Jane's last words to her before she died were a warning that Kate could not deny or ignore. Gripping her hand, Jane had whispered, "I wasn't going to tell you, Aunt Kate. I thought I would be here to hold Rory in check. But now it seems . . ." Her voice had faltered for a moment, then gone on weakly, "Rory will do anything for Beauvais, Aunt Kate—anything to have it. He wants power, and he doesn't care if he sells Beauvais piece by piece, or all together. He . . . he told me so himself. He might act like Beauvais means something to him, but it doesn't. Nothing means anything to him except for what he can get from it."

Kate had been so shocked at this revelation that she hadn't been able to speak. Power? Sell Beauvais? She wanted to ask Jane to explain, but there was no time . . . no time. Jane's face was white against her pillows; even her lips were colorless. Only her dark eyes burned with the effort to make Kate understand, and so she had nodded, not really understanding at all.

Leaning forward from her position by the bedside, Kate had smoothed Jane's hair. The baby had long since been taken to the nursery, a maid had been in to remove all traces of the birth, and the doctor was in conference with Rory and Page in the library. Kate and Jane were alone in the still, quiet room, and Kate had fought to hold back her tears.

"Oh, Jane . . ."

Jane gripped her hand even more tightly. "No . . . please. Let me finish." Her voice was so low now that Kate had to bend to hear. "I told you about Rory because I thought Todd should know . . . Beauvais as it is. I wanted it to be . . . whole for him. Do you understand?"

Kate nodded again, swallowing hard to control her emotion. "Yes, I understand," she said, and this time she did.

Jane closed her eyes, overcome by exhaustion. "Then you'll remember your promise?"

"Of course."

Jane sighed. Her voice was only the merest whisper now, and Kate would have completely missed her next words if she hadn't been so near. "Thank you . . ." Jane had said. "Michael would have wanted it this way, too."

Kate had left her then, and a strained but surprisingly tearless Amelia had gone in to sit by her daughter. Jane had died not long after, and Amelia had sat by the deathbed of her only child for hours by herself, simply staring at the pale face that had finally attained an expression of peace that Jane had not known for many years.

The service was ended. At the stirring of movement around her, Kate looked up. She had been so lost in thoughts of Jane that she hadn't realized the minister had finished speaking. Page gripped her elbow comfortingly beside her, and Kate smiled sadly at him just as Amelia came up to them.

"Amelia . . ." she murmured. There was so much to say, and yet there was nothing to be said after all. Lacking words, Kate reached out, and the two women embraced. "Why don't we go back to the house?" Kate suggested. "You must be exhausted."

But Amelia's blue eyes were resolute when they met Kate's, and her expression was determined. "I would like to talk to you both, if I may."

Page nodded. "What is it, Amelia?" he asked, his voice strong and kind. "If there is anything you need, you know you have only to ask."

A faint smile touched Amelia's lips, and she touched Page's arm in gratitude. "Thank you," she said. "And I do need something, Page, but I'm afraid it isn't what you think."

"What?"

"I need my grandson."

They had all begun walking toward the house, but now Kate and Page stopped with one accord to stare at her. Amelia saw their doubtful expressions, and she smiled briefly again. "Now, don't look at me like that, you two. I'm perfectly capable of taking care of a baby."

"It isn't that," Kate protested.

"What, then? No, Kate, I've made up my mind. I want to take him home with me. I've thought it over very carefully, and Rory and I have discussed it thoroughly."

Kate and Page looked at each other. But before either of them could say anything, Amelia was going on. "I'll give up the boardinghouse, of course, and keep Rory's home in Denver for him and the baby instead. We'll be . . . a family. Jane would have liked that, I think." For the first time, her voice faltered. She looked from one to the other, silently pleading with them to agree, to understand, and helplessly Kate and Page were forced to nod.

Amelia smiled tremulously then, and she said very quietly and with simple dignity, "Thank you . . . both. I know what a sacrifice you're making, and I am more grateful for it than you know."

And so, in the end, Rory got what he wanted once more. By manipulating even these sad circumstances to his advantage, he seized the opportunity to escape Beauvais and his father's watchful eye, and to see that someone else assumed responsibility for his infant son as well. It was an arrangement that suited him admirably, more so than either Kate or Page could know.

34

Jane's son was four years old—a sturdy little boy with reddish hair and deep blue eyes who had unfortunately left behind his fleeting resemblance to Jane to favor his father instead—when Randall married Emily Siddons. George Siddons had died the year before, and Randall and Emily made the

Siddons ranch their home after the quiet ceremony. The ranch was where, a year later, in 1895, Randall and Emily's only child, Marcus, was born. Black-haired and black-eyed from the first, it was Marcus who would so resemble Page, Marcus who was to bring it all full circle.

But while Marcus was to play such a pivotal role, his birth went almost unnoticed, shadowed by an event that overwhelmed the whole family: after a self-imposed four-year exile in England, Adele came home to Beauvais.

Unfortunately, she did not come home alone.

To Kate's dismay, Page's fury, and Olivia's angry mortification, Adele brought home a husband. His name was Varian Winters, and Kate almost fainted when she saw him. Adele's husband could have been the twin of Roger Templeton twenty years before. They had the same faded appearance: pale blond hair, light blue eyes, weak chin, and indecisive mouth. And when Kate's glance met his after Adele breezily introduced them, her spirits sank even lower; Varian was exactly what he looked—out of his class, and certainly out of his depth with Adele. Observing their lopsided relationship from the first, Kate wondered wildly why she had married him, and then, gazing into Adele's triumphant and bitter dark eyes, she knew.

Page had guessed the reason, too, and it was only by the quickest pressure of her fingertips on his arm that Kate was able to restrain him. She didn't need to look at her husband's face to know that he was furious; the letter from Olivia had come three days before, and Page had spent the intervening time pacing the house like a caged lion. Now, with their first glimpse of their new son-in-law, his worst fears had been confirmed. Like Kate, Page knew exactly why Adele had married a man so like Roger.

"Now, Mother," said Adele, bending forward briefly to brush her lips against Kate's cheek, "I know exactly what you're going to say!"

Kate stared coolly at her daughter. "You do?" she said with lifted eyebrow.

"Of course!" Adele laughed. "You're going to tell me that I've been a bad girl, that I've worried everyone—especially Aunt Olivia—needlessly, and that, as usual, I've been thoughtless and inconsiderate. Am I right?"

She laughed again, a high shrill sound so unlike her that Kate forgot what she had been about to say and just stared instead. Adele's glance darted away from Kate to her husband, who was smiling weakly by her side, and finally to Page, who hadn't yet said a word. Like Kate, he was staring at his daughter, who seemed to be, abruptly and unhappily, someone he didn't know at all.

Adele gave Varian's arm a brief squeeze, still looking at her father. "I know I've been simply awful about eloping like this, but really, when I saw Varian, I just couldn't help myself. I was sure, Papa, that you, above all people, would understand that!"

Once again Kate tried to restrain Page, whose arm had jerked convulsively under her fingers at this thinly veiled insult from Adele. She was too late. Ignoring her warning, Page said harshly, "Now, look here, young lady! You—"

"But that's just the point, isn't it, Papa? I'm not a young lady anymore! I'm twenty-five years old, and a married woman—finally! I can't be sent to my room anymore in disgrace—unless my husband sends me there. And Varian would never dream of doing such a thing." Her hard dark eyes flicked contemptuously to Varian's face. "Would you, darling?" But before he had a chance to answer, Adele had turned to the livid Page again. "So you see, Papa, you're just going to have to forgive me, after all. And I *did* come home, didn't I?"

With Page almost apoplectic beside her, Kate decided it was time to intervene. "I'm curious about that, Adele," she said evenly, trying to restrain her own anger in the hope that it would help calm Page, too. "If you felt this way about us, why *did* you come back to Beauvais?"

Adele raised an eyebrow in a gesture that was unconsciously very like her mother's. "Didn't you get my letter? Oh, dear, I see that you didn't. Well, then," she finished airily, "it's really the most tiresome thing—isn't it, Varian?"

"Yes."

So he could speak after all, thought Kate uncharitably; she had begun to wonder if in addition to acting as Adele's shadow, Varian Winters was mute as well.

"What are you talking about, Adele?" Page asked, breathing heavily and glaring at the unfortunate Varian.

Adele affected a yawn. "We had to have somewhere to live, didn't we, dear Papa? And since Varian's family is caught up in one of those confusing, maddening entailed estates, it seems that his two older brothers will inherit everything instead of him. Isn't that so, darling?"

"Well, actually—"

"Varian was supposed to stiffen his upper lip and commit himself to one of those incredibly useless careers like joining the army or whatever it is"—Adele gave everyone a dazzling smile—"but when he found out about Beauvais, he married me instead. Isn't that wonderful of him? To think—he gave up his army career for me!"

"Wonderful," said Kate dryly, wishing she could shake some response from Varian, or at least see if he could complete a whole sentence.

"If you think you can saunter home after the disgraceful exhibition you made of yourself in England—" Page began.

"I really don't think we need to discuss these things on the station platform," Kate interrupted hastily. "Why don't we go out to the house?"

Adele clapped her hands. "That's an excellent idea, Mother! Then we can all sit around and discuss this like civilized people over the tea service. How I do appreciate the English custom of tea now. It gives one the opportunity to be proper and pointed at the same time!"

In the end, of course, Kate and Page had to welcome Adele and her husband. They had recognized the inevitability of it from the beginning, when they had received Olivia's hastily penned letter. Olivia might have been embarrassed by her failure to chaperon properly the errant Adele, she might have been mortified that her great-niece had eloped from under her nose, but she had not been remiss in beginning at once to discover exactly who Varian Winters was and what prospects he presented. Her letter had been brief, direct, and typically Olivia—to the point. Discouraging as it was, what Adele had so blithely revealed was true: Varian Winters was the third son of a fading family that had no real prospects behind an old manor house titled grandly and inappropriately Winter Castle.

Olivia's letter, so terse and dry until the last page, had ended in a private postscript to Kate, in writing that wavered from age and emotion. She was sorry that she had allowed Adele's elopement to occur under her care, she wrote; there was no way of apologizing sufficiently.

"I can't help but feel," she wrote to Kate, "that this is

some kind of judgment on me. Perhaps if I had advised you differently so many years ago, Adele wouldn't have run off as she did. How ironic it is that I had to force you to accept Page's proposal, while if I had known what Adele was planning, I would have begged her to reconsider!

"Sometimes I wonder if it is true that one sees things so much more clearly in old age. I often think back to that time when you were a young girl, and even now I don't know what I might have done differently. You were so headstrong and so willful, Kate!

"And yet, I couldn't have loved you more if you had truly been of my own flesh and blood. I think of you as my daughter, Kate, and I always will. Remember that whatever I did so long ago, I only did because I loved you and wanted the best for you. You're strong, Kate, and capable of such love! You'll weather this storm, as you have so many others, because of that loving strength."

Kate never saw her aunt again. In the winter of 1900, when she and Page were contemplating another trip to England to visit the ailing Olivia, they received word that she had died peacefully in her sleep. A grief-stricken Kate mourned the passing of the aunt who had been more of a mother to her than Augusta Beauvais had been, and yet that was only the first of the blows Kate would receive that year. Adele's daughter, Annabel, who had been born prematurely the year Adele and Varian had come home to Beauvais, was four years old when Kate and Page received the two letters that signaled the passing of one part of their lives and the beginning of another.

In the spring of that year, when the mountain crocuses he had loved so as a child had just begun to bloom, David died in Africa of consumption. A devastated Kate had hardly begun to recover from that loss when another death knell struck, a blow from which both Kate and Page wondered if they would ever recover.

Kate had been waiting for Page on the terrace that day. They had decided to have tea by themselves, a private restful time away from the demands of Beauvais and the friction of Adele and Varian and the fretful Annabel. Consequently, Kate was alone when Page came out; she had been standing at the edge of the terrace, breathing deeply of the light early-summer air, admiring the blossoming flowers in her garden beyond, thinking of David. It was the first time she had been able to remember him without that wrenching sense of loss she always experienced at the thought of his death, so far away in a foreign country. Staring down at the white rose she had plucked, she recalled how he had helped her plant this very rosebush, and she had murmured fondly, "David . . ."

Lost in thought, it was a few moments before she was aware that she wasn't alone. Glancing up, she saw Page standing inside the French doors that led to the terrace. She was about to call to him when she saw his face. It was ashen, almost gray.

"Page! What is it!" Frightened, she dropped the rose and started toward him. What was it? Was he ill? Had something happened to one of the children?

And then she saw the crumpled paper in one of his hands, and the smudged envelope in the other. She stopped abruptly, halfway to him, halted by a terrible premonition that gripped her so strongly she could hardly breathe.

"What . . . is . . . it?"

"Kate . . ."

Somehow he had crossed the distance that separated them and was leading her to the marble bench where the tea cart already waited. She had the hysterical urge to pour tea for them, or to offer him the plate of his favorite biscuits she had ordered just for him that day—anything to postpone whatever it was that he had to tell her. She was just reaching wildly for the silver teapot when he gently forced her to the bench beside him. He took her hand away and clasped her cold fingers in his, and she couldn't look at him.

"Kate . . ."

But she couldn't even respond to the pleading note in his voice. She knew he was suffering; she had seen his face, his eyes. She *knew*.

"Kate!"

"No! No!" she cried. "It's too much to ask! Please, Page . . ."

His voice became stronger, overriding hers. "Kate, listen to me," he said, gripping her hands tightly. "This . . . this letter is from someone named Lily—"

"I don't know anyone named Lily!" Her voice breaking on a sob, she tried to free her hands to clap over her ears. Page held her firmly, forcing her to look at him. His eyes were bright with unshed tears, and she sobbed again wrenchingly, feeling that terrible pain rising, choking her.

"Lily is . . . Michael's wife," Page said.

"No! No!"

"She wrote—"

"I don't want to hear!" Kate's cry was from the heart, from her mother's soul. She felt as if she were screaming into the darkness, into the driving, pelting, unforgiving rain, calling for a son, a child she would never ever see again.

"She says—"

"No! Please—"

"That Michael is dead."

Page sobbed then, a man's cry that was a timeless sound of grief so deep that it could hardly be expressed. It was a father's wordless lament for a son so dearly loved that the loss was almost unbearable.

Kate clung to him, and as he held her tightly, the letter drifted to the flagstones by her feet. Kate saw the misspelled words, the smudged writing, the coarse quality of the paper, and at the bottom of the page, the words she would never forget, the scrawled sentences that would be burned forever in her mind and heart: "He alus took care of us, I want you to know that. He was a hard man, but he was good to, and we miss him. Thot you shud no about his dyin, thats why I wrot. There's no need to wory, we'll get along just fine. Michael's wife, Lily."

And Kate, sobbing, lifted her ravaged face to the mountains that suddenly seemed harsh and cold and unforgiving, and thought: *We'll get along?*

Who was "we"?

It was then that the final import hit her, and she stiffened. Without realizing what she was doing, she pulled away from Page and walked woodenly to the edge of the terrace. Very slowly she raised her fists to her mountains and shook them impotently. She had had him for so short a time, her son. He had come into her life and then disappeared so quickly, like a shooting star that is only glimpsed and never really fully seen. Now she knew she would never see him again, never hear his voice or know what kind of man he had become. She would never know him at all, this son of hers, her first child.

"Have I been so wicked, so evil, that I must be punished with one mortal blow after another?" she screamed to the sky. "Will I lose everything I love until my very soul is sucked dry? I can't stand it—do you hear me? It's too much to ask, too much for one woman to bear!"

Turning, she saw Page coming toward her, and she shrieked at him, "Why, Page, *why*? What have I done? *What have I done?* I can't endure it—I can't! I'm not strong enough . . . not strong enough . . ."

And Page folded her in his arms, pressing her face against his breast, murmuring, murmuring, comforting her in his own pain.

But Kate could not be consoled. She collapsed against him in an anguish so great that it seemed to crush her very spirit. "Michael . . . Michael . . ." she sobbed.

But Kate would have need for the strength that Olivia had long admired, and for the courage that Page loved in her, and the determination that her children so respected. From somewhere deep inside her, Kate would be forced to tap the reserve of strength and will that was hers alone, for the final test was yet to come.

III

35

On July 28, 1914, two months before Kate's sixty-seventh birthday, the world watched aghast as Austria-Hungary declared war on Serbia, accusing that small country of harboring the terrorist group that presumably. assassinated the Archduke Franz Ferdinand. One horrifying event rapidly followed another after that: Germany sided with her ally, Austria, while Russia mobilized to protect her interests in Serbia. Germany was then forced to declare war on Russia, and on France as well, Russia's ally. By August 1914, after German armies had marched through neutral Belgium to crush France, Britain, honoring her pledge to defend Belgian neutrality, declared war on Germany. A bewildered and confused world was suddenly, appallingly, at war.

America's initial reaction was horror, disgust, and a fierce determination to keep out of it. But the European conflict would ultimately touch all nations and all peoples, even fervent isolationists in the United States, including President Wilson, who tried to stand firm in the face of increasing pressure from all sides. And in the end, as it had been planned from the first, America was drawn in. Like so many others who would be compelled to send a son or a brother or a husband or father to fight in a war that had been begun by an unknown assassin's bullet, the Taggart family would be profoundly affected. Like all wars, it was an absurdity, a terrible deadly game that Kate didn't understand and didn't want to understand. In fact, that Sunday afternoon in September, Kate wasn't even thinking of the battle raging half the world way; she was engaged in a terrible struggle of her own. While booted feet marched to war, Kate fought a battle in her own home: Page was dying, and fourteen-year-old Gabrielle Taggart had come to Beauvais to stay.

For a long time afterward, whenever Kate looked at Gabrielle, she would remember that ancient saying that seemed to have plagued her all her life: *Beware the wish, for it may come true.*

And if that saying held any truth, she would think despondently, then she had brought this sorrow onto herself, for she had wished so often to see Michael again, or to have news of him. She had said that she would give anything just to know what had happened to him; she would give . . . anything. But she hadn't meant it, she thought in anguish long afterward; she hadn't really meant it. It was only a figure of speech, something said without realizing the full import of the promised exchange. She would have given anything, she had said so glibly. BUT SHE HADN'T MEANT PAGE.

Sometimes, in the terrible and lonely nights after his death, when she couldn't sleep, she would stand at her window staring out at Beauvais in the moonlight and wonder: Why had it to be one for the other? Why Page for Gabrielle? *Why?*

BEWARE THE WISH . . .

And she had wished that day for Michael, she would remember—she had wished for him that day of her birthday in September, when everyone gathered together for her. She had thought wistfully of him, and she had wished that he were there, too. She hadn't been content, she would realize so bitterly later on; she hadn't been happy with what she had that day. She had wanted Michael, too.

Oh, they had tried to find Lily, the woman who had written to them after Michael had died; they had exhausted themselves trying to find her. Page had engaged the Pinkerton Agency again, and no expense had been spared to locate this unknown woman who had been Michael's wife, their unknown daughter-in-law. But as had Michael so many years before, Lily seemed to disappear completely from the moment she posted the smudged letter that had eventually found its way to Beauvais. It had been posted from New York; that much the detectives were able to decipher from the smeared postmark. But that was all. Michael had been employed by the railroad at the time of his death; that much the detectives discovered, too. But there was no forwarding address to follow up on once the agents had followed the trail to New York; it was as if Lily Taggart had simply ceased to exist.

And then, fourteen years later, on the day of Kate's sixty-seventh birthday, Michael's daughter had arrived unannounced at Beauvais. Fourteen-year-old Gabrielle had walked boldly up to the house she had never seen, and to the family she had never met, and had demanded haughtily to be let in.

It wasn't so much the excitement of discovering that he had a granddaughter he had known nothing about that precipitated Page's collapse; it was the shock of seeing in Gabrielle a young Kate. When he had glimpsed her standing there in the drawing room, he had actually experienced a dreadful kind of vertigo: it was as if the girl waiting there *was* Kate. They were so alike . . . so alike . . .

But to Kate, who witnessed that terrible collapse, it didn't matter what the reason was. She didn't care then; she cared only about Page. One minute he was hers, alive and happy and well, and in the next, he was gone from her, dying a death whose only consolation was that it was mercifully quick and painless.

And Kate had been so happy that day as she dressed for the dinner Page had arranged, so pleased that everyone had made the trek out to Beauvais just for her. She was celebrating her birthday that day, and as she inspected herself in the mirror, she thought with a touch of wry vanity that for a woman who was sixty-seven, she really didn't look a day over fifty-five. Her skin was still clear and unmarked, and the unavoidable lines that had appeared around her eyes and near her mouth didn't age her so much, she thought, as they lent her character. Her hair was completely white now, but her eyes were still the flashing green they had been in her youth, and her smile was just as imperious or mischievous, whichever she chose, as it had always been.

Standing back from the mirror and giving herself a last inspection, Kate wasn't displeased with what she saw, nor did she really mourn for lost youth. The past years with Page, despite the loss of David and Michael and Jane and Amelia, had been the happiest and most satisfying of her life. She and Page shared a deep and abiding love, and to prove it, he had gathered their family together for her birthday. The house would be filled with their children and their children's children that day; there would be ten seated at table for the celebration that afternoon. Much later, when the pain of losing Page had abated slightly, Kate would remember looking around her table that day and thinking what an occasion it was: her family did not often come together all at the same time, and she was proud that they had agreed to come to Beauvais that Sunday to honor her.

There had been Rory, portly at forty-seven, his red-gold hair threaded with gray, his hazel eyes hard and cold until a glance caught his, and then he would smile his charming smile. He was thinking of trying for state politics this year, and Kate thought sadly that if he succeeded, he might not be out of place; there were rumors again about Colorado politicians, and Rory's smile never did reach his eyes.

At Rory's side had been his son, Todd, now twenty-five, and his father's son in character, if not in appearance. His fleeting resemblance to Jane remained only physically; his hair had darkened from russet to deep brown, and he had her nose and mouth. That was all; in other respects he was like his father—selfish, greedy, and wild. Rory had never disciplined him, for he regarded Todd's escapades as boyish pranks, and laughed at them. Amelia had tried to correct her grandson while she was alive, but her efforts had been undermined from the first by an indulgent Rory, so that now Todd was careless, rude, and—worst of all—a coward and a bully, a dangerous combination, especially in one who lacked moral character. Unfortunately, he was also one of the handsomest of Kate's grandchildren, and he possessed his father's easy disarming personality that so charmed those who didn't know him. He permitted few to know him well.

Kate had tried from the first to love Todd, because he was her grandson, and because he was Jane's child. But every time he turned those handsome, expressive eyes on her and smiled that engaging smile, Kate felt herself stiffening inside, wondering what it was that he wanted from her.

She had no such suspicions about Marcus, Randall and Emily's son, for Marcus had captured her heart from the beginning because he looked so much like Page. Every time she saw him, she was astonished anew by his outright resemblance to his grandfather; it was as if some mysterious force of heredity had concentrated on strengthening the link between grandfather and grandson, so that, in the same age, they could have been identical twins. Marcus had the same dark hair and black eyes as had Page; the same startlingly handsome face with its strong features. Like Page, Marcus, too, possessed that intense glance, the quizzical lift of an eyebrow, the sardonic smile. He also had the assurance his grandfather displayed, that confidence in himself that was such a source of admiration or irritation to those around him. At nineteen, Marcus was his father's pride, and the fact that he had argued almost violently with Randall the year before about converting some Siddons acreage from cattle to wheat, and then had reaped a profit that astonished even Page, only endeared him more to his father. Marcus loved the land as his father and grandfather before him, but he studied constantly for methods to improve yield, and he was not averse to trying new experiments that were derided by others less bold. Kate loved him for that, because she remembered the same qualities in Page. She would never admit it, even to her husband, but Marcus was her favorite grandchild.

Kate's glance was troubled that day as it came to rest down the table at Adele and her daughter, Annabel. Adele had become increasingly bitter over the years; she had never recovered from her involvement with Randall, and while she rarely spoke to him, and never mentioned him at all, there were times, as at gatherings like this, when Kate would catch Adele looking longingly at her half-brother when she thought no one would notice. And it was at such moments only that Adele betrayed any vulnerability; there would be such a look of pain in her eyes then that Kate's heart would go out to this unhappy daughter of hers. Over the years, Kate had wished many times that Adele and she were closer, but that single time of shared intimacy at Tremont Hall seemed to have been the first and last of any real communication between them, and Kate knew that Adele would only reject any approach now. She had rejected so many offerings from Kate before.

And Annabel was the same, Kate thought, her glance moving to Adele's eighteen-year-old daughter. Unfortunately, Annabel had inherited none of her mother's vivid coloring, nor even Varian's blond fairness. Her hair was perhaps her best feature, for it was a shining chestnut color, thick and curled, and Annabel wore it in a loose chignon at the back of her small head. Her features were narrow and sharp, with shrewd brown eyes, long nose, and thin mouth that was often petulant and irritable. She was not a happy girl, and her face showed it, but she possessed a formidable intelligence and an astonishing facility for mathematics. She had been educated in the best finishing schools in the East and in Switzerland, for Adele was restless and often traveled, and Annabel had been installed in various schools all over the world while her mother wandered.

In the beginning, when Annabel was very young, Kate had

tried to object to this arid existence for her granddaughter, pleading with Adele to allow Annabel to stay at Beauvais. Adele had refused. She wanted her daughter to grow up sophisticated and poised, able to handle herself in any strange or uncomfortable situation, and she could not, Adele had haughtily insisted, learn such things by staying immured at Beauvais. And the proof that she was right, Adele would point out triumphantly later on, was that Annabel consistently achieved the highest marks in whatever school she had been enrolled in, whether in the United States or on the Continent.

Kate and Page were helpless to argue. They couldn't even deny Adele the funds she required for her travel and Annabel's expensive education, for Adele had inherited a small fortune of her own through the unlikeliest of avenues: Varian himself. Ironically, Varian Winters had been worth far more dead than he had ever been alive. Somehow, through a complicated process Kate had never understood, he had inherited a cousin's estate only days before he himself died of a lung fever he had caught one winter and from which he had never recovered. Consequently, Adele had inherited everything upon his death. That had been years ago, when Annabel was only seven years old, and since then the restless Adele had occupied herself by traveling all over the world. When Annabel became old enough, she often accompanied her mother, and every time they returned to Beauvais, Kate was more dismayed and unhappy at how hard and brittle Adele had become.

What drew the two of them, Adele and her daughter, back to Beauvais several times a year, Kate was never sure. She suspected that Adele's yearning just to see Randall was one reason, but it was difficult to know for certain, for Adele never talked about him.

Instead, she would use Annabel as an excuse, explaining that she didn't want her daughter to forget her grandparents; or she would speak vaguely of seeing to her investments, of which there were considerable. Adele had a shrewd mind and a good business head under her cosmopolitan sophistication, and she had increased her fortune several times already. Unfortunately, Kate thought sadly, she had not increased her happiness or personal satisfaction with it. And so Adele would come restlessly back to Beauvais, seeking a comfort Kate tried always to offer, and then just as abruptly as she had come, she would be off again, searching for something she seemed destined never to find.,

But they were all there that Sunday afternoon in 1914, and as they all sat down to table, no one was aware as yet of the proud figure trudging up the drive, wearing a frayed black serge skirt, patched jacket, and threadbare white shirtwaist. The figure carried a cardboard suitcase, which she shifted occasionally from hand to hand, for with the clothing it held, the suitcase was loaded with books the girl had found too precious to leave behind.

The valise might be cardboard, but the books inside were bound in leather, and the girl's clothes might be darned and mended, but they were immaculately clean. No one watching her walk up that drive to the huge house at the end would have taken her for a servant; the haughty tilt of the head and the determined lift of the chin betrayed her.

But no one was watching, for inside the house Kate was glancing around the full table and giving thanks for those who were there, and sending up a prayer for those who were not: Michael, David, Jane, Roger . . . and Amelia, who had died some five years before.

Kate thought of Amelia now, for some reason, remembering how she had sent for her before she died. Kate had gone at once, for over the years their friendship had grown until they had become very close. They had been through so much together, Kate thought, and had endured so many things, that there had been an intimacy between them the past years as if they had almost been sisters instead of friends. Kate had been so emotional by the time she had reached Amelia's bedside that she couldn't even speak. Amelia's fingers, so stiff and swollen, sought hers, and when Kate took her hand in response, Amelia smiled weakly and with affection.

"Amelia . . ." Kate had murmured helplessly.

"Dear Kate . . ." Amelia paused to catch her breath. The doctor waiting outside had told Kate when she arrived that it wouldn't be long, and Kate stifled a sob as she tried to smile down at her friend.

"Dear Kate," Amelia said again with a sigh. "How we all envied you when we were young—Lucinda and Amy and Ellen and I! Do you remember them? We were all neighbors, friends, and you were the outsider. But we envied you all the same!"

"What nonsense!" Kate said fondly. "Why, I remember you all turning up your noses at me!"

Amelia smiled faintly. "That's because we were afraid of you—I, most of all."

"Afraid of me? But why?"

"Oh . . . you seemed to know so much more than we did. You were so confident and assured, and you never hesitated to throw caution to the wind and do exactly what you wanted to do. I envied that most of all."

"Yes, but that's what got me into a great deal of trouble, if I remember correctly," Kate said. "I was always disgracing myself or doing something wrong. You couldn't have been jealous of that!"

"Yes, even that," answered Amelia softly. "It proved that you weren't afraid to defy stupid rules to . . . to be yourself. I . . . I never had the courage, and I admired you for yours."

"Oh, Amelia!"

Amelia caught her breath again and tried to speak. But her voice was weaker than before, and when Kate tried to quiet her, Amelia shook her head. "No . . . I have to tell you," she whispered. "I've waited years—since we were girls—to tell you, and I can't rest unless I do."

Kate leaned forward to wipe Amelia's face with her handkerchief. "All right, then," she said gently. "What is it, dear?"

Amelia's glance sought hers, and her fingers tightened on Kate's. "Did you ever wonder why I . . . why I never blamed you about . . . Roger?"

Kate stiffened. She wanted to deny it, to say that it didn't matter. But it did matter, she thought. She had always wondered, and yet it had never been mentioned between them. They had spoken of many things, but they had never talked about her and Roger at all. Still, Kate hesitated. Did she want to know at this late date? Did she want to be the cause of any more of Amelia's pain?

"Didn't you wonder?" Amelia asked urgently.

Kate looked into her friend's eyes, and finally she nodded. She had to tell the truth. "Yes," she admitted. "I wondered."

Amelia nodded too. "I should have told you long ago," she whispered. "I always wanted to, but I never had the courage. I . . . I hadn't the courage for so many things!"

"That isn't true!" Kate protested, gripping Amelia's hand.

"Yes . . . yes, it is. And that's what I wanted to tell you, I suppose. I admired you for your courage, and for knowing what . . . what passion was. I never knew about passion, Kate," Amelia said, her eyes very blue. "And I wanted to know. Oh, I wanted to! We used to talk about it, my friends and I, and wonder. And then you came and we knew that you knew all about it. You were so intense—so *passionate!* —about everything, Kate! So alive . . . so vital. I knew from the first moment I saw you that you would know everything I always wanted to know—about passion, about feeling, about . . . being swept away, and I knew that if any of us should have a . . . an affair, it would be you."

"Amelia!"

But Amelia wasn't embarrassed by her admission, or sorry she had said what she did. Holding Kate's gaze, she continued. "That's why I never resented it when I found out about you and Roger," she said, smiling slightly. "I had suspected it for a long time, you know—anyone with half an eye had only to look at David to see the resemblance to Roger."

"But you never said anything!"

"What was there to say? I used to look at David and think: that might be my son, if only I had had the courage Kate did! But I never had the courage, and so if I felt anything about you and Roger, Kate, it was envy—envy that I hadn't taken matters into my own hands like you did and discovered what it was like, for once, to know passion. I envied you, Kate; I never hated you for what you and Roger did that day. Do you believe me?"

And Kate, looking down into Amelia's earnest blue eyes, was forced to nod. She did believe her, and yet that admission was more difficult in its way to bear than her age-old guilt. Amelia had known, Kate thought; she had known, and she had kept her silence all these years. And that, Kate felt, took more courage than *she* had ever possessed. She said so to Amelia, holding that fading blue glance by sheer force of will. More than anything now, she didn't want Amelia to die—Amelia, who had been more of a friend to her than any she had ever known.

But Amelia only smiled at Kate's vehemence, and shook her head. "Oh, how I admire you, Kate," she whispered at the last. "And how I loved you. . . ."

"Oh, Amelia!" Kate cried.

But Amelia was beyond hearing. With a sigh, she drew her final breath, and gradually her tight grip on Kate's fingers

loosened. Her hand dropped away to curl lifelessly on the
quilts, and beside her, Kate wept.

"Here's to you, Kate . . ."

"To you, Mother . . ."

"Grandmother . . ."

Kate looked up, disoriented for an instant at the sea of
faces turned her way. They were all staring expectantly at
her, and she realized finally that everyone had raised their
glasses in tribute to her. She had been so far away with her
thoughts of Amelia that she hadn't even heard the toast.

She was furious with herself. She really must be getting
old, she told herself caustically, to have been oblivious of
such an important moment. She had wanted them all to share
this day with her, and then, when they had all come, she had
forgotten they were here. Really!

Trying to cover her embarrassment, Kate raised her own
glass. It was the right thing to do, for suddenly there were
various smiles all around, and everyone drank. Thankfully,
the buzz of conversation began almost immediately again, as
if no one had really been aware of her inexcusable lapse.
Marcus was teasing his cousin Annabel; Emily was talking
quietly with Randall: Adele was arguing already with Rory
about investing in munitions.

Looking down the table, Kate met Page's eyes. He was
smiling at her, and when he saw her gazing back at him, he
raised his glass again to her in his own silent tribute. He
would be seventy-two years old his next birthday, at the first
of the year, and yet, to Kate, he had never aged at all. His
hair might be as white as hers now, his face seamed with the
lines that never made him look old but only added to his formidable dignity; he walked with more of a pronounced limp
from the injury he had received so long ago that first freight
trip with Colin—but to Kate he was the same man who had
laughed at her that faraway day on a hillside in Sussex. It
was his eyes, Kate thought; his eyes had never changed. In all
the time she had known him and loved him, his eyes had always been the same intense, fierce black. They had blazed
with anger, glinted with tears, shone with love, and she had
been mesmerized from the first time she had been drawn
down, down, into those dark depths. Oh, how she loved him
then—and how she loved him still!

Raising their glasses, Kate and Page looked at each other
in one of those wonderful silent communications between two

people who have shared so many years and memories together. The conversation around them ebbed and flowed, voices rose and fell, arguments escalated and discussions waned, and for a few precious moments there were only the two of them at the table; everyone else had ceased to exist for that one sparkling, breathless moment stolen from time. Kate looked into Page's eyes and saw the love shining there, and suddenly she was a girl again, elated, exultant that the man she had married was everything she could have wished for, and more. She would never change him, and now, after all these years, she realized how they had changed together—how they had grown. They were lovers, friends, companions, and they shared that timeless sense of closeness that only two people who have suffered so much in the past together can know. Page had been the only man for her—then, now, and forever. Without him, everything was meaningless, dry, arid . . . barren.

Page smiled, as if he could read her thoughts. And perhaps he could; they had developed the uncanny ability, over the years of their marriage, of knowing what the other was thinking. They had been together so long, married fifty years on their next anniversary, Kate marveled—so many years, and yet no time at all.

Page seemed about to say something to her over the hubbub of conversation around them, but just then one of the servants came in and whispered in his ear. Kate, watching from the other end of the table, saw him start almost violently and look up at the servant in shocked surprise. She was about to rise and go to him, sure something was wrong, but just then he turned and caught her eye. Shaking his head quickly, he pushed back his chair and gestured for her to stay where she was. An instant later he was gone from the dining room, and after that single moment of seeing him go, nothing would ever be the same for Kate. Seconds later, she heard him call out in surprise, and something in the quality of his voice lifted her to her feet. With the rest of the family staring after her with various expressions of astonishment and confusion, Kate ran after Page. There was something terribly, appallingly wrong, and she knew somehow, in that moment before she saw him, that a flame had gone out in her world.

Two of the servants had already reached him by the time she took the few steps from the dining room across the corridor to the door of the main drawing room. They were bending over him, loosening his collar, putting a pillow under his head. Kate froze where she was, and it was as if her heart had stopped, too—as if everything in her world had ceased. Time seemed frozen, and so did she; she couldn't move.

And then one of the servants moved, and Kate saw Page's face as he lay on the floor. He was absolutely white and still, and with a wrenching cry she ran to him.

He had suffered a heart attack. The doctor wasn't sure why, for from the moment he fell, Page hadn't regained consciousness. Kate didn't care to know the reason; she didn't even think to wonder. As she sat by his bedside, she didn't care about anything but his recovery. He looked so . . . so defenseless lying there, with his face as white as the pillow, his lips a colorless gray as he labored to breathe, and Kate bent all the power of her formidable will on giving him the strength to recover. The doctor waited outside, but he had shaken his head gravely at Kate when she had demanded to know the truth about her husband's condition.

"I'm sorry, Kate," he had said solemnly. "But it's very serious, I'm afraid."

"How serious?" Kate demanded. She was holding hysteria at bay by the merest edge. But she had to know.

The doctor had shaken his head again, and Kate bit her lip to keep from screaming at him. "Answer me, Clay!" she said sharply.

Dr. Wilson had looked helplessly at Rory, and at Randall, who were both standing by her. But it was Randall who said, "Tell her, Dr. Wilson. She has a right to know, if anyone does."

"All right, then . . ." Clay had taken her cold hand and tried to lead her to a chair. She had refused. She stood where she was, her own heart pounding wildly inside her chest, terrified of what the doctor would say, trying to steel herself against hearing what she had known, silently, from the start.

"Page has had a heart attack, Kate," Clay said finally. "And I'm afraid . . . I'm afraid . . ."

"Go on." She spoke through stiff lips, her mouth as dry as dust. Was it only a few hours ago that they had all sat together at the table celebrating her birthday? A sob broke from her, and Randall started toward her. She waved him back. "He isn't going to live, is he?" she asked quietly.

Clay hesitated again. Then he looked at her face, into the green eyes that somehow held his unflinchingly, and finally he shook his head.

It was almost a relief to know. The uncertainty had been more terrifying to her than even the knowledge that Page was going to . . . to die.

She faltered then, swaying a little, so that both Randall and Rory came forward to support her. Again she shook them off. She looked directly at Clay Wilson and said, "You're sure? There isn't any chance you could be mistaken?"

This time the doctor didn't hesitate. "No, I'm not mistaken," he said. His voice broke a little; he had known and admired Page for a long time. "I wish to God I was!"

"Thank you, Clay," Kate said. "I appreciate your being truthful with me."

"If there's anything I can do, Kate . . ."

"No. Nothing, thank you. Randall and Rory will see you downstairs. Perhaps you would like some refreshment before you go back to Denver . . ." Strange, how in times of crisis the mind occupied itself with nonsense. Page lay in there dying, and she was talking about offering this man something to eat before he went home. It was insane, and yet, if she didn't deal with these absurdities, she really would go mad.

"Mother . . ."

She turned stiffly to look at Randall and saw the anxiety in his eyes. Glancing the other way, she saw that even Rory was stunned by what had happened. Gently disengaging herself from them, she put her hand on the doorknob and said, "I'm going to . . . to sit by him now. Please don't disturb us. I'll . . . I'll call you if there's any change."

"I'll be downstairs if you need me," the doctor said quietly.

"As you like, Clay. But really, it isn't necessary . . ."

"Nevertheless," Dr. Wilson said firmly, "I'll stay."

Kate nodded, smiling slightly. Then she went inside and closed the door behind her.

She could hear the murmur of their voices as she stood leaning against the door, trying to gather strength, trying to hold back the agonizing pain she could feel building inside her even now. Listening to their worried tones, she knew even without hearing the words that they were talking about her. She didn't care. Nothing was going to take her from Page's bedside—nothing. If they only had this little time left, she would keep it for herself. Treasure it. Weep over it. But she would not leave Page's bedside while he lay dying. She would not. Page was her life. Her life. . . .

Page died early the next morning, as the sun rose to light the mountains with glorious vivid fire that Kate never noticed. Toward dawn, he had stirred for the first time and murmured her name, and she was instantly alert, leaning over him, smoothing his forehead with hands that shook.

"What is it, my darling?" she whispered. "Are you in pain?" Oh, give her his pain, she thought; she would endure any agony just to hold on to him awhile longer. She couldn't give him up yet—not when there were still so many things left to say! They had been together almost a lifetime, and yet it was no time at all.

Page opened his eyes. Even with approaching death, his eyes were intense, passionate, when they rested on her face. He reached for her hand, his fingers gripping hers in a gesture that he meant to be comforting but which only brought tears to her eyes and desolation to her heart.

"Katie . . . it's too soon, isn't it?"

She couldn't lie to him, couldn't pretend. They had been through too much together for her to feign hope now. One look at his face, and she knew—just as he knew himself. His fingers tightened on hers.

"Oh, Page!"

"Shhh." He had heard the terrible agony in her voice and tried to console her again. "Be strong, Kate," he whispered. "You have to be strong for both of us now."

"But you're my strength!" she cried.

He shook his head. "No, dearest love. And it's you they'll all look to—you know that. I always hoped . . ."

He hesitated, and she said, "What?"

He took a breath, and a shadow crossed his features. Kate wanted to scream, to push it away, but she could sense the approach of death as strongly as if she had seen it coming in a physical form. She could almost hear the hard beating of wings, feel the other-world rush of cold wind against her face. She bent closer to Page, clinging tightly to his hand, not even aware of the tears streaming down her cheeks.

"I hoped that I could be here always for you, my darling," Page said after a moment. "But I've known for a long time that I . . ."

Kate thought of all the times over the years that she had

seen the shadows under his eyes, had noticed the lines of weariness that seemed deeper than they should. Had he always known? Had she?

"Page, don't leave me!" she cried. "I can't bear it if you go! How will I live without you? How will I endure the loneliness?"

The shadow was very near now; it was almost a palpable presence in the room. Page knew it, too, for he said hurriedly, "You will have Gabrielle to help you, darling."

"Gabrielle?" Kate didn't know who Gabrielle was. She didn't care. Death was all around them now, and she tried to stave off the final approach of it by sheer force of will.

"She's so like you, Kate. So like you. I . . . I knew at once that she would be a comfort to you, and a help. Michael sent her, dearest. He's come home at last, in her."

Michael? Kate thought that Page was rambling, confused. But it didn't matter. With each breath, he was going farther away, leaving her behind, no matter how desperately she tried to hold him.

"Katie, my Katie," he whispered. "I loved you always, from that first moment on the hill."

"Oh, Page, don't leave me! God . . . please don't leave me!"

But with a last regretful sigh and a quiet pressure of his fingertips on hers, Page closed his eyes.

The beating sound of those fluttering wings became deafening, increasing to a hard drumming that made Kate cover her ears with her hands. "No! No!" she cried. "It's too soon! Please . . ."

But just as abruptly as it had come, the sound was gone, taking Page away . . . forever. Agonized, Kate stared down at the inert form on the bed. Then, falling across Page's body, she sobbed brokenly into the sudden awful silence of an empty room and a desolate heart.

36

"Kate?"

"Mother?"

She heard the voices, the concerned voices, the voices breaking with tears and shock and grief, and she turned blindly toward the sound. It was an effort to focus on their faces, but finally she saw who was there. Her family. They were there in front of her: all of them. Randall had tears in his eyes, and Emily was weeping openly as she clutched her husband and the stunned Marcus. Rory was ashen, Annabel white with shock, Adele trying not to cry. And they were all looking at her as if they expected her to do something. Even the doctor, who came forward now, to put his hand on her shoulder.

She stood before he could speak, shaking off his hand. Without saying anything, she went from the room. She couldn't speak; her throat felt as if there was a vise clamped to it, her chest too tight to breathe. Somehow she managed to make her way to the head of the stairs, and then she realized that she had no idea where she was going. A servant was just coming up, and Kate stared at the girl as if she had never seen her before. The maid looked up just then and exclaimed, "Oh, Mrs. Taggart! I was just coming to ask . . ."

"What . . . what is it?"

"Well, that girl is back down in the drawing room, Mrs. Taggart. Mrs. Hardesty gave her one of the guest rooms last night, but now she's down again, and she declares she won't speak to anybody but you. I tried to tell her that Mr. Taggart was ill, ma'am, and that you were busy." The servants had not been informed how serious Page's collapse had been. "Anyway, Mrs. Hardesty sent me to ask you what should be done about her. The girl, I mean."

Kate stared at the maid. "Girl? What girl?"

The servant looked puzzled. "But I thought you . . . I mean . . ."

It was odd, thought Kate, how one could engage in conversation just as if nothing had happened. She had lost Page, and yet she seemed so calm inside, almost serene, as if she would look up and there he would be, coming toward her.

But he wouldn't come to her again, ever. Why didn't she feel it? She should feel something for Page, and yet everything inside her was still, empty . . . waiting. Was she in shock? Would they all come and take her away somewhere where she would go quietly to pieces, strangled by the hysteria lurking at the fringes of her mind, swept away by the sound of those terrible wings beating . . . beating . . .

". . . the girl who came yesterday, ma'am. She said her name was Gabrielle. Gabrielle Taggart. Mr. Taggart saw her. I . . ." The maid's voice trailed off as she became aware for the first time of Kate's stillness, her stiff manner, her staring eyes. "Mrs. Taggart . . . ?"

Kate tried to get a grip on herself. "Yes," she said. "Mr. Taggart has just . . . just . . ."

But somehow she knew that if she said the word, she would begin screaming and never stop, and so she paused, swallowing painfully as the maid's eyes filled with tears and her face crumpled. "Oh, ma'am! I'm so sorry . . . so sorry . . ."

"Yes," said Kate. She put her hand on the girl's shoulder. "Tell me about the person in the library," she said. Somehow it seemed very important to keep her mind on these little details. Perhaps if she occupied herself with minor matters, she wouldn't feel that awful agony, the horrible loneliness she knew she would have to endure the rest of her life. Page was gone . . . gone. . . .

With an effort she jerked her attention back to the servant, who was wiping her eyes on the corner of her apron, trying to control her tears. "She's in the drawing room, Mrs. Taggart," she managed. "But I can go and tell her that—"

"No. I'll see to her myself."

Something in Kate's tone made the girl look up. "Yes, ma'am," she said, staring at Kate, who was so calm and still—so abnormally still. "Is there anything I can get for you?" she asked hesitantly. She had never seen the mistress like this, and she wondered if she should run for the doctor.

Kate's lips felt stiff as she answered, "No, thank you. I'm going to the drawing room now, if someone wants me."

"Yes, ma'am."

Kate could feel the servant's eyes on her as she descended the stairs, one hand carefully on the rail. Already the house seemed so empty, so hollow and vacant, as if all the life had gone out of it.

And it had, thought Kate. There would be no more life for her, no joy in living, for she had lost her reason to live. Page was gone, she thought emptily, and her soul was as dry as dust.

She stopped at the door to the drawing room. The girl was there, standing with her hands clasped behind her, staring up at the great portrait of Kate that dominated the space above the marble fireplace. She had her back to Kate, and Kate stood where she was for a moment, her hand at her throat, staring at the girl who could be no other than Michael's daughter—who could be no other than her own granddaughter. Now she knew why Page had been so shocked; she felt the same way herself.

Even with her back to Kate, the resemblance between them was there, so strong that there could be no doubt. Gabrielle Taggart was as tall as Kate, and as slender, and even when she believed herself alone, her head was tilted in the same defiant, challenging attitude that Kate remembered so well from her own girlhood. Fiery red hair tumbled down Gabrielle's back, held away from her face by a blue ribbon—hair as thick and curly and unmanageable as Kate's own had been, and as red.

And then Gabrielle turned, and suddenly Kate was looking into a face that could have been hers fifty years before; she was staring into green eyes that might have been her own even now.

Those green eyes stared boldly back at her—proud, imperious, and just a little frightened, but determined not to betray it. Before Kate could recover from the shock of having a granddaughter who looked so much like herself as a girl, Gabrielle spoke, and suddenly Kate was thrown back in time to herself as a young girl, standing tremulously on the front steps of Tremont Hall after her mother died, trying desperately to hide her uncertainty under a veneer of hostility and defiance.

"Don't think," said Gabrielle, "that I came here because I had no place else to go. I came because my mother"—the

veneer cracked a little to reveal the frightened girl under-
neath—"because it was my mother's last wish."

"I see," said Kate quietly, tactfully ignoring the sudden
shine of tears in those challenging green eyes. "Your mother
was . . . Lily?"

"Yes," Gabrielle answered, flinging up her head so that her
tears wouldn't spill ignominiously down her cheeks. "And my
father was Michael Taggart. I never knew him."

Gabrielle turned away abruptly, flinging one hand toward
the portrait over the mantel, while with the other she quickly
brushed away betraying tears. "Is that you?" she asked in a
muffled voice.

"Yes, it is," acknowledged Kate, glancing at the painting
and seeing a younger edition of herself there, and an older
version of Gabrielle, who was standing below it. She looked
so startlingly like the portrait that Kate felt a moment's regret
for lost youth.

"It doesn't look very much like you," Gabrielle said defiantly.

"It was painted some time ago."

"And it doesn't look very much like me. Mother always
said I looked like you, but I think she was mistaken."

"How would your mother know what I looked like?" Kate
asked. The conversation was becoming stranger by the
minute. And she didn't want to stand here listening to this
rude, hostile girl when upstairs Page . . .

But her mind closed on the last thought, snapping shut
quickly on the pain that rose, like an ogre, ready to claim her
the moment she let down her guard. She would deal with that
agony later, when she was alone, Kate thought, and then
wondered why she stayed here at all. But something held her
in the drawing room, and Kate realized abruptly that talking
with Gabrielle was keeping the sound of those awful flailing
wings at bay. "How did your mother know what I looked
like?" she repeated.

"She had a miniature."

"A miniature?"

"My father painted it," said Gabrielle, as though Kate had
challenged her.

"Your father painted . . .." Kate's voice was choked.
Michael had painted something to remind him of her? She
could hardly believe it.

"Yes, he painted it," repeated Gabrielle with hostility.

"That was how my mother knew where to send the letter about my father dying. The address was on the back."

"Do . . . do you have it?"

Gabrielle glared at her. "Of course I have it. It was the only thing we had of my father's. You can't have it."

"I don't want to take it from you," said Kate with a sigh. "I just wanted to see it, if I may."

"My father never talked about you, you know. Or so Mother said. I told you I don't remember him; he died when I was only a baby. But when Mother told me that, I thought it was strange that he never said anything about his family. About . . ." Gabrielle's hand lifted in an encompassing gesture. "About this place. Why didn't he? Did you make him leave?"

"No," Kate answered sadly. "It was his choice."

"Was it?"

"Yes, it was!" Kate replied with the first sign of sharpness she had shown. Was she really having this nightmarish conversation with a granddaughter she had not known existed until a few minutes ago? She put one hand to her head and said, "I'm sorry, Gabrielle. I'm afraid we'll have to continue this . . . this discussion at another time. You . . . you must excuse me . . ." Her voice faltered; quite suddenly, she couldn't speak.

"It's Grandfather, isn't it?" Gabrielle asked sharply.

Kate had started from the room, but at Gabrielle's pained question, she turned back again. The face so like her own was pale, the green eyes huge, the lips parted anxiously.

"Yes," Kate said. "It's your grandfather." She glanced briefly at the clock. Had it been only an hour since Page had died? she wondered, feeling her emptiness grow into a huge leaden mass. She felt like she had been alone so long, an eternity of barren days and nights, and it had been only an hour. How was she going to endure all the lonely hours to come?

"He died this morning," Kate said woodenly as Gabrielle stared at her. "Your grandfather died this morning."

She had said it; she had finally acknowledged aloud the terrible catastrophe that had taken place at sunrise. The words clanged in her mind, closing that chapter of her life with horrible finality. As Gabrielle looked after her wordlessly, Kate turned abruptly and went from the room.

37

Page was buried at Beauvais, in the family plot that now held four headstones: one for Page, and another for Jane; two more in memoriam for Michael and David, who had not been buried there but who had grave markers all the same.

The news of Page's death had spread rapidly to Denver—and beyond—and there had been a commemorative service in the city that Page had helped to build. But because Kate wished that only the immediate family be present the day Page was interred at Beauvais, there was no crowd of mourners to gape and gawk and exhaust her with their well-wishes and sympathies as they sat sadly about teacups and cakes in the drawing room. Page had wished it this way, and so had Kate.

Rory was incensed at the modest and quiet service Kate ordered; he would have preferred a huge gathering of people, a vast display befitting the passing of one of Denver's finest and most influential citizens. He would have preferred, Kate thought sadly, the pomp and ostentation associated with the transferring of power from one generation to the next. It was their first battle, hers and Rory's, over what took place at Beauvais now that Page was gone, and she won only because the rest of the family sided with her. But it was a sign of things to come, and as she stood alone for a moment of private thoughts after the service ended, Kate wondered what the future would bring.

Would the family always stand behind her? she wondered. And if they did not, would she be strong enough to fight Rory alone over what was important for Beauvais?

But she had to be strong enough, she thought. Rory might be eager to seize the reins now that his father was gone, but Rory hadn't inherited everything—not yet, and not while she was alive. She would fight him if she must, just as she had been forced to battle over something so personal as funeral arrangements. But fight she would, for she and Page had shaped Beauvais together, and Rory was not going to tear down what had taken years of their lives to build.

They had planted a grove of willows at one side of the plot when Jane had died, she and Page, and now she moved over to the stone bench sheltered there. Sitting down, she gazed out at the mountains and realized abruptly that Rory wasn't going to be her only problem. In the three days since Page had died, Gabrielle had succeeded in disrupting the entire household. Even Emily, kindhearted and generous as she was, had thrown up her hands in despair, and easygoing Randall had been sharp with Gabrielle on more than one occasion himself. Rory and Todd had flatly refused to have anything to do with her after she had accused them of being power-mad and wanting everything for themselves, and both Adele and her daughter were incensed because Gabrielle had called them snobs.

Of them all, only Marcus seemed amused by the volatile and prickly Gabrielle, who had made it perfectly clear to everyone that she was there only under duress and that she would prefer to be anywhere else, preferably as far away from Beauvais as possible. Marcus had just smiled and shaken his head at Gabrielle's fourteen-year-old vehemence, but Kate had noticed that his glance often rested speculatively on Gabrielle, and his dark eyes would light with some private inner fire.

Marcus might be tolerant, Kate thought now, but she herself was inclined to agree with the others where Gabrielle was concerned: the girl was hostile, defensive, and definitely a problem. And, Kate thought with a sigh, it was too soon, much too soon, to expect her to manage a volatile granddaughter; she was just too old to cope. It might have been different if Gabrielle had been a loving, gentle, and considerate girl, anxious to please, eager to help or to retire shyly out of the way. But she was none of those things. Instead, she was haughty, imperious, difficult, ill-tempered, and acid-tongued. Not, Kate thought wryly, the model granddaughter, under any circumstances.

Perhaps she should seriously consider sending Gabrielle away to a finishing school, as Adele had already caustically suggested, Kate thought, remembering with a grimace the afternoon before when they had gathered—mistakenly—for a quiet tea hour.

"It would give her a little polish," Adele had said acidly, glancing with a sniff toward Gabrielle. "And heaven knows she needs it, after the appalling way she has behaved!"

That was when Gabrielle had infuriated Adele and Annabel both by accusing them of being snobs. "Well, maybe I don't talk—"

"Speak," corrected Annabel, looking down her long, thin nose with a sly smile that she knew already would infuriate her mercurial cousin. The two girls had disliked each other at once, and neither had made a secret of it since.

"*Talk*," said Gabrielle with a murderous glare in Annabel's direction, "as properly as you do, or choose the right words, but there weren't any fancy schools in our house! My mother worked hard to support us, and I had to help out." Gabrielle thrust her reddened hands into the startled Annabel's face. "And what did *you* do, Annabel, besides learn how to correct someone when they *speak*?"

"Well, really!" sniffed Adele in her best cosmopolitan manner. "There really is no need to shout, Gabrielle!"

Gabrielle wasn't in the least intimidated. Rounding on her aunt, she said, "And you're no better than she is! You're both snobs! You think that because you were born rich that makes you better than the rest of us! Well, I'll tell you something, Aunt Adele—it doesn't make you better at all, just meaner!"

Adele turned furiously to Kate. "Mother, aren't you going to say anything at all?"

Kate carefully put down her teacup. "I'm sorry, Adele," she said, trying her best not to smile at the indignant, outraged expression on her daughter's face. "But I really didn't think Gabrielle needed anyone to defend her. I thought she was doing quite well herself."

"That wasn't what I meant at all, and you know it!"

Kate sighed. "All right, Adele," she said. She turned to the glowering Gabrielle and added, "I think you should apologize to your aunt and your cousin, Gabrielle. There really isn't any excuse for such rudeness."

Gabrielle's green eyes flashed. Jumping to her feet, she glared furiously at them all, but particularly at her grandmother. "How can you accuse me of being rude, when it's they who act so superior! Just because Annabel's been to all those expensive schools, and Adele has traveled so much, there isn't any reason for them to look down on *me*! My mother may have been a dance-hall girl before my father married her, but she had more kindness in her than all of you have put together!"

"Gabrielle!" Kate didn't know whether to be more shocked at her granddaughter's behavior or more startled at the revelation of who Lily had been.

But it didn't matter what her reaction was, for when she saw Gabrielle's mortified expression, Kate knew at once that her granddaughter had never intended to reveal such potent and private information into the hands of those she regarded, inexplicably, as her enemies.

Before Kate could say anything, however, Gabrielle had looked wildly from Kate to Adele to Annabel, and back to Kate again. Tears of rage and humiliation sprang into her eyes, and she shouted as she ran from the room, "I hate you! Oh, how I hate you all!"

That had been only the day before, Kate mused, and a sullen Gabrielle had refused to leave the guest room even for the funeral today. Everyone had been livid at her defiant and unresponsive attitude, insisting to Kate at various times that the girl be forced to attend the service. Everyone had approached her, Kate thought now, except Marcus.

"Leave her alone, Grandmother," Marcus had counseled. "She'll come out when she's ready. She's scared now, and unsure of herself in this new situation, and it's been a . . . a strain for all of us." He paused reflectively. "Perhaps she feels responsible, somehow."

"Responsible?" Kate was surprised. "What do you mean?"

"Well, everything was all right until she showed up, you know. And then Grandfather took one look at her, and he . . ." Marcus looked away, tears glinting suddenly in his eyes. He and Page had been very close. "I don't know," he finished lamely. "I just thought she might feel responsible for his death."

"Yes," Kate said quietly. "I see what you mean. All right, then, Marcus. I think your advice is sound. Gabrielle can come out when she's ready."

And so Gabrielle had not attended the funeral, and Kate, sitting now on the bench sheltered by the willows, sighed again. Gabrielle seemed to dislike them all so thoroughly, she thought; she seemed to hate the very idea of staying at Beauvais, or making it her home. Would it be better to send her away to school? She was nearly fifteen years old now; perhaps a few years at an academy would do more for her than polish her manners. Perhaps, thought Kate, it could smooth a few rough, prickly edges as well.

She was about to get up and start back to the house, where they all waited for her, when a movement to the side caught her eye. To her surprise, Gabrielle was hurrying up the path to the cemetery plot.

Kate was going to call out to her granddaughter to let her know she was there, but just then Gabrielle paused to look hurriedly over her shoulder in the direction of the house. Her whole manner was furtive, as though she didn't want to be seen, and Kate was more unsure than before whether to reveal her presence or not. The low-hanging branches of the willows hid her, so that even if Gabrielle glanced her way, she wouldn't be seen, but even as she told herself how absurd it was to hide like this, Kate sat back again. It was too late, at any rate, to reveal herself now. The moment had passed, and if she said anything to Gabrielle at this point, it would look as though she had been hiding.

Gabrielle, apparently reassured that no one had seen her come, turned to open the low gate that was part of the wrought-iron fence that enclosed the plot. She came through, carefully closing the gate behind her, and as she moved forward again, Kate saw that she held a small bunch of daisies. She felt a pang; the daisies were from the garden, and Gabrielle had obviously hurried out there to pick them before she came. Without even being aware of it, Kate felt a kinship with her granddaughter at the sight of the flowers; daisies had always been Kate's favorite.

Slowly now, Gabrielle approached the mound of fresh earth. Page's grave was heaped high with blossoms, and Gabrielle hesitated. Then she knelt by the headstone inscribed very simply with Page's name and the dates of his life, and once more she paused, reaching out hesitantly to touch the engraved letters in the black marble.

"Grandfather . . ." she murmured, and her voice held such a sad, wistful note that Kate felt tears come into her own eyes at the sound. "I'm sorry, Grandfather," Gabrielle continued brokenly, clutching the daisies. "But I couldn't come to the service. I couldn't! I felt so guilty, so much to blame! Oh, I wanted to know you, Grandfather, I really did! I'm sorry . . . so sorry that you died before we could know each other!"

The flowers dropped to the ground as Gabrielle covered

her face with her hands. Her voice was muffled now, but Kate could hear her clearly, in echoes of her own girlhood, as Gabrielle sobbed. "I don't want to be so mean and awful—truly! I just can't seem to help it—to stop myself from saying such horrible things to everyone. Now everyone hates me here, and I can't blame them, but, Grandfather, I'm so frightened! What am I going to do? Where can I go? Oh, why does everyone have to *die!*"

Without really realizing what she was doing, Kate was moving toward the weeping figure—the girl who acted so proud and defensive and haughty, when inside she was none of those things, only a scared young girl wondering desperately why everyone she loved or wanted to love abandoned her. Something in Kate had responded to that wrenching cry, something that she recognized so clearly from her own youth. More than anyone else could, Kate knew the demons that drove this girl who was so like her; more than anyone else, she understood the twin curses of pride and temper that bedeviled Gabrielle and made her appear someone she was not. Perhaps, Kate thought, that was why she had hesitated about sending Gabrielle away; maybe she had sensed this affinity with her granddaughter from the beginning, had known that the resemblance between Gabrielle now and the girl she herself had been so many years before was more than physical. Perhaps she had known from the start that Gabrielle needed her help as much as Kate needed Gabrielle.

"My dear," she said softly when she reached the kneeling form. She touched her granddaughter gently on the shoulder.

Gabrielle started violently. She had believed herself alone, and now she looked up, frightened, and gasped, "Grandmother!"

Gently Kate helped the girl to her feet. They were the same height, and tear-filled green eyes looked into understanding, sympathetic eyes the same hue. Suddenly Gabrielle was no longer the defiant and hostile and proud girl she had been since her arrival; as Kate put her arms around Gabrielle's shaking shoulders, her granddaughter was only a confused and frightened child begging for the comfort and reassurance that only Kate could give. She understood Gabrielle, Kate thought, so well. Oh, so well.

Drawing Gabrielle gently to the bench beneath the willows, Kate gave her a handkerchief. Quietly she made Gabrielle sit beside her, and then she waited while Gabrielle made a fierce effort to compose herself.

"I want to help you, my dear," she said finally.

"No one can help me!" Gabrielle sobbed. "I make a mess of everything—something awful happens to everything I touch! I'm a curse, a jinx! Nothing comes out right for me, and it's all because I'm so horrible to everyone. Mother used to tell me all the time that my temper would be my cross, and it is—it is! But I can't control it, Grandmother! I just get so . . . so angry . . . at everything! I was wrong yesterday when I said that I hated you—that I hated everyone here! It wasn't true. The truth was that I . . . that I hate myself!"

Bursting into renewed weeping, Gabrielle threw herself into Kate's arms, sobbing convulsively in a spasm of rage and pain and grief she had held inside too long. It was a cleansing, emotional catharsis that she needed desperately to help her over the shock of her mother's death and the sudden passing away of her grandfather she had seen only once before he died.

Kate waited until Gabrielle's wild crying had stilled to shudders. Stroking the crisp, curling red hair so like hers had been, Kate said softly, "Do you feel better now, my dear?"

Gabrielle's voice was muffled. "Yes . . . no . . . Oh, I don't know! I'm so confused, Grandmother. So . . . so scared!"

"But there isn't any reason for you to be frightened, Gabrielle," Kate said soothingly. "You have a family now. You aren't alone."

"That's easy for you to say!" Gabrielle said bitterly. "You never felt alone."

"I think it's time," said Kate softly, "to tell you about someone I knew who was very much like you when she was a girl. Someone who understands what it's like to be frightened and angry at the same time—someone who knows how awful it is to be abandoned by everyone she loves."

Gabrielle raised tear-filled eyes to Kate's. "Who, Grandmother?" she gulped.

Then Kate smiled reminiscently, and proceeded to tell her.

38

Kate's second battle with Rory came far sooner than she had expected, and it was much more serious than the conflict over his father's funeral services had been. It was a bitter disagreement, and one which set the tone for their relationship in years to follow, for in one sweep Rory had made his stand against her and against Beauvais. He also made clear his feelings for her and what she stood for, and Kate had never wished more fervently for Page than she did at that moment, two years after his death, when she faced their son alone and fought for her home.

She berated herself for days after that confrontation with Rory. She should have seen it coming, she would tell herself bitterly; she should have known he was up to something. The very quality of his silence over the past several months should have warned her, but no, she had dismissed her suspicions and had ignored her doubts; she had tried to tell herself that she was only an old woman approaching seventy and inclined to imagine things that weren't there.

But she hadn't been imagining things, and never again, Kate told herself exhaustedly after that battle with her son, would she be such a fool. She could not underestimate Rory, nor the extent of his greed.

Nor, she vowed further, would she ever disregard a warning from Gabrielle, who had tried to tell her for months that something was wrong. Kate might be old now, but she was not so senile, she told herself, as to forget that Gabrielle loved Beauvais as much as she did herself, and that she would do anything to protect the place she had come to regard, in the past two years, as her home. Gabrielle could be a potent ally in the struggle against Rory's quest for power, and although she was only sixteen now, Gabrielle Taggart was already a thorn in Rory's side. She was as strong and as independent as Kate had ever been, and she was unafraid of

Rory, and unimpressed with his son, Todd, who was so like him. What was even more galling to Rory was that Gabrielle had known from the beginning about him and what it was that he was after.

She had told him once, not long after she had come to Beauvais. To his fury, Gabrielle had looked at him one day when he was expounding on something that Kate considered nonsense, and something Gabrielle clearly did not, and she had calmly said, "You won't destroy Beauvais, Uncle Rory—not while Grandmother and I are here to protect it."

And Rory had looked at her with that ingenuous expression that fooled so many, and he had exclaimed, "What do you mean, destroy Beauvais! What an imagination you have, dear Gabrielle! Beauvais is my home!"

Gabrielle had only stared at him, undeterred. "Beauvais was never your home," she had replied coldly.

Kate and Rory had both looked at her, and this time Rory's startled expression was genuine. He could not conceal his sudden unease or the narrow expression in his eyes as he stared at his niece in a new light, and Kate had never forgotten the look on his face. It was almost as if he had seen, and identified, a new enemy.

But if Kate had never forgotten that look on Rory's face, it seemed later that she had forgotten exactly what he was capable of. She had been totally unaware of what he might be planning that day in early October when Gabrielle and Marcus burst excitedly into the drawing room where she was sitting cozily by the fire.

In the past two years since Page's death, she had learned to accept that aching sense of loss that never really abated. She still felt an empty void, a vast loneliness, but she was able to think of him now without that terrible anguish she had suffered so long after he died. And lately, she thought with a smile, she had even found herself talking to him, as if he were there in the room with her. It was a pleasant pastime, pretending he was sitting beside her as she chatted away, and harmless.

Harmless?

Kate's smile vanished as a sudden thought occurred to her. If Rory ever came in while she was conducting these ridiculous little conversations with Page, it would be all he needed to convince himself and everyone else that she was a doddering old fool who had no business at the helm of the great ship that was Beauvais. Rory had been itching for control ever since his father died, and Kate, who knew her son so well, knew that she had to be very careful. One slip of the tongue, one slight sign of hesitation, and Rory would be in court so fast it would leave her breathless. Oh, she knew Rory, all right. And as much as it pained her to admit it, she had long ago come to terms with her son's flawed character. She might be almost seventy years old, she thought, but at least she had learned something. And one of them was to keep her eye on Rory. Why had she forgotten something so important?

Was she really getting too old to run Beauvais?

No! No, she thought fiercely. She wasn't too old—far from it. And she had to maintain control until Gabrielle was old enough to take the reins from her. Gabrielle . . . dear Gabrielle.

Her granddaughter's abrupt arrival, which had caused such an upheaval at the time, had been a blessing in disguise, Kate thought. With Page gone so suddenly, her grief had been almost impossible to bear alone. She had needed an anchor, a diversion—a challenge. Gabrielle had been all three. They had grown very close, she and her granddaughter, and while the transformation from sullen, resentful girl to lively, vivacious young woman had not been easy for anyone at Beauvais—least of all Gabrielle herself—it had been . . . interesting. Now, thought Kate with a wry smile, while Gabrielle rarely deliberately provoked her verbal battles with various members of the family, she had at least learned to control her temper. Or most of the time, anyway, Kate thought ruefully. Gabrielle had as much trouble as she ever had learning to master both her tongue and her temper, and it was a constant struggle for her to control both at the same time.

Especially with Annabel, thought Kate with a sigh. Sometimes the two girls were like cats in a sack, claws drawn and eager to scratch at the slightest provocation. It was a shame that the two of them couldn't get along, Kate reflected. They were so close in age, and now that Adele had gone off again to stay with friends in New York, Annabel was firmly entrenched at the ranch—at least until Adele moved restlessly on to someplace else and wanted her daughter with her. Which wasn't likely, Kate thought with a sigh, with the war still going on.

It was so difficult sometimes, Kate sighed. She could easily understand why Gabrielle became so incensed at Annabel's condescending attitude, for Annabel did have an unfortunate tendency to act the snob. It wasn't really her fault, argued Kate, taking the other side in her private debate: Annabel acted the way she did because she was so defensive. Having been deposited during her childhood in one school after another while her mother flitted about Europe, Annabel felt rootless, adrift, without purpose or direction of her own. Kate had tried to help this withdrawn other granddaughter of hers, but there was so little she could do for Annabel beyond giving her support and love. Annabel had to find some inner strength of her own, some private resources to draw on that would give her her own sense of worth and confidence. And no matter how much Kate wanted to guide her, she couldn't give Annabel that. Still, she felt compelled to try—driven, no doubt, Kate admitted, by guilt as well as love. She was always haunted by the question of why Annabel seemed to lack the initiative to seize her own particular happiness or contentment. Was it Adele's fault, or hers? If she had been a better mother, a more loving or kind or serene mother, would that have made a difference in the lives of her daughter and her granddaughter? Kate didn't know. There were so many questions to which she had no answers, she thought with a sigh.

Had Michael been happy or content? she wondered, her thoughts drifting, as they often did, to musings about her eldest son. Gabrielle had long ago told her what she knew of her father, but her own information was sketchy because she hadn't known him at all. What little she knew came from her mother, Lily, and apparently Lily hadn't been able to unlock the key that was Michael, either. He had been such a private boy, carefully guarding his thoughts and feelings, that it had been difficult even for Kate, his mother, to know him. And from what Gabrielle had told her, it seemed that Michael had grown into an even more reserved, withdrawn, and silent man.

So, after so many years of wondering, Kate was both frustrated that she knew so little about her son and grateful that Gabrielle had been able to tell her anything at all. Michael, she had told Kate, had worked at various times in the coal mines of Pennsylvania, had piloted steamboats on the Missouri River, and captained barges on the Erie Canal; he had been a farmhand on several of the vast wheat farms in Kansas, had driven cattle and sheep and horses up and down the panhandle, and had been a ranch foreman in Montana and California.

It was in California, Gabrielle said, at a ranch near a place called Monterey, where Michael had met the woman he wanted to marry. Gabrielle's eyes had flashed when she mentioned this, and Kate had been puzzled at her expression. Thinking that Gabrielle meant Lily, she asked, "Your mother was at a ranch in Monterey? But I thought . . ."

"That my mother sang in a dance hall?" Gabrielle finished when Kate had hesitated before the glowering expression on her granddaughter's face. "She did. But before he met my mother, my father wanted to marry Julann Fallon. He didn't meet my mother until after he left the Montoya Ranch."

"Montoya . . ." Kate was startled anew. "But I've heard of that place!" she exclaimed. "Why, they raise some of the finest horses in California! Kyne and Ariel Fallon—aren't they the owners of the ranch? And Julann must be . . ."

"Their daughter," said Gabrielle bitterly. "My mother saw her once, she told me, and she was every bit as beautiful as her mother, Ariel, was supposed to be in her day."

Kate hid a smile. She had never had the pleasure of meeting the Fallons, but she suspected that Ariel Fallon was not quite the ancient crone Gabrielle painted her to be. And Julann was her daughter.

Julann, Kate thought: what an unusual name. She was about to ask more about what had happened to the romance between this Julann and Michael, but after another quick look at Gabrielle's fiery expression, she decided to forgo her questions. For some reason, it was obviously a painful subject for Gabrielle, and Kate repressed her curiosity with reluctance.

"But even though Michael might have been involved once with Julann Fallon," Kate pointed out gently, "he did marry your mother."

"Yes," said Gabrielle. But there was a closed, set expression on Gabrielle's face, and Kate never did discover what had happened to end the romance.

After a while Gabrielle had gone on to say that Michael had quit ranching when he had married Lily. He had become a railroad man instead, and he and Lily had moved from California to one place after another: New York, Boston, Philadelphia, New Orleans, back to Pennsylvania again. And all the time, Michael could easily have risen to a position of prominence in the railroad if he had wanted it; he never had. He was more interested, Gabrielle had said proudly to Kate, in finding a way to make the terribly dangerous and difficult job of coupling the railroad cars safer and less perilous for switchmen. Even before he lost three fingers of his own, Gabrielle had told a horrified Kate, he had been preoccupied with this problem, for he considered himself one of the lucky ones: men had lost more than fingers trying to couple cars. It had not been uncommon, in those days, for switchmen to lose hands, arms, legs, even their lives in such a hazardous line of work.

"Mother said that my father was always tinkering with something—a way to make things easier or better," Gabrielle said, unaware of the shock she had dealt Kate. "And this was especially important to him. He wanted to invent a coupler that would end all the guesswork and danger involved in attaching railroad cars."

"And did he?" Kate asked faintly, trying unsuccessfully to shut out the picture of Michael with a mutilated hand. He had had such beautiful hands, she thought, such strong and competent hands, that could wrestle a maddened steer to the ground or gentle a frightened foal.

Gabrielle had looked down at Kate's question, at her own hands clasped tightly in her lap. "Yes," she said in a low voice. "He did succeed. But he died trying to prevent the very kind of accident his coupler would have averted. And after his death, they took his invention and claimed it for themselves. My father never got any credit for it, and we," Gabrielle finished bitterly, "certainly never got anything from it either. They stole it from him, Grandmother! They stole it after their stupidity and greed killed my father. It was too expensive, they said, too much trouble to change the cars or make the alteration that would fit the coupler my father designed. But it wasn't too expensive, after all, or too much trouble, was it? They couldn't wait to make the change after my father died!"

Kate had never forgotten Gabrielle's face that day, nor the tears she had shed in Kate's arms when she related the story of how Michael had died. It had been a cold night, a stormy night in winter, and the rails had been frozen and slippery with ice. As always, the men on the road had been in a hurry to change cars and tracks, for time was money, and no one was more aware of it than the men whose jobs depended upon how fast they could make the trains go. A switch had jammed, a bolt had snapped with cold, a steel plate had come undone—Lily and Gabrielle had never been told what had happened. Lily only discovered, and told Gabrielle much, much later, that by the time the chaos and confusion were over, Michael had been pinned between cars somehow. It had taken hours to free him, and by then it had been too late. The terrible weight of two cars coming together, with the numbing exposure of freezing night air, had taken its toll. Michael had lived, barely, until the next morning, but he had—thankfully—never regained consciousness. Lily, strong, silent, and suffering, had sat with him until the last, smoothing his hair back from his miraculously untouched face, trying desperately not to think of the crushed and broken body beneath the hospital sheets.

Lily, newly widowed, with an infant daughter to care for and very little money in the bank, had buried her husband. Then she had taken the five-dollar gold piece the railroad gave her in compensation for Michael's death and had marched into the president's opulent office and thrown it in his face.

"She always said it was a stupid thing to do," Gabrielle said, wiping her eyes with Kate's handkerchief. "She said it was cutting off her nose to spite her face, since we needed the money so badly, but she had to do it. I never thought it was stupid; when she told me, I could only think how wonderful she was. Imagine! Having the courage to do something like that! I think it was magnificent!"

"So do I," said Kate. She had seen the single miniature of Lily that Gabrielle had, and she had admired the fine eyes, the clear forehead, the generous mouth. But she hadn't seen the fire in those eyes, the sheer bravery it took to make such a gesture, and after hearing Gabrielle's story, Kate's admiration for Lily grew. She wished once more that she had known Michael's wife. Lily Taggart must have been quite a woman. She said so, gently, to the tearful Gabrielle.

"Yes," said Gabrielle in a muffled voice. "She was." Gabrielle raised her wet face to Kate's. "Just like you, Grandmother," she said.

And Kate had been prouder of that single compliment than any other she had received in a long, long life.

"Grandmother! Grandmother!"

Kate started. She had been so preoccupied that she hadn't even heard Gabrielle and Marcus come in from their ride. She looked up, pleased at first to see them, but her smile of welcome faded rapidly when she realized that something was wrong.

"What is it?" she asked sharply.

"Grandmother, did you know that there are men on the north slope taking samples for mineral assay?" Gabrielle demanded. She dropped down quickly beside her grandmother on the sofa.

"Assay?" Kate looked blankly at her granddaughter. Gabrielle's face was flushed as much from anger as from cold, and Kate suspected from her breathlessness that it must have been a hard gallop back to the ranch. "No," she said. "I don't know anything about an assay."

Gabrielle looked up triumphantly at Marcus. "See! I told you so!"

"I never said Grandmother would authorize anything like that," Marcus said mildly, lounging against the mantel. "I merely said we should wait until we asked her."

"All right, then, if it wasn't Grandmother, I know exactly who it was!" Gabrielle cried, jumping up again to pace back and forth. "Oh, I knew it all the time!"

"Gabrielle, please sit down," Kate said. She was trying to understand what this was all about, but with Gabrielle distracting her like this, it was difficult to concentrate. Was it true that she was getting old and couldn't think properly anymore? Kate shuddered at the thought. It was one of her greatest fears.

"I'm sorry," muttered Gabrielle, throwing herself into a chair again and tapping her fingers furiously on the arm of it. "But I'm just so angry! Uncle Rory has no right to do such a thing! He has no right!"

"He hasn't done much of anything yet, Gabrielle," Marcus pointed out.

"How can you say that!" Gabrielle cried at once. "You know just as well as I do what those assays are for!"

"And what are they for?" Kate asked.

Kate glanced from one to the other of her grandchildren—at Gabrielle's furious face and flashing eyes; at Marcus, who was so calm and reasonable—and she was reminded poignantly of herself and Page at the same age. They had faced each other like this so many times in the past: she arguing from temper and emotion, Page responding with logic and judgment. Seeing Gabrielle and Marcus together was almost like viewing a scene of her and Page together when they were young. They even shared the same physical characteristics: Gabrielle with her red hair and green eyes, Marcus with his dark good looks and compelling gaze. Gabrielle, the daughter of her son, and Marcus, the son of Page's son. How ironic that what had begun in shame and guilt and had caused such suffering should have culminated in these two beautiful grandchildren of hers. It was almost as if she and Page were being given another chance through Gabrielle and Marcus.

But she was being fanciful when she should be paying attention to what Gabrielle was trying to tell her. Why was it, Kate wondered irritably, that her mind had this alarming and maddening tendency to wander into irrelevancies when she needed it most? She really had to make an effort to take hold of herself, or Rory might have a court case, after all.

This last thought was enough to strengthen her resolve. Glancing from Marcus to Gabrielle, who was still muttering, Kate said, "Why don't one of you begin at the beginning? I can't make head or tail out of what you've told me so far."

Gabrielle looked quickly at Marcus, who gestured for her to proceed. "We were out riding," she said, taking the initiative without argument. "And we saw this activity on the north slope—you know, where we summer the cattle?"

"Yes, I know the place," Kate said dryly. "Go on."

"Well," Gabrielle continued, flushing a little at Kate's wry expression, "when we saw these strangers poking around, naturally we had to find out what they were doing..."

"Naturally," Kate said when Gabrielle glanced at her for confirmation. She nodded solemnly, trying not to smile.

"...and so we rode up and asked!"

"'Demanded' would be a better word," Marcus said, looking at Kate with a twinkle in his eye.

"Yes," Kate said. "I can imagine."

"Are you two laughing at me?" Gabrielle abandoned her careless pose and sat up straight, her cheeks pink. She glared at Marcus, who wasn't in the least intimidated.

"Of course we're not laughing at you," Kate said. She looked innocently at Gabrielle. "So you asked these men what they were doing, and they said...?"

"They said they were taking samples for mineral assay!" Gabrielle exclaimed. "And that's when I knew you would never order such a thing. We came directly back here to warn you."

"Warn me? But what harm can a few samples do?"

Gabrielle might be impatient with others, or become annoyed or irritated when someone didn't understand immediately what her quick mind grasped so easily, but she was never sharp with her grandmother. Now she jumped up again and went to Kate, sitting beside her and taking her hands. "It's not the samples themselves," she said urgently, "it's the idea behind them. It's not really minerals Uncle Rory wants, it's ore. If there's any tungsten or vanadium on Beauvais, you can be sure Uncle Rory will find it and try to mine it. Tungsten is used for hardening steel, Grandmother—for making munitions! And it's already risen in price from nine dollars a unit to almost one hundred now. There's a fortune to be made if enough of it can be found here!"

But Kate had stopped listening to Gabrielle recite her statistics. The moment her granddaughter had mentioned mining Beauvais, she had reacted with horror. Colorado mining had been plagued with labor difficulties from 1903, and because Beauvais had long before owned interests in the gold fields of Cripple Creek, they had become involved, peripherally, in the violence that occurred there in 1904. A man named Harry Orchard had dynamited the railroad station at Independence in a culmination of difficulties between miners and mine operators. Thirteen had died in that explosion, with many more injured, and finally, martial law had been declared by Governor Peabody. Page, sickened by the violence there, especially since he had tried so hard to negotiate some sort of settlement between the opposing factions, had sold his interests immediately, and Beauvais had sent what aid they could to the families of the miners who had lost their lives. But the experience and the horror of that terrible time had stayed with Kate, and when in 1914, after Page had died, violence erupted in the mine fields at Ludlow Station, Kate had vowed anew that Beauvais would never again be associated with anything remotely resembling mining. Even if she had not loved her land, she would have rejected any proposed mining project, for the Ludlow Massacre, when so many were killed or burned to death in the fire that swept through the tent colony there, had been burned deep into Kate's consciousness, as well. Beauvais would never, she had declared, be mined for anything, for any reason—ever.

With an effort, Kate tried to concentrate on what Gabrielle was so earnestly trying to tell her. Raising her eyes from Gabrielle's urgent face, Kate looked at Marcus. "Is this true?" she asked. "What Gabrielle says?"

"I'm afraid so," Marcus concurred. "There's a lot of money to be made off this damnable war in Europe. And you know Uncle Rory—he's always hungry for more money."

"It's true, you know, Grandmother," Gabrielle interjected glumly. "Uncle Rory would do anything to make money— even destroy Beauvais."

"How do you know so much about this, Gabrielle?" Kate asked, trying to gather her thoughts. "About this . . . this tungsten, and van . . . van . . . what is it?"

"Vanadium," supplied Gabrielle absently. She shrugged. "I heard Aunt Adele and Uncle Rory talking about the war and the increased need for munitions long ago. And then today, when we saw what those men were doing, it all fell into place, I guess. Uncle Rory has been planning this for a long time, Grandmother, and he's going to succeed if you don't stop him."

"He wouldn't dare mine Beauvais!" Kate declared positively. "Not when he knows how I feel about it."

Gabrielle reached over and took one of Kate's hands again. "Uncle Rory would do anything to make money, Grandmother," she said gently but firmly. "Including selling Beauvais—all or part of it, whatever he has to do in order to suit his plans. Don't you know that?"

Yes, she had known it for a long time, Kate thought. She just hadn't wanted to admit it—not really. Jane had seen it as well, she thought sadly, for she had warned Kate about Rory before she died, so long ago. Jane had faced the truth about Rory. Why couldn't she?

"Grandmother . . . ?" Gabrielle said gently.

Kate looked at her grandchildren then, and the fire of the young Kate burned in her eyes. For fifty years Beauvais had been her home. She and Page had built it, and had watched it grow, and had kept it alive through fire and drought, flood and blizzard. Page wasn't with her anymore, but he had left the ranch to her in trust, and she would guard that trust until she died. Fifty years was a long time, she thought—a lifetime of tears and struggle and hardship and sheer determination to survive, to overcome. They had created something valuable here, between them; they had created a legacy, a tradition, a monument to themselves and to each other, and to all the children to follow who would love Beauvais as much as they did. And Rory was not going to destroy all that. No one was going to destroy Beauvais while she had breath left to fight.

"Don't worry, Gabrielle," Kate said, and her voice held all the confidence in the world, "I think your uncle Rory will have a surprise or two when he tries to explain why he wants to assay Beauvais land."

39

Rory was more than surprised when he arrived at Beauvais several days later, assay results in hand. He was taken aback completely by the welcoming committee of his mother and his niece, who waited unsmilingly in the drawing room when he entered with Todd. He saw at once that there was going to be trouble, for Gabrielle, whom he detested, was positively grim, and his mother had that look in her eye that meant he would have to do some fast talking if he wanted to go ahead with his own plans.

But Rory was truly a born politician, a career toward which he had made some progress these past few years, for his expression completely hid his thoughts as he came forward at once to greet Kate.

"Mother!" he exclaimed warmly, bending to kiss her fondly on the cheek. "How well you look today! Tell me, have you had any more problems with that hip?"

Kate hated any reference to her hip, which had in the past several years begun to bother her at times, so that walking was difficult. So far, she had absolutely refused the aid of a cane, but what infuriated her the most was that riding had become impossible for her. She just could not bear to sit in a saddle, no matter how determined she was to ride. Now she, who had found solace so many times in her life in a brisk gallop on a good horse, was confined to the gig, which she hated, or the pony trap, which she despised even more. To her intense annoyance, she was forced to watch others ride, and it was sometimes small comfort to see even Gabrielle, already, under her instruction, so magnificent on a horse, when she herself longed to be in the saddle. Trust Rory, Kate thought blackly now, to find a way to remind her of her infirmities.

"My health," replied Kate crisply, "is excellent, Rory."

Rory had already turned to his niece. "Gabrielle," he said with that false heartiness both grandmother and granddaughter hated, "you get prettier every time I see you."

"And you," Gabrielle replied sweetly, "become more adept at giving out compliments you can't possibly mean."

Rory reddened. But despite the insincerity of Rory's statement, it was true that Gabrielle had blossomed the past two years since coming to Beauvais. Her resemblance to Kate, always strong, was more startling than ever now that she had developed a new assurance and a less hostile and aggressive confidence in herself. Her hair was as red as Kate's had been in her own day, almost as fiery a color as Gabrielle's great-grandmother Augusta's had been, and her eyes were as green and as expressive of her emotions. Those green eyes stared at Rory now with an expression close to contempt, and somehow Rory made himself hold on to his temper. There were more important matters at stake than sparring with his niece, and so he cleared his throat and said, "Don't you have somewhere else to be? Why don't you and Todd go for a ride while I talk to your grandmother?"

Todd started at that, sending his father a sour glance for making such an annoying suggestion. He was a handsome young man, and with his thick dark hair and guileless blue eyes he was a charmer with the young ladies in Denver. Unfortunately, Kate often thought as she looked closely at this son of Rory's, Todd's good looks were spoiled by the same weakness that marred his father—a weak mouth that smiled too easily, and a calculating, sly look about his eyes. Todd had inherited nothing of Jane, after all, Kate realized sadly; he was truly his father's son.

Now Todd tried quickly to extricate himself from the proposed ride with Gabrielle. He had never gotten along with his cousin; she annoyed him with her sharp tongue and even more acute perception. Given the choice, he much preferred the bored Annabel, who could at least be counted on to trade sarcastic quips and to laugh at his jokes. Todd had a quick, clever mind, but unfortunately his humor was often directed cruelly at others. Annabel thought him highly amusing; Gabrielle could make him feel foolish with the derision on her face and the scorn in her huge green eyes.

So while Gabrielle watched with interest to see how he would squirm out of this irritating position, Todd averted his glance from her and said hastily, "I think I'll go find Marcus instead and we can go shooting together." He looked at Kate, deliberately avoiding the superior smile that curved Gabrielle's full mouth. "Is he here, Grandmother, or at the other ranch?"

The other ranch, as everyone called it, was the Siddons ranch, where Randall and Emily and Marcus lived. But Marcus so often rode back and forth between Beauvais and his home that the Siddons ranch had come to be called, affectionately, "the other ranch."

"Yes, he's there," said Gabrielle. "Working—something you never learned to do."

Todd flushed. "Just like you never learned any manners," he retorted nastily.

"Or you any responsibility," Gabrielle shot back. "What are you going to do, dear cousin, when America enters the war? It's inevitable, you know. Are you going to serve?"

Todd had paled. "What makes you think that we . . . we're going to war?" he asked, his voice suddenly strangled. "President Wilson promises neutrality. He—"

"Haven't you been reading the newspapers?" she asked. "Or are you too busy racing those harness horses of yours?"

This time Todd was not so quick to respond. He was staring at Gabrielle, his eyes wide and strained. "You . . . you're only a girl!" he said chokingly. "You can't know anything about America going to war!"

"Even girls have brains!" Gabrielle said cuttingly. "And if you don't believe me, ask Marcus when you see him."

"Even if we do enter the war, I won't have to go. Why, I'm twenty-seven years old!"

Gabrielle shook her head pityingly. "That doesn't matter," she said with contempt. "I read the other day that all able-bodied men will be eligible, and you're certainly able-bodied, even if you are feeble-minded!"

But even this insult failed to elicit a stinging response from

Gabrielle's cousin. Instead, with everyone staring after him in surprise, he turned on his heel and almost ran from the room. Kate and Gabrielle looked at each other, and then Gabrielle shrugged. "I don't know what's the matter with him," she said dismissively. She had never made any secret of how she felt about Todd. "I only told him the truth. If he isn't man enough to take it . . ."

"And how is it," Rory put in sarcastically, stung by Gabrielle's words, "that you're suddenly so knowledgeable about politics? Or were you just talking through your hat, as you so often do?"

"I know what I'm talking about," Gabrielle snapped, "because I make it my business to know. Just like I know about those assays you ordered. Tell me, Uncle Rory, was it tungsten you found, or something else?"

"It was tungsten," Rory snapped back, so taken off guard by Gabrielle's quick question that he spoke the truth without thinking. Seconds later, he realized his mistake and tried vainly to recover. "Not that it's any of your concern!"

"It might not be any of Gabrielle's concern, but it certainly is mine," Kate said, her voice steely. "And I'd like to know, Rory, why you went ahead without consulting me."

Rory turned his back on the niece he could cheerfully have strangled for making things so awkward, and he answered Kate in his most ingratiating manner. "But I am consulting you, Mother. Why do you think I came all the way out here today, if not to talk to you? Although," he added, allowing himself a momentary lapse into annoyance, "if you would have a telephone installed, things would certainly be easier."

Kate wasn't going to be distracted by the issue of a telephone. The argument about the instrument at Beauvais was an old one between her and Rory; he wanted one at the house because it would be more convenient for him, and Kate had so far refused to listen to him. It wasn't that she was old and resisted change, as he had declared once in a fit of anger; it was that she didn't want to listen to someone's voice coming at her tinnily over wires she couldn't even see. Still, she supposed grumpily now that she would have to relent; it just wasn't sensible not to have a telephone in these modern times.

"I'm not going to talk to you about the telephone," she said curtly. "It seems that we were going to discuss why you had these ore assays made without my permission."

Rory had to hold on to his temper again. He hated to be reminded that his mother controlled Beauvais; he had long ago tried to convince himself and everyone else that he was the head of the house. But now he forced a smile and said, "I didn't want to bother you with all the details, Mother; I thought you would prefer results instead." His voice took on an undercurrent of excitement that he couldn't hide. "And the results are even better than I expected!" he exulted. "According to these reports—"

"I don't want to know what the reports say, Rory."

"What?" Rory's surprise would have been almost comical if Kate hadn't been so angry. He stared at her openmouthed, completely taken aback.

"I said," Kate repeated distinctly, "that I don't want to hear about the reports. I'm not interested."

"But . . . but . . ." Rory realized he was sputtering. He made himself take a deep breath, trying to speak with some degree of normalcy when he felt like shouting in complete rage. "But you can't mean that, Mother. Why—"

"I do mean it." Kate barely suppressed the urge to seize the papers he clutched lovingly in his hand and throw them onto the fire.

Rory's face, which had expressed utter astonishment a minute before, became red with anger now. "You don't understand what this would mean to Beauvais, Mother! Why, the north slope alone is rich in tungsten. God knows what else we could find if we looked. We could all be rich beyond our wildest dreams!"

Kate stared at him, sickened. "We have more than enough now," she said. "Your father was very fortunate in everything he did—except for the shares in Cripple Creek, and you know we sold those long ago because of that terrible business with the mines."

"But that has nothing to do with this now!" Rory shouted.

"Nevertheless, your father and I agreed long ago that we would never profit from mining again. I intend to keep that agreement."

Rory shot to his feet, his face congested. He stood over Kate and glared down at her. "My father," he said between clenched teeth, "isn't here now. *I'm* the head of this household!"

Kate made herself look up at him. Her expression was calm, but inside, she was shaken—not with fear of her son, but with despair that it had come to this between them. "Not," she said softly, "while I'm alive."

They stared at each other in a sudden ringing silence, and neither noticed Gabrielle get up quietly from her chair and leave the room, closing the door gently behind her.

The silence lasted a full minute while they looked at each other, and then Rory spoke. With his first words, Kate's despair over her son vanished in a wave of anger against him so great that she was almost enraged. Rory said, and his voice was lŏw and menacing, "There are ways of getting control, Mother. So far I've let you have your own way about running Beauvais. But this is important to me—how important, you'll never know. This damnable war isn't going to last forever, and I intend to make what I can of a heaven-sent opportunity."

Kate couldn't believe what she was hearing. "You think of this war as an opportunity?" she cried, horrified. "I can't believe even you would say such a terrible thing! How can you even think about trying to profit from the suffering of thousands of people, about making money from such misery? Oh, no, Rory! Even if I agreed with you about mining this land—and I don't!—I would never consent to make Beauvais a part of such a hideous nightmare as this war. Never!"

"Oh, come on, Mother!" Rory was unimpressed by her vehemence. "I'm not the only one who sees this war as a way to make money. There are hundreds of men making thousands . . . millions of dollars off what you call 'this misery.' "

"That doesn't make it right!"

"No," Rory agreed with a nasty smile. "But it does make it profitable."

"Not where Beauvais is concerned! If I hadn't been determined to stop you before, I certainly am now! You're not going to mine Beauvais, Rory. You're not going to touch a tree, a blade of grass, a clump of dirt that belongs to Beauvais after what you said today! I'll fight you all the way, and I mean that. I never meant anything more in my life!"

The smile had vanished from Rory's face. Now his mouth was drawn into a sneer as he narrowed his eyes at his mother. Kate faced him, furious and unafraid, not even changing expression when he said so softly, "If I have to go to court to have you declared incompetent to run Beauvais, I will, Mother. I'm not going to lose out this time on such an opportunity to make a fortune. Remember that."

The face that had been so handsome was ugly now—dark and dangerous, Rory's hazel eyes cold like a cruel sea. Gone was the easy smile; his mouth was a hard vicious slash as he stared at Kate. Even his red-gold hair, once so striking a feature, had a sheen of steel gray in the afternoon sunlight. Everything about Rory at that moment was cold and cruel and ruthless. He looked like someone she had never seen before, but someone she had always known would appear—sometime.

Kate stood on shaking legs to face him, trying not to heed the sharp pain that stabbed through her. At that moment, when they faced each other, Rory looked as if he hated her. She knew without question that he meant exactly what he said, and the instant he thought he could beat her, he would do as he had threatened. He would push her aside without hesitation or compunction; he would trample her without a trace of guilt or remorse. Her son was a man without a conscience, and Kate knew that she must never let him think he could snatch victory from her. Once he was sure he would win, he would destroy Beauvais and all that was dear to her.

"So," she said, trying her best to control the infuriating tremble in her voice, "you have revealed yourself at last. How proud your father would have been to hear your threats just now, how pleased to know that his son had so little regard for his family and what they built that he would do anything to destroy it—for money."

Kate's voice strengthened with renewed anger and the force of her contempt. She lifted her head proudly, her expression totally unafraid as she faced Rory with dignity. The challenge had been made, and Kate had never run away from a challenge in her entire life—even from one of her own. "You may think," she said, "that your threats frighten me, or that you will scare me into submission. No doubt you thought—or hoped—that I was too feeble to fight you. Or that I would give in gracefully to your demands because you were a man and therefore entitled to take what you believe is yours, by force, if necessary. Well, unfortunately for you, my son, I am neither too weak nor too old to fight for what is, after all, still mine. And if I were you, I would think long and carefully about going to court for control of Beauvais. There are many who remember Page and all he did for Denver and for Colorado, and if that isn't enough to stop you, I have a few friends of my own I could call on who would be only too happy to help. So you see, Rory, in your haste and your greed, you have rushed heedlessly into a game that is over your head and out of your league. There is one thing you should remember when you play for power, and that is to discover the strength of the opponent before you make your move. You underestimated the enemy this time, Rory. There is no way you can win."

"I see." Rory was tight-lipped and helplessly enraged. He turned jerkily and went to the door. "You have the upper hand for now, Mother," he said, looking back at her in hatred. "But I wonder how long you can keep it."

"As long," said Kate evenly, "as I have to. And remember one more thing," she added as he furiously whipped open the door. "Your father was the head of this house because he deserved the title, and because he earned it. If I was ever in doubt, you have just proved to me that you deserve neither position nor title. In fact," she said coldly, "you deserve only my contempt—and my pity—for what you tried to do today."

Rory stared at her, his face suffused with utter rage. "I won't forget this, Mother," he choked. "And remember, you can't live forever, and then—then!—Beauvais will be mine!"

"We will see," Kate said with absolute scorn, "about that!"

40

The door had barely slammed behind Rory when Kate heard another noise, a shouting in the yard, and quick footsteps running toward her. She had sagged against the back of the sofa after Rory's snarling departure, weak from the charged emotional scene between them, unnerved by the look of hatred she had seen in her son's eyes. Now she struggled to her feet again, forcing herself to face the doorway. She didn't know what had happened, but she recognized the quality of that sound. There was some crisis that would demand her attention, and the luxury of giving in to her despair over the ugly confrontation with Rory would have to wait. In a way, she was almost relieved to postpone that private battle with herself; she had been far braver and had faced Rory with more courage than she had felt.

"Grandmother!"

Kate had known it would be Gabrielle who came for her; she had heard her granddaughter's light footsteps. But she was still unprepared for the way Gabrielle burst into the room, her face white with shock. She stood on the threshold for a moment, holding on to either side of the door, breathing so heavily that for a terrified instant Kate thought it was she who was injured. Her eyes were wide with fright.

"Grandmother!" Gabrielle gasped finally. "Todd's been shot!"

"Shot?" For a moment Kate felt faint. She could hardly voice the words. "Is he . . . ?"

"No, no; he isn't dead," Gabrielle anticipated quickly. But her face blanched again. "But it . . . it looks very bad."

Kate put her hand on the back of the sofa for support, trying, like Gabrielle, to catch her breath. She rallied quickly, forcing herself to be calm. There were some benefits to old age, she thought, straightening; there was no longer an urge to respond to emergencies with a desire for hysterics.

"Where is he?" Kate asked. She hoped by her manner to calm Gabrielle, who looked as distraught as if she had caused the accident herself.

"He's out in the yard; they're bringing him in now," Gabrielle said in a rush. "But . . ."

"Has someone sent for the doctor?"

"Yes . . . no . . . I don't know! Oh, Grandmother, I feel so responsible!"

"Don't be ridiculous!" Kate snapped as she started from the room. "How could you possibly be responsible?"

Gabrielle followed, wringing her hands. "Well, if I hadn't teased him, he wouldn't have rushed off like that. He was angry at me, and maybe—"

"I don't want to hear any more of that nonsense, Gabrielle," Kate said on her way to the front door. "Todd is a grown man, able to take care of himself—or should be. And we don't even know what happened yet. Why don't we just be calm until we know how serious the whole thing is?"

It was serious, but thankfully, not life-threatening. Todd's wound did necessitate an operation, and after hours of anxious waiting, they all learned to their relief that the bullet had passed cleanly through the right thigh, exiting near the knee. But that had caused the most damage. Todd would have use of his leg, but the doctor feared that he would always walk with a limp. How much of a disability it would be, he couldn't say; only time would reveal the full extent of the injury to bone and tissue.

"He was very fortunate, Mr. Taggart," the doctor told a pale Rory. "An inch or so higher, and the artery would have been severed. He might have bled to death before you got him home. As it is, he has lost a great deal of blood, which is why I decided to operate here instead of taking him all the way to Denver. I'm glad someone was sensible enough not to try to transport him all the way to town. How did it happen, anyway?"

They all looked at Marcus, then, who had kept a silent vigil by the drawing-room window during the hours the doctor had labored over Todd. He had been so remote, his expression so strange, that even Gabrielle had not dared approach him. He had said only, in a terse, clipped voice that forbade any questions, that he had met Todd on the road, that Todd had invited him to shoot jackrabbits. There had been an accident; Todd's gun had gone off, and Todd had been shot.

He repeated it all again at the doctor's question, reciting the same story without variation in a flat monotone. Kate, watching him from her position in a high wing-back chair, knew instinctively that something was amiss. Marcus would never have agreed to go shoot rabbits with Todd; he had always considered such a sport cruel and senseless and a waste of time and ammunition.

"Marcus—" she began.

But Rory interrupted just then, his expression hostile and furious as he demanded of Marcus, "And how do we know it was Todd's gun that went off?"

"Rory!" Kate's sharp voice cut through the babble of surprise that rose from the rest of the family waiting there. Marcus' father, Randall, and Emily, his mother, were staring at Rory with identical expressions of anger and shock, and Gabrielle had leaped to her feet, her face red with outrage.

"How dare you say such a terrible, wicked thing!" she cried. "How dare you imply that Marcus was responsible!"

"Be quiet, Gabrielle," Marcus said.

Gabrielle whirled to look at him. "No, I won't be quiet! He has no right to accuse you of something so dreadful!"

"He hasn't accused me yet, and if he does, I can defend myself. I don't need you to do it for me."

Their eyes locked. Marcus was pale but resolute; Gabrielle, fiery with anger. They stared at each other for a long moment, and then, to everyone's surprise but Kate's, it was Gabrielle who dropped her eyes first. She further astonished them all by subsiding into a chair, glaring balefully at Marcus, but not saying anything more.

Marcus nodded briefly at her, then turned his attention again to Rory. "Well? Don't you believe me?"

Rory obviously did not care for the challenge in Marcus' quiet voice. Nor did he like the contemptuous expression in the dark eyes staring so directly at him. Those eyes reminded him uncomfortably of his father, and his expression became even more ugly.

"Todd is an excellent marksman," Rory said. "I find it hard to believe that he could be involved in such a stupid incident."

"Are you trying to say that I'm responsible in some way?"

There was a dangerous undertone in Marcus's voice now, and even Rory, angry as he was, hesitated at hearing it. But he had gone too far now to back down, so he said nastily, "Are you?"

Marcus stiffened. He was about to answer, but it was Randall who spoke before him. "I can't believe," Randall said in a voice that shook with rage, "that my own brother is standing there and accusing my son of shooting someone."

If Rory was taken aback by the rare sight of a furious Randall, he didn't show it. He snapped back, "It's not just *someone* we're talking about, Randall! It's Todd, for God's sake!"

Randall stood. He was as tall as Rory, but a good deal lighter in appearance, for while Rory's bulk came from too much food and drink and too little exercise, Randall was lean and hard, sinewy from constant work at the ranch. But even with the difference between them, no one in that room had any doubts who would be the victor if the two brothers came to blows; they were just all surprised that the easygoing Randall could become so angry. No one had ever seen him come close to losing his temper; and none of them, even Kate, could recall him ever looking for a fight. There was silence while everyone waited to see what Randall would do.

Rory took one look at Randall's furious expression, and he paled. "Now, wait a minute, Randall," he said harshly. He raised one arm as if to protect himself, even though Randall hadn't as yet moved. "You'd ask the same question in my place, wouldn't you? It's possible that Marcus really did shoot Todd, isn't it?" His voice rose higher as Randall took a step toward him. "Well, isn't it possible?" Rory demanded shrilly, completely undone by the look on his brother's face. "Marcus never liked Todd! He—"

But the rest of his sentence ended in a surprised grunt as the infuriated Randall reached out and grabbed him by the lapels. In one swift motion he lifted Rory off his feet, swung him around, and literally tossed him through the air. Rory crashed against the wall, splaying his arms out in a vain attempt at catching his balance, but Randall had thrown him with such force that he couldn't save himself. To his fury and mortification, he slid helplessly down the wall, bringing two pictures with him, and ended sprawled ignominiously in a heap on the floor, his legs thrust out in front of him like an overstuffed doll on a shelf.

"I never want to hear you say anything like that again," Randall said, his voice steely. "My son never shot anyone, accidentally or otherwise, and if he says Todd's gun went off, that's what happened! Do you understand me, Rory?"

Openmouthed, still dazed with the shock and humiliation of what had happened, Rory nodded. The movement made him wince; there was a knot already forming at the back of his head. Struggling slowly to his feet, he put out one hand to support himself and shook his head gently, trying to clear it. Even now, he couldn't believe what Randall had done to him; he felt utterly humiliated and absolutely enraged, and helpless to do anything about either condition. Randall had been surprisingly strong, and Rory was not going to risk another mortifying scene such as had just taken place.

But Randall, once aroused, was not going to let Rory get away so lightly. Standing over his brother, who was beginning to feel almost nauseated from anger and embarrassment, he said, "I want you to apologize to Marcus, Rory. That was a rotten, unfounded accusation you made, and I think he deserves to hear that you're sorry."

Rory looked up, his eyes filled with a sick fury. Randall stared uncompromisingly back. "All right," Rory muttered after a moment. He tried to stand upright, but he felt as though someone had just kicked him hard in the stomach. "I didn't mean anything," he said, his voice almost inaudible. "It's just that I was . . . upset by all this. I . . . apologize."

Emily, who had been silent until now, got up quickly and put her hand on Randall's arm. "We're all upset," she said, looking at Rory, but speaking, Kate knew, to her husband. "It's been a shock for us all, I know."

"Yes," said Kate, taking up the cue. "You're both tired . . . we're all exhausted. It's been a . . . a terrible strain."

The two women, Emily and Kate, looked at each other, and Emily nodded, thanking her for her support. "I think we should go home now and let everyone get some rest. You'll let us know . . . ?"

Kate nodded in turn. "Of course. If there's any change at all in Todd's condition, we'll send someone at once."

Emily smiled slightly. "If there is anything I can do, please don't hesitate to ask."

Kate looked fondly at her daughter-in-law. "You've already helped a great deal, Emily. Thank you."

"Mother," Marcus said abruptly, "you and Dad go ahead. I want to talk to Grandmother alone for a minute first, if you don't mind."

Randall looked at his son. "Are you all right?"

"Yes. I just want to say something to Grandmother, Dad. You go ahead."

"He shot himself on purpose."

Kate stared at her grandson. They had gone to the library after Emily and Randall had left reluctantly without him, and Marcus had scarcely shut the door behind them before he spoke. As Kate gaped at him, he strode over to the fireplace and bent to light the fire. Kate hardly noticed the chill in the room, nor the sudden warmth as the logs in the grate began to burn.

"He shot himself *purposely*?" She put her hand to her forehead in a gesture of disbelief. "But I . . . I can't believe it!"

"Believe it," Marcus said grimly. "He replaced the poker he had just used to jab the logs into position.

"But *why*? How?" She simply couldn't imagine anyone even contemplating such a terrible thing, much less actually accomplishing it.

Marcus became even more grim. "He meant to shoot himself in the foot, I think. But I surprised him, and his arm jerked at the last second. He shot himself in the leg instead."

"But why? Why would he do such a thing?" Kate was still gripped with horror; her mind whirled with questions she couldn't even voice. It was incomprehensible to her that Todd could have done what Marcus claimed, and yet Kate had to believe it, for Marcus never lied.

"I'm not sure why," Marcus said slowly. "I think it had something to do with the war. He was really afraid of having to serve."

"Serve? The war?" Kate felt that she was echoing everything that Marcus said, and yet she couldn't seem to help herself. It was as if she had never heard of the war, and yet they had all followed the reports of it, especially Gabrielle, who read the newspapers avidly and could recite dates and names of battles, and countries involved and the numbers of casualties, which mounted daily. Gabrielle had developed an almost morbid fascination about the war, and Kate didn't know the reason for such unhealthy interest on her granddaughter's part. But why was she thinking of Gabrielle when she should be thinking about the monstrous thing Todd might have done?

"Why would Todd shoot himself because of the war?" Kate asked.

"Because he was afraid he might have to serve," Marcus answered again. His voice was contemptuous.

"But we aren't even involved!" cried the confused Kate, echoing the same words Todd had uttered earlier. "And President Wilson insists that we'll stay neutral!"

"President Wilson can insist whatever he wants," Marcus replied gloomily. "The truth of the matter is that the United States will be drawn in, whether we like it or not."

"Oh, surely we won't!"

"Yes, Grandmother, I'm afraid you'll see it before long. Gabrielle predicts that there will be some incident—some stupid, ridiculous thing that shouldn't even happen—and that will lure us in. For once I agree with her."

Kate stared at him, at her tall, strong, and handsome young grandson, and prayed that he was wrong. She had no need to wonder if he would serve if the United States declared war; she knew without asking that he would go. Unlike Todd, who was so like his father, and therefore a coward at heart, Marcus was without fear. He was brave and principled, and he believed in America and the freedoms offered here. He would go to war, Kate knew, and suddenly a terrible fear touched her. The conflict that had seemed so far away on European soil loomed abruptly and chillingly closer. Staring at Marcus, whom she loved so dearly, and who reminded her so often of Page, Kate knew that the whirlwind was gathering—a storm about to sweep them all into the maelstrom that was war.

She gripped her hands together in an effort to stop their sudden trembling. But her lips shook as she gazed at Marcus, and her voice was only a whisper when she said, completely forgetting about Todd in this new horror, "You're wrong, Marcus. You have to be wrong! There isn't any incident serious enough to make the president declare war!"

But the incident occurred on March 18, 1917, when three unarmed American merchantmen were sunk without warning by German guns with a heavy loss of life. A thrill of horror ran through America, and on April 6, 1917, President Wilson signed the congressional resolution declaring a state of war against Germany. America's nightmare had begun.

At Beauvais, the horror became even more real. As Kate had known, Marcus didn't wait for induction through the Selective Service. While Todd slowly recovered from his self-inflicted gunshot wound, Marcus didn't hesitate. His mind was made up, and Randall and Emily and Kate were helpless to stop him. With Gabrielle tearfully begging him to stay, Marcus went to war. It would be three years before he came home again—three long, empty, and terror-filled years for them all, filled with names that would echo resoundingly through history: the battles of the Aisne, the Marne, and, at the last, the Meuse-Argonne.

41

Gabrielle clutched the window drapery tensely, watching the motorcar as it chugged up the long drive to the house. She had seen its approach from an upstairs window and had stayed there for a few minutes transfixed, following the slow progress up the road icy with new snow. Then she had raced down to the drawing room where Kate sat, and she rushed past her to one of the front windows. The car had turned toward the house, and as she stared at it now, Gabrielle bit her lip, fighting a sudden premonition of disaster. She closed her eyes tightly, and then opened them again, as if the gesture might cause the car to disappear. It was still there.

"Grandmother," she said without turning from the window, "are you expecting anyone?"

Kate glanced up from the book she had been trying vainly to read. She had not been able to concentrate on the words in front of her for some reason; she had been too preoccupied with thoughts of her family. It had been more than a year now since America had gone to war, and they had all been affected in one way or another by the pall that hung over the country.

Todd had recovered to some extent from the gunshot wound he had suffered, although he was still forced to walk with a cane at times, and with or without the support, he walked with a decided limp. Kate had never revealed to anyone what Marcus had told her that day about the shooting incident, but she suspected that Rory either knew or guessed what had really happened. She had tried not to let her own knowledge affect her or allow it to influence her against Todd, but it was difficult. Especially when they hadn't heard from Marcus for a long time and the news from the front was particularly horrifying, and Gabrielle became even more white and strained than she normally was since Marcus had gone away, then Kate would look at Todd and wonder. Had

406

he really shot himself on purpose? Was he relieved that he didn't have to serve, or was he embarrassed by his being excused? Was the sacrifice of his leg enough to unburden his conscience, or did he even have any misgivings at all?

Kate didn't know. It was difficult to read Todd's smooth, handsome face at the best of times; since his injury, he seemed to have become more remote from her than before, more self-preoccupied and concerned with his own pleasures. He and Rory lived extravagantly and well, and in these days of war bonds and increased taxes and war gardens and meatless, wheatless, lightless, and gasless days, that was suspicious in itself.

Rory himself had been quiet of late, Kate reflected. After their last bitter battle on the day Todd was shot, he had never mentioned mining Beauvais again, and while Kate was grateful not to prolong the fight, she knew that Rory hadn't surrendered, he had just retreated for a while. He was onto something else, though, she was sure, and she was almost certain that it had something to do with—her mouth tightened—bootlegging. Colorado had "gone dry" in 1916, anticipating the movement of the rest of the nation toward prohibition, and although the amendment to the Constitution proposed the year before, prohibiting the manufacture or sale of liquor, had not yet been ratified, Kate knew that the Eighteenth Amendment was almost a certainty. Rory had seemed unconcerned at first, passing it off casually, as if it were of no consequence to him. Then, to Kate's initial surprise, and that of everyone else who knew how he liked his wines and his before- and after-dinner drinks, he had actually made a few statements supporting prohibition. His stand was inexplicable to many, but to Kate, who knew him and the extent of his greed and his political aspirations, his motives soon became crystal clear. She was not so old that she couldn't see the enormous profits to be made supplying illegal alcohol to a thirsty country, and while Rory was eager to enter the political arena in any capacity, he was also avid to make money. Prohibition seemed tailor-made for him to do both.

So, knowing what she did about him, it was ironic that she had heard him accuse Randall of being opportunistic. With Marcus gone, Randall and Emily had begun to direct all their efforts to increasing the wheat production of their ranch. Kate knew that this was their way of helping to meet seemingly insatiable demands for food during the war, as well as a means of working so hard that they could almost forget, for a time, the dangers that their son faced in France. But Rory had commented sarcastically once that Randall was only capitalizing on the spiraling wheat prices by rushing to convert so much of his land to wheat, and he couldn't understand why Randall had just looked at him blankly when he had accused him of profiteering. For Rory, such a course would not only have been natural, it would have been a golden opportunity; for Randall, and for Emily, who were so worried about their son, it was a hope that somehow their efforts would help bring Marcus and all the other boys home again.

Adele had not come home since the war started, either. She was still with friends in New York, peevishly waiting for the travel restrictions to be lifted so that she could return to England. She had cabled her daughter to join her a few months after Marcus had gone, but to Kate's surprise and Gabrielle's intense annoyance, Annabel had refused to go. Instead, to everyone's astonishment, Annabel had joined one of the women's councils of defense that had formed all over the state, and she had assumed the responsibility of sending clothing and supplies to war-torn Europe. She was also deeply involved in organizing the Red Cross, and spent long hours at the council headquarters in Denver.

Gabrielle had at first been scornful of this ceaseless activity on Annabel's part, claiming that once the novelty wore off, so would her cousin's interest. But it had been almost a year now since Annabel had moved to her small apartment in Denver, and Gabrielle's scorn had turned to admiration. Annabel had not tired of her work; she seemed to thrive on it, and Kate was both proud and pleased that Annabel had found something so worthwhile to do. Outwardly Annabel was the same—sarcastic, cutting, and curt—but the strength of character that Kate had always believed existed under her abrasive exterior was there after all; despite herself, Annabel's hard work and tireless effort for the benefit of others revealed her better nature.

They had all been changed by the war, reflected Kate; it had touched their lives in one way or another, brought about by the poignant absence of Marcus. It had been months since his last brief, mud-stained, penciled letter, and while Kate would never confess it to Gabrielle, who was already so worried about him, she was anxious herself about her grandson.

It wasn't like him not to write; he had tried to send home letters as often as he could during the time he had been gone. It was rare that a month would go by without hearing something from him—even a line or two; rarer still to have no word in eight weeks. But now it had been almost three months since they had received anything, and Kate's certainty grew that something terrible had happened. Trying not to dwell on the awful possibilities that occurred to her, Kate looked up blankly as Gabrielle repeated her question.

"Expecting anyone?" she echoed. "No. Why?"

"Because there's someone coming," Gabrielle answered stiffly, still at the window.

"Who is it?"

"I don't know. I don't recognize the car."

Gabrielle turned away from the window then, and Kate was struck anew by how thin and pale her granddaughter was. She had lost not only weight and color these past months of intolerable strain; she had lost vitality as well. It was November 1918, and Gabrielle, who had been born with the century, was eighteen years old. She should have been gay and full of laughter and high spirits, attending parties and galas and dress balls, surrounded by dozens of beaux, having the time of her life as she stood poised between girlhood and womanhood, caught like a butterfly in a beautiful moment of transition.

Instead, Kate thought sadly, Gabrielle was a girl who waited for letters that rarely came, a distraught and worried young woman who worked as tirelessly and ceaselessly as Annabel, burying herself in work both at Beauvais and at the community kitchen she had helped establish nearby, where she had taught herself and other women how to prepare war menus and to can fruits and vegetables. With Randall and Emily working so hard to supply food for the constantly growing demand, this was Gabrielle's way of helping to conserve what the Siddons ranch and so many others labored to produce.

But it was still sad to Kate that while Annabel seemed to take a perverse kind of satisfaction in exhausting herself with long hours at the women's council, Gabrielle seemed to feel no pride or sense of accomplishment in what she contributed herself. It was all work to her, a time spent when both her hands and her mind were occupied, when she was distracted enough to bury for a while her ceaseless anxiety about Marcus.

"Marcus is a brave man," Kate had said to her once, trying to offer what little comfort she could when she felt so desolate herself. "But he isn't a fool, Gabrielle. He'll be careful, especially when he knows that you're at home waiting for him."

"But he doesn't know!" Gabrielle had wailed, throwing herself into Kate's arms. "I never told him! I let him go, and never said a word about how I felt. I was too stubborn, too full of pride because he hadn't said anything to me. Oh, I hate myself! Why didn't I tell him that I loved him?"

Kate held the sobbing Gabrielle, and thought forlornly how like herself this prickly, proud granddaughter of hers was. She was so determined to keep her feelings to herself for fear of being laughed at or ridiculed or ignored, and how often that pride worked to her disadvantage! Kate remembered feeling so tragic herself, and not once when she was young had she realized that the fault might have been hers for being so sensitive. But it was not something that could be explained; Gabrielle would have to discover it for herself.

"Oh, my dear," Kate had sighed. "Don't cry so; you'll make yourself ill. When Marcus comes home, you can . . ."

But Gabrielle had lifted tear-filled, haunted eyes to hers. "But suppose he doesn't come home?" she had asked in a whisper. *"Suppose he doesn't come home?"*

"He will," Kate had answered confidently. But the fear that he wouldn't come back after all was as strong in her as it was in Gabrielle, and now that the strange motorcar had chugged to a halt in front of the house, Kate wondered apprehensively if Gabrielle's mournful question had been more of a prophecy than they both knew.

Trying to control her fear, Kate went to the window beside Gabrielle. They both saw the Western Union messenger climb out of the car and pause a moment to glance at the house. He held a yellow telegram in his hand, and instinctively Kate and Gabrielle clutched each other. When the doorbell chimed in the sudden, tense silence, grandmother and granddaughter looked at each other. Then Gabrielle, tight-lipped and trying desperately not to cry, went to answer the door. At that moment, the telephone that Kate had finally surrendered to and agreed to install gave its abrupt, harsh ring. It was Adele, calling from New York, her voice tear-filled and choked and jubilant, shouting over the noise of wild celebration in the background.

"Have you heard yet?" she screamed over the wire at Kate. "Have you heard? The armistice was signed this morning, Mother! The war is over—it's over!"

It was November 11, 1918, and far away in France in a military sector between the Meuse River and the Argonne Forest, a terrible price had been exacted before peace could be negotiated. The telegram that a white-faced and blank Gabrielle held in numb hands and read to Kate said that Marcus had been wounded, as had so many other men, in the massive American attack on the Sedan-Mèziéres railroad, the main line of supply for German forces on that segment of the western front. Cutting that line had forced a retirement of the enemy that included German evacuation of the Briey and Lonwy iron fields, and this terrible battle of attrition had been one of the turning points of the war. It followed such battles as the Aisne, the Marne, the Somme, Rheims, and St. Mihiel—names that would reverberate through history in memoriam to the thousands of men who had fallen. The armistice had brought this final massive offensive to a halt, but while the operation had resulted in the capture of 16,000 prisoners and more than four hundred guns, it had cost the United States 120,000 casualties.

And Marcus had been one of them.

42

Marcus came home in 1920, two years after the war ended, but he did not come back whole. For the first time, everyone at Beauvais had a devastating glimpse into something they had only read about or heard of or imagined. It was a war-induced phenomenon shared by thousands of men all over the world regardless of nationality and irrespective of the side they had fought on, and for those thousands, it did not end with the signing of documents that ended the war. No ink-

stained papers could wipe out the bloodstains of men who
had fought the battles; no agreement could erase the haunting
memories of men who had seen too much and suffered too
much in the cause of peace. Marcus came home, but he
brought two tragedies with him: a useless right arm, and the
memories that would stay with him until the day he died. The
phenomenon was called battle fatigue, but those who suffered
it didn't really care what name was given to it. They only
knew that the nightmare stayed with them, a gangrenous
canker that ate away the edges of their sanity until they either cracked under the strain or buried it under layers of protective amnesia. Years later, Marcus would still awaken in
the middle of the night sweating with recollections of those
terrible last days of the war. And it would be years before he
would even speak of the day he was wounded, about how all
around him, men he had known and become friends with
were bleeding to death, their guts spilled out onto the ground,
splintered bones poking out from what was left of arms and
legs.

But he would never tell anyone, not even Gabrielle, about
how he had crawled over dead bodies and moaning soldiers
and screaming, weeping men to the friend who kept calling
his name, over and over, like some ghastly litany, from a
mouth that was only a bloody hole in a face that wasn't there
anymore. Marcus never even felt the explosion that ripped
through his right arm and shoulder, chopping through nerve
and sinew and bone, until there was nothing left to feel; he
never saw the medics who grabbed him and stuffed bandages
into the wound that wouldn't stop bleeding, saving the arm itself, but not the use of it. The only thing he saw that day was
that tortured hole of a mouth and the barrel of his rifle as he
put it to the head of a man who wasn't a man anymore but
only a quivering, jerking piece of bloody meat begging for
death. Marcus pulled the trigger in a spasm of rage and pity
and pain, and then even the head wasn't there anymore. After a while, the quivering stopped, and the man who had
been a friend to him was a man once more. Marcus had given
him in death what some unknown shell had taken away in
life: dignity.

It was then that the medics had found him, standing un-
protected in the open, his right side red with blood that was
draining away his own life. They carried him off the field, the

two of them, but it took four men and more to take away the gun from his left hand, and it was months before he spoke.

Emily had gone to her son at the hospital in Belgium, where he had been transferred as an intensive case; she had followed him to England, and from there to a hospital in New York. It had taken two years and several operations and countless night-long vigils on her part to bring her son back to Colorado, and long afterward, Marcus would confess that it had been only her determination, her absolute refusal to let him die, that had made him live when he hadn't cared whether he would live or die. She had stayed by his bedside, and the love in her tired brown eyes had given him strength to go on. He had wakened to those calm eyes and that loving face so many times during those nightmare years in the hospital, and she had always been there to comfort him, to enfold him in maternal arms until it was dawn again and the last of the nightmares went away. He could sleep during the day, in snatches; it was the nights that were the longest, the bloodiest—the nights that held the most memories and allowed the monsters he could hold back during the day to come out and take hold of him. It was Emily's love that had given him back the faith he had lost; it was her belief in him that renewed the courage he had left that day on that bloody battlefield in France. But nothing could give him the use of his arm then—not the doctors, nor their surgeries, nor Emily's nursing care, nor his own fierce determination to regain the mobility he had lost. He came home again, but it would be a long time—a tragic time—before he believed himself, if not whole, a man once again.

Gabrielle was there to meet the train that brought Marcus and Emily home. Kate, as anxious as she was to see her grandson, had gone to the Siddons ranch instead, where, despite her age and the infuriating hip problem that hindered her movements and never seemed to leave her now that she was almost seventy-four, she insisted on supervising the housecleaning for Emily and Marcus' homecoming.

"You never did learn how to manage servants, Randall," she had said crossly to her son when he had tried to save her the trouble of coming over that day. "And Emily would be horrified to come home and find her house in this deplorable condition. She was always an impeccable housekeeper."

So Kate had not been at the station when the train pulled

in, and even Gabrielle, who loved Marcus so unreservedly, was taken aback when she saw him. He had been gone three years, and while the physical changes in him were appalling, that wasn't what Gabrielle noticed at first.

"It was his *eyes*, Grandmother," she told Kate later as she wept against her grandmother's shoulder. "His eyes—they look so . . . so *haunted!*"

And Kate had agreed. She had been on the porch at the ranch, waiting anxiously as soon as she saw the car coming up the road. But in the instant before Marcus emerged from the backseat of the car, Kate saw Emily and was dismayed by the hopeless resignation she saw in her daughter-in-law's kind face. Randall, too, seemed strained, and Gabrielle, who had looked forward excitedly to this day for months, was subdued and quiet. She had wanted to go with Emily when she left for Belgium to take care of Marcus; she had begged and pleaded and argued that she was the logical one to go— the person with the least responsibility and the one who loved him and wanted to marry him, no matter what had happened to him.

"But I love him, too," Emily had said gently to Gabrielle so long ago. "And I'm his mother. Randall and I have talked it over at length, and the ranch can manage without me for as long as it takes to bring our son home. You're needed here, Gabrielle—Kate needs you. Now that Annabel has gone to New York to pursue this new feminism idea"—Emily's mouth had pursed momentarily, as if the notion both appealed and repelled—"and Todd is so involved with his own concerns, you're the only grandchild she has to keep her company. She would be desolate without you, Gabrielle . . . and Marcus needs me."

So Emily had gone, and while Gabrielle chafed under the necessity of staying home, she had finally been forced to admit that day that Emily had been right after all: Marcus had looked right through her at the station, and she knew that she couldn't have helped him through the long slow months of his surgeries and recoveries and convalescences. Judging from Emily's exhausted face, it had been almost too much even for her to bear.

But Kate looked away from Emily and Randall and Gabrielle that day Marcus finally came home; she forgot everyone else, for her grandson was struggling to get out of the car. Conscious of nothing but her joy at seeing him at last, of having him home once again, she rushed forward. "Marcus!" she cried, embracing him. Her face was wet with tears.

Marcus bent stiffly, returning her embrace uncomfortably with his left arm. It wasn't until then that Kate fully realized what the war had done to him, for his right arm hung uselessly by his side, the elbow bent at an awkward angle that made her heart twist. "Oh, Marcus," she said sadly, looking up at him.

He gestured, raising his right shoulder an inch or two. "It's the best they could do," he said. His voice was so bitter that Kate winced.

"But you're home, Marcus!" she cried. "You're home! And we're all so thankful for that!"

"Yeah," said Marcus. Then he turned and stamped into the house. The screen door slammed behind him, leaving them all standing there staring helplessly at each other.

"Well," said Kate finally, "I think he just needs more time to adjust."

"Yes, that's it!" Randall agreed heartily. "He just needs time!" He sounded relieved that it could be so simple, and with a heartbreaking smile that included all three of them, he followed Marcus into the house.

Kate met Emily's troubled glance, and what she read there was more discouraging than ever. "Your letters . . ." She faltered. "You never really said how . . . bad it was."

Emily bit her lip. She looked away, trying not to cry. "I tried to be . . . encouraging," she said, her voice breaking. "I wanted so much to believe . . . to believe . . ."

Kate reached out to grasp her hands, trying to comfort her. "We'll take him to the best doctor we can find," she said.

Emily shook her head. "He's had the best, Kate," she said. Her eyes filled with tears again. "They said there isn't any more they can do."

"But there must be something!"

"Don't you understand?" Gabrielle cried then, startling them. She had been silent until now, standing a few feet away by herself, her whole body taut as she struggled to control her emotion. Now she looked at them in shock and horror, her face ashen, her fists clenched at her sides. "Don't either of you understand?" she cried again. "It isn't his arm that's wrong—it's everything else! Can't you see his eyes? It's all in his eyes! Oh, God!" she shouted, agonized. "Why did this damned war have to happen? Look what it's done to him—he isn't Marcus anymore; he isn't anyone! No one at all!"

Before either Kate or Emily could say anything, or even think how to respond, Gabrielle had rushed sobbing back to the car. Throwing one arm over her eyes, she flung herself across the car seat and leaned against the wheel, weeping with the rage and pain and sheer agony they all felt. The two women on the porch looked at each other in silence.

Finally Kate said in a low voice, "She's right, you know."

Emily's face was bleak. "Yes, I know. I tried to reach him, Kate—all these months I tried to reach him. It's a miracle he's come this far." She shuddered, her eyes dark with painful memories she couldn't put away. "If you could have seen him before," she whispered. "Oh, Kate . . . if you could have seen him before!"

But Kate didn't have to see what Marcus had been like before; she had glimpsed the emptiness in his eyes now, and she knew. He was a walking shell of himself, this beloved grandson of hers, and it was only years of practice that enabled her to keep her own emotions under control as she looked steadily back at Emily. When she wanted to surrender to hopeless weeping, like Gabrielle, or to give in to the utter despair she saw in Emily's face, Kate did neither. Instead, she said comfortingly and strongly, "Don't worry, dear. Marcus is home now, and whatever it is that he needs to help him through this, he'll have. You aren't alone anymore, and neither is he. The whole family is here to help."

"Thank you, Kate," Emily answered. But her voice broke as she said it, and it was a moment before she was able to continue. "Will you come in for a while?" she asked. "We . . . we could have some tea."

Kate shook her head. "Some other time," she said gently. "You look exhausted, and so does Marcus. The last thing you need right now is company."

"But you aren't company!" Emily protested.

But it was a token protest, and both of them knew it. Kate smiled. "Thank you, dear, but I think Gabrielle and I will go back to Beauvais. You need some rest . . . you all need time to yourselves to get reacquainted. Perhaps in a few days you can come to Beauvais for dinner or tea—whichever you feel more comfortable about."

Emily was almost in tears again as she reached out and

grasped Kate's hand. "Thank you, Kate," she said simply. "I knew you would understand."

But did she understand? Kate wondered as a silently weeping Gabrielle drove them back to Beauvais. Did anyone understand what Marcus had been through, what it had been like for him, what he had seen and done . . . how he had survived? Kate shook her head, her lips tight as she held back her own tears. She had never seen such desolation, such utter and profound loneliness and horror in anyone's eyes as she had seen in Marcus that day. Not even Page had looked like that when he told her about Colin, or when he had learned that David was dead . . . or that Michael had died.

Would Marcus ever be whole again? Would anything ever take away that despair she had seen in him? Glancing sideways at Gabrielle, Kate saw her granddaughter's strained profile as she concentrated fiercely on driving the car. Gabrielle hadn't made a sound, and yet there were tears coursing down her cheeks as she drove, and her knuckles showed white as she gripped the steering wheel. Every now and then a shudder went through her, a convulsive movement that indicated even more than her silent tears the depth of her emotion.

Looking away from her granddaughter, Kate stared straight ahead, her eyes dry now, too stunned to weep. They rode in silence all the way back to Beauvais, and Kate began to hope that if anyone would be able to draw Marcus out of himself and the horror that gripped him, it would be Gabrielle. Gabrielle, who loved Marcus with her whole being, with all her passionate and intense nature; Gabrielle, who didn't care that Marcus had only one arm, who wouldn't have cared if he had returned home a helpless, hopeless cripple. Her granddaughter was strong and kind and loving and brave. And Kate knew that if anyone could save Marcus, it would be this silent, suffering young woman beside her. For Gabrielle loved Marcus, as she herself had loved Page. And with a love such as that, Kate thought, closing her eyes as her own memories of Page assailed her, anything could be accomplished.

It only remained to be seen if Marcus would give Gabrielle the chance.

43

Marcus had been home two years and more before the first rumors about Rory and "the Klan" began to surface. At first, Kate didn't pay any attention to them; she had always despised gossip-mongers, and she refused outright to believe that Rory could be associated with a degenerate organization such as the Ku Klux Klan. Dismissing the tales as products of overworked imaginations or petty natures, Kate forgot the stories connecting her son with the KKK, as it came to be called, for there were other worries to occupy her mind, other people to be concerned about—Marcus most of all. He hadn't been home more than a few months before he began helping his father at the ranch, small chores at first, but difficult for a man with one paralyzed arm. An agonized Randall had tried in the beginning to protect his son from failing at the more demanding jobs, but Marcus drove himself mercilessly, furiously rejecting any offer of help or sympathy. He seemed determined to prove that his handicap was no impediment to pulling his own weight, and that he could manage as well as the next man—even better. And yet, as time went on, the hard work he took on, and the things he accomplished, gave him no satisfaction; instead he became more withdrawn, more silent and uncommunicative. Helplessly Emily and Randall watched their only son destroy himself with bitterness, and even Kate couldn't reach him. He was like a shell of himself, repelling any human contact or warmth or comfort, locked in a pain that went far beyond the paralysis of a limb. If it had only been his arm, they wouldn't have felt so helpless; a physical malady was something that could be dealt with. But Marcus' illness was as much in his mind as in his body, and this paralysis of his emotions, thoughts, feelings, and needs was impossible for anyone to defy. Marcus was empty, frozen, and more than anyone else, even his parents, Gabrielle was beside herself with worry and despair.

"He won't even talk to me!" she said despondently to Kate one day. "Whenever I ride over to the ranch, he leaves. He doesn't even bother to make excuses anymore, like having to see to the fences or bring some cattle in. He just . . . goes."

"Have you told him how you feel?" Kate asked the question, but she didn't have to hear the answer. Despair was written all over Gabrielle's face.

"I've tried to tell him! I told him that I didn't care about his arm, that it didn't matter! I even told him about my father and how when he lost his fingers, it didn't matter to my mother, because she loved him. I said that nothing mattered but him."

"And what did he say to that?"

"He said . . ." Gabrielle swallowed back tears. "He said that he was only half a man and that I deserved better than that. As if . . . as if there could ever be anyone but Marcus for me!"

"And . . . ?"

"And he just looked at me in that cold hard way he has now, and he walked away. He walked away, Grandmother! As if I didn't matter at all!"

That had been a year ago, and the situation, if anything, had deteriorated even more. Gabrielle rarely went to the other ranch now; it was too difficult for her to see the profound changes in the man she loved, too hard to come into Emily's kitchen and if Marcus happened to be there, to see him get up without a word, put on his hat, and go; too heartbreaking for her to arrive only to see him already mounting a horse to ride away, disappearing into the distance without a word or a glance for her.

"I'm not giving up, though!" Gabrielle would say occasionally to Kate. "I don't care how long it takes for me to make Marcus love me again. I'll wait forever if I have to!"

But it might *be* forever, Kate would think sadly, for in this year of 1924, Gabrielle herself was twenty-four years old. During these past years of strain, with the war and the aftermath of the war, and waiting for Marcus to find himself again, hoping that he would learn to love her as he had before, and worrying about Kate herself, whose own health had not been good of late, Gabrielle had given too much of herself for others. The resemblance to the famous portrait of Kate in the drawing room was fading; Gabrielle was thin to the point of gauntness, her skin stretched over frail bones, her complexion like fine porcelain with blue veins showing near her temples. She had not adopted the new fashion of shingled hair and shorter skirts as had her cousin Annabel, who had stayed in New York working for the feminist cause; instead, Gabrielle wore her heavy mass of hair pulled back tautly from her face, and the invariable blouse and skirt she wore displayed a waist that might only have been a handspan. And yet even the concern and the constant anxiety and worry could not hide completely the fact that Gabrielle Taggart was a beautiful young woman, still. But sometimes Kate despaired that her granddaughter's youth would be lost forever if something did not occur to change the situation soon.

And then something happened that would alter the course of all their lives, and Kate would wonder, as she had so many times in the past, about the power of wishful thinking.

BEWARE THE WISH . . .

She had thought of that ancient saying more times than she could count during her life, and each time she had ignored the wisdom of it, there had been a terrible price to pay. Would she ever learn to stop wondering . . . to stop wishing? Despairingly Kate began to doubt it.

It had begun with Rory, as so much of the trouble did, and when finally Kate was confronted with evidence of his involvement in the growing power of the Ku Klux Klan, her heart was simply not strong enough to sustain the shock and revulsion she felt. She had been so incensed, so outraged and appalled when she learned about Rory, that she collapsed in the middle of that terrible interview with her son, unable to believe his complacent, almost contemptuous attitude and his defense of his friendship with the Grand Dragon himself, Denver physician Dr. John Galen Locke.

"I can't believe," she had gasped, when she had finally asked Rory directly about his membership in the Klan and he had casually admitted it, "that you can actually sit there and tell me that not only do you belong to such a disgusting, dangerous, and perverted group of people, but that you actually enjoy it!"

"Now, calm down, Mother," Rory answered. "Remember your heart."

She had already in the recent past had one frightening episode of short breath and agonizing chest pain; the doctor had warned her then that she must not get excited. But she could not remain calm when her son—when one of her own children—had complacently confessed that he had joined an organization that took such pleasure in persecuting others.

"Never mind my heart!" Kate said now. "I want to know why you belong to such a repulsive group. From what I hear, you're almost a charter member!"

There was an odd, almost frightening light in Rory's hazel eyes as he looked up at her and then down again, examining his fingernails as he lounged back against the sofa. "I really don't understand why you're so upset."

Kate stared at him, utterly repelled. If she had been strong enough right then, she would have thrown him out bodily herself. She couldn't believe that anyone, even Rory, could be so blasé about people who, among other disgusting things, enjoyed dressing in sheets and burning crosses on Table Mountain and Pike's Peak. Oh, she knew that many residents of Colorado, like Americans all across the United States, had been filled with fear after the end of the war—fear of the hard times they had suffered returning to haunt them again; fear of the communism of Karl Marx, or of Eugene Debs and his American socialism—even fear of spies in this country working for foreign governments. She had been alarmed by such thoughts herself. But never had it occurred to her to embrace Dr. Locke's program of "one hundred percent Americanism" that was the cry of the Klan.

Was it because she was an old woman, and therefore couldn't understand or accept such ideas? No, no; age had nothing to do with it, she assured herself as she stared in outrage at Rory. There was no justification, and there never had been, for persecution of Catholics and Negroes and Jews because of their religion or their color or their business acumen. She had heard of attacks on Jesse Shwayder, the son of the Polish Jewish immigrant who had created the huge luggage firm, Samsonite Corporation; she had read about Klansmen advising Denverites to cease patronizing successful restaurants bearing "foreign" names like Pagliacci or Wong or Ciancio. And what was even more appalling and incomprehensible was that the Klan was rapidly assuming political leverage, not only at the precinct level in Denver but also at the state level. And now Rory, calmly sitting in her drawing room, was not only admitting that he belonged to such a deplorable organization, but more—that he actually found nothing wrong with it.

"I don't understand the problem, Mother," he said now. He got up restlessly to wander over by one of the windows. Staring out, he tapped his fingers absently on the sill, knowing that the gesture would set Kate's teeth on edge. He was fifty-seven years old this year, a tall, good-looking man, impeccably dressed as always, with all the assurance that family wealth and position had given him. His once red-gold hair had darkened to salt-and-pepper gray, and his ruddy complexion was more florid than ever, but even with increasing portliness and the telltale beginning pouches of dissipation beneath his eyes, he was still an exceedingly handsome man. Staring at him with a sick, helpless feeling growing inside her, Kate wished that his character had been as attractive as his outward appearance. Where had they gone wrong with him, she and Page, she wondered. Were they at fault, or was it only Rory himself?

Kate shook her head, acknowledging the futility of such thoughts. Whatever it was, whatever the cause had been, it was far too late to wonder, too many years past for recriminations or questions about what she or Page might have changed. Rory was himself; whatever he was or had done or would do in the future, he had to accept responsibility for himself—just as she had to face her own dragons. Not a very comforting thought, Kate reflected soberly, but there were few realities in life that were comforting when faced squarely. Especially, she thought, returning her attention to the immediate problem, this latest venture of Rory's with the Klan.

"Well, Rory, I'm waiting," she said.

Rory turned from the window, his eyes glinting in the afternoon light. "I really don't think I owe you an explanation, Mother. After all, I'm not a child you can take to task; I'm a grown man."

"Then perhaps you should act like one!"

"Oh, come on, Mother! That might have been effective when I was younger—like Todd or Marcus. And that's a thought—perhaps you should be directing your attention to making Marcus act like a man," Rory suggested nastily. "Or haven't you noticed that since he came back from the war, he hasn't been very much of anything?"

"Leave Marcus out of this! It's a miracle he came home at all! He—"

"For God's sake!" Rory exploded. "I'm sick of hearing

about how brave Marcus was, about how patriotic! I did just as much in my own way for the war effort, and so did Todd. But no one thinks to give us credit for that, especially you. It's Marcus—always Marcus! I'm tired to death hearing about him!"

"And why shouldn't you hear about him?" cried Kate. "Marcus went to France against all his principles; he—"

"Don't try to make me believe that nonsense, even if you do," sneered Rory. "He was so anxious to go he couldn't wait, could he? Well, it serves him right, what happened to him. If he had stayed home where he belonged—"

"Like Todd did?" Kate cried. There was a warning pain in her left side, a sharp thrust that made her catch her breath. She ignored it. She was too angry to pay attention to the danger signal she had felt once before. Rory had criticized her beloved Marcus; she only thought of defending him. Her grandson would not defend himself; he retreated farther and farther into his shell with each passing day, and she couldn't help him any other way; she had tried. But she would not stand here and listen to Rory sneer at what he had done, and censure him for what it had taken from him; it was too much to bear.

"Like Todd stayed home?" she demanded. Involuntarily her left hand came up to hold against her side. She faced Rory, shaking with anger. "Oh, don't think I don't know about Todd," she said. "About how he stayed home, and why."

Rory had paled. "What do you mean by that?" he demanded harshly in turn.

But not even to Rory, who had aggravated her beyond endurance, was she going to confess what Marcus had told her that day long ago before he had gone off to war himself and Todd had been carried home with a gunshot wound he had caused himself. Instead, she started to say something about Todd following in his father's footsteps, but suddenly the pain was too intense for her to speak. Gasping, Kate pressed her hand harder into her side, trying to breathe against that awful agony. There was a buzzing in her ears, a terrible pressure behind her eyes, and she was dizzy and nauseous at the same time. Staggering, she tried to put out a hand to catch herself. From somewhere beyond the edge of her darkening vision she heard Rory curse in surprise, and then she was falling . . . falling . . . unable to stand against this sudden agonizing pain. The pain blinded her, surrounding her with a bright light, squeezing the breath out of her . . . squeezing life out of her.

Oh, no, she remembered thinking; it was too soon for this, too soon to die. There were still so many things to see to, so many problems to solve. She had to make sure that Beauvais was safe; she had to find a way to stop Rory in his drive to destroy everything she and Page had so carefully built. And she must help Marcus somehow—Marcus, who had refused all offers of help. She had to see her loyal Gabrielle settled and happy—oh, she wanted to see Gabrielle happy. They belonged together, these two troubled grandchildren of hers; Gabrielle and Marcus were meant for each other just as surely as she and Page had been. She couldn't go until she had helped them; she couldn't go until she knew Beauvais was secure. It was too soon . . . too soon. She had so much to do before she could surrender to the longing she had had for years, that yearning desire to surrender and join Page at last.

She wouldn't allow them to take her to the hospital. If she had to die, and she wasn't sure she was going to, she declared, then she would die in her own bed, in her own bedroom, in her own home. And if she was a stubborn old woman for demanding not to be moved, then that was how it was. She would not go to Denver to the hospital. And that was that.

"But you really should have proper care," Clay Wilson tried to say.

Kate looked at him from her bed. She was propped high on pillows so that she could breathe, and Gabrielle stood silently by, watchful and alert. Kate reached for Gabrielle's hand. "I'll have the best care I could possibly want right here at Beauvais," she stated. "I'm not going to have some stranger poking and probing at me and wanting to take my temperature every five minutes. I won't do it."

Gabrielle recognized that tone, and she gave Kate's hand a comforting squeeze as she looked over at the doctor. "I can take care of Grandmother," she said. Her face was still pale with shock over Kate's collapse, her green eyes huge and frightened. But she spoke with authority.

"I believe you think so, Gabrielle," the doctor said unhappily. "But the fact of the matter is that Kate is going to need a trained nurse."

"I had some nursing training at the Red Cross during the war," Gabrielle replied steadily. "And I'm sure I can manage to follow whatever instructions you leave."

The doctor knew when to admit defeat. He sighed. He had known Kate for over twenty years now, Gabrielle for ten. They were a formidable pair, these two, and when they made up their minds about something, nothing was going to sway them. Shaking his head, Clay thought that one of them was bad enough; with both, a man didn't stand a chance.

"All right, then," he said, giving in without grace. He glared at Kate. "But remember, Kate, that this episode is just another warning—a little more severe than the last one, but more serious for that. You *must* follow my instructions and rest. If you don't . . ." He shrugged dramatically. "I told you before what would happen, Kate, if you didn't listen to me. And apparently you forgot all my warnings, or else chose to ignore them. You simply *cannot* upset yourself or lose that famous temper of yours. You're not twenty anymore, remember that. And since you aren't—"

"All right, all right," Kate interrupted testily. Her voice was weak, but still determined. "You don't have to lecture me anymore, Clay. You've been proven right. I should have listened to you. I didn't. Next time I will."

"I hope so," replied the doctor gloomily. He snapped his bag shut. "But somehow, I doubt it. I've known you for twenty years and more, Kate Taggart, and you have yet to listen to anyone about anything you choose not to."

But Kate did listen. In the following weeks of convalescence, she followed the doctor's orders to the letter. She didn't want to admit it, but the episode had scared her badly. And what frightened her even more was the slowness of her recovery. Her body simply refused to obey the demands of her mind and heal itself again. She had never really felt her age before, but she felt it now, and the aches and pains she had accepted as a normal occurrence before now assumed an ominous overtone. She felt frail and fragile and entirely too delicate, like a porcelain figure apt to shatter at the first rough touch. But she *had* to recover, she *had* to. For now that Rory believed her weak, he wouldn't wait long to set his plans in motion.

She had overheard him that day of her stroke; she had

heard him talking to Todd as she lay on the sofa in the
drawing room while Clay and Gabrielle made arrangements
for taking her upstairs. Rory had mistakenly believed her to
be asleep, or he would never have been so incautious about
revealing his hopes, even to his son.

But she hadn't been asleep, and she had listened in horror
to Rory tell Todd of his intention to take Beauvais away
from her, finally and completely.

"I've got my foot in the door at last!" Rory said exultantly
to Todd that day. "Your grandmother will never recover
from this stroke sufficiently to manage Beauvais; she won't
have the strength; I know it! I'll finally have control at last,
Todd. Do you realize what that means? I'll be able to do anything with Beauvais that I please!"

And Todd, who had never cared for his grandmother because she could see through him with those disconcerting
green eyes that Gabrielle had inherited, hadn't bothered to
ask Kate's condition, or even find out how she was. He had
only asked, "How soon?"

Kate could almost picture a gleeful Rory rubbing his hands
together as he answered, "It won't be long, I promise you,
son. I don't think she'll have the stamina to fight me about
this, but if she tries, I'm sure any court in the state will back
me up. Especially with my Klan affiliations now—the Klan is
so powerful in Colorado now, you know, and I've made such
an effort to cultivate John Galen Locke."

"I can't imagine Grandmother just standing by and letting
you have Beauvais," Todd said doubtfully. "Even with the
Klan behind you."

Rory hesitated, but only briefly. Then he said, "Well,
Mother is, after all, seventy-seven years old. It's a miracle she
hasn't had a stroke before this, after the warning Wilson gave
her before. She's going to have enough to do just guarding
her health. She won't be able to take care of Beauvais, too."

"Gabrielle will fight you, Pa. You know that."

Rory's tone was dismissive, curt, this time. "Gabrielle is a
child," he sneered. "She doesn't have the power or the
knowledge to fight me. Oh, no; Beauvais is going to be mine
at last, and no chit of a girl is going to spoil it for me. I've
dreamed about having it too long to be scared off now!"

"And after you have it, Pa—what then? Will you sell it?"

Todd's voice was eager, excited, and as she listened, Kate's
mouth twisted. She could picture this handsome grandson of

hers, tall like his father—like all the Taggart men—but with thick dark hair instead of the red-gold his father's had been, and guileless blue eyes that had never fooled her with their pretended innocence. He was thirty-five years old this year, and Kate knew that it wasn't the limp he still walked with that had kept him a bachelor this long. He was too wild to get married and settle down; he had too good a time allowing half the girls in the country to run after him. And chase him they did, Kate admitted sourly to herself, for Todd Taggart was good-looking, charming when he wanted to be, and he spent money like it was water. He was also one of the most eligible young men in Colorado, for it was believed—wrongly, Kate thought now with sudden renewed determination—that he was heir to one of the wealthiest ranches in the state.

But not anymore, Kate decided. As she listened to him talking to his father and heard the greedy note in his voice, she knew that she had to do everything in her power to prevent either her son or her grandson from trying to take over the ranch. It wasn't important anymore that Todd was one of her grandchildren, a member of her family; as far as she was concerned, he had renounced any claim in two words. "How soon?" he had asked Rory eagerly. And Kate thought now to herself: "Never."

So it was imperative for her to get well again, for Gabrielle alone could not fight Rory. Gabrielle would enter the fray loyally and without hesitation, for she loved Beauvais as much as Kate did herself, but she would be no match for her uncle, and Kate knew it. Gabrielle would be defeated from the first, because the weapons she would bring to the fight would be truth and honesty and a sense of what was right and just. But Rory had no such compunctions; he was ruled by his greed and his lust for power, and Gabrielle's idealism would be useless against a man who would do whatever he had to do to get what he wanted. Rory's membership in the Klan proved that he was capable of anything to further his ambitions. He wanted it all, and he didn't care who or what he had to destroy to get it.

Kate had not felt so alone since the day Page died.

But Kate and Gabrielle were not alone after all. The family rallied around Kate in the crisis of her illness, and she was never so grateful for their concern and their love as she was at that time, when she had felt so hopeless about so many things. Rory, seeing this support, and opportunistic as always, abruptly changed his own attitude toward his mother—outwardly, at least. If Kate hadn't heard that particular conversation between Rory and Todd, she might have been almost impressed by Rory's dazzlingly false display of filial devotion. He couldn't do enough for her, it seemed, from bringing her flowers and chocolates to buying a new radio and a gramophone with a complete set of the newest record discs. He visited regularly during the long weeks of her convalescence, and if it hadn't been that she wanted to keep her eye on him, she would have told him not to bother to come. The very sight of his hazel eyes resting speculatively on her both aggravated and annoyed her, and it was only by exercising her formidable willpower that she was able to keep her temper under control. She could not get upset or excited, the doctor had told her, and with every ounce of her returning strength, she obeyed. Too much was at stake for her to fail now; she was getting stronger every day, and she hoped that she would soon be able to make the trip to Denver to visit her lawyer and have her will changed. She wanted no one, not even Gabrielle, to know about her plans for revising her estate, and so she made herself stay calm and quiet, spending long hours in bed or carefully reclining in the chaise that was placed by one of the windows.

If it hadn't been that she was so worried about Rory and what he might do, she might have been grateful for her illness, for the Taggart family gathered once again at Beauvais, drawn together in shock and disbelief that the woman they had believed to be so strong and indestructible was frail, after all. And Kate, who would have been irritated and infuriated at such sympathy before, now welcomed these gestures from her family. It comforted her to have them visit, and she didn't even mind the inevitable quarreling and bickering that went on whenever the more volatile of her children and grandchildren got together.

Annabel had come from New York, a surprise in itself, for she was very involved in her feminism, and hadn't visited Beauvais for some time. She was twenty-eight years old now, thin and sophisticated with her brown bobbed hair and "flapper" dress, her incessant smoking of cigarettes and her clipped manner of speech. But because of her work in distributing materials about contraception, she had saved hundreds of women from unwanted pregnancies, and while she had never married herself, she was a staunch advocate of the rights of all women, married or not. She had also, Kate had learned some time before, inherited her mother's shrewdness for manipulating the stock market. Consequently, Annabel had made a small fortune for herself over the years, and Kate suspected that if she hadn't been so passionately interested in women's rights, Annabel might easily have stormed the male bastion and become a stockbroker herself. She might yet, thought Kate, as she raised her face for Annabel's quick kiss after her granddaughter arrived, for there was a restlessness in Annabel that had been in her mother, Adele. But where Adele frittered away her time and her energies and her talent, Annabel had managed to channel hers into one accomplishment after another. Kate was very proud of this granddaughter of hers, with her modern clothes and her advanced way of thinking, and her hard, defensive eyes. She only wished there was some way of relieving the loneliness she had glimpsed behind Annabel's sophisticated expression.

"Well, well," Annabel said at once, sitting down and crossing her silk-stockinged legs and lighting a cigarette. She looked at Kate, gesturing with the cigarette. "I hope it's all right to smoke," she said. "I mean, you're not at death's door or anything like that, are you? In fact, Grandmother, you're looking remarkably well, I think. To hear Gabrielle talk, you had both feet at the edge of the grave and were about to jump in."

Kate laughed. There was something refreshing about Annabel's clipped way of talking, about her irreverence. Anybody else would have been cloyingly sympathetic, asking solicitously about her health, carefully avoiding any mention of future risk. But not Annabel. Annabel had never pretended to be other than what she was: brisk, decisive, abrasive. She was not sympathetic by nature, and never had been. Instead, she was utterly honest about her opinions, and beware the person who asked her what she thought. Annabel would tell him, and not mince words in the process. She proved Kate correct about that now, for she began speaking in exasperation about Gabrielle, who had driven her from the station.

"And speaking of Gabrielle," Annabel said crisply. "What has she been doing to herself? She looks terrible! Can't you do something with her, Grandmother? She looks like some ignorant peasant, for God's sake!"

"Now, Annabel," said Kate reprovingly. "This isn't New York, you know. And Gabrielle has never cared for the latest fashions—"

"I know, but, my God! She looks at death's door herself. What's been going on around here? Surely, she can't be *that* worried about you!"

Annabel saw the smile Kate tried to hide, and flushed. "I really didn't mean it that way, Grandmother," she said defensively. "You know I didn't."

"Yes, I know," Kate answered. This time she couldn't hide her smile at all. Then abruptly she sobered. "She's worried about Marcus, dear," she explained. "It's been very difficult for her, taking care of me and worrying about him."

Nervously Annabel stubbed out her cigarette and lit another with a gold lighter she took from her bag. "I take it that Marcus still hasn't recovered," she said. "Is that it?"

Unhappily Kate nodded. "He works like a demon at the ranch, driving himself night and day, despite Randall's efforts to make him slow down a little. They've converted much of their land back to grazing, you know, whereas during the war so much of their acreage was planted in wheat. Marcus is trying to develop a new strain of beef cattle, but it's all hard work, and with his arm . . ."

Kate paused, and Annabel asked, "So his arm is still paralyzed? It hasn't improved at all?"

"No. The doctors thought that after a while there might be a chance . . . but, no, so far, there hasn't been any improvement."

Annabel got up to wander restlessly about the room. "But Gabrielle doesn't care about that, does she? It certainly wouldn't be like her if she did."

"No," Kate agreed. "Gabrielle doesn't care about his arm. And she has tried to tell Marcus that, but—"

"But he won't listen—right? Oh, men! Thank God, I never married! I simply couldn't stand the strain of having to tiptoe around a man's pride all the time!" She turned to Kate again. "But speaking of marriage—have you heard the latest about Mother?"

"I haven't heard from Adele for some time," admitted Kate ruefully. "She never has made it a habit to call, you know. Nor to visit. The last I knew, she was in England somewhere. I certainly hope she remembered her promise to stop in at Tremont Hall." Kate had always been sorry that

Tremont Hall had reverted to some distant cousins of Olivia's husband after her death; she would have liked it in the family, for she had so many fond memories of her one year there. But since the unknown cousins had inherited, Kate had never returned. It had been sentiment that had made her ask Adele to visit the house; she couldn't bear it if the new tenants neglected it.

"She remembered to see it," Annabel assured Kate now. "I talked to her a few days ago, and she said that the Hall was simply beautiful—windows shining, every blade of grass in place. But that wasn't what I was going to tell you, Grandmother. Did you know that Mother is going to get married again?"

Kate gaped at her. "Married?" She couldn't believe it. After Varian's death, Adele had sworn she would never marry again; it was too constricting a state for her restless nature. And Adele was in her mid-fifties now; still a striking woman, beautiful, in her own way, but . . .

"Oh, I know what you're thinking," Annabel said with her brittle smile. "Mother is a bit long in the tooth for the newly-wed scene, isn't she? But I gather this man is an English peer, Lord Something-or-other, and she was absolutely swept off her feet by him. Can you believe it?"

"No," Kate gasped. "I can't. I can't imagine it at all."

"Well, in fact, you won't have to imagine it, Grandmother, because she's coming here, new husband and all. And what's even more interesting than the announcement itself is that she sounds just like any other giggling young bride—absolutely ecstatic. It's almost . . . nauseating."

Kate hardly heard Annabel's last fond remark. She was thinking instead of Adele marrying again, and to an English lord. She simply could not picture her cold and unhappy daughter blushing like a young bride, no matter how she tried to evoke the image. "Are you sure about this, Annabel?" she asked. "Perhaps she was only joking."

"Oh, it's no joke, I assure you. I talked to her myself, and I know."

"Then . . . when is she coming?"

"I don't know—soon, I think, from the way she talked." Annabel laughed. "I told you that you wouldn't believe it, didn't I?"

And Kate didn't believe it still, even when Adele telegraphed a few days after Annabel's arrival and told them what time to meet her at the station. Kate wasn't allowed to go, of course, and she chafed at the restrictions her slowly returning health placed on her. But as impatient as she was to greet her daughter and her new son-in-law, she wasn't going to lose everything she had gained in these past dreary weeks of following the doctor's orders. She would not risk another attack, for that would give Rory the opening he waited for, and he was already impatient as it was. To his fury, Randall had seen at once what it was that Rory was after, and he had made it clear that he would help Kate retain control of Beauvais if it meant fighting Rory all the way to the highest court in the land.

"Oh, I know what you're up to," Randall had said to Rory one day not long ago when Kate had been brought downstairs to the sofa in the drawing room. Randall and Emily had come that day for a visit, and Kate was tired of entertaining in her room. They were there when Rory came jovially in.

Rory had pretended innocence. "I don't know what you mean, Randall," he said, smiling his charming smile and bending solicitously to kiss Kate's cheek. "How are you today, Mother?" he asked. "You look splendid! And what a surprise to find you downstairs!"

"Yes," said Kate dryly. "Isn't it."

Rory flushed at her tone, but he decided to ignore it. Turning instead to Emily and Randall again, he said, "I see that you finally decided to take some time off from the ranch. Did you leave Marcus there alone? Aren't you worried that something will happen?"

Randall tensed, and Emily put a quiet hand on his arm. Looking up at Rory, she asked evenly, "Why should we be worried about Marcus, Rory? He's perfectly capable of taking care of himself."

"Well, of course he is!" Rory said heartily. His eyes glinted. "I just thought . . . well, I mean, with his arm, and all . . ."

"He manages quite well with only one arm," Emily said steadily. "As well as Todd does, I imagine, with his cane."

Rory reddened at this thrust, and Kate suppressed the urge to applaud. It was rare that Emily was moved to verbal attack, and Kate was proud of her for defending herself and her son against Rory's pettiness.

Randall was proud of her, too, for he flashed her an admiring glance. She blushed and straightened, daring now to stare defiantly at Rory.

Rory hated to be bested; it made him feel both a fool and foolish. He said stiffly, "I'm sorry if I offended you, Emily. It seemed rather a harmless remark, but I understand how sensitive you must be. Next time, I'll be more careful about what I say."

"Do that," Randall said. "And while you're about it, you can reconsider this idea of taking over Beauvais from Mother."

"And what," Rory said sneeringly, "do you think you know about that?"

Randall wasn't afraid of Rory; he never had been. Now he looked directly at him and said, "I know enough, brother. I have eyes and ears; I see things and hear others. And you haven't been particularly careful in town in what you brag about, or to whom. Have you?"

His expression ugly, Rory answered, "You don't know what you're talking about, Randall."

"Oh, I think I do. And I'm warning you, Rory—just forget it!"

And so Rory had been checked again. But only for a while. Kate knew that he would never give up until he had wrested Beauvais from her, and as determined as he was, Kate was just as resolved to keep it from him. But as she waited for her granddaughters to bring home the newest arrivals, Kate wondered tiredly how long she could keep up the fight. She was an old woman, after all, and sometimes it seemed that willpower alone was not enough.

She heard footsteps in the corridor outside just then, and looked up eagerly. Were they back already from the station? She must be in her dotage, if she had lost track of time so easily; it seemed that the car had just pulled away from the house for the train, and now they were all back again. Where had the time gone?

But it was not Annabel and her mother who entered the drawing room where she waited so eagerly; it was Marcus. Marcus, who so rarely visited, who seldom even left the Siddons ranch. He had come to see her only once after her heart attack, assuring himself personally that she was going to recover before he cut short his too brief visit and went back to his self-imposed exile at home.

"Marcus!" she exclaimed, reaching out her hand to him. "What a wonderful surprise!"

"Hello, Grandmother," he said softly. Taking her hand in his callused one, he bent to kiss her cheek. Tears sprang into her eyes. The same gesture from Rory had almost repulsed her; from Marcus it seemed a tender mark of respect and affection.

To cover her emotion, she asked quickly, "What brings you here, dear? I haven't seen you for so long!"

Marcus glanced down. He was almost thirty years old now, and if the haunted look had ever vanished from his face, his resemblance to Page would have been stronger than ever. He had the same black, black hair, the same dark eyes and strong features. As personable as all the Taggart men were, Marcus was easily the most good-looking, Kate thought as she looked fondly at her grandson. Or perhaps she only felt that way because he looked so much like Page. Whatever the reason, Marcus was an extremely handsome man in his own right, and now that he had regained his health, his body was so forcefully built and so strong from hard work that one forgot the useless arm he kept hidden inside his shirt. Anyone looking at him would never know or guess that he was disabled or handicapped; he gave such an impression of strength and controlled power that one never really noticed the empty right sleeve.

"Marcus?" Kate said softly. She had noticed a change in him from the moment he entered the room, and yet she was almost afraid to remark on it for fear that she was mistaken. There had been . . . something in his expression when he came in just now that made her pause.

Marcus looked up again, and for the first time in four years that haunted expression was gone from his face. His eyes were no longer bleak and unhappy and bitter; they seemed to hold a new hope. If he didn't look entirely at peace with himself, he seemed to be . . . more accepting of his situation. It was more than Kate had dared hope for, and yet it was so much less than what she wanted for him.

Then she became angry with herself. It had taken four years for Marcus to come this far, she realized; she couldn't be impatient or greedy for more than he could give, no matter what she wanted for him. Whatever it was that had brought about this change, she had to be grateful and not wish for more.

"What is it, my dear?" Kate asked gently. "Can you tell me?"

"I . . . I . . ."

His voice was strangled. He found it difficult to voice thoughts he had kept hidden for too long, even from himself. "I've been doing a lot of thinking since your illness, Grandmother," he said finally, when he was able to get his voice under control. "And I . . . I finally realized what a coward I've been."

"That's not true!" Kate exclaimed. "You have never been a coward in your life!"

"Yes . . . yes, I have. No, let me finish," he said when Kate began to protest again. "I've never been a coward in the physical sense," he admitted slowly. "At least I don't believe so. But morally and intellectually and emotionally, I have. I just couldn't face what had happened to me"—he gestured toward his useless arm—"and I resented it like hell. I can't tell you how many times I wished I had died on the field like so many others . . . I can't tell you how often I wished I was dead, or how often I thought about killing myself. Oh, yes," he said, seeing the shocked expression that Kate couldn't hide. "I wanted to end it all: my dependence on everyone, my helplessness." His face became bitter again, his tone harsh with self-condemnation. "Do you know that for the first three months I couldn't even feed myself—that Mother had to do it for me?" He closed his eyes in remembered pain and shame. "It took six months after that before I could even dress myself, and then I had to have help with that. Oh, I wanted to kill myself, all right; I couldn't stand the humiliation and degradation I felt. I—who still had an arm, even if I couldn't use it, when all around me men were lying there with no hands or arms or legs . . . or eyes or ears, or . . . faces. And I wanted to kill myself because I was ashamed to ask for help. What a coward I was," Marcus said with loathing. "What a despicable coward! To think how sorry I was for myself when all around me so many were a thousand times worse off than I!"

"But you had never been sick before, or even injured," Kate pointed out quietly. "You had always been strong and able to take care of yourself—and others. And you had been through a terrible experience, something so awful that the rest of us can only try to imagine. You weren't yourself,

Marcus; you were wounded and in shock. It happened to other men; it's not something to be ashamed of."

"In my eyes, it is," Marcus replied grimly. "Looking back on it, I see that I was really no better than Todd, was I? We were both cowards, only in different ways."

"That is absolutely not true!" Kate said sharply. "I won't listen to such ridiculous nonsense! You and Todd are not the same, and you never will be!"

"Not now, perhaps," Marcus said. "But then?" He shrugged. "I'm not so sure. At any rate," he added, responding to Kate's outraged expression, "that's all in the past."

Despite her anger at what he had said, Kate felt a surge of hope. She wanted so badly for him to believe in himself again that she was almost reluctant to ask him to explain what he meant by things being past. Did she dare to believe that he had passed some critical point and was on the way to being himself again? But then she realized that it really didn't matter what answer he gave her now; whatever he said, he would always have her support. She loved him, no matter who or what he was or what he had done.

"You seem so . . . so different, Marcus," she said now. "Has something happened to make you see things in a new light?"

"Yes," he said simply. "I've thought a lot about you."

She was startled. "Me? But I haven't seen you or talked to you for so long!"

"I came to see you that one time after your attack—do you remember?"

"Of course I remember. But—"

"And as weak as you were then, and as ill, you were still determined to get well again. I saw it in your eyes—you weren't going to give in; you were going to fight your illness with everything you had. And you did. That's why I couldn't come again, until now. I was too ashamed of myself for not having the courage you had."

"Oh, Marcus," Kate said helplessly. "You know you never have to feel ashamed with me! You're my grandson—I love you."

He leaned forward, covering one of her hands with his own. "I love you, too, Grandmother," he said quietly. "And I . . . I love Gabrielle. That's really what I came to talk to you about."

"Gabrielle?"

"Yes." He released her hand and stood up again, prowling restlessly about the room. He stopped at one of the windows and looked outside, but Kate knew he wasn't aware of what was there, but of some inner vision of his own. Her heart contracted. He looked so much like Page just then, she thought. How many times had she seen Page stand at a window just so, collecting his thoughts as he stared out at nothing? Too many to count, she thought, closing her eyes in a spasm of pain. Oh, how she missed Page at times!

"I wouldn't blame Gabrielle if she never spoke to me again," Marcus said in a low voice. "I . . . I've been avoiding her all this time. Like the fool that I am, I haven't been able to face her, to tell her what I thought or felt." His voice dropped even lower, so that Kate had to strain to hear. "But I love her, Grandmother. I've never loved anyone else, or even thought of another woman but Gabrielle. Even in France, when everything was so . . . so bad . . . thinking about her and Beauvais kept me sane. But now . . ."

He turned toward her then, his expression agonized. "I've hurt her, I know. And what's even more reprehensible is that I've done it on purpose, trying to drive her away so that I could get her out of *my* mind. I thought that I wasn't . . . good enough for her. with my arm like this. So I tried to forget her because I didn't want to burden her with only half a man. But I can't let her go, Grandmother. I can't."

Kate was silent for a moment, wondering whether to say what had to be said in Gabrielle's behalf. This was the first time Marcus had spoken of his feelings and experiences in the war—the first time he had ever said anything about it at all since he came home. Did she dare speak herself and take the chance of destroying this new confidence in himself? Then she thought of Gabrielle, loyal and loving Gabrielle, who had suffered in her own way just as much as he had suffered in his, and she knew she had to tell him.

"You're not giving Gabrielle much credit, Marcus," she said. "Did you really think she was so superficial that the loss of your arm made you less a man in her eyes?"

Marcus stared at her, and a variety of emotions crossed his face: surprise, anger, guilt. He was silent, too, for an instant; then he shook his head. "No. No, I was the one who was shallow. I see that now. I should have trusted her—I should have talked to her, at least. But I . . . I wasn't strong enough to hear the wrong answer, if she had given it."

"But she tried to tell you how she felt, Marcus. First with words. Then, when you wouldn't listen, with actions. She kept going to the ranch to see you—just to see you—and you never stayed. The instant you saw her, you found some excuse to leave."

Marcus hung his head. "Yes, I know. I've really made a mess of things, haven't I, Grandmother?" There was no self-pity in his voice, only anger at himself that he had been so stubborn and filled with misplaced pride. "Do you think I can ever make it up to her?" he asked finally.

Kate heard the hope and the despair in his voice, and she smiled sympathetically. "Why don't you ask her yourself?" she suggested. "Don't you think she has a right to answer that on her own?"

But Marcus wouldn't wait for Gabrielle to come back from the station. He wanted to see her privately, away from the flurry and confusion of Adele's arrival, and Kate agreed that this was the wisest course.

"I'll come back after I help Dad move some equipment," he said, glancing quickly at the clock. "I should be there now; in fact, since I promised him I would meet him in the south pasture an hour ago. Knowing my father, he will have started without me, and that equipment is too heavy for one man to move by himself."

Hurriedly, then, he kissed Kate good-bye, pausing to look for a minute into her eyes. "Thank you, Grandmother," he said quietly.

Kate was embarrassed. Waving her hand at him, she said, "Oh, go on. I didn't do anything but listen."

Marcus smiled at her. "That was enough," he said softly.

At the door, he paused again. "Will you tell Gabrielle that I came today, and that I want . . . would like to see her? If it's all right, I'll come back later, after Dad and I finish. But I have to talk to her." He grinned crookedly. "Before I lose courage—again. Will you tell her that?"

Kate nodded. "Of course I'll tell her. But don't expect it to be easy, Marcus," she warned. "Gabrielle is just as stubborn and proud as you are, in her own way. And she has a much quicker temper."

Marcus grinned again. "Oh, I know," he agreed. "She's just like her grandmother, isn't she?"

Kate laughed happily, pleased beyond words to see this new change in her grandson. With a quick wave of his hand

and a promise to return after dinner, when he and Gabrielle could be alone, Marcus left, and Kate smiled fondly after him.

Neither of them could know it at the time, but his promise to return would not be fulfilled for almost five years, for later that day, Marcus' newfound assurance was utterly destroyed. An accident claimed his father's life, and burdened him with a guilt that would take years to expiate.

44

They were all unaware of the trouble in the south pasture that day; no one knew, in fact, until it was far too late. Marcus had been gone only minutes when Gabrielle arrived with Adele, and then it was just as Marcus had predicted: utter chaos and confusion as Adele swept in on the arm of John, Lord Fairhurst, Earl of Canthmore.

Kate, waiting anxiously on the sofa, was so astonished by her first sight of her new son-in-law that she barely remembered her manners. Fortunately, long years of social training took over, covering her surprise as she graciously held out her hand to the earl. He was so different from what she had expected that for a moment she thought it was all a joke. And then she looked into Lord Fairhurst's shrewd and confident gray eyes, and she realized that Adele had been truly fortunate with this marriage: this time her daughter had found a man strong enough for her.

Adele's first husband, Varian, had been weak, ineffectual, indecisive, and totally without character, in Kate's opinion. It was still amazing to her to think that between them Adele and Varian had managed to produce as fine a daughter as Annabel. But as she greeted Adele's new husband, Kate knew that he was none of the things Varian had been; the two men were poles apart in character and in appearance.

It was his appearance that had startled her, for Kate knew that Adele had always been attracted to tall, lean men.

Varian, despite his somewhat effeminate demeanor, had stood several inches over six feet, and Randall . . . well, Randall was just as tall. But the Earl of Canthmore was . . . There was no other word for it, Kate thought wryly: short. Standing next to Adele, he was just barely as tall as she. And by no stretch of the imagination could one describe Lord Fairhurst as lean; he was . . . rotund, and frankly so. While he was impeccably dressed, with the finest tailoring Kate had seen since leaving England, still his vest strained over his round stomach, and his shirt collar was hidden under heavy jowls. It didn't matter. John's eyes held hers in that first moment of introduction, and Kate saw an assurance and firm kindness there that Kate realized instinctively were exactly what her strong-willed daughter needed. Despite his deceptively mild appearance, Kate could not imagine this man intimidated or confused or incompetent in any situation. He would take charge swiftly, completely, and with the confidence that his orders would be obeyed instantly and without question. Kate couldn't know it then, but she would be profoundly grateful for those qualities later that day.

"So pleased to meet you, Lord Fairhurst," Kate murmured as Adele completed her introductions.

"John, please," the earl said, and his voice was deep and resonant, pleasing to the ear. "And the pleasure is certainly mine, madam."

"You must call me Kate," Kate said as he bowed over her hand, his lips brushing her fingers in a smooth, continental gesture that was exactly correct. She smiled at him as she straightened. "Unless you prefer to call me 'Mother,'" she added in jest. "And if you do, I doubt that things will proceed smoothly between us."

He laughed. "Then of course I must call you Kate!" he said, pleased.

Adele had greeted Kate quickly, embracing her hurriedly before she turned at once to introduce her husband. Now she said, "How are you, Mother? We were so worried when we heard about your attack."

"Oh, I'm much better," Kate answered. "Although I must confess that it sometimes drives me to distraction being forced to sit here while everyone else bustles around. Still, I've been faithfully following the doctor's orders, despite my impatience, so hopefully, before long, I'll be up myself."

"I know how you are, Mother—so determined that nothing

will get you down. Are you really getting well, or are you just saying so?"

There was an undertone of anxiety in Adele's voice, and Kate looked at her. Reassuring her, she thought that this marriage, however new, had already done wonders for her daughter, for the hard edge to Adele's voice that she had developed over the years had disappeared; her speech was softer, almost gentle—as were the dark eyes that had viewed the world with hostility and unhappiness for so long. There was a new expression in them, a kinder expression, and Kate was grateful to John for whatever he had done to bring these wonderful changes about.

Adele was dressed differently now; instead of the bright hues she had affected before, she wore now a simple, excellently cut dress of mauve silk, and Kate noticed then that Adele had lightened her hair to a pale blond that framed her face attractively in smooth waves and made her appear much younger than she was. She had kept her face and her figure, and as she leaned forward, holding Kate's hands, Adele looked elegant, assured, and—for the first time in years—happy.

"She's doing splendidly, aunt," Gabrielle said, moving to her grandmother's side from her former position behind the sofa. "Aren't you, Grandmother?"

Kate hid her amusement at Gabrielle's protective attitude. Then she watched in amazement as Gabrielle looked at the earl and smiled shyly. It was so unusual for her granddaughter to be relaxed with a stranger that Kate was astonished at first, until she realized that John Fairhurst had that rare faculty of putting people at their ease. Gabrielle, who was so shy and reserved, had responded to that quality immediately, and even Annabel, Kate noticed now, was not her usual tense and abrupt self. In fact, thought Kate, the two girls, who were both so different and so alike in their approach to people, seemed already to regard Adele's husband as a friend rather than as an intimidating title and a stranger suddenly thrust upon them as family.

"How long can you stay?" Kate asked John and Adele, gesturing them both to seats opposite her. She realized abruptly that her question sounded eager and plaintive at the same time, and she made an effort to be more at ease herself. "I mean," she amended quickly, "that it's been so long since Adele visited, and we would all like the opportunity to be-

come acquainted with you, John, before you both rush off to
Europe again."

Adele smiled fondly at her husband and then glanced at
Kate again. "Well, Mother, I'm not sure how long we—"

But she was interrupted abruptly by a commotion at the
door. They all turned in surprise as Todd rushed in, followed
quickly by a young lady that Kate recognized vaguely as
some banker's daughter. She was about to reprimand them
for their rudeness when she noticed their faces. Both were
pale with shock, and the girl was visibly trembling.

"What—?"

But Todd seemed not to notice that Kate had begun to ask
him something. "There's been a terrible accident!" he shouted
wildly. "Marcus sent us! He—"

Kate began to rise from the sofa. "Marcus? Marcus has
been hurt?"

"No, no, not Marcus! It's—"

Gabrielle flung herself forward then, grabbing quickly to
support Kate, who was still struggling to stand, her hand
pressed dangerously into her side. Turning fiercely to Todd as
she held her grandmother, Gabrielle shouted, "That's enough,
Todd! You're scaring Grand—"

But Todd didn't hear his cousin, either. Staring wide-eyed
at them all, he cried, "My God! Don't you understand? It
isn't Marcus who's hurt—it's Uncle Randall! Uncle Randall's
been killed! He was crushed under some equipment they were
moving, and he's dead. *Dead!*"

Kate didn't hear any more. Her hand moving from her
side to her throat, she was trying desperately to hold off that
frightening blackness that was rushing at her again. She
couldn't breathe, and as she gasped for air, she could hear
the doctor's words clanging through her mind: *"I warned
you, Kate . . . no excitement . . . no upset . . . or else . . ."*

She couldn't pay attention to those words, it seemed. Her
heartbeat was loud, deafening in her ears, filling her brain
with a dreadful pounding sound that was all she could hear.
It became louder and louder, expanding inside her head until
that sound was the only thing in her universe. She had to
hold on to that uneven heartbeat; she couldn't lose it, or everything would be lost.

But she had to think about Randall, about her loving and
kind and loyal Randall. She had lost him, she thought in bewilderment; she had lost her son.

And he *had* been her son—from the moment Page had placed him in her arms and his tiny fingers had curled trustingly around hers, he had been her son. Flesh and blood weren't the only things that bound mother and child. There was a love and understanding and a special bond that never needed words; there was a meeting of heart and soul, and Randall had been her child just as much as any of the others who had come from her body. He had been the youngest, and so precious to her because they had found one another when each needed the other the most. And now he was gone, lost to her . . . dead.

"Oh, Randall!" she cried, falling in a heap against the sofa pillows despite Gabrielle's support. "Oh, not my Randall! Not my Randall! He was so good, so dear . . ."

The pain became huge then, too much to fight. It swelled and swelled, driving her down, crushing her with the sheer force of it. Blackness filled her vision, and still that terrible pain increased until she felt she could endure it no longer.

Only dimly aware of Gabrielle weeping uncontrollably and holding her tightly in a spasm of helplessness, Kate allowed the blackness and the pain to claim her.

They didn't tell her about Marcus until much later, when she had rallied a little from this second and much more severe attack, because for a while it seemed that Beauvais might lose Kate, too. She was close to death many times over the following tense weeks, and Clay Wilson absolutely forbade anyone to speak of the double tragedy at the Siddons ranch. So they all tiptoed around her, caught in their own emotions—distraught, worried, anxious, hopeful.

Randall was buried quietly and without fuss, and after the funeral, Emily collapsed. In one sweep, she had lost both husband and son, for while Randall had been killed that day in the south pasture, Marcus might have been dead to her as well.

"It was my responsibility," he said bitterly to Emily the day of the funeral. "If I had been a whole man, I could have saved him."

Emily knew her son; she could see what was coming by the look in his eyes, and with every ounce of strength she tried to prevent it. "No one could have saved him!" she said fiercely to Marcus. "No one! It was God's will!"

"God's will!" Marcus sneered, his lip curling in contempt.

"If it was, then I can't believe in a god who would let a good
and honest man like my father die, while he allowed someone
like Rory Taggart to carry on, contaminating everything he
touches!"

"It isn't up to us to decide such things, Marcus," Emily
had tried to say. "We can't always understand what plan God
has in mind. We can only have faith—"

"Faith!" Marcus was more contemptuous than ever. "I
don't have any faith!" he spat. "I left it, along with my arm,
at the Argonne Forest. And whatever belief I had in anything
was just destroyed the other day, in our own south field. Dad
didn't deserve to die, Mother, just because he had half a son
who couldn't even help him when he needed it most!"

Marcus had broken down then, his tears like acid as he sat
at the kitchen table and wept as a man weeps, agonized and
choked, his sobs strangling him with the effort to hold his
emotions at bay. Emily had tried in vain to comfort him, to
convince him that he had done the best he could—that he
had done the best anyone could. But Marcus refused to listen.

And so, as she had known in her heart, Emily had lost her
son, too. He promised that she would be taken care of, that
he would hire someone to help out at the ranch in his absence. But he couldn't promise that he would come back. His
father's death, and his own impotent part in it, had shaken
him to the foundations of his soul; he had to leave to find
himself again, and it would be almost five years before Emily
heard his step at the door again.

"Gone?" Kate said blankly when Adele and John finally
told her. "I don't understand. What do you mean, gone?
Where did he go?"

How she hated the sound of her own voice now, so thin
and reedy! She resolved to speak more strongly, but words
failed her as she looked from Adele's bent head to John's
compassionate face. "John?" she said helplessly.

"I don't know where he went, Kate," John answered. "No
one knows. He waited until after the funeral and hired a man
to help at the ranch, and then he . . . left."

"But surely he told someone where he was going and when
he would be back!"

"He never said anything, Grandmother," Gabrielle said
dully. She was sitting beside Kate's bed, so still that she might

have been a statue, a figure carved in alabaster. Her voice
was a flat monotone, carrying no emotion whatsoever. The
hurt was deep, her pain too fresh for her to say more than:
"He said nothing at all. And he isn't coming back."

Kate stared at her. "But he must have said something to
you, at least!"

"No."

Gabrielle looked away from her, and Kate saw the convulsive movement of her throat as she struggled with her tears.

"But he was going to talk to you!" Kate exclaimed. "He
wanted to tell you how much he loved you!"

Gabrielle closed her eyes. "He didn't."

John spoke up. "Apparently he felt that he was to blame
for the accident, Kate."

"But he wasn't!" Kate didn't know much about the day
Randall had died; her collapse had come too soon after for
her to learn much detail, especially when everyone had been
under such strict orders not to disturb her. But she had heard
snatches of conversation since then, enough to piece together
the tragic story. Some gear or another had jammed on the
baler, and Randall had crawled under to free it. He was
pinned under the machinery, crushed when it fell on him. A
desperate Marcus had tried heroically to save his father, but
even with his frantic strength, he had been unable to move
the heavy load. By merest chance, Todd and Belinda had
been out for a drive when the wild-eyed Marcus met them on
the road, and they had sped to Beauvais instead of the Siddons ranch because Beauvais was closer to ask for help. It
had been too late by then, of course. And the doctor had
tried vainly to reassure Marcus that it had been too late from
the moment the machinery had fallen on Randall.

"But he couldn't believe that, Kate," John told her now.
"He seemed to feel that if he had been able to use both arms,
he could have saved his father. It isn't true, of course, but no
one was able to convince him otherwise. He felt so responsible, I think, so guilty, that he had to leave. He had to go
away to be by himself, to think things out."

"You talked to him, then?" Kate couldn't keep the pathetic
eagerness from her face or her voice.

John nodded. "Yes. Or rather, I tried. But when a man is
bent on blaming himself . . . well, there wasn't much I could
do. I'm sorry, Kate. Very sorry."

Kate looked down at the satin quilt that covered the bed.

Her hands were clasped tightly in front of her, and she saw
with part of her mind that her hands were gnarled and
twisted, her fingers swollen. She made a deliberate effort to
flex her fingers, trying to divert her mind from thoughts that
carried her back too many years and into too much remembered suffering. Michael had gone away like this, and she had
never seen him again. Was the same pattern destined to be
repeated with Marcus? How could she bear it if it was?

Then she looked at Gabrielle, sitting so woodenly beside
the bed, held erect, it seemed, by sheer strength of will that
she might have inherited from Kate herself, and suddenly
Kate was ashamed of her own selfishness. She had lived her
life, but Gabrielle's life stretched out before her still. Was
that life destined to be arid and barren as she waited for a
man who never came home again? Kate felt the sting of tears
behind her eyes, and this time she wept not for herself, but
for a lovely granddaughter who might never have what she
herself had treasured most: the love of a man whose very
presence had been a flame in her life, a constancy that made
everything worthwhile, even the trials and disappointments—
even the pain and suffering and loss.

Wiping tears from her cheeks with the handkerchief John
pressed silently into her hand, Kate asked him shakily, "Do
you think he'll come back?"

John hesitated. But as Kate had known, he could not be
less than honest with her, so he said at last, "I don't know,
Kate. I wasn't well acquainted with Marcus, but from what
little I know of him, I saw that he was a driven man, beset
by many things we don't understand. But he feels deeply
about all of you, and I think . . ."

Kate looked up eagerly. "Yes?"

But John shook his head. Covering her hands with his own,
he said, "I just don't know, Kate. If Marcus is the man I
think he is, he'll be back—someday. But he won't come home
until he has exorcised his particular demons, and with a man
like your grandson, that might be . . . some time."

"Years, you mean."

Gabrielle had spoken again, turning her head stiffly to look
at them. Her face was waxen, her lips bloodless, her expression so silently agonized that Kate wanted to weep at the
sight of it. But Gabrielle looked directly at John and waited
for his answer, and because John respected Gabrielle's

strength as much as he respected her grandmother's, he was forced to be honest with her, too.

"Yes," he answered unhappily. "It might even be years before he comes back, Gabrielle. I'm sorry. So sorry."

45

Marcus had been gone nearly five years when Gabrielle turned twenty-nine. There was not much for her to celebrate that day of her birth, for after four years of litigation between Gabrielle and her uncle, it seemed that Rory was about to snatch victory from her at last. Another court hearing, this one the last in a long line of such legal battles, was to be held in November of that year 1929, and Gabrielle knew that she had nothing left with which to fight. Rory had kept his promise, made in anger and outrage, four years before, when a failing Kate had summoned everyone to Beauvais to reveal that she had at last succeeded in changing her will. Gabrielle could remember that scene as clearly as if it had been the day before; she would always carry a mental picture of Kate—frail and fragile from her second heart attack—standing up bravely to her son. It was an image Gabrielle would treasure forever, for she had never been as proud of her formidable grandmother as she had been then, that day, when Kate had given Beauvais into her hands.

Kate had insisted on being carried downstairs that day. She wanted to face her family in her own drawing room, sitting on her sofa, saying what she had to say there—not cowering in her bedroom like some senile old woman who wasn't strong enough to sit down properly and pour tea while she spoke to her family. Her wishes had been obeyed, of course, for despite her slow convalescence and continued weakness, she was still the matriarch of Beauvais, and Gabrielle quietly insisted that her grandmother's demands be respected.

"I hope this is important, Mother," Rory said as soon as he arrived. He came sweeping into the drawing room, brushing a smattering of new snowflakes from the shoulders of his fur coat. He looked distracted, almost unwell, thought Kate as she looked at him from her position on the sofa, and she rightly suspected that it was the sudden demise of the political power of the Klan that disturbed him. He had held high aspirations for a governorship or a senatorial seat, and with the power of the Klan behind him, he might have succeeded. But not now. Oh, no; not now. Kate hadn't bothered to hide her elation that summer of 1925, when the Grand Dragon himself, John Galen Locke, had been forced to resign his post after the Denver and other state newpapers, along with federal treasury officials and even national leaders of the Klan, had begun to question Locke about his income. And without his leadership, the Colorado Klan, which had assumed frightening proportions of size and power, dwindled quickly. Leaving Rory, Kate thought with satisfaction, without a power base himself. She couldn't have been more delighted.

"Oh, I think it will be important to you," Kate murmured now. She had practiced strengthening the sound of her voice, so that she would not appear to be a sick old woman, and from the quick glance her son gave her now, she knew she had been successful. She was grateful for any advantage; the next few minutes were going to be difficult.

Annabel came downstairs just then, carrying her cigarettes and a gold lighter—this one with an inscription, "AW from GR"—looking languidly around for a place to sit. She had arrived just the day before, responding to Kate's call to her in New York, asking her to come to Beauvais. Kate had noticed the change in her elder granddaughter immediately, and had remarked on it. Like Adele had been before last year, Annabel seemed less harsh now, her eyes not quite so hard and bright. When Kate had said so, Annabel had uttered a surprisingly girlish laugh and confessed, "You won't believe it, Grandmother, but I've finally met a man who isn't afraid of me."

"You have!" Kate was both delighted and surprised. "Who is he?"

But Annabel only looked mysterious and wouldn't say. "I don't want to ruin everything by talking about him just yet," she said. "I'm superstitious about it, I guess—afraid that he's too good to be true, and that I'll lose him. Or that he'll lose me."

Kate had understood. She had asked only one question then, unnecessarily, because she saw the answer in Annabel's suddenly beautiful face. "Are you happy, then?"

Annabel had nodded and hugged her again with a spontaneity unusual for her. "Very," she said.

Now Annabel looked up as Todd followed his father into the drawing room, and Kate was surprised to see the coolness in her granddaughter's expression as her eyes followed her cousin. Annabel had always gotten along well with Todd; now it seemed that she disliked him thoroughly.

"Well, Todd," Annabel said, "I'm surprised that you actually had the courage to show your face here. Or didn't you know that I was coming?"

Todd started. He obviously hadn't seen Annabel when he entered; now he looked as though he wanted desperately to retreat. "What do you mean?" he muttered, caught.

Annabel stubbed out her cigarette and lit another one with a quick snap of the gold lighter. "You know very well what I mean," she answered through a wreath of smoke. "When are you going to pay me the money you owe me? You promised to repay it, with interest, last year, and I have yet to see a cent."

"Aw, come on," Todd said in a wheedling tone. "Don't you trust me—your own cousin?"

Annabel's eyes were hard again as she stared at him. "No. It amounts to several thousand now, if you've bothered to keep track, and I want it back. Now."

Todd had paled. He was aware of Annabel's reputation for shrewdness; he also knew from experience that she could be cold and ruthless where money was concerned—especially her own. She wouldn't hesitate to haul him into court to make him pay, and he knew it. "All right, all right. You'll get your money," he mumbled.

Annabel had no intention of letting him off so lightly. She was unimpressed with the Todd Taggart charm, for she knew her cousin far better than did so many of the girls chasing after him so blindly. "When?" she demanded coolly.

"Before you leave—is that all right?" Todd said angrily. "Unless you plan to go this minute—which might not be a bad idea, after all!"

"I'm leaving the day after tomorrow," Annabel replied calmly. "That will be soon enough."

Todd glared at her, and then collapsed into one of the chairs, where he stared morosely into the fire. Ignoring Annabel, he turned his back on the rest of the room, muttering to himself.

Her point made, Annabel ignored him, as well. Turning instead to Kate, she asked, "Well, Grandmother, did you get in touch with Mother?"

Yes; Kate had talked to her, finally, that morning. But she related now only that Adele was utterly content with John, traveling between their estates in England and in France; there were no immediate plans to visit the United States again. She did not say that Adele had willingly agreed to the changes Kate wanted to make in her will, requesting only that she and John be allowed to stay at Beauvais whenever they wished.

Relieved that Adele had been so amenable, Kate had happily assured them both that they were welcome at any time; indeed, that she looked forward to a visit soon. She hadn't expected any difficulty from this new Adele, who seemed so delighted with her life and with John, but unpredictability had always been one of her daughter's characteristics, and it was heartening for Kate that the first hurdle had been overcome so easily. The rest, she reflected as she looked from Rory to the sulking Todd, would not be so effortless.

Gabrielle came in just then and took a place beside her, and now that they were all here, there was no reason to delay. Taking a deep breath, Kate startled everyone but Annabel by saying, "I've asked you here to tell you of the changes I've made in my will."

Immediately there was an uproar, for until then, only one other person in the room was aware that Kate had talked with her lawyer earlier that week. Kate had told Annabel when she first called her, because she felt she owed it to her granddaughter to explain. Annabel's reaction had been everything Kate hoped for, and more.

"Of course I don't object," Annabel had said over the telephone from New York. "As much as I love Beauvais, I'm quite content to stay here where I belong. If I inherited Beauvais, or part of it, it would only be a burden. This way I can come and go as often as I like and just enjoy myself without worrying about all that responsibility."

"Are you absolutely positive, Annabel?" Kate had asked her anxiously. "After all, Beauvais is your inheritance, too."

"I know. But as much as I hate to admit it, Gabrielle will take care of it much better than I." She laughed mischievously. "Of course, that doesn't mean I renounce all financial claim, you know!"

Kate laughed, too. "I would have been disappointed in you if you had," she admitted. "But there isn't any need to worry about that, dear. I've taken care of the financial end of it in a way I know will please you."

"There is just one thing . . ."

Kate felt a pang of alarm. "What is it?" she asked apprehensively.

"I'd like to be there," Annabel said, and Kate could just picture the evil gleam in her eye, "when you tell the rest of the family. Especially Uncle Rory. Can you give me time to get there before the great denouement?"

"Oh, Annabel!"

Kate had laughed, but she had waited for Annabel's arrival before calling the family together, and now, looking around the room, she saw their faces as she had known they would be: Annabel, watchful; Todd, worriedly speculative; Gabrielle, surprised; and Rory . . .

"What the hell do you mean, changes in your will?" Rory demanded sharply as the hubbub of surprise subsided a little. "I hope you're talking about small things, Mother—like bequests."

"No, Rory," Kate answered quietly. "I'm afraid the revision I've made is a major one."

Rory blanched. "How major?"

Kate reached for Gabrielle's hand. "You might all think I should have discussed it with you first . . ." she began.

Rory shot to his feet. "You're damned right I do!" he erupted.

Kate stared at him, and her voice was cold when she said, "Sit down, Rory. You might wait until you hear what I have to say."

"I don't have to hear it!" Rory snarled. "You've been waiting a long time for this, haven't you, Mother? Oh, I can see it all now—you lying upstairs with so much time on your hands, time to think and plan, to plot against me!"

His voice was shrill toward the last, and Kate watched him carefully. His face was so congested that she hardly recognized him, his rage so apparent that she saw the throbbing of a vein near his temple. "No one plotted against you!" she said sharply. "And whatever has been done has come about because of your greed and your selfishness—remember that, my son. If you hadn't wanted to destroy Beauvais, I might have decided differently. But I told you long ago that I would never leave Beauvais to you unless you proved to me that you would care for it as Page did, as I have . . . and as Gabrielle will!"

She could feel Gabrielle's violent start beside her, and she grasped her granddaughter's hand more tightly. The contest was between Kate and her son now; everyone else in the room was completely silent, surprised and stunned by Kate's revelation, awed by the fierce battle of wills taking place before their eyes.

But Kate had not lived for over three-quarters of a century to be intimidated now by a son she neither respected nor admired. She had gathered all her strength for this day, and nothing would make her reconsider. She was right, and she knew it, in her mind and in her heart; what she had done was proper and just.

But Rory was standing over her now, breathing heavily, staring at her with wild eyes. "I won't have it, Mother!" he shouted. "I won't surrender everything that should belong to me to this chit of a girl—to this nobody, who doesn't deserve it and who never has!"

"As you deserve it?" Kate asked. If she was afraid of him and what he might do, she didn't show it. There was contempt written on her face as she looked at him.

"Goddammit! I'm your son!"

"And Gabrielle is my granddaughter."

Rory laughed then, harshly. "Your granddaughter!" He sneered. "The daughter of a saloon girl and a coward who ran off because he found out he was a bastard!"

"That's enough!"

"No, it's not enough! I'm not going to give up Beauvais this easily, Mother—you can be sure of that! I'll break that will of yours if I have to go all the way to the Supreme Court to do it. You're over seventy-five years old; you've had two heart attacks. Surely there's one court in the land that will agree that you're an incompetent old fool who doesn't know her own mind!"

Before Kate could stop her, Gabrielle had leaped to her

feet. "How dare you!" she cried. "How dare you speak to Grandmother that way!"

And before everyone's amazed eyes, Gabrielle's hand shot back and she delivered a ringing slap right across Rory's suffused face. The sound was loud in the sudden silence, and Rory stared at her in utter shock and surprise. His hand went to his face, where the imprint of Gabrielle's hand showed red against his suddenly white skin. Behind him, deep in her chair, Annabel snickered. No one heard her; all eyes were riveted to Gabrielle and her uncle.

"You'll be sorry for that!" Rory shouted.

"I'll never be sorry for it!" cried Gabrielle. "It's what you deserve, and more!"

"You'll pay—"

"And so will you!" Gabrielle shrieked. "You'll never have Beauvais now—not while I have a breath left in my body to fight you!"

Rory stared into those blazing and unafraid green eyes, and this time his voice was abruptly lower, a menacing snarl that raised the hair on the nape of Kate's neck. "It will take more than breath to fight me, little girl. Are you really prepared for that? By the time I finish with you, you'll wish that you had never set foot on Beauvais. You don't stand a chance against me—just like Michael didn't. I beat him, and I'll beat you, too!"

"Don't be too sure of that!" Gabrielle shrieked after him as he grabbed his hat and coat and strode furiously from the room. "Don't be too sure!"

But Gabrielle, despite her bravado, was shaken by Rory's threat, and Kate knew it. She was shaken herself. Rory's expression just then had been truly frightening. He had looked murderous, absolutely enraged, and almost insane with jealous fury.

46

Gabrielle fought her uncle for four years, in court and out of it. When the day came that she turned twenty-nine, she collapsed in the hallway outside Kate's bedroom door while she was carrying a tea tray in to her grandmother. The doctor diagnosed nervous exhaustion and prescribed complete bed rest, but of course Gabrielle wouldn't hear of it. As soon as the doctor had gone, she was struggling out of bed, ignoring Kate's pleas to follow Clay's orders and rest.

"No, Grandmother," Gabrielle said, resting a moment on the side of the bed before she pushed herself upright. "I can't stay in bed; I have too many things to do."

Kate, who knew that her own failing health was just one more cause of worry for her granddaughter, said pleadingly, "Let someone else manage for a while, Gabrielle . . . please. You're running yourself ragged, trying to do so much all the time. Someone else can take over, can't they?"

Gabrielle stared at her, eyes bleak. "There's no one else," she said flatly. "Uncle Rory has seen to that, hasn't he?"

Carefully Kate lowered herself into a chair. She had been eighty-two years old her last birthday, and sometimes she felt it was all too much for her, too—keeping up the facade of getting stronger so that Gabrielle wouldn't worry about her so much. But the face that looked back at her from her mirror was even more seamed than before, and more marked with lines of pain and concern, and—she had to admit it, as much as it hurt her vanity, she thought wryly—with age. She was eighty-two years old, she would think, older than anyone had a right to be, and she was tired. So tired. Her bones creaked and ached; she had trouble getting up and down; she had to make herself eat, for she had no appetite. Sometimes it seemed an effort even to lie in bed and stare at the ceiling; she, who had once been so full of youth and vitality that nothing had stopped her. It all seemed so long ago now, she thought as she rested her knotted hands on the cane she was forced to use; it all seemed so long ago, and she was so anxious to be with Page again. Sometimes she fancied that he was waiting for her, just out of sight, calling her name softly, asking her if she was ready to join him.

But she wasn't ready, she thought; not yet. And she didn't know why, really. It was just some feeling she had, some urge that said she had to wait awhile. There was something unfinished in this long life of hers, and she couldn't leave it until she discovered what it was and set it right.

Sitting in Gabrielle's room now, staring helplessly at her granddaughter, who had stood up shakily and belted a dressing gown about her thin waist, Kate almost laughed at herself. What a foolish old woman she was, she thought, for thinking such ridiculous things. Page was gone; he had been dead now for fifteen years, and if there was any unfinished business in her life, it would have to stay undone. She had done enough; there wasn't any more she could do for anyone.

Except, possibly, for Gabrielle.

Kate sighed again, watching as Gabrielle went to the mirror and began brushing her hair. Her movements were quick, abrupt, and tense as she hurriedly divided the strands and began plaiting two braids to wind around her head. Suddenly, with the coronet only half pinned up, Gabrielle stopped and stared at herself. Her eyes were wide and very green as she leaned slowly forward, examining her pale face.

"I'm getting old, Grandmother," she whispered. "My life is passing me by, and I'm not doing anything about it except watching it go. Do you realize that I'm twenty-nine years old today? *Twenty-nine.* When you were my age, you were married and had five children."

A sob escaped her, and she put her hands quickly over her face, shutting out the sight of her reflection in the mirror. "Oh, Grandmother," she wept, "I can't stand it anymore—the waiting and the not knowing! How could he do this to me? How could I let him do it to me? I love him; I thought he loved me!"

Kate struggled to her feet. Leaning heavily on the cane, she went to Gabrielle and put her hand on her granddaughter's shoulder. "He did love you, Gabrielle," she said steadily. "I know he did."

Gabrielle dropped her hands. She stared at Kate with ravaged eyes. "Then why?" she cried. "Why did he go? Why hasn't he come back?"

Kate shook her head. "I don't know, Gabrielle," she answered sorrowfully. "I don't know."

"Oh, Grandmother!" Turning around on the seat, Gabrielle flung her arms about Kate's waist and buried her face, sobbing. Her thin shoulders heaved, her body shook with the force of her tears, and Kate held her close, stroking her hair as she had done when Gabrielle was a young girl and had sought comfort from her in just this way. But there was no comfort Kate could give, and so she remained silent as Gabrielle wept. Her own eyes were misted, too, and her face was sad and bleak.

47

Gabrielle's birthday depression, as she later scornfully called it, had taken place in September. In early October of 1929, they received the only sort of communication they had ever received from Rory since the day Gabrielle had slapped him and he had stormed out of the house: a court order summoning them to appear for a final hearing in November.

As Gabrielle opened the heavy envelope containing the information to appear, her face was speculative. "He thinks he has the upper hand," she said after she read the document, giving it to Kate.

While Kate pretended to glance over these latest formal papers Gabrielle had given her, which lately had only confused and bewildered her, Gabrielle got up from the edge of the bed where she had been sitting and wandered over to the window. "I wonder why?" she murmured.

Kate followed her with her eyes. "What did you say, dear?"

Gabrielle turned back toward her. "I said, I wonder why Uncle Rory's so confident this time. There's something going on; I can feel it."

"But what?" Kate was even more confused. "What do you mean?"

"I—"

But the telephone rang just then, interrupting whatever Gabrielle had been about to say. They had had a phone installed upstairs after Kate's last attack, in addition to the one in the library, and now Gabrielle ran out into the hallway to answer it. It was Annabel calling from New York, and her voice was excited as she greeted Gabrielle.

"How goes the battle?" she asked breezily.

Despite her preoccupation, Gabrielle smiled. She had never become accustomed to Annabel's brisk entry into a conversation, and it always amused her the unique way her cousin had of turning a phrase. The two of them had become quite good friends over the past several years; the old animosity was gone as they discovered their mutual dislike of Rory and his son, and now they were two women united in a common cause against a mutual enemy. At least, reflected Gabrielle, that was how Annabel phrased it.

"It doesn't go well," she said now, answering Annabel's question glumly. "Uncle Rory has just now sent us a final court date. I really think this time he believes he's going to win."

"Oh, really!" Annabel's voice still held that curious undercurrent of excitement. "Well, I'm not surprised. The man is absolutely flushed with success, you know—or he thinks he is."

To Gabrielle's astonishment, Annabel actually giggled. Annabel never giggled or became coy; it was too at odds with her sophisticated image.

"What do you mean, Annabel?" Gabrielle asked suspiciously. During the past four exhausting years, Rory had tried everything he could do to take Beauvais, and Gabrielle was afraid suddenly that he had stumbled upon some new plot to harass her. She had never told her grandmother, but she knew that Rory was somehow behind the mysterious loss of some Beauvais cattle and the death of several valuable foals; somehow he had contrived the mold in the stored hay, and the downed fences, and . . . But there had been so many things, she remembered, disasters large and small, too many to count. To Gabrielle, though, they all added up to one thing: Rory's absolute determination to take the ranch from her, even if he had to destroy it in the process. It had been one headache after another, one crisis on the heels of the one before. Gabrielle wondered wearily what Rory had decided to do now, that Annabel had apparently found out about.

"Listen," Annabel said in her quick, businesslike tone. "I think I've helped solved your problems with Beauvais at last."

"You have?" Gabrielle spoke absently, still speculating what Rory had planned for her now.

"Are you paying attention to me?"

Gabrielle shook herself mentally, recognizing Annabel's impatient tone. "Yes, I'm paying attention," she said. "You just haven't said anything yet."

"Are you quite finished with sarcasm? Good. Now, listen. You know how involved our uncle is in the stock market, don't you?" Gabrielle had only a vague idea; Annabel was the one who had always had a head for stocks and bonds and issues and margins; Gabrielle herself had never been interested. "Yes," she said uncertainly. "But what—?"

"Just hear me out!" Annabel said impatiently. "Things aren't looking too well here on the exchange. There's been a boom you can't believe, all over the country, and it made me nervous, so I decided to do a little checking. Giles helped . . ." Giles was the GR of the inscription on Annabel's gold lighter. Kate wasn't aware of it, but Annabel and Giles had been living together without marrying for the past two years, and Annabel had never been happier in her sinful state. Gabrielle envied her unreservedly. ". . . and we discovered an ominous trend." Annabel's voice lowered conspiratorily. "I've unloaded all my stocks, and so has Giles, Gabrielle. Something has to break soon, and I think there's going to be a crash!"

"A crash!"

"Yes, you know—a terrible drop in stocks, with everyone unloading at once in a panic. Giles and I aren't the only ones who believe it's coming—Alexander Noyes, of the New York *Times*, agrees, and so do many other important economists and financiers. There's been too much unchecked speculation and more than a little double-dealing going on for too long. The market won't be able to stand up under it for much longer."

"But what does that have to do with Uncle Rory?"

Annabel laughed in delight. "I knew you were too honest and truthful a person ever to take matters into your own hands and play Uncle Rory's game—you wouldn't be able to live with that overactive conscience if you did. Fortunately for you, I'm not bothered by the same moral considerations!"

"Oh, Annabel, what have you done?"

"Oh, nothing much," said Annabel airily. "I just advised our dear uncle to invest heavily in companies like RCA and Cities Service. They're rolling high right now—but just wait! It's going to be a disaster, and even though I made sure to sound a little warning note when I talked to Uncle Rory, I knew he was just too greedy not to take a chance. He thinks he can get in and get out again before he's hurt, but he won't. He won't. He's going to go down with the market, and all your problems will be solved!"

"But how can you be so sure?"

Annabel was affronted. "My dear child!" she sniffed. "Haven't I been playing the market since I was in pinafores? Do you think I haven't learned anything during the time I've made my own fortune several times over? Uncle Rory is like a babe in arms compared to those who really study the market. He can't see a thing except the chance to make money! His own greed will destroy him, and I couldn't be happier! Oh, yes, and don't worry about Todd, in case he decides to try something funny after the sudden decline of his father. Todd owes me enough money for me to keep him hacking at a rock pile for years, if I choose!"

"Oh, Annabel!" Despite her misgivings about what Annabel had done, Gabrielle had to laugh. It was the first genuine amusement she had felt in so long that it felt wonderful.

Annabel laughed with her. "And the best part about it," she said gleefully, "is that no matter who warns him about overextension, he won't listen. Uncle Rory thinks money is the key to everything, and he'll take any chance to make it—even mortgaging everything he has to the hilt!"

"Annabel . . ."

The sudden seriousness in Gabrielle's voice made Annabel pause. "What?"

"Annabel, why are you doing this? You don't get anything out of it."

Annabel was silent for so long that Gabrielle thought the connection had been broken. She said hesitantly, "Annabel . . . ?"

"Yes, I'm here." Annabel's voice was suddenly subdued.

"Did you hear me?"

"Yes." There was another long silence, and then Annabel

said, "I am getting something out of it, Gabrielle. I'm helping to save Beauvais—for you. You belong together, you and Beauvais. I always knew it. You're so much like a Taggart, so much like Grandmother. I . . . I always respected you, Gabrielle—even when we used to quarrel. I often wished I could have been like you."

"Annabel—"

But Annabel had broken the connection purposely this time, and Gabrielle would not talk to her again until after those four terrible days later that same month when Annabel's prophecy came true. On October 23 there was a spectacular drop during the last hour of trading on the New York Stock Exchange; the next day, the infamous twenty-fourth, when almost thirteen million shares changed hands, became known as "Black Thursday." Spokesmen for bankers and brokers insisted that the worst was over then, but October 28 and 29 were even more terrible days, from which there was no recovery.

And Rory, who had invested so heavily, who had overextended himself in the hope of cashing in on the spectacular profits to be made during that unprecedented stock boom, was utterly, totally, and completely ruined. Like so many others whose greed outran their common sense and their sense of proportion, he had invested wildly, without regard to consequences. The fortune he had hoped would enable him to buy whatever he needed to take Beauvais from Gabrielle and his mother never materialized. He had become fanatical about what he considered his inheritance during the past years, and the only thing in his life had been his desire for Beauvais and his revenge against Gabrielle, whom he had come to associate somehow in his mind with Michael, the brother he had always hated so desperately. In his last days, Rory might have been even a little insane, and surely on the day he realized his complete ruin, he was more than a little mad with grief and fury and despair.

He had to have been out of his mind, Kate would reflect sadly at a later time, for fastidious, immaculate, particular Rory, who was always so meticulously groomed and impeccably dressed, who hated dirt and disorder, had calmly climbed into his Cadillac car and had propelled it at high speed toward an embankment. The resulting collision had been one of the messiest the police had ever seen: filled with blood and gore and twisted metal grotesquely scattered over the entire road and even into an adjoining field, where a gasoline fire erupted and burned everything into a horrendous mass.

The final irony was that Rory came back to Beauvais at last, to rest in the family cemetery that was part of the home he had tried so desperately and fanatically to claim. In the end, the land claimed him, and his headstone was simple, like the others there, carved only with his name and the dates of his birth and death. The cold marble gave no hint of the pain and anguish he had caused so many, nor did it give a clue to the demons that had driven Rory Taggart all the years of his life.

48

Gabrielle sat by Kate's bed the day after Rory's funeral, trying not to cry. Events had been too much for the frail Kate, and she had suffered a third—and final, the doctor gravely told Gabrielle—heart attack. She was dying, and Gabrielle sat helplessly by, clutching the gnarled hand in her own, as if by some miracle she could infuse some of her own young life into Kate's failing one.

Despite her efforts to be silent, a sob escaped her, and Kate stirred, opening her eyes. "Don't cry, Gabrielle," she whispered. "It's time for me to go."

"No!" said Gabrielle fiercely, bending over her. "I won't let you die; I won't!"

Kate smiled at her granddaughter's protectiveness. She had been in some pain before, but it had gone now, leaving behind a wonderful lassitude. She didn't feel tired anymore, or weary. Just . . . lazy. It was a delightful feeling, to know that she never again had to force herself to get up, to walk across a room, or to look in a mirror and wonder where her youth had gone. She had been beautiful once, strong and vital and full of life. Now she was old and wrinkled, and glad that she had lived the life she had. It had been grand, all the things she had been part of: building Beauvais, helping Colorado achieve statehood, knowing Hill Flower and Jane and Olivia and so many others who had influenced her in so many ways. She had fought blizzards and droughts and fires and floods, and had won; she had raised five children and lived to see her children's children grown and on their own.

She really didn't regret that it was time to go, for her life had been full, rich, longer than most—with perhaps more than her share of pain. She couldn't even quibble about that, though, for she had come to believe that fate sends only what one can manage. It was just, she thought with a touch of humor, that sometimes fate was a little too heavy-handed; it was hard to manage so many things at once.

If she had one wish, she thought now, it would be to see Marcus again before she died. She had hoped . . . But then, she should have learned sometime in her life that things seldom worked out quite so neatly as they did in books, where everyone came together at the end and lived contentedly ever after.

No, there was no use hoping, and she had been disappointed too many times in her life to think Marcus would appear now simply because she wanted him to. And every time she had ever wished for something, it seemed, a malignant fate had granted that wish—only to exact a penalty of some kind. No; she wouldn't wish.

But she could be a little wistful; surely she could be granted that small concession. She wasn't even wistful for herself; it was Gabrielle she thought about—dear, loving, and kind Gabrielle, who had been such a joy and comfort to her all these years; Gabrielle, who had proudly given up so much, and who was sacrificing still. Would Beauvais be enough without Marcus? It had to be, for it was all she had to give Gabrielle now.

Sadly, Kate wanted it to be more, much more. She had known such heights with Page; he had been her love, her life. Would Gabrielle never know that ecstasy of loving and being loved by such a man?

"Grandmother . . ."

Gabrielle's voice was strangled, choked, the fingers clutching Kate's beginning to grip convulsively, as if Gabrielle had had a terrible shock. With an effort, fighting the lassitude that made lying here so pleasant as her thoughts carried her driftingly along, Kate opened her eyes again.

Gabrielle was still sitting by the bed, but her face was absolutely white as she looked toward the doorway. Her eyes were wide and staring, and her throat worked as if she wanted desperately to say something, and couldn't.

Slowly Kate turned her head to look in the direction that riveted Gabrielle, and then her laboring heart gave a twisted leap in her chest when she saw who was there.

BEWARE THE WISH . . .

But she didn't care what penalty she had to pay now. Like Gabrielle's, her joy was so great at seeing him that no punishment would have mattered. She would have welcomed anything, just to see him again.

"Marcus," she whispered.

"Grandmother," he said. But he was looking at Gabrielle, drinking in the sight of her, his eyes hungry, his face taut with emotion.

"Marcus," Gabrielle breathed. She half-rose from her chair, her eyes shining, her lips parted.

He came forward then, tall and strong once more, his face shadowed by too many memories, but his eyes clear and direct and compelling again—Page's eyes, thought Kate, and her tired heart convulsed again.

She could hear him, she thought in sudden wonderment. She could hear Page calling to her. "Katie . . . Katie . . ."

They were all there, she saw now: her beloved Page, and David, and Jane and Amelia, and Olivia, and Randall . . . and Michael. They were waiting for her to come, and she was almost ready to obey.

With dimming eyes she looked up at the grandchildren she loved so dearly. Their hands were clasped across the bed, Gabrielle on one side, Marcus on the other, and Kate saw then that it was Marcus' right hand Gabrielle held—his right hand, which had been paralyzed and which now gripped Gabrielle's fingers so strongly. Together their hands formed a bridge across her, generation over generation, and Kate thought that now it had truly come full circle: the daughter of her son and the son of Page's son, united at last, as she and Page had been so long ago, and would be again in the space of a few heartbeats.

She had done all she could, she thought, as the sound of fluttering wings rustled and grew louder, claiming her, calling her, taking her to Page. She had saved Beauvais for them, for these two who were so like what she and Page had been. The rest was up to them.

BEWARE THE WISH . . .

But this time, Kate thought, as the fluttering wings enfolded her and began to carry her away, there was no penalty to pay. Fate had finally relented, and granted her last wish for free.

About the Author

JANIS FLORES was born in Fort Benton, Montana, in 1946. After graduating from Immaculate Heart College in Los Angeles with a degree in Biology, she obtained a license as a Medical Technologist in 1969. She spent the next few years supervising various medical laboratories in Los Angeles and Santa Rosa, California, and in 1976 began a second career with the publication of her first novel, HAWKSHEAD.

Currently occupied full-time with her writing, Ms. Flores also enjoys her husband of thirteen years, their country home in Sebastopol, California, a menagerie of pets that includes four horses, and a determination to finish a sampler quilt by spring—any spring.

Janis Flores is already at work on a new book, and HIGH DOMINION is her sixth novel.

The Best in Fiction from SIGNET